A Novel Idea

A Novel Idea

Author F. Bradley Reaume

Penshurst Publishing (Books) 2025

First Edition — November 2025

This is a work of fiction. Any resemblance between actual events and those herein described is purely coincidental. All characterizations and names are fictional. Any use of known historical figures in the text are presented to conform to their known traits, histories and general facts of their lives.

ISBN — paperback — 978-1-998193-03-5

ISBN — electronic book — 978-1-998193-04-2

A Novel Idea

For my mother

Leila Patricia (Harris) Reaume

Table of Contents

Chapter One

"I need an idea. You know something different; I want to stand out from the crowd."

"Doesn't everyone, but I'm pretty sure every zipper, every fabric, cut, length, ornamentation, everything has been done."

"Thanks for your encouragement." She tossed it back to me. "How about you? Come up with a new plot for your next novel?"

"Everything has been written a million times. There are no new ideas in fiction. It's all about the twist on the familiar, maybe in clothes, too."

Sitting in a café with my best friend, lamenting my writer's block, I was trying to shake loose a new approach. Theresa and I met on Wednesdays to catch up, get on the same page with each other and generally start or finish the day with a little social time.

The café was downtown, on a corner, with windows facing either street. Maybe a dozen tables and usually half full, though there was a bustling walk-in crowd, taking their joe to go. The area was full of high-rise office buildings, a hospital a block away, several banks and insurance companies.

Both of us did business in the area frequently and it had become our stop of choice. I often arranged my freelance meetings on Wednesdays because I knew I'd be in the neighbourhood anyway.

I was dressed for a business meeting. Nothing out of the ordinary, I blended in with the downtown crowds, people going every which way and all with a destination. I was a copy writer, freelancer and an aspiring novelist with a couple of books to my credit and a steady trickle of free-lance work that paid the bills. My aspiration was to make fiction my full-time gig. That's a tough road, but without a viable idea for a novel, it was impossible.

Theresa was a clothing designer, recently gone out on her own, with a line of urban wear, both for the office and for the town. She usually wore her own designs, understated, utilitarian with an unusual mix of colour, just a touch.

A Novel Idea

I tried to dedicate at least 60 minutes per day to my fiction, a plan that was increasingly becoming its own fiction as I found myself blocked from any idea for a new story. Sixty minutes staring at the screen, or starting a few paragraphs only to have the narrative peter out and be erased, was not my idea of quality work time.

"Just start something. The ones that die just become short stories, right?"

"That's the problem, I can't even focus on a genre. I'm just tied up in knots."

"Okay, I'll help. Romance. You haven't written a romance and they sell pretty well."

"Yeah, okay, sure. Because they sell well everyone writes romance. I don't write romance. If you haven't noticed I'm single and kind of like it that way. And every possible story has already been written over and over again."

"That isn't stopping anyone else, why let it stop you?"

I just looked at her. The 10-mile stare. Apparently, she had not been listening to my rambling complaints for several weeks.

"It's the nature of writer's block, I guess. I've got nothing."

"Not even a hint?"

"Nothing."

"And either do I," she said, looking down into her empty coffee cup. "But I soon will. You want another?"

I nodded and handed her my cup. "You'll have something by the time I return." I was going to retort that it was going to be coffee, but I let it go.

As she busied herself at the counter, my eyes rolled over the entire shop. She was speaking and laughing with the barista. Maybe there is something there I thought, before dismissing the most obvious of tropes. Then I gazed outside through the window. I wondered if I could marry the craziest elements within my sight and imagination. Then I realized a corner coffee shop was pretty lame, and my imagination had dwindled to zero, limited to my own sightlines.

I had just finished a long historical account of two women, left behind in rural Virginia as their men went to fight in the Civil War. Keeping all the elements in my mind for the 18-month duration of the project, I hadn't yet completely cleared my mind of them. That was my crutch. However, I usually had two or three solid ideas rolling around in my head, developing, but this time, nothing.

There are a few weeks where finishing one project felt good, because I no longer had to keep all the details in mind. That time had passed.

I had checked my "Story Ideas" file but found little more than crazed gibberish. Tropes upon tropes and not an idea to develop. I now had three novels to my name, and I'd like to think they all had a significant freshness in their approach. And I didn't want to admit it, even to myself, but I was improving. Fiction is really hard.

Theresa was right, everything has been written a thousand times. But not by me. 'Okay', I thought, sitting upright as Theresa, across the shoppe was pouring the cream into one cup. 'Coffee, coffee – people are coffee importers, and they are trying to break into a market already full of coffee shops and grocery brands. It's a tough nut to crack', I thought, and then grinned at my own accidental pun.

"I need a novel idea," I said as she sat down, sliding a steaming cup in front of me.

"That's where we left off." She looked a bit annoyed. "You were instructed to have something by now."

"Let's just move on to other things. I'm trying too hard."

"Okay. I have a meeting with a fabric importer, that's where I got the cloth I used to make that coat I wore the other day."

"I remember it. What's the deal?"

"I'm thinking of starting a second line. More of a brand actually. I want to work with the overseas suppliers, take their designs, add a little swish of my own and brand them."

"You aren't going to stop doing the full designs are you?"

'For this line, yes. But I will still keep my own design side going. This way I have two lines, totally different branding and I can branch out a bit. Hopefully I can tap into bigger sales."

"And a lot more work. So, it's a marketing thing, mostly?"

"Absolutely. You do some of that for your clients, right? What can you tell me?"

"Well, it's like writing novels. Everything has been done a thousand times. These days branding is a bit of a niche kind of marketing. You have to very clearly define your style and market and then relentlessly move your marketing to that end. It can be pretty expensive."

Theresa said that her urban line of clothing was pitched at a higher end clientele, office workers and those who spent time on the town. That wasn't news to me, I was wearing one of her skirts and had a few other pieces in my closet. She offered several items for men, a line of outdoor jackets, useful for business guys who do not do the whole suit jacket thing and guys who do work site visits. Her new line would be suburban and even small-town casual, hoodies, khakis, golf shirts and light dress shirts.

"What about casual dress clothes, working man's stuff, you know?"

"I need to do a bit of research and find out what-is-what in suburbia, and in small towns. I was thinking of making a little trip out of it. My brother lives in the suburbs, so I can start there. I was planning to go for a visit anyway, my nephew is in a big regional high school baseball tournament in a few weeks. From there I was thinking of continuing on into some of the small towns a little further out."

"Sounds like a plan."

"Want to come?"

I tilted my head back, caught off guard, but the idea seemed like the perfect antidote to being squeezed into my usual routine. "When?"

Theresa smiled, "I knew I could count on you."

She had already planned the whole thing. Winter was behind us and the spring was well advanced and promising. A few weeks later we jumped in her small car, and made our way out of the city. Wednesday afternoon traffic was pretty typical for rush hour.

"I can't remember the last time I left the Big Smoke."

"I don't go often, but my brother usually hosts all the holiday stuff. My place is too small."

"So, we are staying with him and his wife, what's her name again?'

"Charlene, though he calls her Charlie. We get on pretty well. Their son, Oscar, is playing baseball for his high school team. Big tournament. We are going to watch their game. Though I will be scoping out the adults and what they are wearing. If you don't mind, take a few pictures of anything unusual. Subtle-like, you know."

We were headed to a distant suburb so as we approached our off-ramp, traffic had lightened considerably. Theresa's brother was an engineer, working at a mid-sized firm, located on the cheaper real estate in the suburbs, complete with free parking. We both marvelled at the expanse of paving, as we drove by the large, but low-slung office building.

A twist here, a turn there and soon enough we were at Thomas Jefferson High School, and wheeling into the back parking lot near the baseball diamond. We found Charlene on the first base side of the small grandstand. She said David would be along after work. Charlene was ensconced in a fold-out field chair with a fixed umbrella to block the sun. She had done this before. We had no such equipment.

Charlene motioned to the empty chair beside her. "That's Dan's chair, but he won't get here for a while yet."

Theresa offered it to me, but I politely declined. She seemed poised to take it but remained standing with me. There was a metal bleacher with five rows of benches just a few yards behind us.

"Oscar plays third base usually, but the kids get moved around a fair bit. The coach likes to broaden everyone's experience, so he keeps changing things hoping to find the perfect combination. At least that's what Oscar says."

Oscar was a lean kid. Not too tall, nor too small, his defining feature was massively broad shoulders. Unfamiliar with baseball, we did not notice the speed in which Oscar could throw the ball to first. It only became apparent when Charlene mentioned it, and I watched the other kids throw. Apparently, Oscar pitched sometimes as well.

I kept one eye on the game and constantly scanned the spectators looking for some kind of suburban style. A few innings of this and my feet were getting tired. I was just about to take the chair when Dan arrived. Some small talk ensued and Theresa and I found ourselves on the metal bench seats with Dan.

"Oscar is likely to pitch in the tournament but I don't know when. Most likely as a reliever."

I nodded, and Teresa continued to speak to her brother as my eyes roved around in search of style.

After some time, it became apparent that there was no suburban style to hang on to, or at least, I wasn't astute enough in the details of clothing to notice anything common that stood out. It seemed to me that everyone there had come from somewhere else, jobs, meetings, and the like. One guy stood behind the right field fence in an orange safety vest and work boots. My general roving gaze had turned quite intentionally into a choice to take in each person with a hard, critical look, make a mental note and move on. This way I could cover the spread of spectators and eventually be done. The systematic approach fit my personality.

Oscar's team seemed to be winning and Dan was distracted by the game, his conversation trailing off any time there was action. I did notice that action seemed rare to the non-baseball fan but to Dan and most of the spectators, action seemed almost constant, with defensive positioning, individual pitches and who was playing where.

I did notice that Teresa was not conducting the systematic research into clothing styles that I was. She and Dan spoke mostly about their other family members, some of whom I had never heard mentioned. There was a throw to first and everybody began to converge on the pitcher.

"Hey that's the game. Good stuff. A win. When do we play tomorrow?"

"You don't know already?"

"No, it depends upon whether we won or lost," he said. "Hey Charlie, when do we play tomorrow?"

Charlene was still in her seat, collecting up her stuff, getting ready to head to the parking lot. She looked up, "I think it's the 7:30 pm time, second game, but you'd better double check that with Oscar."

"So, head on over to our place. You know how to get there? And I've arranged for Chinese for dinner. I will pick it up on the way home."

The crowd was collecting their progeny and making their way to the parking lot. We stood up waiting for Oscar to amble by.

We all made our way to the lot with Charlene and Oscar breaking off to her car, Dan taking a few more steps and breaking off for his car, leaving Theresa and I alone. "Well, what stylistic revelations have you found?"

"Well, these suburbanites seem to have solutions for everything. Field chairs are better than cold metal benches, the sunshade for Charlene's chair, equipment bags for the kids, parking lots close enough to the park but far enough away to avoid getting hit by stray balls."

"Clothing, Teresea, clothing is your business."

"Yes, it is but there are so many other things to see. I guess if I could draw any early conclusions . . . "

"If they are early, they aren't conclusions."

Theresa gave me a short withering look. "In my early estimation, suburbanites are first drawn to the comfortable and necessary. They are not concerned with style, they are concerned with practicality and comfort."

"Sounds like me, and I live in the city."

"Yes, but practicality in the city is a different thing. Sometimes you have to look sharp."

"We will continue our research tomorrow. I will jot down a few observations I had and give you the whole thing once we are headed home. I took the time to look very carefully at everyone to try to discern patterns in what they chose to wear."

"I knew you would be useful on this trip. Let's make a quick pit stop for a few bottles of wine on our way to Dan's."

"Now you are speaking sense."

We enjoyed a lovely dinner with her brother's family, including two younger children, Patty and Bryson. The whole confusion surrounding dinner finally gave way to some quiet as the kids wandered off to do their own thing, enjoying the lack of parental attention that came with guests.

The adults all settled into a cosy, typically suburban room, with a fire-place, lots of pictures of the kids, big old heavy comfortable furniture, and a little music playing in the background, something to fill in the gaps of conversation.

“I’ve heard that before, it’s from a movie I think, can’t remember which one,” said Theresa.

Dan laughed. “Dad used to play this stuff all the time. It’s the Rolling Stones, ‘Shine a Light’. He played this stuff so much it sunk into me. I listen to some modern stuff, but I keep coming back to the oldies. And there are a lot of oldies. You hear it in commercials, movies, music at sporting events. It’s everywhere.”

“Well, I like it. I probably heard dad play it as well. I just wasn’t paying as much attention.”

“So how is the big city these days? I don’t get there as much as I used to, what with video calls and stuff.”

“You used to live there. It’s pretty much the same, just more so. A little louder, a little busier, small changes happening so fast that if you leave for any period of time, you feel like you are returning to a completely different place.”

“We’ve come to like the ‘burbs, eh Charlie?”

She took another sip of wine, “This is very good. You must have known about it. Or was it just luck?”

I laughed, “No, it’s one of my favorites. I was actually a bit surprised they had it here. It’s not too well known in my neck of the woods.”

“The ‘burbs can be surprising.”

“Sometimes the surprise is that there is no surprise.”

“How very Oscar Wilde of you. I’m just reading ‘A Picture of Dorian Gray’ and that sounds like something Wilde would say.”

“Cassie here is a writer; she just published her latest book.”

"Tell me about it, maybe I'll pick it up."

I had to bite my tongue. Trying to describe a novel in just a few words and make it sound like all the work that went into it, is a writer's nightmare.

"It's a lengthy tale of two women in rural Virginia who have to keep things together after their husbands go off to fight the Civil War." Good thing I had a short answer already worked up.

"Sounds interesting. Is it written from an historical perspective or a modern one?"

I had not expected that question. "It's historical but I guess, everything is written from a modern perspective, or at least modern in the time it was written." I thought for moment. "I think that is true always. Maybe that's the whole point."

Charlene seemed intrigued and asked for the title. She wondered if I might have a copy with me. Everyone, it seems, is intrigued by a story that they get for free. A blind entry by an unknown author into any genre rarely commands any money, unless it has been recommended, or some third party talks it up.

"So, are you working on a new book?"

"Well, I have a day job, so I'm getting back on track with that. Taking a break from the long nights, and considering my options," I lied gently. I looked at Theresa and she gave me a slightly dark look, squishing down her brow.

"Well, I picked up 'Dorian Gray' from one of those neighbourhood libraries, you know, the box of books in someone's yard. It caught my eye because of 'Oscar'."

"Are you liking it?"

"Yes, it's quite witty. And the story, a bit gothic, I guess. It's been made into a movie, long ago."

A little more conversation and we finished the wine and headed for bed. The next day Theresa and I drove to the local shopping district, a good place, Theresa thought, to scope out true suburban style. We shopped and dabbled and ate a light breakfast and lunch before heading to Oscar's second game.

I recognized several of the parents now and tried to compare today's styles with yesterdays, but came up blank. I couldn't remember. One mother was sporting a very stylish light bomber type jacket, with lapel flaps, zippers and pockets galore. She wore tight fitting slacks and high heels.

I nudged Theresa, "What do you make of that?" I nodded in the direction of the woman.

Theresa's eyes widened. "Well, it's a style, I guess. I wonder what she has been up to?"

I shrugged and looked around some more. "Where does the other team come from? She might be one of their parents."

Theresa wandered over to Charlene returning to our bench spot, settling down before saying, "The other team is from Springfield, about 90 minutes from here. It's a mid-sized town, kinda out there."

"And so is it's style apparently."

Thersa grinned. "That's what we are here for. Research."

That night we repeated our evening, this time Theresa bought steaks for Dan to barbeque and we sipped through several bottles of wine. We took our leave after a quick breakfast.

"So, where are we going? Are we headed into the great wide open?'

"Of course. Springfield it is. We will hit a mall or whatever is there and decide what is next."

The drive to Springfield was actually pleasant now that we'd left all the suburban traffic behind. Rolling hills, farms, and two small settlements, cross-roads really, with a few commercial buildings and not much else. Then we rolled into Springfield, immediately finding a small outdoor mall, really a series of plazas, spread before us.

A bit of time checking out the stores and we returned to the car, both commenting on the lack of shoe and clothing stores. The stores were a range of kitchen stuff, hardware, automotive and small restaurants, fast food and mom and pop family spots.

"I am getting a whiff of suburban style, I think," said Theresa. "Let's find the downtown."

We did and it was more of the same, with a few professional offices mixed in, a lawyer, a dentist, a realtor, two banks and a financial planner. We passed one guy wearing a tie.

Back in the car I waited for Theresa to announce our next move. She was silent. I was silent as well, though I was beginning to think we should decide where we were going to stay for the night.

"Are you good with another night of this? I think I have a handle on it, but one more place, a little further out, I think is a good idea."

"Okay. Where are we staying tonight, and what are we doing for dinner?"

"I have a plan. But it doesn't include those very practical needs," Theresa said.

I had to laugh, "We could stay in that little inn we saw back near the out-door mall. Or we can carry on and see what we find. We have a fair bit of daylight left."

"There is nothing else we need in this town, save a bottle or two. Then we can head out. I think I remember, there is a well-known rural inn, a way on. If we find it, we can stay there. It's supposed to be nice, lots of conferences are held there."

"Sounds good to me, as long as you are right, and we find it."

And find it we did, just before concern about not finding it set in. A sign led us off the main road and a few miles later, into a long driveway and a really sharp looking Victorian mansion. There was a golf course that looked very well maintained, and a few other outbuildings.

"Okay, this nice. I can't help but be concerned about the cost."

"We're in now, cost be damned. Maybe you can use this for your own research. Make a great setting for a romance."

"I don't write romance."

"You know, two city girls, on a research trip, floundering a bit, lost in their next steps and unsure of where they are going . . . "

"Oh stop. Let's find out if they have any rooms."

The clerk at the desk looked a bit surprised at our request, "You aren't part of the wedding party?"

"No, just passing through and looking for a room for the night."

"He looked at his screen with concern, "Ah, yes, there is a suite left. I can give you that."

We nodded in unison, happy to have a room in the gathering dusk, and not really caring about the price.

Until I heard it, then my mouth went dry, but Theresa did not balk, agreeing without looking at me.

We signed in and went to get our things, deciding to get dinner at the inn's restaurant. There were well dressed people milling about, no doubt attached to the wedding that had been mentioned.

"Who would have a wedding way out here?"

Theresa shrugged.

"It will be a different aspect to our research. Let's get something to eat. Perhaps we can even crash the reception."

I gave her a dirty look. I did not like doing such things, but she was less uptight. I mentioned that we had no formal wear with us and that seemed to settle the issue.

We spent that evening and the next morning in the public parts of the hotel, the lobby and restaurant mostly observing.

So absorbed in our research, we failed to notice two young men slide into the next table at breakfast. One was anxious to catch an eye and when he did, he asked if we enjoyed the reception.

"The ceremony was lovely and the reception was wonderful," said Theresa.

I just nodded dumbly, caught off guard by her bald-faced lie.

"I didn't see either of you two ladies at the reception, and I know most everyone. Glenda is my younger sister."

"We are distant family of the groom, up from the city. This is a lovely place, though a bit hard to find."

The young man dominated the conversation and Theresa masterfully used the information he provided to push into things she knew nothing about. Soon she knew the groom's name, where he'd gone to school and for what degree, some of his family members names and backgrounds and a touch more about Glenda, the bride.

Still, every moment in the back and forth provided a doorway which might quickly close on her if she said the wrong thing. They asked after us and Theresa was vague but segued into our fashion mission which got the two men talking business. One was employed at a brokerage downtown and the other worked in engineering process design with a manufacturing company located in the eastern suburbs.

"Any insights into the difference between city wear and suburban styles?" Theresa asked.

Both men pursed their lips. You could tell it was exactly the last thing they had ever thought about. The first one, the broker, who's name was Markus spoke up, wanting to make a good impression.

"I'm not sure there is a major difference in the style at all. What there is, is a difference in the need and desire to wear specific clothing in your own space."

Theresa was about to counter this observation with a touch of acid, as her entire business revolved around the differences. But Markus beat her to it.

"For example, Brandon here works in the suburbs but is expected to be in a shirt and tie every day at work. In that way he's ready for city visitors, carries the look of management around the plant, and can easily pick up and head to the city for meetings or after work fun."

"And I can always take the tie off. It's actually really easy. I just make sure I don't break the knot," he laughed.

"And what about you Markus, are you in a shirt and tie all day?"

"Absolutely. In the brokerage business it's expected, well maybe not expected anymore but certainly a business look is necessary. Some of the older guys wear a lot of sweaters and skip the tie."

"Yeah, it all started with the IT guys 30 years ago. They were in such demand that they generally dressed how they wanted, tossed all the old, staid business apparel aside and began the slide to a more comfortable day."

"So the sweet spot for an upscale urban look is comfortable, with a touch of panache but not too formal. I take it cravats are out?"

Both men laughed. "Sashes too," said Markus.

"And stiff collars," said Brandon.

The guys invited us to join them. I was reluctant, as I expected we would expose ourselves as not being part of the wedding, but Theresa did not consult me. So I dragged my jacket and purse over to the other table and waited our breakfast orders. Strangely the commotion of changing tables seemed to stifle the conversation and I wracked my brain for something to keep it away from the previous evening's festivities. It never dawned on me that the groom might happen by the table and expose us.

"I never did hear where the honeymoon is."

"Aruba, I think, that's what they eventually settled on. You know Ollie loves the islands and Glenda was happy to accommodate him as long as it was an adventure and not a resort."

As they ate the girls spoke about their own professional lives and Theresa asked after each of the men's lives, finding they were cousins.

Markus slipped Theresa a business card, saying if she wanted to talk more about fashion she could call him. I'm in the city so we could meet for lunch or after work. Give me a couple of weeks though, I have to do some observing in the meantime."

The girls had been watching a steady stream of people come into the restaurant, dressed in casual but not sloppy clothing. Theresa pointed this out and Brandon said it cemented his thesis, that people wore what was appropriate no matter where they were.

The girls finished and escaped the table without knowingly giving themselves away. They checked out of the inn and turned onto the main road away from home.

"We have to be back tonight. I have to work in the morning."

"I know, I know. We will be back. I've given this a lot of thought and decided that we need to go to Hasseldon College. It's in a little town about an hour from here. It might give us a different perspective on fashion."

"I'm not sure a bunch of college kids on a Sunday morning will provide the kind of insights we are looking for."

"Fashion isn't all about business or pleasure. The kids often lead the way. Let's check it out. We can wander the campus a bit and maybe hit a coffee shop. Then we will head home. It's going to be a long drive."

We found the college predictably empty, the kids likely sleeping off their previous night. There were a few university workers in uniform and a couple of joggers and early morning types, dressed in sports togs.

We found the campus coffee shop and sat down to observe.

"You know, I sort of miss college," I said.

"It's a nice time in life, but I was anxious to move on. In my work, you learn a lot more in the field than in the classroom."

"That might be true about everything."

"I know there are a few things I learned that were useful, but I probably could have learned them in a month out of school."

"But did school open the door that allowed you to learn on the job?"

"It did. But you know, it's odd that I have very few friends remaining from college. Most of my old friends, the one's I keep up with, are from high school."

"That's because you returned home after school. You had a line of established friendships already in place."

The drive back was lengthy and mostly quiet. As we approached the city the late Sunday night traffic buzzed around us. We agreed to be prepared to go over our findings when we met for coffee at our usual time later in the week.

I rumbled into my place, tossed my bag on a chair and flopped on the couch, with visions of jogging suburbanites dancing in my head.

I was thinking of what we had seen but couldn't get past Theresa's brazen deception of the two guys at the inn. No harm, no foul, I thought. Nobody will ever know. I wondered how much that kind of thing happened in social situations.

Chapter Two

A couple of days later I had arranged a meeting with a client for the following morning – expecting my noon meet up with Theresa to work perfectly. However, I spent more time than I expected with the client and had to beg off continuing the meeting over lunch, to get to the coffee shop a few minutes late.

"Ah, there you are."

I explained my predicament but Theresa brushed it off. "You could have let me know. Especially if the lunch was a good idea."

"It's okay, I said. I can send my proposals to him in a couple of days. I need to mull over things before I commit to anything."

We chatted about our workweek before Theresa moved to the main event, "Okay, spill on our trip."

"It's not terribly complicated. That guy, Brandon, was on track when he talked about the places you would go rather than the geography you were located in."

"Yeah, that hit me too. Funny that some random guy has a great insight." She reached down and pulled up a few rolled-up sheets of drawing paper. "So, I took the liberty of drawing up a few ideas."

She unrolled the papers, weighed the top down with her coffee cup, leaving the corners to curl up, and we looked at drawings of a jacket, blouse, some slacks and a skirt that were intriguing. "I'd buy these. I really like them. The lines are a touch urban, formal, but not too much and they have a ready made, comfortable look to them. Sort of like your favourite clothes, the ones you look forward to wearing."

Theresa smiled broadly, "That's exactly what I was aiming for."

We talked about the design elements for a bit, before I remined her that she had originally talked about very comfortable suburban styles with a touch of the city, not city styles with a brush of the suburbs.

"I'm not seeing any hooded pullovers, or light jackets."

She smiled and reached down again to a second sheaf of papers at her feet. A deep sip of coffee, which allowed the first pages to roll up, and she replaced them with the second scroll. Sure enough, there were two hooded pull overs and a jacket.

"You can wear these anywhere. What I got thinking about was the branding. Especially on the suburban styles. Every damned person on campus had a Hasseldon College logo on what they were wearing. At the end of the day, it's the branding that will attract buyers and the quality, comfort and panache of the styles that will keep the customers coming back."

Theresa spoke of some of the branding ideas she had. "The city stuff should be knowing, wise, a little dangerous and sneaky in a smart way. The suburban stuff needs to emphasis space, elbow room."

I nodded, she had sketched out a few ideas but stressed they were preliminary and she really wanted my feedback before continuing. I was struck how Brandon's point and the branding approach really crystalized my thinking.

"The style is the comfort, I think, within the confines of where you are and what you are doing. Choices are a bit of an advert for the wearer, unconscious in a way."

Scrolling up the drawings she changed pace, "How about you? Still having writer's block? Have you had any time for fiction in between the client meetings?"

"Funny, I hadn't even thought about it since the weekend. Too busy with clients. Working on an entire product catalogue. It's a huge undertaking and as usual, the client wants it print ready yesterday."

"But they just talked to you about it today."

"Exactly."

"I guess it's that way everywhere."

I took a sip of my coffee, now a bit tepid. I'd have to keep at it, or it would go cold and lose the touch of joy it brought.

"Maybe the break from fiction will do the trick," Theresa said.

"Maybe. Though I can't help but thinking that our meeting of those two guys was right out of a made-for-TV Christmas movie. I mean Markus as much as asked you out in a clever left-handed way. Are you going to call him?"

Theresa hesitated. "I could I suppose, but that seems a bit forward."

"It's the 21st century you know."

"Yes, but if this is going to be a Harlequin Romance, it must follow the protocol."

I had to laugh. "It was a strange way to meet someone, and if you pursued it, you'd have to fess up that we didn't know anyone at the wedding. A lie, no matter how little or seeming inconsequential, is not a good way to start something new."

"I would like to let him see these designs. At least then he'd know we were honest about our real purpose. Given that the ideas are in his head, he might offer a touch of something when he sees the drawings."

"You are giving men a bit too much credit, I think. They rarely consider anything fashion oriented unless they are directed to wear things."

"Maybe. But something makes me want to have him comment. Where did he say he worked again? Maybe I can run into him. It's more random than calling him direct."

"Now who is playing the TV movie card?"

Theresa laughed. 'We will see, I can let it go for a few weeks before I call."

Then it hit me. I didn't want to say anything, because it was merely a flashing thought. It was a TV movie. It was a cheesy romance story, practically ready made. It entirely did not suit me nor my approach to writing fiction, but maybe giving it a go for fun would break me out of my block.

"You must update me on whatever happens."

"Update you? I might ask you to come along if I can get him to a coffee commentary. I was thinking of asking him to meet us here."

We headed our own ways, agreeing to meet the following week as usual, but Theresa would not commit to calling Markus before that.

She headed east to her small office loft in an old building, just far enough from downtown that she needed to catch a streetcar. I had another client meeting for a public relations retainer. It was supposed to be a little light press contact, and an on-call retainer for public relations concerns. The client was venturing outside their usual business paths, and wanted some assurance their approach was comfortably controversial and that they had a plan in place should it blow up in their faces. Everyone was trying to get an edge, and get noticed more than their rivals for all the right reasons, and none of the wrong. Problem is, you can't always call the public mood or reactions, which can snowball, despite your best guesses and pushes.

Home that night, I was mulling over my approach to the cheesy romance that Theresa was getting into. I jotted down a few ideas, a few things to make the story a bit more interesting without leaving the genre, nor conforming exactly to it, the bane of most writers. Well, not all, but a lot. Many successful novelists find a niche that works and they keep mining the same vein in every conceivable way. Hence the cheesy aspect of the made-for-TV romance. I hated that approach and feared I was moving in that direction. I reminded myself that it was popular, and for me, just an exercise to break my writer's block.

And so, I began writing.

Chapter Three – Behind the Façade

I turned the car into a long driveway and was instantly confronted with sculpted ponds and lawns, framed by large trees. Trimmed topiary appeared as I approached the main building. Not far from the city, this Inn catered to an exclusive clientele.

As an event organizer, I was there to stage manage a fashion show. This show featuring both clothing and jewelry. In my capacity, on top of the runway section of the show, I had to arrange the red carpet, the food and drink, manage the press, and set up speaking introductions for the designers and the models. It was going to be a busy weekend despite all the preparation I'd already done. Virtually everything was complete, media accredited and only the small tidbits remained.

The Inn sported a golf course, tennis courts as well as a small lake for water sports. There was ample time for most of the participants to take advantage of these amenities, but not me, as I was scrambling to fill in the gaps in my research, and write it into notes and show introductions that worked for the clients.

I'd been to the Inn before and couldn't help but notice the lobby had been redone, gone was the more rustic approach, changed to a modern, clean and classic vibe. I checked in, and sought out the principal sponsor of the show to make sure everything was proceeding to plans. I required a final list of all who would take part, including room numbers and contact information. I had 36 hours to speak to everyone, from the sponsors to the designers and models. There were to be three shows. One of stylish but comfortable clothing. Another of more urban designs particularly suited to the office, and a third which incorporated the jewelry accents into the apparel.

I set to work immediately and managed to get a serious head start on my interviews that afternoon. I was comfortable with my approach as I'd done this before. I knew I could meet the deadlines, as most of the background work was done.

I sat down to dinner in the Inn's dining room, by myself. I had tried to get an interview with the show's main sponsor set for this time, but they declined as they were hosting a cocktail party for the designers and models. I thought maybe I would get an invitation but I did not.

Sitting down alone at dinner I had my notes and scribbled some preliminary remarks for formal speeches by the red carpet and catwalk host and emcee. It crossed my mind that I had taken on too much, hosting the event, organizing it and doing most of the post event editorial for the magazine write ups.

In truth the sponsor was the host, I was really the stage manager. The sponsor's hired face would do the actual public speaking, introductions and light commentary as the models took the stage.

I faced a busy evening and early morning collecting the last quotes and tidbits of information for the show and the following press release. Dinner was light as I had decided to crash the cocktail party in order to do my job. While I hadn't received a formal invitation, they hadn't barred my attendance.

Dressed in my finest little black dress, a look I could still carry off, I strutted into the reception room as if I owned it, a tiny voice recorder and miniature notebook tucked into my clutch.

I mingled at first, getting a sense of the room and where everyone was that I needed to speak to. My first few interviews were discreet, as I mentioned who I was and what I needed to know. Catching my quarries alone was the trick and telling them I needed them only for a brief minute. I managed to get much of what I needed before I was approached by a tall guy in a tuxedo.

"Miss Abernathy?"

I nodded. I had decided to be bold, so now I had to fill myself up with bluster.

"I'm afraid I'm going to have to ask you to refrain from collecting information from the guests."

"I'm being as discrete as I can. I require this information for the catwalk tomorrow afternoon. There is very little time to get it."

"I understand, but several of the designers have pointed out that the press was not invited to this affair. They feel unprepared and somewhat ambushed."

"And for that I am sorry, but I am not the press. Not strictly, anyway. I am show staff and I'm preparing information for the catwalk announcements and the follow up press release of the event."

"I understand. However, please stop for tonight and I can help you make any arrangements tomorrow morning for anything else you require." He smiled and his eyes widened, looking for cooperation, with a tilt of his head. I decided I did not need a revolt by the show's subjects so I agreed.

I told him I would remain without asking any questions and would leave if I could not get anything I needed. Rather than cause a scene, he nodded, saying he would meet me at breakfast to facilitate anything I needed.

I mingled a few more minutes but without the direct approach I was unable to get the details I needed. The next morning, I rose early and sought him out. Looking first in the lobby and then in the hallways leading to the pool, weight rooms and breakfast room. I found him on my second look through the lobby.

"Ah, there you are." I handed him a short list of people I need to speak to, explaining my requirements.

"Perfect. I will require all this information to be written up."

"You? Who are you?"

"I should have said, I am the Master of Ceremonies at the catwalk events."

I rolled my eyes. "Really? I'm busting my butt to get this information, and the guy who needs it, is making my job more difficult?"

He bowed his head a touch. "I am sorry. My boss asked me to do the event and said the background information would be provided. That is standard procedure. I've done this before."

Despite my exasperation, he wasn't wrong. I took a deep breath and decided to get a bite to eat, telling him we could plot our process as we ate. "The people I need to speak to can have a few more minutes before I start."

I sat down with a tea and a few croissants. "I'm a bit run off my feet. You'll have to forgive me but your boss significantly enlarged the show from what I had initially signed on for. Freelancing is hell sometimes."

"Oh, so you work for yourself. I thought you were an employee of the magazine."

"I've done these shows before. However, one catwalk session turned into three and the designers invited to the show pretty much tripled."

He picked up the sheet, giving it a quick scan. "Hey the top two are sitting over there. I'll go and see if we can talk to them now." He rose before I could object.

He beckoned me over and I asked forgiveness and managed to collect what I needed in only a couple of minutes. He scanned the dining room while I spoke to them, and once I was finished, we managed to knock three more off the list, which was now pretty short.

He offered to contact the last few on the list and tell them they were needed for a quick info session in the dining room, if I would wait.

Pretty soon the job was complete. He seemed to have an easy way with the participants and was able to coax them into quick interviews at will. I thanked him and left for my room, where I would add the gathered information to my notes and start crafting the formal remarks.

Not long after I set up at the room's desk, there was a knock on the door.

He held two coffees. "I thought maybe you could use a coffee and perhaps my help setting up the notes, especially since I'm the one speaking." He gave me a crooked grin.

I was momentarily miffed, completely unprepared for this twist, "Okay, I suppose that's a good idea."

I motioned for him to push another chair to the desk and I started in on the agenda. "Here are your opening remarks," I pushed a page at him. "Here is a shout out to your boss and the lesser sponsors," And I pushed another page. "And here are the notes on each designer and model. My plan was to do a little introduction of each designer at the beginning of their models portion of the show. And then to follow up with a short introduction of each model. I know that's unconventional, but there are some famous models here, and a quick mention of their careers is a nice touch."

"That is a nice touch. Can I read them all through. I am going to make some suggestions as I read because I want it to sound authentic and natural."

I must have grimaced. "You don't want me sounding like a twenty-something freelance press agent, do you?"

"Aren't you the charmer."

"Sorry, I guess. I was just trying a little levity. You know, humour. It's nice sometimes."

"I'm on a deadline. I will leave the levity to you. I guess it's funny that I'm doing your work."

"Hey, I've helped. And don't forget, you took the assignment and I have only been told I was to take on the MC role, two days ago."

"Okay, okay. I'm sorry. I'm just feeling a bit of pressure."

"And I have tried to relieve that pressure by setting up this mornings' interviews and coming by to help."

"There would have been less pressure if I could have finished last night."

"That was not my call. I just did what the boss-man asked."

"You could have explained the situation."

"I didn't know it."

"You did once I told you."

"Okay, okay. You are right, I am a cad. Can we put it all behind us now?"

"Okay a little levity is good," I said. "And I'm not a twenty-something."

"A career girl? I had you pegged as a model want-to-be. You know, get a job in the industry and hope to get noticed."

I must have blushed, and I wanted to retort, but could not think of a snappy comeback. He took my silence as an affirmation of his characterization. I felt I had to say something.

"I'll take that as a compliment, but no, I was in the hard news business and was shuffled out for the flavour of the month, a few years ago. Media is brutal, especially for women, so I took up some freelance work. And here I am. And what about you. Set up as a pretty-boy, doing his masters bidding without thinking?"

"Okay, I deserved that. Actually, I have been a model from time to time. Mostly when they are desperate on short notice. I'm not the right body type, or so I'm told."

"So you are, what you accused me of being?"

"You could see it that way. But I had no intention of getting into that end of the business. I was a finance major in school and landed in the industry due to family connections. My uncle is Yves Dellarosa."

"Your uncle?"

"My mother's older brother. He has no children so I am being groomed to head up the business."

"Are you a designer?"

"No. Making the grooming difficult. I am a businessman. I can hire designers. We learned that in school."

"Wow. Okay. Wow." I had to shake this new knowledge through my brain cells. "Are we done here? I have a number of other things to do before the show."

"Okay, let me read through these and I'll let you know if I think we have to make changes. Or do you want me to wing it?" He leaned back in the chair. "I'm familiar with this stuff as my uncle wants me to try everything associated with the business."

"Are you sure you can handle it? Standing in front of a crowd throws some people. They freeze."

"I think I'll be okay. I've had to speak at board meetings. And standing up in front of a bunch of people who have money invested and ideas of their own can be intimidating."

"When you have to make the decisions, it can be."

"You are right there; my uncle is still fully in charge."

"Well, I have to go," I said. "Things to check on, remember?" He looked at me oddly. "And this is my room."

"Oh, oh yeah. I'll just go to my own room. I'm in 455 should you need me."

He left and I sat down to make a list of the things I needed to check on in the three hours before showtime.

It did not take long to make the rounds to see that everything was in place for the show. And after it was over, I just had to fashion a press release featuring the new designs and a magazine article. That reminded me I needed to check on the photographer.

As showtime approached, I hadn't heard from the MC, whose name I had forgotten to ask, so I assumed that everything was in place from his end.

With the show about to start, he strode up to me, behind the stage curtain. "Ah, there you are. The lectern is just outside the curtain, stage right?"

I nodded, "Everything in the notes is okay?"

"Yup. I made a few very minor changes, so it sounds more natural coming from a guy."

"Okay." I looked at my watch. "Just about ready. Five minutes people," I said with whatever authority I could muster while keeping my voice down. Activity behind the curtain was hot, with models in temporary cubicles fashioned from office dividers, and carts of clothing being wheeled up to each space. Each one had a show listing and the cubicles were arranged in order of appearance.

A peek through the curtain showed the room was almost filled. I wanted to see the reactions of the audience to the show, so I could weave it into the follow up communications. Back stage was not ideal for this, but I had to stay as I would certainly be called upon to help the models as they made their way through the stage and back to the change rooms. And if there were issues, they would occur there.

"Okay, here I go." He nodded and stepped out through curtain, moving to the right side of the stage. The crowd noise lessened and then stopped altogether.

"Good afternoon. I'm Piero D'Antonio your Master of Ceremonies for today. I'd like to welcome our designers, Yves Dellarosa, Pierre Cartu, Marcasi and Sons, and Carl Huvon." There was a polite round of applause. "As you know there are three portions to this event. Clothing for comfort and style, urban wear and our designer's fancy, incorporating pieces from our dream collections with jewelry from our partners.

Piero launched into a bio of his uncle as the curtains opened to a painted street scene out of some nameless European city. Some of the paint was still wet, which gave it a glistening tone, like a recent rain, rather than tipping off the audience that we'd only barely met the deadline for set construction.

The first model emerged from the left side of the stage, and began her walk, as Piero described the clothing, its use while stylishly conducting one's daily routines, shopping, meeting friends or touring galleries.

'A far cry from my life,' I thought.

Piero mentioned the model's previous work and hometown, including a show or magazine cover highlight. He went through the entire show in much the same manner, as the models paraded up the catwalk into the crowd, posed in several configurations and walked back down the raised walkway to exit on the right side of the stage. The pandemonium behind the stage was managed perfectly and I thought to look in once or twice, to make sure everything was working in perfect synch.

In the audience I noted the presence of a famous movie director, and a couple of producers, whose faces would be unknown to the general public, but who had enormous influence in putting movies together, especially on choosing the stars.

The room was dotted with a few B list stars, and a couple of well-known character actors, there to be seen mingling with the smart set.

Peiro announced a short break before the second portion of the show began.

"So, how'd I do, boss lady?" he asked. He wore a finely tailored grey suit with a subtle dark grey tie.

I gave him a veiled look. "You've done this before. You lied to me."

"Lied. That's a bit dramatic, isn't it?"

"Perhaps. But you let me believe you'd never done this before. A bit of honesty would have saved me a lot of worry."

"Don't worry about me."

"I was worried about me. A major mistake falls on my head."

"You are right. Let me take you to dinner tonight to make up to you."

I was caught off guard and all I could do was nod before turning away.

The rest of the show went perfectly and I knew I had Piero to thank, as his delivery was flawless and his mastery of timing obvious. Fortunately, there was no drama with the models, who all managed to stay upright and on the stage. Sometimes these makeshift stages were uneven and difficult for the models to do their dramatic strut.

Piero even managed to inject a bit of humor into his descriptions of the clothes in the final stage of the event, where the designers paid heed to their whims. Piero did explain that many of the whimsical clothes were really tests of fabric and designs for use in future pieces. Nobody was going to wear a dress with shoulders four feet across, but the fabric and design elements that kept those shoulders in place might be used later. Some in the audience nodded.

As the show ended and the designers and models mingled backstage after taking their curtain calls, Piero whispered in my ear that he would come to my room to fetch me at 7 pm.

I had to put my press release out and so spoke to his uncle as lead sponsor, for some thoughts about the show.

He provided the usual comments and I pushed for a bit more. “Piero did a wonderful job as MC,” I said.

“Yes, he does that. A very capable boy.”

“Your sister must be proud of him.” He looked at me oddly.

“Yes, Katerina. She is dutifully proud of him. I think she wanted him to be a doctor but the boy is a born salesman. It’s not the most glamourous job nor the most dignified. But success lies in sales, even if nobody wants to admit it.”

“Well, I thought he was very professional. Experienced. A natural.”

Dellarosa nodded and excused himself to speak with another designer who had been waiting for us to finish.

Back in my room, I was getting ready after issuing the press release, when a knock came on the door. Through the peephole I saw a messenger, who confirmed he had a note for me.

I took the note and apologized that I had no cash for a tip as I had not been expecting anything. He nodded curtly, saying he was an employee of the Inn, and not to worry. I expected some sort of service charge would be added to my bill.

'A change of plans. Meet me in the lobby at seven.' Piero.

I had not given any thought to where we might go for dinner, vaguely thinking we'd stay at the Inn.

Half an hour later I arrived in the lobby to see Piero talking with his uncle and another man and two women. They were very much dressed up and I was not. I moved toward the group and Piero said something to Dellarosa, who turned to look at me.

"No, no, that will not do, my dear. Go back upstairs and make a quick change. We can wait," said Dellarosa. He turned and spoke to Piero, "Didn't you tell her where we are going?"

Piero muttered something and without further instruction I quickly headed for the elevator. Before the elevator came, I turned back around, I realized I had not come prepared for an elegant dinner. I told Piero.

Dellarosa cut in, "Piero, just get one of the dresses from the second portion of the show. How about the blue one?" He looked at me, "No, not blue, the red one. Yes, that will suit her much better."

Piero shooed me to my room and promised to deliver a dress. I had not been waiting for more than a moment when there was a knock at the door. Piero stook waiting with a long, elegant, fiery red dress, over his arm.

"How do you know it will fit?"

"My uncle chose it. It will fit. I will wait for you in the hallway."

I quickly donned the dress, touched up my make-up to match the red and met Piero waiting in a chair at the elevator. "Look, I have to be straight with you. I mentioned this dinner with you, and my uncle insisted we join his party. The other man is his chief tailor and the two women, are their wives, the taller is my Aunt Bella."

"Bella? She looks familiar."

"She should. She is the former Bella D'Antonio, fashion model. Some would say, icon."

"She has your last name, but she is your Aunt?"

"Yes, my mother, Dellarosa's sister, married her brother. It's a close-knit family."

"Okay," I said slowly as I tried to put it all together. "So where are we going for dinner?"

"My uncle's favorite restaurant is in the city. Walden's is a three star and has been on the Michelin list forever."

"Isn't that the top tier?"

"It is. My uncle says they should have fourth tier and Walden's would be on it."

"What makes it so special?"

"You'll see."

We arrived in the lobby and a limousine was waiting for us. Dellarosa simply nodded at Piero when we first arrived, but I thought I detected a hint of a smile as he directed us to the waiting car. Once we were all seated in the limousine, facing each other, introductions were made all around.

"Piero has told us about you, my dear," said Aunt Bella. "You took on quite a task with today's show, and managed it wonderfully."

"Thank you, I said, declining my head. I did not want to talk about me and was content to listen to conversations that I was normally not privy to. They had other ideas, as I was the newest thing. They focussed on me, as there was nothing new or novel between them.

Piero could sense my discomfort and asked them to stop the interrogation.

"Now Piero, we need to know more about this young lady that you've taken to."

And Piero blushed, not expecting such a direct appraisal of his previous conversations with his uncle and aunt. He changed the subject rather awkwardly.

"So have you been to Walden's before?" Dellarosa asked me.

"Actually, no. I'd never even heard of it until about 10 minutes ago." Perhaps not the most politic thing to say, but honest.

"I hope you like it, my dear. It's long been my favorite. You can order off menu if you'd like. They know me."

"I think its because they know Aunt Bella," said Piero, with a smile.

We arrived at the restaurant and were swept inside, greeted like family, and taken to an elevator to a smaller dining room and a table overlooking the city. I recognized several famous faces at some of the other tables but managed to keep my mouth shut and my eyes averted. I figured wide -eyed shock was a poor approach.

Dellarosa nodded to a few tables and stopped only once to say hello, but I did not recognize anyone at that table. As Dellarosa spoke to his friend, I followed Piero's lead and moved off, heading to our table near a high corner window.

I was in far over my head and almost wanted to roll up into a cocoon. Aunt Bella saw my discomfort.

"Yves always mixes business with pleasure, I'm afraid," said Bella. "It's his biggest vice and perhaps the key to his success."

The waiters appeared moments after we sat down, placing a few appetizers on the table and enquiring about something to drink, while promising menus once we were settled.

I was content with water and the waiter nodded, eventually bringing a bottled water that I'd never heard of. Bella asked for champagne and Piero hesitated a moment but decided on water as well.

The elder Dellarosa sat down, and told us that his friend was in town for a large charity affair, and was unaware of the fashion show.

"Sarah, I hope you are hungry, as Walden's specializes in appetizers. We will order several and after that, the main course. They are widely known for their lobster seafood alfredo and their choice cuts of beef."

"Thank you so much for inviting me. I am still processing Piero's skill as the Master of Ceremonies. He was wonderfully able and very professional, though he claims he hasn't done much of it before."

"Piero has a number of latent talents that seem to pop up at opportune times. He tells me it's the finance training, as they had to do mock business presentations and learned a range of sales techniques."

Bella beamed and seemed ready to say something but Piero interjected, "As I've said Uncle Yves, if you take advantage of the opportunities presented to you, you can stretch your comfort zone and skill set. At school, so many of the students saw their courses as something to conquer rather than something that would push them."

"And Sarah? Piero says you were in media before moving into the fashion industry."

"I was. I loved that world, as everyday is a new day and few things repeat themselves. Though I must confess after a time I tired of reporting on the things other people were doing, and seemingly doing nothing of substance myself."

"You left the business?"

"No, it left me. Media has a way of chewing up and spitting out people, especially women. And with new media, there is a constant erosion of the old ways, resulting in a short shelf life for most of us.'

"Aye," said Yves, "I've seen some of that as my safe old media contacts have disappeared."

"So now you do freelance things, like our show?"

I nodded, "Things like this show require a lot of hours to get right and some experience in the industry. A lot of background work goes into the public stream of information. Piero helped me gather some of that at the last minute."

I found myself trying each of the half dozen appetizers that were presented to the table, especially after the first one was so delicious. When it came time to order dinner I deferred.

"You must have something dear. Steak or seafood?"

"I really can't. I am already so full."

"Seafood for the young lady please," Bella said to a waiter. "Just a very small portion and cut off a slice of my prime rib for her to try." The waiter nodded.

"You will enjoy them both, and if you have a bit of mine, you will help me as I too am rather content with the appetizers."

"Now that the show has ended, where are you headed next?" I asked.

Bella looked at Yves, and Piero cleared his throat, "I believe Uncle Yves has some business to conduct here in New York and then he is headed to another show in Los Angeles."

That comment hung in the air long enough to become uncomfortable.

"I will be going as well," said Bella, "but Piero is remaining in New York a few more days and then, I believe, he will head for home."

Piero nodded. Yves nodded.

"And where is home?" I asked.

"Italy for us," said Bella. "Our main residence is about an hour from Milan."

"And for me," Piero said, "I am currently homeless as I've been on the road on business trips for a long time. I guess, I'm headed to my family home in Venice."

Bella sighed deeply. "I have told you Piero, that you need a home base. All this wandering worries me, and your mother."

"There seems little point to buying a home that I will hardly ever use. I will sometime, but for now, I can use company residences in various places that I'm likely to be, and I've always got my old room in Venice in between trips."

I was lost in the swirl of travel, thinking it all quite glamourous but seeing beneath the façade to the practical things in life, knowing the transitory nature of such a life was difficult and more than a little exhausting.

"You must collect quite a few air miles," I said, trying to find a light touch.

"Actually, most of my business is in the United States and while I do fly most of the time, I like to drive through the country when I have the opportunity. The USA is huge and empty. If I'm not here, I'm usually in Paris or Milan."

We finished the meal and the limo took us to their hotel. I noted they had stayed in the city rather than the Inn. Yves directed the driver to take me where ever I wanted to go. Piero said he would accompany me to ensure I arrived safely. He had a room at the Inn, but I wondered if maybe that was just for show needs.

Once we had made our goodbyes and I had thanked the older couple many times and wished them success in Los Angeles, the door closed and

I breathed a deep exhalation. Piero smiled, "You handled yourself beautifully, well, except for the question of our next adventure. I had quite forgotten how different our lives are from normal people."

"I did sense a bit of discomfort at the question."

"Similar to my discomfort now, as I have to direct the driver where to take you."

"Oh, oh, Upper West Side please, 39 West 74th Street."

"That's not far from the Museum."

"It's a nice neighbourhood, close to the Park and a quick subway ride to most places I need to be."

"Have you been to the Museum?"

"Oh, yeah, but not for a long time now."

"We should go. I have most of the afternoon off tomorrow. I have never been."

I hesitated, but thought, why not?

"Okay," I said rather timidly. "I have an appointment in the late morning. I can meet you at the main entrance at 2 p.m."

Peiro nodded, "Perfect. I will be there."

The limousine rolled through the always crowded streets of New York from the midtown hotel where we had dropped Yves and Bella. A few people turned to look, but most people were used to fancy cars and didn't take notice.

"I have a meeting with the show sponsors tomorrow. Necessary stuff, I'm afraid."

"Me too," I blurted out. "They want to know that everything was done up to specs."

"Your meeting must be after mine. Why don't we meet at the Inn, since we will both be there, and maybe I can take you out to lunch before we go to the museum?"

"That makes too much sense,' I said. "Okay."

We turned the corner of Broadway onto 74th Street and I pointed out my building. Well, thank you for an eye-opening evening. It just occurred to me that my things are still at the Inn."

"Get them tomorrow before your meeting, and I can arrange to put them in the car."

"Okay, until tomorrow." And I slipped out of the car quickly, headed for the stairs of my brownstone and gave a quick wave as the limo began to roll away. Up the lift to my apartment on the third floor and I sat down heavily, only then remembering I was wearing one of the gowns from the show. My friends would never believe my day, or maybe two days, as tomorrow promised its own memories.

I arrived at the hotel mid morning and looked in on the ball room. It had been completely cleaned and changed over night, ready for the next event. I decided to get a coffee in the hotel restaurant after I had gathered my things and checked out. I sipped at my coffee with two bags at my feet, thinking of where I could store them, should Piero fail to show up. Then I remembered I had my little car in the parking lot. The previous evening seemed like a dream.

Just as I was becoming anxious, Piero appeared and sat down. "Do I have time for a coffee?"

"I have half an hour before my meeting, sure if you want."

He returned and shortly a porter arrived at our table, "Please take these bags to my car."

I must have looked relieved, "It might not have been a good look to take those into my meeting. And oh, the dress is in one of them. Remind me to give it to you."

"Don't worry about the dress. My gift to you. You looked quite fetching in it."

"Fetching? Well, thanks, I guess."

Piero mentioned that his Aunt and Uncle were still in the city at a business meeting, but he had begged off. They had been a bit nonplussed at that, until they found out why.

I headed to a suite to conduct my post-mortem on the show. It all went very well, especially when the sponsors heard me mention my conversations with Yves and Bella Dellarosa. The models were happy, the designers pleased, the sponsors keen to redo the event the next year and apparently Dellarosa, the biggest sponsor, had commended my efforts. I spoke up for Piero's skill as an MC, and said the press releases had been sent and press kits distributed. Any follow up would go directly to the specific designers.

Peiro was waiting for me in the lobby. He enquired after the meeting, and indicated the car was waiting outside. We were whisked to the front door of the museum. We toured the various exhibits including the famous gem room. The museum was much more interactive than I had remembered it.

Piero suggested we go to dinner after the museum. A quaint Italian pizzeria and family restaurant was only a block or two away and we enjoyed a bit of downscale New York. At least to him. For me, the Pizzeria was a once a season kind of place. Very nice without being too over the top.

He offered to walk me back to my apartment and as we arrived, I noticed his car glide up.

"Well Sarah, I have enjoyed our afternoon together. May I call you next time I am in New York?"

"Yes, of course. As a freelancer, I'm always looking for the next gig."

He frowned. "I have enjoyed your company. I am required in LA or I would stretch my time in New York." I gave him my business card explaining there was no formal office, the phone number was mine.

And with that, he turned and got into the car without so much as a wave. Perhaps I'd insulted him. I wasn't sure, and while I wished our parting had been more amiable, I could not help but think my presence was only a passing fancy to him, as he lived in a different world.

The car rolled away and I stood on the sidewalk feeling odd, like something important had brushed by me, only to slip away again, unacknowledged. I shrugged and walked up the brownstone steps, wondering if I'd ever hear from him. Given his business itinerary I figured it would be many months, if at all.

And so, I was surprised to hear from him two nights later. He called to chat about the Los Angeles show and share a laugh about one of the models tripping on the makeshift stage.

"I think she was a bit out of her element," he said, "she caught her heel on the hem of her dress, and it tore slightly and caused her to fall."

"That's not funny, Piero. She must have been mortified."

"Actually, that's when I knew she was a professional. She bounced up, smoothed her dress with one subtle pass and continued on her way. A little bit less exaggerated in her step, perhaps."

"Other than that, the show went well?"

"Yes, indeed. But LA shows are much different from New York. The models are more on display, the whole red-carpet thing is big in LA. The designers are decidedly less prominent. My Uncle mentioned it. He wondered if your approach could be accomplished in California?"

"I'm sure it could, but I don't know anyone out there well enough to recommend."

"Is it necessary that they be local?"

"It sure helps. Contacts are good to grease the editorial wheel and they help things go smoother, especially when there are last minute fixes."

"I'm going to be back in New York in a week. Can we meet so I can pick your brain on this?"

"Sure, let me know the day and I'll try to keep it open."

A week later I received a message to meet Piero at a mid-town restaurant. I was surprised at the last-minute approach. I told him I was expecting a call, so I was unavailable until after 8 pm. As usual his limo pulled up to my apartment and he escorted me to a lovely restaurant at the top of a non-descript skyscraper not far from Wall Street.

We chatted mostly about California and the whole way of life there. I had some experience with the place as I'd vacationed there and had a few assignments in San Francisco in my media days. He never once spoke of the LA show or any organization.

I returned home not entirely sure what had happened.

The next morning Piero called and asked for a lunch as he'd forgotten to speak of the LA show details. I begged off having a business meeting at 1 pm. He suggested the next day, and we met at a place he knew just south of the Park.

I arrived, a bit surprised to not be driven, and he was already there waiting for me at a table. He rose and greeted me and motioned me to sit, saying he was just back in the city after a day trip to Miami for a meeting. Asking after my recent few days he launched into a recitation of the menu, almost as if he had worked there at one time.

We spoke of the Los Angeles show and Piero expressed concerns about the way the press was handled.

"We had nothing in the papers, and there was decidedly no buzz. One of the local LA television stations had a single camera there and posted 10 seconds of video on the late news. That was it."

"What about notables? Who was there?"

"All the usual designers. We had mostly picked up the New York show and took it to LA."

"Not the designers, silly, the stars, the famous faces. Who was there?"

"Oh, you see? I don't think like you do. In fact, there were a few people there that I'd seen before."

"Like in movies? Television?"

"Yes, maybe at Cannes."

"Okay, that's a start. Though, Cannes does not impress Angelinos."

"My uncle was unhappy and came to the conclusion that our publicity staff in Italy is simply unequipped to handle our North American business."

Then Piero slipped into a discussion about South Beach in Miami. I had been there, in fact I'd done press for a celebrity golf tournament there, something which perked Piero up.

"So you know the golfers and the local personalities in Florida?"

"I wouldn't go that far, but I have had some exposure. Frankly, it isn't hard to get a bunch of men to play golf with the professionals. Even the famous guys are star struck, on both sides."

"How did the press go?"

"Same thing really. You get a bunch of well-known celebrities playing golf with golf celebrities and the press run to you. The charity aspect gives those events a lot of shine. The press loves it when you are not flogging something, at least not directly."

Piero mused. Our meals were served and Piero asked after my family. And I his, especially his mother to whom he seemed close and far away at the same time.

"She loves it when I come to Venice. But sometimes I feel like I'm 12 years old again. But there is no way I'm going to take down my poster of Buffon, my all time favorite."

"Buffon?"

"Gianluigi Buffon, the greatest keeper in the World, at least when I was a boy."

"Ah so he was a soccer player?"

"Football, the beautiful game, and he was the best. A maestro. I should take you to a match. You would quickly see the poetry of football."

Piero admitted he as a fan of several sports, but none so passionately as soccer, er ah, football. He asked me if I had any mad passions, especially as a child.

"No, not really. I was a dancer. Though mostly because my parents felt I should pursue something. I tried a bit of music but I was unwilling to put in the time. Too often the music comes from the collective group and each player only contributes a little bit. The joy is in the melody or the fullness of the music which one person really cannot achieve."

"It's sort of like that in all team sports. One of the reasons I preferred tennis as a teenager."

"Where you good?"

"Yes. Yes, I was. But only good locally, among my peers. And for me that was okay, I had no passion for beating people I did not know. My mother pushed me to compete in some All-Italia tournaments, but I was crushed, beaten soundly, and it wasn't my lack of skill, it was my lack of interest in getting better, because I really felt I was as good as I wanted to be."

Piero dropped me back at my apartment and said he was back to Italy for a few days and then in London before coming back to New York.

"Why don't you come meet me in London? You could use a holiday. And I could use a companion. Someone to help kill the boredom."

"With sales skills like that you will go far, Piero."

He flushed and blurted out an apology. He said he'd been to London so many times there was nothing new to him there. When I said I'd never been, he was insistent that I meet him there.

And so I found myself on a plane 10 days later heading for Heathrow. Piero was there to meet me and we took a cab to his hotel where he had a suite, giving me a room of my own.

He shook his head, when he saw me, "Why did you book the over-night flight? You should have let me do it for you."

"It made sense at the time. Getting here first thing in the morning sounded good. Wilted like a week-old daisy is not what I expected." He laughed but sported the necessary sympathetic expression.

"I've been in meetings for the last two days and have three days without anything, before a couple of follow up meetings before we head back to New York."

I nodded, struck dumb by the effects of jet lag. I had not slept well on the flight.

"That's standard," he said with a grin. "Now just like I said, you have to do anything necessary to stay up until at least 9 pm then you will sleep like a baby and wake up without a trace of jet lag."

We decided to take in the less strenuous sights as my brain was not up to processing anything too complicated. Piero obviously took great joy in showing me things for the first time.

The three days were a whirlwind. And the last two very nice for me as I was able to retrace my steps and see some things again, in more detail, while Piero conducted his business obligations.

We flew back to New York, this time first class. A much more enjoyable trip that the overnighter I'd come in on.

"Sarah, I've always wanted to go to a baseball game and an American Football game. Both New York teams are playing. I can easily get tickets; can I count on you to explain it to me?"

"I can try. Baseball is probably more up my alley. Football is a world unto itself."

"Baseball it is."

So we went to a baseball game, and I was beginning to wonder why Piero, seemed very interested in me, but had refrained from taking the next step.

We went to dinner after the game.

"Sarah, my Uncle asked me to meet with you in the light of our experiences in Los Angeles." I nodded. "As you might understand the fashion business is, at its heart, run by families. It's so cutthroat that the designers like my uncle rise to prominence and only trust close relations to manage the affairs of their world-wide businesses."

"And that's why you work for him and are going to take over the business at some point," I said.

"Yes, yes, that's it exactly. My own mother is a fabric buyer for Dellarosa, and two of my cousins are involved in manufacture and sales. We are no different from the other designers, most of whom pick one or two relations for their public face, but actually have many more in key positions out of the public eye."

"So, you are about to take over the company?"

"In time. My uncle has already moved into a designer emeritus position, having elevated two family members to manage that part of the business as he teaches them and maintains the last word on new projects. He is very much interested in his legacy and the continuity of the company."

"He seemed very much in control during the show here last month."

'And he still is, that's why he asked me to speak with you."

The waiter approached and asked if we were ready to order.

"My uncle wants you to accept a position as Public Communications Officer of Dellarosa House."

"Wait, what?"

Piero slowly slid back in his chair, allowing me a moment to collect my thoughts. I had not expected his offer, rather expecting he was going to tell me he'd been transferred to Europe or maybe permanently posted to the United States.

"But I thought the fashion houses all relied on family?"

"They do."

Now I've not had a concussion before, but I've imagined it would be similar to my state of mind at that moment. I did not want to take any leap that would embarrass us both. It was obvious that Piero and I got on quite well. Things between us had been natural and comfortable, but that was because it had never occurred to me that he was anything more than a friend. In some ways I felt that he enjoyed the juxtaposition of our lifestyles. Not that he was showy, more that he liked the less formal approach his uncle demanded and he liked sharing luxury. And I still wasn't sure, as we lived in different worlds. I was too stunned to say anything, which was probably a good thing.

"Sarah, I have very much enjoyed our time together. However, my business schedule is heavy and pursuing you in an ordinary way would take many months. I propose you take the job with no expectations. If things work out, wonderful. And if they do not, then we can remain friends."

"Piero, I like you very much, but this is all a bit too much. We haven't even kissed yet."

"That can be rectified easily."

"Where would I be based? How often would we be together? What about my other freelance contracts?"

"Accept the arrangement and we can begin to answer those questions." He leaned over to kiss me. It wasn't awkward, but it seemed like a necessary step to be accomplished.

This was not what I had imagined. I had crossed the threshold but I had little idea of what was behind the door.

Chapter Four

Theresa put it down.

I took another sip of my coffee.

She looked at me and I stared back at her.

"Well?"

"There are several ways to go about this."

"Go on."

Theresa smiled ruefully, "I know you want the truth but I have to know if you will pursue this story based on what I say."

"I don't know, it depends on what you say."

"Fair enough. You are not a romance author."

I laughed, "You think? I knew that before I started."

"Where is all the description of how tall and handsome he is? His chiselled features. And how beautiful she is when she dresses up for dinner."

"Romance can only happen to beautiful people?"

"In books, yes. Remember you are trying to sell it. It's romance, it's not hyper realism."

"But that's not me. I'm trying to find my writer's voice, not copy some industry standard."

"Okay, sure. I thought you were trying to sell books? I think you ruined it right from the start. What if you took the idea seriously?"

"I can't. I just can't. The whole genre is a trope. I can't do it. I think I was looking to prove my point or alternatively, write a parody of the form."

"So, write a romance that isn't a trope romp."

"I can't put myself out there like that."

"Didn't Hemingway say something about bleeding on the page?"

"Yeah, yeah. But it's not bleeding. It's more like breaking your own heart.

I think that's why so much of this romance stuff is light hearted tropes, nothing too serious."

"Okay so if it isn't romance, what is the next thing you will try?"

I took the sheets of paper containing the romance story, folded them in half and put them in my bag. I couldn't take a chance that they would be lost and end up in the hands of some nefarious shyster.

"It doesn't really matter if I'm going to try them all."

"Really? That seems a bit too much, if all you are trying to do is find a good idea. Are you trying to have a go at the genres you are least comfortable in?"

"Well yeah, that's part of the exercise. But I will not end up in one of them with my next novel. I think I'm going to shake it up and go science fiction."

"That's a bit of a leap for you."

"A bit, I suppose, but it seems more open, more possibilities are there to break new ground."

Theresa laughed, "Break new ground? You said yourself that everything's been written a million times."

"I have a new approach," but I couldn't help but giggle at the absurdity. "I'm going to do an analysis of great novels and try to figure out what makes them great. Okay, I've already conducted my research and concluded it is good writing, quality characters, something novel, and a depth of approach."

"Oh, is that all?"

"Listen, I have an idea and I will bring it back to you when I have it completed. I'm just going for shortish stories, no length specified. Maybe just the opening of something longer."

Theresa nodded, and I asked her about her own fashion design plans.

"It's coming. I did something of what you did and tried to distill the essence of the home style I'm trying to find. Frankly I think it comes down to branding. A logo, a backstory maybe, you know, to push sales."

"Have you got anything yet?"

"I've tried a few and rejected them, so, no, but I'm somewhere down the line of the process."

"Suburban people have rebelled against city living. Try something rebellious."

"I thought of that, Theresea said. "But that is just a way of thinking that city people have. I want to brand from a suburban perspective."

"Suburbanites used to be city people."

"Not all of them. There are generations that have grown up in the burbs, you know. They don't think of themselves as rebels."

"Doesn't everybody want to be a rebel? Even the most straightlaced, conforming suburbanite must have a streak of rebel in them. What other approaches do you have?"

Theresea walked through a few ideas of branding approach, the outsider, the rebel, the conservative, the countryside, sporty, and a few more.

"You can't pick them all for a logo, and I would think that if you tried too hard to cram too many together you would end up with a hot mess."

"Precisely. So, I looked at successful product branding. Frankly a lot of it is simply repetition. But admittedly the best ones have a little style. Either in subject or in presentation. Hopefully when you show me the science fiction, I'll show you a logo."

Theresa was convinced that the logo would dictate the style and had not really tried to put anything together in the design.

I went home and decided to sit down and start writing. It was a dismal failure. I sat staring at the wall trying to center on something sciencey to riff on. Flying saucers, government knowledge of ETs, a new invention, they all flitted through my mind without catching fire.

How about a character, I thought, and went through the tropes of a mad scientist, a professor, a future man doing his future job, and came up empty.

Then I started . . .

Chapter Five – Science Fiction – Choose Your Overlords Wisely

Forget first contact, that had already happened, one cold and rainy September day, our governments broke the world. Or at least the world that had not really been paying attention.

An announcement was made that people on the Earth were not alone in the universe. Period. The President would follow up with more details in a television address the next morning, before taking questions from the media.

And each head of state, or government in every nation on Earth, did the same.

The world stood still. Various media quickly cobbled together all the near misses and near proofs that something was out there, and speculation was at a fever pitch regarding the details, through the media, on talk radio, in personal conversations and in the minds of virtually everyone on Earth. In the absence of little green men, it seemed that the media wanted to find out which of the thousands of UFO sightings were real.

Finally, at 10 am Eastern Time, from the Oval Office, the Presidential address began. And it began from 10 Downing Street at 3 pm London time, at 7 pm Moscow time from the Kremlin, 10 pm Beijing time from the Forbidden City and everywhere else in between at the co-ordinated moment. Of course, the President explained all this, as Presidential addresses were usually done in the evening.

"My fellow Americans, this announcement is being delivered to everyone on Earth at the same time, through their national leaders. Permanent members of the United Nations security council, The United States, China, Russia, France and The United Kingdom have all been in contact with civilizations from other worlds since the end of World War Two.

"These civilizations are obviously more technologically advanced than we are, given their ability to travel the huge distances of interstellar space. They have been adamant that their existence should remain undisclosed, until now. It may be noted that our level of technology has grown significantly since 1945. We have also, mostly successfully, managed to work out our differences and philosophic approaches to governance and societal norms. Everyone has acceded to accept capitalism and citizen input at some level. This was a necessary requirement of our visitors before the truth could be known.

"There are three Extra-terrestrial civilizations that have made contact with us. They are all aware of each other and co-exist in peace. They want us to choose among them, which civilization we would like to join.

"Much more detail will come later, to explain historical incidents and encounters. But for the purposes of this announcement, know that a non -binding, World Wide plebiscite will be conducted approximately one year from now, to help determine which off-world civilization we should join.

"While much more background will be presented in the near future, I will now outline the nature of these civilizations. All are peaceful, having long ago understood that peace and understanding are preferable to violence.

"One of them identify as "The First" in our language, as they have determined that their civilization is the oldest they have encountered. They fully expect that their understanding of their origins will continue to evolve and that perhaps they will find an older civilization. Among the three groups they are the most inclined to exploration, science and knowledge.

"Another civilization would be called 'Neighbours' in our language. They are centered not far from Earth on a star system about 30 light years away. They are the most similar biologically, and consist of a number of settled worlds of similar beings. They believe their civilization was seeded by some spacefaring culture in the past, with the plan of creating a larger multi-planet civilization in their future. That has occurred.

"The third group is 'The One' or 'The Singularity' in our language. Their primary interest is finding the centre, the start of the universe, believing that finding that, will lead to a complete understanding of all things.

"It's important to know that all three of these civilisations are broad and wide, their nature is simply a way to identify them, as they are broadly concerned with all things, the potential of our species, the nature of our concerns, the broad improvement of living and understanding.

"Which ever of these civilizations we choose to join, it will have an effect on the singular approach to our future development as we seek to bring ourselves up to their level of achievement. That goal will likely take a few generations of human lives to manage. I encourage everyone to consider this choice carefully. Do your due diligence on these civilizations, and understand that your voice, however small, matters.

“Thank you, and may whatever god you worship, bless you. I will take questions from the media in the Blue Room in 30 minutes, giving everyone some time to digest this news.”

For the first time in human history, there was a moment of complete global silence, before a cacophony of voices began to chatter, though nobody really noticed the profundity of it, separated by miles and oceans.

“Well, now they know,” said Marshall Everet, CEO of Global Defence Contractors, sitting in his boardroom high above Manhattan. “And our business is dead. I hope everyone here was able to cash in their shares and options months ago.”

“They know shit,” said Kerry Hamil standing beside him. Hamil was Vice-Chair of GDC’s manufacturing business and a former Lieutenant Colonel. “They think they know. They know what the establishment wants them to know. And after the press conferences and future press conferences, and rounds of editorializing in the media, they will vote, still not really knowing.”

“One step at a time Kerry. We have to ease humanity into the next phase of our history.”

Hamil had expressed his disbelief to Marshall before.

“This is so huge it’s going to take a while to get every little thing squared away,” said Hamil. “They have to manage the malcontents who will scream that government cannot be trusted as this announcement is proof the government has been lying to us for decades, concealing vital information, and lying directly when questioned.”

“We’ve been over this. It’s all going to take time. There will be a fallow period for us, perhaps more than a few years. Bringing the real truth to light, the whole truth, is going to take time.”

"Don't forget, the fact that we know there is more to this, means that the government has already lied to the public, lied to them about telling the whole truth," said Hamil. "Yeah, yeah, it's got to be done in stages or the shock will crumble the whole enterprise. I fully expect that someone, somewhere will suggest a fourth alternative, that we simply opt out of any civilization."

Evert looked at Hamil with a touch of pity. "Stop fighting all the possible battles. Fight the one in front of you. Sometimes you outthink yourself."

Hamil smiled, "You aren't wrong. But I cannot help myself but to think ahead, you know, think of the implications and what they might mean."

"Shift to thinking how we can tank this company but still keep it ready for a revival when the time comes. Our key engineers are going to have to be retained and let in on the secret, at least in part. As for our workforce, unemployment insurance and the like will carry them over for a while, but perhaps not long enough. I think our plan, to shift our production from defence products into consumer stuff, cars, trucks, tools and the like, is a good approach."

"I know, we've already had this conversation, remember. I have some of those plans on my desk already. We will wait a bit so it doesn't appear that we had advance knowledge. A press release in a week saying we are looking at our options and hope to retain our employees should buy us some time."

Months went by with life continuing much as it had, though international concerns seemed to get ironed out and trade issues solved to everyone's satisfaction.

It was obvious that the referendum, slated for September 28, would return a fairly easy win for 'The Neighbours" civilization. While campaigning had been subtle, and all civilizations treated equally, the notion of aliens that were not too alien in appearance, and their central concern being the welfare of the general populace, was a winning formula. 'The First' and 'The One' seemed fixed on goals that were too esoteric for the population of Earth. Especially a population barely into the computer age.

"It's our nature to seek comfort," said Evert. " 'The Neighbours' will win easily, especially after the big alien reveal a few months ago. A lot of people were unnerved by that."

'The First' were tall, almost angelic beings. Bipedal, they had four eyes, two on the sides of their heads, creating stereoscopic vision almost in any direction. They were able to process the multiple views forward and back, without confusion. They also possessed the ability to speak to each other without verbal language.

'The One' were entirely alien in body stature. They had three 'legs' for motion and stability, but really functioned with two at any time. It gave them incredible speed and agility. They also had three appendages for manipulating their environment, something like arms and fingers. A pair of eyes in the front and a second in the back, meant that functionally, they had no front or back.

In contrast, 'The Neighbors' were very human in appearance, perhaps a bit taller on average than humans, and with larger, more oval heads. They possessed two arms, two legs and two eyes. They did have two hearts which beat in syncopation, apparently because they believed they originated on a large, high gravity planet.

Hamil and several board members had gathered for an update and planning session as the vote would be held in two weeks.

"All I'm saying is we should have a general sense of what we will do, should the vote go against 'The Neighbours'," said Hamil. "And there is the possibility that the choice will require a run off if no civilization manages a majority in the first ballot."

"Let's hope that doesn't happen. The logistics of the first vote have been almost impossible and there are numerous reports of irregularities."

"How long after a civilization is chosen, will it take to reach the next stage?" one of the engineers asked.

Evert shook his head, "That, I cannot tell you. We are in the loop with Washington, of course, but we are simply a cog to them. They cannot afford to let this slip out of control. This is a very volatile time in our history, and not for the reasons that people in the street think."

There were nods all around the table. Hamil continued to wonder if they were in the true insider's loop, or if there was more to the situation than had been revealed. He'd said so privately and managed to collect some intelligence on the issue, but he had to keep his head down and not raise too much suspicion. Already there were reports that several unexpected deaths of senior defence and military contractors were engineered as those people were off-side with the plan.

September 28th came and went without incident. 'The Neighbours' managed a runaway victory and its representatives spoke to the United Nations, an address that was broadcast world wide.

Two beings strode to the dais, in front of a bank of television cameras and microphones. All the major languages and broadcast companies insisted on their own feed.

They were alien for sure as they almost glided in their movements, apparently due to a third joint in their legs. But otherwise they looked human, a touch off, to be sure, but human nonetheless. Their body shape was the same but they wore dark sunglasses due to the fact they had evolved underground. The bright light hurt their eyes, which were large to capture as much light as possible, like the eyes of nocturnal animals on Earth.

"I am Elodom, a representative from the High Council of Zeria, which you call 'The Neighbours'. My companion is Keralee. We want to thank the citizens of Earth for their trust in us. We speak in English, the language of Diplomacy on Earth, which we have long studied in preparation of this moment. Between us, we speak most of the major languages on your planet."

"Our friends, 'The First' and 'The One' will still be involved with your development and there are efforts being organized right now to facilitate visits in both directions. They will both establish embassies on Earth, and invite you to do the same in reverse. Think of Earth as a Province of Zeria, you are the 39th planet to join our federation. All are very similar to us physiologically, and we believe we were all seeded by some other civilization in the distant past."

"We do have disagreements with our friends but we seek to solve them to our mutual benefit, much as you have recently done here on Earth. And it is anticipated that we will find other civilizations in the large portion of our galaxy that has not been explored. Fear not, we have found it a hard truth, that for any civilization to reach the stars, it must be able to conquer violent tendencies. We have evolved to seek inner peace while our friends in 'The First' and 'The One' are seeking peace in a greater understanding of the universe."

"It is also universally known that the more we learn about our universe, the less we understand it. Our physics has evolved into local, planetary, galactic and universal physics, essentially four branches of the science of Order."

"There are plans to have a large number of your citizens colonize some of our planets, adding your essence to our civilization. Likewise we will live among you here, for greater understanding and social development. There are currently two other planetary civilizations that we are monitoring, with the idea of integrating them into our whole, when the time for them is right. You will be part of that process."

Elodom referred to a press package with photos and an accessible data base of Zerian arts that might be explored by Earth humans.

The boardroom at GDC was silent, as those invited, watched the address. One of the engineers broke the quiet.

"How long do we anticipate for this phase?"

"We are being told it might be 10 years, perhaps longer, but of course the length of time is not in our hands, but rather in the hands of the unexpected alien contact."

"And our factories?"

"Are running well with an almost complete retention of our work force. Some of our production was changed into civilian security equipment. Of course, a few people used the retooling to make their own changes, but that was anticipated."

"We have been gifted some advanced technology from our Zerian allies."

"And we have retooled our factories to produce it."

"Yes, of course, the real issue is the raw materials needed for production. We have most of them but two elements we need are rare on Earth, and another, Solarium is unknown here and has to be imported from a far world," said Hamil.

"I worry about what we do not know," said Evert.

"Nice to have you on board, sir," said Hamil. "I have worried about that since the beginning of this transition. "I cannot help but wonder when the other shoe will drop."

"There is no evidence of any deception."

"The evidence is all around. Particularly in the notion that there is a fourth alien civilization. What worries me, is that it is obvious that the raw materials we are collecting, appear to be for a very powerful weapon."

"Or some power source we do not understand. I agree, we must be ready. The contact to Zeria was made by these new aliens, and the Zerians are not used to that, having studied all the civilizations they have encountered before initiating contact."

"So, if it's a major weapon why are we being entrusted to produce it? Why would the Zerians not do it themselves and let us in on the process of their preparation for this new First Contact?"

"Ask them. I have asked around official circles but have just received nice little pats on the head. People thought their worlds would change once we were integrated into Zeria, but that really hasn't happened, save at the upper levels of administration."

"Oh, come on, food and industrial production have altered significantly and, given time, will alter almost entirely. People are still required for services, though mostly to manage the Artificial Intelligence that does the work. Perhaps the raw materials we are collecting will build a powerful creative force that we need to more fully integrate into Zerian culture?"

"I am not surprised that many of the same cultural touchstones are covered by all or most of the planets in the Zerian system. Music, art, writing, philosophy, all have similar antecedents in all cultures. And the nice part is that makes us all seem much less alien to each other."

"And then there is the new group."

Part Two

A streak of light smeared the sky just before sunset. Kerry Hamil was sitting in his condominium high above Fourth Avenue on the Upper East

Side. The large windows admitted the light.

These streaks had been occurring now for several days, sometimes one, then two and once he even noticed the light during the day. The news networks finally reported them, saying they were meteors from a new asteroid cluster, which had snuck up on Earth's orbit. The news anchor said there was nothing to worry about as the International Space Agency, working with its Zerian counterpart had investigated the phenomenon and found it posed no danger.

But the light streaks had continued with the occasional one seemingly bolder and brighter. Background chatter said there was a battle in Earth's deep orbit, somewhere near the Moon. Hamil enquired but was told through back channels that it was just some live fire experiments and there was no issue.

Two nights later all Earth communication was disrupted and off-line for most of an hour. A world wide power glitch, said official sources.

Hamil knew this was a lie. Something was happening but he could not penetrate the information bubble despite his security clearances and senior position with a major defence contractor.

He received an urgent call to meet with Evert and senior members of the Board of GDC. Entering the building he was given a very thorough security screening, a process he usually breezed through. His eyes were checked, he was full body scanned, even his ID card was subject to testing for authenticity.

The elevator doors were opened and he faced four armed guards. Not just armed with pistols they were dressed in SWAT gear, with menacing looking rifles and vests bristling with equipment.

Inside the meeting room, the windows had been covered in thick black fabric and cardboard, there was a hum of white noise in the background and the lights had been turned down low.

"I apologise for all the security gentlemen. We are entering a dangerous phase. As you know, our terrestrial communications system was compromised three days ago. Our technicians were unable to halt the breach so the entire system was shut down by our Zerian allies.

"Overlords, you mean," said Hamil. "Something about all of this does not smell right."

"Aye, Mr. Hamil, you are right to question the official narrative. We have been informed that our Zerian friends are currently engaged in a battle with invaders who, they say, seek to harm Earth in their quest for resources."

"Is this the other shoe that we were expecting at the beginning of all of this?"

"Perhaps. The Zerians seem to know about this entity, who they call the Xerons, but have stuck by their story that they had no idea they were in the neighbourhood nor inclined to violence. The names of the civilizations are eerily similar. So far, the skirmishes have been mostly minor, as ships dodge between the Earth and our Moon. Apparently the communications breach was the Xerons trying to hijack the grid to deliver a message to Earth."

"So what's the message?"

"The Zerians say the Xerons want to buy some of our resources and have offered to ally with us for our own protection," Evert said. "Meaning they don't trust the Zerians."

"The administration is parroting the same line. At least they are claiming the light streaks and such are weapons tests meant to help defend the Earth. I heard it on the news just before I came here."

"That's the official story. And one the administration of Earth still stands by. However, one of our communications guys managed to record the Xeron broadcast which still occurred, even though the global grid was shut down to prevent anyone from receiving it."

The room looked at Evert expectantly. Evert sat down and collected his thoughts, reminding everyone in the room that what he was about to say could not be repeated in any form outside the walls which now surrounded them. And that in the wake of the knowledge they were about to get, they would have to formulate a plan. He stood up.

"The message said, 'The Zerians are slavers. They have enslaved 30 other worlds, stripped their resources, while maintaining a benevolent face. No one is allowed to travel to the other nine, central Zerian home worlds.

They have used the Xeron arrival in a dozen different systems, to sow fear, dig their social and economic control deeper, and keep us from getting a fair price for our elements. The claim to seek nothing from the Earth itself, only wanting access to mine distant planets in our system."

Evert said they Xerons offered to meet with Earth representatives, but of course that message did not get through as the Zerians censored it.

"It would appear we cannot trust anyone," said Hamil. "Imagine that."

"Has anyone sought the advice of our more distant allies, 'The First or 'The One'?"

"In this early stage of apparent revelation, no, but your idea is sound. There are fears that those two civilizations have dismissed us. When we did not opt for them, they shed the façade that we were equals."

"And what of the promised population exchanges?"

"There have been reports of such things but my network cannot find any actual proof of migration by our people, though there are a large number of Zerians on Earth."

"Who is to say the Xerons are telling the truth? What is the truth and how will we know it in time to make any defence?"

"All we can do at this point, is watch and wait and remain skeptical of any claims, until there is hard evidence," said Evert.

"By then it may be too late."

"I remind you all, that it is already too late. We are weak and can easily be conquered by any spacefaring culture as we are barely off-world and they are interplanetary. We have no choice but to play along and try to weave a path between these civilizations."

"But somehow we need to get word to these Xerons that we are friendly, while still maintaining our relations with Zeria."

The room lit up with a flash of light and everyone stopped. Evert waited until the flash had subsided. "Perhaps wait and see has been superseded by another action." He moved to the windows and peeled back the card-board and fabric. The city sprawled around him, but on the southern horizon there was a glow, a light peeking over the horizon like the rising sun. Evert described the scene and those present moved to peek out of the window.

"We need to know what is happening," Evert said. "Moody, get your tech guys on the broadcasts. Hamil, check with your government contacts, fish, go hard, be skeptical, but don't let on our level of disbelief. Attwater, check with our engineers on what they have learned from the Zerians. We may need their technology if the Xerons are aggressive. Who knows how much fire power the Zerians have at hand."

There was a knock at the boardroom door. The room went silent.

Knowing his voice would not carry, Evert opened the door. A man outside spoke, "Sir, I think you need to see something. It has just been broadcast across all frequencies."

Evert moved into the anteroom where there was a big screen. "It's just about to start again."

". . . . for that reason to come and liberate your planet, should you ask. Greetings people of Earth. We have been blockaded by the Zerian Empire from speaking to you, our close neighbours." The figure that spoke could have been anyone from Earth. It spoke perfect English. "The Zerians are slavers. They gain control of planets through cooperation and good works, slowly sealing control, bringing in millions and if necessary, billions, of their kind, before converting the planet into a resource stripping operation. We seek mutually beneficial trade and resources only from your outlying planets, to maintain the natural balance on your home world. We will provide a portion of those elements for access. We seek a mutual advantage."

"What you have seen recently is Zerian aggression against our diplomatic mission to Earth. So far two of our ships have been damaged. It appears they are being somewhat restrained and are trying to force us to leave. We have not yet countered their aggressive actions."

"We have a report of a major explosion in Washington DC. As we have discharged no weapons, that explosion is not the result of any aggression by us," said the video image. "It is either an errant shot by the Zerians or more likely, a calculated false flag attack which they will blame on us."

"In the spirit of future cooperation, we will withdraw, but invite you to contact us for future discussions. And we encourage those discussions while you still have leverage with the Zerians, whose refusal to allow diplomatic relations would lay bare their true agenda. The resources in your outer planets are valuable to us. If the Zerians do not allow you to contact us, we would be prepared for that reason to come and liberate your planet, should you ask."

There was a pause and the message began to repeat.

Evert motioned everyone back into the boardroom. Once seated they all looked to Evert for direction. Finally, he spoke, "As I said, work your people. Let's try to find out the truth about the Zerians. This could all be a ruse. Having said that, diplomacy is a fair approach and should be pursued. We are on the knife edge. We sit between two powerful civilizations and we may not be able to trust either. I am hopeful that we can set up some industry out of sight; to build defence components in the event we will need them to maintain our independence."

"I'm not sure this is a battle that we can win with weapons. We have to think about other ways of imposing our desire," said Hamil.

Part Three

'The First' and 'The One' had been contacted to weigh in on the Zerians. They were surprisingly uncommitted, as we'd made our choice and they did not want to interfere. Diplomats came and went but little of substance was accomplished. Their true nature seemed to rise as they treated our concerns as the fears of pets.

It was apparent that the Zerians were going to keep the Xenons away from Earth. And equally apparent that the Zerians were prepared to play the long game, allowing Earth culture to change as young Earthlings began to mature and outnumber those who had lived before the Zerian age.

Incidents with the Xenons were supressed though the Xenons had infiltrated second tier echelons of Earth authorities, content to provide a second perspective on the Zerian take over of Earth, through an underground operation of mutual contact.

Hamil had retired, the last of the Board of GDC who had been serving when the First Contact announcement was made. But his skepticism remained fully ingrained with existing Board members. GDC had built a secret underground test facility where they worked on weapons that might be necessary should the Zerians or anyone else decide to supersede Earth's wishes.

The Zerians maintained very strict controls over specific metals and other natural resources which made GDC's testing facility difficult to operate. There were established back channels with the Xenons for information and resources.

The Zerians slowly pushed their control, first over currency, then movement, and finally over actions and speech. They did it all with a smile, and all with the illusion that they were controlling only the vestiges of bad and violent elements of the population. The constant refrain was that development and progress were not possible with violence.

Some delegations had gone to Zerian planets and returned with positive impressions of their societies. Some wondered how much of the visits were stage managed.

There was an on-going dialogue among intellectuals. "We on Earth evolved in several ways, some of which the Zerians are trying to push out of our psyche."

"The command-and-control approach seems to be their default. They prefer a populace which knows its place and limitations, which has considerable latitude in its day-to-day as long as it doesn't cross the line of challenging authority and upsetting the generally pacific nature of people."

"There are a considerable number of Earthlings that evolved with a very independent streak, living as they wish without any rule, save one, don't make rules for anyone else. This is often explained as don't bother anyone else or have your choices affect their lives. However, even this 'Don't Tread on Me' approach has its problems, as anyone can complain that your choice, no matter how esoteric, is bothering them, no matter how distant."

Other thinkers believed differently. "The Zerians are using the compliant nature of Homo Sheepius, to curtail the fundamentally natural approach of Homo Sapiens toward individualism. It is that desire to strike out on your own and be self-reliant, that makes humans, human. We must preserve it."

As governments tightened their control, pockets of resistance grew. It was there that the Zerians fomented rebellions so they could crush them, not with violence, but by smothering them with those who were compliant. The compliant were inclined to have protests peppered with violence, which the governments ignored, essentially challenging the individualists to be more violent in response. Either approach by the individualists gave government the opportunity to crush dissent either by fomenting violence against it, or avoiding it all together.

And then one day, the tendency to violence by the compliant ones, forced the hand of a group of individualists who saw through the charade.

Seeing protestors setting fire to police cars and blockading traffic in the name of peace at any costs, a small group of local individualists finally broke at the hypocrisy. Surrounded by protestors and unable to get an injured person to hospital, they simply drove a vehicle through the protestors, killing three.

Protests ramped up but this time, instead of being cowed and avoiding confrontation, the individualists came out in force and engaged in pitched battles with mindless protestors, who believed their right to collective action and control superseded those of the individualists.

At first, the Zerian authorities tried to gain control by attacking the individualists, but they failed as more and more people refused to be pushed into compliance with hypocrisy. The pitched battles began to go the way of the individualists and the Zerians called in some heavily armoured troops, a robot army that they had held in secret reserve.

This escalation, and revelation that all was not as it seemed, brought many of the peace-loving compliant silent supporters onto the side of the individualists. By nature, the rebels were uncoordinated but after a robot force mercilessly destroyed a group of rebels, they realized they had no choice but to organize.

Appeals to the other space faring nations went unheeded, except the Xenons, who swooped in and took part in several major confrontations on the rebel side. It appeared they had created several caches of weapons on Earth in a secret operation of their own. Light streaked the sky.

Kerry Hamil had risen to become the lead voice of the individualists. Grey haired, with stiff joints, he moved slowly but his mind raced. He met with a Xenon delegation.

“We warned you that the Zerians meant you no good, save for their own purposes.”

“We are concerned that you may just be a reflection of them. The same in a different guise,” Hamil countered.

“A reasonable assumption. Judge us by our actions, if you are uncertain of our words.”

“How do we rid ourselves of these parasites? Most especially, without tearing our own world to bits?”

“With the years you have given them, the Zerians are deeply embedded into your world. They control most of everything and are quite willing to invoke violence, the same violence they pretend to despise, to achieve their ends. Greater violence is not the answer but it is an agitation that can lead to salvation.”

“Forgive me, but violent rebellion won’t work, but keep violently rebelling? That’s your answer?”

“No, it is the reality on the ground. You must find a way to expel the Zerians to their advantage.”

“Well,” said Hamil, “I’m all ears.”

“As we said, keep up the opposition, maintain your determination for individual choice. Once it is seen that you will not be cowed, demand they leave and give leave to any of your population which prefers the social credit compliance approach to citizenship, to leave with them. A society divided against itself will not flourish but will engage in endlessly repeated battles of choice. Encourage people of this ilk to leave by making it a better choice for them. Maintain relations with the Zerians but push them to a distance. An embassy, sure, thousands of Zerian administrators and Zerian robot workers, no.”

“But those robots now do much of the hard drudgery of society.”

“Build your own. Restart your own society built on your own values. We can help. We would like to come to an understanding with you and with the Zerians who we have no wish to fight. We can be your partners, mostly in resources, in hopes that the Zerians will take note and back away."

And so Hamil arranged for a meeting with various resistance groups and came away with that plan, to parlay with the Zerians, push them away from the tight control they had been working for, but maintaining them as partners and friends.

It would take a generation perhaps longer to rid the Earth of the controlling nature of Zeria and put in place a mutual approach to administration. The first order of business was to study the other Zerian planets for signs of how they had developed and battled this dichotomy of choice.

The second was to allow the Xenons to mine the outer planets and share that wealth with Earth, for the privilege of taking the needed resources. When Solarium was found on Jupiter the Zerians disavowed all knowledge of this rarest of elements. The Xenons suggested there was evidence there that Solarium had been mined from Jupiter in the past, the recent past. But in the huge universe, they conceded, it was unknown who might have been behind the operation.

Earth had survived the initial stages of First Contact. But it emerged wary. Treated like livestock by 'The First' and 'The One' and like an army of workers by 'The Neighbours', the people of Earth had no choice but to navigate the new reality of their existence with a healthy dose of fear mixed with excitement for a future they would have a limited ability to direct.

Chapter Six

I sat back. I didn't have to convince myself that the story was good, but I did check my sanity. Some tropes were there to be sure, but with a bit of difference in approach. But now what? I could expand this into a novel, I thought. Much of the third part was really a road map for continuation of the story. Conspiracy, mystery, exploration, thriller; the possibilities were endless. In fact, with that science fiction approach, I could keep the entire story Earthbound, if I chose.

Meeting Theresa a few days later, I still hadn't decided if I should expand the story or move on to something else. I leaned to shelving the science fiction for now, and move on to another genre. My desire to try other things kept changing, but I decided I should consider a western, contemporary literary, historical, thriller, mystery, gothic, war, sport or even a multi-generational saga. Of course, the latter could be filed under historical fiction, and maybe I should consider marrying two genres.

Sitting in our usual table, Theresa read the story, handed the papers back to me, as I grinned at her confusion.

"I am not a science fiction reader, so my assessment is flawed." The smile of triumph faded from my face.

"That's okay, I need to know if you were at least interested in reading more?"

"Where is it going?"

I shrugged. "How the hell do I know? I agree with you, it screams for a longer treatment and it could go anywhere."

"Well, maybe you need to flesh out the plot a bit more. It seems like a good start but I can't say anything now until I know."

"I'm afraid to make a choice. Frankly I want to avoid all the tropes, so devolving it into a mystery or thriller seems like the easy way out. I need a new approach to my new approach."

Theresa smirked. "Good luck. Keep me in the loop."

"Okay, okay, where are you? Got a logo yet?"

Theresa bent to her bag and pulled out a folded sheet. "Before I show you this, I want a quick visceral reaction and then something that is a bit more considered. This logo thing is tough, but I'll say no more until I hear from you."

She unfolded the sheet, creasing the folds backwards to make it flat, and placed it between us.

At first, I wasn't sure what I was seeing. But it came clear, it was a representation of the New York skyline, with a submarine on the surface of the Hudson River in the foreground. Circled around the image was

'Suburban Style' with the first word arched on the top and the second word bent underneath.

I was complete caught off-guard. I did not know what to expect, but this was not it.

"First impression?"

"Confusion," I said, "Well that's not quite it. "It's striking but not immediately obvious."

"I have to play with the graphic some more. I want it mysterious but not scary. Putting it in silhouette leaves out some identifying detail. But I don't want too much detail – too expensive to reproduce."

"You know I really like the idea of it, but I'm not sure of the execution."

"Yeah, me too. The whole rebel thing is there. The underground nature of style, and the city – suburban dynamic. But I need to find the right elements, and I'm not sure I have them yet. I like suburban – hits the whole thing on the head with a twist. But gotta find another word rather than 'Style' its not subtle enough."

We both sat there sipping our coffee and gazing on the graphic between us.

We agreed to think on the graphic and I promised to bring back my next effort.

So far, I hated the romance bit and kinda liked the sci-fi starter but could not think of the full plot line without descending into the usual tropes. Normally when I wrote fiction I started with an idea and a sense of the plot line, characters and story progression, often with the big reveal, twist or big finish very much in mind.

I resisted the idea of plotting out the whole thing, chapter by chapter, because usually the characters and situations suggest new directions when they are fully fleshed out, and I need the freedom to pursue those tangents to add richness to the story and the characters.

And this failure seemed the big part of my writer's block. I could dream up a situation and a character or two but the broader story eluded me.

With that rolling around in my head I sat down two evenings later with several hours to give to my next attempt. Full gothic, modern gothic, neo-gothic? I didn't know. So where do gothic stories take place? A castle? Lovely and evocative but too obvious, I thought.

And so I plunged in . . .

Chapter Seven – Modern Gothic – Hello, I've waited here for you.

I grew up in a city neighbourhood. One that was built years ago as the city grew, so it has houses on small lots, each with a bit of garden space, a shared driveway between the homes, usually leading to stand alone garages in the back, and a little patch of patio or something between the house and the out building.

Some of the neighbourhoods had a laneway behind the houses, between homes on one street and homes facing the parallel avenue a block away. The garages faced this laneway.

I had longed for such a space after years living in the sky, in a series of high-rise apartments that matched my waxing and then waning circumstances.

I often drove or walked through the streets near where I grew up hoping that maybe a small, suitable home might come on the market. Several larger, more elaborate ones had come and gone, without me really being able to hope I might get it, given my means.

My parents had long ago abandoned the neighbourhood, but something always drew me back, despite there being a number of other city neigh-bourhoods which fit the same style and description. Invariably these homes were old. The better ones had been fixed and upgraded beyond my means, but lesser prices were attached to those where the owners had lived happily for decades without seeing the need to upgrade or modernize much of anything.

My husband and I liked the proximity of living in the sky close to our jobs. Not having any children, it was a choice that worked. He knew of my desire for a little more space, and while not actively seeking a change in abode, he did not fight my desire to at least look. Occasionally he accompanied me on my strolls up and down the 20 or so blocks of the old neighbourhood.

My father had died some years before, a victim of the social acceptance of tobacco. My mother, never a pillar of health, entered a nursing home a few months before and was still adjusting to the rhythms of the place. I visited regularly, and she would often ask after the old neighbourhood, even though she had left when my father coughed his last. There was never much to tell.

My husband and I had entered the long service portion of our working lives. He, a financial analyst for a mid-sized bank, and I, a teacher at an inner city primary school, we weren't likely going anywhere, with maybe a bump in responsibility and a few extra dollars our only possible alternative lives.

It was the beginning of the school year, with the bounce between warm and cool days, and a hint of grey winter on the morning horizon, and I hadn't been able to go for a walk anywhere. As we all settled into our new classrooms, one of the other teachers, Alice McFadden, with whom I was a work friend, suggested a meet up for coffee one Saturday.

We settled on a coffee shop in the area of the old neighbourhood. She seemed to want to talk about something important to her, and I thought, if we walked while we talked, I would at least know my way around. She lived a few miles past the neighbourhood, so it was a logical halfway point.

I arrived at the shoppe, and saw Alice already there with a full mug of coffee and a muffin. I waved hello and got my own, black coffee, which I preferred, and a double chocolate donut, which, once I spied them in the display case, were hard to resist.

I slid my tray on the small table and sat down across from her.

"Little cool this morning, glad I wore a heavier coat."

"Yeah, but once you start walking, you warm up pretty quick, then its just your fingers that get cold," I said. "That's what pockets are for."

"Nice to see you outside of the precinct. Among all the noise and confusion it's hard to get a word in," she said.

I nodded, still wondering if she had something important to address, or if this was merely a social call. We chatted a bit about the usual students, a couple of curriculum changes and the new vice-principal. He was young, inexperienced and on the rise within the Board of Education. Alice figured he'd be around for two or three years and then off again, probably as a principal, and sooner than later, a super-intendent and maybe even a director of education.

"There is little need to steer him straight, excepting any strange ideas he might have. These newbies are always full of idealism and plans to reinvent the wheel."

"I'm not worried, Principal Evers will keep him in check. There will be the usual grand plans that are thwarted by reality and come to dust when the inevitable push back comes."

Alice laughed, "Yeah, you are probably right. I've talked to him a bit, and that's exactly how he comes off."

I stared into my coffee cup, figuring if this was the moment for a more serious subject, Alice would tee it up right here.

"Phil asked me to marry him."

"You are still involved with him? I thought you'd broken it off."

"We did for a while, once Evers found out we were together, he wasn't too happy. Board policy you know. But we got back together and kept it very low key, so nobody would suspect."

"So if you get married one of you will have to transfer schools."

"Maybe both of us. Phil has an opportunity to go to a high school near here as a Department Head, they want fresh blood."

"Then you don't have to go," I said, somewhat relieved that Alice might stay. Then the other shoe dropped.

"The commute is too long for him. He wants to move. Into one of the older neighbourhoods near the school."

"Making a longer commute for you?"

She nodded.

"So first you have to decide if you want to marry him, and then if you want to accommodate his new job location. You could try the commute for a while before making the big leap."

She admitted that she had considered all the permutations of the choice, convinced as she was that she would marry Phil.

"I'm just looking for a bit of insight as to where we should look and how I should go about it. I'm comfortable at our school. I know its rhythms, I know most of the families, and Evers is a good boss, fair, balanced and sort of flexible."

"Seems to me you should stay where you are and see if you can handle the commute. If you are thinking about children and take some time away, that would be a good time to look for another school. You can work some days as a substitute and then select a school you like."

"As long as a position comes up."

"Of course. Not everything falls in our laps, but you'd be surprised how many opportunities pass us by, some we don't even know about. "

Alice nodded, "You are right. Go slow, don't jump in with both feet and you can always step away."

"So when is the wedding?"

"Don't know yet. I haven't actually decided yet. Well, Phil thinks I have. I said yes but I am still mulling it over. Didn't want to upset him, and I think it likely is the right choice. I just decided to myself that I'd give myself a week to weigh the whole thing in my mind."

"It's a big step. Were you not expecting him to ask?"

"Yes, I was, but I wasn't sure of how I would feel about it. It's a major choice, a huge life decision and I don't want to have any regrets either way."

"So what's wrong?"

"Nothing. I'm just not sure if I'm ready. You know, settled and comfortable with the decision. And frankly, having someone else's job offer be the catalyst to my life, just doesn't sit right. But Phil is great, he's wonderful to me, doesn't have any black marks, you know, and marriage seems inevitable and proper. Just not this way."

I pursed my lips. "How old are you?"

Alice blinked and said she was 25. She had been at the school a bit too long to have graduated teacher's college only four years before. So she was likely at least 27, otherwise, why lie. I didn't say anything.

"I started school a year early and went straight to teacher's college," she said.

"Either way, life has presented you with a decision to make. Be thankful that the choice is in your hands. I think you know what you want. Just accept it, make the choice final and don't look back. You must remember nostalgia is one thing, but living in the past, or constantly going back to it, is unhealthy. Don't look back, you aren't going that way, life is a one-way street."

"But there are twists and turns. And side streets," she laughed.

"Yes, there are, but they are usually just obstacles to whatever is at the end of the road."

"Death?"

Now it was my turn to laugh. "A life well lived. Family, friends and memories."

"Oh, that. So where should we look for a place to live?"

"Right here. It's close to Phil's new school and not too far from ours. Remember, you might be presented with other opportunities at any time that require new choices. I've been looking for an appropriate home here for a few years. I grew up on Chalmers Street, a few blocks away. It's familiar."

"I didn't know that. Maybe we'll be neighbours."

"Maybe, but we haven't found the right home yet. I'd really like a fixer-upper, but nothing too dramatic. Unfortunately, the neighbourhood is perfect for large rebuild rather than renovations."

We chatted about the neighbourhood, the future wedding, honeymoon plans, and extended family. While I knew Alice before our coffee that day, I felt much closer to her after our lengthy chat.

We decided to go for a walk through the neighbourhood. A few homes were up for sale, but the whole idea of taking such a leap, when an hour before, she was unsure of her own choice, was too much for Alice. Me, I saw a couple of homes I kind of liked, and said I would look into their asking prices and property details before bringing my Jimmy into the conversation. He did not like expending mental energy needlessly and only wanted to know about real possibilities, not pipe dreams.

We turned the corner onto Chalmers Street, where I grew up. There was a small parkette on the corner, where once there had been a house. I think it burned down. Some benches, gardens and a few pieces of children's play equipment. Low maintenance. Realtors I asked, said it was torn down a few years back as the former owners took the insurance money and sold the property. The city bought it eventually and decided on the parkette, a common thing in these old neighbourhoods, which were built before park access was mandated by city planners.

As we walked down the street I commented on most of the old homes, giving a bit of my history with them. A childhood friend lived here, a mean boy lived there. A grandma lived in this house and as we approached my own home, I saw a little hand made sign, 'For Sale'.

I gasped a little, caught off guard. I had never really considered my old home as desirable. But that 'For Sale' sign, written in bold black letters on a piece of plywood, stabbed my heart.

"Oh my God, I didn't know it was up for sale. This is where I grew up." The Arts and Crafts look, with three pillars holding up a significant porch roof, a single wide door on the left side and a large window, completed the look. Absolutely typical for the neighbourhood, with nothing to distinguish it from dozens of other homes in the surrounding blocks, save a mailbox and choices of paint.

Alice and I finished our walk, but my mind was elsewhere, as I wrestled with telling Jimmy or researching the home first. Alice and I parted finally, with me suggesting we meet for coffee again in a few weeks so she could catch me up on her thinking and potential wedding.

At home finally, I began to look around for real estate information. I was pretty familiar with the places to go but there was no realtor attached to the home. I was going to have to knock on the door. First, I decided to ask a realtor that I had worked with on occasion, if she knew about the home.

She said the home was not listed, which squared with the hand made sign and suggested I knock on the door. I was reluctant and felt a bit strange begging at my old home. The walk up the path from the street, brought back memories.

It wasn't as bad as I thought. On the surface it seemed worse, but I wasn't sure.

My knock was answered by an old woman, who spoke through a screen door she did not open. I immediately mentioned the sign, saying I was interested. The woman hesitated. She did not appear to know what to do. And, frankly either did I. My mind was swirling with details as I was going to have to describe it to Jimmy.

"That sign just went up yesterday. I'm going to have to speak to my husband, he will know what to do."

"Is he here? I can wait."

I really wanted to know the asking price as that alone was the primary determining factor.

"I'll fetch him." And sure enough a few minutes later she returned with a man of the same vintage, who did not seem happy.

"You interested in buying?"

"Yes. Do you have an agent and some details of the house?"

"No agents. Don't trust 'em. And don't want to pay their crazy fees."

"Well, I am interested. What can you tell me about the place?"

His eyes shifted back and forth, and then he looked at me carefully. I was happy I was not dressed particularly well, as he seemed to be assessing my ability to pay.

"What makes you interested?"

"My husband has taken a job near here and we are looking for more space. I've been looking at this neighbourhood for a while."

"Ahh. Well, it's got three bedrooms upstairs, and the usual living space on the main floor. Three bathrooms, one is an addition. A bit of space out back, including a small shed and one car garage."

Of course, I knew all of that. I was hoping he'd mention the price. I looked at him expectantly. He did not offer to have me look around.

He mentioned a price that was higher than I expected, but I got the feeling that he was setting up a negotiation, and the quoted amount was only his opening salvo. He was no fool, as the price he quoted was high, but not outlandish for the neighbourhood.

"That seems like a good place to start," I said. "I'd like my husband to see the place and if we continue to be interested, I'd like to set up a home inspection. You know, to make sure it's solidly built and everything works."

He gave me a withering gaze, but asked when I could come back. We found common ground two days later and set a time.

"Can't guarantee that it won't be sold by then."

"And I can't guarantee I will still be interested. I'm going to have to take my chances."

That evening Jimmy was not thrilled with the prospect of dealing with such a major purchase in such an unconventional way, saying he would have to engage an agent or lawyer or both to help facilitate the sale.

I shrugged. I certainly did not want to simply hand over cash and of course wanted a clean, legal sale process.

Late in the afternoon, two days later we found ourselves walking up the path to the front door. I explained to Jimmy that this was my old home, but did not want to tell the current owners that, for fear they would jack up the price.

He nodded. The day was windy and I could not tell if a change in the weather was coming, or whether a major storm loomed just over the horizon. The wooden stair to the front porch creaked as we both ascended. I knocked confidently, but there was no response. The windows rattled slightly in the wind as we waited.

"This is the time we agreed to. I wonder where they are. I was just about to suggest we look around back when the door opened and a young woman answered.

I was taken aback, expecting one or both of the older couple. "I'm here to look at the house. I had an appointment with, with the owners," whose name suddenly escaped me.

"Yes, my father said to expect you. My parents are not here right now. I can show you around."

She opened the door and allowed us to enter. Typical of homes from that era, there was a half wall to partly separate the entrance from the main room. It was typically furnished, but the couch and chairs were old and in need of repair, or better still, replacement.

She introduced herself, but made no excuse for her parents. We made a slow tour of the house, looking at the room sizes in particular, with Chris taking in the details. Lighting, electrical outlets, heating. He asked about the age of the windows, but the young woman did not know. It appeared that little had been done to upgrade the house since I had lived there almost 15 years before.

"Your father is asking a lot for a home that is in serious need of upgrades and modernization."

The woman shrugged. "He sees what other houses in the neighbourhood go for and judges mostly on location and size."

"I think we'd like to make an offer, but keep in mind that we will have to do a lot of work before moving in. Floors, some electrical, the kitchen and bathrooms all need upgrading."

"My father would say, that's on you, as everything here works and is in good repair."

Jimmy quoted a figure fully 30 per cent lower than the asking. I had to stifle a gasp. The young woman allowed her lip to curl into a sneer.

"My father would throw you out. But I understand it's a lowball offer and likely just the beginning of negotiations."

"We can edge, back and forth, or you can give me your best price now, and I will let my father know."

"Too often I've seen that tactic set a new target to start the back and forth, forcing me to go much higher than the halfway mark between our suggested prices. You have to understand that we will have to spend a lot of money, making upgrades which have been neglected. That adds to the cost of the home."

"And you need to know that my parents do not have to move. They are looking for something a little easier to manage. The sign has only been up for four days," she said, "and already several people have inquired."

I was ready to interject when Jimmy asked her to name her bottom-line price, trying to turn the tables on her.

"I will tell my father of your offer. Can you come back tomorrow and speak with him?"

We agreed, though Jimmy mentioned the need for a home inspection, in advance of agreeing to a final price. The young woman nodded but she did not seem pleased.

We returned the next day and decided that the inspection of the home should come first. The old man did not want to discuss lowering the price based on the inspection once we'd come to an agreement.

We hired an inspector, who agreed to do his work a week later.

I admit to liking the idea of moving back into my childhood home, the memories there were good. But I wasn't married to the idea and I refused to pay a premium for the home.

I showed the inspector's report to the homeowner and he pooh poohed it, predictably. Three days later I had my agent present an offer, detailing the deductions from the asking price, necessary to bring the house up to date.

He signed back a counter offer with a substantial increase and the agent told me that he had said my upgrades and ideas of style where not his responsibility. And while I understood his position, his lack of regular maintenance and necessary work had to be accounted somewhere.

I signed back a counter to his counter, coming up in price to reflect his position. I heard nothing. My real estate agent was getting a bit antsy but I instructed her to leave it be. He would either come back with another price or we would let the offer expire, and, if she wanted to let the sellers know, I was prepared to walk away. We had no house to sell, we did not need to buy and the price of this home was reflective of houses with substantial upgrades and remodels.

The offer expired. Two weeks passed and I began to believe the owner had another buyer or decided to wait out the market.

Then the call. He would accept our offer if we pushed up the price $5,000. A face-saving bid on his part, according to my agent. He told her that he had looked more closely at the inspector's report, which I had gifted him, even though I paid for it, as it was of no use to me if I did not own the home.

I waited two days and we accepted, setting the move in date to six weeks later, once the fall school term had ended and we could give notice on our condo.

"You are sure about this?" asked Jimmy as the pen hovered over the contract. "I like the idea of homeownership but it scares me too."

I nodded. The condo was feeling a little cramped and the three bedrooms and small backyard felt like a luxury we should take. Live a little while you are young, one never knows when life will change.

Fortunately our meagre possessions did not take up too much space, so after we were moved in, we set up shop in a secondary bedroom and began the process of upgrading the master and the rest of the upstairs.

A lot of sweat equity and the judicious use of professionals, and we managed the renovations in three months. With the upstairs finished we began the real work.

Rising one morning with the task of cleaning out the kitchen in front of me, and setting it up in the living room while we renovated, I heard a rustle from the third bedroom. We had moved from the other bedroom back into the master and loaded up things to store in the third bedroom while we worked.

Thinking something had fallen over, of slipped off the place where it was leaning, I sleepily walked into the third bedroom to see a bunch of photos and framed pictures that had been piled on a rocking chair, were now spread on the floor like an avalanche. The rocking chair was just sitting in the middle of the room. It was one of the few pieces of furniture I had acquired from my parents when they downsized. That chair had been in much the same place when my parents owned the home. I quickly scooped up the accordion flow and put it back on the chair, before heading downstairs for coffee and a plan on where to begin.

Downstairs I sipped on my coffee, waiting for Jimmy to wander down and get ready to help. We'd only put those things we absolutely needed into the kitchen, the rest was in boxes in the dining room. I heard noise from upstairs and figured Jimmy was on his way. But as I finished my coffee, he had not appeared. Nor had I heard any running water. Getting annoyed with waiting, I decided to wake him up. We had planned to get a lot done this day as the new cabinets were being installed three days later, and the new appliances were due in at the end of the week, all after the floor was laid the next day.

I headed up the stairs trying to decide what level of anger I should compose when I looked into the third bedroom and again saw the pictures and photo pile strewn across the floor. I was sure I had picked that up, I thought.

And I gathered it again, and angled it back into the rocking chair to discourage its falling again. By the time I managed to enter the master, Jimmy was up and making a show of cleaning the laundry up.

"You know, a laundry chute would be wonderful," he said. "I've been trying to visualize how we might do it. Lugging the laundry up two flights of stairs is a pain I had not anticipated."

"If you think it will fit in, then come up with a plan. In the meantime we have a lot to do in the kitchen. Come on down and we can have a bit of breakfast and get started."

He nodded, absentmindedly looking at the closet, thinking about what was below it. As I pivoted to go back downstairs, I heard the avalanche of photos strike again. Entering the room the chair was still moving. Thinking the momentum of the slide had accentuated the movement of the loose pile on the seat, I took the stuff and piled it together but left it on the floor.

Jimmy finally joined me and we quickly finished breakfast. I put on a pot of coffee and began to work. First, we emptied a number of drawers and cabinets, and once several were ready, Jimmy took a screw driver and hammer and began to remove them.

We had agreed to put any that survived their removal into the basement to increase storage. After several hours we had most of the cabinets pulled and the majority in the basement waiting their turn to be reinstalled there.

"You know, these are likely the same cabinets that were here when I was a kid, but I cannot remember them. I guess kids don't pay attention to those things."

"Does the house seem smaller to you now that you are back in it, as a larger person?"

"I was thinking about that, but no, we haven't filled anything in yet, so it seems huge to me. Once we stuff it full of things, I'm sure that will change."

We finished the rest of the job, leaving the floors for the next day. Electrical was due in on Monday along with the floors and the painters. It was a tight dance to be ready for the cabinet installers in the middle of the week.

We set up a rudimentary kitchen in the dining room and ordered pizza for dinner. I contemplated getting started on the floors while I ate but waited to see if Jimmy would make the same suggestion. I could see him staring at the rough edges of flooring under the old cabinet spaces but he didn't say anything.

With so much physical work done, and more to do, we slept soundly and then repeated the process the next day, pulling up linoleum and tiles and exposing the old subfloor. We agreed to ask our flooring contractor to replace some of the old plywood boards before the new floors went down.

At the end of the day, our tasks complete, we decided to go out to a local pub for dinner, agreeing that we needed to make our own meals at home as much as possible, if only to save the cost. Neither one of us wanted to tally up the cost of the renovations but we both knew it was into the six figures.

Coming home from the pub I heard a strange creaking from upstairs. Jimmy stood beside me but he claimed not to hear it. I skipped up the stairs and glanced into the third bedroom as I went by. The rocking chair was moving back and forth.

That made me feel a bit creepy. Home inspection had detected no vermin in the house, but chairs don't move that much on their own. The window was open, so maybe it had been a gust of wind. As I went to close it, I could feel the air, which carried the scent of a spring storm. Moving into the master, I heard a peel of thunder and then a loud crack, as if lightening had hit nearby. I managed to close the window in the master a moment after the skies opened up.

"Good timing on getting home," Jimmy said, entering the room. "I managed to close a couple of windows downstairs as well. I don't remember opening them all, but I guess we must have as we got warmer and warmer pulling up the floor."

I nodded slowly, as I couldn't remember opening these windows upstairs. Something wasn't quite right, but I couldn't put a finger on it.

We had timed all of this for the spring break at school, and Jimmy arranged a few days off from the bank. The next morning he headed off to the hardware store to buy cabinet pulls and a couple of light fixtures we had decided on. I remained home waiting for the electricians, expected late morning.

"Thank you so much," I heard a voice whisper. I looked up but the room was empty and there were no electricians standing at the door. I gave my head a shake, wondering if I was daydreaming.

"I do love that rocking chair. I've missed it so."

My head snapped up, fully expecting someone in the room. It was empty. Looking outside I could see the electricians van pull into the driveway. In the hustle and bustle of the electricians setting up, asking questions and eyeballing their task, I forgot about the quiet snippet of conversation.

Jimmy returned and said the flooring guys were delayed but would be by late morning. They were sending a guy by to inspect the sub-floor before they started. When he arrived, he had a pick-up truck full of boxes of hardwood. Jimmy helped him unload. They could get started before the bulk of the order was delivered a few hours later.

The next couple of days were a whirlwind of whirring saws, cracking wood, and general labour. New electrical outlets, pot lights, wiring throughout the kitchen. A new plywood subfloor, doubly screwed down with a foam strip laid down on the floor joists to stop creaking, the floor installed and the new cabinets being delivered. Amidst the chaos, Jimmy managed to lay down two coats of paint but didn't get the ceiling done.

I went to bed on Thursday night expecting the cabinet installers the next day and knowing once they were done, we were going to take a break on further renos. Eventually we would replace the flooring in the whole downstairs and redo the small bathroom on the main floor.

As I lay partly awake the next morning, a few days from Easter, the light outside seemed too dim to indicate the time to get up, I heard Jimmy say something.

"Now that everyone is gone, can we have tea?"

Jimmy doesn't drink tea. I rolled over to look at him and he was still asleep, his lips quivering as if he was in a dream. "Jenny, I'm so happy you came back."

"I never left, Jimmy," I said.

"Yes, you did. I've been all alone." Jim's lips did not move.

Out of the corner of my eye I glimpsed the figure of a little girl. I knew her. My memories flooded back.

"Lenora? Is that you?"

"Yes, I've missed you so."

I was at a loss. Lenora was my friend when I was very young. She had faded away when I became more involved outside the house, with school, choir, music and the like. I thought she had moved away, as she didn't attend the same school I did.

"Mr. and Mrs. and their daughter were no fun. They just ignored me. You won't ignore me, will you?"

I shook my head, "No Lenora, we just bought the house." Jimmy stirred beside me and I turned my head to look at him. Looking back at the door-way, the frame was empty, Lenora was gone. I shook my head violently and grabbed my ears. Was I dreaming?

Over the next few weeks I had several encounters with Lenora. All mild as she pleaded for attention. I had to let Jimmy know as he had caught me speaking to her on a few occasions, and I could see in his eyes he thought I was crazy.

I decided to tell him one evening when we went to dinner. Predictably he took it in stride, but I could tell he was more than just skeptical. I told him I wanted to research the ownership of the home, which had been standing for about 50 years before my parents bought it.

I checked at city hall and found the tax records and the names of three previous owners. I decided to look back at newspaper reports in the year preceding the change of ownership. On my second try, with the middle owners of the house, I found they had a daughter who had fallen down the stairs and died of head trauma eight months before they sold to the people my parents had purchased the home from. The accident happened 75 years before.

I told Jimmy. Still skeptical, he suggested I mention it to Lenora when she appeared again. The way he made his eyes big and round was off-putting, as if he was indulging my madness.

Three days later Lenora appeared again. I saw her sitting on the rocking chair slowing moving back and forth, this time with a big bruise on her forehead. I stood in the doorway.

“You’ve been hurt.”

“But I’m alright now. I keep telling my mommy that, but she doesn’t say anything. Then I didn’t see her anymore, and had nobody to play with until you came.”

“Lenora. I think you need to go and find your mommy. She is probably looking for you.”

“I heard her voice. She was calling to me. But I couldn’t see her. I see you though. I’m afraid.”

“Don’t be afraid Lenora. Go looking for her. You can always come back here. Even if you find her, and want to visit me, you can.”

Lenora smiled at me and she looked down into her lap. “You won’t be mad at me if I leave?”

“Not if you go where you want to be. I will be here for a long time.”

There was a knock at the door. My eyes averted to the stairway and when I looked back Lenora was gone. I waited in vain for Lenora to return, fearful that she might not find her way. Several years passed, our renovations were completed. Jimmy switched jobs and I remained teaching until we had a baby. Then two, and eventually three. Two boys full of life and the youngest, a girl with the prettiest smile that burst forth every time one of her parents entered the room.

Jimmy had taken the oldest boy to hockey practice. The younger boy was in their shared room reading or playing a game, and my baby was doing a puzzle on the family room floor as I busied in the kitchen.

"Hello again," my baby said. "You look happy this time."

"I am, I found my mommy and she was so happy to see me."

I looked into the room and my baby was sitting on the floor looking in the direction of the rocking chair. It moved.

As I stared at it, Lenora materialized slowly into solid form. She looked at me. She no longer had the bruise. "You were right. Thank you," she said. "I was so scared they would not remember me."

"I remember you, and it seems little Beth here remembers you."

"You said I could come back if I wanted."

"I did."

"I'm just here for a visit. I like this place. It's warm and makes me feel happy."

"I'm glad you came."

"I'll be back now that I know you are still here." And with that she blinked out of existence. Beth watched in wonder but I said nothing.

"Any time little one," and I looked at my child and wondered if I could ever bear to be parted from her. My heart got so tight, that I could feel the beats.

"Thank you for loving me when I was all alone," said a quiet voice. Beth looked at me and I scooped her up and walked upstairs to see my middle boy concentrating on a puzzle. He looked up at me and smiled, just happy I was there, I guess. Just them I heard Jim and my oldest son, blunder through the door, tossing a hockey bag on the floor and taking off their heavy coats.

At the sounds, Beth struggled in my arms and I put her down but didn't leave the room. "What do you want mom?" said my boy.

"Nothing," I said, "I have it all here."

Many years later, Beth and her husband came to dinner. They announced they were having a baby.

I brightened up, very happy for them. Jimmy, more than a little grey, was subdued but I knew he was happy.

"We've had the ultrasound and they said it's a girl," said Beth.

"That's lovely, but don't get too invested in that. I've heard plenty of stories of rooms painted pink and all the baby clothes bought, when things change."

"Oh, I know. But I'm pretty sure, the doctors are quite confident. Anyway, we thought we'd go neutral, you know, in case the next one isn't a girl."

"Smart thinking."

"And we've decided to name her Lenora." My breath caught in my throat.

"Now, now, you decided to name her Lenora," said Beth's husband Paul. "I haven't said anything as it was my Great Grandmother's name."

I managed to keep my expression placid, surprised by the name but not wanting to say anything in front of Jimmy or Beth or Paul. I could wait.

As we were cleaning up from dinner, Beth and I were alone in the kitchen. I probed her a bit, wondering why she'd chosen the name.

"It's a lovely old name, which seems to be a bit of a trend these days."

Beth looked at me oddly. "It just came to me in a dream. Sort of like Edgar Allan Poe, quite persistent it was. I was reading an old book, sitting in that old rocking chair you gave us, when I heard a tapping on the window. I thought it was a bird, or maybe a tree branch in the wind, and then I stirred. I'd fallen asleep and when I woke, I knew I was pregnant and that the baby would be called Lenora."

"Wow, that's quite a story all things considered."

"I didn't want to say anything to Paul. He might think I am crazy. But I knew you would understand, mom. I knew."

I nodded. I did understand, entirely. And after Beth left the room, I said a little prayer, just loud enough to be heard. "Please Lenora watch over my child and her child. Keep them safe."

There was a combination of sounds. Me, sliding a dish on the shelf, a rustle of paper and a creak of the wood framing from the front room which combined into, "I will."

Chapter Eight

Theresa and I met as usual. She put the pages down.

"Gothic, eh? Where's the spooky?"

"It's in there, creaky floors, odd old people, storms' a-comin', wind and rain, all the stuff."

Theresa made a face.

"Tropes. Yes. But it's just in the set up."

"Are the horror elements in the house or in the people?"

"How do I know, I'm just the author. I have to turn the page and figure it out. I need to shake off the usual suspects."

"Aliens in the attic?" She suppressed a laugh.

"I already did science fiction."

"You already started science fiction. At this point you've done nothing but a strangely abrupt short story."

"Now come on, I think the process has at least loosened my pen. The writer's block is over, sort of, even if I still don't have much concrete in a novel sense. You have to admit the sci-fi thing has some promise."

Theresa nodded.

"The next one, I think, is a western. I'm trying to break away from the usual tried and true. A western is not in my bag of tricks yet."

"A western romance? A western thriller? A western mystery? A western family saga? Which will it be?"

"Wait, wait, wait. I still have to get my head around a western. Maybe its modern. That breaks the tropes and I don't want to go to the old genres, that have been done a million times."

"Okay, fair enough. I eagerly await the next installment of 'Outlaw Truckers on the High Plains' or whatever you decide upon."

Now it was my turn to laugh, "This isn't easy you know. Not like slapping together a logo."

Theresa blanched, "I didn't slap it together. I thought about it long and hard. I'm trying to get as many elements of the subject in as I can without being too confusing."

"Are you happy with what you've got?"

"Yeah, I am. But I'm not entirely sold on it either. Still trying to push it in one way or another. I like the subversive 'Suburban' bit as it points to the target market, but I can't think of a second word – 'style' isn't it. It's too urban, too city oriented."

I thought for a moment, and then another one. Then Thresea sipped her coffee. She didn't say anything.

"Imagine that, tropes in logos."

"What? I'm thinking. I told you the second word eluded me."

"How about . . . ." my voice trailed off. "I honestly thought something would hit me, but you're right, it's not an easy thing. How about 'Unlimited' you know, rather than 'Limited' in a company name, 'Suburban Unlimited'.

"I don't think so. Sounds too forced."

"So did you ever hear back from Markus?"

"No."

"That's too bad, he, they seemed nice."

"I didn't hear back, but I took your advice and called Markus. Asked him to comment on some of my designs."

"And what did he say."

"He seemed a bit surprised to hear from me, but we chatted and agreed to coffee."

"And what did he say."

"That he'd meet me here in about half an hour."

My smile stayed put but my eyes betrayed my surprise. "Look, I know you know him and would provide me some cover. All very professional."

"Okay, I guess. I sort of wished I'd have known in advance."

"Me too. I just spoke to him this morning. Sorry."

"We will see what he has to say. Maybe he can think of the second word for the logo."

"I guess I should show him that too. I brought a couple of initial designs but didn't think of the logo, though I think I have a rough copy of it in here somewhere," she rummaged her portfolio bag.

And as if on cue, Markus walked into the coffee shop. He looked a bit older than I remembered, dressed in a business suit, and clean shaven. He scanned the shop looking past our table. Theresa waved and he made his way over.

"Nice to see you both again. Hopefully I can help."

"When we first spoke, you said you didn't often wear business formal, but here you are."

"True, I do most of my work on the phone or at my desk. Though, like today, I sometimes meet clients face to face. Company policy is a suit and tie. Most of us keep a change of clothes at the office, in the event of an unexpected meeting. I usually dress so I only have to put on a jacket and maybe a tie, given short notice. The junior guys in the office are often meeting clients and the more senior guys usually meet their long-standing clients in a less formal atmosphere. I guess that's a bit counter-intuitive."

Theresa took a sheaf of large format papers, unrolled them, and put a weight at the far end while scrolling out and holding down the other. There was a drawing of a young man, but it was his clothes that were drawn in detail, while he was only a sketch.

"Tell me about this."

"This is Suburban casual. The pants are fitted loosely with an extra bit of fabric, just an inch or so, in the upper thighs."

"An elastic waistband?"

"No, God no. The legs are trim but not tight. If you make them too tight, not only are they uncomfortable but they look like riding pants, especially when you first get up."

Markus nodded.

"They have extra deep pockets, where the extra fabric allows you to comfortably keep a phone in the front pocket. They do have back pockets, but they are mostly decorative."

"A lot of guys still keep their wallets in their back pocket, though that's not as universal as it once was."

Theresa nodded, making a mental note. "And the sweater he's wearing is knitted in a pattern. As you can see it's nothing too elaborate, just a bit of stitching to give the sweater some body and visual appeal. The sleeves are tighter than standard so the wearer can roll them up without it being too bulky or can wear them down and not have to worry about extra fabric if he's working with his hands."

"Nice. What about the shirts?"

Theresa allowed the top sheet to curl itself closed, revealing the same figure, this time in a shirt.

"This is the button up Oxford and on the next page is the collared golf shirt."

They apprised them and Markus commented that nothing she had presented was strikingly new.

"It's fashion. Everything has been done. That's why you see the outlandish stuff in the big Paris runway shows. They are trying to be eye catching, hoping their more pedestrian designs will be considered. It's a form of branding."

"And what about your brand?"

"That's the whole thing. Branding is the key. First, I need quality designs that are comfortable. Comfort is the number one consideration in suburban casual wear. Style that hides the comfort level. The branding sells it."

She pulled out a folded sheet and placed it on the table facing Markus.

"Ah, the logo." Markus stared at it a long time, cocking his head back and forth. "I like it. It seems a bit too detailed, but when I think on it, it's actually not detailed enough, if you know what I mean. I think it's the silhouetting."

"Frankly it's done that way to most easily reproduce the image. It does take a second to process what you are seeing."

"I like it," Markus said enthusiastically, "the more I see it, once I've realized what it is, the more I like it. It's got an urban cool vibe, and a subtext that the burbs are really cooler than the city."

"Thank you. That's the feel I was trying to get."

"But what about the lettering," I said. "Suburban what?"

Theresa looked expectantly at Markus. "I see your point," he said. "And the word suburban. I think it should be hyphenated or something."

"Hyphenated? That's an idea. But Sub-urban what? Apparel? Sub-urban Apparel? What about just spacing out the lettering to go most of the way around, but still be readable. Like from 9 o'clock to 3 o'clock?"

"Or maybe just go with Sub' at the top and 'Urban at the bottom. Let the reader put the two together."

"Let me think on it. Both suggestions are better than anything I have."

"So, what about you Cassandra? What have you been up to?"

Hearing the full version of my name I had to cringe a bit. I usually went by Cassie, or Cass to almost anyone. Though, to be honest, it didn't sound as bad coming from a guy in a business suit.

"You know, plugging away. Just dealing with my usual clients, who have been less busy than usual. That is nice in the summer but it doesn't pay the bills. Things should pick up shortly."

"I thought you were writing fiction, too."

"Oh yeah. On the side. It's difficult to talk about that though, as questions are hard to answer, when I haven't really decided the details yet. I'm trying to break a writer's block with Theresa's help."

"Can I help?"

"Well, I don't . . . . yeah, why not. What I've been doing is exploring different genres of fiction, writing just a short story and letting Theresa comment."

"And that's breaking the blockage?"

"Yes, but frankly in three attempts so far, I think I have only one that might be worth pursuing."

I explained to Markus that I had already tried Romance, Science Fiction and Gothic. His eyes betrayed his interest in the sci-fi, but he offered to read all three.

"At this point I'm just going to plow ahead. I'll come back to anything that seems promising after I've covered all the genres I can."

"Okay, so what's next?"

"A western."

Markus smiled broadly. "That's an unusual choice."

"So was the romance and the science fiction. I'm trying to stay away from my usual spaces by pushing some boundaries."

"Any idea of subject, time period, locality, characters, plot story line, themes . . . "

I had tried to interrupt him but he had kept pushing, almost in defiance of my desire to stop him. He grinned at my discomfort.

"No, nothing. I have been focussed on the gothic story until the moment you walked in here."

He looked puzzled, but I let it stew. Theresa collected her scrolled pages and secured them in a tube, asking us both to forward any additional thoughts if we came up with something. She mentioned that she would be actually making several pieces and had her eye on a few fashion shows in which to show them off.

"The problem is, the key to the clothes, is the way they are made, rather than the look. It's coming down to the logo. I can get that on the collared golf shirts easily, and maybe even the buttoned shirts on the breast, but the pants are another thing."

"Feature the logo prominently at the shows," Markus said. "I can help you set up, if you'd like. Let me know when they are."

Theresa's eyes moved slightly. I'd seen it before. She was surprised at the offer and pleased.

We chatted amiably about the city without the wedding ever coming up. A couple of times I almost fessed up, just to clear the air. Markus mentioned going to a baseball game, and Theresa mentioned a concert she attended. We asked after Brandon. Markus said they were old friends and cousins but didn't see a lot of each other anymore due to the distance, though he did say Brandon had met him in the city for the ball game.

Theresa said she would message him about our next meeting and he reminded her to let him know if she needed help on any show she might enter.

I met with two clients that afternoon. Preliminary meetings on pre-Christmas and early New Year promotional things they were planning. Most of my clients had a good grasp on technical deadlines for promotional work, that had to include printing costs, ad booking and delivery time lines. Some did not, despite my efforts to educate them.

As I walked between meetings I began to consider where my western story would go. I didn't really get anywhere, conjuring up some scenarios and then dashing them on my own ignorance and lack of desire to do a lot of preliminary research on what was really just a flyer, an exercise to get writing, rather than a serious effort.

"No!" I said out loud. A few people around me looked at me strangely. I realized I had to take the exercise seriously if it was going to have any value. But I did not look forward to the background work I was going to have to do on something that probably would not work out.

I sat down at my desk that night – determined to at least make a start.

Chapter Nine – Western – Before the gold rush.

Moving up the steep hill, the wagons creaked and groaned under the strain of the weight they carried. There was already a track here, rutted deep. We weren't the first to pass. At the top of the rise, after a long steady climb to a plateau, I saw the crosses.

Dotted, without any organization that I could understand, crosses dotted the land on the right side of the track. Most crosses were on the top of a pile of rocks. I counted eight before deciding that the real number was at least double that.

Jeb had seen me looking at the field. "Most of them are pretty rudimentary. I'm guessing they didn't expect to die."

"Who are they?"

"Wagon trains come through here regularly. I think the top of the mesa is just a nice place to rest, for the travellers and those who don't finish the trip."

"How do they die?"

"Oh, lots of reasons I expect. Some are young and not hearty enough. Some are old and face a difficult challenge but don't want their families to go without them. Some are snake bit. Some get injuries without a doctor around to help. You know, the usual stuff."

"Why would people make the trip if they are not up to it?"

"You don't always get to chose the timing of these things. Many people who come this way, are forced by circumstances to take this chance as they have nothing left for them back East."

I looked at the crosses, wondering if they had names and dates carved into them. I didn't want to ask that we stop and look, but the caravan walked on a bit and then stopped for a rest. Seems like the lead man didn't want to stop too near the makeshift cemetery but knew that a rest was needed after making the arduous climb.

I considered walking back to look at the graves, but it was pretty apparent that our rest was going to be short, and the walk back would have taken at least 20 minutes. The crosses were barely visible through the dust of our passing.

"Where do you reckon we are?" I heard one of the woman ask.

Her husband looked at her laconically. "About half a day past where we were yesterday."

"But then you said you didn't know, exactly."

He gave her a long look, the reality finally setting in, then he tossed her a bone. "If the land is rising, like it appears to be, we can't be far from the mountains proper. In fact, I think you can just make out the ridgeline on the horizon. We are several days journey at least from them. And that's where things will get really interesting."

"So where are we?"

"Like I said, several days from the big mountains. There is no name for this place, if that's what you want."

She pouted before turning away. He went to check on their horses, those pulling the wagon. It was likely he would change them with the other pair the family had brought. The four horses shared pulling duties. The farmers were content to live off the land as much as possible, saving their supplies for those times they could not provide for themselves or their animals. The top of the plateau was pretty barren. Fortunately, they had taken what they could from the lower lands and the river valley they had crossed two days before.

They had left St. Louis in March 1844 and travelled up the Missouri River before lighting out across the prairie headed for South Pass and eventually Fort Hall in Oregon Territory, and from there they could choose to go north to Portland or south to San Francisco.

The mountains got larger each day, shimmering in the heat of early summer.

"We've been lucky, I'm thinking, as we've encountered no Indians, and aren't likely too once we reach the mountains."

The man he spoke to spat into the dust. Indians don't generally come after large wagon trains like ours, unless we provoke them. And with a group as big as ours, it would take a lot of provoking to get them to attack us."

Jeb nodded slowly. It was tough to get anything concrete out of the wagon masters who had been hired to lead the train. He reckoned it was because they did not want to say anything too specific in case things turned out differently.

"So we follow the ruts all the way to San Francisco?"

"Something like that." The man was checking out his rifle, making sure it was in working order before loading it with a couple of rounds. "The trail runs pretty true but it doesn't account for anything unexpected. That's what I'm here for. You get a flood or a bunch of Indians blocking the way, well, you have to know where you're going."

Jeb nodded, "Let me know if there is anything needs doing. Any way, I can smooth our passage I'm happy to do."

"Like I said before we left, we will do some considerable hunting in the woods of the mountains as we pass through. With any luck we will replenish our supplies of meat."

With a nod, Jeb tilted his head down and headed back to his wagon.

"How are the horses doing?"

"Okay, I guess. Good thing we can spell them off each other, but four are getting hard to feed."

The whole trip had taken on a routine that was about to change. It was uncertain on any particular day if they would be climbing or descending through mountainous territory. Eventually they crested South Pass and turned northwest with the trail headed for the Hudson's Bay Company trading post of Fort Hall.

A few more days journey and the little Fort appeared over a prairie hill, its palisade a welcome sight of civilization to both the migrants and those in the Fort, who could welcome mail, supplies and even new people to the job of the trading post.

The guides went to speak to the Captain of the garrison, explaining they were passing through but had some deliveries for the Fort, and wondered if they could purchase some supplies.

A few days later the wagon train resumed its journey, breaking up a few miles west of the Fort where the trail diverged north and south. Jeb and I had already decided we would head south as the call of California and rumors of good farm land were strong.

With the Oregon question still up in the air, as the United States and Britian negotiated the future of the territory, we decided we'd rather not take a chance of falling under the Crown should negotiation favour the British.

"California is still Mexican, sort of. But a lot of Yankees have headed that way and word is they are the majority."

"So is there going to be violence?" I asked.

"Not if they leave us alone. We just need to find a bit of open land and we will settle. A bit of ranch land, a bit of wood, some water and a few acres of rich soil, and we are set."

"You are a dreamer, Jeb."

"Maybe so. Not sure what we'll find once we get there but if we can find land with some of those things in abundance we'll do just fine."

"Seems to me we've passed a lot of land with at least two of these properties, already."

"Now we've been over this. With that prairie land, you have go get permits and titles and all of that from the various governments. But California is unregulated for the most part and we can just lay claim and a few markers, and we are in business."

I nodded, I'd heard it all before and was amazed by Jeb's complete unwillingness to deal with any official body. It might have been his defining characteristic.

"I gotta feeling that something big is going to happen. Probably in Texas, as that's where all the noise is aimed at. Out here in California it will be peace and quiet until the Mexicans cotton on to the numbers of settlers coming in."

"But if the States and Texas get into it won't that spill over into California?"

"It might, but I doubt it. We won't be waving any stars and stripes, we're just peaceful farmers, and hopefully any land we cultivate will be far enough away from any town to keep it quiet."

The party moved slowly through the Sierra Nevada mountains, as ranges seemed to grow out of each other as they headed west and south. As June was nearing its end, they had several days of hard rain and the travelers simply hunkered down among the trees, awaiting drier conditions. And sure enough the sky cleared and they were able to move again, even if the sky showed dark clouds to the north, day after day.

"The clouds are there again today."

"Just be thankful they are up there and not overhead. Can't go anywhere in the rain, not with wagons and mud."

I looked ruefully north to the dark roiling clouds. The wind was gentle enough and blew eastward, pushing the clouds away. On the whole it seemed we'd dodged a bullet by getting off the prairie before all that rain came. There would have been no place to hide in the great wide open.

Soon enough the wagon train began to break apart as families headed in their separate directions, towards San Francisco or the nascent Sacramento, or further south into the great Valley of California. We stuck to the trail, determined to get to San Francisco, resupply and reconnoitre before heading south to find some unclaimed land.

Most of the coastal lands had been claimed by the Spanish missions, located about 30 miles apart, or one day's journey. Twenty-five years before, the Spanish had forced the Spanish operators of these missions to leave. The El Camino Road ran from San Francisco south to San Diego. American migrants were told to stay away from the coastlines and make whatever arrangements they needed to with the native Indians of the interior. Many of the old missions were subdivided and converted to ranch properties. The Spanish put up with American settlers as Russian interest in the area, primarily for hides, was well known, and included a Russian fur trading post in northern California, wedged between San Francisco and Portland.

Jeb was certain that he wanted to move south even though the land north of the great bay was fertile and rich. And so we made the decision to bypass San Francisco on the other side of the bay, and work our way down the valley. Only the rills of mountains on both sides of the expanse suggested a valley, though there were several small languid rivers that fed the bay.

We made our way along the San Joaquim River until we found a ford to cross the river, and headed south eventually running into another river flowing north. A few more days found us in a place where this Middle River connected to the San Joaquim providing ample water for farming. As there were already several settlers in the area, we spoke to them and staked out a fairly large plot and immediately set to work.

There was still some good, watered land to the east which also supplied the trees and a bit of ranch land that Jeb wanted. His first move was to buy a breeding pair of cattle from a rancher nearby. Everyone there had started in much the same way, and the rancher made us a very fair deal. Being friendly with the neighbours could mean life or death.

Jeb planted and hunted and somehow we made it through. Our two little ones helped where they could but they were unable to do anything heavy, so their help was mostly domestic. Cavan, the oldest was able to help with the sawing of the wood, which was done a mile or two off the ranch. The felled trees were too heavy to move until they had been cut up, so that had to be done on site. Cavan was able to steady the logs as Jeb sawed and he was strong enough to carry the smaller boards back to the homestead site.

Our younger boy Willie stuck to my side and helped me establish our home. First we just lived out of the covered wagon and accumulated wooden boards. When Jeb and Cavan were away felling timber I started to dig a foundation, scraping the dirt away in the rough shape of a home. Jeb warned me to not be too ambitious as getting a shelter built was our priority. It could always be added to in the future.

And so I dug down a foot or so in a rectangle about 20 feet by 15 with a little side room of about eight by five. I deepened the perimeter and then started to gather stones to fill the foundation. That effort also helped to clear the fields which had been quickly planted. The river provided much of the stone. Next year's crop would be much larger.

Towards the end of the summer, just as I noticed the weather getting a bit cooler, Jeb decided he had better head north to San Francisco for winter supplies. We had the frame of the home built and it was on track to be completed by November. The beginnings of a stone fireplace were also taking shape. The trip for supplies was going to take more than a week.

Jeb set off one morning taking Cavan with him. I took on the task of bringing some of the finished wooden boards back from the sawing area. I trussed up the wagon for the task knowing it would not make it all the way, and I'd have to walk the last portion of the journey.

Abandoning the wagon half a mile short of the mill, Willie jumped and ran along the path that Jeb and Cavan had made and we arrived at the saw mill faster than I thought. The last portion of the path was impossible for the wagon, running up a ravine, winding through trees up to a rise above a creek. The creek would have been a good source of stone, but I figured that Jeb had ignored that as transport would have been difficult, and removing the stones from the crop lands was a priority.

Willie was carrying two four-foot lengths of four-by-four posts, one under each arm, dragging them behind. I told him he'd be best to just carry one, but he insisted and I figured if he had to drop one, we'd just retrieve it later. I had to smile at his determination. The wood lengths were bigger than he was. I managed two larger planks about eight feet long, which I expected were supposed to be for the outer walls of the cabin.

Halfway back we rested a spell and then took up the task again, though I wasn't sure how often we could make this trek. Certainly, taking the wagon as far as we could, then loading it with shorter trips was the right idea.

On our way back with a substantial load of wood and about a quarter mile from the cabin, I knew something was wrong. One of the horses had broken loose and wandered free. I dropped my desire to move quickly to the cabin, not sure if anyone was still lurking about. Willie sensed my fear and he started crying.

Reaching the compound, I realized we'd been robbed. One of the horses was gone. The other was running free. Our supplies had been overturned and rooted through and all the meat was gone. Nothing else seemed amiss. The cabin framing had not been damaged. Some of the food was still there. Thankfully I had taken the wagon so it was safe. I imagined the difficulties we would have had if I'd left the wagon and it had been stolen. Now I knew why Jeb had insisted we tie it down with stakes to keep it stable.

I squatted down to rest without a chair and Willie finally reached me, launching into my arms, not sure why I was upset. Fear was rising in me. Jeb would not return for several days. I thought to go to our neighbouring ranch but that meant I'd have to abandon our cabin again. Perhaps it was fortunate that neither of us were there when the thieves raided our camp. Jeb was gone and he had all our money. Cavan was safe with him. In the end we had little to steal. Hopefully they would not return.

As I squatted in front of the cabin, I decided to unload the wood and considered making a return trip to the mill. At this point there wasn't anything left to steal at the compound. Jeb would be disappointed if we couldn't get more of it. And I worried that our heavy tools lay strewn around the saw mill site. I decided that we would rest a bit and go again for some more wood, and secure the site, hide the tools and bring back what we could. If they came back to rob us there was little I could do even if I was in the camp to object.

I collected the stray horse, which seemed happy to be tethered. I considered using the horse to carry the wood but it seemed too precarious to arrange. The horse seemed spooked so I decided to let it walk with us to the sawmill site, forgetting how difficult the final climb up the ravine was.

By the time we returned I had calmed down, realizing that if we were going to be robbed, we had gotten off fairly lightly. The meat could be replaced. No tools had been stolen, at least none that I knew of, and we were all uninjured. The horse was the biggest loss. I got to thinking what kind of thieves would just plunder easy pickings. Indians? Mexicans? Settlers?

I was anxious for Jeb to return.

A few days later he rolled in just after the sun set. I breathed a heavy sigh, thinking I was facing yet another anxious night.

"Did the horse die?"

"We were robbed. They got the horse, all our stored meat and other odds and ends."

"Who were they?"

"Don't rightly know. Willie and I were at the sawmill collecting wood and arrived back after they'd gone."

"Thank God for that. No further sign of them?"

"No, Jeb. It happened the first day you were gone."

"I wonder if they'd been watching us, waiting for a chance."

"We went to hide the tools after they'd gone. Except the horse and the meat, they didn't seem to take anything of value."

"Of value to us. I'll go to Robinson's place tomorrow and ask around."

"How was your journey?"

"Fine, we got what we needed. It was nice having Cavan with me. Stopped a lot of the rough types from approaching us, and the boy and I had a lot of time to jaw. Did run into a few other travellers. They said they'd heard that Texas and Mexico are at it again, mostly because Texas is joining the United States. Might be war. We should probably be ready for trouble."

"We've already had it. I was so scared they would come back."

"I left you a rifle."

"I didn't see it. Maybe it was stolen too."

And Jeb reached over into the wagon's back trunk and pulled out a rifle. He was shaken. He looked at another trunk in the cabin and saw that much of the ammunition he'd accumulated was also missing.

"I'm going have to beg Robinson for some bullets. We have some left, the ones I took with me, but not enough to get through the winter hunting season."

"The crops are about ready for harvest. The corn did not do too well though. I think the land is a bit too swampy for it."

"We will make do, Clare. A couple of years from now we will look back at this and know we did the best we could."

"Once we get the crops in, I will try to shore up the cabin. We'll be wanting it badly in a month or two."

Mr. Robinson said he wasn't surprised the homestead was robbed. "The damned Mexicans come by once or twice a year demanding rent from me. I chase 'em off by waving a gun around. Two of my boys are old enough to be armed as well. Gotta a bad feeling it's going to get worse with this Texas thing."

Jeb told him what he'd heard on his trip north. "Look we need a signal we can use when they come back. We can help each other, and I'm guessing they will hit you up before trying to mess with me, again."

Robinson thought hard. Their two properties were about three-quarters of a mile apart. Eventually they settled on smoke signals, like the natives. Three puffs of smoke meant trouble.

"Proper smoke signals would be a might difficult once you are in the middle of battle," said Jeb.

"Well, you got a fire going almost all the time, right?" Jeb nodded. "Just make sure your wife knows the signal and how to make the puffs. It only takes a few minutes to get to your place. Signal at the first sign of trouble."

So 1845 bled into 1846 as Jeb and Clare survived the winter in their new cabin. Jeb realized the fireplace needed some improvement and resolved to take on the task after the spring planting. He still needed planking to finish the second room of the building and to double up on the roof and walls.

Word spread in the spring of 1846 that the United States and Mexico were at war. All the American settlers hunkered down, expecting violence. American troops clashed with Mexicans in several places without either side able to claim significant victories.

In the summer a group of ragged Mexican bandits rolled through the area. They came seeking rents, through Robinson later said they were also looking to see if the ranchers were helping the American troops.

As the party of Mexicans slowly rode along the river toward the cabin Jeb told Clare to send the smoke signal.

As the horses reached the cabin Jeb stepped out with his rifle. He waved his arm and the party stopped about 40 yards away from the cabin.

"What do you and your friends want?" yelled Jeb.

"We come seeking rent for your land. You are on Mexican territory." They let the horses move slowly forward.

"This land was empty when we arrived a year ago," said Jeb.

"And we came by to collect our rent but no one was here."

"So, it was you who robbed me."

"No, senior, we did not rob, we collected payment."

"It was a pretty dear payment. A horse, my ammunition and a store of meat. I do not recognize your ownership of this land."

"You had better. It is registered with authorities at the Mission. Once we send off the Americanos we will do a complete land survey, and set the rents more formally."

One of the men on horseback behind the speaker was loading his rifle. Jeb raised his, calling for the man to throw his rifle down, to replace the one that was stolen. The man at the front laughed.

"Senior, you have no standing here. This is Mexican territory. We decide who lives here."

A second man began to load his rifle and the speaking man moved forward. "The rent is 1,000 pesos or goods worth that amount. We have come to collect."

The smoke signals had been sent. Clare opened the front door and saw the standoff. Jeb directed her back into the cabin and told her to keep the boys close.

"We want no trouble with you mister," said one of the other armed men.

"Then leave. I do not owe you rent. And I do not want you on my land."

A shot rang out and wood on the door jamb splintered. Jeb fired at the lead man, who jerked back as the bullet caught him in the shoulder. A second horsed shooter fired as Jeb retreated inside the cabin. There was a jagged, splintered hole in the door. Jeb's first thought was finding a replacement plank for the door.

He quickly reloaded and grabbed a second rifle thrusting it at Clare. "Stay here. If they try to come in shoot the first one."

Jeb put a handful of bullets into his pocket and moved to the door of the unfinished storage room. He could get out and move into the yard, if they hadn't yet surrounded the building.

He tried to count how many of them there were, thinking back on the confrontation. Six or seven he thought, one injured and probably all armed. He crouched at the side of the cabin, in the notch where the storage room did not reach all the way to the back wall of the cabin. He had to pick which way they would go.

A bullet in his hand for a quick reload, he peeked around the back wall. Boom. His rifle exploded and the man went down, his horse dragging him with his foot still in the stirrup, creating a trail of dust. Jeb quickly turned around and saw a horseman coming from the other direction. He moved quickly to the back of the cabin for a little cover.

Boom. A shot rang out and some wood behind him splintered out. It was not a shot from the horseman who was still trying to get a clean shot, it was a shot from inside the cabin. Jeb leaped out, his rifle at the ready, but there was no horseman there.

He turned quickly and saw a second man coming around the corner of the cabin on foot. He swung his rifle around but was too late. A second boom echoed off the back wall and the man on foot went down. Another shot sounded from inside the cabin and then there was silence. Jeb crept around the back side of the cabin on the other side from which he had exited. There was no one. But someone had shot the man on foot. There was nobody in sight and he knew he needed to get back in the building to make sure Clare was okay.

He saw a wave from behind a tree. It was one of Robinson's sons with a rifle. Two shots fired quickly. Both from inside the cabin. Jeb rushed around the front and seeing the door open he ran in behind his gun barrel. Two Mexicans lay on the floor though one was still moving. Jeb kicked his rifle away thinking he'd at least gotten his stolen property back.

"Clare?" he yelled. She emerged from behind two barrels. "Are you okay?

Where are the boys?"

Two wide-eyed boys poked their heads up, "I'm here Daddy," said Willie. Cavan looked shocked.

"This is two of them. There are two more outside in the yard. I reckon there are two or three more about."

A shot was heard from outside. And a moment later Robinson yelled if it was safe to enter the cabin. Hearing the affirmative he came in and said they gotten another one, leaving the last two to ride off. "If you are okay here I'm heading back to my place. They were moving in that direction. Come with me if you can."

Jeb nodded. "I'll be along shortly. I gotta get my horse ready."

Robinson left and quickly road off. "I gotta go Clare. Keep the gun at hand. I must return the favor and I will be back, hopefully fairly quickly. I expect the Mexicans will retreat and I hope Robinson gets them."

The Mexican who had been moving on the floor had stopped moving though he was moaning low. Clare kept her eyes on him and directed Cavan to the front door to act as a look out with instructions to hide again if anyone he did not know approached.

Two hours later Jeb returned.

"We got one more but the last one got away. I think it was the man I shot in the shoulder."

The next day Jeb saw a cloud of dust rising above the river. He ran inside. There had been no signal from Robinson. He came back out armed and had set Clare with a rifle of her own.

The cloud of dust suggested a large party was approaching. Clare was right, they were in the middle of a war they wanted no part of. Jeb was not going to flee. He waited in the door jamb.

A horse broke away from the main pack about 100 yards from the cabin. Thirty yards away the man on horseback yelled, "John Fremont, United States Army."

Jeb lowered his gun. Fremont approached. "Sir, I spoke with your neighbour. He said you'd had some trouble here yesterday."

"Aye, and with his help we saw them off. I don't know if they were banditos or Mexican soldiers. They wanted rent."

"We are here now. Anything we can do for you?"

"I've got four Mexicans out back. I could use your help."

Freemont looked a bit panicked, "Why didn't you say so sir?" He looked behind him and made a few hand gestures to men to flank the cabin. They raised their rifles.

"Cause they're dead. Need help burying them." Freemont was visibly relieved.

"We are at war with Mexico, sir. You need to prepare for trouble. My men and I are looking for battle but we will not always be nearby to help."

Freemont dismounted and shook Jeb's hand. He directed several of his party to begin to bury the bodies. In the tall grasses flanking the river, a pair of eyes watched the scene. These settlers were helping the American soldiers.

They buried the Mexicans in a row in a communal grave at the bottom of a small rise about 100 yards from the cabin. Jeb would have liked to have Fremont haul the bodies away, wanting nothing to do with them nor any reminder of their battle.

"I'm going to suggest you refrain from marking the graves with a cross or anything, though you might want to put a few stones at the corners so you know where it is. You can put something more substantial up when all of this is over. Fresh graves when some of their comrades have gone missing is just a marker for more trouble."

Jeb nodded.

"With the troubles in Texas it could take years for American justice to reach us."

"No sir, it already has. We are United States Army though I'll admit we are but a few, covering a huge territory."

"I just want peace."

"Sometimes you have to dictate the peace by removing the impediments to it." He gestured to the freshly turned earth. "It appears you have made a good start."

After Fremont and his party had moved on, Jeb rode over to the Robinson place, knowing the army group had gone through the area.

"What did you think of Fremont?"

"I welcome the Americans, but they are here as a token only. I doubt they will be of much use to us save as a deterrent to Mexican violence. I've heard that a group in San Francisco want to set up an independent Republic. Saves face for the Mexicans some of whom are still not happy they broke with Spain."

"I'd be happier with the Americans. You know what you are getting with them. The Mexicans who abandoned the Spanish, are less predictable."

"Aye, I hear you. Those behind the independence movement are largely Americans. Fremont's bunch will help, but I'm guessing it won't take long before the Americans lay their claims. Right now, they are more concerned with Texas but soon enough they will look our way."

The last of the Mexicans made his way back to the coastal mission area with news of the determined Americans and the force of army regulars who appeared on the heels of the battle at the ranch. The missions were loosely administered by Mexican authorities who had usurped the Franciscan monks after the Mexican War of Independence a generation before.

The Mexicans were engaged in a losing battle with fewer people, less determination to hold the land and a better armed and more willing defensive force opposing them. They had relied on native labour but the natives were no longer cooperating and were leaving the area.

Several of the Mexican settlers near the coast had decided they were more interested in surviving the American invasion and holding their properties than they were in pushing out new settlers. They found the Americans were quite willing to honor their claims as long as they were working them, and despite their differences they could exist as neighbours. Californians declared the California Republic but with Fremont and the Americans intervening on their behalf, they quickly became a territory of the United States as the Mexican – American war ended and territorial issues were settled.

Before the Mexicans could catch their breath, gold was discovered north of San Francisco and 49ers flooded the area leading to the Americans making it a state in their union only a few years later.

Jeb and Clare continued to work their stake and built a substantial ranch. And predicably they looked back on the early days with pride and a reminder of their tenuous hold on the land.

Chapter Ten

Theresa wanted to get together earlier than our usual so I trundled down to the coffee shop sporting my rough draft of a Western.

As had become our custom, she took the sheets to read while I managed to get my coffee fixed the way I liked it, one sugar, two creams.

I had barely settled down before she put the pages down. “You weren’t kidding, saying this is a rough draft.”

I shrugged, “You wanted to do coffee early, so it’s on you.”

“Do you have any idea where this is going?”

“Some. But I’m not entirely sure at this point. The whole war with Mexico thing was a bit of an eye-opener. I think it has to stew a while and more of the story will jump out.”

“So there’s a novel here?”

“There’s novels, novels everywhere,” I said shifting my eyes and looking about, “But mostly plots that stink.”

“Really? You need your coffee badly. I guess your writer’s block is an albatross of sorts. What’s next?”

I explained that I thought I should give a crime mystery a go.

“And how has Markus been? Did he help you at the trade show?”

Theresa explained that he did help her, coming in on the Thursday morning to help her set up her booth and displays. The show was in a hotel downtown.

"He really fussed with the set up. I thought he'd be all over the building of the booth and stuff but he seemed more interested in the placement of the promotional materials. He even lugged in two mannequins. He said they belonged to his aunt, who used to be in retail."

We both knew what Markus' actions likely meant. "Are you happy he helped?"

"Absolutely. The booth looked great, and I made a significant splash with some of the buyers. On Markus himself, I still don't know. He helped with the set up but was nowhere to be found the rest of the weekend, though he did arrive Sunday afternoon with a couple of coffees to help disassemble the booth."

"Well maybe he's trying to avoid coming on too strong."

"Could be, I certainly did need his help when he came, but I wish he had stayed some, to see the reactions. You know, to improve the set up and pitch the next time around. I was thinking how I could show some appreciation without it being misconstrued."

"I guess it depends upon how you want it to be construed."

"Well, I didn't tell him about today, I figure I'll invite him along next week and at least thank him then."

I nodded sagely, though I wasn't sure how Theresa felt about him. She surely showed no signs of keeping him at any distance.

"What's your next genre?"

"Like I said, crime mystery. I've not tried it before, but what the heck, it's going to come up eventually."

We finished our coffees and headed out into the urban wilderness.

I arrived home to a message from my mother, wondering about my attendance at Thanksgiving dinner. My older brother had decided to make a trip of it, coming in from Atlanta with his small family.

I carefully unloaded the few groceries I had purchased while thinking on how I could avoid the crime mystery tropes or at least make them less obvious.

Putting the butter away, I briefly thought of using butter as a weapon.

The evidence would melt. Or would it? I glanced at my butter dish, still with half a stick, soft to be sure, but not melted.

How about using food as a weapon? I went through the various foods that were dangerous, thinking that peanuts would kill, but only someone who was very allergic. Then I shifted my thinking to who would die, why they needed to die and who might kill them. The whole thing swirled around in my head until I sat down to some paid work after cleaning up from dinner. Maybe I just needed to have a bit more experience with these things, I thought, determined to read the news each day in order to soak up the details of major crimes.

Finished with my paid stuff, I'd let it stew until I could review it in the morning prior to submitting it to my clients.

I opened a new document and stared at the screen. I stared a while, kind of hoping for the phone to ring or an email to ping its arrival.

Then I began . . .

Chapter Eleven – Crime, Crime Everywhere

The gray metal elevator doors opened on the second subterranean level of my building, the middle level of the parking garage. It's all concrete, dim light and motor oil.

I briskly moved through the doors and turned left toward my car, parked about halfway along the way before the right hand turn that leads up and eventually out onto the road above.

I was never too comfortable with this walk, but in the mornings, I never got too concerned, even though the artificial light remained the same. Daylight just lends a different atmosphere, even if you can't see it.

At first it looked like someone had dumped a suitcase between two cars, but I looked a bit closer and gasped, it was a body, crumpled under a mess of other clothes.

I looked around to see if anyone else was about, called at it a few times without response, save the echo, and then steeled myself, got in my car and dialled 911. I explained everything as much as I could and was told to sit on the scene as 911 dispatch would contact the building security and ensure the door to the parking area was open.

I sat patiently looking for anyone else to come by, but there was no one, though I could hear a few cars fire up and move off, in some other locations in the garage, out of my line of sight.

Enough time passed that I was compelled to phone my morning meeting, explain the situation and reschedule my presentation two days later. My client was understanding, but with an edge of annoyance in her voice. Clearly she was busy and had set aside this time for me.

I heard a short burst of a siren and a moment of flashing lights so I got out of my car to flag down the Emergency Medical Team.

Slowly rounding a corner, they saw me and moved up to where I indicated.

Two uniformed EMTs exited the van and one came with me between the cars while the other began unloading equipment.

The EMT with me, bent to the body, without moving anything that lay around and on top, and felt the neck of the middle-aged man, for a pulse. He checked the eyes, flashed a light in them and stood up.

"DOA. No need to rush."

The second EMT visibly slowed down, methodically pulling the gurney out of the van and arranging it for use.

"He's dead," the EMT said to me. "Hard to say how long, but a few hours at least. I can't see any trauma to the body, but that doesn't mean there isn't any."

"So you will take him away and I can leave?"

"Not right away. The coroner has to sign off on removing the body and the police are on their way, they will want to speak with you."

I nodded. I had caught a glimpse of the face when the EMT did his work, but it was nobody I knew or had even seen in passing. I wondered if the parking assignments were set up in the order of the condo spaces above. If they were, this guy might have lived on the same floor as me, but there was no way of knowing unless I asked the question of the property managers. And I wasn't sure I really wanted to know.

Might have been a heart attack, except where was the suitcase, if all the clothes were still there?

Murder? I guess we'd find out when the doctors looked more closely at the body. In the mean time, I leaned against my car, waiting for the police. I didn't drive often and only had a little compact car for any journeys I made. The truth is, I drove whenever it was more convenient than taking public transit. Most of my work was done for people outside the central core of the business district. Downtown businesses had communications and promotional departments of their own. I worked mostly for the smaller businesses and on occasion as a counterfoil to another hired gun to see what we might come up with.

Working in those situations initially bothered me, but I found going head-to-head was actually beneficial as I produced more detailed stuff, knowing it wasn't the only option out there. I won these competitions more often than not, and either way, I got paid.

Soon enough the police car crawled into the parking garage, displaying the same behaviour as the EMTs. A quick burst of siren which echoed around the place and then some flashing lights, but not the full array.

A resident came out of the elevator and saw the commotion before slowly walking to his car and easing it out in the wrong direction, though he was unlikely to encounter anyone else leaving in the hundred yards or so it would take to find the ramp.

The police stopped and spoke to the EMT who gestured at me. The policeman stayed a moment with the EMT and then made his way over to me, bristling with equipment attached to his uniform.

"Ma'am," he nodded, "I understand you found the body?"

I nodded, explaining that I was heading to my car and had seen the pile of clothes as I walked to it from the elevator. He asked if I'd touched the body and if I had any idea who the deceased might be. I shook my head both times.

"Did you see anyone else down here, either in the elevator, or walking to or from a car?"

Again I shook my head, though I did mention that I'd heard the noise of a few cars leaving the lot while I had waited.

The policeman took my name and contact information and handed me his card. "If you recall anything please give me a call. You will likely be contacted by a police detective, who will go over your discovery."

"Am I, am I able to go now?"

"Yes, just track back away from the scene."

I thanked him, and made my way to my car, which fortunately was beyond the area taped off by police, so I could exit the car park in the normal way. I left the garage with my mind swirling about what had just happened, and what other details I could remember, noises, shadows, movements, but there was nothing. I forced myself to shift into presentation mode, but I kept coming back to the disheveled pile on the ground between the cars.

I remembered the car on the right side of the body was one I'd seen a middle-aged blonde park and leave, maybe a month before. I only remembered because it was evident she was trying too hard, and she was parking her car mid-morning, even though she was clearly dressed for something important. She should be going, not coming into the building. And her car was a little sport coupe, a two-seater, maybe the only two-seater in that whole section of parking garage.

'So, the guy must have been getting into the other car,' thought I, almost aloud. 'But that would mean he was trying to get into the passenger seat. Or he was putting something into the car. Or he was jumped and dragged back between random cars. Or he was getting into the sporty coupe.'

I smiled to myself, despite the circumstances, I would likely make an imperfect detective, give that virtually anything could have put that particular man between those cars, and, something I didn't know was what left him there in a crumpled heap.

By now I was a few blocks from my building and about to turn onto a major street heading uptown to my late morning appointment, more sprawling spaces and easier parking. I glanced down, to reassure myself that my portfolio clutch was still on the seat beside me, and then strained to remember putting the clutch of pages into it before departing my apartment and engaging in all the drama.

"Well," I said aloud. "A call from the detective and then I can forget the whole thing. It has nothing to do with me."

I punched on the radio, expecting the notes of some old familiar song, but got a strange feeling I was on the wrong station, as news chatter filled the air. I glanced at the radio and saw it was on the local all news station, something that I rarely listened to. When was I last in the car? Why had I switched stations?

I had merged onto a short internal freeway that followed a ravine uptown, taking those who really wanted to get out of the clutches of city traffic a couple of miles north, where city traffic was still an issue, but the intersections were larger, and the space between stop lights increased.

I knew where I was going. I'd done work for these people before. I readied my excuses and apologies for being late, and turned into the parking lot, finding a spot about as far away from the main doorway as was humanly possible. At least I didn't have to circle the lot nor did I have to go to a neighbouring business and sneak a spot. I'd had to do that before.

In the lobby I mentioned the person I had an appointment with and was directed to the elevator and eventually ushered into an office. My meeting seemed to go well but I knew I was distracted by what had happened that morning.

"Frankly you come highly recommended from our ad department. I'd like you to consider a retainer situation. We would pay you a small regular fee to put us first in your work schedule and of course pay you for your time when we require your services."

"How much work do you expect to need?"

"Honestly I cannot say exactly other than when we need you, we need your services badly and often for some substantial period of time, days for sure, weeks more likely. What I can say is those times are very predictable, and of course other issues may arise unexpectedly. For the retainer you would be expected to react immediately to our need."

We chatted a bit more about the scope of the work and the busy time periods and I agreed to take on the task, wringing a few more dollars out of the pay for necessary work while retaining the original retainer fee.

We agreed the arrangement could be ended at any time by either party with a month's notice. I was told there would be a small job on the near horizon, with the expectation it could be turned over in less than 24 hours.

Back in the car, out of downtown I was footloose and wondered if I should visit a local shopping center since I was already so near.

The mall seemed busy and I pulled into an empty parking spot at the back of the huge lot. I was riffling through my messages when a person ran beside my car on the passenger side. There was a muffled bang and he went down. Thinking he had tripped I got out to investigate when he didn't immediately rise into view. Moving around the car there was a body, blood streaming from the head, fallen in the most uncomfortable position, its torso doubled up and over a pair of twisted legs.

I automatically looked up and around, more to see if anyone else had seen what happened. I noticed two men in overcoats walking away, now halfway down the line of cars, headed for the mall entrance. It seemed a bit warm for overcoats.

A blue pick-up truck rolled by me, the driver leaning out of the car. "Did you see that? They chased him. Then he ducked and they turned away."

"He's been shot, I think."

The man in the blue pickup looked stricken and quickly turned and drove off, with a momentary burst of acceleration. I caught the license plate ARQ051. I got back in my car and punched 911. I stood beside the body, surrounded by parked cars and looked for someone to flag down. As I waited, I noticed an envelope on the ground beside the body. It had my name and address written on it. I picked it up and tossed it in my car thinking it had fallen out when I got out of the vehicle. A mall security team arrived a few minutes later and said police were on the way.

Two murders in close proximity to me in one day? I was going to be a suspect. No matter what I said. I waited patiently and was not actually surprised to see the same cop exit his car after being flagged down by the security men.

"You again, Miss D'Angelo? This is most unusual."

"For me too. Never having seen or been near a major crime, and now to have it happen twice the same day."

The security men looked at me closely, like I was going to spout an evil laugh or something.

Checking that the man was dead and letting the ambulance know there was no life-or-death rush, the policeman came over to me. "Okay, so how did you end up here?"

"After I left my building, I went to a meeting uptown. A business meeting. After that meeting I decided since I was in the neighbourhood, I might do a little shopping, or at least looking around. I really wasn't in the market for anything in particular."

"How did you find the victim?"

"He found me. I had just pulled into the space and was checking my messages when he ran between the cars and went down. I did hear a low bang but saw no one. Of course I wasn't really looking. I thought he tripped. When he didn't get up, I got out to look and it was obvious from the blood he'd been shot. I called 911. And here you are."

I described the two men in overcoats walking away, though there was no reason to believe they were involved, other than their proximity. I mentioned the witness in the blue pick-up and gave the license plate number, commenting that my experience in the morning was the only reason I had to have taken note.

"Did any other cars leave after you called 911?"

"I think a few. I really wasn't paying too much attention outside the immediate area. One or two people came out of the mall and drove away, and yes, a single car drove out as I was calling you. It wasn't in this block of cars but the next one over and a little closer to the mall entrance," I pointed to the general location. He asked what kind of car it was but my memory was not sharp. A few more questions and it sounded as if it must have been an American car, beige or off-white, four doors. I have never been very good at identifying auto makes, it's just not something I think about.

"These two murders do not appear to be related," he said. "But that's not up to me to determine. There are some similarities. I believe the detectives will want to talk to you further. Have you been able to remember anything more about this morning's event?"

I mentioned the blonde woman driving the sports car but admitted there was nothing else as I only came upon the scene after the fact. "Was he shot?"

"Yes, the man this morning had been shot at what appeared to be close range."

"You're are free to go Miss D'Angelo but expect a call or visit from a detective."

I slowly exited the scene wondering if the next place I went would mark yet another murder. I mean, I knew I had nothing to do with either one, but such a strange co-incidence seemed very odd to me.

The phone rang that evening and I fully expected a detective at the other end, but it was only a contact at H and G. This person, Frank Faraday, would be my immediate supervisor and contact within the company. He said he would forward the details of a job the next day and required it to be complete for public release at 9 am the following morning. I agreed to send the completed press release to Mr. Faraday during business hours the day before release, to make sure they were happy with the content.

I sat in my one easy chair and looked out the window. Newer buildings filled my view, save for a sliver of space between them that revealed a stretch of a major downtown street. From action on that stretch, I could often figure out how busy the city might be. Even though the hum of the city was very predictable there was something about seeing it in real time that was comforting.

With the expectation of the detective's call in my mind I contemplated my dinner choices, settling for cutting up some meat and adding it to a bit of left over salad. I turned on the news but there was no mention of either murder.

Just as I finished my dinner the phone rang.

"Miss D'Angleo? This is Detective Ross, I understand you were told to expect my call?"

"Yes, how can I help you?"

And I went over all the details of both murder scenes that I had witnessed with detective Ross moving away and coming back to many of the same details, over and over.

At the end he thanked me and signed off, giving me his contact information should I recall any additional details.

The next day I received the assignment from my new employer and managed to send the completed press release to Mr. Faraday just before noon. I made some lunch and Faraday messaged me asking for two minor changes, which I completed and fired off to him.

An hour later, he contacted me to say it was all good and he would contact me again when I was needed. Satisfied I decided to go for a walk. I stopped by my car to gather my gym shoes and headed outside straight from there, leaving my street shoes in the car. It was then that I saw the envelope I had picked up, sitting on the front passenger seat.

I did notice that the little sports car was not there, as I sat sideways in my car and put my shoes on with the door wide open.

A brisk walk around the block and I returned home feeling much better. I decided to watch a movie and studiously avoided any crime drama, looking hard until I found a comedy. I was distracted as my mind flicked back and forth between the two incidents.

The next day I was planning on staying home as I had a fair bit of work for a regular client. I was putting together a small catalogue which would be mailed to preferred clients of the store in two months time. I was ahead of the curve on this one, still waiting for a couple of photos from the client and some pricing details but much of the lay out and copy were already complete. I picked away at the details.

By mid-afternoon I had done everything I could on the project and packed it up for the day. I'd had a message from my friend Addison to meet her for a coffee at a shop a few blocks away, when she finished work. I figured I'd go early and do a little window shopping as I walked over.

"Hey Addie, how are things?" I asked once she sat down.

"Good, and you?"

"A little strange." She perked up. "A couple of days ago I was at the scene of two murders."

She smiled, "Like who got fired?"

"No, actual murders. One in my building parking garage and the other uptown at a mall."

Her face fell. "Oh my god." She inquired about the details.

"I've never even seen a crime take place before, and now this. It has definitely thrown me, but how, I'm not quite sure."

"What do the police say?"

"They don't think they are connected but that's about all they've said. If you asked me, and I'm no expert, they looked like professional hits."

She asked a few more questions and we eventually moved on. My new retainer came up and I mentioned I'd already done one job for them but there was nothing else at the time.

"They pay me every week no matter, so I'm okay, unless they flood me with assignments and my other clients are affected."

Addie worked at an insurance company down the block and took the occasional shift in a local gym tending the front desk.

My phone rang but I let it ring through, content to get the message later. I headed home. Another coffee later I saw the envelope sitting on the counter, which reminded me of the phone call. It was Detective Ross so I returned his call right then.

"Miss D'Angelo. Thanks for returning my call. I wanted to let you know that the man shot in the mall parking lot worked for H and G. That's the company where you had your interview, correct?"

"Yes. I only saw a couple of people when I was there. I spoke with a Mr. Faraday. Frank Faraday. I had done some freelance work for H and G in the past and they wanted to put me on a retainer for quick turn arounds of small assignments. I also spoke with the receptionist."

"So, you've worked for H and G before?"

"Yes, as a freelancer. Doing communications work, mostly press releases and some ad copy. Once I helped to script a television commercial, but I only provided the initial pass at the copy. Someone at H and G took over the final edits and I never heard anything more about it. That was about a year ago maybe, I'd have to look."

"Please do. I'll be straight with you Miss. D'Angelo, our department has been informed by the FBI that H and G has been under investigation for money laundering and corporate espionage. It turns out that the man killed in the underground parking of your building had connections to H and G as well."

I was wide-eyed. "I can't think of anything else I might be able to tell you."

"It's still very much an open investigation. Given that there is a connection between the two murders and a connection to you, we would like you to report to us any interactions you have with H and G."

"Okay," I said. "I did a small job for them the next day but haven't heard anything more." I described the nature of the press release.

Once off the phone I saw the envelope on the counter. I opened it and inside was a single folded piece of paper with ten 100 dollar bills inside. I opened the paper to read.

"Miss D'Angelo, I would like to pay you a retainer to have you relay to me any activity you have with H and G. Simply call 555-5309 and deliver the details as they happen. This money is a first payment for your trouble."

I decided to think on what it might all mean, now that it was obvious the dead man intended to deliver this to me and must have followed me from my meeting at H and G. And he must have also been followed. It didn't take long for me to call Detective Ross and explain what I had.

"You didn't mention the envelope when we first spoke."

"No, I thought it was something that had tumbled out of my car when I got out to look at the man who had fallen. It has my name and address on it, but now that I have it in my hand, I notice there is no postage stamp. I didn't notice that before."

"And the payment? You said it was five 100 dollar bills."

"Yes."

"Can you bring the money and the note down to the station. Don't touch the money, it will be fingerprinted."

Once at the station, the detective told me they would have to fingerprint me, to eliminate any of my prints that would be on the letter and bank notes. I nodded meekly but was humiliated as they inked my finger tips and pressed them onto a form identifying which finger was which.

"Well it appears you are involved in this problem. I'd like you to make the phone call and provide the details of your assignments for H and G. Keep me informed of future contacts with H and G. We will trace the line and hope to make a connection in the case we are building. The second man worked for H and G and now it appears he was delivering a payment to have you spy on them. There is every possibility that the man in the parking garage was looking for you as well. He must have known you were going to a meeting there and wanted to catch you before you left."

"I don't want to get involved in this. I'm scared. These people are willing to kill and they all want a piece of me."

"The first man must have been coming to speak to you only. We didn't find any note amongst his things. As for the second man, just do what the note asked and we will do the rest."

I hung up the phone and started thinking of having to enter the witness protection program. Three days before I was working hard to pay my bills and juggling social engagements, and now I was involved in a corporate spying game, and being used by who knows which side and for what end. My instinct was to flee, change jobs, move away.

I spent the entire weekend looking over my shoulder, expecting someone to pop out of the shadows for some nefarious reason. On Monday around noon, I received a message from Mr. Faraday about another assignment. He wanted me to design an ad campaign for an apparel manufacturer. It was to be in two parts, one with an unlimited budget and the second, a saturation campaign over one month.

I dutifully phoned the number and dropped the details of the assignment to an answering machine. I sat in my living room, the TV on, in fear of the phone ringing. I sat at my screen and plunked through an assignment from another client, deciding to plough through and get it done, so I could completely reconsider my work in the morning, once the initial worry about the H and G assignment was over.

I made dinner, thinking of what an unlimited ad campaign might look like. Radio, television, social media, even newspapers and some selected on-line sponsorships. The media landscape was very fragmented, but those shards allowed a very directed approach to any campaign. I messaged Mr. Faraday asking for more details on the client. In order to design an affective campaign, I needed to know who the target audience was.

Faraday messaged back, saying it was for a clothing retailer, for smart office and out-on-the-town wear for 30 and 40 somethings. He added that he needed the campaign plans back to him in a week. Friday if possible and no later than Monday morning.

I called Detective Ross to let him know.

This went on for several months. I had a number of assignments coming my way. Often just corporate planning for potential options for H and G clients. Some were just press releases and other internal media. I detected no pattern, though H and G had a wide variety of clients. And my own stable of communications clients kept me busy. At least my bank account was getting bigger.

Then I received a call from Mr. Faraday for an in-person meeting at H and G. I relayed the information to Detective Ross. He wanted to wire me up, but I firmly said no. While I was willing to help, I would not put a target on my back, or under my sweater.

I arrived at the H and G offices and was ushered in to Mr. Faraday's office.

"So glad to see you, Miss D'Angelo. If I may say, your work has been exemplary. Several of my colleagues have commented on it."

"Thank you. What's on your mind for today?"

"That's just it. We are pleased enough with your work that we would like to offer you a full time position."

I breathed out heavily, "Oh, well that's nice of you, but I have a number of other clients that I work for."

"That's fine. You can decide how much of that work you want to take on, outside of your assignments here. Frankly it's that kind of dedication that has drawn us to you. We will make it well worth your while to join us."

He named an astonishing figure. One so lucrative that I immediately knew it was designed to pull me in no matter what my misgivings might be. I supressed a gasp but something in my expression must have given me away.

He smiled. "Think it over. I'm quite confident you can find the time for your other clients if that is your wish. Let me know by the end of the week."

Returning home I dutifully informed Detective Ross and made the anonymous phone call. The heat had been turned up and I didn't know what would happen. If I turned the job down, Faraday would suspect something, but I didn't want to be dragged into the abyss of whatever crimes were being committed.

Ross seemed almost gleeful when I told him. "You are right Miss D'Angelo, things are changing and we may get a break in this case."

He was quite adamant that I take the job, as turning it down would send a signal to H and G.

"If they drop me entirely, I wouldn't be upset. I do not like this spy stuff."

"I think if you take the job, this operation might be soon over. If you don't, I'm not sure where this will go."

I took the job.

Three weeks later I was sitting in the board room awaiting a meeting with several senior staff regarding an ad campaign for a major golf manufacturer. I fully expected the more senior guys would take on the project, and perhaps ask a little advice from me regarding the targeting of 20 somethings.

The door opened and two men came in who I was not familiar with. I smiled and said this was the golf client meeting. They nodded and sat down across the table from me.

I was trying to think of something bright and on topic to say when one of them spoke.

"Miss D'Angelo, we are not here about the golf client. We arranged this meeting to talk to you in private."

I am not a trained actor, but I did my best to appear completely clueless about any nefarious activities at the company.

"We are senior vice presidents of H and G. Our names are not important. We have been authorised to give you an assignment for our most important client, who also shall remain unnamed."

The second man spoke, "Our client seeks to influence opinion in several important countries, Iran and by proxy Iraq and in Jordan and their ally Egypt."

"We would like to send you to these countries under a diplomatic seal, knowing that you would otherwise have difficulty moving about freely, due to their local . . . customs."

"To do what?"

"To ascertain the mood of the country, especially the women, and to collect as much information as you can in the way the people there think and act. All part of putting together an information campaign designed to influence public thought."

"This is way beyond my experience level. I am not the person you want for this assignment."

"Actually, you are our first choice. It is precisely that lack of experience which would serve to deflect attention from you. As a woman you will be viewed with some suspicion by the men in charge but you may be able to gain the trust of women you encounter. You can use the cover story that you are working for a clothing manufacturer seeking to get into the large market in these countries, specifically in women's wear. What you are really doing is trying to figure out how to effectively message people there to change their minds."

After much back and forth I agreed to think about it. I told Detective Ross and despite my misgivings, I phoned the number I had been given to report my interactions with the company. I had received another $1000 in the mail a week before. I decided not to inform Detective Ross about the letter, but decided to admit it, if he asked.

After I agreed, the assignment was laid bare. I would be putting together a subtle campaign to subvert the theocratic government of Iran and also to message the Jordanians and Egyptians that western countries were friendly and open to a moderate approach to their faith.

So, I headed to Tehran after being in contact with the Embassy and setting up some meetings with local apparel manufacturers.

Tehran was a surprisingly modern city. I'm not sure what I expected but steel and glass towers and endless traffic made it seem normal to my sensibilities even if local customs lurked beneath the veneer.

A couple of awkward business meetings later and I was told I could meet with a women's wear buyer from a large retail chain. I was operating under the Italian Embassy, with their blessing, as the US had no diplomatic ties to the Iranians. I was travelling around with embassy officials in tow. I was most uncomfortable as nothing had been said by my handlers about my true mission. Maybe they didn't know.

Winging it works on those occasions where you are confident, and I was decidedly not. I attended a fashion show and I went through the motions of seeking information about local needs, styles, wardrobe pieces, manufacturing, customs and taxes. It was all women, and after the runway event, we all repaired to a different room for some tea.

After some small talk, one of the more senior women, the wife of a major retailer, called me aside to look at some Persian art she had recently purchased which hung in an adjoining room. She spoke perfect English, with only the slightest British Midlands accent.

"You speak so well, were you educated in the United Kingdom?"

"Yes, I much prefer it there, but my husband likes Tehran. His business is here and his family. I was born in London. My parents fled when the Shah fell. I met my husband on a buying trip he took to Paris, where I was on holiday."

"Oh, so very romantic."

"I suppose. But the difficulties of life here are hard to bear." She pointed to a large mosaic installation.

"It's beautiful, very detailed. But your clothing is simple in style."

"That's not what the majority of women prefer. They like the high style and the details."

"So, help me out here. How can my company appeal to women who are shut out of everyday discourse in this country?"

"Radio, delivered media I suppose. Most women have access to that. Things like point-of-sale displays and store windows are not an option."

"Is there significant opposition to the imposed religious customs?"

She almost gasped at my brazen approach.

"I ask that as someone who is trying to break into a new market in a significantly unfamiliar country."

"I think we should get back to the main reception," she seemed rattled. "We can talk later, if you want." And she led me back into the reception room and spoke loudly about the glass and metal details of the mosaic.

Two days later I found her at another reception and she suggested we meet later at a women's wear retail outlet. I agreed.

I was directed to a back office and told my driver and security man to wait in the main room. I found her in an office, ten paces down a hallway, with papers strewn all around as it appeared she was significantly involved with the chain's operations.

"People here are . . . no, women here are . . . unhappy. The rules under which we live are onerous to say the least but the men see nothing unusual or wrong about them. I long for a regime change but I am powerless to enact it. As you have seen, there are morality police everywhere, often disguised as old women to get us to put our guard down."

"I have wondered how any ad campaign I design might help ease the restrictions you face. Starting slowly, and moving bit by bit towards a greater change is possible, though it will take many years."

"And it will never happen if we do not start."

And with that the doors burst open and several uniformed men moved quickly to block us from any exits.

"Excellent work Minerva, you have exposed a spy." And they grabbed me roughly by the upper arms and bound my wrists behind my back.

Minerva smiled at me with a wicked grin and was gently ushered out a side door. She did give me a little wink just before she disappeared.

"Much as we suspected, you are an American spy intent on stirring subversion in Iran."

"I am the representative of a clothing manufacturer based in Italy, on a mission to sell clothes."

"Minerva Ghistmalus was wearing a microphone."

"I must talk with my Embassy."

The oily uniformed man merely smiled, "Of course you will. At some point."

As they carried me, or dragged me away, it struck me that the policeman spoke unaccented English. Was he specially chosen for this assignment? I was bundled in a car, lights flashing, and quickly taken to an ominous looking building in central Tehran. I was hustled into a cell on the main floor. My driver and security man seemed to have disappeared, likely detained as well.

Whenever anyone wandered past the cell, I called out that I was there on a diplomatic visa to improve trade between countries. I was ignored though I did catch one uniformed man making a crooked smile.

I sat in the cell for at least two hours and was beginning to wonder if I would have to ask for a private space to relieve myself as I had no intention of doing it in the Turkish toilet in the corner of the open cell.

Keys rattled in the lock and the door swung open almost soundlessly. "Come with me please," said a man with a heavy accent wearing a dark blue business suit.

"I need to use the facilities." He nodded and took me to a doorway, indicating I should go inside. He was waiting for me as I exited and he grasped my upper arm to forcefully direct me. A few twists and turns later I found myself in an interview room with a desk, some chairs, an old land line phone and one wall entirely covered by a mirror. I might have laughed at the absurdity if I wasn't so unsure of myself.

"Now look here, I am on a diplomatic visa and demand to be handed over to the Embassy."

The man in the suit said nothing. He sat down.

"Miss D'Angelo? You are an American citizen?"

I nodded. "Here on a diplomatic visa. I promise you if you do not deliver me to my Embassy there will be grave consequences."

The man smiled. "Like what?"

"Like trade embargoes, economic sanctions, denunciations at the United Nations . . . ." my voice trailed off at the absurdity of my own pronouncements.

"You work for the Central Intelligence Agency. You are here to subvert our customs by influencing Iranian women to throw down their morality and service to the Prophet."

I shook my head. "I'm just trying to sell some clothes."

"By your own admission, remember we have a recording, you know women's clothing in Iran is very standardized and without much style."

"I also know that women in Iran dress differently in the privacy of their own homes, much differently than they are allowed to on public streets." I was defiant, still believing the Embassy would swoop in and scoop me up at any moment.

The interview went back and forth and I stuck to my instructions to reveal nothing, nor admit to anything nefarious. The interviewer became tired of the whole affair and I was taken back to a cell, this time in the basement of the building. A cell with only a small window and a slot for inserting food trays. I had the feeling I would be here a while and was tempted to come clean, as I really had nothing to do with anything and was only a pawn in whatever game was being played.

Two days later I was retrieved from the cell, without a change of clothes or a shower, and handed over to diplomatic officials from Norway. They explained they were there as proxies for my own countrymen. I had thought the Italian Embassy would rescue me.

'So, how was I acting on behest of an Embassy that didn't exist?' As I wondered this, the Norwegians delivered me to the airport and out of the country.

After a stop at the US Embassy in Rome, I was flying home and had some time to consider my next move. That I would tell all to Detective Ross, and then drop out of this affair, was obvious. But part of me wanted to know what was actually going on. Who were the two H and G vice presidents, who was Frank Faraday and who was Detective Ross? Who was I calling with details of my H and G dealings and who were the two men murdered as they tried to contact me?

Back at H and G headquarters two days after I touched down, I asked the two apparent VPs all those questions. One smirked the other turned his head to hide his reaction.

"Suffice to say Miss D'Angelo you are far better off not knowing. In fact, that was one of the reasons you were chosen for this mission, you could not betray us, because you know nothing."

"I am out. I will not be a part of this organization without knowing what might happen to me."

"Well, Miss Dangelo, you cannot know for the reasons I have just outlined, and no, no, you cannot be 'out' as you demand. Without our protection you are in grave danger."

"Sure. You just said I know nothing, how can I be in any danger?"

"Our enemies do not know that."

"At least explain all the connections to me."

"No, then you would know things. And you are better off not knowing. Plausible deniability."

It was obvious that H and G was much more than just a Business Affairs company, that they had some government connections and that there was an internal war inside the organization. Were the police involved or at least told to back away?

I went home and sat in my apartment for a few days, picking away at assignments from my regular clients, and hoping that H and G would leave me alone. For two months, they did.

I saw Mr. Faraday's number pop up on my phone. I hesitated to answer but decided I would resign my retainer and refuse any assignments no matter how benign.

"Hello, Miss D'Angelo. I have an assignment for you."

"Sorry Mr. Faraday, but I have decided to resign from H and G."

"I see. You realize that if you do that, you are no longer under our protection, and those who would wish you harm will not know you are no longer associated with us."

I resisted the urge to simply hang up. "I cannot continue. I do not like what this has become. I will take my chances. Please do not contact me again." I broke the connection. The fear I had been holding back now burst and I cried and gasped, overcome with fear, and an empty feeling.

After a few hours I called the number to report my dealings with H and G and also signed off, saying I had resigned from the company. I also called Detective Ross and reported the same thing.

Ross was nonplussed but I could tell he was unhappy. I didn't care. I wanted nothing to do with the company, with corporate espionage, with international relations or with murder.

I barricaded myself in my home for nearly a month, having food delivered, refusing any assignments that required me to leave my condo. Eventually I had to have a face-to-face meeting with an old client, so I agreed to meet uptown.

To say my drive was harrowing would be an understatement. I drove expecting intervention at every corner, every stop light, and I ran from the parking lot into the building.

After my meeting I had the same problem returning home. I was prepared to dig in for as long as it took to be rid of H and G. I considered leaving town, but I'd also have to leave many of my clients. Starting over seemed to be the best solution.

Chapter Twelve

A week later I met with Theresa, again at our usual spot and in fact, at our preferred table.

It's funny how people gravitate to a familiar spot, be it a seat in front of the television, a spot at the dinner table or even the same section at a baseball game.

I was no different, moving without thinking to our usual table and taking my usual seat facing the main entrance and service kiosk, with the two floor-to-ceiling windows behind me.

I was halfway through my coffee before Theresa arrived, I could see her almost running to the entrance, so I couldn't be too hard on her for being late. Curious, that's all.

She looked right at me, and I waved a cheery hello. She gathered her coffee and brought a pair of chocolate dipped donuts with her. It was an unusual touch.

"What are we celebrating?"

She looked confused. I gestured to the donuts.

"Oh, that. I was just hungry and thought I'd get you one as a peace offering. I'm late."

"I didn't know I was so hard on the tardy."

"Oh, you are. You are on time to a fault. It's admirable but hard to match your dedication sometimes."

"Then I won't ask why you are late. I wouldn't want to add to my reputation."

"You can't, but I will tell you. Markus called me this morning just as I was headed out the door. In fact, I had decided to let it go through to message but picked up anyway. I was expecting a call from my mother."

I expected her to go on about the call but she didn't. I wanted to know the details but after being chastised on my annoyance of tardy behaviour, I let it go.

Theresa looked at me while taking a sip of her coffee. Then a bite of her donut. Then another sip of coffee.

"Well?" she said.

"You haven't changed the subject," I laughed.

"Nor have you."

"Okay, I'll bite. I wouldn't want my reputation to be hurt. What did poor Markus want?"

She shot me a look. I waited.

"I wasn't sure at first. He was sort of shy, just the usual platitudes, then he asked about the aftermath of the trade show. He had apparently seen an advert for another one in Philly, and wondered if I was going, and if I needed help."

"Awfully nice of him. I think he's interested in you."

"I'm not sure it's the kind of interested you think. He offered to invest in the clothing line. He yammered off a whole streak of business stuff, markets, cutting edge finance, investment opportunities and he even said, with a successful launch, he expected buyers to line up to make offers. He said, fend them off for at least a full season, maybe two, as the more successful the launch, the higher the sell price, should I so choose."

"That's an earful. What do you think? That's a heck of a way to ask for a date."

Theresa laughed, "I'm going in 10 directions on this. Remember, this just happened, not half an hour ago."

"Well, think about it. In the meantime, here's my crime mystery story. I'll go and get another coffee. Want one?"

She waived me off, as hers was still fresh, and I rose and got in line, which seemed to be moving quite slowly. Something about the first person speaking the same foreign dialect as the coffee person, and them reminiscing about a far away home.

I returned to the table and she was more than a little into it. I cupped my hands around the coffee and waited. I tried not to watch her for any indication of what she was thinking. I knew she didn't like that, and I knew, from previously trying to root out the clues, that I could never really put a quizzical expression to an exact passage in the story.

She made a show of putting the last page down and straightening the pile.

"Okay. I think I say it every time, but where does it go from here?"

"And I say, I'm not sure. I'm not writing novels here. But are you interested enough to continue reading?"

"We've established our parameters, then. I do want to know what happens next, but I always do. I'm not enough of a literary critic to say anything, but every time I wonder if you shouldn't be a bit more forceful, a bit more dramatic in the opening sequence?"

"That's not my style."

"Maybe it should be, if you want to grab the reader, that is. Especially in a short story."

"Maybe that's the problem. I'm aiming at novels, but only writing shorts. The pacing is all mixed up."

"Well, there are a lot of loose ends."

"And it's likely to stay that way. I think my mission in crime drama has been accomplished."

I stared in my coffee. Like all criticism, I deferred it, I rationalized it, I disagreed at first vehemently, then with ebbing reasons. And, I knew that by the time I sat down to write again, I would have absorbed the criticism entirely, moving on a creative tangent to embrace it as my own, never actually agreeing out loud.

"I wonder if we should ask Markus what men like to read?"

"You can, I can have him come by next week if you like. But, men don't read. At least not nearly as much as women. So why write for that market?"

She was right of course, but I had always tried to bridge that divide. "Yeah, get him to come by. Perhaps he can read it and offer a perspective?"

She nodded. "What's the next one?"

"In keeping with Markus potentially coming, how about fantasy?"

"I'm not sure what you are saying there, but whatever you want."

"Are you going to Philly? When is it?"

Theresa said she had already signed on and was going to check out the details once we were done. It was three weeks later, but she didn't have the heart to tell Markus these things are done months in advance.

"Any mention of his friend Brandon?"

"Funny you should ask. He mentioned that Brandon had family in Philly and might be enticed to help out, if I should need it."

"As I recall, he was a nice sort of guy. But we might want to come clean about our brush with that wedding. At some point the happy couple will be mentioned and we will look bad if we have to confess."

"Yeah, you're right. Once in a while at the coffee shop is one thing, but the both of them for a few days in Philly means it is almost certain to come up. I'll fess up for the both of us, next time I talk to him."

I looked at her.

"I promised I'd let him know if I was going to the trade show."

At home a few days later, I half expected a call from Theresa with Philly details. And maybe the fall out from Markus after she confessed the truth.

Fantasy. God almighty, how I had avoided fantasy. It was all Tolkien. You couldn't write fantasy without a nod to Tolkien. I confess I had first encountered JRRT by watching the movies. My boyfriend at the time loved Tolkien and dragged me out. I was expecting something akin to the paintings on the sides of vans owned by aging stoners. Muscled men brandishing oversized swords amongst a group of odd humanoid creatures conspicuously blocking out the interesting parts of a scantily clad female warrior type, or not.

Then I saw the movies. I was mesmerized. Okay, it kinda had that same feeling of the van, but in a good way. Big swords, check. But nothing else really. Except well dressed noble women, okay. Odd creatures? Yeah, yeah. But there was something else, some sort of majesty. A mythic quality to it that seemed buried in the details of architecture, conversational references, place names and more.

My pre-writerly self, devoured Tolkien and started to search for more. And slowly, I realized there was no more. Fantasy was a weak genre, given shape by the writing of Tolkien and never more than a mist of him in the hands of some other writer.

I eagerly read the follow up stories that came after his death, and to be sure, some of them were great, almost as great as the Lord of the Rings. But even they were not the same. The Lord of the Rings was the final chapter in his legendarium, and it was the culmination of a lifetime of writing, creating and dreaming.

So how could I possibly approach fantasy with anything new or at least not entirely derivative? Too much fantasy was firmly rooted in medieval stuff and dragons. Even Tolkien used dragons, but had the good sense to reign it in, so to speak.

I opened a new file on my computer. I had been thinking about this for three days and had promised Theresa and probably Markus something to read.

And so I began . . .

And then I ripped it up. Figuratively of course. I just deleted it. Two paragraphs in, and I had my doubts as it had too much mist and bold expectation. Two more paragraphs proved me right and with only a moment's hesitation, zap.

I tried again, and again, and again. I started to believe it was impossible. I considered moving to another genre but I had promised Theresa some fantasy.

Okay, I rationalized, something that normally doesn't talk, has to talk. What?

New humanoids? Maybe. Animals? Been done. Toys? Been done. Plants? Not as a main story, roots being what they are. I watched a lady bug crawl across the window screen. Insects? Been done. Okay, I thought, it doesn't have to be novel length.

Buildings? Do they have a soul? Surely some do, I thought. I've been in some of them. And if some do, then why not all? And in this case the story comes to them, rather than them going on adventures. Buildings cannot move, a limiting detail. 'Sentient buildings are the foundation of the story', I thought out loud and almost gave up, fighting a grin amongst my despair.

Of course, that led to a deep think about the kind of story I wanted. A buddy story was right out. Didn't seem to me that buildings would have friends. They are more like monolithic demi-gods, dictating life and death. Okay, I enthused, perhaps I'm on to something.

I certainly had never read anything like this. But that doesn't mean it doesn't exist, I thought. But the hole in my experience was enticing. I would not be influenced by anything else. I was certain not to write anything derivative. Though it struck me, unsaid, that if I'd never heard of anything like this, that I would probably be drawn into writing the most obvious, the most elemental thing that the sub-genre of speaking, thinking buildings, could offer. And if this genre did in fact exist, I would be walking right into its walls.

With a shrug, I opened another file. I wrote the story, feeling that it was spiralling in on itself. The conceit was very limiting and so, upon finishing the tale, I set it aside and started something much more conventional.

Chapter Thirteen—The Thrall

"What aileth thee, good Sir Knight?"

The merchant, walking beside his pony and cart, had overtaken a tall knight, in light armor, astride his large battle horse. The road bent, avoiding something unseen, as it passed through a stand of trees.

The knight's horse was moving, but only in a slow walk. The pair seemed to have no purpose, no plan for their journey.

The merchant slowed to fall into step with the knight, though he had not responded. It was past full light, and rays of sunlight snuck through the leaves and high branches, dappling the pair, and danced upon them.

"Sir Knight? Are you wounded? Are you lost?"

The merchant repeated his questions, before the knight seemed to notice his presence, and turned his face to him. "No, not lost on the road, but lost perhaps in my mission."

"On that I cannot help you," said the merchant, relieved at last to have a response. “I am not privy to knightly deeds, or regal assignments.”

The knight turned to him again, colourless of expression, confusion in his eyes. “I seek the castle of the Grey Lady. I know it is among these woods and hills, but cannot find it. I’ve traversed this area for many days without success.”

“I know not of any such castle, Sir Knight. Not near here, nor anywhere else in the realm. And I do travel far and wide, good sir. Can I interest you in some of my wares?”

The cart jangled lightly with metal cooking gear. Pans, knives and spoons combined to produce a sound that was not quite musical. There were also linens hung from the cart. They made no sound as there was no wind to swish through them.

The knight did not even gaze at the cart, which bumped along the road noisily enough. “The Grey Castle is real enough, my friend, I have dwelt there many months, though I return from a mission for the Lady herself.”

“Well, ask of me what you will, and I will try to lend a hand. Have you eaten? Perhaps together we can parse out where this Castle might be.”

“I’d ask nothing of you, if you know not of the Castle, but if you can spare a bit of meat and mead, I would be in your debt.”

The merchant stopped his pony and cart, rummaged around under it’s cover and pulled out a bit of fowl, and a mug into which he poured a liquid. He handed them to the knight, who accepted with a bow of his head.

The merchant knew not what to say, so he watched the knight, who crossed himself and moved his lips soundlessly, before eating quickly and drinking fast. He handed the cup back to the merchant, who thought the knight looked more alive and more awake than he had only minutes before.

“Aye, I thank you, and God, for I was in need of that. I can continue my search.”

“Perhaps you are in the wrong place. This is Wiltshire, though not far are we from Berkshire or Hampshire, depending upon which road you follow.”

“I am where I ought to be,” said the knight. “I will continue my search. I thank you for your generosity.” He moved off at a brisk trot.

The merchant shrugged. Never hurts to help a knight in need, he thought. He replaced the cup and jumped into his cart, seeking a ride as he urged his pony forward. He was headed for Glastonbury where he would sell most of his haul to local shopkeepers, before heading to the sea to get salted cod for shipment back to Oxford and St. Albans. From there he wasn't entirely sure, sometimes heading into London or moving towards Yorkshire in the north. It all depended upon what he might buy cheaply for markets he could count on.

The merchant shook his head as he thought of the time he had a load of fish and nowhere to sell them. Oh, he had eventually found a buyer, a fisherman looking for some chum, as the fish had begun to rot. He was lucky enough to take a large loss rather than a total one.

The merchant had not been entirely honest with the knight. He had heard tell of the Grey Lady but in truth did not know where her seat lay.

The knight had moved ahead and was now only a small blot on the road, and gone entirely when the road bent.

"The Castle of the Grey Lady?" the merchant said aloud, and shook his head. The tales of the Lady were mysterious. She held men in her command, and gathered them to her. They came willingly, but seemed unable to leave her service once they agreed to join it.

And as the horse picked up its pace, moving too slowly for the knight, he began to hum a tune, under his breath at first, as he was unsure of anything, and even the words to it came only sporadically to his lips. He was familiar with it, and soon a phrase or two, a touch of melody passed his lips a time or two, and he mouthed the tune louder and with more command. His horse, picked up his optimism and increased its pace.

With the tune on his lips the knight, as he trotted, noticed far ahead, a pair of huge oak trees, old and spreading across the road. There was something in his mind that thought the oaks important. As he reached them, he could see a small break in the rushes on one side of the road. A path, at the foot of the giant oak. He turned his horse and gingerly nosed his way onto the path, moving slowly through the overgrowth, unsure of his mount's footing as it twisted through the tall reeds.

He felt confident but his horse did not. The soft ground and high reeds provided no certainty. The knight, his head just high enough to see over the reeds urged the horse forward. The steed moved a bit quicker, trusting the rider, but it was unwilling to plunge ahead through the tall rushes with any speed.

The rushes broke at the side of a clear, but soundless stream. There, the path followed alongside, and the horse turned upriver without any prodding. It picked up the pace into a trot. Trees lined the small river, perhaps fifty feet across. It was hard to see beyond them.

Now with the tune running through his mind the knight followed a turn in the path, that skirted a small hill, the stream still on his right. As the path turned, he could see a castle in the distance, sitting astride a much larger rise, its walls seemingly built into the cliff.

The castle was formidable, made entirely of grey stone, tightly laid with a skill and precision that amazed anyone who looked closely at them. Few did. The castle displayed few decorations or embellishments. As he neared it, he crossed a stone bridge, built with three segments arching over the stream. From there the path wound its way up, doubling back in a series of loose hairpin turns, though it never felt steep or dangerous.

The horse was moving as if familiar with the place and the knight himself was feeling lighter of mind, though heavier of heart. Soon they faced a latticed metal gate. The knight sat on his horse barely able to remember why he had searched for this place. About to call out, the great heavy gate began to lift, pulled straight up into the barbican. The gloom inside the gatehouse all but oozed out to the path, but the knight did not hesitate, spurring his horse into the opening. There were no torches to light the way.

But his horse did not hesitate and after only a moment or two another heavy metal gate had already begun to rise at the other end of the long entrance hallway. His eyes adjusted to the low light, and the knight could see a large double wooden door, it too slowly swinging outward, a sliver of silvery grey light peeping through the widening crack.

He passed through the double doors. Still nobody challenged him or greeted him. It was as if the castle was empty.

As he passed the gate he felt a collar around his neck, that he had not felt before. The metal was cold and it was the change in temperature that he had noticed. He put his hand to the metal band. This was no decorative chain, it was a substantial metal collar, fashioned to fit properly around his neck without choking him.

The tune in his mind had changed, now bereft of all joy. It was a martial song, slow and heavy, meant to inspire great deeds and duty.

The castle, from the outside was austere, but inside the stonework was beautiful, with carvings, crenelations, and turrets at every corner. There were several large trees built into small garden areas, all surrounded by low stone walls which doubled as benches. The stonework construction inside was equally impressive as the façade. Opposite the entrance was a wide stone stair, perhaps 15 steps high, wide at the bottom, narrowing as it reached a porch with an elaborately carved doorway at its center.

He moved toward the door, dismounting on the way, and tethering his mount in front of a ramp down into the castle. As he left the horse and moved toward the staircase, one of the double doors swung open and a groom came out to take the steed.

“She is waiting for you.”

The knight took the steps deliberately, due in part to the heavy kit he wore. Light chainmail, his helmet, metal leggings and a sword girded about his waist. The rest of his armour stayed with the horse, upper thigh pieces, heavy gloves, various bits of metal cladding for his arms and feet, and his shield.

The shield as a marvel. He knew it to be his and not a captured trophy but he could not place the sigils painted upon it. A crest divided into four with additional sigils top and bottom and a sprig of thistle at the top. The top portion of the crest was a picture of the sea, with an isle in the distance. The bottom part was another picture of the sea but this time filled with land from edge to edge, featuring the hints of castles and stone buildings.

The central part of the crest, divided into four showed a red lion, a harp, an oak tree and a dragon. The knight had puzzled over this combination but he could not remember their significance. He decided that he was English and his family had been landowners in Ireland and that they had some connection to Wales. But of course, perhaps he was Irish, or Welsh. Either way, the oak tree suggested strong, deep roots, but where those roots might be, he was at a loss.

Without thinking, he stripped himself of his helmet and chainmail as he climbed the steps, leaving them outside the door. He entered the castle, torches lining the walls. He proceeded through the entrance and under a grand staircase to a doorway. It opened on a large room with a very high ceiling, carved with ornate figures, that made up much of the stone vaulting.

On a throne at the end of the chamber sat a lady neither old nor young. She sat upright, elegant in her posture and dress, detached it seemed from the hoary old furniture, and emptiness of the space. She sat on a carved wooden chair, with a high back, and crimson cushions, on a low dais.

"Sir Mithras. You have come at last."

It was then that the knight remembered his name and the mission on which he had been charged.

"Yes, My Lady, I had some trouble on the road, finding the castle, but all is well." He touched the collar around his neck.

The Lady shifted in her chair, her silvery honey hair mingling with the silver, grey and white of her raiment.

"I spoke with the Earls at both castles and they were intrigued with your proposal, but wary of entanglements."

She tilted her head in inquiry, the silver in her hair seemed to disappear, and younger she appeared, and she laughed gently. "Any agreement between us is an 'entanglement' even if it is disavowed, broken or fulfilled with honour."

"Both Earls asked for time to think and both suggested an arrangement but one that was non-binding. I am convinced they anticipated my visit and were in agreement in advance."

The Lady smiled again. "As they wish. I merely suggest some help defending my lands. If I fall, there will be a wave of knights washing over this land and threatening their fields. I can provide little in return save a bulwark against violence."

'I will deliver the message my Lady."

"No, I will send another, more fully versed on finding his way home. I fear for you Sir Mithras, you seem disengaged with your purpose. Some time in the Castle should set you right. I will send a messenger to you with a new assignment."

And with that the knight bowed deeply and turned to leave the chamber. But now he saw that it was now entirely filled with knights and squires of various ages, dress, and stature. He had perceived no noise behind him in his conversation but now the room was brimming with voices. He turned back to the throne but the Lady was gone.

And now he remembered. He had pledged his life to the maiden he had rescued from highwaymen. She had brought him back to this castle, where he expected to meet her father or brother, but found she was the liege lord, and she had many other pledges of service.

He left the room and exited the castle, collecting his armour along the way. He secured it in his chamber, started a fire, and changed into lighter clothing. He decided to go and check on his horse and perhaps find something to eat in the castle hall.

Making his way into the Great Hall, he passed groups of knights, much as himself, talking about the plans for some campaign ahead. They all seem to have consulted the Grey Lady and come away with a mission.

Food was laid out on long tables. He filled a plate and seeing no one he knew, he settled at the end of another table filled with chattering knights.

He was ravenous after his journey and tore into the meat and bread. After eating he found his desire to see his horse was overcome by fatigue. He slowly made his way through the castle and entered his rooms, where he flopped on the narrow bed.

The next morning, he rose with the rooster, and unsure of what to do with himself, he lay awake, replaying the events of his meetings with the two Earls.

They had expressed a reluctance to become entangled with the Grey Lady and her castle, vaguely assigning past experiences as their reason for holding back. Both Earls acknowledged that there were raids on their lands, assigning blame to an enemy which threated first the Grey Castle and then their own.

Earl Cardoman had submitted to sending a troop of knights through the Grey lands to take on the interloper directly, but he would not join with the Grey Castle's knights, nor would he agree to be provisioned or supplied by the Grey Lady. Mithras had been on the verge of agreeing to the terms when Cardoman backed down a step and begged time to consider the plan, wanting to consult with his neighbour and kinsman Earl Westershire.

Mithras had decided to let the matter stew and return to the Grey Lady for direction. He wondered if he should have negotiated further. Back at the Grey Castle his days were filled with caring for his mount and repairing his armour, a task he had put off for too long. Gazing at his shield he wondered again of its origins and thought, not for the first time, that perhaps he should paint a new heraldic sigil upon it.

He could not think what he might use to replace the old crest and the plan bobbed along in his mind, formless. As he finished his meal, the thought of a new sigil in his head, heralds announced horses and knights approaching the castle. Sir Mithras found his way along the parapet to watch. The retinue reached the top of the hill beside the metal lattice gate and stopped. The gate opened but they did not enter, sending a messenger ahead who loudly beckoned a parlay to come and meet them.

A rider exited the gate a few minutes later, in half armour, as if hastily exiting the Castle.

"Hail there," said the rider, "you have arrived at the Grey Castle, perhaps unknown to you."

"We have heard tell of this place, but it is difficult to find, even the locals seem not to know where to look."

"Come, enter, I will inform the Grey Lady of your visit, she is eager to welcome new guests, and share news of the outside world.

The visiting rider, looked at those on each side of him, giving them time to speak. Hearing nothing, he nodded in assent and moved his horse at a slow walk toward the barbican. His retinue followed on, almost reluctantly, as if pulled by his choice.

Their horses were fed and watered, and they were invited into the Great Hall for food and refreshment, and told they would meet the Grey Lady after they had taken their needs.

"Why does everyone here wear a metal collar?"

The hosting knight looked around. "You know I never noticed, before. For me, it is a sign of fealty to the Grey Lady, a more significant device than a painted shield.

The retinue ate their fill, feeling weariness from their journey, but more interested in meeting the Grey Lady. They trudged off, through the castle courtyard and up the wide staircase which led to the throne room. As they crossed the yard, the whinnies of contented horses could be heard. A wedge of silent swallows arched across the sky, speedily moving away from a hawk which pursued them.

The Lady was there, waiting until all had entered before waving them closer. As she gestured the torch light flickered and dimmed.

"Welcome my weary travellers. From whence do you come and what might be your destination?"

"We are from the far north, beyond Yorkshire, travelling at the behest of our Lord, the Duke of Eddingsworth. His seat is Castle Arwend, located not far from Carlisle, a town under his banner."

"I have heard tell of the Duke and his Castle. Old is his seat and long has he himself been on it."

"Aye, fair lady, we had heard much the same of you, but one glimpse shows we were misinformed as you appear much younger than we expected."

The Lady declined her head at the complement, and as she did, her yellow hair ripened almost imperceptibly and silver highlights became more visible.

"Care you to join us before continuing on your way?"

"By your leave we will take refuge here, before retaking our path to secure the release of our Lord's cousin, cruelly held against his will by Earl

Bothingham, who apparently has lands in this area."

"Well, sir we may have common cause. That very Earl is threatening my lands, conducting raids and stealing livestock. We are engaged in talks with other nearby Lords to take the battle to Bothingham. If your negotiations are not successful, perhaps you might consider joining us."

"A fine suggestion my Lady, but first we must attempt a measured and peaceful approach to the conundrum."

"An understandable approach. You, my fine knight, please stay and parlay with me. Your friends are free to go and explore the castle. You can rejoin them when our discussion has finished."

The lead knight nodded and his companions collected themselves and exited the room led by he who had shown them in.

As the door closed behind them, the Grey Lady, rose and beckoned the remaining knight with a shy smile, to a doorway behind the throne.

They entered a much smaller parlor with a fireplace, rugs, wall hangings and several armchairs in a half circle around the hearth.

"Sit, and be comfortable. You have just eaten but I will fetch us both some refreshment." She clapped her hands gently and a servant appeared from behind the fireplace with two glasses and a pitcher on a tray.

She poured his drink first, and then one of her own.

"To new acquaintances."

The knight tipped back the glass and drank a sip at first and then a healthy gulp of the slightly sweet, cold drink in the mug. The Grey Lady held the mug up to her lips, tasting the sweetness.

"My Castle is threatened. Bothingham has conducted raids and sent messengers demanding I hand over the Castle, my family seat for generations. We are not as strong as we once were. Most of my knights are mercenaries. They seem content to fight for me, but with mercenaries, one never knows where their loyalties lay."

"I notice they all wear an iron collar."

"They do. My oldest, most trusted knights took to it as a sign of fealty. The others seem to have joined in that tradition. I can offer little but a secure home, and so I have collected many a lost knight, men who by one reason or another have no home, no other loyalty, and so they seem to flock to me, I who can offer that."

"My Lady, you have been most gracious."

"Stay with us until you are ready to face Bothingham, and return to us before facing your journey back north. I should like to hear of your dealings with the man, it may help our own."

After a few days the retinue from the north collected itself and went to demand Duke Eddingsworth's cousin. Several in the group wore the metal collar, showing loyalty to the Grey Lady for her generosity at no cost to the itinerant knights.

Three days later they returned, a smaller group, battered, bloody and unsure of what to do.

"Bothingham was most unhappy with us. He refused to even acknowledge that he was holding the cousin and he became quite enflamed when one of his attendants noticed the metal collars on a few of us. He demanded to know our affiliation with you, who he called his enemy, and called us spies when we said we had met you and enjoyed your hospitality for several days."

"You are welcome to join us or if you prefer simply lend your strength to ours as myself and the two Earls Cardoman and Westershire, my neighbours to the east, are planning an assault on his stronghold."

And the knights of the north agreed to stay as the assault was to be arranged shortly. The knights did not want to go back north without something tangible, even if it was only a failed assault on the castle.

Sir Mithras was engaged in setting the plan for the assault, parlaying with both local Earls and the knights of the northern Duke. They would take a formidable force to the castle, and lay it under siege while seeking the inevitable breech in its defences.

The Grey Lady was adamant that any siege could not last for more than one turning of the moon. She feared leaving her own castle undefended for longer.

The weather closed in and a hard rain fell for several days. At last the war party left the Grey Castle, riding two by two through the barbican, into the grey mist which sucked the colour from everything it touched. They gingerly descended the switchbacks down to the riverside. Crossing the bridge, they broke into a light trot and turned up the path away from the main road. The deep green trees hung with water droplets and the sky, though lighter, still provided a misty rain. The wetness and tangled underbrush and the thick wood kept them on the path, the river always to their right. The knights made a miserable camp and rose into a weak sun, hampered by a gloomy sky and the thick woods which lay all around. At least the rain had stopped.

Squires and camp followers managed to cook a meal. They carried enough to last many days but if the siege continued, they would be forced to forage from the land.

Breaking camp they moved slowly north until at last they came within sight of Bothingham's castle on a small rise beside a widening of the river. On the land side of the castle the woods had been cut back some distance from the walls. The knights decided to encamp inside the wood to hide their numbers.

The next morning, they sent a group to parlay with Bothingham in the castle, demanding the Duke's cousin and an end to any aggression against the Grey Lady and her lands and holdings.

"The Grey Lady is a menace. Your very presence here is proof of that. And as for Duke Eddingsworth's cousin, the Baronet Dunhelm, he is here of his own free will."

"Please show us the man and let him speak for himself."

And duly a youngish man was presented on the parapet. "I am here as a guest of Lord Bothingham. And from what he tells me of the Grey Lady, you should forsake her service."

"The Grey Lady has been gracious. You may be a guest of Bothingham but your own Lord Duke Eddingworth has sent us to secure your return."

"And I am quite content here for now."

"I'm afraid Eddingsworth commands your return. If you do not return and are not a prisoner of Bothingham, then you are a fugitive from your Lord and will be returned to him unwillingly."

The young man merely shrugged, dismissing the parlay.

"And then there is the issue of the threats against the Grey Lady."

Bothingham spoke, "The Grey Lady is a menace, gathering to her itinerant knights and men of arms, seeking to enlarge her lands and influence. I am commanded by the High King to curtail her activities and to reduce her influence on these lands."

"Would a pledge to remain within her own boundaries suffice in peace between us."

And Bothingham thought a moment, "Yes, but those boundaries would be smaller than at present and any breach of terms would produce war."

"Provide us with our northern man and strict boundaries for the Grey Lady and we can retreat in peace."

"I cannot breach my hospitality by forcibly handing over your quarry. Those boundaries I will respect, shall be sent to you tomorrow." He turned and retreated into the castle.

"You are giving in to their violence, My Lord?"

"To them perhaps, but if I can satisfy the Grey Lady's knights and those of her allied Earls, I might be able to have them retreat, splitting the party of attackers and provide a rebuff to the northern knights."

He spoke to the cousin privately. "Why will you not return north, good sir?"

"Tis a complicated business, my friend. I would pledge my fealty with you and forsake my cousin as he has done me wrong."

"Aye, you have been a worthy knight in our dealings, but I am loathe to make an enemy of a knight as powerful as your cousin, even though the distance is great."

"I understand. Would it change your mind if I told you he will likely have me imprisoned or worse, should I return?"

"What is your crime?"

"His daughter and I were forbidden. We were secretly married and planned to leave his castle, but he found out and kept her, and I only just managed to escape the same fate."

"Aye, we shall have to think on this. I do wonder how you managed to come to me rather than the Grey Lady? She seems to possess an ability to draw itinerant knights to her, those without a clear purpose or home. Those like yourself."

"I know little of her but was warned away from her castle when I made enquires as I travelled the road. They said she gathers knights and is growing her lands by using the knights to control the farmers, extracting taxes, livestock and more, for a protection they do not need, or already have from other Lords."

As Bothingham and Dunhelm spoke the siege party fanned out around Bothingham's castle, encircling it, save for the river to the east. They spoke of the rising siege works. The main body of knights remained in the forest, to hide their true strength of numbers.

Knights moved back and forth between these positions giving those who did the hard work of building works a time to idle in the wood, gather what foodstuffs they could.

Bothingham had sent a retinue from the castle to the Grey Lady's party providing the terms of peace. Her Castle was to be isolated from the road and the wood, with her realm extending no more than a bow shot from her walls. And never could she send more than half a dozen knights beyond this boundary.

Itinerant knights of the Grey Lady, accustomed to freedom of the realm, refused these provisions outright. And upon learning that Bothingham refused to surrender Dunhelm, those who came to fetch him, decided to remain with the siege hoping for a breech in the walls or the terms.

In siege fashion, the next two weeks were a stalemate as both sides watched and waited. The Grey Lady's force began to run low on provisions and they foraged off the land, fortunate that it was rich with game. They avoided raiding nearby farms as that would set an already unhappy citizenry against them.

Mithras felt his steadfastness waver, as if distance from the Grey Castle and time away had clouded his belief in the Castle and its mistress.

One evening he was summoned by the Earl Cardoman, and he entered a tent where both Cardoman and Westershire, and their northern allies were already at parlay.

“Ah Mithras, the castle has been betrayed, at least it will be if we are bold enough to take advantage of the breech.”

“You have been discussing this opportunity without anyone present representing the Grey Lady?”

“Aye, apologies Mithras, news of the breech came to our northern friends, and as our tent was nearby, they passed it to us. Westershire and you were summoned immediately and, he arrived before you. We have only just spoken about it as we waited. The breech and our plan seem obvious.”

“Speak, please.”

“A disgruntled guard approached my tent two hours ago,” said Earl Cardoman. “He said there is a tunnel from the castle to the dock area of the river, emerging in one of the small storage buildings by the wharf.”

“And he is disgruntled, why?”

“Disgruntled is not proper, we paid him for information. He said there is a plan afoot to smuggle Dunhelm out of the castle, in hopes of splitting our forces. A way out of the Castle is also a way in, however the tunnel is narrow necessitating a clandestine operation to capture Dunhelm rather than an assault from within. If we could fetch him Dunhelm quietly, we could alter the sticking points of the siege with no loss of life.”

“It seems logical to make the attempt. Even if it is betrayed, the loss of a small party would not cause us to lift the siege. The Duke’s men have said that a diversionary frontal assault of the castle might be a wise way to disguise our extraction.”

“And you want the men from the Grey Castle to affect the assault?”

“It makes the most sense. Of course, the knights and bowmen of both our retinues would be involved in supporting roles. The Grey Lady’s knights would lead the attempt to breech the gate. We just have to look like we are trying for perhaps two hours in order to make the plan work.”

“The plan will solve the issue of Dunhelm but the main issue for us is

Bothingham's unacceptable terms," said Mithras.

The two Earls were in agreement on the clandestine operation so Mithras felt he had little choice but to agree if he wanted to keep the alliance together. Wanting a look inside the Castle, Mithras himself insisted he be part of the tunnel operation.

They set the operation for dawn two days hence.

It was obvious inside the Castle that something was afoot. Their fears were justified, when at the appointed time torches were lit, siege engines readied and a canopy moved into place, to cover the men trying to smash open the gates.

The Grey Lady's men had a better plan. While they took a battering ram with them to use under cover of the wooden canopy, they also brought a number of wedges. The heavy gate was wood, reinforced with metal, a natural for a battering ram. But they would use the canopy to hide their true purpose, they would wedge wooden beams under the gate and try to force it up inch by inch, adding additional wedges into the gap as they lifted.

At the same time, a small party of five knights, lightly armoured, would descend into the tunnel by the river, await the heavy door at the Castle to be attacked and would use the distraction of move into the Castle, and find and extract Dunhelm. Two of the Eddingsworth's men, Mithras, and one each of the two Duke's men would take on the task, hoping that they would not be betrayed.

As the sun peeped above the horizon the operation began. The canopy was shoved up against the main gate. A rain of debris was dropped upon it from the second level of the barbican, as defenders hoped to break the canopy and render the invaders vulnerable. Twice torches were thrown upon it, but they bounced off and were quickly put out.

The rammers began their pounding, more intent on making noise than actually battering the gate. Many castles had heavy doors that swung on hinges but some castles had heavy gates that were raised and lowered by ropes, pulled up into the ceiling to allow people and horses through, and dropped back into place to bar entry.

As the men worked under the canopy, archers stood back some distance taking cover and shot arrows at anyone who showed themselves above the gate.

The attackers wedged up the heavy gate and slid a beam underneath it. With the battering providing cover for their activities, they wedged up the gate, and slid several heavy planks under it, holding it up. Repeating this process, they managed to raise the gate three and then four feet, all the while expecting those on the inside to retaliate once they saw the gate rise.

A few men scrambled under the gate when the gap was wide enough, returning to say there was a second levered gate at the other end of the barbican. There was no resistance from anyone above them, save the attacks on the canopy. They had expected more resistance.

A party of men were gathered to first secure the barbican and see if there was any way they could capture the gate mechanism and lift the second gate quickly.

There were slit entrances, barely noticeable in the low torchlight of the passageway, that led to stairs up on either side of the main tunnel into the castle.

They had been at this work for almost an hour, when the first knights ran up the stairs and engaged in combat with the defenders of the Castle in the space above the entrance pathway.

One defender ran to an opening on the castle side of the barbican, and from the second storey shouted at whoever might be listening, "They have breached the barbican." He started to say more, but a sword cut him down. The battle was short, with the invaders simply pouring more men into a small space, taking their dead and wounded and wearing down any resistance.

But the defenders of the castle could see that the interior gate was still intact, and believed their men had fought off the invasion. But then the inner gate began to rise. The invaders had captured the entire barbican and now controlled the entryway.

Inside the Castle, Mithras and his companions had been let in through the tunnel door, and they quietly as possible moved into the Castle, staying in the undercroft as long as possible. They were forced to kill two men, one a groom for the horses, whose stables were on the ground floor, and another a man of undefined mission, who they surprised and who began to shout.

Moving into the Castle, they were directed to the cousin's tower room. They slew the two guards and ran up the circular staircase until they reached the top. There a sleepy cousin awaited them.

"Thank you for coming to get me."

"We thought you were free to go."

"So did I, until I tried. I think Bothingham was trying to ransom me to my cousin Eddingsworth, once he understood my reason to remain here."

"And how do you know we will not try the same thing."

"I don't. With Bothingham I knew I was a prisoner. With you, I can offer to join your retinue, with the Grey Lady or with one of the Dukes, her allies. Not a foolproof plan, but better than simply waiting to be ransomed."

"But we have you now, my Lord and we are commanded by the Duke to return you."

"You know my reason for escaping Eddingsworth. Have mercy upon me, allow me to go in peace."

The Duke's men were silent and the sounds of the battle at the main gate penetrated the turret room.

"We can decide these things later, once we have secured this man." Mithras nodded and motioned the cousin to the door. The sounds of the attack and breech of the gatehouse grew louder.

"It seems our brethren are having some success."

"Aye, let us fulfill our plan and perhaps we can join them."

Mithras pointed to Eddingworth's two knights, "You escort your quarry to the river and secure him in our camp. I hope Cardoman's man and Westershire's man here will join me in attacking the defenders of the Castle from behind. Even three of us should be able to sow great discord among them."

The two northern men took the cousin into their charge. "We are sworn to uphold our duty and return you to your Lord."

Dunhelm appeared to be resigned to that fate, but he used his time to find a breech in that plan.

Mithras and the Dukes' men moved toward the barbican, now captured with the beginnings of a swarm readying to move into the Castle proper.

The Grey Lady's knights had taken charge and were moving in several directions, to capture the armory, the stables, and the main hall.

Skirmishes here and there, the clash of weapons and soon Bothingham himself was brought out, his hands tied behind his back. The two Dukes, the northern men and Mithras met in a tent to decide his fate.

"We have captured the Castle and our man. The question is what do we do?"

And then a breathless knight, one of Eddingsworth's men who had been assigned to escort Dunhelm out of the Castle entered the tent, a guard behind him holding him by an arm. My Lords, I must speak, Dunhelm has escaped." The rest of the northern knights were up in arms immediately.

"Where? How? We must pursue him."

"As we escorted him out of the tunnel, he drew a dagger, slammed an inner door on us, wedged it and fled to the river, where he captured a small boat and made his escape. We had no bowshot to fire, equipped with swords only, and he escaped."

"We want our Lord's cousin so we can escort him northward. As for the Castle, it is yours if you want it, but we should like some form of reward for helping you capture it."

The two Dukes looked at the ceiling, and refused to look at each other, trying to read the others thoughts.

"As for your man, you can have him if you can catch him, despite the potential reward we might get for turning him over." I would say that Dunhelm is your reward for helping us. That is until you let him slip away. We had not expected the castle to fall and were merely helping you. A reward, something beyond mere good will should be paid to us. Your forces involved in the siege were negligible."

"We still do not have Dunhelm. We will give up any claim on the Castle."

"While you all fight over the apparent spoils, the Grey Lady provided the bulk of the forces, took on the most difficult part of the siege, and suffered the most casualties."

"She has achieved her objective. This castle and Bothingham no longer threaten her realm."

"Mithras is right. Perhaps we should parlay with her regarding our good fortune. She is after all, allies with both of her neighbouring Dukes and would want to see them appropriately rewarded," said the northern man. And there is the matter of Dunhelm that is unresolved."

"Did you witness him on the boat that escaped?"

"No, come to think of it, we just assumed that he was on the boat floating away. It certainly does not make any sense that he would cut the boat loose as a diversion to remain in a fallen Castle, with a Lord he no longer trusted."

"Aye, you are right. We must pursue the boat, though we are more than an hour behind its departure."

The Dukes and Mithras made to provision the Castle, taking on any who would serve them and allowing any northern knights who wished, to pursue Denhelm. Theirs was an unlikely pursuit, as Dunhelm could beach the craft anywhere along the river, or ride the current far downstream.

Many days later the bulk of the Grey Lady's party and those knights loyal to Cardoman and Westershire saddled horse and made their way to the Grey Castle, where the Lady awaited having been apprised of the victory.

The Dukes would not enter the Grey Castle, and the Lady would not leave it.

"I have a Castle, and do not require another. What I do want is peace and good will. While I abide by your assurances, I fear setting a precedent of weakness. It was my good knights that largely carried the day, so I require something more."

Mithras remained with the Earl Westershire's retinue and had gained the trust of several of those knights. He wondered aloud why the both Earls refused to enter the Castle.

"Mithras, have you not seen what becomes of knight upon entering the castle? Look at yourself. What is the iron collar you wear?"

"It's an expression of loyalty to the Grey Lady. We are mostly hedge knights, seconds, thirds and more down the pecking order of our Lords, and we choose to roam rather than sit idly in our ancestral castles watching our elders enjoy the fruits of being the eldest. Knights here are free to go, but rarely do, as the Grey Lady has promised protection and has other missions she requires completed."

"But do you not notice the lethargy of your brothers, especially within the Castle walls?"

"Not lethargy my good sir. They have returned from missions and they require rest and good food to regain their strength."

"You Sir Mithras, have not partaken in food from the Castle for many days. How do you feel?"

"I, I, I feel strong and ready to conqueror. In fact, I believe I should engage in a far journey."

The Earl's knights nodded in unison. "Perhaps good sir, you are coming out of the fog of control that the Grey Lady has imposed. That is why none of us will enter the Castle. We prefer our freedom."

"But we are free to come and go as we please."

"But do you?"

"I've nowhere to go save where the Grey Lady directs me."

The knights nodded in unison again. "Remember, we live not far, and we have seen the denizens of the Grey Castle often. We believe that if you leave her realms you may begin to see things that have been hidden from you. It has likely already started, given our recent sojourn."

Mithras considered their words. He thought back to his history with the Grey Lady. She rarely sent anyone on a long journey, content to maintain her own lands and rarely parlaying with other Castles or their Lords. And he did feel better, more energetic, more aware, since he had not been in the Castle nor had eaten its provisions for many days.

"Okay, I will remain with you if you please, and see if your predictions pass by."

"And what shall we offer the Grey Lady from our spoils? She has a point about her knights being the main force which brought Bothingham down."

"Offer her exotic foods. Offer her knights to solidify the bonds between your Castles."

"Food, okay. Knights? Have you not heard what we have said?"

Mithras left the tent to find his own bed. He looked at the Grey Castle and contemplated his life there. Was there more? It did seem shuttered and limited, once he considered his life there.

"The offers of foodstuffs were made and a suggestion that the Lady ask what she required, as payment. She asked for two small ships to patrol the river. The Earls complied. She asked for knights to serve with her in rotation, so they should all come to know her Castle and serve as allies in times of need. The Dukes said they were too short of manpower to allow that.

During the negotiations the Grey Lady sent a knight to Mithras asking when he would return, as the Grey Lady wanted to speak with him.

Mithras felt a tug on his shoulders, as if the collar was summoning him. But he remained outside the Castle saying he wanted to conclude the talks and maintain his new found friendships with the Earls' knights.

At the conclusion of the talks, he sent a message that he would go with the Earls and perform the act of fealty with them, since they were reluctant to send any of their knights to the Grey Castle.

A messenger from the Grey Lady caught him as they were breaking camp, heading to the Castle of Earl Westershire. "Sir, my Lady seeks to speak with you urgently, prior to your leaving."

"We cannot wait any longer, Sir Mithras. You are expected at our Castle, pray thee, follow on and catch us if you may. We are but one camp away from our own lands. We travel by the main road."

Mithras was torn. He did not want to enter the Castle, but he could see no reason to refuse the Grey Lady. The Earls began to move out, and Mithras remained on his steed, unmoved. As the last of the baggage carts trundled down the path from the Grey Castle, Mithras remained still. The Earls now gone, he turned his steed toward the road with the idea of circling back around to the Castle.

As he tuned, he could hear the faint sound of bird song. There was no other noise and the song hung on the air, sweetly beckoning him down the road. He took a tentative step away from the Castle and the song grew more obvious, the individual notes now discernable. He turned back to the Castle and the music faded. The gates were open and he felt a pull to speak to the Grey Lady, to assure her of his loyalty and set a date for his return.

He took a few more steps and the birds went silent. He noticed the greenery around the Castle looked dark and twisted, as if it grew on poor soil. He turned once more to the road and galloped a way down its length. The undergrowth seemed more alive, the trees taller and the bird song returned. It was the same fading tune he remembered from the moment he exited the main road at the oak tree markers, as he returned from speaking to the Earls about the threats of Bothingham.

The tune then was slower, but the melody unmistakable. And now, leaving the Castle, the same melody seemed faster, brighter and more alive. He was somber, but a slight smile creased his lips at the sound of the birds. He paused and then with a shrug, spurred his mount down the road, in an effort to catch the knights and their supply train.

Chapter Fourteen

Okay, I'd settled for a more traditional fantasy story. I had written a sentient buildings short story and abandoned it. It was just too out there and didn't really work, except as an exercise. I confess, I cut it when I thought of Theresa reading it. I wondered if my desire to avoid the cliché and the tropes of fiction had led me to a dead end. I knew that many people loved the predictable expectations that the tried and true gave them. Expert authors used these expectations, while embracing them, to tangle their readers thoughts.

Strangely the words had come quickly once the idea had been given substance. But it quickly boxed itself into tighter and tighter places where there was no air for the story to breathe.

Theresa got the knight's tale instead and was reading it when Markus appeared. I had not seen him enter, but there he was coffee in hand and three apple Danishes on a dish. He smiled, nodded a greeting, so not to interrupt Theresa and sat down. She put the final page on the pile, and handed the pages to the new recruit.

Markus eagerly started and seemed to settle into the tale.

Theresa and I had remained silent and both of us tried not to stare at him, but only catch his countenance as our gazes swept the coffee shop.

"Okay, that was nice."

"Remember, this is an exercise to try to loosen my writer's block."

Theresa nodded. "It's not a finished product Markus, it's a story within a proscribed genre, not an attempt to break new ground."

I nodded with the little enthusiasm that remained. "I tried something more adventurous and had some fun with it, but there was no novel there. It was a tale of sentient buildings. Animating things which do not move is limiting."

"Why not allow them to move. You could have a great building chase scene, where the people are running through the buildings which in their own turn are running somewhere, for some purpose, yet to be determined." He grinned.

I had to smile in spite of myself.

"That doesn't mean I don't see the potential in the buildings talking and such." Markus could not keep a straight face and soon let out his held breath. It was that which caused Theresa to laugh and despite my annoyance, forced a smile to my face.

"Okay, smart guy, remember, I dropped the idea as unworkable. Tell us what men like to read. I'm all ears."

"In which case you might be on to something. Men like most things, save romance, perhaps they lean to action, and not just in the plot but in the writing. Too much description and too much dissecting the inner thoughts of those in the story are uninteresting. Men prefer to leave those details out unless they vary greatly from the standard expectations. You know, if I'm being chased, I'm likely afraid, no need to spell it out. Lean, short stuff."

"Like Hemmingway?"

"Perhaps, but Hemmingway was a touch short of fullness. He is too curt, though that might be because his protagonists are uncomplicated. Yours, decidedly, are not."

"Should I trust your judgement when it is delivered as a double negative?"

Markus looked confused and then it dawned on him, that the form of his response made it thus.

"It's no surprise that men like things a bit more straight forward. A gun is a gun, a death ray, a death ray, a chase needs to have a couple of cool elements."

"Cool elements? You mean like complications?"

Markus smirked, "Yeah, I guess. Maybe we like our complications where they need to be overcome, quickly and then discarded, where women like there complications to be turned over and over, in order to figure them out."

"Men like science fiction and fantasy."

"So do women, they just like the science of psychology and the fantasy of interpersonal circumstance, where men like flying things, explosions and worlds to be understood, and if necessary, tamed, controlled, and used for the common good."

"Or world domination?"

"Yes, world domination has its charms, and not just in fiction."

We all took a moment to sip our coffee. Both Theresa and Markus took a bite of Danish.

"I hear you are going to Philadelphia? I'm not very conversant with that city. Liberty Bell, navy yards, what else?" I asked.

Markus perked up. He began to espouse the glories of old Philadelphia, and happily admitted it all sounded much like old Manhattan, but pointed to the smaller crowds and the cheaper, in fact, actually affordable prices.

He admitted his family was largely from Philadelphia, his own branch being the renegades that escaped for the bright lights of New York.

"So you can show me around?" said Theresa.

"Of course, if we have any time. The show has long opening hours, early, very early to, I think, 7:30 pm. Not a lot of time for tourist stuff."

Theresa shrugged and took another bite of her Danish.

"These look pretty good," I said before taking a bite.

"They are. My guess is, they must be very fresh. That seems to be the key element in Danishes."

Markus asked how long it would be before I completed my next novel. I hummed a bit, returning that I needed a solid foundational idea, a story arc, and quality believable characters who act out a tale fresher than our strudels.

He nodded, and I could actually see him swallow down a sarcastic comment, unsure if his observation would be seen as funny or cutting. He saw me notice his restraint and gave me a knowing toothless grin.

"Well, I wish you well in the Philadelphia part of the story."

"Why don't you join us?" Markus said. "I'm trying to get Brandon to come, and if there is someone there without Trade Show responsibilities, he might be enticed."

My mouth made the beginnings of excuses while my mind ran over the expectations of my weekend. I ended by completing the excuse, but neatly reversing and suggesting that I might be able to wiggle out of my invented plans if my tasks were completed.

"So, I'll tell Brandon you might be there?"

"Tell him, that if he goes, I'll try to make it work. I am in the same boat he is, not really wanting to be a third wheel in a city I know nothing about."

"And what about your next effort? Writing wise I mean."

"Frankly I was thinking of expanding the sentient buildings one." I laughed when I saw their expressions matched perfectly. "No, I've been thinking about a dystopian tale of something or other."

"I'm glad you are on track."

"I gotta start somewhere."

I went home to a phone message from a client asking me to return his call the next morning. In the mean time I could consider my approach to my next genre.

Usually dystopia begins with an end-of-the-world scenario, so that's out, I thought. What kind of bad social outcome could I base things on? The list seemed endless and mostly mined by others, or too ridiculous to approach, especially in light of the reaction to my almost fantasy story.

I sat down and began to type . . .

Chapter Fifteen – Dystopia – One Storm begets another

The rolling, boiling front edge of the surge advanced fairly slowly down the oversized creek that ran through town. Those who saw it were at first amazed and then concerned with the ominous, black oozing.

The front edge passed through the town as people watched from bridges across the deep channel. They'd seen this before. The result of flash floods from all the rain upstate. And then the water began to rise. Still, those in town were not too worried as the creek was 30 feet below the level of the banks on which the town was built.

And then the black and brown swirling mess crested the bank and ran through the streets. Within hours everything was a swirling brown, smelly mess. The entire city had been swallowed in an explosion at the water treatment plant, conveniently located near the center of town.

Now Westerville was not a large city by standards of the time and place, it was home to 23,459 residents, give or take, and had a sizeable down-town center surrounded by a few pre-suburban streets, with small yards, separate garages and bits of vegetation, unproductive in the front and hopeful in the back.

Central to this disaster was Westerville's location, nestled into a creek valley of what was once a more significant river, now reduced to a meandering creek with a centre stream among the larger rock formations left by what ever had come long before. Something to do with a dam upriver, built in the 1930's to harness electricity.

Of course, it was the rain that caused the treatment plant to over flow. Okay, not the rain specifically but the trees and debris that had been swept by the flash flood, down the creek valley into town.

The debris clogged the intakes and other systems, and an accompanying power outage stopped the mixers and digesters. Plus, our illustrious plant was built to hold a large amount of sewage so that it could be consumed properly and then used to spray agricultural fields. An elegant solution to our issues, thought all who were charged with considering such things.

So, when the plant ceased to function there was much more effluent stored on the property than anyone really knew, until they came face to face with it.

Contained by the valley walls and the debris which clogged the now massively swollen creek, Westerville was awash in excrement. A shit show of epic proportions.

Fortunately, the width of the valley, and bend in the river, prevented the buildings from being completely covered. Unfortunately, the rest of the surrounding area was digging out from the series of storms and could offer no assistance. Even if they could, they had no way of getting to Westerville as the main route followed the river. And getting there just brought you to the edge of the flood.

People gathered on the tops of buildings, in the top floors of the tallest buildings in town, a foursquare of five-storey buildings at the central intersection, built some years before when an entrepreneur bought up the old building on each corner, added some property and built the complex, leaving room for traditional retail on the bottom floors.

So nearly 23,000 people were gathered on the top floor of several buildings and were spread across town on the roofs of others, in a slowly swirling sea of brown and yellow and green.

When, on the second day, the sun broke through, those who knew were not pleased. Within four hours the heat pressed down the gathering odour, from which there was no escape.

Sitting on the roof of one of the central buildings, people conjured all sorts of solutions.

"Somebody has to pop the debris dam, if this stuff is going to move."

"You're welcome to try Fred."

Helicopters had come through to survey the area and a few people had taken to boats to find higher ground, but the boats rare and full, and the helicopter solution would take days. It did pluck a few people off low roofs.

Talk among the stranded suggested that authorities were trying to break up the dam that held the water high, but of course nobody really knew it this was true. And they sat. And slowly the relative calm of these people began to break. Two days on, without their daily medications, some people began to suffer. The very young began to act out, ratcheting up the tension hour by hour.

Late that day there was a muffled explosion somewhere down the valley. Hopes rose just as the sun began to set.

"I think they got the debris dam, maybe by tomorrow morning this will all be over."

"The water might be gone, but it is really just beginning. Nobody here will have anything to go home to. Everything is destroyed."

Those within earshot, all smiles a moment before, dipped their chins and stared at the floor. The realization of what had happened hit hard.

"Our town is gone. What's left will have to be plowed under and everyone will scatter to whatever safety they can muster."

"Surely the government will help?"

"Maybe in the short run, but disasters like this are over for the government once the public health issues are cleaned up. It's more about the insurance companies and sure enough they will find a way to reduce any payouts."

By the next morning the early risers could see that most of the fetid water was gone. Pools still held in low lying areas, and the entire town was coated with a nasty film somewhere between green and blue. And it stunk.

A car drove into the main intersection with a public address system on its roof, repeating the same instruction. 'Stay in place. Buses are on their way to transport people out of the valley. National Guard units have been dispatched to stop any looting.'

"Fat lot of good that will do. Stopping people from taking shit covered crap." People were alive but their lives had been overturned.

Other vehicles arrived to help evacuate people from the edge of town, where the flood waters had been the lowest. However, the first rumbles were not buses. Army personnel carriers rolled into town, with the soldiers either heavily armed or wearing hazmat suits.

"They have suits but we've been breathing this air for four days now."

Again, the orders were to stay in place as authorities determined who should be moved first. Late that day the first busses arrived and they left full of people in distress. Army personnel switched out and still most of the population waited.

Bales of food were brought in by helicopter as those people dotted on roofs here and there were brought to the tall buildings downtown.

Late that first evacuation day, word filtered through the makeshift camps that the rest of the town's people would be moved the next day. A few water street cleaners moved through the main streets, trying to remove the fetid scum from the streets. Not that it really mattered but it gave the illusion of progress. The air became noticeably better.

And a line of busses did appear the next morning, and the shuttle began, with busses filling up with refugees and trundling off down the block to turn out of sight. Followed by another and another. This continued all day, and by the end, the pressure on those strong enough to wait, was greatly relieved.

Anna Black and her three children had lived close enough to the four tall buildings that they ran to them when the water started to rise. Of her husband Frank, she had an indication that he was in another of the tall buildings. She and her brood were evacuated and set up in a camp for sorting out the homeless. She hoped Frank would soon join them. He had a brother that lived upstate and that's where Frank would go looking for some immediate help.

She walked with her children to a tent that they had been assigned with a mix of relief that the air was fresh again, and fear that they had nothing, not even Frank, yet. She tried to go over every scenario of her next few days but the jumble of things swirling around her mind stopped her from coming up with any real plan.

She really wanted to go back to their home and try to salvage anything they could. She had no idea how bad the damage was, but was being told by every authority that everything would be plowed under, that there was nothing that had not been destroyed.

"I expect you are right," she said, "But I have to see it for myself. Believe me I have no interest in rooting around for salvage, but I need the closure."

The camp worker looked sympathetic and mumbled something about passing Anna's sentiments on to those in charge. It was a long shot as the logistical nightmare of trying to get homeowners to their properties was almost impossible.

In the mean time Frank had dutifully arrived, counted his blessings and suggested that he would try to go back to their home to see. He was prepared to walk if necessary, and kept pressing camp officials to provide means.

It began to rain and the family huddled in the tent, thanking God that it was summertime. Frank figured the rain would begin to wash away the remaining scum from the town. It would still be a dangerous place to go, but with each cleansing of rain, it was a little less so.

Two weeks later, Frank had managed to contact his brother who came to the camp to fetch them. "We don't have a lot of room Frankie, but we will make do. I have already fetched a couple of mattresses, though I had to travel a bit to get them. It won't be pretty, but it will do for a while."

Eddie and his wife were all in on helping. Mattresses were slung into open spaces at night and hiked up and leaned against walls in the day.

Frank gave Eddie all of the emergency money that he received from the town authorities.

Frank had been a county by-law enforcement agent and he returned to work fairly quickly as the town needed its people to assess the damages.

"I don't know how long we will be able to pay you all," said the mayor. "We have money in the bank for the rest of this year, but there is no town left to collect much property tax from. In the mean time, we have to assess all the town property and help federal agencies do whatever work they want."

Riding with a crew of town workers assigned to inspect each property, the men decided their first stops were their own homes, even if they would not mark the properties to show they were there, rather leaving them to the process as scripted by the town.

Frankie's home was last, as it was nearest the downtown, and furthest from the municipal works depot.

The first home they visited looked okay from the outside. Stained from the scum which formed a line about a foot below the top of the front door, and obviously not tended for a while, the owner almost smiled as he bounded from the truck, his front door key in hand.

The men slowly followed him up the drive and could see his shoulders visibly slouch once he opened the door. He moved quickly out of the way as a thin stream of water flowed out the door and down the walkway. There wasn't much of it, and it seemed clear, but its presence did not bode well for the home.

The man entered the house and came back out quickly. "It's all over."

"What about upstairs? Clothes, kitchen stuff, keepsakes, important papers?"

The man nodded and plunged into the home again. The other men followed entering the home but staying on the main floor.

There was a ring of scum on the walls at about the six-foot level, just shy of the ceiling. One of the guys pointed to it. Another shrugged.

The homeowner came down the stairs. "It doesn't look like the water reached up top. I assume things up there are salvageable but I'm not an expert. We need to speak to people who know these things if we are going to be marking up buildings and assigning damage levels."

"Well, the home itself is pretty much a write off as everything on the ground floor is damaged or destroyed."

They repeated the effort at each of their homes, finding much of the same thing. At his own home Frankie saw that Anna had moved several downstairs items upstairs, in a frantic effort to save them. It was lighter objects and some kitchen stuff. She probably made a dozen runs before abandoning the house. Furniture, appliances, housewares were all underwater at some point, just like all the other homes.

At the end of the day the crew filed their report, suggesting strongly that in many homes things on a second storey might be salvaged, including clothes, keepsakes and maybe even beds and other furniture.

After the crews had established that this appeared to be true for the entire town, efforts were made to allow homeowners into their properties to salvage upstairs effects. Much of the town was built with only bungalow style homes where nothing could be salvaged.

Homeowners were allowed to scout out their properties and given 48 hours before signing off on abandoning them.

"It is remarkable how little I really want to take out of our home," said Anna as she took a break from running items down the stairs and into a rented van. "One whiff of those old mattresses and I had no trouble tossing them."

In the end they took as many clothes as they could muster, figuring they could try to clean them as they had no contact with the effluent, and failing that would dispose of them later. They took three bedside tables, four dresser cabinets, some cleaning supplies, pictures and framed wall hangings and still had room in the van.

"That's it?"

"That's it. What's left of our lives packed neatly into a large van. We can take it to the storage unit and unload what we don't need. Any luck on finding another house for us? Eddie has been great, but every day eats at me a bit more."

"I found a small house in Centerville, just a bit north of here. The price is reasonable mostly because its too small for us. We should probably take it for a year. By then we should know where we stand. And your job situation should be sorted."

Frankie nodded. He took pride in providing a comfortable home, and now was resigned to just having a functional one. Anna said they could move in almost immediately. So Frankie decided to forgo the storage unit, leave their stuff in the van and pay to rent the van for two more days, so they could secure the lease on the house and move in.

A few days later Frankie closed the door of the small house after waving goodbye to his brother who had come to help him move.

"I owe you Ed, thanks."

"Let's hope you never have to pay. I can't imagine."

The next stage of their lives would begin now. The light unease of their new situation had gnawed at Frankie and was forming an idea, and idea of leaving entirely and starting over. He broached the idea with Anna, not sure what to expect.

"All I can say is pick a place and try to find work there. If you can then we have an option. It's probably best for now to simply carry on, see what happens to our insurance claim, the town rebuild and other stuff. We are good and safe for now and you have a job. We can endure almost anything for a year, especially if we can see the light at the end of the tunnel."

Frankie nodded, she was right. They were in on the lease of the small house for a year, so he had that long to plan and look and hope.

Months had passed and the insurance settlement had been presented, covering a significant amount to rebuild the home, but not covering its true value as they still owned the land and that land was now worth considerably less. The State had suggested they would make a bid for the property, but warned everyone it was a lowball as there would be no building allowed. There were speculators trying to by up property but they offered a pittance.

Frankie took some off days to travel a few hours to nearby cities and large towns hoping to find work. He came up empty.

"Anna, I think our only hope is to abandon this state entirely, go where the work is, and be willing to start again from nearly scratch."

He could see her shoulders slump but her face did not follow their lead. He marvelled at her ability to move past the worst of things and simply march on.

"I think maybe you are right. I hate to uproot the kids again, but perhaps its for the best. An attachment to a place can be unhealthy. They will learn to be resilient, and learn how to make new friends."

Frankie began to look at booming States and settled on Texas, Florida and a smattering of other places in hopes of finding some work. Municipal enforcement was not a growth industry in those States so he looked at civilian jobs within the police departments, or works jobs with municipal government and eventually settled on a warehouse job.

The family moved to Florida, settling on the southside of Jacksonville. Anna took an office job and they were able to cobble together enough money to survive. Frankie's hard work got him a couple of promotions, to shift lead hand, shift supervisor and eventually as an assistant to the warehouse manager. The hours were tough but the work honest and oddly fulfilling as the dominoes of warehousing and moving goods and packages, felt like solving a puzzle.

Anna was able to get a bit more pay and some better working hours as the kids took a bit less time. She worked in a real estate office, mostly handling initial contacts, follow ups with clients and day to day office needs. The only downside was she was required to work some weekends.

They had put the trauma of the flood behind them, with the kids mentioning their old home very infrequently and even forgetting much of the time in the small temporary house in Centreville.

And then Frankie was offered a job managing a new warehouse facility several hours away in the booming new cities north of Orlando. He struggled with it, wanting to keep his career track moving but worried about uprooting the kids yet again. They were now approaching the end of their middle school years and about to enter high school.

Anna suggested he talk to them and to his employer about his future should he remain in Jacksonville. She said she could get another job fairly easily but did lament the credibility she had built with her current employer.

Frankie had determined that he did not want to move his family again.

"It's only a few hours drive. The kids can maintain their friendships and continue to spend some time with their friends if we want to make it work. What have they told you at work?"

"They encouraged me to take the job in Orlando and pointed out that Jake, my manager is many years from retirement, so opportunity in Jacksonville is limited. If we move, it's the last time. At least willingly. And frankly with the job opportunities for the kids in the entertainment complexes in Orlando, and the nearby universities, when the time comes, it's hard to say no."

"So yes, it is," Anna said, forcing a smile. "I'm with you Frankie, and this hopefully will be it. Maybe we can consider buying a home and putting down some roots."

They had rented for their entire time in Jacksonville, partly because they waited for an insurance settlement and partly because that settlement had been inadequate. Now, they could consider a real home.

Frankie took the job, doing the brutal commute for a month, while they kids finished out the school year and while he and Anna started to search for a home using what off days they could spare.

They found one in the far eastern suburban part of Orlando, away from the tourist action, and close to the university where Anna landed a job in administration. The warehouse was so far to the north side of Orlando, it was really another town. But the commute was easy and the kids found their new school to their liking. A couple of trips to Disney and other tourist haunts helped ease the transition.

Frankie got used to the insane street pattern of eastern Orlando, obviously just an expansion of old rural roads that had been inundated with new residents as Orlando grew from a town, to a modest sized city, to a metropolis of several million people, all within a few decades.

Frankie wasn't sure if he would ever live to see he cacophony of commuters tamed in any meaningful way. It was a mess and it wasn't likely to get better. His company decided to open a new warehouse facility on the south west side of the city and wanted Frankie to take charge. His commute was going to be better, he thought, so he took it.

He settled on going into work very early and leaving fairly late, reserving himself the option of leaving correspondingly early should he be needed at home. It wasn't ideal, but he made it work.

The destruction of their home in Westerville was now five years behind them and both kids were firmly into high school. Both he and Anna knew that they were going to struggle to put the children through university should they choose that route. Bobby was a bright kid, but not particularly academically inclined, constantly disappointing his teachers with middling grades when it appeared he should do better. And Rose, his daughter, seemed unfocussed, being more interested in pop stars and movies than anything that might be turned into a career.

"You are supposed to be obsessed with singers and movies when you are 15," Anna said. "Weren't you?"

"Not particularly, I was more into sports, football and baseball."

"Tell me," Anna smiled, "what CD did you have playing in the car yesterday when we went to the market?"

Frankie thought for a second, "Pink Floyd. But I was never obsessed with them. My brother was," he laughed. "Okay, okay, I guess we won't worry just yet about Rose. But Bobby is an issue, he's not obsessed with anything."

"Except Penelope."

"Who or what is Penelope?"

"A girl who lives a couple of blocks away. Bobby seems to be spending time with her."

"And that's bad?"

"No, in fact it means he will have to start thinking about his future, even if he doesn't seem focussed on it right now."

"It's that serious?"

"No, no. Well, I don't think so. But sooner or later it or someone else will be. I'm going to suggest, you have a little 'plan for the future' talk with him. At least get him thinking about what he's going to do after high school."

"Okay, I can do that. I live for that kind of thing."

Frankie was determined not to make the talk a big deal, rather a series of comments tucked into normal conversation. And by no means was he going to mention Penelope.

Both kids had avoided jobs at the big theme parks, mostly because they were a difficult commute away and because those places preferred older students. Bobby had a job with the maintenance crew at the University of Central Florida, which Anna had found for him. Rose worked for a small restaurant that catered to older students and suburbanites, located just off the campus.

Life seemed pretty good, their troubles behind them and whatever troubles that loomed in their way, were standard concerns of middle-class families. And then the hurricane hit. Not a standard hurricane but the largest ever recorded in the continental United States. Making land fall at Cocoa Beach just south of Cape Canaveral, it pushed a huge storm surge into Florida just south of Orlando. The low lying areas were inundated with salt water even if the Cape had shielded much of the area from the surge.

The surge had not reached too far inland, but it had affected the water table. Several college buildings were faced with significant water damage. The University managed to remain open but there was much concern about rebuilding efforts.

Anna's hours were cut back at UCF along with most of her colleagues in an effort to save money to help pay for the repairs to campus infra-structure. It was hard for people to believe there was anything wrong or broken in the aftermath, but sewage systems had taken a beating, a few roads had crumbled and several buildings had flood damage around their foundations, not from water pouring in, but rather, from the rising water table pushing up through drains.

"At least the damage didn't reach the west side of town," she said.

"It didn't but there has been a slow down in usual business volume, as dollars are being redirected to repairs across town, so our business has taken a hit."

"Next thing you know we'll be hit with a fire," Anna said.

"Now don't say such things. That's all we need. Maybe we should have moved to California."

"And face the earthquakes? No thanks." They both laughed, but deep down knew that life had just thrown them another curve ball. "I wonder when things will just calm down?"

"Maybe never. And that's okay, as life would be too boring if things never happened."

"Things? Why is it always bad things? Why can't it be good things?"

"Sometimes bad is just a catalyst to get to the good. "I'm pretty happy here in Central Florida, well, except in July."

"You don't miss Westerville? I do. I liked the pace of the place. I liked our neighbours. Here, I hardly even know them. When was the last time we had a drink or a BBQ with friends and neighbours?"

"Not sure I'd like to socialize with our neighbours. They are an odd lot."

"That's entirely the point. In Westerville they weren't odd."

"I'm not sure we can change all the outside forces which impact our lives."

"I know that. I'm just tired of fighting the forces of evil. You know, work, work, work and never feeling like we are getting ahead."

"But we are, slowly, the mortgage is being paid down. We are about ready for a family holiday, which we've put off for too long, and the kids seem happy and well adjusted, despite the turmoil of the last few years."

"But where does it all end?"

"It's life. It ends when you stop breathing. And caring."

"Well, I'm doing both," said Anna. "So where do we go from here?"

"Well, five years ago I would have said a beach vacation. But living the beach life such as we do, I'm thinking of something different. Big cities, historical places, the mountains; you pick."

Anna just stared at Frankie. Either he did not understand her angst or he understood perfectly and had moved on, but she didn't know which.

"Let me think about it."

"It probably depends on when we decide to go. And who is going?"

Life, it appeared, was one big shit show, she thought. How you navigated the storm was the whole point. Calm could be had when you were dead. A lot of calm.

Chapter Sixteen

"I'm not going to let you read this one. It's a mess."

"Well at least tell me about it."

Cassandra related the basics of the dystopian tale she had written.

"Okay, it is a mess, but isn't it supposed to be?"

"Oh yeah, but this has so little elegance. It's worse than my typical vometic flow of a first draft. There is nothing redeeming about it."

"So, what's next," Theresa asked as she prepared to bite into her croissant.

"Not sure yet. What are the details for the Philadelphia show? You still want me to come?"

"Well, Markus and Brandon are coming and they are expecting you. So yes. We are loading up on Wednesday and planning to leave early Thursday to get there around noon and set up. Show opens Friday morning."

"You know, guys don't do these things without some kind of ulterior motive."

"Whatever are you suggesting?"

I looked at Theresa and blinked my eyes rapidly a couple of times. She laughed. "Nobody has said anything about anything. Markus does call me to chat every now and then."

"Be careful," I said, "There is a point of no return."

"Funny, I've never thought about Philadelphia that way."

I changed the subject. "Any new items to show off?"

"Of course, that's the whole point of attending. In fact, I have two new jackets for my urban collection. I thought they would contrast nicely with the sub-urban pieces, of which I have added some pants for women and men."

Theresa rummaged through her small portfolio and slid a sheaf of pages on the table between us. I quickly flipped through the pages and then went back again to look at the finer details.

"You have a discerning eye."

"I just imaging myself shopping and thinking of actually paying for these clothes," I explained.

"So would you buy them?"

"I really like this one,' I turned over two pages and pointed to a half-zip front sweatshirt. "Of course, it depends on the cost and the fabric, but I love the style and the feel."

"Maybe you should move out of the city."

"I like it. It's got a comfortable feel. Not business clothing to be sure, but something for a weekend, absolutely."

"Maybe we will dress one of the mannequins in it. Anything else?"

"I am finding myself drawn more to the comfortable clothes and away from the high style. It's probably the circles in which I travel. It's not every day I need something for the Met."

"But you do need business clothes when you make a presentation or proposal? And what's that, twice a week or so."

"Give or take, I guess. But the rest of the time I'm crouched over a computer monitor and I need the appropriate dress for that."

"I don't do pyjamas."

I laughed and Thresea smiled without showing her teeth. I had been outed, but that was okay.

"What's the next story about? You have to be running out of genres."

"I am, but there are still others to try. In the meantime, I've had a brain-wave and decided to include all the story archetypes as well, like buddy stories, quests, rags to riches tales, voyage and return – that kind of thing."

"Aren't they part of the genre thingy?"

"Yes and no. Each tale is one or more of those archetypes and is run through a particular genre, although they can bleed into each other as well."

"Sounds complicated."

"It's only as complicated as you want to make it. Some people say there are only five genres and only a few archetypes, but I like the slightly expanded take."

"So if you write in each genre and each archetype you have a pretty large number of story tropes you can access."

I thought for a second. "Yes," I had been thinking about this and was trying to do the math in my head. "I count about 120 story types, give or take. Of course, other people would say there are more. And my plan is just to tackle one in each story, so I'm looking at around 23."

"Or less."

I nodded. "It's no different than the possible types of clothing designs."

"Okay, I guess. But there are only so many things you can do with pants, or a shirt."

"Well multiply it out, I bet its hundreds depending on where and how you want to define and limit the design elements."

I went home that night and began my next story try, but only after packing my overnight bag for Philadelphia. Theresa and I were taking Amtrack and the boys were driving, first picking up the trailer full of show elements at Theresa's east end business space.

I figured I could get a head start with an evening to spare.

Chapter Seventeen - Pursuit of Happiness - California calling

I don't really remember much of it. I was young.

They said my parents died in a car accident and I had no other family. So,

I was bundled off to a series of foster care arrangements, most of which lasted only a week or two. Until they placed me with Mrs. James.

She was a widow, her husband having died in Vietnam, though the circumstances were murky, or maybe that was my limited understanding. I guess I was too young to wonder about the details.

Mrs. James was involved in the theatre scene. She was a small-time actress, and a big-time costume designer and creator. New York was a giant hustle in those days, Broadway and off-Broadway productions were opening and closing regularly. By 1966 Mrs. James had steady work, occasionally farming out some of the seamstress work to other independents scattered across Manhattan, mostly in Soho or Little Italy.

Mame, Showboat, Breakfast at Tiffany's and Annie Get Your Gun were all available to theatre goers as were several dozen other mostly forgettable productions. Mrs. James had a hand in the costume design of some of these shows, and she herself would take up some work to help out when another costume designer was overwhelmed.

It was right about this time that she began to use me as a delivery boy, taking designs on paper to who ever needed to see them, or dropping a completed costume at a theatre or even going to get fabric or some other order from local shops.

Mrs. James treated me like an employee. Well enough, I suppose, but there was no love, no affection. If she was concerned about me, it was to ensure I was available for errands. I attended school when I could, and found out later that Mrs. James took me in because of the stipend provided by the State of New York. She found out later that I would work for food, so to speak.

After a time, Mrs. James took on another ward of the state, a little girl who she set up much like me. I was now 10 and used to making deliveries to various stages, even getting to know the doormen and some of the theatre managers and show directors. I had been given a few roles as a crowd extra in a few shows, and Mrs. James, to her credit, insisted I put the money in the bank. The new ward was Lilly, and she said she was eight. I showed her around the shoppes and soon Lilly was doing the fabric pickups and costume deliveries that I had done.

This went on for several years. One particular summer evening, I was sitting out on the fire escape of Mrs. James apartment building when she came and sat with me. She often did this to prepare me for whatever I needed to do the next day, and get a sense of the timing.

By now, The State of New York was watching our school attendance closely, so most of Lilly and my deliveries were done after school, which suited Mrs. James, as she worked through the day to get the costumes completed.

On this particular day she told me that I was nearing my 18th birthday and at that point the State of New York required that I set out on my own. She waved a letter that she had received from the State outlining the procedure. I could transition to a group supported home, or merely set out on my own.

Mrs. James told me I should contact the youth social worker listed as a contact on the letter to get more details.

It turned out that the State would give me some monthly money and put me up in a transitional group home for as much as a year while I found my feet.

Not having much choice in the matter, I followed along and found myself sharing a room in an old tenement with another orphan who appeared to have had a much rougher go of it than I.

At first his rough demeanor repelled me, but I soon figured out that he had been mistreated and did not trust anyone. Mrs. James had never mistreated us.

He constantly talked about saving enough money to get out of New York, but he had little idea of the world and no real plan on where to go. In New York he had a series of odd jobs, many of which seemed more than a little sketchy, but I didn't say anything.

For myself, I first worked the theatre district and managed to land a gig as an usher at a small Broadway theatre which had a promising show. I learned to hail cabs, watch out for people who needed help and most of all, run cover for the actors. Everything came with the promise of a tip, but the result was hit and miss. I once scored 20 bucks from a leading man for running him out the back door and into a waiting cab, and I often took quarters from little old ladies who needed help exiting the theatre into their waiting limos.

My bank account steadily rose, from the few hundred I had saved as a child extra, to most of my wages and tips from six months of ushering.

With six months left in my State of New York stipend I had to figure out where to live and how to stay alive. My group home roommate had calmed a bit, at least towards me as I tried to be kind and understanding of his outbursts. I got him a job cleaning the theatre, but he didn't last. I think it was mostly the late hours, which interfered with his other paid gigs, which consisted mainly of being a go-fer for the regular customers of several bars.

I scoured ads looking for roommates and found a few with students at Columbia. The school was way uptown, but the rent was reasonable and the people a little less rough than those in Bowery and Little Italy. Okay, maybe a different kind of rough.

The counter culture thing was something dismissed by the New York I travelled in, but the Columbia folks ate it up. Of course, by now it was 1974 and the psychedelic era was peaking, 'Hair' was still running on Broadway, but the shock had worn off.

Vietnam still raged but mostly as a side story on the evening news as the United States had withdrawn the year before. The steam had left the hippie movement with a bunch of lost sheep looking for the next cause to back.

With my background I became something of an establishment figure to the students I encountered, though my roommates tried to convert me in a good-natured way, as I was certainly sympathetic to their way of thinking. I'd like to think that I was in a perfect place, on the good side of the staid old conservatives who kept going to see 'Hair' and its ilk, despite saying it was detrimental to our national values, and the youth, who saw every thing old as outdated and mired in conventional jingoistic Americanism.

In between ushering on Broadway, I started a tee-shirt business, knocking off shirts for various occasions and spending much of my free time hawking them near the University and in tourist haunts. I tried to set up at the exit to the Staten Island Ferry but found mostly frowns and annoyed looks from the passersby. I found out that tees with a protest message weren't popular with suburban commuters.

However, it was at this time that I ran into Lilly again. She was now nearing 18 and was soon to leave Mrs. James. She said another ward had taken my place once I'd left and she fully expected someone would replace her. I picked up my display of t-shits and we went to a nearby coffee shop where I explained all the wonderful things she had to navigate as the State released its hold.

She seemed resigned to her fate and even had a few ideas for jobs. She liked my plan for getting age-appropriate roommates up near Columbia and even expressed an interest in attending. I had heard there was aid money available but really had no idea of the process. I had heard my roommates speak of such things and it didn't seem too complicated.

As Lilly prepared to head back to Mrs. James place, and I told her to thank Mrs. James for me, and tell her I was doing okay. Lilly said she'd heard tell of me from some of the theatre managers, then she laughed and said Mrs. James was up in arms at all the counterculture shows that featured nude scenes.

I had not thought of Mrs. James as being old-fashioned, as she was on the cutting edge of Broadway. I must have looked quizzical as she leaned in and said, "You can't make costumes for naked people."

I leaned back in my seat with a wide grin.

Lilly walked out the door and I wondered if I would see her again. She had a tough transition to make, but maybe she would turn up near Columbia.

The tee-shirt business was experiencing a turn as the weather cooled. Something I had not figured into my thinking. So I began to find some other odd jobs, after running into my old roommate. It was pretty sketchy stuff, taking packages between bars, and dropping notes to various nefarious types.

I could hardly wait for the weather to turn and my t-shirt business to pick up again. I believe I was ever fully trusted by the gang leaders for whom I worked, but that was okay as it kept me looking for something more legit.

In 1975 I started with band tees. I'd copy logos and pictures onto cotton tees and sell them near concert venues. Got a good deal on the silk-screening due to volume. The only difficulty at the start was getting the quantities right. Though I did learn to drop the price dramatically after the shows to get rid of any extra inventory. Still, doing that, if concert goers figured it out, was death to the business, so quantities were hugely important. Just the right amount of scarcity meant I could charge top dollar and sell out 15 minutes before the show.

Concert promoters cottoned on to what I was doing and they tried to push me away. So often I moved from a prime selling location 45 minutes before the show to a lesser spot, but that gave me first shot at the buyers. A hand written sign suggesting that my prices were slightly better, seemed to work.

By this time, I'd amassed a nice little fortune and wondered how I could use it to move up the economic ladder. Service and short-term product sales did translate into real business skills, but convincing a legitimate company to take me on, was not easy.

Slogging through the streets one night, carrying my little wheeled display case from the subway to my building in the 140s, I happened upon a group of students starting their night out.

I maneuvered to let the group pass and as I did, I saw Lilly and called her name without thinking. She looked up from her conversation with some guy and called my name, rushing over to me and giving me an unexpected hug.

The guy she had been talking to seemed pretty put out, so I asked her for an introduction. Her group had paused its march down the street though some were trickling onward, saying they did not want to be late or they would not get seats.

"I'll catch up, I won't be long."

"Nice to see you Lilly are you a student?"

"I am. This is my friend Roddie, and that mob are also friends. We're on our way to The Pleb, a band of our friends is playing tonight. Why don't you join us?"

Roddie had nodded at the introduction but the sour look on his face when Lilly invited me along made my decision for me. "I would love that, but I've been working and I'm tired. Gotta get this gear home. If you live around here, maybe we can meet for a coffee sometime?"

I didn't have a piece of paper and told her I'd just remember her number but she seemed reluctant to say it aloud. I did have a pen handy so she wrote it in little numbers on my forearm, before waving goodbye and moving quickly to catch her friends. I heard her tell Roddie that we were friends, though whether she told him that we were both orphans, I never heard.

I watched her head down the sidewalk with Roddie, noticing that they were not holding hands or anything.

I shrugged and continued on to my place where I decided to take a shower to get the grime of the work day off me. As the water rolled down my arm, I saw the phone number and leaped out of the shower to find a paper on which to scribble it down.

A week later, on a rainy late fall night, I gave her a call. One of her room-mates answered and took a message for me, though I had the feeling I was being screened, so I was surprised when I got a call to meet her at a coffee shop off-campus two days later.

She was waiting for me when I arrived.

"So, what are you taking?"

"Oh, you know, just a general set of courses, well, a bit unusual maybe. I am mixing arts and sciences, taking a bit of fine art and a biology course. I have no idea what I'm interested in until I try it."

"I have much the same problem, but so much so, that I wouldn't even know where to begin."

"How about your friend Roddie, what's he taking?"

"He's in general science too, that's how I know him, from biology, but I think he is leaning towards engineering. At least that's what he says. And he's not really a friend, more of an acquaintance."

"Not sure he feels that way. He was awfully annoyed that you even knew me?"

"Yeah, I guess. There's an awful lot of that going on at school. People pairing up. I'm not really into it. I want to experience life for a while and see where it goes."

"How about Mrs. James? How is she?"

"I went back to see her a few weeks ago. Feeling a tug for a bit of familiar, you know. She looked at me like she didn't even know me. At first any-ways, then she offered me a cup of tea and we talked a bit, but it was very stilted, uncomfortable. A little girl wandered in and she introduced me. The little girl was maybe seven or eight and she looked at me with big eyes, almost as if she saw the future flash in front of her. I left shortly after. Mrs. James told me to visit again sometime, but there was no warmth there, just a bit of obligation."

"I went back once," I said, "And it was pretty much the same, though she asked me to drop off an envelope at a Broadway theatre and to deliver a bolt of cloth to one of her seamstresses. I laughed, but she didn't seem to get the joke, just asking me if I'd do it."

"Did you?"

"Of course I did. Mrs. James was never warm, but she was safe and honest and frankly, I came to believe she held back any affection so she wouldn't have to show it."

"I never saw it."

"I did, once in a while. I do remember her being quite concerned one time when you were late bringing back a cheque you'd gone to pick up."

"You took that for affection?"

"Affection for money maybe, but I thought I detected a twinge of fear that you might have fallen into harm's way."

Lilly laughed. "That's a new one. Don't get me wrong, Mrs. James was fair and faithful to her responsibilities, but never once did I feel any concern from her, other than making sure my assigned tasks were completed."

"So, you expect to graduate from Columbia?"

"As long as I can finance the degree, why not? It seems like a ticket to a better life. What about you?"

"I'd like to do some school, but I think it's passed me by. I looked into a trade, but there is so much rigmarole that I pretty much dismissed that. Well, not entirely. What I'm thinking is trying to get something more solid, though I'm have no idea what. My tee-shirt business and other odd jobs pay the bills."

We parted with an awkward hug, and I left feeling pretty good, like I actually had a real friend in the world. It felt even better two weeks later when she suggested another meeting at the coffee shop.

In the mean time I had been running some messages for bartenders and their customers uptown just south of the Park. One of those messages was a cryptic series of words which I was told not to write down and to deliver immediately.

A few days later, I was back to see if any messages needed to be sent, and I was hustled behind the bar.

"Holy shit, I can't believe you came back."

"What do you mean. I've been running for these guys for months."

"You didn't hear? Mickey got shot. Dead. Ran into a trap. Suds thinks you tipped off the cops. Something about you being willing to do anything for money. Maybe being an informant so the cops lay off your street sales."

"Me. I never even talk to the cops. Stay as faraway as possible."

"Suds is looking for you. Tell him that and maybe you're off the hook or maybe he does something drastic. Your choice."

"I got nothing to hide. I'm clean."

"Clean? Nobody's clean in this racket. You're here, ain't you?"

"You tell him I'm clean. Tell him I'll talk to him. I got nothing to hide. But I don't need to be looking over my shoulder for ever more."

"If I was you, I'd just bust town. You got nothing here. I'll tell him what you said, but don't take a chance. All you need is Suds wanting to make an example out of you. And who's going ask any questions?"

I left the bar shaken and worried. Why would they think I spilled to anyone. There must have been some sort of leak if Mickey was dead. But was it the cops? I hadn't heard anything but then I didn't read the papers too often.

I kept my head down for a week and then went back to the bar, early like, when I figured it would be empty. Caught the barkeep's eye and he told me Suds was really mad, crazy even, and that I should get lost, there was little I could do to redeem myself.

"What do they got on me?"

"One of the cops, told one of the boys, after the shooting that they'd figured out what Mickey was up to. An informant."

"Well, it wasn't me."

"Suds don't know that. He's purging all the hangers on. Don't trust nobody. Talking ain't gonna do you any good. Hike it outta here."

I left the bar and headed home. They didn't know where I lived or they'd have got me already. I was going to meet Lilly the next day but I wasn't sure what I was going to tell her.

In the end we sat down for a coffee in the same shoppe as the previous meeting. Eventually I spilled the story, a little at a time, as I was unwilling to tell her the whole thing.

"I think I might leave New York, and stay away from bad places."

"That's awful. I don't know what to say."

"It's probably best if you forget you know me. I didn't do anything wrong, all those years of working for Mrs. James and I know how to speak nicely but say nothing."

"I'm going to miss our coffee talks."

"So am I. Somehow you are the only person I feel I can trust in the whole world. I'm not sure Mrs. James wouldn't cave in to pressure, if she got leaned on."

"Oh, don't say that."

"Either way, don't tell her anything. I will let you know where I land, once I figure it out. Maybe we can at least talk by phone."

She agreed, and we parted again with a hug. "Take care of yourself," she said. "I think you know how, but I won't be happy until I hear you've found your place, far from the City."

The next day, I collected my few belongings, packed them in a duffle bag, made arrangements with a storage place frequented by students for the kitchen stuff and bits of furniture, and hightailed it out of New York by bus. I didn't have much but decided that waiting until I could sell it, was likely a mistake. I could get Lilly to take it when she was ready. I was actually scared at the bus terminal, wondering if any of Suds' guys were watching it.

Once the bus crossed out of Manhattan, I felt a bit lighter. And once we were on the interstate heading south, I used a rest stop to scope out the other riders looking for someone that might be looking for me. There was no-one and I fell into conversation with a girl about Lilly's age who was headed to Florida and then on to California. She was at loose ends and wanted to become an actress in Hollywood.

"I was the lead in the school play like every year. I took a few theatre classes and had a few bit parts in some Broadway stuff. Well, mostly off-Broadway. But I still did it and they called me back a few times, so I must have been okay."

"Good luck. Why are you going to Florida first?"

"My mom lives there. She and my dad divorced 10 years ago and she moved to Tampa. She said I could stop by on my way."

"Well, that's nice. Do you have any friends in California?"

"Yeah, a couple of the chorus girls from one of the shows I was in, went out there. That's actually why I'm going. They said there's lots of work. Small stuff but enough to keep the dream alive, I guess. Commercials pay pretty well, they said. And, you never know, I might get lucky, hit it big."

She asked where I was going. And I said I was tired of New York and had no ties there or anywhere else. I was just looking for opportunity and maybe a cheap place to live. Warm weather seemed a likely way to save on living expenses.

She smiled. Our bus was headed to Miami but at Daytona she said she was changing busses to go to Tampa and asked me if I'd like to tag along. "Not sure if my mother would care, if I brought a friend. I've liked talking to you."

I was reluctant to become involved, just because of the imposition, but I had no where else to go, and Miami seemed like a bit of a dead end. I figured if I wanted, I could double back to Atlanta and try to get a job there and keep my tee-shirt business going.

It turned out that Amanda's mom met her at the bus station in down-town Tampa, and drove us to her condo in St. Petersburg, well actually Clearwater, though it was hard to tell the difference. Amanda's mother was striking looking. She worked as a waitress at a tourist hotel. She looked me over and seemed okay with me sleeping on the couch for a few days, stressing that it was nice to have Amanda around, 'for a few days'.

A master of between the lines communications, I heard it loud and clear. Three days later, I asked Amanda when she planned the next stage of her journey.

"Two days, on Friday, there's a bus from St. Petes that heads west. I'm planning on that. I was going to tell you today."

I nodded, realizing I had a decision to make. Amanda and I had become fast friends and I definitely had the feeling that she was pleased to have a male companion and her mother seemed equally happy that Amanda appeared to be travelling in tandem.

"So, if you two are headed west we should have a nice dinner before you go. I can drive you to the station early, in time to catch the bus."

I caught the implication that Amanda's mother thought I was travelling west as well and Amanda didn't correct her.

We did have a nice dinner in the hotel where Amanda's mother worked, and as we were finishing a man came up to the table and was introduced as Amanda's mother's good friend. Amanda did not seem surprised so I followed along.

Mr. Walters seemed a bit greasy, but that might have been the Florida heat. He said he knew about our travels and said he had a few friends in California. He wrote down a few names and some contact information and assured us that he had spoken to these people and they would be happy to set us straight on the Los Angeles scene.

"You know. Where to live, job opportunities, a bit of insight on the studios and the like. Not going to kid you, what you two kids are doing is a long shot. The entertainment industry is cutthroat, mean, and it tosses people aside for very petty reasons."

"Like everything else," I said.

"Yeah, I guess," said Mr. Walters. "Just don't have too many expectations of help, even from my contacts. Truth is, everybody is on the hustle. They can help you with information, and anything more means they are likely doing a favour for someone else, filling a need or whatever."

We had dessert and a drink to finish the evening, with Walters speaking of his time in California where he managed a talent agency and worked in hotel management.

"Truthfully, I'm not sure which was the main job and which was the side hustle. Kinda went back and forth."

He explained the hotel company had asked him to manage a few of its properties in the Tampa area, so he took the gig and got out of the hustle in California. "Florida is the next big thing. Easy drive from up north and lots of places for the older set to find some warmth."

Amanda and I boarded the bus the next morning, with a cheery goodbye from Amanada's mother, who encouraged us to write and let her know how things were going. She did say that Mr. Walters had suggested a trip out west at some future time, so she might meet us out there.

I didn't let on that Amanda and I might not remain together in any meaningful way once we arrived, but I did expect that we would at least stay in touch.

The bus was mostly uneventful save for the switching of drivers and the stops for food and presumably fuel. The rest of the passengers fell into two camps. Aging people who saw the bus as a mobile camp and who were willing to trade time to save money. And young people like Amanda and I who wanted a fresh start in a place with good vibes.

Riding the bus, mile after mile, and seeing much the same thing over and over, was eye opening to a boy from the city, who had never left Manhattan until he was pushed. The sheer size of America was hard to deal with, and of course, my background meant that I needed people in large numbers to ply my businesses. I wondered about life in the small towns, without any comprehension. My experiences had nothing to stick on.

I couldn't help but think of Paul Simon's song 'America' about two young travellers finding their fortune. Not that we saw any likely spies but we did eyeball our travelling companions and I certainly spent some time looking at the passing landscape.

And then we pulled into the bus station in Los Angeles. Like so much out there it was pretty new and glitzy on the surface but not too nice when you really looked at it. Chrome, steel, and grime.

We squatted with two of Amanada's chorus girl friends for a couple of days and did the rounds of Mr. Walter's contacts. We approached the magic moment. I could take my leave of Amanda or we could try to find a place together. I had the feeling that she was welcome to stay with her friends, and felt that pull, but I was not, largely because of the space available. There wasn't any. I told her I was good with whatever she wanted.

In the end she agreed to help me find a place. I knocked around a few shoddy neighbourhoods and eventually found a small bachelor basement apartment, one room, furnished with just enough to get by, in Boyle Heights, not far from Los Angeles' alleged downtown. I took the place and settled in. Amanda stayed with her friends but visited most days. She told me I needed to get a telephone, though I'd been loathe to spend the money, until I really needed it, and was happy to remain in the basement for an extended period. A telephone was like an anchor and I wasn't too keen on having ties. At least not yet.

Once I secured a job, I arranged to have my few remaining things in New York shipped. It didn't take long to get a delivery job, mostly taking small packages and business envelopes here and there around LA. It certainly helped me to learn the city layout and find the good and not so good places to live.

I wrote to Lilly but didn't hear back. I wondered if she had changed addresses and even if she was still at Columbia.

Amanda wandered in and out of my life, almost a surrogate Lilly. We'd shared the ordeal of cross-country travel and the uncertainties of life without an anchor. Of course I was used to such things, and she had had enough experience with it, that she was not uncomfortable. She got a job at a dry cleaners and she waitressed on the side.

She was trying to save money and more than once hinted at finding a less crowded living arrangement. Apparently, her roomies didn't mind the crowding as it helped to keep the rent down.

Amanda was earning enough to squirrel some money away and she was making contacts in the entertainment industry. Not a classic beauty she was striking in an odd way, and her efforts had managed her a few jobs as crowd extras in several television productions. She even had once close up, as a bar patron in a cop show, where she eyeballed the detectives entering the bar, with a knowing and dismissive expression. The two seconds of screen time were her calling card and she practiced her expression endlessly before the shoot.

She attended a number of cattle calls and toyed with getting an agent, finally taking the plunge after the close-up and a suggestion by one of the show runners.

Seeing her struggle, I had no interest in the entertainment industry, except as something that might pay me. My deliveries took me inside some of the studios to drop packages, contracts, and messages, and I struck up a friendly banter with some of the staffers.

I didn't have a television, nor did I have much time for movies, so I likely brushed shoulders with a few famous faces, but I never knew it.

Weekends were spent mostly hustling larger deliveries. I made my self permanently available to my bosses so they'd call me first with last minute things, as they were the most lucrative. I'd get a little bonus and often a decent tip for my efforts. And yeah, I was attracted to the beach when I had some off time. Amanda and I went as it was a cheap day out.

They offered me a job as dispatcher, but I turned it down as it came with no tips. I was attracted by the predictable hours but the experience of an offer made me reconsider where I was going and what I wanted to do.

Amanda and I, and occasionally some of her friends, would go to see new bands play on the strip. It was fun and cheap entertainment if you didn't drink too much. My experiences with bar types in New York kept me on the straight and narrow for the most part.

I got talking to one of the musicians in between sets and learned something about the hard scrabble lives they led. Just getting gigs was tough and getting paid fairly was tougher.

At the end of the night, I jumped up to help load some of their equipment not expecting any money, just the opportunity to speak to these guys. When they slipped me $20 and asked if I'd be around the following week, I was pleased and felt I'd made a couple of friends.

I fell in with them for a few months helping do the background stuff on their gigs, usually once or twice a week and began to hang out with them in their cheap, rundown place up in Laurel Canyon. This side gig was good as it was usually done at night and didn't interfere with my day job. Not far from Hollywood Blvd, Laurel Canyon was a winding road up into the mountainous landscape, with a lot of run-down houses precariously perched on hillsides. It was almost an old cottage type area for Los Angeles. It offered cheap rent, a bit of quiet inside the city and an eclectic spirit that drew a lot of musicians and hopeful actors.

I met a lot of up-and-coming people there but always felt like a hanger on. I enjoyed talking to the musicians about their work, but I never had any talent or inclination to take part, something I believe they appreciated as the place was crawling with hopefuls in a constant stream. Not surprisingly I gravitated to the business of music, especially concerts and promotions.

One year bled into the next and my lease was up. I was inclined to stay in my place a while longer. It was really just a place to lay my head. I was too busy and too footloose to become involved with anyone, though from time-to-time Amanda would hint that we should move in together.

I didn't take her seriously and had no interest in limiting myself in any way. For all I knew something would come up and I could leave town in a week or a month.

Amanda was getting a steady stream of call backs for various roles, mostly in television. With all the productions being shot in LA, there was a huge number of actors needed to fill all the bit parts. She managed a few speaking parts, took acting classes in the evenings and we talked about her dreams. I didn't really have any, though I'd brought my tee-shirt business to LA. As soon as I became friendly with the bands, I didn't have the heart to horn in on their trade. I did give them a few sales tips and they seemed to appreciate the insight.

I advised them how to score in the business and one or two of the promoters hired me to run that end of their business. I was involved in band logos, selling the shirts at concert venues and even running small crews to sell 'authorized' stuff for some of the bigger bands. I began to hang around the stages and venues and spoke to the promoters and even band managers, occasionally filling in as an assistant when needed.

"I'm so close to breaking in. I can feel that big break coming."

"You've been saying that for a while now," I said as I reached into the basket for another soda, offering Amanada one at the same time. She took it.

We were lounging on a blanket on the beach with swimsuits underneath our shorts and tees. With me, it was always a tee-shirt as I had access to a lot of them.

"My agent keeps my hopes up, you know. He said my role as the daughter in Mannix last month had some people talking. You know, fresh face and all of that."

I rolled the towel back down across the sand. "Sooner or later, it will happen. I think you've got the look."

"Well, that's the nicest thing you've ever said to me, I think," she smiled. "Amber said she'd be here by now."

"She might be having trouble finding us, it's crowded today."

"Yeah, I guess. So what is the 'look' that I've got?"

"I've told you before."

"But I like to hear it. Struggling starlets need constant reinforcement."

Now it was my turn to laugh. "You are very pretty, but in an unconventional way. Certainly, at certain angles you look like a conventional model.

At others you look almost foreign. You know I've told you there is a market for unusual looking people, especially girls."

"Well thanks for that, I guess."

I hadn't been quite as direct as that in the past, but the truth is the truth. "The real issue is, how long are you going to play the game, and how are you going to make the leap from fresh face to established actress?"

"That's for my agent to figure. First things first. I have to keep getting roles and keep getting better, more substantial ones. In the mean time I'm auditioning for a play. Small venue, low level stuff. He says experience is valuable."

"Where is Amber?"

"Who knows. Keep your eyes up and you might spot her looking for us. I'm getting mighty warm, might take a plunge in the sea. Wanna come?"

"Not if Amber is looking for us. We aren't too far from our usual spot."

"Okay, I won't be long. Just want to cool off." I stepped out of my shorts and pulled the tee over my head and walked down to the surf.

And when I returned a few minutes later Amber had arrived with a guy in tow that I'd never met. She introduced us and he seemed like a pleasant guy, who said he was involved with a cinema prop business, sourcing things needed for movie and television sets and making what they couldn't find.

Turns out he did some of the actual prop production himself which was almost an art, to hear him tell of it. He admitted that most of the props were recycled and were kept in a pair of huge warehouses in Long Beach.

"It's a business," he shrugged. Amber must have given him the lowdown on Amanda and I, as he did not ask.

Amanda got chatting to him about the various studios and the sound stages she was familiar with. He said he had tried the same route but had given up when bit parts dried up and the prop business got bigger.

"The way I see it, there is a very good living to be made servicing the entertainment industry here in LA. The glamor jobs are hard to come by."

When he heard Amanda talk about my efforts in the service industries, he figured it proved his point. The girls went along with it, but were clearly unmoved to change their course. They were both still on the upswing as fresh faces.

After a few hours, I excused myself as I had promised a band manager I would help with the set up at the Whiskey A-Go-Go for a new group he was managing. They'd gotten some airplay on local radio and had even had one of their songs used in a film.

Amber, Amanda and Jon seemed happy to stay and said they might come by the Whiskey that evening but I could tell from Jon's half-hearted promise that he had other plans.

At my apartment I quickly got ready for the evening, stylish enough to be presentable as an audience member at the Whiskey and comfortable enough to do some heavy lifting. Fortunately, the band's equipment was already loaded in their panel van so all I had to do was go for the ride downtown or even just meet them there.

I came out of the shower to a blinking light on my answering machine. It was a reasonably cheap alternative to a pager. I had to be home to get the message but that was alright as I could reasonably dodge calls I didn't want to take for as much as 24 hours.

The message was from Lilly. She was headed to LA and expected to be in town in two days. She was calling from a pay phone in Kansas City.

She said nothing else, only hoping I would be able to meet her at the bus station when she arrived. She gave the bus number saying her trip had started in Pittsburgh, which was unexpected, but likely cut down the confusion about bus arrival times.

I decided I would go to the station the next day to see if I could get more details about the probable arrival time of the bus. It would be nice to catch up with her, and find out what she was doing in LA.

The bus rolled in about 10 minutes before it was expected. Late night traffic being light, they must have made good time. I watched the people disembark, smiling at the usual bewildered look of the cross-country travellers. Buses were not used by glamor travellers so the rag tag group that got off, uniformly carried backpacks and small clutches. They milled around waiting for the bus to empty and the driver to open the luggage compartment.

I saw Lilly only a second before she saw me. Stepping down onto the platform her smile exploded. And so did mine, as she told me later.

I gave her a quick hug and asked if she had luggage to carry.

"I tried not to, but I do have a small case I have to get."

I hung back as she waded into the group milling around the bus and claimed a small squarish box, not really a suitcase, more of a presentation box, in hard plastic, with a handle on the top. I picked it up and it weighed a ton.

"What the heck have you got in here?"

"You'll see."

"It's late. I imagine you haven't got a place to stay. Come to my place. It's small but you are welcome, unless you have other plans."

"If I had other plans I wouldn't have asked you to meet me, especially when I realized we'd likely arrive so early in the morning."

"So, what are you doing in LA? Are you staying here? How is school? How is New York?"

"Slow down. I came to visit you. I don't know how long I'm staying. I graduated but have an offer to go back and do a graduate degree. New York is New York, and the desire to get out, is mostly why I'm here."

"Is everything okay?"

"Absolutely. I ended up with a degree in biology and wrote my medical school exams. Lo and behold I passed and was offered three places to go to medical school. Not going to start until the fall, so I had some time and figured I needed a change of scenery, and my lease was up, so I bugged out of Manhattan, and came here."

"You might have written ahead."

"I might have, but I didn't decide until just a couple of days before coming. I gave up my place and was in Pittsburgh, where one of the medical schools is, and decided instead of going back to New York I'd just come here. It is further than I thought."

"Well, it's nice to see you. All your stuff is going to be okay even though you've gone?"

"Oh yeah, I'd packed up and told my roommates I was moving out, so they are watching the two boxes of stuff, and said they'd forward it or wait until I came to fetch it."

"Nice to have friends."

"That's why I'm here. How are you doing?"

"Okay, I guess," and I thought about it. "Good actually. Really good. Got some money in the bank, regular employment and a few hustles on the side."

"Thanks for being here for me. I thought you would but I couldn't find out if you even got my message."

"How's Mrs. James?"

"The same. I drop by every couple of months and she never changes."

"That's good, I guess. Come on along, we can walk. I don't live far from here. Lots of highways here and there, but that's kind of the defining thing of LA. Cheap digs, you know, just east of old Chinatown. And I'm not home much anyway."

Lilly saw a road sign. "Dodger Stadium, wow."

"We are going the other way."

After threading our way through a couple of underpasses and past some industrial sites, I began to wonder if it wouldn't have been better to take a cab this late at night. But I had so rarely done so, the whole idea wasn't really formed in my mind as an option. Lilly didn't seem to mind the walk after being cooped up on the bus for four days.

On the way, Lily described the trip out and a few of the people on the bus that she had spoken with. I recounted my own journey and wondered if anyone had come looking for me. Old Suds was long gone but the reason for fleeing New York lingered.

"No, I didn't hear anything about you from anyone. Of course, I had no contact with that side of New York, what with being a respectable student, and all."

"What about Mrs. James, she had some contacts that I had?"

"Now that you mention it, she did wonder what became of you. She didn't let on that anyone had asked, but I said I had no idea, and that was that."

"Not entirely comforting, but I'll take what I can get."

We entered the apartment and stowed her things. I was too hyped up from the walk and seeing Lilly to go straight to bed. We talked for a few hours and eventually drifted off, with a plan to go to the beach the next day, though I mentioned I had a job in the evening that she could tag along with, if she wanted.

We spent the next day enjoying the sun and surf, though Lilly had to buy a bathing suit before we got there. It is a must have item in LA, but not even thought of in Manhattan.

Lilly was trying to decide what to do for the evening, as I was on a job for a band playing the Hollywood Bowl. Set up, tear down and directing the tee-shirt sales runners in between. Given that it was the Hollywood Bowl she said she'd tag along and look around. I figured I could get her in on my say so, especially if she was carrying a microphone stand or something.

The next morning, we slept in late as the show clean up took a while and we had attended the post gig party, for a few hours. Lilly was amazed at the famous faces she encountered but I warned her that things in LA were just as bad or worse than New York.

There was a knock at my door and I sleepily got up to answer. My rustling had roused Lilly who sat on the sofa as I answered the door.

Amanda burst in full of news. "I got the part. I got the part," she said as she came in through the doorway. I'd never blocked her way before, and didn't do it this time.

"Oh, oh, sorry," she said, catching a look at Lilly sitting on the sofa under a blanket. "I can come back," she spluttered.

"No, it's okay. This is Lilly, a friend from New York. She arrived the other day and had no where to stay. It's okay."

Amanda stopped and looked confused, unsure of whether she should simply leave but my okays got her to stay. "You want me to come back in a few minutes?"

"It's okay. We were at the Bowl last night. I had a job there, and Lilly wanted to see it. We got in late."

I turned to Lilly, "This is Amanda, a friend of mine. We travelled here together on the bus from back East and have stayed friends. Amanda is an actress."

"So, you got the part? said Lilly. "That sounds wonderful."

"Yes, that's what I came to tell you. I just heard from my agent. I'd been at auditions all week and it was down to three of us. I was so nervous, but I got the part, a significant role in a new movie being shot next month, starring . . . wait for it . . . John Wayne."

She was triumphant. "Shooting on location in Arizona. It's a western."

"So what's the role?"

"I'm a young wife of a rancher and he is shot and I'm holding the fort with my young family from outlaws. Small but significant part. Most of the film is a shoot 'em up with Wayne and a posse of lawmen."

"That's great. And I imagine it pays?"

"Union scale. They wanted a new face and someone fairly young."

"Wow. I'm so happy for you."

The shoot starts in a month. I'll be on location for a few weeks and have to remain available for any retakes for six weeks after that. And the best thing is, they pay a small retainer."

"How much screen time? How much dialogue?"

"I don't know yet. I guess some of that depends on the editing. I am supposed to get the script in a few days," she beamed at the thought. "I finally feel legit."

"We should go out and celebrate," I said. "I was thinking of heading up into the Canyon tonight to a party I've heard about."

"I would love to see more of the city," said Lilly. Amanda tried to disguise a sour look. "You two go, maybe I'll just cool it a bit. It's been a real whirlwind the last few days."

After much wrangling both girls agreed to accompany me, mostly on the promise that there would be a few well-known faces there. I had to warn them, that things sometimes got a little wild.

Both girls attracted attention from the party goers, not all the kind of attention they wanted. Lilly seemed utterly fascinated and alternatively shocked at the seediness. Amanda was used to it, and even saw a few of her own friends there.

Lilly indicated she'd had enough, and frankly, when the drugs came out, so had I. We took our leave and Amanda decided to stay, the pull of well-known faces was stronger than staying with us. I shrugged.

Lilly made the rounds at USC as she had been offered a spot there at medical school. Probably the real reason she came to California, but she never said. She had a couple of weeks to decide and wanted to visit the third university that had made an offer before she chose. She said she'd hit that campus on her way back east.

Two days later Amanda showed up after dropping me a call that she was coming. We talked about the party and she mentioned that she'd run into Arthur Mendel, a concert promoter who I'd worked for. He had been looking for me.

"Odd. Mendel has my number. He could call."

"Maybe he just wanted a social chat."

"That's it. He had been talking about using me as an assistant on a big tour he was trying to put together. If he needs me, he'll call."

And he did, three days later. I was asked essentially to be the head man putting together a US tour by Led Zeppelin, a hugely popular band from England. Mendel would be the name under which we'd do everything but he wanted me to handle the everyday stuff, all of it. It was a big ask, and paid pretty well, well considering most of what I'd been doing was either union wages or cash in an envelope, real money was nice. Problem was I had to travel with the band which meant a pause in my day job.

Lilly seemed please for me, and she was headed back east in a few days. We agreed to see if our schedules might mesh, putting us in the same city at the same time. Lilly was stopping in Chicago on her way back, as that was where the third medical school was located. Amanda was pleased for me, but could not help but caution me as to Zeppelin's reputation. I was well aware, and frankly too concerned about doing a good job to even consider getting involved in the extra-curriculars. It did cross my mind that I'd have to be present at least, to be ready to fix the inevitable problems.

"I've seen those guys up in the Canyon. They are pretty wild."

There was little I had not seen in my days working with the business of music. I shifted focus, turning to Lilly.

"Have you managed to decide on a medical school yet?"

"I haven't been overly impressed by either so far but I'll reserve judgement until after Chicago. I could also try applying in other places, I guess. Maybe I'm not supposed to be impressed by anything the schools say, medical school is medical school."

Much of Amanda's movie shoot would take place when I was on the road, but that was left unsaid. Lilly went to Chicago and Amanda seemed a bit distant, but I put that down to her getting antsy about the location shoot. She insisted on accompanying us to the bus station. I could see Lilly taking the suggestion with a smirk, but I refused to share it with Amanda so close.

I must confess, I was looking forward to hitting the road and being a bit footloose. The two girls did not compete directly, but they seemed to be constantly circling one another, like prize fighters sizing each other up. And all the while I had never shown any preference, nor anything but friendship to either of them. It's true that Lily and I shared a deeper understanding, but we were practically brother and sister. Amanda didn't quite believe that but she seemed happy that I was her reserve. She had made no attachments that I was aware of, but she had a lot of male friends in the industry, and made no attempt to hide them or their interest in her.

She was wise enough to know that such attachments were incredibly transitory in the entertainment industry. I thought that our connection outside of those things, is what kept her close.

The next few months would be interesting to us all. Amanda would have her moment. Lilly would decide her location for the next few years and maybe more, and I would, I would, maybe find a little more stability, or not. I didn't mind moving from one gig to another but deep down I understood that it was no way to live and wasn't sustainable. But I was content making money and content having connections to people who seemed to matter, even if I was so close to it, that I didn't realize how unusual that was.

Choices are good, especially if they are reversible. It's the ones you cannot change that are life-altering.

Chapter Eighteen

And then I was in Philadelphia, walking around with Theresa after we first arrived just before noon on Thursday. It was likely the only tourist time we would have. We found a nice bistro on a narrow cobblestoned street and settled in to eat.

"So, I was thinking about your project," Theresa said.

"Funny, I've been thinking about yours. Isn't that why we are here."

"Okay, okay, just let me make one point so you have something to stew over." I nodded. "You are going about things one genre or story trope at a time. Why not combine them?" she said.

"I guess I could, but if I were to complete the cycle, it would be endless, especially if I was to add more than one to each mix. Good God, I'd be left in trope-land, in a never-ending maelstrom of possibilities. Funny, but writer's block is bad, that sounds worse."

Theresa grinned. "Oh, don't worry, I imagine that most stories contain more than one category, otherwise they'd be pretty dry."

"Dry is what I'm trying to get past. Perhaps I will take up your challenge but I have to count each story as a genre and if any other stuff that sneaks in, just happens."

Two guys asked if they could join us at our table, but Theresa quickly shut that down, saying we were meeting our boyfriends a little later. The guys just moved on.

"Boyfriends?"

"Well not in the commonly held sense. But you have to speak their language. And we are meeting Markus and Brandon tonight to do the set up at the convention centre. That's later, isn't it?"

"Tell me what's the plan at this show?"

"Nothing different from what we first spoke of, save that Brandon and Markus are going to be wearing some of my pieces . . . ."

"And, you, want me to, as well?"

Theresa smiled her gotcha smile, "Well if you'd like, sure."

We arrived mid-afternoon to do the major part of the set up. Brandon and Markus showed up on our heels half an hour later with coffee and bagels. Markus stood back and surveyed the assigned presentation space. They had brought the booth elements with them in a trailer and we quickly unloaded all the stuff and began putting it together. I didn't want to admit it, but it was nice having a couple of strong, agile guys available for the heavy and awkward stuff, especially the upper beam across the front of the booth.

Theresa fixed her company name to the beam and we started in on the mannequins. We decided that the urban part of the collection would be displayed on one side of the booth, with the suburban elements on the other, separated by a table and some large drawings of various pieces on easels. Theresa also had a four-page brochure of her urban and suburban collection. She admitted that several of the pieces were just drawings at this point, but she wanted to present a larger, fuller line to potential retailers. She also decided on a raffle, as a way to get names and contact info for her mailing list.

"What's the prize?" asked Brandon.

"You two to help take down the winner's booth."

Brandon looked stricken, but Markus laughed. I'm guessing its not the addresses of your competitors that you want."

Some of the other companies doing displays had sent scouts around. Theresea was cordial and Brandon thought at least some of them were likely big-wigs who were allowed a sneak peek before the show opened.

Two such passers by seemed to take an interest in our booth, but they said nothing.

We finished the set up, Brandon and Markus had made sure their pieces fit properly, and we all decided to do a little tourist walk before going out to a late dinner. The show started at 8 am on Friday and finished at 2 pm on Sunday. Theresa pushed us toward a local shopping district, rife with small restaurants. She eyed the merchandise, without being too obvious, and I looked at the colonial architecture and streetscape. Brandon somehow kept us all entertained with a running commentary on Philadelphians, or at least those he was related to.

We found a likely restaurant and I insisted we cut the night short as we all were expecting a busy two days.

The show went well for Theresa. She chatted to several buyers, and explained that her collection could be had as a whole, both urban and suburban, or split, if a retailer wanted to take on only one side of her output. One buyer from Atlanta wanted to see more summer attire and Theresa was caught off guard. Fortunately, Brandon stepped in and said that that part of the collection was at the tailor's and would be unveiled at the next show in Nashville, a few months later, in February.

Theresa caught on and asked for a mailing address to send the show details and a full sales brochure, once it was printed. The buyer hesitated, but then complied after Brandon asked if she attended the Nashville show each year. She admitted she did not, and happily handed over a business card.

They chatted for a bit, Theresa saying she would be open to a collaboration with the southern buyer if she had particular pieces in mind. It turned out that she represented a small chain of clothing stores, pushing more urban designs but from a southern perspective. She was looking for very comfortable business clothes for women in particular, with an eye toward the standard sizes of normal women, not the pencil thin model types.

Theresa jotted down her comments and said she would have some drawings to her shortly, emphasising that she would happily modify her initial designs based on what the buyer wanted.

Another buyer walked slowly past the booth, seemingly uninterested in it, but casting a side-eye as he walked. I didn't think much of it until I saw him later a few booths away with an older woman, indicating our booth with a nod, and saying something to her. She eyed us from a distance, and I tapped Theresa, letting her know there was interest approaching.

"Good afternoon," I said. "Can I interest you in one of our brochures?"

The younger man nodded, and took it without looking at it. He moved closer to the older woman. "Well, Aunt Marylynn, what do you think?"

She shot him a withering look and tilted her head down, without speaking. Even I got the message. There was no value in saying what you were thinking with the sellers standing within earshot.

This guy was in for a dressing down once they were away from the booth. It appeared to me that she was teaching him the business.

I let them look a bit, and managed to get Theresa to engage them before they left the booth area. It turned out my instincts were not too far off, as Aunt Marylynn was the buyer for a modest chain of retail stores in the mid-Atlantic states – some 25 stores in all from Baltimore to Richmond with a few new outlets in North Carolina.

"I was hesitant at first to move into the Carolina market, but the population growth there is undeniable. I think your collection might fit in well with their aesthetics." She said the last word oddly, as if she had read it, but never actually heard it spoken.

Theresa nodded vigorously, and the woman asked about wholesale prices, return policies and restocking times. Fortunately for Theresa she had researched some of this, and was able to be convincing with her answers, as they conformed to the industry standards, though she did let on the caveat of being a small manufacturer, and potentially requiring a few extra days notice for restocking.

The woman seemed satisfied and they agreed that Theresa would ship 100 pieces, split between the urban and suburban collections, mostly women's blouses and jackets, with a smattering of pants as well. Theresa beckoned Brandon and Markus over, to model some of the men's casual attire, but Aunt Marylynn did not bite.

The woman left, and Theresa beamed. "The smaller retailers seem to be focussed mostly on women," said I.

Theresa nodded, absently rearranging the display table, and thinking so hard I imagined I could hear the gears turning in her head.

"There are literally no men's wear stores for casual clothes." She turned, "What is wrong with you guys?"

"We buy from department stores. One stop shopping and all that. Don't like having some sales person staring at us while we decide what to buy."

"And sports stores for our casual clothing. Okay, I went into a tailor to buy a couple of suits once, but that's a rarity, as is wearing a suit these days," chimed in Markus.

"Sport stores, eh, I might have to modify my collection to appeal to them. Tell me, do I have to license the pro team logos?"

Markus looked hurt. "Give us a bit more credit than that."

"Yeah, at least during business hours. Pro team stuff is very frowned upon."

"Except for casual Fridays."

"Except for casual Fridays. And Saturdays and Sundays."

"Which is nearly half the week."

Markus grinned.

A few more buyers came through and Theresa managed a few more small orders, though she confided in me that filling them quickly was going to be tough. We all went for a casual dinner that evening.

"How are you going to fill all these orders?" asked Brandon.

"I've been thinking on that. At least in the short term, I will be very busy. I think I'm going to have to expand my facilities and hire."

"That's a big step."

"Yeah, but a good problem to have. I also realized I can forward my southern style sales brochure to that mid-Atlantic buyer. The stuff might not all catch on with her, but given her expansion into the Carolinas, some is likely to catch her eye."

"Two birds, one stone. Smart," said Markus, on the verge of mocking.

Theresa gave him a withering look.

Dinner was good, mostly because we didn't have to move. One day of the show had been tiring and we had the longest day in front of us.

"Sunday shouldn't be too bad, except that we have to pack everything up."

Saturday, the busiest day of the show came and went, with many people stopping by the booth and a few more small orders for single stores being made. Theresa knew enough about the business that the terms for these retailers were a bit more favorable to her, as they did not have the volume leverage that the larger chains had.

What she really wanted, and feared, was an order from a major retail chain. She was very ambivalent about such an order coming from a more pedestrian chain, rather than something a bit more upscale, as the latter was her niche.

"What if Walmart comes by?" I asked during the lunch time lull.

"Oh, don't put me in that position. Though I have considered it, strangely enough. I would happily go there, but use a different name for the collection, so I can preserve my brand. Those who have bought from me already, did not buy from a supplier to Walmart."

"Good answer. You are much wiser than I thought."

Brandon was talking to a pair of youngish men and I was trying to visualize what kind of retailer they represented, when he broke off, coming over to me, and beckoning the men over to speak to me. Theresa was engaged with another woman, looking at the large drawings.

"This is my cousin Chuck," Brandon gestured to a brown-haired, blue-eyed guy in his mid-twenties. I shook his hand with a nod. "And this is his business partner, Allan."

I repeated the gesture. Allan was black haired, with the slightest hint of grey. At first I thought it was highlights, but the wrinkles around his eyes suggested he was a bit older.

"Are you two in the clothing business?"

Chuck looked at Allan, expecting him to field the question. "Yes, we are.

Well, we want to be. We are developing an idea for a men's store, for stuff guys like, and want to include some clothing options, things you can't find everywhere."

"Well, that's an idea. You should speak to Theresa. Are you ready to buy?"

"It's exploratory at this point," said Brandon. "They have two locations already leased, but not open yet. They are looking for stock." The two men nodded.

Theresa came over, having finished a conversation with another potential buyer. She was apprised of the situation and said she was open to supply them, at the usual industry terms.

Chuck spoke up. "Theresa, my cousin Brandon confided that you were just starting out as well, and so we imagined we could help each other."

Allen chimed in. We do not want to dive in too deeply and have trouble with our cash flow and debt situation. We envision a steady growth in this business, once we are firmly established in the minds of the buying public. A process of probably two years."

"Well, I can't supply significant clothing for free."

"No, no, not for free. We wondered if you would be interested in teaming with us, as a shareholder, part-owner, entitled to a share of all the profits, in return for supplying our two stores with multiple pieces. We would promote the store and your brand."

I had never seen Theresa caught off guard. She stumbled and hummed as the three guys looked at her expectantly.

"Think about it, Theresa, I think it could be mutually beneficial. We are planning to open in two months, once the interiors are complete. Our ad campaign starts two weeks before. What we'd like, if you agree, is a complete line of casual and business casual. Our stores are north west in the Philly area, in good retail spaces. Chuck's dad was able to help us, he's connected in commercial real estate. He got us good terms too."

"Well, I'm interested but of course it depends on the terms."

The boys looked relieved and they exchanged business cards, and planned for a more detailed discussion after the show closed the next afternoon."

"Things are really looking up for you, missy," I said after the boys had gone for a walk about and coffee.

"So far it's better than I thought, and I believe, I can still handle most of the orders myself, especially if I can stretch the delivery times a bit."

"What about the men's store thingy?"

"I'm beginning to think I need a business agent. I can likely handle this myself, but if I get any bigger, I'm going to need to hire someone."

On Sunday, Theresa met her future. Two buyers for Costco came to the booth. They stood hunched over a mannequin and then moved to one of the easels, their heads together, speaking in low bass tones. Theresa stood nearby, expecting them to break the ice. They chatted and told Theresa they were from Costco, explaining what they were after. Theresa agreed to supply their stores under a new brand name. They would start out at a dozen locations and go from there. They agreed to get their business agents together in following week.

Once they left, Theresa sat down at the back of the booth. "I need an agent, now. Know anyone?" She smiled weakly. "I did not expect this to go this well."

We closed up the booth a few hours later and once it was all packed away, and plans were made for delivery, we decided to have a celebratory dinner, Theresa's treat.

We went to a downtown steakhouse and lived it up a bit, our payment for helping, though we limited the drinks to a shot apiece and a glass of wine. The boys were driving back to New York and we had a train to catch.

"And what about your latest project Cassie," it was the first time either of the guys had referred to me in the diminutive. I never really liked it and did not encourage its use. Theresa used it on occasion. I guess close proximity for a weekend, knocks down walls.

"Only my closest friends call me that, you know." Markus looked hurt. "I've been focussed on Theresa's gig this weekend and haven't really thought about it."

"You'll be back at it this week, I imagine. Theresa has a lot on her plate now. What's your plan?"

"Not sure but I've been toying with an adventure story or a quest."

"Or both," said Theresa, a bit too loud.

"Can we read it? Like once it's done? Markus told me you've let him read a couple."

"I suppose. I'll be at the coffee shop at the usual time if anyone wants to come by. Theresa and I have been meeting there forever, every second Thursday morning 8 am sharp."

"I may be pressed to make it this time." Theresa said. "I've suddenly got a lot on my plate."

"You will, if only to let us know how you are doing."

We all laughed at Theresa's predicament, now she headed a large clothing manufacturer but had no staff, no factory, no national exposure and no profits.

"You have a busy week my dear."

"We have to hammer out a game plan on the ride home."

"But it's less than an hour's trip. You need to be in go-mode on Monday morning. That's a little more than 12 hours from now."

Once on the train we chatted back and forth about hiring a business agent and how to find some clothing manufacturers who could take her order quickly. She wondered if she should get Markus to get the ball rolling while she looked for a more permanent solution. I gave her a long look.

I arrived at my apartment, very glad to see the inside again after a busy week. At first, I was content to sit on the couch and melt. I hadn't been so active in many months. And then a germ of an idea started though my brain and I shrugged, figuring I could be tired and sore in front of the keyboard, and so I opened a new file. At first I just scribbled the ideas down and then they began to take shape.

Chapter Nineteen - A Quest

It was a very odd message. A scavenger hunt? Not really, more of a quest to find the Holy Grail, or something like that.

Let me backtrack. I had applied for a position with an accounting firm. Seeing as how I was studying to write my Chartered Accountancy exams, it was a natural. I went through the usual selection process and it had gone well. I seemed to click with the interviewer who confided to me at the end of the first interview that he would recommend my application proceed. When I asked how long the process was likely to be, he deferred, saying only that these jobs were highly sought after and there were several steps in the process, as they wanted a particular type of person, and maybe more than one.

I gave the usual trope that I was also interviewing elsewhere, but that seemed to have no effect. It never seems to, but it's obligatory that I say it, and the company representative ignore it.

After a second interview which delved into my interests outside of accounting, my interviewer said they were wanting to hire a forensic accountant, who would be assigned exceptionally complex and sensitive files. He thanked me for my time and said the firm would be in touch.

So, when their name appeared topping a message notification a few days later, I wondered if I'd made the grade. I wasn't scheduled to write my exams for another six months, during most of that time I would be studying.

As I said, the message was odd. It thanked me for my interest and time. Oh, here we go, I thought, the gentle let down. But the message continued, saying that I had been selected as one of a group of applicants to move to the next stage of the process. I shook my head.

I dreaded another interview, not because of the time, but the process was making me think that I'd rather not work for this firm, a company which seemed exceptionally picky and precise. Realising that that is the nature of accountancy, I smirked to the wall above the screen.

The rest of the message detailed a search, throughout the city, with a series of clues hidden in plain sight, leading to a conclusion. My candidacy's success rested on my willingness to participate and my result. A link in the message led to the first clue.

I had questions, but questions were not allowed. Clicking the link meant I was in the hunt which was expected to take as much as a week to complete.

I sipped my coffee and realized that I might do well in this endeavor. I liked puzzles and this one intrigued me. I clicked the link.

I was immediately taken to a page identified as part of the firm's own system. It was an orphan page, as there were no links to their website configuration. Only the URL identified it. I took a screen shot, just in case and copied the page URL into a separate file.

The page showed a picture of our local major sports stadium, focussed on much of the structure, but taken to feature the ticket booths. 'Ticket booths', I thought, 'they are kind of outdated now, aren't they?'

I copied the picture to my own screen and increased the size considerably. Then I took the time to scour every inch of the image looking for something that stood out. The image seemed pretty benign with a few signs in the ticket windows referring to a concert that day, a show by a musical group popular with the older generation.

'They could not fill a stadium anymore, could they?'

I took a closer look at the signs; they appeared to be one standard page in size and appeared to be fixed to several ticket windows on the left but not all of them. They said "Tonight – The Rolling Stones – additional tickets still available."

'When was the last time those guys played here?'

I zoomed in on the signs and realized they did not look quite right. The angles were wrong and it dawned on me the signs were photoshopped into the picture. I looked more carefully at the people in the image and saw members of the band, or at least younger versions of Mick Jaggar and Keith Richards, standing around, loitering in the crowd, away from the windows.

Okay, I had to look even more closely and found that the man who conducted my first interview was also in the photo, way off to the right, in three-quarter face, holding a clip board with the company logo partly visible.

"So what does all this mean?" I said out loud.

Young Rolling Stones, my interviewer, a show from God knows when and who knows what else I might find? I needed to stew on this a while. So, I looked up the company and saw they had sponsored a Rolling Stones show at the stadium 20 years before. It was part of the Licks Tour, to celebrate a greatest hits collection release. They had played the city four times on that tour, once in the stadium, right in the middle of the series of shows.

I wondered if the other shows might hold some clues. One was a huge outdoor event at a temporary stage. So that was likely out, unless the name meant something.

The other was at a small refurbished dance hall called the Palais Royale. Interesting I thought as the company I had applied to was called Royale Accounting. I scoured the web for pictures and figured I'd pay the place a visit.

Down near the lake, west of the city centre I managed to find a bus that took me to the front of a sprawling, fancy tennis and athletic club located next door.

The wind was brisk coming off the water and I trudged in front of the venue, hoping the wind would calm a bit for my return trip. The dance hall was only a few hundred yards along. I reached the front and there was a listing of several events posted in a glass fronted message board.

The third one down was mention of a private event, closing the public building on a date a week later. There was no information about the private event.

I circled the building looking for something that might jump out but not much did, save I noticed I was being watched from inside. Two people holding what was presumably coffee, started out at me, or maybe the lake behind me, as they sipped at their cups. One of those cups, appeared to sport the company logo. I ended up at the building entrance again and tried to enter, but the door was locked, and it dawned on me the clues were supposed to be hidden in plain sight.

It was then I noticed the event board again, and a drawing of dice, mid-toss, to highlight a casino night the venue was hosting, sponsored by a local brewery. 'Dice, dice?' I thought, then remembered that the encore song played at the stadium concert 20 years before had been Tumblin' Dice. I gave a silent thank you to the detail obsessed mega fans who provided such precision to the web. I made a mental note to check the lyrics.

There was a menu posted including an ice cream cone with three scoops called the 40 licks cone – same as the Rolling Stones greatest hits release which spawned the tour.

Okay, there appeared to be connections but where did it go next? I scrolled through the lyrics of Tumblin' Dice but nothing stood out except the oft repeated phrase, "You've got to roll me." But that seemed a dead end. What else are you going to do with dice?

So maybe the other concert venue was the ticket, so to speak. It was held at a large outdoor urban park, with temporary facilities, and was attended by as many as 500,000 people with a variety of bands including the head-lining Rolling Stones. It didn't seem likely that any clue would emerge there so I returned home to think it through, keeping the words 'hidden in plain sight' foremost in my mind.

And then, there it was, in plain sight. As the bus rolled past the stadium it passed a pub across the street, 'The Staring Snake' with a stylized drawing of a cobra. Dice formed the eyes with both showing one pip, the proverbial snake eyes roll.

I was sure that the pub would lead to another clue so I exited the bus and went in. It took a while for my eyes to adjust. And as they did, I wondered why the first clue was so roundabout, so mushy, with so many possible threads.

I sat down and a waitress approached with a smile. "Yeah, I'll have a glass of red house wine please."

That should buy me some time to try to put things together. I could only assume that the pub itself was a clue and so were the plethora of things the previous clues had put forward, namely the Rolling Stones, and the specifics of snakes and dice.

I looked around while I sipped and scrolled through a list of Rolling Stones song titles, album titles and tour names.

The pub had a few pictures and drawings of classic snake charming, among them a hooded cobra moving to a charmer's flute in a striking pose. I looked at some Rolling Stones' lyrics but nothing jumped out that seemed connected to forensic accounting. I tried to pick songs that appeared on the surface to have some connection to what I was doing, 'Rip This Joint' mentioned a lot of place names, 'Shine A Light' seemed almost a wish for a better life, 'Under My Thumb' is about shifting power dynamics in a relationship. I looked through other albums and song lyrics but found nothing that jumped out at me, especially since I really didn't know what I was looking for.

The waitress wandered by asking if I wanted a menu. I nodded, thinking I might get a bit to eat while I mulled things over. There were no mentions of snakes in any lyrics I had scrolled through.

I ordered a burger and looked more carefully at the menu. Under specialty drinks, 'Sympathy for the Devil' jumped out at me. It was a non-alcoholic concoction aimed at designated drivers, sympathy for those revellers who were driving the devils home, apparently. I went back to the lyrics and found that the song ended with a kind of devil's chorus repeatedly singing 'Woo Hoo.'

"Bingo," I said aloud. Woo Hoo was a Chinese investor who had just finished negotiations to buy up the assets of a large bankrupt retailer. He had been called a 'snake' in the business press, due to his reputation for slithering into companies and emerging as the sole owner. 'So is Woo Hoo a snake,' or is he rolling the dice, or is his investment somehow tainted?' I thought to myself.

Once home I started in researching Woo Hoo finding his full name was Shah Woo Hoo. A little more digging and I found that Shah was the Mandarin word for snake. I was pretty sure I was on the right track now, but I did not know where that track was headed. On a hunch I went back to the accounting firm's website and was amazed to find a picture of Woo Hoo with the company CEO.

It turned out that Royale Accounting was the company handling the retailer's divestment and sale of the company. A news story said Woo Hoo had bought the remnants of the retail chain for pennies on the dollar, speculating that he was really interested in the company's real estate holdings. Having been in business for decades, the retail chain actually owned several of its key locations, and that property was worth a large sum.

I wondered where I should go from here in my less than wild goose chase. Should I respond to the company with what I had found? I'd managed it all in just over two days and they had suggested it would take a week. Without any obvious next step, I decided to forward my findings.

In the mean time I did a preliminary lay out of the transaction and Woo Hoo's other holdings to see if there were any potential pitfalls. Other than Woo Hoo having to push his board of Directors hard to complete the purchase, I found nothing. At least nothing that was public.

The next morning another email arrived from the firm with another link. It said to use the knowledge I had gained to open an additional link. I clicked on it and entered Snake as the password. Nothing. Then Rolling Stones. Nothing. Then Woo Hoo. Nothing. I had one last shot. I entered Shah Woo Hoo. Boom!

The link took me to another page. This time I was congratulated for getting this far. Now I had to investigate the source of Woo Hoo's funding for the retail purchase. 'The Devil is in the Details', was the final line of the email. Should I find an answer, I was to forward it to an email linked at the bottom. It was anonymous but had a Royal Accounting domain. I had two days.

I looked up every possible story about the sale and purchase I could find in the financial press. Sifting through mountains of information there was only one mention, in a New York financial newsletter that mentioned a partner company that Woo Hoo's company was working with. He was the front man for the transaction and held, apparently a fairly small stake, though details were sparse.

I dug a bit deeper, searching out the company name, and found it had only been recently incorporated. The Board Chair was unfamiliar to me, but one of the Directors at Large, was the former CEO of the retailer. Well, well, I thought. Could it be that the retailer was buying up its own assets at fire sale prices, leaving the old debtors high and dry, while letting in some Chinese investors through Woo Hoo? And why was Woo Hoo doing this? Surely there was some profit for him to front the purchase. But if Woo Hoo was a snake, might he be arranging to pull a fast one, to somehow double cross the Director at Large who was probably the representative of some of the failed retailer's old owners?

I looked at the background of the Director at Large, and found he sat as a director on the board of several companies in which Woo Hoo held a large stake. Maybe there is no double cross then, I thought, maybe they are just content to scoop the assets of the failed company, having tanked it themselves.

I typed in the name of the Director at Large as the answer to who was funding the purchase and figured I'd done about as much as I could. I wanted to include the possibility of a double cross and after some thought, sent a second email to that affect.

With no answer forthcoming for a few days, I stopped looking anxiously at my messages and went about my life. A week went by and I stopped thinking about it, figuring I had failed the test. I was somewhat annoyed however that I had not received at least a thank you for participating from Royale Accounting.

Another week went by and I saw a story in the financial press saying the transaction for the purchase of the failed retailer had been finalized, and the new owners would announce their plans for the enterprise before their annual financial reports were posted a few months later.

I shrugged. I had my Chartered Accountants exams coming up and while I was still looking for a job, I had slowed that process, thinking to wait until the exams were done.

Sitting at my screen a message notification hit, something from Royale Accounting. I didn't even open it right away, expecting the inevitable let down note. But curiosity got me and I opened the message which consisted of a link. I did not need another wild goose chase. I was too close to writing my exams and was annoyed with the game playing.

I got myself a coffee and sat back down, hitting the link, so I could be done with it and move on.

A video link opened. "Greetings" said Woo Hoo. "And congratulations," said Royale Accounting CEO Robert Williams.

"You both have passed the test and if you are still interested, we will offer a position at Royale Accounting, handling the Shenzdong Global accounting business. There were 23 people who began this test. Two have completed it successfully. Both of you will be supported by the firm in attaining your designations and once completed, you will be handed the Shenzdong account working under a senior partner in the firm. All the other details can be ironed out if you accept. Please respond to this message and further instructions will be forwarded.

I smiled broadly. I really wanted to celebrate or at least have someone to tell that I had found a position. I immediately responded, and was told to attend a meeting the following week.

That week was very pleasant. I had a job in my back pocket and the notion that I was somehow suited to forensic accounting. I went over the whole chase and wondered what the bottom line might be. Surely the accounting firm trusted Woo Hoo and he was not implicated in anything nefarious.

I reported to the address that was given to me, which turned out to be a coffee shop in a small, innocuous eight storey building a few blocks away from the main financial district. Okay, I thought, it can't be the coffee shop it must be one of the offices in the building. I looked at the building tenants but there was nothing that stood out.

Getting worried I sat down for a coffee, and as I sipped the man who had interviewed me entered the shop. I was determined to speak with him and he headed my way.

"Hello. Congratulations on passing our screening process." He reintroduced himself.

"It's a bit of an odd way to check out candidates, but it worked for me, so what can I say."

"You and one other, who should be here by now." And as if on cue a young man entered the shop, scanned the tables and headed our way.

"Mitch O'Hearn," he said. "I'm supposed to report to this address and Royale Accounting. I recognize you from the interview."

"Sit down Mr. O'Hearn. This is Megan McDaniel, she also passed the screening and has been hired."

"It's a bit unusual to start a new position in the coffee shop?"

"Yes, yes it is. Our offices as you know, are several blocks from here. We also have satellite offices in several other locations. We are meeting here because the job is not office based. And in fact, you will remain unknown to almost everyone in the firm. You report to me, and your work is known to our CEO Robert Williams. That is all."

"It all seems sort of cloak and dagger," I said, trying to illicit a laugh.

"Yes, I suppose it does. Your lives are not in danger. At least any danger we are aware of. We want to keep you out of the loop for several reasons. First, there is concern that there is a stray employee at Royale. Second our work with Shah Woo Hoo has turned up some inconsistencies in his business practices and third, we have been in touch with federal regulatory agencies and law enforcement, and they want us to investigate these issues so as not to tip the hands of anyone who might shut things down if they found police were involved."

"Oh," I said, trying to process this information. O'Hearn sat stoically but I could see his mind working behind his eyes, despite his best efforts to remain calm.

"You are to work together chasing down business deals, stock purchases, land transfers and personnel movements which might shed some light on whatever might be going on. As far as Woo Hoo knows you've been hired, and are working on your designations, prior to taking on his company work with Royale. That explains your absence from the firm's offices."

"Do we have any connection with law enforcement."

"Yes, you will have a contact at the DA's office who you can use in your investigations. You must be discreet with the contact because if you divulge too much, they are obligated to act when they are certain a crime has taken place."

The man pulled out two folders, stuffed with files about an inch thick. "These are identical dossiers on the case. I'm going to suggest you both become familiar with them and talk between yourselves on how you will proceed. You will be given company cell phones and business cards in the name of Palais Accounting, so your investigations cannot be connected with our firm."

He said he understood that both of us were studying for our accounting designations and encouraged us to use about 20 hours per week of company time to prepare. The other 20 hours should be dedicated to the investigation.

"We are well aware that in the quest for information sometimes there is a latency period where you sit and wait. We are confident in both of your abilities to sift through the pile of papers and dealings and at the end of this investigation you will be offered permanent employment with Royale Accounting, assuming you pass your exams and get your Chartered Accountancy papers."

Any questions were deferred until after we had both read through the files and met to whittle down our queries and concerns. There wasn't much more to say. He gave us contact information and suggested we contact him once a week to ascertain progress and with any questions.

O'Hearn stood up. "Thank you. I accept your offer, and will work with Ms. McDaniel to lay bare the dealings of this company and its officers."

I echoed his sentiments and he left, saying he would contact me in three days after having looked at the files. I nodded and made a mental note to be completely through them by that time.

After O'Hearn had left, my contact also made ready to leave, apparently giving Mr. O'Hearn some time to melt into the city. Sitting alone in the coffee shop, I was struck by what I'd apparently already found out about Shah Woo Hoo and his dealings, and thinking that Royale Accounting believed there was enough they did not know that they hired two accounting students to investigate.

'And accounting is supposed to be dry and boring,' I thought to myself. As I finished a second cup I began to sift through the files, just taking a scan of what was there. It ranged from press clippings and official company earnings statements, to tax information and a lengthy list of company officers.

I was in for a few days of deep reading and a lot of cross checking. Once I arrived home, I made myself dinner and collected what I believed I would need for my searches.

As any accounting student would do, I made a grid file to keep track of everything I knew and found out. I also began another file outlining Woo Hoo's business dealings and those of Royale Accounting.

I arranged to meet with Mitch O'Hearn at the same coffee shop where we had been given our assignment. The meeting was scheduled three days later.

"Hi, nice to see you," I said. He nodded and mumbled something similar.

"I take it you've looked into the files?" He nodded again.

"Frankly I can see all the things that were revealed in the initial scavenger hunt leading up to the job offer. There is a lot there, but I'm at a loss as to what more there could be."

"Obviously, Ms. McDaniel, there is something, or at least something suspected or we would not have been hired."

'Okay' I thought, 'this Mitch guy is a bit brusque. Maybe that was why he was hired'.

"So, they must be looking for corroboration of the likely connections we already know about."

"And the details of who is involved and to what end," he said.

"Right. So where do you suggest we start?"

And Mitch O'Hearn made a complete 180 degree change in his personality, he laughed, "I had hoped you might suggest something."

"How far along did you get in the initial investigation as part of the interview process? I found cross connections with Royale employees and Shenzdong Global I also found some issues with the purchase arrangements with their recent offer on the derelict retail chain, and a few other details of potential funny business."

"Yeah, me too. I did see that Robert Williams appears to be in the middle of this. Given that he's in on the investigation he must be trying to clear his name, or help the District Attorney get more in exchange for some favor from the G-men."

"I'm going to suggest we split our efforts. We have to find connections between the people in both companies and we have to chase financial records. Which half would you like to take on?"

"That seems reasonable," he said. "If it's just the same to you, I'll go after the financial records."

"So I'll take on the personal connections. I suggest we meet each week and apprise each other of our progress, and pick each other's brains for some angle we might have missed."

We chatted briefly about the direction each of us would take and what we knew so far. I asked him where he had gone to school. He looked at me strangely, almost as if I had breached some red line.

"Um, ah, I graduated from the University of Pennsylvania in Philadelphia."

"That's Ivy League, isn't it?"

"Yes, but I went there because my father is a professor there and I was able to attend with a much-reduced tuition."

"No Ivy League for me. I went to UConn, the University of Connecticut. Just outside Hartford, it's a fairly big school located in a very quiet, almost forgotten state. I'm from Connecticut and my parents both went there, in fact they met there."

"Was is a big accounting school?"

"Oh yeah, Hartford is the home of a number of insurance companies, so accounting and actuarial work are big. How about UPenn?"

"It's a very big business school so accounting is prominent. My father is a math professor."

We chatted a bit more. Neither one of us was too long out of school and so we talked easily about our experiences.

"Are you hoping this assignment with Royale will lead to something?"

"Frankly, I'm happy for the work and for the opportunity to get my designation. As for Royale, we will see what comes of it. It seems like a solid firm and being in New York has its charms," he said.

"Me too, I suppose. I'm not committed to anything, though I must confess this forensic stuff is interesting. We will see how I feel about it at the end of this process."

We went our separate ways agreeing to meet again in a week. I decided to put most of the next week into my investigation so I could get ahead of it and so the studying I did for my exam would not be lost among my other responsibilities. I returned to the coffee shop a week later with Mitch already there, waiting for me.

"Have a good week?"

"Oh, yeah. I got a lot of stuff. The problem is I don't know how far down the rabbit hole goes."

He outlined a web of financial machinations that were blinding to normal people. Money switching back and forth, into and out of companies, companies starting up and being used to park assets. It was all bewildering. He handed me several pages of names of Boards of Directors, and pencilled in details of company ownerships and the like.

I had gone through the personal records of anyone I had connected to both Royale and Shenzdong and found many connections, through Boards of Directors, schooling and even family. Mitch's investigation had added to the total number of people I would have to check up on. And the details of connections I found meant that Mitch would have a number of new companies that he would have to investigate through their financial records.

"So far there is ample evidence of nepotism, corporate padding and even possible tax evasion, though some of that is legal," I said.

"Another week chasing down the avenues of investigation that we found for each other and we should probably report up the ladder."

"Agreed."

The meeting was set with Mr. Hwang saying we should meet in Brooklyn, far from the financial sector and any prying eyes. He chose a restaurant and we met for lunch.

Mitch and I presented the reams of detail we had accumulated.

"Okay, what the long and the short of it, before I wade into all the details?"

We looked at each other willing the other to speak. "It's a rabbit hole," we both said in unison. It was a phrase we had used in conversation regarding our findings.

"It's deep and detailed. There is obviously something there. Some conspiracy to avoid taxes, to hide corporate allegiances, and maybe use corporate funds for private endeavors. Of course, all of this is alleged and while suggested by the evidence, we do not have check stubs, or bank records to prove it," I said.

"The detail of who is in who's back pocket is so cross-hatched with relationships, and partnerships and stock holdings that it is tangled beyond belief, likely on purpose," said Mitch.

"You two have done a lot of work in only two weeks."

"Well, to be honest, I wanted to get ahead on this stuff, and put off my efforts into studying for my exam closer to the actual test day." Mitch nodded.

"Please take the next week to study. I will present your findings to Mr. Williams and we can meet in a week to decide how to proceed."

Mitch and I spoke on the phone twice during that week. He had uncovered a bit more detail and admitted he was hooked on the investigation. I had no new facts, but I had been thinking of the possible connections and found a couple more that were not immediately obvious.

Our meeting was set for the following Tuesday. My exams were only three weeks away and I was getting antsy. I almost didn't want to waste half a day talking to Mr. Huang as there was nothing really new. But I went anyway, hoping that the investigation had come to an end.

"Excellent work you two. We have presented your findings to the DA. They will take it from here. There are very likely charges that will come up and a grand jury will be convened. Write your exams and we will talk some more once the results of both things are known." He left.

"That's it?"

"Yeah, I was looking for some more detail."

"I feel like we've been dismissed. At least we get paid to study for a few more weeks and who knows after that."

Mitch seemed lost. I felt much the same way, but was not surprised by it. He seemed completely caught off guard by the fact the investigation had been taken from us.

"It feels wrong to do all the background work and not be involved in the outcome."

"Maybe we will be. Wait until after our exams, after the grand jury and see who is still standing at either Royale Accounting or Shenzdong Global."

"Or a half dozen other companies."

"I'm not sure I want to conduct another whole investigation just to find out who is holding bag."

"The worst part? I'm not sure we can list our connections with Royale on a resume, should we be looking for other employment. With the investigations on-going and half the company under suspicion who is going to pat us on the back?"

"Maybe we don't want them too."

Chapter Twenty

Two weeks later I finally caught up with Theresa. I ran into the coffee shop a little late, just a combination of things, but I had some time as I didn't have an appointment until later in the day.

"Oh, there you are, so nice to take a break."

"You've been busy."

"I'd say. Well, first I secured a bank loan. They were fairly accommodating especially once they found out I had substantial orders already. I outsourced the manufacture to a company in Texas and found a business manager. I had to deal with the designs and approve the manufacture of each piece before they would manufacture in bulk. That took a while and a lot of couriers."

"There's nobody closer to home that can make the stuff?"

"Yes, but the cost was prohibitive. Texas was the best fit for cost and proximity, otherwise it was going to be done in Asia. Frankly, that's where I'll probably look in the future when I have a large order. The cost is much better."

"What about the quality?"

"My manager says that in Asia you generally get what you pay for. Too cheap and the quality suffers."

"What's next?"

"Delivery and then some advertising. My manager is working to try to get us into some fashion magazines and websites."

"Have you heard anything from Brandon and Markus?"

"Markus called to see how it was going. We had a nice conversation and he wanted to meet to give me a break and get together, but I had to put him off. I was just too busy. I think he was a bit miffed, as he said I couldn't be working all night as well, and a break would do me good."

"And Brandon?"

"No nothing from him, though Markus mentioned him in our conversation, related mostly to his cousin's men's store business. How about you? What's your latest?"

"I've had to back off as well. A number of jobs have come through and I have to pay the bills. I did get something scribbled down but its really rough."

"So what's next? Are you determined to finish the project or have you found an idea you can work with?"

"A bit of both I think. I am finding this approach stimulating. Forcing me to step outside my comforts. I am writing again, even if most of it seems rough."

What about releasing your output as a collection of short stories?"

"I thought of that, but short stories don't sell."

"I never knew you were chasing sales. If that's the case, stick to romance, that's what sells."

"You're right, I don't chase sales, God knows, but writing something that has no audience seems to be pointless, except as a writing exercise. Actually putting in the work to clean up the stories and get them ready for publication seems like a waste of time."

"Then the whole thing is a waste of time. Now that you've broken the writer's block, start something with legs."

I was a little miffed with Theresa as she was so pushy. Perhaps her own success had emboldened her. I searched for something to change the subject.

"The boys were really helpful in Philly."

"I have to keep reminding myself that they sort of invited themselves. Truth is, I think Markus at least is interested in one of us. I just don't know which one."

"Maybe he doesn't either. How many times have you met a guy who you like but the whole thing just doesn't catch fire?"

Theresa nodded. "You know, the funny thing is we know almost nothing about them. They surface in our lives but we don't know much about them."

"Do you want to? Ask."

"Yeah, okay, but I don't want to appear too inquisitive."

"If I know anything about you, I know that you can be subtle when you choose. And not so subtle, like today when you pushed me on my novels."

"Yeah well. I'm finding in the business world; it's a lot better to be straight to the point and firm. You need a push, just like I did. At least I didn't sign you up for a writer's conference, or something."

"I went on one of those a few years ago. I still am not sure what to make of it. The problem is nobody is on the same path, or even at the same point on the path. Those ahead of you, like the speakers and published authors are working the room and have no time for the up and comers, who they often see as competition. And there are a lot of wanna-bes."

I sipped my coffee.

"That's why I have avoided those events and even ignored a few writer's groups that have invited me in. I figure if they are too new to the process, I don't want to be their teacher, and if they are too far ahead of me, they don't want to be mine."

A loud noise erupted from the counter. Somebody just dropped something.

It was interesting to see the various reactions, from horror, to sympathy, to humor.

"The industry is changing rapidly, being turned on its head really. Small publishers are turning into paid-for expertise shops, where they will take on your project and sell you the necessary services, cover art, editing, pagination and even uploading to various retailers. They will even engage in marketing, for a price."

"It's all about marketing, and marketing costs money. And, if that wasn't enough, almost all of the skills necessary to book production are learned, so anyone can call themselves an editor, an artist or a paginator. You never really know what you are getting until you've paid for it."

"It sounds like a miserable business. Maybe you should try something else?"

"Yeah, maybe, but now that you have experienced the tribulations of wholesale fashion marketing, product returns, and the like, are you likely to give up and try something else?"

Theresa nodded her head as my point was made.

"As for Brandon and Markus, perhaps we arrange a dinner with them, you know, to thank them for their help."

"We already did that."

"Yeah, I know, but it would be nice to see if anything comes of it, and perhaps we can grill them on their lives."

Theresa said she would call, as she had already promised Markus a call back. I went on to my appointment, to consider edits for a corporate speech I had written. My client was a nice guy, who rarely made significant changes. On this day, however, he wanted a whole new section added which addressed an item in the business news about loan availability and interest rates. I had some research to do and had to have the copy to him by the end of the week. My fiction project sat still for a few days until I was able to give it a few hours on Friday evening, just after Theresa had called saying we were meeting the boys the next night downtown.

I badly wanted to write comedy, but I did not feel very funny, which appeared to be a significant roadblock. I reminded myself that the humor came from the context, from the interplay of elements, so I started searching for a ripe place to start.

What is ripe for comedy? A situation? A funny person? Slap stick did not work in print. I mulled, and mulled, and mulled. Then I poured myself a glass of wine, and sipped, poised above the keyboard, I twitched, and then went for another sip. Maybe I was not ready for comedy.

And then . . .

Chapter Twenty-one – Horror- Stuck in a time loop

A few years back, when we were all younger and just finding our way, my friends and I attended a wedding of one of our group, in a small town. A group of closer friends had been invited, the wedding being in his fiancé's home town of Passau, several hours distant.

It was a lovely place, a classic small town, almost plucked from the past. It was a place that slips into memory once you've left, making you wonder if any of it was real.

Unbeknownst to us all, the area was heavily German, settlers of course, from generations before, but despite this, little had changed across that time. The architecture was German, what North Americans think of as Swiss, with half-timbered buildings, stone on the main street, cobbled roads, and signs in a Germanic style, even if they were in English.

I knew something was off once I saw Kingstrauss street and then Oak-enstrauss Avenue. At first it seemed quaint and a bit affectated but when every street in the town was thus named, it was obviously something the locals liked.

I tried to think of a joke but nothing came and I was struck by the blank looks on everyone's face in the car. Almost as if they were awestruck by this little town and were rendered speechless.

We pulled up to a guest house that the groom had arranged for us. We were warmly welcomed by the proprietor, and warned that any funny business would be dealt with harshly. Yes, there was a bit of disconnect there, but I dismissed it. I wasn't one for funny business anyway, so the threat seemed like a bit of comedy. The proprietor smiled.

The guest house included a bar as part of the restaurant, which worked for all of us, as we were on holiday, didn't know our way around, and really badly wanted a drink, or two.

We collected our stuff, found our rooms and met in the pub area. A few more of our group had come together and were already there. One of the other guys decided that we couldn't start drinking until a bit later, especially as we all had to be up the next day for the wedding. So, we decided to go for a little walkabout in the small and picturesque down-town area.

Older brick buildings, right out of the 1800s were everywhere. It all seemed very surreal, especially as our little posse did not encounter a single person. Now to be fair, we didn't venture into any of the shops which were surely staffed, but there was no one else on the street. And it stayed that way until a car pulled up beside us. Out climbed the groom himself. We all greeted him with genuine affection, but he was all business. It was probably the stress.

"Ah there you are. I have to outline the details of tomorrow's events, so meet me in your hotel pub in an hour."

We continued our strange tour and made our way back to the hotel. Someone in our group said they saw someone far down the block get out of a car and enter a house, but it happened so fast nobody could believe it.

As we sat down, the proprietor of the hotel approached us. "How did you like our quiet little town?"

We looked a each other and someone chimed up that it was nice but very quiet.

"Not the hustle and bustle of the big city. We like it that way."

We all nodded and then I changed the subject by ordering a pint of Pilsner. "Chuck should be here soon and we'll get the details about tomorrow."

And as if on cue, Chuck materialized at the door and approached our table with a big smile on his face.

"There he is, made to order. This place is a bit odd. Like it's right out of a movie or something."

"Like a movie set," someone else said.

"Yeah, like its all a facade. You know, nothing behind the storefronts."

"I'm aware of what 'facade' means, but I can assure you its real enough. Just a little old fashioned."

At that point our pints were delivered to the table.

"Are you and Greta going to live here after the wedding?"

"No, we have a place in the city. That's where my job is and she works in the city suburbs."

"That is strangely comforting," I said with an exaggerated look around. "This place is . . . odd."

Chuck dismissed my conspiracy theory and sat down. "Okay, the ceremony begins tomorrow at 3 p.m. at the church down the street. You can walk from here, first steeple on the right. Okay, only steeple on the right, a bit more than a quarter mile. The reception is in the church yard. Apparently, the weather is supposed to be good, so there will be a few tents erected and a temporary dance floor."

"And polka music?"

"Lots of polka music," Chuck said.

The mood was light hearted, but brooding, as we still had not encountered anyone except the barman and Chuck. Chuck asked about each of our own doings. There being little real news, that portion of the conversation ended quickly.

"You've only been gone a couple of days. What's going to happen in that time?"

"Uh, yeah, you're right. It feels like I've been here longer."

"Okay Chuck, why does this place seem so odd? I mean I'd never heard of a German town here in the middle of the state."

Chuck took a sip of his beer, and looked around the empty pub. "Okay, it's an odd place, tucked into the folds of hills so much that it seems to disappear."

"It seems odder than that. Too quiet."

"It's sort of a magical place really," he said, looking around to see if anyone was listening. "What if I told you, Passau is only accessible only in high summer, for three days each year, June 20-21 and 22."

"Well we got here easily enough," said on of our group. "Oh, today is June 20 and the wedding is June 21."

"And you will all be gone by midnight on June 22."

Most of the people at the table laughed, "Okay now we know about it. What if we come back in a week."

"You'll never find it. You will pull off the interstate and drive around in circles expecting it around every bend. But it will not be there." Chuck did not smile.

Now everyone at our table had big grins on their faces, expecting a punch line, and we'd all gone quiet in anticipation. The oddness of the place, the lack of people milling about, and the oddly blue sky, started to make Chuck's claim seem real.

We all simultaneously took sips of our pints. Then we all noticed we'd all taken sips at the same time, and we all shifted our eyes left and then right.

"Stop it" I said. "This is a joke. You're all in on it. Where's the hidden camera?" I looked about frantically.

Chuck laughed, "Sorry my friend. It is no joke. This place is odd and I've become initiated into it. And you all, have been exposed. But don't go trying to break the spell. You will just look insane to the outside world."

"So, if you and Greta will not be living here, then she will not see her parents for a year?"

"Correct."

"So that must be the case for everyone in town."

"Yes, they often live on the outside for many years and then retire here, run a small business, like this guest house."

"So, these are the only days the guest house can rent rooms?"

"No, they often rent to people coming back who arrive in June and sometimes stay while as they sort out their retirements and such."

"So this beer is a year old?"

"No, it was delivered this morning."

****

Cassie typed the last word. 'Okay,' she thought to herself, 'this is not a comedy. Maybe an adventure story or crime or horror. Or maybe it's a rebirth story or a voyage and return. Who the hell knows?'

She went to the fridge and grabbed the whole bottle of wine before sitting down again, and thinking about where the story would go, and which genre or story type it was going to be. Then she started typing again.

****

"So, all the food for the year is delivered during the summer solstice?"

"No, we have farms here, and we process food. A lot of supplies are brought in for the year. The people here are very self-sufficient."

"Are they Amish?"

Chuck laughed, "Well they are German, aren't they. They aren't Amish, but they certainly maintain some of the characteristics of the Amish."

The next morning, I awoke, pretty much believing that our conversation with Chuck was a dream. We all went down to breakfast, where Chuck's revelations were alluded to, but never vocalized directly. I was determined to ask our hotel staff about it but my girlfriend Alice said not to bother, it would just make us seem weird, and they were sure to deny it.

"Well, that's easy for you to say, you've probably been here before, being a close friend of Greta."

She nodded slightly and cast her eyes to her plate. "We've got a bit of time before the wedding, perhaps we should take another look around."

So, we all finished breakfast, and agreed to go for a drive to look around and have a bit of lunch when the time came. That would give us plenty of time to get back and get ready for the wedding.

The five of us piled into the car and down the main street we went, but not without a warning from the guest house proprietor to give ourselves lots of time as sometimes the roads were confusing and we might get lost.

“Don’t worry, we aren’t even going to leave town,” I said.

“You don’t intend to leave town, but sometimes road signs can be confusing. Take care.”

We wound our way through the maze of streets, which were not laid out in the usual grid pattern. We circled around coming back to the same intersection several times before the driver decided to take a left and cross an old arched wooden bridge.

“Did anyone look down. You can barely see the creek at the bottom,” I said. “It goes down a long way.”

“So we must be up pretty high. I do remember the road sort of going up and up as we drove in here from the interstate.”

“Wow, I had no idea. It looked like a creek at the bottom but it had to be at least 100 feet down, maybe more.”

“Perspective is difficult as you flash by in a moving car.”

“Oh hey, look, there are a few more streets over here.” The Road from the bridge led to a circle from which several streets spoked off at regular intervals.

“We can explore them, if they aren’t too long. We should stop for lunch at some place soon.”

“I don’t want to eat too much as we have a wedding reception coming up.”

And so we turned to the first street on our right, soon coming upon a property with a lot of things displayed for sale. Kind of an emporium of collectables. We decided to stop and look around.

As the car rolled to a stop a stooped old guy, bald on the top with a fringe of thick white hair looking like a collar from ear to ear on the back of his head, emerged from one of the barns and ambled up to us as we spilled out of the car.

"Morning to you all. Lost? Or looking to buy?"

"We'd like to have a look about and maybe buy something, if it catches our fancy."

"Ach, do that. I'll be in here if you have any questions. Everything is for sale, but there are no prices on them. Talk to me if you want to buy."

We thanked the old guy and he ambled back to the ramshackle barn. We headed to another building across the compound. Ducking in, I saw that in the front of the building things were displayed on shelves and on each other in a pleasing way. As you moved further back the items were stacked and even further back, they were really just a jumble of stuff, with items almost impossible to discern from one another.

Chrissy took a liking to an old desk clock, shaped like a gothic arch, its face sporting black roman numerals on a gold backing. Archie's girlfriend saw a small table she liked. We went back searching for the old guy and mentioned the items. He knew them exactly, and knew where we had found them.

"For the clock, $50. It needs to be wound, but don't overwind it or you will break the spring. As soon as it begins to feel tight, stop. One more turn may break it."

Chrissy accepted the price without bargaining.

"And for the table, $50 but it doesn't require winding. Are you going to be able to get it into your car with all your stuff?"

"You know we aren't from around here?"

"I know pretty much everyone and you lot look like wedding guests for the Berkshire wedding this weekend. "I'll be there you know. I'm Greta's Great Uncle Mikal."

Annie paid for the table and we went back to fetch our new purchases. We wanted to explore some more and agreed to come back the next day before we left town.

We kept going around the circle looking for a place for lunch. On our second time around Archie pointed out a doorway with a sign. Parking and getting to the door we saw that inside was a staircase up to the second floor. At the top it opened into a modest reception area, behind which were a number of tables.

We all sat down when a waiter emerged from a doorway and motioned for us to select a table.

A few moments later he came out with a pitcher of water and began the ritual of handing out menus and making sure we knew that the special of the day was veal schnitzel. I smiled, but couldn't think of anything witty to say.

Having selected our meals, we all sat back to enjoy with beers being served. We all kept watch on the time and were just about to pull the plug on an enjoyable stay in the restaurant, when Chuck burst in.

"There you are, I've been looking for you. You're cutting the time a little close, aren't you?"

"We were just getting ready to settle up. We've got time."

"Ahh, okay, then. Sorry I am a bit frantic. Seems like Greta's mom decided without telling her that the bar at the reception would not have any beer, just wine and spirits. I wanted to let you know and I'm prepared to go out a buy some beer if that's what you all wanted."

"No beer?" echoed three of us, laughing as we managed it in an unpracticed unison.

"Okay, okay, I'll get some. Just get a move on. You still have to get ready for the ceremony and its more than a short walk to the church from the guest house."

Chuck herded us out of the restaurant and insisted we follow him back to the main street. I must admit, he took a couple of odd turns on the streets but we did get back to the road and passed the church on our way to the hotel.

The ceremony was pretty standard, Chuck's best man was his older brother, he had admitted to me in private that it was a choice he made to avoid annoying any of his group of close friends. The church emptied out and people milled about on the lawn, speaking to each other and congratulating the couple and their parents.

Soon Chuck and Greta were directed to a copse and fancy stone bench in the back corner of the churchyard, where they posed for photos and family shots. Anyone who wanted a picture of, or with the happy couple, were invited to step up.

As that was happening, people were gently being encouraged to move to the other side of the church property where three large tents had been erected. On one side were tables for dinner. On the other was a dance floor with some small tables and a number of chairs surrounding it. And in the middle was a service kitchen on one side and on the other a place for the band and necessary audio equipment for the dance.

Pretty neat I thought. These people have done this before.

A small white van rolled up. The caterers started to unload trays into the kitchen service area. Finger foods were passed around and a line formed at the bar.

The sun remained high, it was June 21st after all, and the standard wedding announcements and procedures went off perfectly. The air was fragrant with lilac which framed much of the area. There was no graveyard, despite the age of the church, and everyone ate with gusto, a very German dominated affair with slaw, veal and pork cutlets, potatoes with onions and peppers.

The speeches and toasts were winding down as the sun became noticeably low on the horizon. A lovely red streak filled the space between low clouds and the rim of land.

"This is picture perfect," I said aloud. "I almost think we need to start a ruckus or something so there will be something to remember this by. Perfection has a habit of melting details away."

A few of my friends snickered and the girls looked cross, annoyed that we would even think of upsetting the perfection of the day.

An announcement that the dance would soon begin had guests moving to the other side of the central tent. And we were assured that the bar would remain open and that some small nibbles and sweets would be available throughout the night.

Music rose slightly from the dance area, but it was just happy tunes, not yet the hard-core dance numbers everyone expected. Some announcements, the standard groom and bride dances with parents and in-laws and the music picked up a bit with some traditional classics to woo the older generation into tripping to the floor. The inevitable polka music was wound in.

And the party was underway as the last of the natural light bled away, several arc lights positioned around the dance floor became more apparent. The music rose again with a popular song designed to fill the floor. It did. Even some of the older people, determined to strut their stuff, remained on the floor while everyone with a girlfriend or spouse was pulled onto the floor by the familiar gravity of the music.

I don't remember much else of the night as it all went perfectly. Chuck and Greta remained a bit longer than most probably thought they would, and then took their leave with the best man driving them to the airport.

Before they left Chuck thanked everyone and those in town who had helped. He reminded everyone from out of town that the roads were expected to become difficult late the next evening and to avoid lingering, lest they be stuck.

I looked at my companions but nobody seemed to notice what he had said. I did notice a few of the older locals eyeing each other and saw that when Chuck and Greta left the party they did so after a lengthy conversation with Greta's parents, and some deep heartfelt hugs. I put that down to the happy couple showing their gratitude.

We all went back to the dance floor and occasionally wandered back to the kitchen area to sample some sweets or take an extended rest from the hyper-active party side. The evening ended with a few polkas and the older folks reprising their early lead on the floor. People started to trickle away and some of us, stayed, got a drink and found a table on the kitchen side.

"Where are they going on their honeymoon? Anyone know?"

"I heard they were going to New York City for a few days. They are cutting it short and planning a longer holiday in the fall, California I think."

"That all sounds nice. New York is quite the place."

"I thought it an odd choice, being that it's a tourist town, not really a honeymoon capital. Too much to see and do, not like a lodge or resort, which is what I thought they'd do."

"Too each their own, I guess. Perhaps that's what the fall trip will turn into."

Our group retired to the inn we were staying at and gathered for a final drink before heading to bed. It was late and we were all tired.

The next day after breakfast one of the three cars we all came in, left town. The second car went after lunch with Archie and Annie grabbing a ride as they didn't want to stay. Chrissy and her clock had gone with the first car. I thought we'd poke around and get dinner before we left. We only had a two-hour drive so we'd still get home at a reasonable time.

There was something about the town that attracted me. The architecture and layout were fascinating and I enjoyed moving about just trying to get used to the layout. We ran into the antique shop again and greeted the old proprietor like old friends. There was an old Coca Cola sign I kind of liked. A bit big, but it was a classic, round, in red with white lettering. I offered $100 but the old guy just laughed. Those signs go for upwards of $1000 and that one is in good shape and larger than normal. I'd be hard pressed to let it go for less than $1800."

"That's out of my range. And frankly, I'm not sure where I'd put it." He shrugged.

We drove around town, Alice wanted to look at some furniture and clothing, more for ideas, not real purchases.

We decided to stay for dinner and found a lovely family style restaurant. The waitress chatted about the wedding the previous day, as she, and most of the town had attended. She said the forecast was for heavy fog to roll in late in the evening, making the roads treacherous and difficult.

I looked out the window of the restaurant and it was a clear and perfect late spring day, well, early summer now, I thought. I could hear a bird chirping.

We lingered a bit over dinner and left, headed for home. I had a bit of trouble finding the road out of town, but I did and turned onto it, more than a touch relieved as the sun was now fully down and it was a moonless and even starless night. There were hints of the fog in low lying areas, and apparently no breeze.

We drove a few moments after making the correct turn out of town when there was a large pop. It was quickly evident we had a very flat tire. I got out to look and slowly began to pull the spare and jack from the trunk.

It was a bit tough working the in pitch dark but I managed to make the change and put on the temporary tire. I worked up quite a sweat. Turning the car back on it was evident that a thick fog had rolled in, as the headlights could not penetrate it. We rolled back onto the road and started through the fog moving much slower than the speed limit. There was no one else on the road going in either direction. I turned where I believed I should to hit the main highway but we didn't intersect with it where I thought we would.

I thought of backtracking but was beginning to get anxious. Chuck had warned about this. I had no idea where we were and the thought of driving around the rural area for the next year, rattled in my head. Were we in a neverland between the town and the rest of the world? Were we clear of the town itself?

Continuing to drive would take us further and further away, I figured, so I kept going, saying we would have to hit the interstate at some point, but panicking more and more inside as the clock ticked past 11 pm.

Then there was a turn in the road to the left and I followed slowly barely being able to see past the hood. We rolled on and could see some faint road lights. Where were we? We went over a bridge, which I only knew because the sound of our tires was different, and then the fog cleared enough to reveal that we were back in town.

My heart leapt into my throat. It was now 11:15 pm. And while not hopelessly lost we were unsure of ourselves.

As I stopped at a streetlight trying to get my bearings, an old pick-up glided up beside me.

"Son, I thought you'd left town hours ago."

"We did, but I had a flat, and then this fog confused the way. How do I get out of here?" I tried to remain calm but my voice rose with enough panic that Alice beside me, looked at me oddly.

"We're not going to get home until really late, and I have to work tomorrow."

The old man pursed his lips. "You'd better follow me, I'll show you the way back to the interstate."

And so we did, following faithfully behind the truck in the thick fog, we eventually found the interchange and glided onto the highway at 11:45 p.m. The old guy waved cheerily and then cut across the median in his truck, an unusual move, and with a spray of grass and dirt he sped off back towards town.

The fog lifted a few minutes later and when I looked at the clock it was midnight. "That weather cleared pretty quickly."

"It did. Almost unnaturally so," said Alice. We looked at each other.

My heart was beating fast and hard, with each thump echoing between my ribs. I sighed deeply, and Alice looked at me.

"Do you believe that stuff about the town disappearing?"

"No, but I didn't want to chance it, you know. Either everyone there is in on the joke or there really is something to it."

"Why don't we come back next weekend. I'd like to check out that antique place again and well, if we find it then . . . we can go there anytime."

"Okay let's. Should we bring a trailer? Did you have your eye on anything too big for the car?"

"No but you liked that sign."

"Not at that price, I didn't. Besides, where would I put it?"

"Well, check out the prices. Maybe you can flip it and make a few dollars."

The next Saturday, June 28th we had other commitments and decided to go the following weekend. So it was that morning we found ourselves cutting off the Interstate with only a few miles to our destination.

I made a turn onto Route 39 and then another onto Route 445 and we rolled through familiar farm country. Up ahead there were a few horses pulling wagons, a couple of Amish going shopping or some such thing.

We drove and drove, turning, twisting, crossing some of the same territory over and again. The town was not to be found.

We decided to just drive until we found any town and perhaps find some lunch and some answers.

Sure enough, a town emerged round a corner and spread down a dip in the road which bridged a small river. The sign at the town entrance announced 'Spandau' with a population of 3,363.

"That's oddly exact," I said. "Usually, those population signs are rounded off.

"Hey, there's a restaurant. I'm starved."

We went in and found it was a family style place, with a standard menu of schnitzel, salad, soup, burgers and the like. Alice ordered a schnitzel with French fries and I, a large farmer's salad, with meat, egg and, well, just about everything else.

After ordering I beckoned the waitress over and asked her about 'Passau'. A very odd expression passed behind her eyes, and she looked away, feigning to adjust her apron.

"Passau? Passau?" She shook her head slowly. "I've heard that name, but there is no 'Passau' around here."

"We were there two weekends ago for a wedding, and found a lovely antique shop we wanted to see again."

"Sorry, I'm unfamiliar with anything like that and I've lived here most of my life."

We both nodded and thanked her, and tucked into our lunches. "You know, this salad is exactly what you would make at home, if you had all the ingredients, which of course you never do."

"My schnitzel is really good too. Not sure what makes it taste so good though. Maybe its just fresh. And the fries have a different, very pleasant taste. Just like those fries I used to get downtown, at my old job."

"I remember you talking about them. These are the same?"

"Yeah, crispier than usual but only on the outside, with a great taste. Maybe it's the oil. I wonder what they were cooked in?"

We ate in some silence. I was listening to conversations around us. More to glean the nature of the place than anything else. Alice didn't speak and I thought maybe she was doing the same.

The couple behind us, spoke in low tones about a wedding they had recently attended. That perked up my attention, but it didn't seem to be the same one we went to. And then I heard the word 'Passau' clearly, but from where I did not know. Alice perked up considerably, and her eyes widened. She had heard it too.

I shrugged but turned up my listening, putting my finger to my lips. Nothing. No mention of any town, any wedding or anything out of the ordinary. We finished our meals and settled up.

"Well, now what?"

"We should just explore at bit. Drive around, see what we see."

And sure enough, we wandered into another town several miles away, and blundered into the middle of a Fourth of July parade. This town was significantly larger than 'Spandau' and the parade sure showed it. There must have been hundreds of people participating and many more than that lining the streets. We parked and found a spot to watch, and I counted three marching bands, half a dozen floats depicting scenes from American history, and the requisite number of clowns and gymnastic dancers.

The parade ended at a large park which skirted a wide river. People hunkered down and barbeques were hauled into position commencing a large tailgate party. A man came around with a hat asking for donations to help pay for the fireworks, which would start about 9:30. I dropped $10 and got a thank you, but no indication if I was above or below the expected contribution. I should have asked.

We had a blanket in the car and spread that out, and a few snacks but no chairs or anything so it was a bit uncomfortable. Alice got talking to the family beside us, who quickly identified us as outsiders. Alice mentioned we were from the city and had come looking for an antique dealer we had seen on a previous trip.

The lady she spoke to couldn't think of any business that matched the description so Alice mentioned 'Passau'.

I was watching some kids throw a football around and only vaguely listening to the conversation. At the mention of 'Passau' I could hear the catch in the woman's throat.

"You were there?" she asked quite incredulous.

"Yeah, we were there for a wedding."

"Passau? Are you sure?"

"Yeah," Alice nodded. "Two weeks ago. Nice place, but strange."

By this time, I had shifted my attention to the woman, and I could see here mentally calculating the time frame.

"The wedding of Greta Berkshire and our friend Chuck. It's her family that lives there."

The woman blanched. "You've come back to find it then? You know you won't, it's hard to find."

"We've heard such things. And we've had no luck. You're the first person that seems to acknowledge that it exists."

The woman scootched over from her blanket to ours, getting very close to Alice. She bowed her head and spoke in very low tones. I couldn't hear what she said and determined to find out after we left. Alice looked at me with wide eyes.

The fireworks started and the women moved back to her blanket as her kids returned from romping around the park. Her husband was on their tails.

"Those boys can really run you down," he said. The woman introduced us and told her husband that we had been looking for an antique dealer in 'Passau'. He definitely missed a beat, but recovered quickly. "And you said?"

"It's a hard place to find."

Alice changed the subject, commenting on the fireworks, "Does the town do this every year?"

"Yes, there is a baseball game between us and Breslau, a neighbouring town, then the parade and the BBQ with the fireworks. Standard stuff, really, but everyone here likes it."

"I certainly do, it's nice to hear the rockets go off and know for certain that a blaze of light will follow, rather than wonder it they were gunshots, which sometimes happens in the city," said Alice.

Back in the car, I asked her what the woman had said.

"She admitted that 'Passau' has an odd reputation and admitted to me that her family had originally been from there, leaving years ago to regularize their lives. She suggested that we should not go there, especially if we were just looking around. The locals do not like people messing with their thing."

"That's what she said? 'Regularize their lives' and 'their thing?' "

Alice nodded. "I'm not sure if I want to figure this out, or if we should leave well enough alone."

"Either way we have some time to think on it, we can't get back for another year."

"Maybe we should talk to Chuck and Greta when they get back."

"And maybe we should just forget the whole thing."

And Alice would not let it go. Her conversation with Chuck and Greta, a couple of weeks later, did not go well. Of course, they were planning on visiting the following June but did not seem to be interested in Alice and I tagging along. She was adamant, and would not be swayed.

"They are clearly uncomfortable with us going. The last thing we want is to be in 'Passau' and have the whole place hostile to us."

"Why would they be hostile? They were all perfectly pleasant last year."

"Then we were there for a happy occasion. This time you just want to burst their bubble."

"No, I don't. I'm just curious. I feel a real need to know."

"And they don't want you to."

"I'm going either way. You can come with me or not."

And I must confess, when she said that I had a strong tug saying let her go on her own, with an underlying feeling that if I did, I might never see her again. Or at least for a long while.

"I have to go, but I'm not sure I want to."

"You don't have to come."

"If you go alone and do not come back, I will be the number one suspect."

Alice laughed, "Don't worry I have no intention of staying."

"Famous last words. Remember how we almost got stuck there last year."

"I'll just get Chuck and Greta to escort me out. Easy, peasy."

"Easy if they want you go get out."

"Oh, come on, they would never. They will be leaving too."

So we arranged to go, much to the consternation of Chuck and Greta, who were clearly not happy with us. They said they would be busy with family when they were there and would have no time for us. It was a major brush off, but they tried to mollify us by saying we should get together few weeks later in the city.

"Look we'll go on the 20th, stay overnight, find that antique dealer and leave the next day. That gives us 24 hours or more to find our way out," Alice said. I nodded, siding with our friends but unwilling to let Alice go on her own.

June 20th fell on a Sunday, so we would be leaving after dinner on the Monday. Our mission completed and hopefully Alice's curiosity satisfied.

"I'm not even sure what you want to find there. We've as much as established it's a town lost in time. Chuck wasn't kidding and everything we've done to prove that, has fallen into place."

"If we find the place easily, that will prove the point, won't it?"

"And if we don't, then what? This has been a year long dream?"

"Come on where's your sense of adventure?"

"It certainly isn't in the fourth dimension?"

"This isn't the Twilight Zone, you know."

"I'm afraid we might find that out."

A few weeks later we were on the Interstate honing in on the turn off. Alice was beside herself, barely able to contain her excitement. Me? I was not sure what I thought, only that I'd be happy once we were back on the Interstate the next night.

One turn, then two, then three and four. We couldn't find it. I was relieved and getting ready to suggest we head home, when we rounded a curve and saw the sign, 'Passau – population 3,365.'

"Again, with the oddly exact numbers."

"Is that what it was last year?" she asked. I shrugged.

We entered the town and stopped at the guest house securing a room for the night. The proprietor did not seem surprised to see us, but said nothing. I thought it odd, as we were clearly outsiders.

And then we headed out to find some lunch and eventually find the antique dealer. It took some doing and a bit of memory that didn't seem to quite fit and we saw his sign. The property looked the same, a few large trees festooned with signs, a dirt driveway through them and once inside a large courtyard surrounded or formed by a number of outbuildings and barns.

The old guy popped his head out of one of the buildings and ambled over to our car.

"Remember us?" Alice asked. "We are here last year looking around."

"Bought a table and a clock. Inquired about a Coke sign."

"And I'm back about the sign."

"Same price I'm afraid."

But we never settled on a price, you just gave an estimate."

"So, I did. I can't take less than $1800 for it."

"So, you said. Do you have any others, maybe a bit smaller?"

"I do, back in that barn. Take a look. I'll be here if you want to talk."

So Alice and I wandered back into a large barn and were struck by the huge number of items inside. Every thing from toys, to farm equipment, to vehicles to advertising.

There were two large, round Coca Cola signs hanging on the wall. I was interested, and at about four feet in diameter, I figured I could fit them in the car.

She spied a pair of candle sticks, probably pewter, with a gothic design, and an old bread box in pretty good shape and labelled with a brand I'd never heard of.

We made our way back into the courtyard and the old guy emerged as if on cue. We mentioned our interest and bought the bread box for $75 and the candle sticks for $60. Then we talked about the two signs.

He hummed and sighed, blowing his breath noisily while he thought.

"$1500 each."

"How about $2500 for both?"

We bounced back and forth and settled on $2750 for the pair.

He seemed pleased. "You can get these into the car, I hope. I won't be here next week, if you have to come back."

I gave him a knowing look and I could see Alice was going to say something, so I spoke up, saying I figured they'd fit easily. And they did. I paid the man, cash was all he would take, and we loaded up Alice's items and drove off.

She wanted to explore the town some more and stay an extra night. We swung by Greta's parent's place to see if we could catch our friends there but there were no cars in the drive. As we made our way out of town the next day, I became disoriented as the streets did not seem to connect up the way they had the day before.

The sun was going down and I was getting a bit antsy but Alice was convinced that someone would appear to help us find out way out of town. She suggested just taking a main street and driving away from town until we were far enough away. With no better plan that's what we did, but in two tries, the main roads petered out a mile or two out of the main settlement area.

"Okay, so where did we come into town when we got here?"

We tried that approach to leaving, and found the same dead ends and twisted connections with other roads that only led back to town.

A few minutes to midnight and we were not going to make it. Nobody had appeared to save us, and the town appeared exceptionally quiet with few lights and no traffic. We sat in the car at a down town bank parking lot as the clock ticked into the next day.

There was no flash of light, no big bang, nor anything unusual. "I guess we just make our way out of town in the morning, unless you want to keep trying."

We hunkered down for the night, sleeping in the car. A car door slammed and I stirred into the full morning sunshine.

I opened my door and got out stretching. Alice was just stirring.

Everything looked fresh and bright. Another car pulled into the lot, evidently the bank staff was arriving to work. I sauntered over to the car and asked for directions out of town. The person just looked at me and shook their head slowly.

"That road has been blocked. You can't get out now."

The fear that had been deep inside me rose quickly into my throat and I looked around frantically. The person had turned and was almost inside the bank entrance.

"Okay Alice, now what?"

"Let's try to get out of town. It's not a problem until it's a problem."

"It was a problem last night. It was a problem last year."

"Just drive. Maybe we can get a coffee for the road."

Having something to do settled my rising nausea. What would happen if we couldn't get home?

Alice took a job at the local school and I managed to find some accounting work. The people of Passau seemed to all know our situation but never spoke of it. We were definitely dealt with at arms length.

After spending a year trying to fit in, I awoke on the morning of June 20. I wanted to get out of town as fast as possible though Alice seemed to want to linger to say some goodbyes. Not everyone had treated us as outsiders. Some seemed to want us to have sympathy for Passau.

I could not wait. We'd had plenty of time for goodbyes. I took the main road and made a couple of turns and a sign for the Interstate appeared along side the road. I was giddy.

Two hours later we were in the city and headed for home, not sure what to expect. I pulled into an ominously empty lot. As I took the elevator up to my floor I heard a voice.

"Hey, I thought you went away?"

"Well we did, but we got lost."

"And now you are back. Well, things are a bit different now."

I feared they'd declared us dead or something. Given away my apartment and wiped us from existence.

"Yep, the super said everyone had to park over at the mall and walk for two days. The pavers are due here around noon."

"Oh. I remember that. That's why we left for the weekend, but they haven't started yet?"

"Not supposed to. Starting to dig things up at noon, should finish in two days and then will lay the pavement. It needs two days to firm up, then we can drive on it. But all of that is in the flyer they sent around."

Now I was confused. It was like we had never left. The work that was supposed to be done a year ago hadn't even started.

"What day is it?

"Sunday. Just like it was this morning."

I smiled weakly. "Indulge me. What is the date?"

"Um, June 20. Getting the job started on a slow day to give everyone a chance to get used to parking down the road. You alright?"

"Yeah, I'm just fine," I said. "Just fine."

Chapter Twenty-two

I arrived at the restaurant and Theresa and the two guys were there ahead of me. It was an upscale place but not fine dining. We planned to go to a comedy club afterward. I thought I might find the key to humor, so I was all in.

"So how is your project coming along Cassie?"

I hated talking about my stuff in too much detail. When I'm in the middle of it, its so unfinished that there are no details worth sharing as they will probably evolve, and when its complete and for sale, I worry about over-selling it and disappointing any readers.

"It's coming, but it is still very unfocussed right now." I had always felt that talking about such things is like letting people into my brain, outlining my thought process and leaving me very exposed to judgement. In any fiction worth reading the author is trying to find a pithy way to describe universal experiences.

"I try to avoid time period cliches, especially if I'm writing about something happening right now. Nothing says 'dated' like pulling out your mobile phone and plugging it into your car's cigarette lighter."

Markus laughed. "My dad's old car had one of those. I had no idea. But then of course when I wanted to plug in a music player, he thought it would burn."

Theresa outlined the steps she had taken in setting up her business, saying that some of the women's jackets and blouses were in the production process right now in Texas. Other pieces were still in the pre-production stage with proof pieces or designs flying back and forth by courier. I figured it was a good time to turn the tables.

"So Brandon, tell us about your gig?"

He looked shocked to be asked. "Well, I'm a process engineer. Actually, graduated in mechanical, but landed with Bruce Manufacturing, you see their name on large warehouse style buildings all over the place. We make a number of things, often under contract. I help manage and design the processes for that manufacture."

"It changes that much?"

"Oh yeah. We do some things on an on-going basis and of course we are always looking to improve the process. However, much of our business is in contract manufacturing, whatever the clients might want built. I help design the process that gets things made. Ever seen that show 'How it's Made'? I do a lot of that stuff, getting machines mixing plastics, cutting wood and steel, fastening things together and producing things to specifications."

"Wow! Your work must be different each day."

"Yeah, it is, but I'm usually working on several projects at a time, some in the design sequence, some in the machining and others in the conceptual space with clients. So from your perspective Theresa, I wear a lot of different things, sometimes having to change during the day. The industrial plants can be quite dirty, and of course dealing with clients in downtown offices requires a certain approach."

I switched gears and asked Markus. I think he was ready for me.

"I'm down in the banking part of downtown. Banks and brokerages and the main stock exchange are all there. I've often wondered what a three-D rendering of the entire downtown would look like without any of the street level stuff visible. Those bank towers have multiple levels of offices and things many storeys below ground."

"Is your office underground?"

"No, but some of the computer banks are located there. I know the bank brokerages are located all over the place, in fact one of the bigger ones just moved uptown a mile or so, citing congestion. In truth I think they felt that their connectivity would be a bit better as everything is tied together, and the slightest issue cascades through the system. And for Theresa, I'm always in a shirt and tie, though I often take the jacket off, so much so, that its really just a prop most of the time."

"Pretty much what I expected," said Theresa. "Dress standards have come way down in the business district in the last generation, or so I've been told. The desperation for computer guys was the undoing of the entire fashion edifice."

"A fashion edifice? I had never really thought of fashion in those terms before, but you know, it fits. There is a bit of a step ladder of proper dress for places, times and situations. And there still is, even if it has become relaxed in recent years."

"Don't they say dress for the job you want, not the job you have?"

"I've heard that. It seems to be a form of imagining yourself doing something and pretty soon, you will earn the opportunity."

"In that case, I think you can imagine all you want, but the stepped-up grooming level, is noticed by those around you, even if it is very subtle."

"So what do you do all day?'

Markus considered a moment, "I'm talking to clients, making some buy and sells on their behalf, talking to colleagues, parsing the news, which often drives the market and always keeping an eye on the 'ticker'. The market is so interconnected. One move here, forces counter moves there, and they aren't always predictable."

"Seems like a fair bit of pressure."

"There is, especially first thing in the morning as we are reacting to other markets around the world and to our own news stream. Some of it is fairly predictable but good lord, when something unexpected happens, the markets go crazy, with money sloshing around trying to find an equilibrium. Most money is in for the long term, but there is a substantial segment that is trying to sniff out short term profits."

"Maybe I'll set my next novel idea in the stock market, if I can pick your brain. I'm looking for something in the Thriller genre."

I guess there is a Thriller to be had there somewhere, but that is exactly what we are trying to avoid everyday. Have you done a Crime story yet?"

"Theresa has been trying to get me to combine genres so maybe I should tackle a Thrilling Crime drama centered on a stock market segment that is hidden deep under ground in a lonely part of the banking district?"

Theresa gave me a look but Markus laughed. "Where people dress nice but not as nice as the decade before. Now that's something I would read."

"So you aren't much of a reader, then?"

Markus looked sheepish, "Not too many people are these days, what with all the entertainment choices they have. I do read regularly but it's only a small portion of my free time. Sorry."

"The truth hurts I suppose, but I enjoy it and there is money to be made, its just that the success pyramid is very steep, with a very few ultra-successful writers, a few modestly successful and the rest of us chasing a smaller and smaller readership."

We kibbitzed over dinner, with everyone seemingly more comfortable with each other. Theresa seemed to be warming up to Brandon, who had not been around as much as Markus, but even that conversation seemed to center on Brandon's cousin and the new business venture. Theresa let slip that the clothing designs for their store would soon be in the manufacturing process and she was very hopeful for some early sales to help balance out the bottom line. She admitted she was a bit concerned with this opening round of debt as nothing had really been sold yet.

The comedy club was a lot of fun. It was in an old theatre, which sat perhaps 500 people, and was set up for young, up and coming acts. Most of the show was an improv set of sketches, some involving the audience, and some featured stand-up performers, mixed in to give the cast regulars a bit of a break.

I recognized one guy from some local TV commercials and another looked familiar but I couldn't place him.

Markus laughed loudest and both Thresa and I had a lot of fun. Brandon was subdued but when Markus called him out on it, he just said he was thinking of his drive out of the city.

At the end of the show, we all decided to go to a local coffee shop for something hot, before calling it a night. Before we finished Brandon bowed out, saying he needed gas before heading home, leaving Markus with us. He offered to walk us home but we both declined, saying we'd get cabs.

It turned out that Markus lived in the same direction as me, so we ushered Theresa into her cab and Markus hailed another that we could share. I fumbled for some money to pay my share even though I was unsure how far he had to go.

I could see that he wanted to say something to me, but could not bring himself to do it. As the cab pulled up to my building, I patted him on the shoulder and thanked him for an enjoyable evening, saying, "I know Theresa appreciates your help quite a bit. It was a lucky chance that we stumbled upon each other at that wedding."

"It's Brandon who has helped her the most. I must admit, the two of you make for a lively evening, lotsa fun. I haven't laughed like that for a long time."

I smiled and scootched out of the cab, closing the door with a wave. The cab glided away and I found myself watching it head down the street for a moment before I turned into my building.

I found a message from Theresa on my phone when I finally sat down.

"So, what did Markus say? Call me."

I shook my head, I did not want to call, but I knew if I didn't, I'd either get a call later or I'd be dealing with a seriously annoyed Theresa.

"He didn't say anything."

"I don't believe it," Theresa said.

"I'm telling you, he said nothing, though I had the feeling he wanted to, but with the cabbie there, he was stuck. Certainly, getting out with me would have been awkward."

"Like I said, he's interested in one of us. If he'd truly said nothing, then it was me he likes, but given that he obviously wanted to say something, it might well be you."

"He didn't ask for my number. He didn't bring up my work, or my writing. He had every opportunity to say something casual, but he didn't. I'm guessing he wanted to ask after you."

Theresa was silent, processing my words. After a moment she said, "Yeah, but he can say something to me anytime, he has my number. It can be casual."

"Who knows how the male mind works? Why don't you call him."

"I've got nothing to say on that account. No spark, remember?"

"Maybe he's wanting to say something about Brandon?"

"Come on, these guys are not 14, they can handle themselves."

I hung up, with the decision to just wait out Markus, who would eventually say something if he wanted to. I started to think that maybe he wanted to help Theresa's business in some way.

A week later, a few days before my coffee with Theresa, I sat down to tackle my next genre. After the soft horror of Passau, I decided on something different, and stared at the screen trying to conjure up something funny, but couldn't. I then slid into the stock market story I had mentioned at the dinner a few nights earlier. It came surprisingly easily. After all, Thrillers are usually mostly chases and crime is everyone's villain.

I jumped in . . .

Chapter Twenty-three – A Mastermind – Crime Thriller

"We are being followed."

She turned the wheel and halfway through the turn, hammered the accelerator. The blue sedan made the same turn behind them and seeing the lead car farther down the block, pushed their speed as well. The follow had turned into a chase.

"I don't know where they picked us up. I don't want to abort, but I can't have them on our tail, or Jimmy will never get away."

She raced on, thinking how she could best approach the square. "Call Jimmy, let him know we are three or four minutes out, and he should position himself just inside the square from the Avenue entrance. We will toss the package out the window and continue past. Hopefully our company will not see."

She made another left and a quick right.

"Okay, Jimmy's in place. His contact is supposed to meet him on the other side of the street, for the hand off, but they haven't made contact yet."

She sped up as the blue sedan was closing on her. Then she figured the speed up needed to be in the last turn before the square, to get some distance between the cars at the right moment.

She heard a siren in the background. Looking in the rearview mirror she could see a patrol car several blocks back, lights on, and gaining. "Shit."

"We're almost there. Get the drop done, scoot and take the speeding ticket a few blocks later."

A man in the blue car looked into his rearview mirror. "Crap, it's the cops."

"Either way this is bad. If I slow and they pull me over, we'll never catch her. If they go after her, we'll never get a shot at finding the memory drive."

She made a final right turn and was headed for the square a block away. The blue sedan turned, with the cop car still far enough back that it wasn't evident who he was chasing.

She was driving way too fast as she flashed into the square, lined with cafes and restaurants, and full of people, standing, talking, sitting at tables and wandering along the roadway.

Ready with the thumb drive, Ken pitched it out of the car at the moment they entered the square. He thought he caught sight of Jimmy but he wasn't sure. He didn't want to turn around or leave his arm hanging out of the window. It might tip off the chasers that something was up.

She kept her speed but rammed on the brakes where the roadway turned left, leading to the exit of the square. After the left turn she hit the gas to take on the straightaway.

The hard braking and quick turn were too much.

There was quiet, shocked silence, though the horrific sounds of the crash still echoed in the ears.

The car lay on its side, held up by two tables it had slammed into. Smoke rose from the hood. The foremost tire still spun with the motion it had carried.

A blue sedan glided in behind the overturned car. "Quick, that cop will be here in a second."

The two men scrambled out and made a quick search of the overturned car. The two people inside kept their heads down.

A police car slid to a stop on the roadway where the car had left the street.

Carlos made some gestured like he was trying to help the victims, but he was really looking for an envelope or a package of some kind. There was nothing.

Next thing he knew there was a policeman standing beside him. "Are you a doctor?"

"No," said Carlos, "But I have some emergency training."

They both assessed the crash. "I don't think there is any danger of fire. We shouldn't move them. I will request EMTs," said the cop.

Caros nodded and he waved in his partner for a few more seconds of search. It was then that he heard the screams.

The initial shock was passed, and chaos slowly grew as everyone in the patio took stock of the aftermath. One of the tables holding up the car had been mercifully unoccupied. The other was now surrounded by smashed bodies, though all four revellers were moving.

Stray bits of the crashed car had been flung into another table. Two of its occupants appeared gravely injured, covered in blood, and two more were unscathed and trying to formulate a plan to help in the slow motion of shock.

At the far end of the square, away from the carnage sat two men calmly finishing their coffee. One rose, and approached the crashed vehicle. He looked around and yelled for help, twisting back to look inside the car before moving around it, and then melting into the growing crowd.

Two people in the car sat transfixed, shock beginning to set in. One was bleeding heavily from the forehead and the other sat still strapped into the passenger side, the seat belt having done its job.

Another policemen slowly approached the car. The first one had taken charge of the crowd, the second spoke to the injured. Ascertaining the victims in the car were in no immediate danger, he moved about the patio looking for other injuries, radioing for several ambulances.

As he moved around the patio, the man from the table calmly approached the car, quickly scanning it for an item but he saw nothing.

Distant sirens got louder, he was going to have to arrange for a search once the car was impounded. Jimmy had seen the two men from the far part of the square stand up and begin to move towards the crash.

He targeted the second man who held back as the first made a scan of the site.

"Excuse me, I am looking for Senor Augustus Meltiades."

"That's him over there," the dapper man said, pointing towards the crash. "Nasty business. Why would anyone be going so fast through the square?"

"I have a delivery for Senor Meltiades." Jimmy held up an inch long piece of plastic with a metal end. "Can you please see he gets this. It is what he's looking for."

The dapper man took the small thumb drive and put it in his pocket. He nodded at Jimmy, and moved with surprising speed toward the crash. He moved without running or even looking like he was determined to get somewhere quickly. Jimmy watched as he took the other man by the arm, spoke a few words and led him away. Two ambulances entered the square, shutting down their sirens but leaving their lights flashing.

EMTs swarmed the crash site, made a quick assessment and began to move to help the more critical of the injured. A policeman started to canvass all the witnesses.

Jimmy, concerned for his friends in the crashed car, was frozen to his spot, but knew he should exit the area quickly. But he wanted a look at the two men in the blue car. Eddie would want to know who they might be.

An EMT loudly announced to the crowd that the blue sedan would have to be moved. Jimmy watched as the two men who had arrived in the car, looked at each other and moved toward the car to move it out of the way. The policeman asked everyone present to remain calm, and to please wait as police would collect their witness statements.

A policeman sidled up to the car as they were moving it and spoke to the men.

"I was in pursuit of the crashed car. So were you."

"No, no sir. We were following on and couldn't find a proper place to pull over to let you pass."

The policeman tilted his head down and looked over his sunglasses. "Right." He asked for license and insurance and instructed them to move the car into a loading zone entrance and wait for him.

The blue car glided along the street, giving the accident scene a wide berth. The driver thought of just leaving, but knowing the police had his license and plate number, he backed the car into the service entrance, which gave both men a forward view of the scene. Jimmy was in a building alcove as the blue car moved past.

"Carlos, did you find anything?"

Carlos shook his head, "No. But I did note the two men who also seemed interested in the crash. The big one even went over to it and looked around. I think he may have spoken to the people inside."

"He could have been checking to see if they were okay."

"It seemed like they knew each other. Didn't hear any words though, the conversation was quick and the big guy seemed satisfied. Then that other guy came up to him and they left the scene."

"So that's it. Where did the other guy come from?" He started to look around the scene. "And how did he have the package? We gotta find him."

They both scanned the scene and even exited the car to look further, but didn't stray too far as they didn't want to raise the cops' suspicions. The two men were gone.

Jimmy considered simply leaving the square but didn't want to be seen by the two men in the blue car, who were standing beside their vehicle and were scanning the scene. As they moved into the roadway, Jimmy dodged back inside a restaurant.

"Sorry sir, we are closed now due to the accident."

Jimmy mumbled something about needing to use the facilities and moved down a hallway. He burst into a run, slipped through the kitchen before anyone could stop him and exited through a back door. He was in an alleyway and realized he had only one way out. He ran.

Hitting the street he quickly looked both ways and casually walked in the opposite direction of the square. After a block he increased his speed, crossed the street and took a side block to the main street. There he entered a subway station, made his usual train connection and emerged a few minutes later several miles away.

He made his way down the block and went into a high-rise condo building. Buzzing a flat he was admitted.

"Eddie. I delivered the goods to Senor Meltiades though there was a glitch." Eddie looked at him to continue. "Sarah and Ken were in an accident just after dropping the drive, they were being chased and flipped it out of the car as they entered St. Gaius Square. They messaged me that they would flip the drive out so I was able to retrieve it pretty easily. Then they crashed into a restaurant patio. Meltiades went to investigate and I was able to identify him and pass on the delivery."

Eddie seemed relieved. "You were sure it was him?" Jimmy told of identifying him. Then Eddie asked about Sarah and Ken.

"They seemed okay. The car was flipped and there were injuries on the site but they were strapped in to car and seemed shaken but not seriously hurt. The cops were there instantly, lights flashing. They seemed to have picked up either us or the chasing car and were in pursuit."

"Damn it. Things never go smoothly, do they?"

"I got a look at the two men in a blue car that were right on their tail."

Eddie looked at Jimmy waiting for the description.

"Um, ah, it was a blue car and there were two men in it. They got out to look around the crash. One was tall and the other not so tall. Um, let me think. One wore a golf shirt and slacks, the other had a jacket on, undone. Like a windbreaker, not a suit jacket."

"What did they look like Jimmy?"

"Like anyone. Both had dark hair, clean shaven, white guys, they seemed sure of themselves," he spoke slowly, trying to picture them to add to his description. "The cops asked them to move the car and they did, but they stayed with it. When I realized they were scanning the site for something, I slipped into a restaurant and out the kitchen door to the alley."

"If Meltiades has the thumb drive then our job is done. We just have to lay low for a while. I'll pass your account of the situation upstairs and let them handle it. I'd like to send you to see if Sarah and Ken are okay, but I think it best to wait. If they are unhurt, we will get a call, in due course. Stay close to the phone and keep out of trouble for a few days. I'll be in touch."

Eddie turned and went into an office, closing the door. Jimmy, stood a moment and then left.

"McGonagle?"

Eddie switched the phone in his hands, "Sir. The package has been transferred."

"Good, anything else?"

"Yes, two of my people were in an accident at St. Gaius Square. They were being chased and the chasers remained on scene."

Eddie relayed the details. "The police will likely look to charge Sarah Lorenz with a serious traffic violation. Speeding at least. Dangerous driving more likely, and worse if anyone in the square doesn't make it. I need that reduced as much as possible or outrighted. Like an improper lane change or something, at most."

"I'll see what I can do."

"And sir, the chasers? See if you can have them charged with something."

"Not likely possible Eddie, we can't be that obvious. Agency business. But we protect our own."

Three hours later Sarah called, "Eddie? I take it you've heard?"

"I have spoken for you. I do not think you will be charged with anything serious."

"Okay, thanks. Jimmy got the drive I believe . . . "

"And he passed it to Meltiades. All is good. Are you and Ken whole?"

"Yes, they checked us out in the hospital. We spoke to the cops. I said something about hitting the gas instead of the break as we entered the square. Didn't want to let on about being chased. More questions that way."

"Good girl Sarah."

"I'm on my way home now. Got a bad headache, but didn't say anything to the emergency doctors. I didn't want to be kept in the hospital for observation."

"Don't go home. Go to the Fifth Avenue coffee shop we've used before. I'll send a car around in two hours. I don't want you followed. Ken too."

A few hours later Sarah received a call to get in the car at the curb, and sure enough as she was leaving the shoppe, a car glided up and she got in quickly. Ken had begun to walk up the block against traffic. Sarah's car moved away and turned right. Then two more right turns and they were back on the street in which Ken had started walking. They stopped and picked him up.

"I think we have a tail," said the driver looking in the rearview mirror. That grey SUV has followed us around the block. He's backing off now which is a tip off."

The car was silent as the driver made a series of turns, lane switches and double backs, before emerging in the Park and slowing. "Now we'll see if he's still on us."

They pulled over for a minute or two until the driver was satisfied. "Eddie wants you in Brooklyn tonight. He's taking no chances."

"There were a few people at the scene who got a good look at me," Sarah said. "I didn't recognize them but . . . "

"Best to stay safe tonight. Eddie will monitor the coms and hopefully you can head home tomorrow."

"Gotta admit I've never seen the like of this before on any other job. Deliveries are usually smooth."

They crossed the Queenston Bridge at 59th Street and wound their way into Brooklyn, pulling up at a tall residential building near Jamaicia Plain. The driver turned, "Here are the keys. Suite 1504. Stay there until you get further instructions."

Sarah and Ken arrived in the suite and double bolted the door. Awaiting them was a change of loose clothing, gym wear mostly, tee shirts, sweat pants and hoodies. Sarah checked the bar.

"I can always count on Eddie."

Ken motioned for her to pour him a drink as well. She managed to pour two stiff double shots of scotch and handed one to Ken before sitting down opposite him in a large overstuffed chair.

"Well, that could have gone better, but here we are."

Ken nodded, not in the least perplexed by the turn of events. "Whatever was on that thumb drive, somebody wanted it almost as bad as the people we delivered it to."

"This Agency work is edgy, you know. Doing drops for brokers and bankers and their mob seems easier."

Ken laughed, "All the same. I think we will appreciate what the Agency can do for us, regarding any further entanglements. I almost laughed after the cop got off the phone and looked at me like I was James Bond or something."

"All I got was, 'You're free to go. We'll be in touch if necessary'. And they were gone."

"You okay?"

"Apparently I got me a contusion," said Ken, rubbing his side above the belt line. "Seatbelts really do work."

At that moment across town, Senor Meltiades was handing the thumb drive to his own man. He had carefully taken the opportunity, as he was instructed, of copying it onto his own computer, labelling the file, House Plans.

The man with the drive boarded a small jet at JFK and proceeded to settle in for the overnight flight to Barcelona. He managed a few hours of sleep and was met by a car at the airport, which whisked him into the city. He did not pass through customs, which was good because he was not carrying a passport.

Once in the city he could see the Cathedral Sagrada Familia looming over the city scape, its odd stone work was not visible in the distance. His destination was a small café several blocks away. There he met with a familiar face and handed over an envelope with the drive inside. They exchanged pleasantries, and sipped a coffee until a car arrived to take the man away. The deliverer decided to go to the Cathedral for a visit before reversing his travel and heading back to New York.

The man with the drive was taken to Madrid and there he boarded a flight to Riyadh. And the drive was successfully delivered. Now Saudi Arabia possessed the technical drawings and specifications to construct a small nuclear weapon. With a 10 kiloton yield it could be carried in a suitcase.

Looking at the dripping stonework, the man from New York, having completed his work, entered the Cathedral, and wandered up the nave. Looking up he never saw the dark man approach him and was dead only moments after hitting the marble floor.

He was quickly pulled into a row of benches and searched. He had nothing on him, no wallet, no identification, no receipts, nothing. The swarthy man tucked the pistol in his side holster, took a quick look about and moved off, leaving his victim in a growing pool of blood, hidden among the pews.

Eddie received a call. Their security had been breeched. Everyone was suspect and needed to remain where they were until further instructions. Eddie passed the order on to Sarah and Ken, and then to Jimmy.

"Eddie? McGonagle. I don't think it was any of your people. They didn't know anything. But we are keeping a lid on this until we figure it out. Tell them to shelter in place. Let me know ASAP any contact you have with anyone, your people, our people, anyone, we need to know."

Two hours later Jimmy called. "Hey Eddie, I got things to do. I can't be hidden forever."

"Jimmy you are being well paid. Shut up and don't go out. If you are in need of any supplies let me know. Don't even order delivery. I expect this will be sorted out in a few days."

And Eddie dutifully passed on Jimmy's complaint to McGonigle. Sarah and Ken were silent. There was no unusual activity at the Brooklyn address nor outside of Eddie's building.

Eddie's phone rang. It was Senor Meltiades.

"I understand the DA is asking questions as to why your people have not been charged with dangerous driving and why the standard DUI tests were not carried out."

"There is nothing I can do about it, Senor."

"You need to be aware sir. There had been a breech and the time your people were in the hospital in the custody of NYPD, we do not know anything about."

"Well, sir, they didn't know anything about the contents of the delivery, only that it was to be given to you in St. Gaius Square at or near the time it was actually delivered. They were being chased. I take it you were able to exit the Square without raising suspicion? I understand the chasers were looking closely at everyone in the Square."

"I did not receive the delivery."

"What?" Have you reported this upstairs?"

"Of course. I checked the accident scene to see if I could get the item from your people but they said they had dropped it to an associate of theirs. He was to give it to me. A young man. I never saw him. And I left the scene before it was obvious that I was too interested."

"I've been told that my man approached your companion, as you were busy speaking to the car occupants, to ascertain your identity and he personally dropped the item to you."

"I can assure you sir, I did not receive the delivery. I was at the scene alone."

Eddie abruptly ended the call and telephoned McGonigal. It was a short call.

McGonigal dispatched four agents to Jimmy's apartment. Jimmy did not answer the door, following his instructions. They were about to break it down but a relay call from Eddie, suggested Jimmy open the door. He did and retreated to an armchair.

An agent trained a small rifle on his chest. Another one spoke.

“James McKendrie?”

“Yes.” He had been able to tap out a quick message to Eddie. It wouldn’t make any difference.

“I’m special agent Charles Overholt. We are all special agents of the Secret Service. We need to speak to you about your recent involvement with Edward Demitrius.”

Jimmy reached for the badge and pulled it in closer. “These things can be faked. My instructions are to say nothing to nobody.”

“He contacted Demetrius,” one of the other agents said, a phone to his ear.

“Listen Jimmy, I have been sent here on the instructions of Edward Demitrius’ boss and that bosses boss. The drop you made to Senor McGonigle was intercepted. I need to know the details.”

Jimmy remained silent. His phone rang. It was Eddie.

“Jimmy. There has been a huge mistake made. Senor Meltiades said he never received the item. The men there now are on our side, they just want to know what you know. Answer their questions the best you can.”

The voice seemed right. The number the call came in on was right. The gun had been stowed away and the agents had a less threatening look to them.

“Okay, what do you want?”

“Tell us what happened.”

And Jimmy related the drop and transfer from his perspective. The delivery had been compromised, there was a car chase and a wild drop at the entrance to the Square. He had retrieved the dropped package. He had seen a large man, matching Meltiades description, eyeing the wreckage after the crash. That man had been speaking to another before he approached the overturned car. Jimmy said he approached the man who appeared to be running a screen for Meltiades as he spoke to those in the accident car. He asked for Meltiades, to corroborate identification.

And not wanting to be seen by the men in the blue car, he dropped the item with the second man. He explained he took a bit of time to eyeball the two men who were in the chase car, as Eddie would want to know, and then fled through the restaurant into the alley.

The asked him a number of questions regarding Meltiades and his friend. And then they wanted info on the chase car and its occupants.

The agents relayed the information to McGonigle, including a video of the interview with Jimmy. Experts would comb the video for missed alley-ways, double talk, and body language.

The agents left, warning Jimmy to remain inside and contact only Eddie. He wanted to know what had happened and they would only tell him the item had fallen into the wrong hands.

Jimmy thought back over the interview trying to figure out what had gone wrong and if it had been his fault. He fixed his memory on the car accident and all the people at the scene.

Across town, McGonigle stood awkwardly in an office suite.

“Somehow the item was intercepted, by someone passing themselves off as Meltiades,” said McGonigal. “Or Meltiades himself is compromised. For three days we thought the item had been safely delivered, despite the problems. Now, either our security had been breached to allow the deception, or Eddie’s man is lying, or is a plant.”

“Thank you for the update McGonigal. I will be in touch.” McGonigle left.

The man in the suit turned to another man sitting in one of three armchairs at his office desk. “There are several possible places the breech occurred.”

“Find out which one and eliminate it. I don’t have to tell you how bad this is. We don’t even know who stole the item and where it was taken after it was acquired.”

“There is a report from one of the field offices that a known Spanish agent was found murdered in Sagrada Familia Cathedral in Barcelona, yesterday.”

“Is it possible that Meltiades is lying, that he did get the item and forwarded it to the wrong people with someone stealing it on the way?

That would be a convenient cover story."

"My god, someone who shouldn't have it, has plans for a nuclear device. It would take anyone with the necessary background and the required enriched uranium only a few weeks to engineer a working model."

"At this point it doesn't matter who has it. We have to assume everyone has it, and anyone could be ready to use such a device."

The agency knew it had been compromised but couldn't find out how. Some believed Meltiades was a double agent. That he received the item and simply sold it. Others believed the breach occurred in the transfer in Spain. And still others believed that the crazy complications in the transfer of the item allowed the breech to occur. The problem to them was that too many people handled the item, an arrangement made to obscure the origins of the information. The evidence of a breach was with the dead agent in Sagrada Familia Cathedral.

"Why was he killed? He wasn't supposed to be in the Cathedral. Did he drop the item to someone there? He was apparently driven from the airport to a destination several blocks from the Cathedral. He was found in the nave a few hours later, dead from a gunshot."

"Like I said, it almost doesn't matter how the breech occurred, only that it did. We are going to have to inform the President at some point."

"Politically, who has the drive is irrelevant perhaps, but knowing what went wrong and narrowing the search to who might have it, helps us decide what our next steps will be."

"I'm on it, sir."

"Please keep me informed about anything you find out."

A month later the trails had gone cold, with several potential breech possibilities investigated. They remained open but were still speculative, and Meltiades, Jimmy, and the dead agent, all still in the mix as potential problems. Jimmy was released from his apartment in hopes he would do something that might indicate his involvement. Meltiades was under surveillance, and the actions of the driver in Barcelona were watched.

Two months later, a nuclear device exploded in St. Peter's Square in Rome on a sunny Sunday.

The Pope, speaking to the crowd in the Square, and an overflow crowd of locals, tourists and several delegations scheduled to meet him later that day, were vaporized. Experts decided the small device exploded with the force of about eight kilotons of TNT, perhaps half the size of the Hiroshima bomb. News agencies were not informed that the likely delivery method was a suitcase. Speculation centered on a van in the Square.

Film of the event was mostly destroyed but some tourist videos were eventually retrieved and there were too many people in the audience that could have carried the bomb for there to be any definitive determination on who did it.

The blast destroyed most of Vatican City. As the explosion occurred at ground level it remained localized in its devastation. St. Peter's was all but flattened, only its great bulk stopped much of the shock wave from destroying a much larger area. The Sistine Chapel was gone, battered into pieces too small to put back together, its great artworks consigned to history. The Vatican Museum and library were badly damaged, but shielded from the blast by the other buildings, and as they were largely underground, they remained intact and their contents safe.

There was no claim of responsibility.

The world was in shock. The usual suspects were lined up in news talk shows and conspiracy theories emerged with reasons, opportunities and likelihoods debated and questioned.

The Pope was dead, his body scattered. An estimated 10,000 people in the square that day shared his fate. Many of the Vatican's most important churchmen were also dead.

Known enemies of the Catholic Church topped the lists. Any country or group that benefitted from the destruction was also scrutinized.

Many cardinals were not at the Vatican that day. They met in secret, three days later on an island in Lake Como in northern Italy. The great Cathedral of Milan became the focal point of the Catholic Church, with official information and announcements coming from there. It's Cardinal, Vitoli Isbnza, was the unofficial voice of the church until such time as the conclave of remaining Cardinals elected him as Pope John Paul III.

In the ensuing days more and more people were identified as likely dying in the blast, as those who had gone missing and were supposed to be in Rome at the time, were consigned to victims lists.

It was speculated that many people used the event to slip out of official view, change their identities and their lives. One was Senor Meltiades, who was supposed to be in Rome on the fateful day, and did not emerge after the blast.

"I'm convinced Meltiades is our man," said McGonigle. "He went to Rome, knowing the blast would take place. His hotel room was searched and little of consequence was found there. He made a big show of going to Rome, lots of people were very sure that he was there, and his hotel only had personal effects. He was also on the list for an audience with the Pope.

"And I am skeptical McGonigle. Could Meltiades apparent demise been engineered by someone else, trying to cover the tracks?"

"Sure. I could have been anyone with the influence to get Meltiades to go to Rome, I guess. However, the simplest explanation is usually the correct one. Occam's Razor, you know?"

"Don't guess, McGonigle. Find out. Or at least exhaust the options. I needn't tell you, if this could happen once, it can happen again."

"People are not surprised that our national security has been hardened like never before. The area around the White House has been emptied and plans being made to permanently move the seat of government to a secure facility, leaving the White House itself as a symbol."

The world had been forever changed. Security concerns were everywhere. Officials were paranoid and nations instituted various programs to reduce threats. Some were concerned that these changes would be too restrictive. Others did not care.

The movements of everyone involved were traced, retraced and examined in minute detail.

Jimmy, Ken and Sarah had a feeling that what they were involved in, had triggered the world altering events. Eddie had instructed them to lay low, very low.

And Eddie, for his part, thought the same thing, that the memory stick that had been inadvertently passed, apparently, to the wrong man, was the key to who conducted the bombing. McGonigle would not say, when Eddie asked directly, saying the issue was highly classified and that it was better for him if he did not know.

Jimmy was brought in several times to identify photos of various people he had dealt with on that day. He had identified a grainy security camera still of the man he'd talked to, and another photo, much worse, of the man identified as Senor Meltiades. The two men in the blue car were identified without his help as members of a shadowy intelligence agency of the US government, called Overlord by some but known officially as USOC, United States Operational Command.

"If Overlord is involved, and I'm not surprised they are, then why haven't we been called off the investigation?"

"McGonigal, until you have been relieved of your assignment you will carry it out to the best of your ability. And you will focus on the details and stop trying to piece together the whole conspiracy. Is that clear?"

"Yes, sir. I only speculate because knowing the nature of the crime might help in identifying the perpetrators."

"At this point McGonigle, it's a dead end. Meltiades is either dead or disappeared. The operation to transfer the files to him was compromised or he was. And apparently Overlord knew about it, and it appears, was actively trying to stop the transfer. My question is why hasn't Overlord taken action on what they knew. Surely, they could have made arrests?"

"Do they even make arrests? And what of the Spanish agent killed in Barcelona?"

"Obviously someone who represented a loose end, if it's related at all. There is no way to know. We have security footage from the coffee shop and it appears the dead man handed another man an envelope. They do not stay long, like they would if they were friends meeting for coffee. He's been identified as an intelligence agent with special clearance. As far as anyone knew he was in New York. There is no record of him leaving the country, nor arriving in another. The other man is unknown."

"So this is a dead end?"

"All we can do is keep looking, keep searching out connections. And pray whoever did this has no further designs on western nations."

Chapter Twenty-four

I headed to the coffee shop, camera and photo gear in tow, as Theresa had asked me to take a few shots of her and her creations for her new website.

"You really need models, you know. You have to be legit. Modeling your own designs is low . . . key." I wanted to say 'class' but I didn't want to be so harsh.

"Oh, don't worry. The shots are just for the men's shop guys, not for publication. They want some idea of what they are going to sell."

So, you aren't going to wear them?"

"Of course not. I do need a headshot for my web page if you can muster it. Even something in the shoppe if you can set the camera so the background is very much out of focus. The idea that we are in a public space if what I'm looking for, without it being too obvious, or having recognizable people who might complain."

"Okay, I can do that, but first, I thought about your message the other night."

"And . . . "

"Shockingly, that was what I was going to ask you."

"Well Markus never mentioned Brandon at all. As I said, I thought he wanted to say something, but in the end, he said nothing. And no, I didn't kiss him good night."

"You said that. Well, I thought Brandon's exit was odd. Very abrupt. I think I heard his phone beep in his pocket."

"Well, he didn't answer it. I could have been anyone's phone nearby. We were surrounded by people."

"Or maybe he has a girlfriend, or a wife."

"And if he does, he certainly has not stepped over the line."

"From our perspective I suppose, but what would you think if you were the girlfriend?"

"There was no indication of a girlfriend at the wedding."

"Were we really paying attention then? And who were they waiting for when we met them?"

"Look Theresa, I'm not going to condemn anyone on the basis of imagined innuendo. Who knows what they are thinking. From my perspective they've been immensely helpful, friendly and not pushy in any way. That's supposed to be good, isn't it?"

"Too good if you ask me. I'm naturally suspicious. I've been burned."

"Let it rest. Remember that guy you used to hang out with a couple of years ago? You said the two of you got on great but nothing ever caught. That was what you said, but it was also obviously his perspective too. Neither of you had the willingness or inclination to seize the day, even as you saw it rolling away. Have you spoken to him since?"

"No. Once we stopped running into each other, we just never picked it back up outside of work."

"I'm guessing Markus likes our company, and he includes his friend Brandon to balance things out. Perhaps Brandon is uncomfortable with the arrangement. Perhaps Brandon just started seeing someone so his perspective has changed. Something will happen, or it will not. Either way, I'm quite confident they are not CIA agents."

"Well, maybe we are about to find out." She nodded toward the shop doorway where Markus had just entered and recognized them in their usual seats.

"I thought I might find the two of you here." He looked worn. His clothes were rumpled. His face unshaven.

"Markus, what's happened?"

"Brandon. He's been in a car accident. Bad. He's in hospital with a broken everything. Some guy t-boned him last night."

Both girls were speechless, shocked. Then finally Theresa managed to squeak out, "Will he be alright?"

Markus took a deep breath. He was obviously trying to formulate his answer, "There is every possibility he will be, but he has to undergo several surgeries, his pelvis and a leg are broken. He has internal injuries and his head and neck have been immobilized, though they say that's just precautionary. He's been put into an induced coma. We will know more once the surgeries are completed and he comes out of the coma. Either way, he's going to have a lengthy recovery period."

Theresa had covered her mouth and slowly let the hand fall as Markus added more detail. I was wide-eyed and feeling bad that my first thought was how did the news affect me? Not very much, I concluded, perhaps a bit too quickly. My two friends seemed wrapped up in the event.

Eventually I arrived at home with visions of Brandon laid up in hospital, machines beeping around him. Markus told us that there would be no point in visiting him for at least a few weeks, and he would keep us informed as he was in touch with Brandon's family.

I started in on my next project with all this swirling in my head.

Chapter Twenty-five – Perfect Crime

The perfect crime. I had just managed it. I had $5 million in cash and precious metals. My victims never even knew they'd been robbed.

I smiled to myself. Of course no one would ever know the brilliance of my crime, but that was the price I paid for riches. Now I just had to convert the metal into money and skip away from the scene.

I had already given notice and while they asked me to stay for a week to clean things up, I was gone after that with a week's pay for my labours.

I had shuffled some documents from my employer to a contact in exchange for the reward. Not really industrial sabotage, I guess, as there was little more than information involved. Timely information.

See, I worked for the Department of Labour, buried so deep in the government that nobody even looked at us, and few even realized we were there. Hidden in the documents we handled was a trove of insider trading knowledge. Ever wonder how politicians get so rich?

After a complicated process of finding the right contact, I was able to get a good payday, a finder's fee, if you will, for the knowledge that a major player could use to cash in on the market. I had played the market a bit with my own money, but the amounts were too small to really score. And I didn't want to leave a paper trail.

I had cashed a series of cheques for $10,000, the banks no-reporting limit, and I had been paid in gold and silver with a few diamonds tossed in. It was going to be a job just to cash it all with small transactions, in several different places. But I would do it, and simply disappear into the mass of humanity once it was accomplished.

The accumulation of cash was one way I could be traced, but by opening a series of accounts, no one place had so much money that it was unusual, and I had made efforts to invest my winnings in retirement and blue-chip stocks. Most of the gold was in coins and a few wafers. I put them in a safety deposit box and slowly cashed them in.

Now with a week left on the job I avoided any inappropriate stuff at work, happy to blend into the background. I'd accumulated about $350,000 in cash in various banks with the bulk of my net worth still in gold, which was an investment of its own.

I had given some thought as to what I might do going forward and small-time stock investor seemed like a natural fit. I had a nose for sniffing out insider information through financial reports. I now had a substantial stake to work with, and I could do it from anywhere in the world.

I planned to leave the DC area, and first move to California. I'd secured a place in San Jose so I could blend in with all the remote computer workers. I figured a few years there and I'd move on, hopefully with much more of my gold converted to stocks and cash.

I began to frequent a café not too far from where I set up in San Jose and managed a few acquaintances that were regulars in the shop.

Of course, we all got talking and I mentioned that I was a stock trader. Two of the others were computer programmers and another was a beach bum who had a substantial inheritance. He asked me to help craft a portfolio for him, to invest his money.

I tried to avoid that but he was good natured and was really only asking for a basic outline, so I gave in. Turned out, he knew much more than he let on. I had outlined a strategy where he would balance his money in various areas, food, utilities, finance, services, high tech, and he said that was what he was already doing. What he really wanted was a strategy for day trading.

"Well, you have to be up pretty early in the morning to accomplish that," I said. I was not a day trader, more of a quarterly reporting trader, chasing good earnings reports and buying and holding stocks for a few weeks or months.

"Because the market in New York opens at 6:30 am California time?"

"Yeah, that's it."

We talked several times a week, and he tried diligently to pick my brain, but I was not willing to go along with it, as I told him, because I did not want to be responsible for any issues that arose from his trading. That didn't stop him from pushing. The truth was, I was a blue-chip investor, who mostly bought and held, but would sell when the news suggested a dip. I believed that a once a year, 10% gain plus the usual slow rise in blue chips was enough. I had tried the greedy approach and abandoned it quickly as it never worked the way it was intended. The market was too hard to read with any accuracy.

Nearing two years in San Jose, I began to get restless. I wanted to go back to DC to cash in some of my gold, so I arranged a quick in and out trip where I could hit several of my banks and spread my selling around. I managed to divest myself of another $75,000 and realized that I wanted to complete the entire laundering scheme much quicker. So I took several of the two-ounce wafers, and some of the gold and silver coins with me and went to Florida. I cashed them in for another $50,000 by moving around through the state, cashing a little at a time.

By now I had come to realize that it was going to take me a while to sell off the gold and silver, and while I was a bit anxious about it, I was not going to do anything foolish. I stayed in Florida a year and managed to cash another $100,000 after driving up to DC twice to retrieve my stake.

Then I moved to Texas. I liked the idea of large, populous states where I could blend in, and where banking rules allowed me some freedom.

I found the best place to sell gold was to acquaintances. They would usually buy it for the weight value as it was an investment item for them.

I sold many coins this way, simply by being honourable and cutting the price a touch off the current spot gold price. They saved the fees, and I did too, as well as the scrutiny and paperwork of dealers and pawn shops.

This process was taking a long time. I was now almost four years out from my old job and found I had sold off less than a quarter of my gold and silver.

More and more I wanted to complete the transactions and get out from under any evidence of scrutiny. I started to believe I was being followed, and any untoward glance in my direction sent me into worry.

Of course, my rational mind realized I was just a little anxious. There was no way I could be caught if I just stuck to my plan. But it seemed that my plan for cashing in, was everything I lived for. I had not been able to settle, nor create any roots in any community, and I was rapidly getting to the point where my choices would be limited.

I moved to New York, well, actually New Jersey, but just a quick trip through the Holland Tunnel to Manhattan. The hustle and bustle of the city ground me down and I completed yet another series of transactions and cashed another portion of my take.

I was looking for another place to go, to cash out, and was thinking of Chicago, and researching other jurisdictions where gold was easily bought and sold.

I was tempted to go back to California, perhaps somewhere in the LA area and begin again, this time settling a bit. I rented an apartment and scoped out the city, eventually buying a small house in Orange County, south of the city. I figured the real estate was another way to launder the cash.

I made several trips back east to retrieve my gold and sold it, here and there, by now I'd managed to divest about half of what I owned.

I realized that holding the gold was an investment in itself. So I began to think in terms of how much money I wanted to have as cash or easily convertible investments. I dabbled a bit in the market, and managed a standard sort of return, though that was made up of significant gains and losses rather than slow growth.

I was looking for a place to settle, perhaps to take on a bit of work for some additional cash and I decided to investigate Montana and Idaho. I had considered an overseas location but the issue of language and culture were off-putting. I wanted to put down some roots but wasn't sure where. A city boy at heart I wasn't interested in ranching or farming but property acquisition, with the idea of developing it in 15-20 years captured my imagination.

So I bought some property in Texas and in Florida, just a few acres, and in both cases, not far from existing developments.

I then had the brainwave of developing these small plots into golf courses, as a way to make some cash while the property gained in value over time.

I found myself a couple of entrepreneurs and set up 20-year leases. The courses were local cow pastures, suitable only for beginners, but that was their charm, as they could be run by one or two people and generated a steady cash flow, especially in warm climates.

I arranged to pay off the bank loans on these properties a little ahead of schedule, getting the banks paid in seven years.

I had a notion that I'd laundered the money I'd been paid and that now that seven or eight years had passed, I was free and clear, nobody was going to find the insider trades done so long ago, nor would they trace back the info to me, a long-gone minor cog in government. Though I did cringe a bit every time the news reported insider trading issues or scandals.

Driving out to the golf course one particular day not long after it had opened, I got pulled over for speeding. The police ran my plates and asked me to come into the station, just an inconsistency they wanted cleared up.

Upon arrival, I was sent to an interview room and told to wait. There was a mirror which I expected was a two-way view and that I was being watched. They hadn't even issued a speeding ticket so I was lost to why I had been called in.

"Son, you are Travis William McCharles?"

"Yes. What's this all about sir."

"Truth is, the FBI has a Travis William McCharles on their ten most wanted list. You fit the description well enough."

"And what has this Travis McCharles done?" I was visibly nervous, I tried to control myself and was hyper, thinking that being nervous is a natural reaction, and trying to stop it too obviously might show some guilt.

"Murder, embezzlement, fraud, and a few minor things."

"I can confidently say you have the wrong man. It's not that uncommon a name. In fact, most names are held by hundreds of people."

"And how do you know that?"

"Just search anyone on Google and you'll find dozens of people with the same name, at least you will if its conventional."

The policeman asked me several questions about my doings and movements. He seemed concerned that I had moved around a lot, but I made it seem that I'd just not found my roots yet. He did seem visibly calmer when I mentioned I was developing the golf course property.

"So you are going to settle here in San Antonio?"

"Truth is, I'm not sure. I like Texas. It seems like a good place to invest. I also have a small course in Florida, near Sarasota."

"So you are a developer?"

"Sort of, more of an entrepreneur. Looking to see where I can make a good return in a reasonably short span. The golf courses are my longest play yet. More often I'm in stocks and I've even acted as a middle man for importers, buying the goods overseas and selling them at a small profit to wholesalers in the US."

In Texas, importers were met with suspicion. "I have contacts mostly in California that I have worked with."

The policeman had sent an assistant out of the room while we talked and that person came back and entered the room with a slight shake of his head.

"It appears you are not the Travis McCharles the FBI is after. But we did find you have an outstanding parking ticket in Dallas. I'm going to have to get you to pay that before you get on your way."

I nodded making some excuse that I'd never been issued a ticket, but of course it did not play.

"Given that you've missed the court date, I'd advise you to simply pay the ticket and walk away. I will see what I can do about reducing the late fees and the fee for paying out of jurisdiction.

In the end the ticket came to $60. Relieved, I paid it in cash and took the receipt, looking for reassurances that the payment would remove the apparent offence from my record.

I left the station happy to be free of official scrutiny but also concerned that if I was ever looked at again my shared name might be an issue. I wanted to go back into the station to see if my own license or SSN had been marked as not the man they were looking for, but I decided to stay away.

The perfect crime, was not so perfect as I had thought. I still had substantial assets that still had to be converted to greenbacks and while I had laundered much of the windfall, I had little trust in anyone and no real roots anywhere. My smarts had led me into a life I did not want to live. Not exactly a fugitive, I was consumed by the thought that I would be caught, that I could not explain my wealth very easily and that I had to remain quiet for the rest of my life.

Day to day, that was not a problem. But year by year, even as my scheme faded into the background, I was not the upstanding citizen everyone thought I was, and I could never really let down my guard.

"What's done is done," I often told myself out loud. "Move on, have a life." But friends and family eluded me.

The perfect crime was leading to a life I no longer wanted to live, but could not get out of. I had dated a bit, here and there, but knowing I would move on, especially in the early years of my disbursement, I didn't take anything seriously. As I aged, I wanted more.

I needed a place to settle. Close enough to my two golf course investments that I could keep an eye on them. In a place populated enough that outsiders were accepted. I looked here and there, often getting out a big old map and poking at it. I had it narrowed down to three places. Nashville, Charlotte and Atlanta. I had identified Houston, Columbus and Tampa as well, but they were just lesser options.

I decided to travel to each place and get a sense of it before deciding. I liked the idea of a college town, because those places, especially when they are of moderate size, had a churning turn over of people which suited my purposes.

Nashville was culturally not my cup of tea, though it seemed a good choice. Charlotte also was nice but not quite right, though I couldn't put my finger on it. As I travelled to Atlanta, I considered expanding my search. Dallas maybe, Oklahoma City, Birmingham, or maybe Jacksonville?

None had any appeal. I staying in Atlanta and decided to give an old friend a call to show me around. He was someone I'd gone to school with and hadn't seen in more than 10 years. He was surprised to hear from me and agreed to take me through the city for a day, all he could spare from his job and family.

I drove to his home in the suburban hills, a lovely sprawling place on a big, not quite rural lot, surrounded by large pines and a rolling landscape.

He greeted me at the door, introduced me to his wife and two little kids, who seemed curious that some guy was going to consume the time of their father.

"So Travis, are you considering a move to Atlanta? What business are you in these days? Last I'd heard you were working for the feds in Trade and Commerce."

"Yeah, I left that job a long while ago. Learned a lot there and sort of became an entrepreneur, dabbling in anything that might make me some coin. I'm looking to settle down a bit as I've travelled much of the country in search of a good deal."

"Atlanta is a good choice. It's a big, sprawling city of more than 6 million if you include the suburbs. And we've got almost everything from schools to the arts, to sports and a bunch of corporate head offices. The major downside of Atlanta is that it's hot but that's also good, because it never gets too cold either. We have winter to be sure, but very little snow."

"That's an upside. The humidity in DC was awful. I think it's built on a swamp. Everything around it would be pleasant but DC was a cesspool in the summer. I was just in Charlotte and I was told it gets pretty hot too."

"We are not so bad here in the burbs, there are lots of trees that provide a nice shade. People from other places often comment on it." He turned to his wife, "Remember what your sister said?"

His wife nodded, "She's from Chicago and was amazed at the number of trees we have, even in the city center."

A couple of days in Atlanta and I was hooked. And I'd even found a lovely little property in a suburb that needed a golf course. So I bought a modest home in an older suburb and drove out each day to supervise the construction of my course. Nine holes on an old horse farm to start, with an option to expand to 18. Nothing fancy, and easily maintained.

As a golf course superintendent, greenskeeper and manager, I spent most of my time working the course, especially for the first two years. I did a little stock speculation on the side. And investigated other avenues of making a bit of money, but my course took almost all of my time.

In the third season, I hired a couple of college kids to help with the course maintenance, and made plans to expand to 18 holes. I found it impossible to get away back north to cash some more of my gold, and equally difficult to get to my other properties in Texas and Florida, just to have a look around, as they were rented to the operators. And those operators were faithful in making their rental payments, and I was happy to keep the rents reasonable.

Still, I wasn't too concerned, as taking the job in Atlanta allowed my investments to grow and my comfort level to rise. By now I was over 30 and had established some roots in the Atlanta area.

I had a girlfriend and life was chugging along nicely. I decided to go north to sell a little gold and bring some back to sell in Atlanta. Not much really, but enough to leave only the amount of gold I wanted to hold as an investment.

I calculated I had liquidated almost $3.5 million in gold over the years and that I still held nearly that amount of money in cash and land investments, despite paying my living expenses all those years.

I was a bit concerned as I was going to take 100 ounces out. Cash 10 there, cash 10 more on my way south and bring the rest to Atlanta to cash a bit at a time.

Leaving the bank in DC, I reached for the door handle of my car when a voice called my name. I turned almost involuntarily and saw my accomplice from years ago, approaching me on foot.

I smiled and straightened up. "Mr. Smith, how are you doing? Imagine seeing you here."

"I barely made it, Travis. I paid the bank manager a tidy sum to let me know if you came into the bank."

"I haven't been here in several years."

"I know. Listen, I know we had a deal, and I must admit I cashed in pretty well thanks to you. How have you been?"

"Okay I guess. Well, the truth is, I find I can't settle down anywhere. Not that I'm paranoid but I just haven't found my calling."

"I'm a little skint these days. I was wondering if you had any other insider tips, I might use."

"Sorry Mr. Smith, I left the Commerce Department not long after our deal was completed. I have no contacts there. I just live modestly, taking jobs here and there."

Smith nodded and backed up a step. "Listen Travis, I'm a bit desperate. I'm going to have to turn you in, unless you give me some of the windfall you received. That's what you're here to retrieve, right?"

"Mr. Smith we had a deal."

"And now we will have another one."

I stood there wondering what to do. Last thing I needed was attention or some sort of a scene in the parking lot.

“Okay, what do you want?”

“I’m told you just cashed 10 ounces of gold. That’s what, about 30 grand, these days?”

I nodded.

“I’ll take 20k and leave you alone. That should get me back on my feet.”

I thought of the additional gold I still had in this branch in a safety deposit box and realized any effort to retrieve it was being watched. I had to think quickly.

“I have no cash on me. The gold transactions take a few days. Your insider will verify that.”

“Then write me a cheque.”

“I don’t have any cheques with me.” He looked at me sort of desperately. I was beginning to think I might walk away.

“Then I’ll take the car.”

“I’ll just report it stolen.”

“No you won’t. I’ll implicate you.”

“Doesn’t matter, the statute of limitations has passed.”

“You know the feds, they’ll dream up some other charge.” He pointed to the Georgia plates. “Taking the proceeds of crime across state lines.”

I caved. “Look, I took all of my gold out of here so all I can offer you is a small amount and trust that will help you get past your present difficulties.”

I had put the gold coins in various pockets to spread out their weight. I reached into my pocket and pulled out a small envelope with 10 gold coins.

“There are 10 gold coins in here, worth more than $30 k. That should be sufficient to conclude our business.”

I could see the wheels working in his brain. He knew I must have more, significantly more, but he would have to threaten me from a very weak position, unless of course he pulled a gun. I held the envelope out to him and rattled it a bit.

He took it, commented on how heavy it was and thanked me for helping him and being more than reasonable. I took the complement and wished him well, grabbing at the door handle and quickly exiting the bank lot before he could do anything else.

I was furious as I drove away. I had been robbed. I was now under some scrutiny by thieves and probably worse. He had seen my license plate. I had to move, I thought. And even though I had decided to leave 50 more gold coins in the safety deposit box how could I get them out without being tipped off.

He must live or work near here, or he couldn't get here quick enough to catch me, I thought. But how did he know this is the bank I used to hide the stuff? He must have tracked me right after the pay off.

"Fuck, how could I have been so stupid." I yelled at the dash.

I had a lengthy drive back to Atlanta to decide what to do.

The first thing I did was purchase a fire arm. I contemplated selling out and leaving Atlanta, but I would have to hide, all the worse for knowing they are looking for you.

So I waited. A year later Smith came looking for me. Fortunately, I was tipped off when the kid in the pro shop said an over dressed guy had come around asking after me.

The next day Smith showed up at my front door. We talked and soon enough Smith demanded more money. I told him he needed to get himself together and suggested he look for another mark inside the Commerce Department.

He appeared to consider it. I maneuvered Smith onto the back deck when I went in to retrieve the gold. He appeared to have no idea that I might turn on him.

I did.

Two bullets. One in the back of his head, another in his chest, just to make sure, though a scan of his cranial injuries probably rendered the second bullet wasted.

I wrapped his body in a bed sheet and dragged it under the deck. Covered it in a thick coat of lime and waited. That evening, I took the keys to his rental car and drove it through the back streets as far as I could without passing a major intersection, one that might be covered with traffic cameras. I managed to get a few miles out, and walked back, taking a divergent route in case anyone saw me.

Back home I started digging in the back yard the next evening. I was going to put in a bit of garden in the otherwise austere acre. The lots out here in the suburbs were nicely spaced. I stopped at an appropriate time and started up again the next day, working hard, but not during unusual hours.

I checked the body. Nothing seemed amiss so I stretched the 'garden' dig out another day. As the sun went down, I had managed to dig down more than three feet. Just after midnight, I put another few minutes into digging a bit deeper, and very quickly managed a trench another six inches deep. I dragged the body, which stunk as soon as I moved it, and got it in the hole. I covered the body with enough lime and dirt to look like I was still in the business of building a larger garden, making sure the remaining hole was only about a foot deep.

The next day, I enlarged the garden and used the dirt to fill in the grave. A s I worked I managed to create a small garden in the back corner, about 20 feet by 10 with the grave in the back, left corner. It was arched along the side fence, widened in the corner and arced to a point along the back fence.

I planted an oak tree in front of the grave, out from the fence enough to allow it the necessary space to grow. A few native bushes and some flowers and the garden was complete. None of my neighbours said anything. I then decided to build another small garden in the front, to make it look like I was working on the landscaping of the property.

Of course, I considered if Smith might have partners or accomplices, but I never heard tell of any, nor did I receive any indication of somebody snooping around. I figured the rental company retrieved their car, wrote off the abandonment and moved on. While the police were likely involved in finding the car, with no missing person reported there was no cause for investigation.

Still, I was wary, looking for a second accomplice. I decided after a few years to retrieve the last of my gold and if necessary, sell out in Atlanta and move to Florida. I still held the lease on the property in Florida and the course operators were talking of buying the land. Being in the property development business, I had named a premium price as developments had creeped closer to the property over the years, but it seemed a long way off to when the property might become valuable.

The retrieval of the gold went perfectly. I left the safety deposit box empty, thinking it prudent and deciding to close it over the phone a year later.

The tree was growing in the garden, and the other plants had taken shape. While everything seemed peaceful, I couldn't shake the feeling of being watched. I couldn't live this way, and decided to sell out in Atlanta and Florida and try to disappear into the great unwashed in some unlikely place. I considered foreign countries but the lack of regular status worried me. I thought of becoming a reverse snow bird, moving to Canada and coming back to the States in winter.

The tree grew. I avoided complications and connections. My seemingly perfect crime and devolved into a perfect murder, with only my conscience and my fear remaining. I had little conscience about Smith, he had threatened me and I was justified. But the nagging concern that he wasn't alone never left my head.

After a time, I sold my home in Atlanta, hoping the body would never be discovered. I sold my property in Florida and in Texas, for a nice profit. I started to consolidate my bank accounts and investments into a more manageable arrangement.

I moved to Sacramento, California and bought some property, thinking of doing the golf course thing again. I was pretty good at it, building short, simple courses for families and new golfers. Too many courses were aimed at the high-end player, but the relative costs, ease of maintenance, and desire for a quick sale made the lower end stuff ideal. Throw in a driving range and a mini-putt course and I was making money.

I asked my girlfriend if she wanted to move with me, but I knew she wouldn't, as she had family all over the Atlanta area. Our relationship had been nice but it was not deep, and we parted ways fairly easily. I told her

A Novel Idea

I was moving north to be closer to family and had sold my Georgia and Florida investment properties.

I'd selected a spot in Sacramento southeast of town near the airport, figuring that land there would gain in value quicker than other spots. The land was flat and barren, and dry. That was my major concern as golf courses needed water and water was scarce.

I was able to get the zoning for the course by promising to only water tees and greens, which meant I was building an executive style course with almost every hole a par three. Perfect.

I didn't attempt to look up any of my previous acquaintances in the San Jose area and settled in, hoping to finally dig some roots.

The weight of my adventures was heavy, but slowly lifted as the golf course business took off and I opened another similar course to the north west of town. The courses could be operated and maintained by a small staff, usually two or three people, though I had a few part timers who relieved my regulars from time to time.

All my investments were concentrated north of San Francisco. I had sold out in Texas, Florida and Georgia and had no reason to return to DC. I breathed a little, but once all those transactions were completed, I moved house, just to put a little distance between me and the address of the seller in the property transactions.

I had it in my head to move again, just to be safe, but realized that I would likely never be completely rid of my past actions. I had to let them go.

And so I did. I took a long trip after Christmas, a month in England, to clear my head, to plot a course moving forward. I decided I wanted a family and I needed a vocation, something to compel me to push forward everyday.

I even considered moving to England or some other country but in the end such a move had little long-term appeal. Even Sacramento seemed wrong to me and I thought of moving north, but there really wasn't a place that seemed comfortable. I wanted to be nowhere near DC. My life style had centered around small-time golf courses for much of the last 15 years, and I was now approaching 40.

I decided to set up shop as a golf course management consultant, taking contracts on building, setting up, and operating small golf related businesses, like driving ranges, mini putts and local executive style courses.

Turned out there was a business there, although it started slowly. I divested myself of my own courses, making a tidy sum. And as my business grew, I could live anywhere. I settled on Dallas as a nice central location for my business which included not a small amount of travel.

I kept my consulting fees reasonable, not so low as to appear desperate, but on the low end as I really wanted the work to be steady. I worked out of a cell phone and a website, with no office.

On one particular job I met the sister-in-law of the course developer, who had taken a job with her brother-in-law as the front person for the operation. She and I worked fairly closely as we put together the course and I schooled her on maintenance, staffing and all the little things that go into small course operations.

Our friendship blossomed and eventually she moved in with me. I was wary of the marriage commitment, mostly because I could not shake the feeling that roots made me a target.

On one hand I was pretty sure I was free and clear, but on the other hand, I always had an eye looking over my shoulder for the unusual or concerning. Everything that popped up in that regard was fine, even if it shook me. I was recognized by one of the two guys to whom I'd sold my first Texas course. I'd been out on a site visit and he was there as he wanted to sell some of his old maintenance equipment. The new course was happy to get some necessary mowers on the cheap.

"Travis, nice to see you. How have you been."

When his voice boomed out as I walked to the construction trailer, I jumped. Turning slowly toward the voice I tried to settle into as casual a frame of mind as I could. Fortunately, I recognized him quickly and we fell into conversation. I wanted to see if anyone had ever come looking for me at his location, but a couple of weak efforts to push the conversation that way were fruitless so I didn't try harder, again, not wanting to tip him off that I thought nefarious types would be looking for me.

"I'm good Rick. Nice to see you. Are you still operating Breezy Pines?"

"I am, and I've opened four more courses in the San Antonio and Houston areas. It's a good business."

I agreed with him, noting that I'd moved into consulting, which is why I was on site.

We chatted briefly about potential add-ons to the business, especially the driving ranges, which he did not like because of the large amount of property they required. He leaned much more to mini putt.

I realized right then that my criminal life had become mundane and while I was likely clear of any follow up by law enforcement, I would forever be wary of any official contacts. My perfect crime had succeeded but the cost was my peace of mind, and the fear of a tap on the shoulder.

Chapter Twenty-six

Three weeks later, Markus was sitting in the coffee shop when I arrived. Theresa was only a few minutes late. He had been keeping us up to speed on Brandon's progress and today was the day we were going to visit him in hospital. He'd come out of the coma a week before and had been transferred out of intensive care.

We all took a cab to the downtown hospital. These places made me anxious as I had spent a lot of time here after my father's stroke. He never really recovered and a series of additional strokes eventually killed him, a few years later.

Brandon's room was festooned with flowers and other nicknacks of home. His mother had cleared off for the morning to give us some space to visit. I think she was really just downstairs in the coffee shop biding her time, but we appreciated the gesture.

Brandon was watching television when we got there, a book by his side with a bookmark just a few pages deep.

"Hey," Theresa said as she entered. We all came through the door with wide, forced smiles. Brandon smiled weakly.

"Thanks for coming. I need a few different faces."

"How are you feeling?"

"I could make a joke or point out that I'm basically a prisoner here, but the truth is, not great, but a bit better every day."

"How long are you going to be here, any idea?"

"Doctors aren't sure. They are guessing another two weeks at least but making no promises. It's all about being able to get around. My total recovery time is likely to be measured in months. I'm not even expected to report into the office on my progress, for at least two more months."

"Wow!" I said, "But there is light at the end of the tunnel?"

"I guess, but my dream of being an NFL linebacker is over." Brandon remained straight faced, but Markus broke up. That seemed to relieve the tension. "My mom has been here every day and my dad drops by in the evening, which gives her a bit of time to take care of the home front."

"So what happened?"

"I got hit by a car."

"Yeah, I get that. What happened?" Only Markus could be so blunt.

There was still a machine for blood pressure and heart rate attached to Brandon. They beeped like an ellipsis between the questions.

"I wish I knew. I can't remember much actually. Apparently, I left work and made a left turn out of the office driveway, and was t-boned by someone driving very fast. The driveway is at the top of a small rise, and while you can see the cars approaching, their speed is disguised by the elevation, or so the police told me."

"The other guy?"

"Walked away. A few cuts and bruises. Airbags work apparently. He was charged with dangerous driving. I got a ticket for making an unsafe left turn. Three points and $75."

"What's the last thing you remember?" Theresa chimed in.

Brandon looked at her, seemingly for the first time. "I know you." And then he switched his gaze to me. "And I know you, for sure."

I felt a little awkward, but Markus reminded Brandon who we were and of our trip to Philadelphia a month before his accident. Brandon nodded, admitting he'd forgotten about the trip until it had been mentioned.

"I remember the office and the project I was working on, but the details remain hazy, as there was little of consequence to focus on, before the accident. I do remember Philly now that you mention it.

He looked at Theresa, "You were at a fashion show." He looked at me. "And you, you were there too."

'So was I," said Markus. "I trust you remember me?"

"Oh yeah, you are my brother John."

Markus made a strange sound but Brandon, beat him to it. "I'm kidding, you are my cousin Chuck." He waited a heartbeat, and laughed. "You're my friend and cousin Markus. We grew up together. Same schools, same friends, including these two lovely ladies."

Markus looked visibly relieved. "Well, it sounds as if all the important stuff is still in your scrambled brains. Have the doctors cleared you of brain damage?"

Brandon nodded, "They say I had a major concussion, that's one of the reasons the curtains are drawn, sunlight is a bit of an issue. But it's getting better."

We chatted a time, bringing Brandon back into our lives, explaining who we were and how he knew us. More often than not, he would nod at a tidbit of information as if it was clearing the cobwebs in his mind.

"So you are a writer? He said looking at me. "Have I read anything you've written?"

"Mostly I work in corporate communications as a freelance contractor. There are a lot of businesses who need people like me but are too small to employ someone full time."

"She writes novels on the side."

"Oh, I could use a few novels right now." I promised to bring him one the next time we visited.

At that point Brandon's mother came into the room. Being his Aunt she of course knew Markus and was introduced to Theresa and I.

"You are the clothing designer that is working with Chuck. I've heard about you and the show you attended in Philadelphia. Brandon was impressed with your designs. Okay, he was really impressed with the interest in your designs."

"Yes, I was, now that I think of it. People were very interested in them," Brandon said. "But I'm sitting right here, mother."

"Yes you are, but you have some memory lapses."

We all chatted amiably about the care Brandon had received and his prognosis, before we left with a promise to return early the next week.

We went our separate ways, with me catching a subway, Markus heading downtown and Theresa to her hybrid office and manufacturing space in Brooklyn.

We planned our usual coffee meeting and another visit to Brandon for the following week.

Once home I sat down to punch out a few words to begin my latest genre effort but I found the words came easily and I managed much more than I had intended.

Chapter Twenty-seven

Her head bounced with an unworldly crunch. The sound of a head hitting stone, was something I'd never heard before, and did not want to hear again. It rolled over twice and lay rocking, trying to find an equilibrium. Fortunately, I could not see the eyes.

And we were all expected to carry on as if everything was all fine, normal, everyday. And, in a way it was. The Queen was apparently engaged in an affair, and was eliminated, executed by royal decree. What that affair was: sexual, treasonous, or something else, was never spoken aloud.

To us, as staff in the royal household, we were largely unaffected, but wary, as it was obvious that there were spies everywhere. Even the slightest indiscretion was avoided and we walked and talked carefully.

A Novel Idea

When the King announced he was going on a Royal tour we were all quite relieved. Without a king to tend to, things around the castle would be much more relaxed.

However, I was selected to attend the King, despite my lowly position, or perhaps because of it, and made ready to travel with him. I said my good-byes to those I knew around the castle that were not travelling, and we left two days later.

The King took the lead position in the procession. I realized four miles from the castle that it was entirely for show. Once away, a strong guard of 20 armed knights took the lead, with a dozen out about a quarter mile in front as a lead guard. The rest stuck with the King and appeared to be chatting with him. Behind that were several more lightly armed men, archers for the most part, and following on were the attendants, then the baggage train. It was difficult for me to see how long the train was, as it stretched out of sight. Of course, sightlines were not long, as no road or track ever went straight for very long through the countryside.

I was a minor attendant of the King, a scribe really, often called in to write a letter, make a note about something he wanted to deal with later, or merely provide a foil for him to think.

He was a large man, a bit corpulent as he moved out of his youth, but strong, agile and scary in a physical sense and because of the power he commanded at his own hand, and by his word. The former Queen knew that first hand.

I wondered if we were going to camp for the night, but was quickly disabused of that notion when we were announced at Windsor Castle, which rose up on a high point of land not far from the river.

Fortunately, I had not said anything of my thinking to any around me, keeping my thoughts to myself, and our sojourn at Windsor was entirely expected. And I avoided looking foolish. It took a day just to get settled in the castle, and though I had no idea of our length of stay, it was obviously going to be of some time.

On the third day I was summoned to the King.

"A lovely place Windsor," he said after greeting me with a nod. "I really should come here more often, but it is just far enough from the Tower to be inconvenient."

"It is my first time, My Lord."

He raised an eyebrow, "Is it. How long have you been in my service?"

"Since you spoke with my grandsire, Sir William Makepeace, a bit more than a year ago."

"Ah Makepeace, there's a fine gentleman. Have you heard anything of him lately? I believe I'd heard he was sick."

"He fell off his horse, My Lord. Broke an arm and damaged his liver. He's recovering well, I'm told. My mother and father live with him near Bury St. Edmonds. My father is his steward."

"A knight falling off a horse is not a good look, my boy. Let's just say he was thrown."

I gulped, the King was right, I should never have let on that my grandsire was a weakened older man. I kicked myself mentally for the mistake.

"Yes, Your Grace. In fact, I do believe he was trying to break a young foal, that had henceforth appeared quite docile."

"That's the spirit, my boy. Now get your quill ready, I have a bit of work for you to attend."

The King wanted me to write him a letter to the Earl of Bath, saying he would be in progress to that city in three weeks. The King never said, or asked for lodging. It was inherent in his message of arrival.

"Add a few flowery lines to the bottom and send it off in the name of Sir Thomas Cromwell, my chief minister."

"Yes, my lord."

"And please come back tomorrow after Terce as I will have some notes you need to take."

I bowed and retreated from the Royal presence. Two men swung their shoulders to get past me as I left through the narrow hallway. I heard the echo of the King giving them a rousing greeting.

I spent the rest of the day composing the letter and searching out the chief minister to affix his seal. Once that was complete, I wandered the public areas of the castle and marvelled at its size. I did see the king in the distance, as I walked out of the forecourt garden, he was speaking with a few attendants, including a few ladies, some distance away in the large walled space.

The next morning, I announced myself to his guard and was shortly escorted into his rooms. He had just completed dressing for the day and was being fitted for some new armour.

"Ah, there you are young Makepeace. You have come prepared I trust."

I nodded and looked for a small desk I had seen the previous day. "May I sit to write, My Lord?"

"Of course, of course." He clapped his hands and an attendant slipped into another room and with a few helpers, brought in a small writing table and chair.

I thanked the king profusely, and took my spot, my pen held in ready.

"First make a note to the chapel builders here at Windsor to lengthen the size of the building. It is currently too short in the nave. I'd like it to be wider as well, but given that the foundations are done, I think we will have to pass on that. I want the building completed without delay. So, a second note must go to the Minister of the Exchequer, to authorize funds to speed construction of the building."

He went on to dictate letters to his chief minister regarding military preparations for the castle, and two notes to ladies who accompanied him on his garden walk the previous day. He thanked them for their attention and asked to walk with them again.

"The letter to Bath has gone?"

"Yes, My Lord, I committed it to the rider last evening, once Sir Thomas had affixed his seal."

"Excellent. I do love it here, but I need to get a better feel for my realm. I have reports that all is not well in the north."

"You are well loved My Lord. The kingdom is secure and people are prosperous."

"Aye, but there are rumors in the North. Have you heard any of them?"

I grew wary, having never been taken into the King's confidence before, I immediately wondered if this was a trap.

"No, my Lord, I hear very little from outside the castle, save when I speak to the riders delivering the mail."

"So that is how you know my people are pleased with me?"

"I suppose My Lord, I never really thought of it that way. The couriers I speak with have good things to say. Should I speak with them further to search out anything else they may know?"

"Never mind. Just be aware that there is a great swirl of things going on outside the castle walls. And verily, if you hear such rumours, please pass them on to my attendants or me directly."

I nodded, "Did you enjoy your walk in the garden forecourt yesterday?"

The King looked at me abruptly, "You knew I was there?"

"Yes, my Lord. There are your notes," I nodded to a pile of papers. "I was also there, leaving the garden, I noticed your party at the far wall. I was taking the time to become familiar with the castle."

Henry softened. "Thank you for your honesty. I am afraid that I am sometimes unaware of the notoriety of my presence. It comes from being left on my own so much as a child. One becomes used to being ignored in certain circumstances. I shall be more aware in future."

I nodded and took my leave, going immediately to write the notes and have them delivered. I could not help but think that much was happening in the kingdom that I was unaware of, and I chided myself, much as the King had chided himself. I thought I should ask more questions and be more concerned with things I heard, but then I might be considered a spy, and that had its own consequences. Still, as a spy for the King, I might be of use to him and perhaps even rise to a more trusted position.

And while that notion warmed me, I quickly realized that those who came too close to the King, or knew too much, often ended badly.

A few weeks later the King moved on to Bath by way of Salisbury. He took the time to visit Old Sarum. The ruins gave him pause.

"It's all dust," I heard him say. I was in the group of attendants that climbed to the top of the tor with him, but I held back, ready to be summoned at any moment.

He and his confidents trooped around the remnants of the Cathedral, robbed of most of its stone since it was moved into the town below.

We stayed three days at Salisbury where the Bishop provided a guest house for the King, as the rest of his retinue found what accommodation they could. Stewards were unwilling to unpack everything only to pack it back up shortly, as word had gone out that we would shortly be proceeding to Bath.

Henry of course knew this, but didn't much care, though his requirements for his stay, seemed sparce and limited. He met with the Bishop. He met with local nobles, and made ready to depart.

We ignored the rock pile of Stonehenge and headed west to Bath, taking two days to get there.

The King proceeded into the city like a conquering hero, with citizens lining the streets as he made his way to the new Abbey church that was nearing completion.

"These people seem to have unlimited funds."

Riding beside the king, a guardsman said, "The old Minister is slated to be restored. It is much larger than the new abbey church."

The King was in deep consideration as he looked around the city. Placed by the Bishop in his own dwelling, the King met with the usual round of local nobility, churchmen and even a prosperous merchant or two.

I wandered the town and marvelled at the Roman bath complex that had been embellished by local works. It was obvious the town relied on the bath complex which drew travellers from great distances.

Standing near the great pool, a man sidled up beside me. "It is nice to see the King here in Sussex. We so rarely see the Royal personages, and sometimes wonder if they really exist."

I turned and saw what appeared to be an older man, likely a merchant. "The King is trying to give people the opportunity to see his Royal Majesty, to feel as one with the great seal of the kingdom."

"Well, that's good I suppose. Rumours and speculation abound here in the hinterlands. The execution of the Queen was a shock to us all."

"And a shock to her no doubt. And hopefully to any traitors or intrigues that might still flourish."

"Do you come often to Bath? I live here much of the time but take a lengthy journey to London, going into Kent one year and Yorkshire the next."

He had mistaken me for a merchant. I was about to set him straight but knew that if I confessed to being in the King's service, he would be a changed person. So I spoke without lying, "I reside in London and rarely get out to the countryside."

"So you are used to seeing the King about?"

"Well, he doesn't make himself public in London often, staying usually at Westminster or the Tower."

"The word is he is shoring up support in the shires. I've always wondered about this approach, as no one involved in any intrigue is going to show themselves during such a Royal Progress."

"I suppose not. What do you hear in your travels?"

The man looked about, but spoke mildly, "There are concerns with some public needs. They have been ignored in the past decades as the nobles fought among themselves. The King, it appears, is popular, at least in the places I go. But there are those who are fiercely opposed to the new Church of England and think the King a heretic."

"And yet the issue is solved and the King placid in his application, save to his chief ministers, or so I've been told."

"In London, too be sure. But in some paces where the King's authority holds less weight there are many who seek to return to Rome. They are not obvious, but they exist, and perhaps in numbers that may surprise you."

"Indeed."

I parted from my merchant acquaintance and returned to my encampment. There I was given a message from the King to attend him the next morning and bring my paper and quills.

"Ah there you are young Makepeace," he said, freshly scrubbed and filled with breakfast. He sipped a cup of mead, the preferred drink of court as its fermented nature rarely upset the stomach.

"I have audience with a number of merchants who have petitioned me. I'd like you to sit with me and take note of their concerns so we may address them later."

The doors of the Bishop's chambers opened and a flood of perhaps 20 men moved in, and were stopped by guards some 20 feet from the dais where the King sat.

"Greetings men of England. The King is keen to know your minds. Your leader may approach the chair."

And one man moved forward and with a bow, said, "Your Majesty. Profound greetings from us, the merchants of Sussex. We would like to address a great need. Bridges, roads, direction posts and distance markers are in grave disrepair. We would like the Crown to advance some funds to fix these issues."

The King said nothing. He tilted back his head as if thinking. "Explain the need, good sir."

The man spluttered a little, "Travellers have become lost as ancient markings crumble. On at least two great bridges, one over the Severn near Gloucester and another over the Avon near Amesbury north of Salisbury, the piers are weak and while they are still in use, should they collapse, it would be catastrophe."

"Would not rivermen take their place?"

"No doubt they would my lord, but given the traffic that uses these routes, all commerce would be choked and goods would become more expensive to cover payments to the ferryman."

"And what of the cost of the bridges?"

"None would object to a small toll, my lord, if it meant getting the bridges rebuilt and strong. The Crown can wait on its return of costs much longer than a man. A tiny toll would eventually return the expense to the Crown and if kept in place, would add to the Royal coffers."

"What about local lords and those more intimately engaged with these areas?"

"By all means Sire, use these men as you see fit, they would benefit from the enhanced commerce as well."

The King turned to me, "Makepeace? Make a note to send letters to nearby nobles to propose a meeting to get these works completed. We will send out a royal representative for the conference. We would entertain a toll arrangement in return for construction. And as for local markers and such, a general note to all landowners requiring them to restore land markings within a year, and to repair roads that traverse their lands."

As I listened to the proceedings, I noticed the merchant I had spoken to was staring at me. I smiled at him to reduce his fears.

A number of other petitioners paraded through the double doors and found the King engaging, questioning, prudent and apparently willing to make what changes they required to various laws, statutes and personnel.

Dismissed by the King to begin a large number of letters that must go out in his name, I left the Bishop's chambers. Just outside the building I saw the merchant, who had already spied me and was moving briskly in my direction.

"Ah, my friend you are a king's man, a scribe it appears."

"I am, and a busy one after all of that. Who knew how busy things were in the shires?"

"I am afraid I mistook you for a merchant yesterday and I must confess I am concerned about what I told you regarding the acceptance of new Church."

"Fear not sir, I have not said anything to the King as what you said was perhaps not surprising, once some thought had been applied to the situation. I can, if you would like, arrange to have you speak to one of the King's advisors, one of Thomas Cromwell's men."

"I thought I already had."

I smiled, "No, no. I am merely a scribe to the King. He barely knows my name."

"Ah, but he does know it."

"I must leave you, as the King will want to see the letters by tomorrow. What would you have me do?"

"At present, nothing. But let me think on it. Speaking to someone in the King's circle might relieve my conscience. I will seek you out tomorrow."

And with that I left, wondering if I should speak to one of Cromwell's men myself to ascertain the interest the great man might have in exploring what the merchant had to say. Deep down, it seemed obvious there would be pockets of resistance to the New Church and that those pockets would be especially popular outside the confines of officialdom, where the veneer of royal authority was a bit thinner.

I managed to write the letters with enough time to have Cromwell look at them before they were set before the King for his approval. It was dark however, and Cromwell's man simply took the papers and said he would follow up if anything needed to be restated.

"I am, of course, at your service."

I left the hall, walking slowly through the flickering torch lights. It was not often I saw such fires, as the great run of people could not afford such extravagance nor wanted to take the chance of a general fire, but the King's business never ceased, and so the Bishop's hall was alight.

Once out on the street, there were a few torches lit at street corners but only nearby to the King's dwelling. Each torch was attended by an armed swordsman, ceremonial perhaps, but wary and able to raise an alarm if needed.

I recognized one such guard from the Tower, and was familiar with him, having chatted as we made our way from Windsor to Salisbury.

"Ah, Mr. Makepeace, what are you doing out on such a dark night?"

"The King's business, as I expect you know. He has much to say and many people to say it to."

"You have seen Cromwell then?"

"Not a few moments ago I was in his chamber, but no, I did not see him."

"He is wary, tis said, there's trouble afoot."

"There is aways trouble afoot, or at least the fear of it. Otherwise, you might not have a job."

The guard laughed. "Aye. Still, in these provincial towns, tis hard to know one thing from another."

And Makepeace moved on with a wave, heading to his tent along the river. He had perhaps a half a mile to walk without any but the half moon light. People moving to and fro made the way seem less foreboding.

And then he was approached with a wave. It was the merchant from earlier.

"Hail there, King's man."

I stopped and let him approach. He came at me with a smile and said he'd been thinking on our conversation.

"I should like you to introduce me to Cromwell. As I have said I have urgent business with him."

"Well, sir, I cannot get you into Cromwell but I can introduce you to one of his secretaries, who shall hear your report and decide what steps are next."

Having said I would be at the Bishop's House early the next morning, I arranged to meet him there when my business with Cromwell and the King were complete.

And sure enough, he awaited me across the cobbled street from the Bishop's residence, lingering in a portico and making himself known once I stepped into the open air.

"Come with me. What is your name, good sir?"

"I am William, William St. Albans, as that is my home city, or was when I was young."

And so I took the man inside and confronted a King's guard. "You know me, sir, and this is my acquaintance, William St. Albans, who was in the merchant's delegation at yesterday's audience with the King. He seeks urgently to make himself known to Thomas Cromwell."

The guard nodded, and looked at a squire sitting against the wall. With a nod the squire rose and moved back into the depths of the House. We moved out of the way and stood against the opposite wall, waiting.

Soon enough the squire returned and beckoned us to him. He led us inside the next set of doors and into a side chamber, likely the guard-house and once the public cloakroom.

"Wait."

I was not expecting Cromwell himself, and I was not surprised. One of Cromwell's junior clerks, entered the room, his face tilted back in a mask of arrogance, but his body movements indicating his unease.

"I am the King's scribe, Thomas Makepeace. I have become acquainted with this man who has asked for an audience with Sir Thomas regarding urgent information he is privy to."

"Well, do go on then," said the clerk, his squeak belying his haughty demeanor.

"Um, ah, well, sir . . . " St. Albans turned to me. "You are certain this is the correct person I should be speaking to?"

"At this point it is the only person you can speak to."

"Well, um. At great personal danger to myself, I want to inform you, I mean the King, that there is a plot brewing against him."

"Sir, is that all? There are plots brewing all the time. This is not news."

"Details then. It is the Bishop here, who is taking the measure of the King and his retinue is in league to hatch an attempt on him in the next stage of his journey, or perhaps the one after that."

"The King has not said where he will go next."

"The plot knows he will go to Gloucester. And after that, the small market town of Stratford."

"I see," said the clerk. "And what of the plot?"

"They have arranged to capture or kill the King and restore the Church of Rome as the religion of England. They have already received dispensation from his Holy Father in Rome to act against the heretic, their words not mine."

"And how will this act be carried out?"

"The conspiracy is studying the King's Progress to decide. It is likely to be a swift ambush along the road, but if no suitable place can be found, alternative approaches have not been ruled out."

"Who is behind this plot?"

"The Yorkist, Baron Henry Pole. He has a distant claim, as you well know."

The clerk paused, considering the words of St. Albans. "I should like you to remain in contact with me, as we progress. I shall tell the chief Minister of your concerns. You should inform me of any additional details as they come to your attention."

The merchant nodded with a slight bow. "I am risking much already being here. And further, I had planned to be on the road with the King's retinue as they move to Gloucester, where I have business. But from there I will journey to Amesbury and then London with a group of other merchants. If I changed those plans, I would be suspect."

"As you wish. Thank you for your help and if necessary, speak to Mr. Makepeace here. That will keep you a distance from explicit contact."

The clerk left the room, and St. Albans made ready to leave, but asked conduct to another door of the Bishops House to disguise his presence. Seeing no issue, I agreed to accompany him. He knew his way.

As we moved through the House, past guards and members of the court, I noticed St. Albans walking particularly slowly and looking at each room and passageway with some attention.

My senses up, I hurried him along the corridor, down some steps into a dank basement and out a delivery passageway in the back of the stately home, with the Avon River flowing not 100 feet away. There were no guards.

At the door, he gave a quick look around and with a wave, headed north away from the Abbey Church and into a copse of trees and bushes framing the Bishops House. I certainly wondered if I'd ever hear from him again, and turned, retraced our steps and decided to find the clerk, to whom we had spoken and inform him of the unguarded back passage.

As I did, I was summoned by Cromwell himself who directed me to make changes to two of the letters I had written, and bring them back to him immediately.

Thomas Cromwell was not without humor but he used it sparingly. Generally, he was a difficult task master, likely because he acted for the King, who was his equal in that regard. With the intrigues of the court swirling around him, Cromwell was on point all the time.

"Mr. Makepeace, my thanks for turning such a volume of work back to me so quickly. The King was pleased."

"My duty sir, and my pleasure. I serve at the pleasure of the King, and yourself, of course."

Cromwell nodded and seemed to be taking me in. He turned his head and with a slight wave dismissed me. I could not hold back.

"Sir, when I was summoned, I was on my way to seek out one of your clerks, to whom I had presented an informant who approached me yesterday."

Cromwell turned back to me, his eyes at attention.

"I wanted to inform your clerk that my acquaintance asked to be let out of this place by an alternative doorway, so as not to be seen. That passageway appeared to be storage and delivery way, through the back of the manor." Cromwell said nothing but remained looking at me. "This man appeared to know the House well, well enough to know the passage. And, sir, the passage was unguarded. We saw nobody from the time we entered the basement, nor along the passages, nor at the back exit."

"Thank you, Mr. Makepeace. Please inform my clerk of your doings, but do not mention to him that you have spoken to me. I don't want him thinking you've broken protocol."

I thanked Cromwell and left him to complete the rewritten letters he had asked for, once I had spoken to the clerk. I returned with the letters for Cromwell and asked if I was needed.

"For the King. No. But Mr. Makepeace, Sir Thomas has asked to see you."

Brought before the Chief Minister he seemed pleased to see me, saying, "I would like you to keep your eyes and ears open, especially as you already have some knowledge of the plots surrounding the King. An extra set of senses can only help."

Later that day, word was handed down that the King's Party would proceed to Gloucester on the next stage of its Progress. It was quite the effort by those making it, to truss up all the Kings needs and begin the long procession north.

In time we would stop in Kingwood Abbey but not unpack the train. Immediately the next morning we resumed our travel, expecting to reach Gloucester by evening. The monks seemed relieved. I was wary and watching most of the time, especially as we approached towns and after we left them.

The villagers came out of their homes and walked down to the road to watch the King's passage. He spent some time riding and greeting those he passed, but soon grew tired and retired to a covered carriage. Cromwell and two knights rode with him.

As the sun set, we entered Gloucester and proceeded to the Cathedral close, where the King's Party would stop for several days. Again, the Bishop made space, giving up his lodgings to the King.

I was expected in the audience hall the next day. I was charged with taking some notes on local complaints, including a petition for a major bridge on the Severn. The King had it in mind to demand the work be undertaken by the local lord, and granted the right to toll the bridge once it was built.

Local ferrymen complained the bridge would kill their business, but the King bade them find other places to ferry people, and gave them King's license to ply their trade where ever they saw fit on the River Severn.

Once the audience ended Cromwell himself beckoned me aside.

"Mr. Makepeace, your informant's prediction did not come to pass."

"He said it could be on the leg of the journey just passed or the next one. He seemed to know where we are going next."

"Makepeace, I have heard rumors of plots all around. I have sent men ahead to plan our way and look at possible staging areas for such a raid. In truth there are many. I am particularly watchful as we are now in De La Pole lands, he is invested at Tewkesbury Abbey, just north of here."

"But surely De La Pole is a relative of the King and one of the accusers of Queen Anne."

"Of intrigues you know little my dear Mr. Makepeace. However, I need you to remain vigilant. The King is aware of the threats as are some in the court, but the whole party cannot be aware or the whole Progress would be jeopardized and our travels would not have the intent we hope from the run of Englishmen."

And Cromwell was right. I was approached again by St. Albans and we spoke in some code, or at least I ascertained it to be, saying nothing plainly. As we walked between the main camp of King's attendants and the Cathedral close, he said that his information suggested an attempt as we were early in the trip, less than halfway to Stratford and only a few miles from Tewkesbury. Our goal for the morning was Evesham Abbey where we would make a quick stop and continue on to Stratford.

The baggage train left first as the King had more business with the Bishop. I wondered if this was a plan, to keep the King at the back of the procession, where he would not normally be. And yet another Abbey as a stop over. I did not understand why the King preferred such places, save that they were made with stone, but usually housed some of his less ardent supporters, those churchmen whose world's had been shaken with the break from Rome.

Cromwell asked me to ride with the advance guard. But as we approached Evesham, he had me sent for, so I dropped back in the procession, and became more concerned with my ability to fall back among the lengthy train of carts and horsemen, and those with less watchful eyes.

I had reached back some distance into the train, partly by waiting for it to pass and by hurrying backwards along the road when an opening presented itself.

Still without the King's carriage in sight, I heard a commotion behind me. I wheeled my horse around and saw a group of horsemen charge out of the forest, near a side road I had just passed. Two mounted guards were raising the alarm, one with an arrow in his thigh. The guards had been surrounding an ornamental covered carriage, one which did not seat the King, but did contain several of his chief attendants.

With a whoop more men descended on the carriage from the other side of the road. They surrounded it and those closest swung their swords while a group on the embankments poured a steady stream of arrows at anyone who fought back.

I was unarmed, though even if I was, I doubt I would have made any move. Fighting was not something I had an experience with. Realizing that on horseback I was a target, I swiftly rode back down the road in hopes of informing the King's Guard.

A few of them passed me, evidently word of the attack moved swiftly down the baggage train, faster even than a man on a horse.

With the King's carriage in sight, I was accosted by a heavily armed guard. I stopped immediately showing my hand to show I was not armed.

"What say you?"

"I am a King's scribe, riding up the procession at Minister Cromwell's request. We have been attacked. The carriage holding the Earls has been surrounded and by now likely those inside have been taken or worse."

"Stay here." The guard hefted me a short sword and rode off.

Feeling very naked should an attack come, I held the sword across my legs, edge up to avoid hurting the horse. Then flat as it was two sided. Hopefully the sword was visible to anyone thinking of violence. However, its short nature did not lend me any quiet, as, a skilled swordsman I was not, and with an inferior weapon, I would have been cut down like wheat.

The train had stopped and I kept a constant watch for any attacks. More guards rode past me and soon the baggage train began to move again, in short order moving much faster than its usual plod.

We arrived at Evesham and the King's carriage was whisked past the rest of the train into the Cathedral Close where armed guardsmen circled in behind it.

Cromwell's men came out of the Abbey lodgings and told everyone to make ready to overnight there, directing us to pitch whatever tents were necessary, but to be ready to move again the next day.

We did not move. Apparently, a garrison was called in to accompany the King's travels, and it required several days to arrive.

I was called to take letters for the King. As I arrived the King was raging.

"Thomas, we must continue our progress. We cannot be scared into returning to London. I am the King, not a rat who scurries away."

"Sire, we do not have the means to protect you against a determined assault, even with the garrison at Warwick coming to help. In fact, I am wary of Warwick. It has been granted to Tutor supporters but the country around it completely untrustworthy, turning with the tide in the not so long ago Rose wars."

"The progress must continue. I am not afraid."

"I know that Sire. Alas, the Crown must be protected. Allow me to root out what I can and then we can determine if it is safe, or prudent to continue your travels."

Henry made indiscreet noises about not being caged, and sat down in the Bishop's seat. I was summoned to him, trembling like an entire oak tree in a storm.

"Ah, Makepeace. I understand you had some foreknowledge of this affair."

Cromwell interjected, "He informed my men and me about certain conversations and movements he was concerned about. If it were not for Makepeace, you might well have been riding near the front of the train as is your custom."

"What about the Earl's who have been dispatched?"

"If the plot was to expose itself, there had to be a prize available. They were informed that their carriage might be mistaken for the King's. They were armed."

"In a tiny carriage and on foot." Henry tilted his head down. "I am grateful to their service. Their families shall be rewarded. Arrange to have their sons meet with me in London. Do we know who did this?"

"The rumor is De La Pole is behind it, and we were very near his seat in Tewksbury. Though, he has been faithful, despite his claim, and I am inclined to believe it was someone else, seeking to implicate him with location and idle talk."

"Do keep me informed of your inquires on the matter. As for Makepeace, please follow up on his informants."

"But Sire, the main informant took a route back to London once we left Gloucester. Or at least he said that's where he was going."

"Ah, Mr. Makepeace you are beginning to sound like a seasoned king's man."

I flushed with pleasure at the compliment. Though I did not guess where it would lead.

My notes and letters for the king finished, I returned them to Cromwell's men, but was asked to meet with the Chief Minister. I was ushered into his chambers and brought forward to a raging fire in the hearth.

It roared but Cromwell motioned me in closer. He moved his lips to my ear. I was frozen, despite the heat of the fire.

"Mr. Makepeace, you have proved useful as a spy for the Crown. I would like you to act on that presumption in the future and will have you speak shortly to my chief man on these matters. He will help you to better understand the role and what is expected of you."

"But I am the king's scribe, my lord."

"And that you will remain. A perfect cover for your other, more significant activities."

He pulled away and nodded. I returned the gesture. Then he loudly asked me about the letters I'd written and sent me off to have them delivered by horsemen.

I was now a spy and was soon introduced to an older gentleman I had seen lurking in close proximity to the King. He was the Duke of Wrexham, a distant relation of the King, but addressed only as Wrexham and treated as an advisor to the king, never as a kinsman.

Wrexham took me aside and said that Cromwell had asked that I be tutored. Two days later the garrison arrived and the King, expecting them, was ready to depart. I had been told that the King would continue his progress but curtail the length of his trip. We headed to Cambridge, Bury St. Edmonds, Chelmsford and back to London. It was decided that certain personages would make a trip on the King's behalf to the Midlands and into the north. From that trip various noblemen would be recruited to visit the King in London in an attempt to build a network of loyalists in the north.

"Isn't that the same plan that failed so spectacularly with Neville and the

Earls of Northumberland, not two generations ago?"

Wrexham jerked his head up from his task, "Aye, my young charge. But Cromwell knows it and against his better judgement has determined to try. Best for you that you remain silent and learn unless you are asked directly for your thoughts. The first rule of serving the King is assume nothing, deal only with what you are assigned."

I nodded. Wrexham went back to his task. He was hammering a chisel into the back of a small broach with a red jewel of some kind, likely a garnet, surrounded by a lovely filigree pattern in an oval.

I stood without speaking, until finally he lifted his head. "There you are," he handed me the broach. "This is your pass inside the king's circle." He showed me the back where he had stamped into the metal, 'WTCVHIII'. Tell no one what this is unless specifically asked for your token from me or Cromwell. Most will recognize the garnet and pattern of the setting, but the inscription identifies you as a King's man under the service of me and Cromwell. If it is lost or stolen, tell me immediately, even by fast messenger if you are far away."

I nodded and took the broach, inspected it for a moment, and pinned it to my cloak on the upper left shoulder, as Wrexham indicated. Not used to it, it seemed quite ostentatious.

It was our time to join the procession to Northampton where we would stay with the local earl and garrison the poor Abbey in that town.

Eventually we made our way back to London visiting those nobles on the way. In Colchester word reached us that William St. Albans had been accosted on the road to Birmingham, not the route which he had told us he was taking. He told a story of meeting a fellow merchant on the road who told him there were several manufacturers of woolens that were keen to sell off their last seasons' wares before harvesting this year's wool.

He was let on his way but told to report to the king's men at Stratford on his return journey as they might be interested in purchasing the woolens for the garrison. I smiled when Wrexham told me this, as I recognized the plan to call St. Albans at his word.

Wrexham scowled at me, "Keep your thoughts to yourself Makepeace, even the slightest expression can give information."

Back in London I was to meet with Wrexham twice weekly to learn the arts and sciences of spy craft. And soon I was added to observer teams often as a bystander, but one with knowledge of proceedings. I was tasked with following the movements of those surrounding the mark that Wrexham had put a mission on.

And then a rumor came to me that the King would make a northern progress, visiting the estates of northern lords who were often more powerful than the king himself in their far-flung realms.

"Isn't this a most dangerous passage?"

"Not at all. The Lords we seek are doubly loyal, trusted and perhaps most important, investigated and immune to temptation. Those lords whom we suspect will be invited to attend their neighbour's castles to visit with the King as he will proceed fairly quickly.

"The idea is for Henry to meet with locals and be seen by all manner of Britons," said Wrexham. "And you will be tasked with watching these meetings to see if all is well among the lesser attendees. Your usual duties will be largely dispensed with, save a few assignments for show, to suggest to those in attendance that you have the ear of the King and his Ministers."

And so north we went, by ship, in a surprising move. We were taken from the Tower to the Royal Docks on the Thames and thereby set sail up the easternmost coast of England to New Castle on Tyne.

The ships sailed into the Tyne estuary and docked near the ancient castle. The Earl was there to meet us and escort the King to his lodgings.

They consulted for the whole next day while word was sent that the King would receive petitioners the following day.

From there we boarded ship and continued up the Tyne to Prudhoe Castle where we met with the Earl of Northumberland.

And from there we visited Aydon Castle and then Langley Castle before abandoning the ship as the South fork of the Tyne turned away from our preferred travel direction. We moved overland to Hadrian's Wall. From there we continued on to Carlisle. Several ships met us on the River Eden there and we began our journey to London via the Irish Sea. On the way we stopped briefly at Drumburgh castle, recently rebuilt by Baron Thomas Dacre as a small but heavily fortified tower. Dacre met the ship and had an audience with the King.

From there we sailed to Birkenhead Priory and stayed with the monks for a few days. Again boarding ship we moved south, and, keen to avoid Bristol where all the previous unpleasantness had begun, we rounded Land's End and headed for Portsmouth. The King wanted to see the progress of several naval vessels he had commissioned. And thence we headed north over land to London.

Kent was a funny place, at once more docile than the north, there were still strong feelings about the break with Rome. The King avoided known areas of discontent at Cromwell's insistence and the trip back to the Tower was uneventful.

It was nice to be back in London where my involvement seemed to be reduced. Not quite sure what to make of that, I was wary when I was summoned to Cromwell a few weeks later.

"Young Makepeace, the King has been pleased with your work. The Earl of Amesbury agreed to rebuild the bridge there and cited the co-operative tone of the King's letter in his response."

"Thank you, Sir Thomas."

"Henry has also mentioned your work alongside Wrexham," he fingered his garnet broach.

"Again, Sir Thomas, thank you, but I cannot help but believe I have much more to learn."

"Aye, you do. Wrexham tells me that you have quickly taken to his instruction."

Chapter Twenty-eight

Theresa read the story and liked it, but then she had a thing for spy novels. I thought of it as historical fiction but the mix of genres was more typical than I had believed. We went to the hospital where we met Markus in the lobby.

He asked if he could read my draft as well, after Theresa mentioned it to him. I shrugged, not really liking that my unfinished work was being parsed but not having a good reason to say no, given he'd already gone through a few of them.

We saw a much-improved Brandon, sitting up and reading a book. He explained that getting into the reclining position was painful still, but once there, he could handle it for several hours. And the reading occupied his mind, but he had to take breaks as prolonged concentration brought on a headache. They were trying to get him up and walking but it was painful.

He mentioned that he had spoken to his cousin and that there was interest in Theresa's sports wear. They had purposely priced it for bare profit margins to help stimulate sales. Theresa nodded, she explained she had been in touch with Allan, and they had plotted the strategy.

"Of course, that means more work for me as they need a steady flow of product. People seem to like the stuff, particularly the men's light jackets, and there has been more than one comment that someone came into the store after seeing a piece on a friend."

"They say I might get out of here in a week or two."

"That would be right on schedule. Have you been up and about yet?"

"A little, they want me to keep my muscles limber, but its pretty painful."

Brandon wanted to see my story as well, and Markus said he could drop it off, and we could pick it up the next time we visited. I wasn't too happy about that, but what could I say, Brandon was desperate for something to do and it seemed cruel to exclude him when Markus was already involved. I presented him with one of my novels. He nodded enthusiastically and said he'd tackle it next.

I was more than a touch miffed that he did not enquire about the subject or plot. But then, part of me was relieved.

Theresa said she was planning on doing another fashion event, this time in Dallas. Both of us had to beg off as the timing of the trip was impossible.

Theresa said she could manage as she had recently made a couple of hires who would help her.

"This whole business thing is not really what I expected. She laughed at herself. "I thought success would free me up to do more design work, but really, success is just more and more administration."

I thought that somehow success seemed backward. Winning the game meant doing less and less of what you love. Applied to my own business, I enjoyed most of the actual writing work I did for my clients, and liked the business management part of it the least. But I was not big enough to hire a business manager, nor did I really want the headache. I still dreamed of making it big as a novelist, but the difficult truth of that business was seeping into my brain everyday.

Technology in the 21st century had made publishing very easy, but it had made getting exposure for marketing, infinitely more difficult. There was more and more product, with less quality assurance in a shrinking marketplace. I wondered if reading for pleasure would ever make a comeback?

I also considered writing for television or film, but a look into those industries was perhaps even more daunting than print. My comfort zone called me back, and I went willingly.

While I waited for Markus and Brandon to give me their feedback on my Elizabethan spy tale, I dove into another.

Chapter Twenty-nine – Italian Adventure

I was off on an adventure. Packed my bags, paid my ticket, locked the apartment and I was gone. Rome, the eternal city, and all that stuff. I had cultivated an interest in Roman history, which I had long ignored, mostly because it was, like the city, seemingly eternal.

Histories in the modern west stretched back a few hundred years, maybe a bit more, but Roman history encompassed 2,000 years, give or take, and touches on so many people it is hugely difficult to keep it all straight.

But I tried, first looking at the major periods of Roman history on their own. The Republic was perhaps the most interesting, and then Imperial Rome, which is the best understood. I filled that in with some of the Etruscan Period, and a bit on the move of the capital to Constantinople.

And then I tried to stitch it all together. What a mess, I thought, and then realized that was a metaphor for Rome itself.

I took the Red Eye flight from JFK and landed in Rome mid-morning the next day. I found a shuttle to the city center, from where I could walk to my hotel, or at least that's what the map suggested. I was hauling a heavy bag and I trundled through the streets, at first on a mission to find the hotel and then doing a bit of sight-seeing on my way.

The shuttle had let me out at the Roman Forum but my hotel was near the Spanish Steps, a hike of a bit more than a mile, as the crow flies. I am not a crow. And trudging is not flying. In Rome, even a crow would have trouble staying on course.

But I got to my hotel, fortunately at the bottom of the steps, which I'm not sure I could have managed without a significant rest. The hotel did not allow me to check in, but did take my bag and store it in the office.

I thanked the clerk in pidgin Italian, and decided to find a café for a rest and a look at my phrase book. Fortunately, I had been practicing basic Italian phrases for a month before I left and really just needed a refresher. Of course, having checked in, most of the phases I'd practiced were now behind me. And the rapid Italian of the natives was difficult to process.

I ordered a Café Americano to the lopsided grin of the waiter. I took a deep sigh, as the trip to this point was arduous. The main part of the adventure was that I was on my own. Exploring a city like Rome, in the kind of detail I imagined, was not going to work well with compromises. I knew from experience that staring at some pointless exhibit in a museum, to satisfy a companion could be exceedingly painful especially if it went even five seconds longer than it captivated my own imagination.

The coffee came and I said a very heartfelt "Gracie" feeling perfectly Italian. The waiter still grinned. Then asked if I wanted something to eat. Of course I didn't understand him, until he produced a menu and the light-bulb went on in my foggy head. Red eye flights and foreign languages do not mix.

I had to stay up until at least early evening, 8 pm or later, if I wanted to avoid the pitfalls of jet lag.

The coffee braced me and I considered going with an Italian coffee, or even an espresso, but decided to save that jolt until mid-afternoon.

I left the café after another Americano, and walked to Piazza Navona, famous for its fountains. I had decided to avoid any difficult touring as my brain was not ready for any real thinking. I tired easily, not entirely used to long walks, and parked myself on one of the fountains and took in the passersby.

The Piazza was long and narrow, with fountains at both ends and renaissance buildings lining the edges. A few of them were churches, but my travels in Europe made me think twice about entering them, as churches were a dime a dozen and once you'd seen a few, there was little left to inspire awe. I had mapped out several churches I did want to visit but these were not among them.

I toyed with going to St. Peter's across the river, but decided against it, as I was simply too tired. I wandered around the Piazza and managed to move a few blocks away from it, mostly to get my bearings and ready myself for the next day's exploring.

Back to the hotel I got my room, and lay down for a moment to stretch out my back. I started to doze and leaped up, refusing to succumb to sleep. I rushed back out the door and decided to look for a restaurant for an early dinner.

Italians do not eat early. I was stymied. So, I wandered up the Spanish Steps and stood in the spot Gregory Peck stood when Audrey Hepburn wandered by on her Roman Holiday. I did notice, I was not the only one who did it, as a number of people seemed drawn to that spot halfway up the steps. After that I figured it best to ascend the Steps and make my way past them, as there were many tourist hotels in the area, and hopefully restaurants which catered to the earlier eating times of English speakers.

Being alone, I decided on a fast-food approach, so I prepared my phrases and strode into the lion's den. After I butchered the language enough, the cashier switched to English and took my order. I found a little table to sit at and daintily ate my meal while trying to watch the people around me. Most were tourists like me, though many of them managed a bit more Italian than I had mastered.

Unilingualism has its charms, mostly when you are at home, and I decided we Americans were at a decided disadvantage. I did engage in a short conversation with two women at the table beside me. They were on a graduation trip to Europe, the first week was a bus tour of Italy and the second week they were on their own, scheduled to fly back to England from Paris.

They were trying to decide the best way to move about and where to go. They had decided on trains but were still working out their itinerary.

"So how much longer do you have in Italy?"

"Oh, we got here yesterday, after a day in Pompei. Our tour is nearly over with two night in Rome to finish. From there we are trying to figure out where to go. Any suggestions? We want to end up in Paris?

"I'm in Italy for the first time, but I have been to Paris and The United Kingdom. Where in England are you two from?"

They looked at each other oddly. "We just graduated from the University of London. I'm from Winchester and Katy here is from Birmingham." Amanda spoke with an odd precision.

"I'm from New York, but not the city, the State, actually Long Island, about 35 miles from Manhattan."

"Ohh, I've always wanted to go to America. In fact we wrestled with the idea of going there for this trip, but airfare is much cheaper here so we decided to stay in Europe."

I nodded and as I had finished my meal, I started to collect my garbage and rose to leave. "Have a good trip."

They nodded in unison and I wandered away.

After a good night's sleep, so good that I almost missed breakfast at the hotel, I happily made my way to the Vatican, wandering first to the Mausoleum of Augustus not far from the hotel, and then walking along the Tiber before crossing at the Pont d'Sant Angelo, across from the

Castel Sant Angelo, originally the mausoleum of Emperor Hadrian.

I wandered with the tourists into the ancient building and eventually left to make my way up the triumphant roadway to the nearby Piazza and the grandiose colonnaded space in front of St. Peter's Cathedral.

It was impressive on the approach, as a huge baroque church might be, when stacked up against the Gothic cathedrals of northern Europe. Inside was simply awe inspiring. The nave seemed to go on forever, and the arches that made up the bulk of the building were hugely substantial and graceful at the same time. I wandered towards the main altar and saw a service of some sort being conducted, before I doubled back to take in the artworks on display.

Standing a moment in front of Michelangelo's Pieta, a statue of Mary and Jesus, I was in awe of Michaelangelo's skill as a sculptor. It simply belied belief that such perfection was possible with stone. One accidental chip and the whole thing would be ruined.

"Oh, it's you again," a voice said beside me. I looked and it was the two girls from the hamburger joint the night before.

"Hello, it seems tourists are drawn to the same things."

The one called Katy laughed a bit nervously, which I put down to them thinking I was stalking them, or something. "Is this your first stop with the tour?"

I looked around but there was no sign of a large group nearby. Usually these tours have guides which show people around the sites and sometimes even have privileges to get into areas that are not as obvious to individual travellers.

"Yeah, I guess," said Amanda, looking at Katy with a confused expression.

"We walked here, though we looked at the Piazza with all the fountains first. After this we are on our way to the Piazza Argentia, apparently a group of old temples which are difficult to get into."

I nodded, "I want to see those too. Maybe if I just tagged along with your group, I could sneak in. They don't take head counts, do they?"

Now Katy looked panicked, so I backed off, "It's okay, if you are worried about it, I won't do it. At least not with your tour group."

"Have fun," I said, wandering up the nave. I looked back at the Pieta after waling for a minute, and saw the girls still standing there. Katy, turned and looked me straight in the eye from 30 yards away, through a crowd. She said something to Amanda, who then looked my way. I pretended that I didn't see them, and moved off.

I figured they were probably smart to be a bit skittish in a foreign country without a lot of experience in the world. Heck, I was happy to remain unattached as even I was wary what with a number of sharp-eyed touts hitting up tourists to act as guides for them. I'd heard rumors that these people were usually honest, but some used their newfound connections with the tourists to rob them. And pickpockets were supposedly every-where.

An hour later, I'd mostly forgotten them, as I was approaching the front of the huge cathedral and was preparing to leave, though still unsure of where I was headed.

"Eric?" came a voice behind me.

I turned and sure enough the two English girls were standing there, now just across the nave from where I'd left them. Now I was beginning to feel they were stalking me.

"Eric, I was wondering if you could help us."

"I can try, but I'm still learning the city myself, you are probably best to speak to your tour guide."

"Umm, it's not that Eric."

I looked at Katy, perhaps about to reveal some personal need.

"We are being followed."

"Italian men are like that, very persistent. Just stick with your tour group."

"It's not that simple Eric. She leaned in. "Can we all go for a coffee and we will tell you?"

I shrugged, "Sure, I passed a place at the end of the Colonnade."

We wandered together through the piazza and went into the coffeeshop. It did not escape me that they carefully positioned themselves near enough to the door and facing it so they could watch who came in.

“Okay, you two what’s up?” I had been thinking of various scenarios that might be at play but couldn’t think much past either approaching the police or the Embassy.

Katy looked around, and then right at me, “We are MI5.”

I was shocked only momentarily, “Yeah sure. And I’m CIA. Look, if you were MI5 you would not be asking for my help, as I am just a tourist from New York. I don’t know what game you are playing but stop.” If I didn’t have a full coffee in front of me, I would have gotten up and left. I should have.

“No really, Eric, surely you have descriptions of us. You said, ““I’m in Italy for the first time, but I have been to Paris and The United Kingdom. Where in England are you two from?”

And I answered, “We just graduated from the University of London. I’m from Winchester and Katy here is from Birmingham.”

I starred blankly.

“That doesn’t mean anything to you?”

I shook my head. “I was in Winchester once, saw the Cathedral. Never been to Birmingham, well, I think I took a train through there years ago.”

The two girls looked at each other. “He looks exact.”

“An American.”

“Alone.”

“Said the right words.” They ping ponged back and forth. “Eric, you match the description of our contact and you said the right words to verify your identity. If you aren’t our contact, then he is missing and we are in some sort of danger.”

“I’m not big on danger,” I said. “Nor am I big on practical jokes. Which one of you is wearing the camera?”

“I can assure you this in no joke.”

“Well, it is to me. If you two have a problem, some random guy from Brooklyn is not your solution. Go to your embassy, or contact MI5 in London.

They'll tell you what to do."

"Some random guy from New York is our contact. And if you are truly not him, then we do have a problem." She turned to Amanda, "Maybe this is some kind of training mission. You know, throw up some road blocks, some twists and turns and find out how we respond."

"We were told not to approach police or our Embassy. Come to think of it, it's almost like they anticipated trouble," said Amanda, narrowing her eyes.

I drained the last of my coffee, thanking God for the small portions of Italian cafes. "Good luck, girls, give my regards to James Bond." And I stood, and quickly left the table and the café without looking back.

Out on the street I wanted to shake these two so I retraced my steps to the Castel Sant Angelo and then back across the bridge and into the streets of Rome. They said they were going to the Place Argentina so I avoided that, and even stayed away from the Pantheon, heading instead to the Trevi Fountain and the Roman Forum beyond.

The fountain itself had the usual tourist groups tossing coins and taking photos. I moved on quickly wandering down a side street and moving into the church of Ignatus Loyola, cruising a few retails stores and eventually ending up face to face with the Victor Emanual Monument, a huge stark white colonnaded space which framed off one end of the Capitoline Hill. Ancient Rome obstructed by a modern monument trying to look old.

I moved around it and worked my way up a broad staircase to the Piazza above where I took the opportunity to sit down and look around. Watching the world go by I simply shook my head at the antics of the two British girls, who by now, I expected, were plying their trick on some other unsuspecting tourist. I plunged into the Capitoline museums and became immersed in the lengthy history of Rome. Fortunately, I had done a bit of studying about the ancient city before I left, and was able to vaguely place most of what I saw, at least into the Republican Period or the Empire. Given that each lasted for centuries, I was not too confident on understanding anything much more specific.

Eventually I moved out of the museum, the sculptures and artifacts all becoming a bit of a blur. I wandered the Capitoline Hill a bit and then descended into the ancient Roman Forum, now not much more than random ruins. I begrudgingly paid my entrance fee and joined a tour group. In the end that was a good plan as I had no idea which bits of stone and pillars belonged to which. The guide was actually pretty good at conjuring the grandeur of the spaces at the height of the empire. Seeing that some of the buildings were more than 100 feet tall, the height of an apartment block in New York, I was impressed.

Then, like a moth I was drawn to the Colosseum, which loomed over the eastern end of the Forum ruins. I figured I'd go west to visit the Circus Maximus and the Baths of Caracalla the next day, and maybe wander over the river to the Travestore neighbourhood.

Dodging all the costumed touts outside the Colosseum I was prepared for nothing inside. Taking a hint from my tour group in the Forum I paid the fee and took a tour of the huge edifice which proved worthwhile. I'm not sure I would have missed anything the guide pointed out, but I certainly would not have been able to put it into context. By this time the sun was headed down and I figured if I was going to walk back to my hotel I'd better get moving.

I flopped on my bed and drifted off trying not to actually sleep but I couldn't help it. I had had a long day and a lot of walking, coming on the heals of the overnight flight. I woke up once during the night and seeing the time, just drifted back to sleep, hoping that the jet lag would be behind me the next morning.

I was famished, not having had any dinner so I had a continental breakfast at my hotel and then, as I passed a McDonalds, I decided to supplement my hunger with a touch more breakfast. I had planned a busy day.

As soon as I sat down the two girls walked in and spied me immediately. Katy did not make to speak to me, but Amanda sat down at my table.

"Apologizing?"

"Umm, no. We were telling you the truth." Katy made her way to the counter and was ordering. "We did find our man at the Pantheon. He repeated the required phrases. Interestingly he does not look like you at all."

"I thought I matched the description?"

"The description was vague. Anyway, both of us are convinced it's a training exercise. We are to meet Carl at the Trevi Fountain today for our assignment. Sorry to have bothered you."

"So, it is an apology. Accepted. Sit with me if you want."

Katy brought a tray back and sat down after Amanda waved her to the table. "Eric seems okay with us now and I hope he won't give away our misidentification of him, if Carl or anybody asks. It was just a coincidence that you said what you did."

"Of course. Have you decided where to go once you've finished in Rome?"

"It will depend on what Carl has to say to us, I suppose."

"Well, good luck and I hope you have a lovely time." With that I crumpled my wrappers and stood, taking the tray with me. If they still wanted to play their game they could, but they seemed to understand I wanted no part of it.

I took a city bus, with some confusion, to the Circus Maximus and poked around there and the nearby Baths of Caracalla until mid-day. From there I toyed with heading back into the Palantine Hill or across the Tiber to the Travestore neighbourhood.

The later won, and I found myself on some leafy streets and among galleries and churches. A different kind of Rome but lovely. There were a few old manors converted into museums, some interesting shops, though I was not much of a trinket buyer, and a much more relaxed approach to daily living.

I decided upon a big dinner back at the hotel, as I was still hungry. Then I would wander the area around the Spanish Steps, and perhaps just plant myself there for a little tourist conversation.

Sitting on the steps with a full stomach and a lot of Rome swirling in my head I was beginning to think of my trip home. My week in Rome was almost up, and then it occurred to me that the English girls had said they were on a tour that should have ended, but they were still in Rome. Now I was convinced they were just toying with me, and who knows who else.

The next day, I decided to visit the Pantheon and the Piazza Argentine, after making arrangements with a guide through my hotel.

I marvelled at both sites, deciding to take the tours slowly and not try to cram too much into my day. Leaving the Pantheon I spied Katy and Amanda in a café across the square. I was far enough way that they didn't see me. They were sitting with a short, older man, who seemed very engaged in the conversation and then, who, abruptly rose and left.

'Just like me, I thought, another victim of their joke.'

I hung out on the Pantheon step to see what they would do, and to make sure I did not run into them. Watching them, I failed to notice the older man come up to me from my left.

"Eric? I am told that you are with the American government."

I ignored him but he persisted. I denied knowing anything. He persisted. "My two contacts assure me that you are their man in Rome."

"What ever are you speaking about?"

"Look Eric, I've spoken to your boss. It was very clever of you to deny being their contact. It worked for a bit but Katy in particular was not fooled."

Now it was my turn to be confused. I had received no information about my trip from my own boss. He had told me only to go to Rome and have a nice holiday. The leave had come after a particularly difficult and harrowing assignment in Charlotte, North Carolina of all places. Something about Mexicans and drugs and such.

I needed to find out what was really going on here, and denied having any idea what he was talking about and shook him off, with a touch of real anger. The last thing any agent wants is to be dropped into the middle of an entirely unfamiliar situation. If this 'Carl' was right, I was about to have words with my boss. And if the two girls were simply continuing their elaborate ruse, then I might have to sic the constabulary on them.

As I worked my way back to my hotel I thought about the bits that led to my leave. As a detective with the DEA I worked the back half of cases, collecting evidence and speaking to those involved in drug trafficking and sometimes human trafficking cases, as the two often occurred together.

In Charlotte, I'd been involved with the interviews of several witnesses and those charged with lesser involvements in a drug case. The DEA had crushed an organization that operated in the near south, using Universities as their cover. Offering reduced charges for information and testimony, it was a pretty routine assignment, until the attack on our facility where gang members tried to spring several of those we had in custody.

The location had heavy security on the inside to keep the prisoners at bay, but on the outside, there was little as the location was supposed to be unknown and unofficial.

The attackers managed to breech the building and several of our prisoners were sprung. In the bloodbath four DEA agents were shot to death, six of the attackers and two of those in custody. Mostly unknown to the local press, the incident had caused an internal hemorrhage within the local DEA office and most of us who were there were sent away on leave while it was being sorted out.

Now that I thought of it, my boss suggested I take in the sights in Rome. I thought it was only because he knew I was interested in the history.

I did know that I was nobody's contact. Now it was time to phone home.

"Okay Eric this is a complete f-up. Yes, you were sent to Rome as a back-up agent in case we needed someone to help interrogate probable smugglers. Carl is the lead agent, and you should not have been contacted except by me, on the off chance we needed to activate you. Bloody MI5, sending in a couple of amateurs."

"Can you call off Carl and the two British girls. This whole affair has not been particularly relaxing, you know?"

"Aye, aye, Eric, and sorry this happened. If you'd like to extend your holiday, just let me know. The investigation here is going quite slowly. Apparently, there was a breech in our security precautions which tipped off the gang where to find us."

"Well, I will admit, I've sometimes wondered why investigators are required to carry, but I was plenty happy to have a piece on me when that attack went down."

"You shot one of them?"

"You've read the report." One of the thugs had burst into the interrogation room and I fired without thinking, putting a fist sized hole in his chest. The man I was speaking to had risen up and looked to do some violence to help his rescuer, but sat down quickly once it was evident I was armed and willing to shoot.

"I will take you up on the longer stay, though I think I'll leave Rome. I will let you know when I arrive back in New York."

"Okay Eric. I hear you. And again, sorry that this worked out this way. MI5 is going to get an earful."

I had one more day in Rome and I figured I'd stay and give myself a chance to decide where I'd go next. I really didn't need to think I was being followed and my movements traced by anyone. I even thought about resigning from the DEA. I could find a nice little DA's job in a nice quiet part of the country.

The next day I headed for the Palatine Hill and the Baths of Caracalla. Wandering around there for a time, with my mind flitting back and forth between the dramas in North Carolina and Rome, I was leaning more and more to resigning. At one point I thought I saw Carl, but I kept my head down and he never materialized.

As I was leaving the Baths the crowd squeezed through the exit and dispersed, revealing Amanda waiting, apparently for me.

"I just wanted to apologize for real. Nobody will admit to this being a set up or training exercise or whatnot, but Katy and I learned a lot. The agency is not happy with us."

"And I'm not happy with them, or my own boss. Apparently, he sent me here on the off chance I might be needed."

"Well you looked the part. Really you did. And you said the code words. You just looked too out of place to not be our contact."

"Didn't they teach you that spies are always set up to blend in. Anyone that sticks out will never be an agent. The thing is, I just work for the government, I'm not a spy."

"Yeah, well, we figured reverse psychology, you know, standing out is more of a disguise than blending in. The stiff could never be the spy, right? You just said that."

"Okay, okay. Look, it's over. I've had it out with my boss. You can deal with yours. Good luck to you."

"Are you heading back to the Spanish Steps? I'll walk with you."

"No, its okay. I just want to be done with all of this. Good Luck. Good bye." How many times had I said goodbye to these girls, only to have them bounce back into my life?

I left and returned to my hotel, walking through the streets of Rome and trying to decide where to go next. Milan was out. And by virtue of that decision I figured I'd decide by eliminating those places I did not what to go, leaving only the place where I was going.

I eliminated Switzerland, and after some consideration, Austria. Then I considered Spain or Portugal but dropped them along with most of Eastern Europe. I'd spent too much time in the UK so that was out. How about Russia? I thought, but no, I didn't need that hanging around my neck so I was down to France, Holland or Germany.

Holland, or at least Amsterdam, was a drug den, and Germany had little historical appeal, so I decided on France. Besides I could get there easily from Italy and I'd not spent any time in the south, so France it was.

I decided to take a train to Nice and rent a car from there, and explore the smaller towns and cities between Nice and Biarritz. St. Paul de Vence, Aix-en-Provence, Arles, Nimes, Avignon and Carcassonne were all on my agenda and shifted my interest from Rome to the early medieval period, with some of these places starting as Roman settlements. I took a hotel near Nice and poked around there for two days before finding myself in Arles, where I engaged a hotel for four nights to explore the local area. I had intended to find a flight from either Nice or Lyons back to New York.

Wandering through the streets of Nimes, I started to forget the odd chance that brought Katy, Amanada and even Carl into my life. Nimes has a large Roman amphitheatre and a few nice streets and parks oddly integrated into the modern city scape.

I had almost decided to quit the DEA and take a nice quiet job somewhere with little crime, Montana, Idaho or even west Texas. Of course, as a city boy, none of those places really appealed to me, but it was nice to imagine. A ten-gallon hat, a pick-up and a ramshackle place out in the country. It all had an appeal, at least until I actually had to do it.

In the mean time I walked up a hill in Nimes, part of an old park system with a canal running down it. I thought the view might be nice.

It wasn't. As I made my way down and decided to find my car by taking a different route than I had arrived, I saw a group of people gathered along side the canal. The water was moving much more rapidly than I had expected and I found myself wondering about how it had gained such speed. It must have cascaded down the hill. I looked around and the stream seemed to appear out of nowhere and disappear, buried under the city streets.

Eventually I found my car and decided to head to Avignon, mostly because the street signs all pointed that way. I found a lovely medieval town center and I poked around it for a time before heading to Pont Du Garde an ancient Roman aqueduct, not working but still standing, a few miles away.

An impressive sight, I walked along it staring down into the river below and thinking the flow must be more impressive in the spring.

I got back to the car and there was a message on my phone to contact my boss. It realized my moment of truth had arrived. Without much hesitation I messaged him that I was resigning once I had used up my holiday entitlements.

My phone rang within a minute.

"Eric, please, reconsider. I need you now. The situation has heated up with Carl and he is waiting in Annecy in the French Alps for you. It's just an investigation. The drug runners have been arrested. They were couriers, taking hashish from Marseilles to Turin."

I could feel the bile rise in my throat, "Sorry, I've decided to resign. I've had enough of running around and exposing myself to gangs and violence. Charlotte was the last straw."

"Come on Eric. Help me out. I promise there is no difficulty in this assignment, straight investigation, when ships arrived, where they came from, and connections to car rentals and such. It's going to take two days maximum and it will take me a week to get an agent in place if you won't do it. I can make it worth your while if you are determined to quit at the end."

It was hard to say no, with a dangling incentive, substantial pay and an easy out with the agency. With a deep sigh, I agreed. I got the co-ordinates and made my way to Annecy, most of a day's drive away. I arranged to meet Carl mid-afternoon.

Chapter Thirty

By now Theresa's escapades were becoming routine. Business is like that, once the thrill of success passes, it becomes a bit of a grind. Yet, Theresa seemed to be enjoying it, and even had some time to dabble in design again. The design request came this time from a client who owned a small chain of women's wear stores in North Caroliina, but it fit with the program she had laid out.

We met for coffee at the hospital coffee shop. Brandon was going to be released and we were going to drive him home. Well, Markus was going to do the deed, but Theresa and I were going to see them off.

But first they all decided to weigh in on my story from a couple of weeks back.

"I think you need to put in a bit more background about Tudor England."

"Oh, no, it's just right. I immediately got it, it's Henry the Eighth, right?"

"I liked it, a spy story in a historical context. What's next? What happens if you break your writer's block? Do you just abandon all the work you've done?"

"Maybe I can put them together in a short story collection."

"Well, they aren't that short, are they?"

"Short is in the mind of the reader. They aren't novel length, or even really novella length, so I'll call them short stories. In fact, I think I'm learning the knack of the shorter style, but I really want to get back to novels."

"Your writer's block seems broken, now you've just got to find a story line."

In between all that, we talked about Brandon. Which was nice as he was sitting right there. He appeared to be able to move with ease, but sitting and standing still were an issue, with the grimace on his face and the slowness of the movements giving it away, despite his declarations.

The hospital staff insisted he be moved through the building on wheel-chair, though they were happy to deposit him in the lobby on his own. Brandon insisted on walking out to the car, rather than wait for Markus to bring it up to the door. We all made our way though the parking lot with Brandon only slowing down as we approached the car. He got in gingerly and smiled.

"I have to get used to this," he tilted his head back and closed his eyes. "The fresh air and sunshine are nice."

"When are you back to work?"

"Maybe next week, or the week after. It's going to be like starting all over again. Eight weeks is a long time to be off. I'll likely be starting from scratch as I will have no projects on the go, though maybe I'll take one or two from the other guys going on holiday or something."

Theresa invited him to meet us for coffee if he was able, and with a wave, off they went to the burbs.

Theresa and I looked at each other, "Might as well stop here for coffee, rather than hike it back to mid-town."

"Well, what are you thinking?"

"Markus asked me out. Yesterday, by phone when we were arranging this."

"And you accepted?"

"Yes, I'm not sure how I feel about him, but I've grown used to having him around. Brandon too, but to a lesser extent."

"I hope it goes well. Any idea what his plans are?"

"Movie and dinner. Stock traders are not the most creative people on Earth."

"Why, what did you have in mind? Ziplining though the Amazon? Rock climbing? I'm not sure if you are cut out for those kinds of dates."

We both laughed. "I'm glad to see Brandon almost back to normal. I have to speak to his cousin today, and might schedule a run down to Philly to check things out. He's selling a lot of jackets and wants to expand the line due to some requests he's had."

"That sounds good. Maybe you can entice Markus to drive you."

"I was wondering if you wanted to come as well. If you do, I will mention it to Brandon. He might want the change of scenery."

"I'm not sure I like where this is going."

"It's not going anywhere if you don't want it to. Brandon has never said anything, has he?"

"He's been in a coma for a month. He hasn't said much of anything, other than 'Ouch'."

Theresa gave me a look but I was defiant, bouncing the look back to her. "There is no guarantee that anything will develop with Markus. In fact, I'd like to make sure that if it doesn't, we all remain friendly."

"Nice try, you know how that usually goes."

We split up and I made my way home, having some work to do for a client and wanting to take a crack at my latest genre. I really wanted a shot at comedy, but funny was elusive. Strange, as most of my friends considered me at least mildly amusing.

Chapter Thirty-one – On the Road with Literary Fiction

I stared into the glass, watching the light bounce off the curved surfaces and sparkle on the etchings. I moved the glass around, in and out of the chief light source seeing how it changed the look.

"Why don't you dance? The music is wonderful."

"Nobody asked me."

"What kind of excuse is that?"

"A damn good one. You know I'm not inclined to dance."

"I do know once you start it's tough to get you to stop. Dance with me, and that will attract a few watchers and maybe some requests."

"No, no thanks. I'm quite content here."

"What happened to your date?"

"He's over there talking to a few guys he used to go to school with. I remember them a bit."

"A date of convenience?"

"Yeah, we were both invited and neither one of us had dates, so we came together. Cindy makes a nice bride."

"And Joe a dashing groom. Though I expect it will be some time before he's in a tux again."

"Maybe the next wedding."

"What kind of thing is that to say. He just got married."

"I was thinking of one of his friends."

"He won't wear a tux to that."

"Oh, I hadn't thought of it that way."

"Well, you never know. I'm not sure how committed Cindy is."

I suppressed a tortured feeling. I had heard rumors that she was not entirely sure of her decision, but felt that she had little choice, especially as she had been dating Joe for several years and their families were close.

"You know something?"

"No, not really. Just the talk among our mutual friends."

I looked back at the drinking glass and saw the shards of light breaking apart as the beam hit the etching, a design logo for the hall we were in.

I felt a bit of longing for something more permanent in my life, and sort of envied Cindy that she had the choice and had made it. Of course, if it went poorly, then she would have another sort of melancholy to deal with, especially if there were kids involved.

My date was on my shoulder now and he asked me to dance, as a slow song had finished and the tempo had picked up.

I nodded robotically, and followed him to the dance floor. We jittered around a bit, neither one of us having their heart in it, though he seemed to be having a bit of a time, wearing a crooked grin and glancing around the room to see who was watching.

I kept my eyes on him or on the ground and the nearby dancers, one of whom was swinging around wildly. Though not in any danger of crashing into me, it was certainly on my mind.

Two songs ended and the DJ launched into a toast to the bride and groom, as we took the cue to sit down. He got me a drink, a touch of wine as my first drink had been nursed to its demise. I looked around the room, maybe a dozen large round tables littered with glasses, plates of dessert and used napkins, jackets on the backs of chairs, the whole ritual of a wedding reception. Everyone looked at least sort of happy, and I wondered if I would recognize the father of the bride from the father – daughter dance or from his glum expression realizing he had to pay for all of this.

“There you are. I’m so glad you were able to come.”

Cindy slid into the seat beside me, settling her dress as she did. Her make -up still held, despite the heat, and the long day behind us.

“It’s been a wonderful day. Where are you going on the honeymoon?”

“She sighed loudly, “We had wanted to go to Europe, but just could not find the time, so we are headed to a resort in Mexico, Ixtapa, all-inclusive. Only a week, but it should be fun.”

“That sounds nice. A nice getaway to forget all your responsibilities and stuff.”

She looked at me as if I’d said something odd. “You know, once you get back you have a lot of decisions to make: where to live, dinnerware, linens, and even glassware.” I picked up the glass I had been reflecting light with, for emphasis.

"Oh, silly. All those things have already been decided or bought or borrowed. Joe goes back to the Bank. I'll be back at the library and we figure out how to live together."

She smiled and so did I. She put her hand on my knee, just as my drink arrived.

She stood, "Oh you two are together." Of course, she knew my date, we'd all gone to school together, several years before.

"Together tonight," he said, "for this evening's festivities," he corrected himself. Cindy looked bemused, and I could feel myself redden. "You look lovely, Cindy. And Joe can work a tux, you know."

She nodded and moved off, "Nice to see you both. I hope we can catch up once we are back from Mexico."

"Thanks for the wine. Are you having a good time?" he asked.

"It's nice to see everyone again. I'm only a couple of hours away now, but it seems like a whole other world. Is anyone still in school?"

"I think a few stayed in the town, but have regular jobs. Those college towns are hard to beat. In the end, a lot of us just drifted back home. And here we are."

"Home has it's charms you know. I was happy to see my folks. Hadn't seen them in a while. And you, it's nice to see a familiar face."

"Like those guys from the football team?"

"Yeah, everybody you know. You forget the people you used to know well. Times change I guess."

"Or you do, when you are in a different situation."

"Do you think so? Have I changed?"

"You didn't used to like to dance, I seem to remember."

He laughed, "Still don't but I thought you might want to. Well once you loosen up, it's actually kinda fun."

"Well, that makes me feel better, I guess."

He looked at me oddly and seemed ready to say something but choked it back.

Just then a quick number from Elvis chirped up, and he grabbed my hand, pulling me to the dance floor.

'Jailhouse Rock' seemed appropriate somehow and I let my feet and hips move to the music. He had a big grin on his face as I seemed to enjoy the sound.

Eventually Cindy and Joe left to a big, though seemingly forced hoopla, and people began to drift out leaving more room on the dance floor for the hardcore dancers.

Billy and I had agreed that since we didn't have far to go, we'd stay a while. He dutifully dragged me to the dance floor, stood and spoke to his friends and sat with me for a bit. A few of our old friends drifted over to me and we unsatisfactorily chatted a bit. I'm not sure what I wanted. I sure wasn't going to get anybody's angst, I thought, before giggling to myself.

"What's so funny there, missy?"

Charlie Smith-Corella, and old acquaintance saddled up beside me. I had always called him Charlie Smith-Corrona, but never to his face or anyone else's. He had confessed to me one night long ago, that he wanted to be a writer.

"What are you doing these days?" I asked, genuinely interested.

"Well, I'm working in corporate communications. Mostly putting together annual reports and staff circulars. It pays the bills. You?"

"Nothing as exciting as that. I'm working at Walmart, managing the women's wear section. Are you in town, still?"

"No, there's no corporation around here big enough to have a dedicated communications guy. I'm in Dallas, well just outside of Dallas."

"Isn't everywhere in Dallas, just outside of Dallas?"

He laughed, and I felt I'd finally scored one, despite not trying all evening. My date had pulled himself from his friends and sat down on the other side of me. "Hey, Charlie, nice to see you."

"And you. I've actually had a good time tonight. Wasn't sure I would. But seeing everyone again, well, it's almost been like a school reunion."

"I hear ya."

Charlie looked at my date and then me, but he said nothing. "Come on, I said to him, lets shake." I grabbed him by the hand and pulled him to the dancefloor. It was a quick familiar tune, though I could not remember the artist. And then a slow number came on, and Charlie began to move back to the table, but I pulled him back and we danced and talked.

"Billy won't like this. I think it's the last song of the night," he said.

"Billy and I aren't together. We just came together out of convenience."

"Oh, in that case," he began to sway a little more aggressively, and then laughed at his joke.

"You dance divinely."

"I'm happy for Cindy and Joe. They've been together for a long while," he said.

I nodded, unwilling to stir any intrigue.

"I'm in town for the weekend. Feel like catching a movie or something tomorrow?"

I nodded, not willing to admit I'd already seen the film that was showing in our small town.

We headed back to the table and Billy was there asking if I wanted to stay.

I left it up to him, and turned but Charlie was gone. He'd find me if he wanted to, I thought.

I sat waiting for Billy to make up his mind and lifted the empty highball glass once again. The shards of light seemed a bit brighter now, but that was because they'd turned up the lights, our signal to end the evening.

We gathered our things, said our goodbyes and thank yous, and headed out into the cool night air. Billy drove me home, humming a tune under his breath, "Thanks," he said in my driveway. "It was a good idea to come together. Made things easier, you know."

I nodded and got out of the car, "Bye now."

As soon as the car door closed, he was sliding backward down the asphalt. I gave an offhand wave without looking and skipped up the steps to the door.

'Mexico' I thought to myself. 'How different is that from this one stop town?'

My mother was sitting at the kitchen table reading a book. Not the most comfortable place to settle into a story, and she looked up as I moved down the hall.

"You're in. Was it fun?"

"We stayed to the bitter end, but it wasn't bitter. Almost like a high school reunion. Everyone seems to be moving on with their lives."

"Unless there is some earth-shattering news, I'm going to bed. I can hear all the details tomorrow."

She popped an old business card between the pages and headed up the squeaky steps. The squeaks came dutifully on the first, fourth and eighth steps, the pattern almost a tune.

I went to the fridge looking for something cold to drink. I dropped a few cubes in a glass and poured a bit of fruit juice, then cut it with water. I wasn't ready for bed, but I had nothing that needed doing, save to sit there, sip my drink and think of Mexico. How easy it was to get to these far-flung places. Jump a plane and within a few hours, almost as long as it takes to get settled in an airplane seat, you emerge into whatever odd and foreign place you've chosen. And then you haunt the places that are purposedly less odd and foreign than the rest of your country of choice.

The idea of taking one of those mystery tours almost sounded fun. The ones where you sign up and don't know where you are going. There were so many places I'd never been, tackling the list was daunting.

I sipped at my juice until it was gone, reading the exotic ingredients on the label of the juice bottle. And then switching to the ketchup bottle that had been left on the table.

There was nothing exotic about Winslow. Well, the Walmart had been exotic when it first opened, a huge array of products brought to the door-steps of people who used to have to drive miles for such choices.

But even the Walmart became old hat. Winslow grew a bit, with a couple of subdivisions popping up in farm fields on the edge of town. But it had stopped there. The same economy which stopped the building in Winslow slowed my chances at any kind of satisfying job.

Now a few years out of school, I had a degree, once cherished by every parent in America and now reduced to very little value. I still didn't know what I wanted to do, and envied those who had it all figured out.

I rinsed the glass, put the juice back in the fridge and headed upstairs. Turning off the hallway light, the house was dark and silent. I crept into my room, turned on a table lamp and got ready for bed in the low light.

Billy was not going to call again. And that was okay. A nice boy but we had nothing in common a decade before and still didn't. Except Winslow, I guess. I smirked, somewhat taken with the fact that our lives both seemed so mundane, and tonight was our closest shared experience.

Charlie was really no different. I think I liked his lack of pretence. Like he knew that life was pretty mundane and was okay with it. How easy is it to get on a plane and end up in Mexico? At a resort, but it wouldn't take much to venture out to a Mayan ruin, would it?

Cindy and Joe were more the resort types. Mexico was probably just the best value for money. Mayan ruins were for other people, dreamers maybe, explorers. Given my complete lack of adventure, I wondered why I kept thinking of Mayan ruins. What about the Aztecs? Their society was in ruins too. A thought I found oddly comforting.

I nestled between the sheets with visions of ruins in my head and drifted off to sleep. I wondered if Charlie or Billy liked ruins. Sometimes people surprise you.

The next morning, with no reason for rising, I tried to sleep in. To no avail. At least it didn't feel like it, but the clock showed I'd been trying for nearly an hour. I was starting to get warm and flipping down the covers to cool down, which just suggested getting out of bed.

I crept downstairs and saw my mother at the stove. "Eggs and bacon?"

"You read my mind. Not much to tell about last night. Cindy and Joe looked great and are off to Mexico for a week."

"That's nice. A resort I'm guessing?"

"No, they are driving through Mexico with stops in Acapulco, Guadalajara, Tiajuana, and Mexico City."

"I would not have expected that of them."

"No, you are right, they are going to a resort in Ixtapa. But a driving tour sounds more fun."

"Fun? I'm not so sure. Alice Cranston's sister was down there a while back. She and her husband were looking to retire there but found it a bit lawless. They said it was uncomfortable constantly looking over your shoulder."

"I've heard that leaving the resorts can be a similar experience."

"I do like the idea of seeing other places. But only safe ones."

"That hardly seems to be the point," I said.

"Getting robbed or worse is not a life experience I'd care to have."

"The same can happen to you in New York, or Chicago."

"Yes, but at least I'd understand the robbers demands." My mother giggled. "Maybe staying right here in good old Winslow is best?"

"You think so?"

"Well, we're here. Life is okay, if not good."

"You don't yearn for more."

"No honey. With the edgy and interesting comes a lot of uncertainty and worry. Would I like to take a garret in Paris? I'm not a painter. Mine you a wander around Paris might be interesting, but I don't think I'd like to live there. Well, who knows?"

"That's what I saw last night. Everyone I know just doing regular jobs, living pretty much the same as we did in high school or university."

"It takes time to find your way. I don't expect you'll stay at Walmart your whole life."

"What if I love it there?"

My mother looked at me, bemused. "I am hopeful that everyone gets what they want, within reason, of course. After all there can only be so many Presidents of the United States."

"I don't know what I want."

"Not many do at 25."

"Problem is 25 has a way of turning into 30 and then 35." She slid a plate of fried eggs and bacon in front of me. "Toast will be a minute."

She asked about several of my other classmates, who she could remember me speaking about. There was not much to tell.

"Remember you are the manager of ladies' wear. You've always liked clothes. Maybe you should explore becoming a buyer for Walmart?"

"Yeah, the manager of ladies' wear, in a Walmart that only exists because it serves the tri-county area. In the middle of nowhere because all the other nowheres are within easy driving distance."

"Now that sounds positively exotic."

The phone rang and I answered. It was Charlie. He enquired as to my joy level the previous evening, reminded me that we were going to a movie.

We had a brief conversation and I agreed to be picked up for the early showing.

My mother looked at me expectantly, but I ignored her.

After an uneventful day in an uneventful town Charlie pulled into the driveway exactly on time. I didn't want him coming up to the house, so I scooted out with a goodbye and got into his car.

"Hey hi," he said. "We've got two choices, a superpower mash-up or a slower paced international drama."

"I'm for the superpower thing."

"You sure?"

"Absolutely, I'm just not that into drama."

With a smirk Charlie tooled onto the main street and eventually into a parking lot behind the old theatre.

"I really like this old place," he said. "You just don't see the old marquees in front of theatres anymore."

We watched the film, and entirely forgettable sugary concoction of action, explosions and an allegedly world saving plot. He suggested a coffeeshop and I agreed but was determined not to have a late-night caffeine rush.

"So what did you think of the wedding last night?"

"What's to think? It was lovely and predictable and nice to see people I haven't seen for a while."

"Yeah, I guess."

"You didn't have a date?"

"Nobody in a position to ask, especially given the stay over and time with my folks."

"I hear you. Lucky for me, they decided to come home to do the deed."

Charlie laughed, "I heard they are off to Mexico."

"Yeah, a resort in Ixtapa. I'm sure they will have fun."

"So, you seem to be the only one from the good old days who is still here in Winslow."

"You know, I just can't seem to break away from the familiar stuff. I've toyed with taking a Walmart job in a larger town but the cost of living, the lack of any real future and the same old pay, just make it unappealing."

"What about going back to school?"

"A great idea if I was fixed on some particular career."

"Sounds bad. You're in a rut that even caffeine can't fix."

"How about you? Is there a path forward for you?"

He looked into his cup and swirled the contents a bit. "You know. Like everyone else I'm dealing with the high expectations that come out of college and realizing that everyone on Earth has my background and the rat race has begun anew."

I nodded, mirroring his swirling cup.

"What about doing something crazy?"

"Like getting a coffee and staying up all night?"

"No. You and me. Let's go. Practically, let's quit our jobs and go to California or New York or someplace else. Impractically, let's go right now. Pack a few things or if you really want to be nuts, jump in the car and just go, right now."

I looked at him for signs of a put-on. They weren't there. I allowed a smile to slowly invade my face. He sat expectantly and then did the same.

"You want to go right now? Don't you?"

I looked around the shop, "And leave all this?"

He laughed, a little manically. "New vistas, new choices and new opportunities. They aren't coming if you don't go out and grab them."

"You know it seems like a plan. But . . . ."

"But what? We both need a change. Let's just do it for a holiday, something different."

"Okay, maybe. Can we do it in a few weeks? I have some time off then."

"It's way more memorable to just jump in the car and go."

"So, you've already taken the next couple of weeks off?"

"No!" He looked wounded. "Crazy has to be spontaneous. A plan to go in a few weeks isn't that."

"Okay," I said. "I'd like a job to come back to, you know, in case I fail to meet my destiny, and all that. Give me a week and off we go. You choose. And don't tell me. Well, let me know the day before, so I can pack appropriate clothes."

Charlie smirked, "You for real?"

"I am. We leave at dawn next Saturday."

We spent the next two hours talking about possible destinations. Charlie, to his credit, was less fixed on the end goal and more interested in places we would happen to pass on the way. Unfortunately, he talked more like a tourist, and less like someone interested in getting to the reality of places we might find ourselves. I had to fight him and almost pulled the plug when he couldn't think past the sights.

My mother thought I was crazy. And that was the point. I needed a jolt and this was going to be it.

"You are going to take a trip with Charlie who you have said repeatedly is about as adventurous as the nightly news."

I nodded. "Who knows what will happen."

On Saturday morning Charlie pulled into the driveway at 6 am, and I jumped out the front door, one suitcase and a backpack in tow and leaped into the front seat. My mother, in a hastily donned pair of sweats and a tee shirt, followed me.

"Charlie? Are you certain you know the way?"

"Hi Mrs. Turner. I don't have any idea, because if I knew the way there would be no point in taking this trip."

"You two be careful and please check in every couple of days."

"Sure mum. Love ya!" and I waved as Charlie backed down the driveway.

"New York here we come."

He had told me it was New York the previous evening, and I had been able to cast off my thinking of the west coast and try to consider all the things in between, things that weren't tourist attractions. And frankly, that was trouble, as the world has conditioned you to think in terms of sights rather than experiences.

Leaving our own neck of the woods, where every town was named after some other better-known place, we finally ended up in Texarkana. Not the most imaginatively named place, but it did have a ring to it. It wasn't until I saw the signs for Memphis that I felt we were free. It didn't immediately dawn on me that Memphis was itself, a borrowed name. But I did feel that the freedom came with ties back to jobs and family, familiar places and routines. Breaking those connections was the key.

Charlie and I sat in silence for a long while, he was afraid to say anything specific and I was just looking at the countryside. I think he was wondering if I'd change my mind while we were still in Texas.

As we drove, I noticed that the place names had a distinctly Southern feel. My understanding and knowledge of the War Between the States was never good, but I did remember that Arkansas was late to the southern cause, and largely out of the fighting early on as the Northern troops captured Little Rock before they captured much else.

But we didn't even discuss stopping in Litte Rock and crossed the Arkansas River with barely an acknowledgement. We pulled into Memphis determined to look around a bit. The signs for Graceland were everywhere but I was determined to avoid that place at all costs. Tourism was not the point of our adventure.

We rolled through some neighbourhoods in the dusk of early evening and quickly realized that we were completely out of our element.

"Finding sketchy places that we did not expect, is part of the journey, right?"

"Right," I said, trying hard to convince myself. "Can we find a place to stay first, and then maybe look around a bit more?"

We had not discussed the overnight arrangements, but I believed it was implied since we were friends only. I decided to be firm. We took a hotel room with a couch and decided that we would flip flop between the coach and the bed each night of the trip. Charlie looked relieved at my suggestion.

We checked in, and piled back into the car to roll around the streets before it was fully dark. Memphis did not seem too inviting, though I kept thinking we were just unaware of where to go for a meal. Going to the tried-and-true fast-food places was out, per our, or at least my, determination to cultivate experiences.

The next day, after a look at 'places of interest' in the hotel brochure, we rolled down to the Mississippi bluffs, saw an old French fortification, really just a line of stumps in the ground and got back in the car and headed for Nashville. Modifying our travel code, we decided that 'Places of Interest' qualified as an experience as long as they weren't amusement parks, there was no charge for access, or a line-up of tourists in front.

Once on the road to Nashville we had to decide, north through Ohio or West Virginia or east through North Carolina and the big cities of the Mid -Atlantic, Washington, Baltimore and Philadelphia. I scrolled through an electronic map and for the first time understood what my father had always complained about, that paper maps gave you the bigger picture, while the digital ones only showed you the next 50 miles. Unless of course you scaled up.

A long lunch in Nashville turned into a look about that lasted so long we decided to stay until the next morning. Nashville was full of young people and we mingled a bit at a bar and wandered back to the hotel, exchanging stories of people telling us Nashville was a wonderful place.

I didn't see it, particularly, but then I had little idea of what wonderful would be or look like.

"Except for people telling me how great Nashville is, I didn't see any wonderful."

"I guess you have to live there."

The next day we dutifully left the wonders of Nashville and almost by accident headed east, the highway exit took charge and we were on our way. We passed Knoxville and then headed into the hills before having lunch in Asheville. We ended the day in Durham, North Carolina. The big buildings of Greensboro almost repelled us after the college town of Asheville which seemed nice but insubstantial. I was struck by my use of these terms when there was little to point to what created the belief. Passing through, and living, really living there, was completely different.

We looked around Durham and nearby Chapel Hill, drawn to the universities which guaranteed a pleasant stroll. And we talked about where to go the next day.

"I know New York is the goal, but I'm just as happy to share our time with the other major cities on the way and keep New York to a few days."

"That will save us some cash as well" Charlie said. "Of course, this adventure isn't all about saving cash."

"Nor is it all about New York. Maybe we should get off the Interstates. I'm thinking on the return trip we should go back a different way and open up the country."

Baltimore seemed like an urban jungle, Washington like a bureaucratic one, and Philadelphia was a place that the highways seemed to want travellers to avoid. We took a couple of days there and poked around, drawn a little bit to the tourist places or at least near to the tourist places.

The harbour in Baltimore was interesting, the National Mall in Washington was impressive and the old city of Philadelphia was eye-opening to a pair of Texans.

The next day we rolled through New Jersy and simply marvelled as the miles rolled away and the city never really gave way to countryside.

As we neared Manhattan, we decided to ditch the car at a commuter train station and head into the heart. The island was shocking to us; it's sheer size and heavy development were mind-blowing.

"Good thing we prearranged the hotel. I wouldn't have the first idea of where to start."

"Me either, and that goes for looking around as well."

Our hotel was on the upper west side so we checked in, after some finagling with the subway system, and then decided to walk south as much as possible to take in the city.

Block after block of high rises and significant urban landscapes, we were drawn to Times Square, more because the roads led there and the bright lights attracted our eyes. I didn't know whether to love Manhattan or hate it. It felt so oppressive, pushing down on my heart with great weight. I certainly did not want to leave and did feel a touch better when escaping to Central Park, even if it felt like a cage.

We wandered the streets, sort of like tourists but staying away from the bus tour hot spots. We did take in the Metropolitan Museum of Art and the Natural History Museum. I cringed at our choices but neither of us fussed about it. The choice of restaurants was mind blowing but my craving for barbeque was unsatisfied.

I had caught Charlie scribbling in a notebook on our second evening before we turned in. He picked it up each night and wrote for half an hour or so.

"Yeah, I'm just trying to record my impressions of the places we've been. You know, I'm likely to forget the details and have the entire experience boiled down to one or two major feelings."

"I'm not opposed to that actually," I said. "But don't let me stop you. In the end, your approach might be best."

"I figure we have three more days in New York, four if we want to make a run for home, rather than stop and look around."

"I'm inclined to stay here the extra day. It feels as if we've hardly scratched the surface of the place."

"So you are willing to throw Columbus under the bus?"

We laughed together. "And Cincinnati. Sacrifices must be made."

"You know, some of those smaller cities were nice. I'd go back."

"To live?"

"Maybe, but not for any significant length of time."

"Drawn any conclusions on our trip so far?"

"Not really. I'm not sure I'm going to find any meaning in all of this until I'm back among the routines."

"In the end, where you live and what you do with your time are defining. I still have a lot, barring some accident of fate. And you certainly cannot live your life with the expectation of accidents changing its course."

"Let's go down to the hotel bar and nurse a drink. Maybe we will meet some fascinating tourists from some mythical place. Like Buffalo. And that might be our next trip."

"Slow down. We still haven't finished this one nor determined its meaning."

"Right now, I am craving a shot of bourbon and a beer."

I looked at the clock, "Okay, it's not late. Let's go. But early to rise. We have explorations to conduct."

I knew I looked like a tourist, baggy pants, a loose-fitting top and running shoes. But I didn't care. Not that New York was the epitome of fashion but there were certain expectations for going out on the town. But then again, we weren't going anywhere.

The hotel bar was pretty empty as it was a Sunday night. We sat down and Charlie got us a couple of drinks. "What are we doing tomorrow?"

"Okay, don't get upset but I was thinking we should split up tomorrow and just pursue our own thing."

He looked a bit shocked. "New York is a crazy place. You sure of that?"

"Yeah, I'm not even sure what I'm going to do, probably just walk down Fifth Avenue and check out the clothing stores. I didn't think you'd be interested in that."

"You're right. But now I have to think of what I would be interested in if you aren't going to be there. Something that you aren't interested in seeing or doing. Help me out here."

"Wall Street? Maybe Trinity Church? The 9-11 Memorial?"

"You aren't interested in those things?"

"Like I've said, I want experiences, not sights. Although some sights have been worthwhile. I've wondered if we shouldn't have taken in Graceland when we had the chance?"

"I never expected to hear that out of you. Graceland? You have definitely changed your tune."

"The more I see, the more I realize that Graceland is an anomaly in Memphis and maybe in America. Think of all the titans of American culture who have lived in New York and yet there are no lasting monuments to them. A plaque here and there but no real big memorials."

"New York doesn't stand still I guess," he said.

"It most certainly does not. It's the constant churn, that's what I feel everyday, that's what seems to grind me down. The weight of constant pressure to grow and change and be different, erodes what's already there. The constant looking ahead seems to denigrate the reasons things are as they are."

"Do you like that?"

"I don't know. I certainly do not like the pressure. It seems to be change for its own sake, as if there is always something better on the horizon. Maybe I'm just too used to the slower pace of Winslow, you know, to the belief that the marquee on the movie theatre has value."

"Uh, oh, I think your adventure is in danger of pushing you back into the tried and true," he said.

"Like I said I won't know about that until I'm home and settled and back to the routine."

"Excuse me. I couldn't help but overhear your conversation," said a youngish woman, pushing 30 maybe, with long, long hair and a thick Scottish accent. "Your accents are familiar. If I'm not mistaken you are from North Texas."

We must have looked shocked as she laughed. "Yes, we all have accents, even you."

She turned toward our table. "I used to work as a maternity ward nurse in Dallas. I went to school in Texas and stayed until I got homesick."

"And now you are back in the States?"

"I'm here on holiday, meeting a couple of friends from Texas here. It's kind of halfway."

We chatted about Dallas for a bit, with Charlie doing most of the talking, as he was living and working in its shadow. And sure enough two people entered the bar and their faces lit up when they spotted their quarry.

The young woman introduced her friends and explained we were from Texas. We introduced ourselves and quickly, everyone joined the same table. The new Texans were very tired and we too were out of gas but we talked about Texas for an hour before agreeing to meet for dinner the next day.

We talked of the familiar Texas ways and the oddities of New York, putting much of it down to the geography. Sprawling plains versus a small island makes people different, I guess.

The two additional Texans had never heard of Winslow. They were both from the Dallas area, Fort Worth for one, and the northern suburbs for the other. While Charlie spoke to them of home I turned and asked our new friend Beth where she lived in Scotland.

"I'm from Inverness, which is north, but not all the way into the Highlands. But the jobs are south so I live in a small town outside Edinburgh called Bonnyrigg. Rents are cheaper and the pace of life a bit slower."

"You don't like the city? But you came to New York?"

"An experience. If you are going to spend time in the city, you might as well pick a big one," she laughed.

I told her we were in New York for the experience but so far the nature of the place had not agreed with me.

"It's all about your expectations, at least in my experience. If you go somewhere with few expectations, you are almost sure to like it."

I picked up my glass to take a sip and glanced over at Charlie who was laughing at something that had been said. He noticed my look.

"Oh, something Tamara here said about football day in Dallas, and the seriousness of the tailgaters." He could not supress a big grin. Beth looked a touch confused but then the recollection of the event dawned on her and she broke into a smile as well.

The hotel bar seemed to fill up a bit, and then drain away. Revellers were getting ready to go out on the town, or like us, and those who stayed, tourists who would rather not battle the elements outside.

"So would you come back to the States?" I asked Beth.

"I would, but I'm in no hurry to. I enjoyed my time in Texas. I also like Scotland. Two sides of the same coin, I suppose. Something different and something familiar. My parents are happy I've come back, though they sill live north. I can get there for a weekend once in a while, and they like visiting Edinburgh too."

Charlie and I were going downtown the next day just to poke around. Trinity Church, St. Patrick's and everything in between. We decided to walk from our hotel down to St. Patrick's, perhaps not the wisest decision but we skirted Central Park most of the way and that was nice, like a box holding the chaos of the city at bay. Once inside the huge cathedral we were transported out of the city again, almost as if the huge stone walls were sound proof.

A few others were there wandering around and we took our time and sat a while in the nave, just taking it in.

"Honeymooners?"

The voice had come from the steps as we exited the building. I turned and a street performer was just setting up. I looked around the few people that congregated there but saw no one that matched the description. I wasn't sure what I expected to see, a man in a dark suit and a girl in a white dress, perhaps, but that was crazy. The newly married change for their post-nuptial trip.

"Honeymooners?" the performer asked again, looking right at me. It took me a second to understand and less than that to flush. The guy with the guitar launched into 'A New York State of Mind' while I stammered and shook my head. Charlie just thought it was funny, and pushed my shoulder towards the sidewalk.

"A lot of young people footloose on a working day in New York, are probably on a honeymoon, or something. Hey how about some lunch. All that walking has made me hungry."

I nodded, and began to look around for a likely restaurant. I glanced at the time and realized we were still a touch early for lunch. "What do you want to eat?"

"The truth? Barbequed ribs, biscuits and some greens. But I'll settle for anything. Bacon and eggs? You think we might be able to still get that?"

"Charlie. We can get anything. There is sure to be an all-day breakfast place close by. We just have to find it."

As we crossed the street, still walking down Fifth Avenue, I started laughing. There was a sign in the street, well, two of them actually. One said 'Texas BBQ' and the other 'All Day Breakfast' and both had arrows pointing right.

Charlie started laughing too, "Come to think of it, I think I'd just like a burger."

"No, no, no you have to choose. Ribs or eggs?"

"Isn't a burger a choice," he asked innocently.

"But not one you are allowed to make. Come on?"

"Eggs sound awfully good," he said as he reached for the door of the Texas BBQ place.

"Wrong door."

"Is it?" He flashed a huge grin. "I don't even care if they Yankify it. I really need a taste of home."

The ribs themselves were okay, certainly made better by the location and our yearning. We both rolled our eyes at the local push for authenticity, even if we were secretly pleased at the attempt. The biscuits were dry as sawdust but rescued with a little butter, and oh, so good.

After the meal, Charlie confessed he just wanted to lay on a couch for a while but we soldiered on. The big buildings of New York loomed above us, and the crowds of people on the streets, scurried to and fro with some kind of internal purpose that seemed entirely natural. Like blood flowing through your veins.

Soon enough we were walking down Broadway and noticed the sidewalk plaques embedded in the sidewalk along side the road, with a date and a mention of who or what was being celebrated.

"I'm certain seeing these plaques is not much of an experience, but imagine being here for a ticker-tape parade?"

"I guess all you have to do to get one, is do something spectacularly memorable."

I turned and kissed him, "Like that?"

And glib Charlie was at a loss for words. After a moment he spoke very slowly. "Um okay. I'm not sure how I'm going to get the offices to toss out their confetti."

I grinned maniacally. "Maybe I should have done something else spectacular."

"No, no, that was quite spectacular itself. Not sure how you could have beaten it."

"Think nothing of it. It was entirely spontaneous. Like this trip was supposed to be."

He saw the sign for the Staten Island Ferry and mentioned that it was free, and offered a good view of The Statue of Liberty. We made our way to board.

Sitting down for a while was nice after the huge hike we'd had all the way down Fifth Avenue, despite the pit stops. More than the Statue, the view of The Battery, with the buildings of Manhattan sprouting from the river, was even more spectacular. I took a few photos.

"I thought we were avoiding the tourist thing?"

"We are," I said, "the view is an experience I may never forget."

Back at the hotel that night we had to decide on one more day in New York or the beginning of our journey back to Texas.

I looked out the hotel window and saw the streetscape. The window did not offer any broad view, just a close-up of the retailers across the street, the traffic in front of the hotel and a few neon reflections.

"New York is really just a whole lot of small neighbourhoods stitched together into something massive. Like if Winslow and a whole bunch of other towns were all jammed together. If one got boring you could just go a few blocks to another, similar but different."

"So why does it feel so weighty?"

"Maybe that's just it. You can't get away from the everyday. There is nowhere to go that's truly a different experience, just variations on the same theme."

"So you want to leave tomorrow?"

"Yeah. I think I'm done with New York. At least Manhattan."

It took some doing, making all the connections to get back to the car parked in New Jersey, but we did and were back on the highway headed west by mid-morning. The open road seemed to sweep away the heaviness of the city. We were headed toward Allentown, Pennsylvania, and Harrisburg and eventually Pittsburgh.

What was interesting was there was a whole lot of fields and hills and stuff, in between.

"You know. It strikes me that all the people in these places are like us, beholden to something local and either too happy or too scared to move away."

"Speak for yourself, missy. I moved away."

"But you miss it, I know you do."

"Not really. I miss the familiar and my folks a bit, I guess. But I like that things are different."

"But Dallas is like New York. A whole lot of neighbourhoods stitched together."

"I guess, but that is the charm. If you don't like your surroundings just move a bit until you do."

"I'm going to hope that is not the pithy wisdom that comes out of this trip."

"I'm still taking notes. History is written by the victors. Or something. I'm writing it down, what I write becomes the detail."

"Or something. I'm going to have to include a footnote to your journal."

"You already did. But feel free to add another one. I'm just not sure what wisdom comes out of travel, but it certainly comes out of change."

And as we drove I just watched the country roll past. Gliding through the hills of Pennsylvania we saw farms, industrial buildings, towns, interchanges and trees broken up by the occasional lake.

I took it all in without much thought. This was America. Or at least Pennsylvania's version of America which didn't diverge much from every other version, save in landscape. Signs by the highway proclaiming an affinity for Jesus, for politicians, and occasionally sports teams. Of course, there were billboards selling everything from legal advice to fireworks to booze. Directions to a store or restaurant or hotel. Gas stations. Roadside memorials.

I certainly saw America, in fact I thought in one place we'd gotten back to Winslow as the layout of the highway, Walmart, gas station and nearby town, was an exact match.

But pretty soon that rolled into my memory as more of the same kept coming in the kaleidoscope of scenery. I never once had any emotion, okay, in the Winslow duplicate I was momentarily amazed. But emotions as the world rolled by didn't exist. Charlie said nothing, save an occasional mention of our progress.

We stopped for lunch at a burger place and I noticed the similarity of those who worked there with Charlie and I. Obviously locals, they didn't seem to be eager to leave. I wanted to ask one or two of them about their lives, their circumstances, and why they chose to be in that place. But doing so seemed forced and odd, an invasion of their privacy.

I was definitely looking for some sort of revelation but I knew I wouldn't get it. Mostly because I was too scared to break social protocol. So, we got our burgers and sat talking about New York and thinking we should have stayed the extra day.

Allentown came and went. Harrisburg had a nice river but that made the highway connections a bit dicey. I wondered if we should go to Gettysburg, but never said anything. Gettysburg didn't have to be for tourists, but it was set up that way. I wondered what battles, military, legislative or activist, really changed the nation? As was my wont I tried a top five and thought about asking Charlie.

"What's on your mind," I asked him as we flashed by a curtain of billboards covering a substantial hill.

I think he was thinking about something as I had to repeat my request.

"Umm, ah, what's on yours?"

"Just watching America roll by and wondering where we will stay tonight, and where we will head from there?"

"Pittsburgh or someplace near there is the most likely, especially if you want to look around. All the steel stuff is gone but what is left might be interesting. I've seen pictures of the three rivers spot and wonder what that would have been like to find as an explorer?"

We passed a few small towns and then a sign directing us to Frank Lloyd Wright's 'Falling Water' a house he designed for a Pittsburgh industrialist. I wanted to see the house, its uniqueness but I didn't feel like another tourist trap.

Charlie was enthused. "Oh wow, that would be cool. I've read some stuff about Wright. Odd guy, and had some interesting ideas about design."

"Let's go if you want to." So we exited the highway and followed the signs about 25 miles south, passing through a small town of Normalville.

"Makes you wonder what abnormalities forced them into naming their town that?"

Charlie laughed. "Maybe we don't want to know. We are some distance from the normality of the interstate."

We ended up at the house, took the tour and hung around the place a while. I was much taken with it, more the setting, cantilevered over a creek in a lush forest.

"Funny, I'd always read that Wright was all about practicalities, making sure things blended properly, seamlessly and in a pleasing way. Building over a creek is not too practical."

"So there is more to Wright than practicalities."

"I guess, but we are talking about a man who not only designed the houses he built, he also designed things inside them, tables, chairs, and such, to blend with the style and layout of the home."

"It's a mystery." I wasn't meaning to dismiss Charlie like that, more Wright, but I think Charlie was upset. "I was talking about Wright. Maybe you just need to know more about him. He's pretty famous."

"And from what I know, fairly notorious. Couple of marriages, headstrong and determined in his professional life and quite willing to trample people who got in his way."

Back on the road we headed into Pittsburgh, thinking we'd have dinner near the city center, wander about a bit and get out of town for a cheaper hotel.

We talked about our route. Columbus was next but then we could vary things, going to either Indianapolis or Cincinnati on our way to St. Louis, with a potential pit stop in Louisville if we took the southern route. And from St. Louis to Oklahoma City and home.

"St. Louis is the forgotten city of America. It hosted an Olympic Games, think about that. It was the gateway to the west, with everything in the interior of the country moving through there either east-west, or north-south on the Mississippi. And now, what?"

"So, what are the happening cities today?"

"Texas cities are growing and Florida, and some of what we saw in North Carolina."

"So, America grew from chasing beaver pelts, to panning for gold in California, to using the miracle of air conditioning."

I smirked, "To think, AC is the biggest driver of growth. I wonder what that says about us?"

"Wait a generation or two and find out."

Both of us fell for the college atmosphere of Columbus. And both of us were repelled by the urban blight in St. Louis. We chatted about our impressions of these places based on very scanty and specific experiences in these places. My family had lived in St. Louis a few generations before and I wanted to explore some of the older areas they would have known. Big mistake. The very definition of urban blight.

As we rolled south of Oklahoma City and past Norman, things became clear. We rolled around Dallas, which seemed to take forever and headed to Winslow. Getting home was a nice feeling, as home produces a feeling no other place can.

"Take a break in Winslow for a couple of weeks and then come see me in Dallas if you want. Somehow, I think we need to cap this road trip with a bit of urban Texas."

"I grinned. I guess I could do that. I'll call you, but it may be a few weeks, got some catching up to do."

We exchanged an awkward hug, and I turned with my case up the drive-way. He pulled out slowly and I turned and waved before disappearing inside.

"I'm back," I called out.

"Hi," I heard coming from upstairs. Pretty soon my mother appeared on the staircase. "Well, let's get a look at you. Any revelations?"

"Not yet. I haven't had time to process it all."

"Once you do, it will all fade into the background."

"One thing is for sure. Seeing Winslow after a few weeks away makes it seem fresh and new. Like I'd forgotten all the details that used to blend into the background."

"Well that's something, I suppose. What about Charlie?"

"I think he had the same experience as we passed through Dallas."

"So what stands out to you? My mother asked.

"Here or elsewhere?"

She gave me a look.

"The towns are all made up of the same things, jumbled together in a different way, sometimes due to geography or history, I suppose."

"So Winslow and New York are the same?"

"Yeah, in an odd way. The three blocks around our hotel in New York were like a small town, just that there are a whole bunch of other small towns marching on and on like a ripe field"

"So your wanderlust is satisfied?"

"Oh, I don't know. Maybe it's just lit. Maybe Europe is different, or more of the same with a language barrier. I really don't know. Strangely, despite wanting to avoid the tourist places, it was the tourist places that defined the character of each place. The practicalities of life were just built around them."

Chapter Thirty-two

A road trip to Philadelphia was arranged with just one overnight.

Brandon was on board, as his aunt wanted to see him and he needed a break. He was still a bit ginger in his movements but able to get around fairly easily, as long as we kept it slow.

The boys arranged to stay with Brandon's aunt and Theresa and I took a hotel on the outskirts of the city. The first day we arrived like a gang at the main retail location of the men's store. Theresa had seen pictures of her clothing display and I could tell she was unhappy. I toyed with the idea of being an intermediary but it felt better to leave it to her. The photos she had seen highlighted her display but did not show it in the context of the store layout. The store was large and the clothing section made up only a small part.

We were greeted warmly as we arrived late morning. There were a few shoppers in the store. One was looking at the men's pants so Theresa stealthily made her way over to the ranks to observe. She came back disappointed.

"That guy murmured a bit, but he didn't say anything."

"So you expect people talk to themselves and conduct a running commentary on their browsing?"

She laughed, "Okay, okay. I was hoping for more. You know, appreciative noises, happy humming, revelatory exhalations. I think your writing has begun to rub off on me."

"Oh, what is it this time?"

"Well, Brandon, if you must know, I took a shot at literary fiction. Lots of description, inside thinking and not so much plot as beach books that you favor."

He looked wounded, "I hate beaches, boring as hell, though I imagine that is why 'beach fiction' is so full of plot. Something to balance the monotony of the waves."

"Okay, I admit I don't know your literary preferences, and perhaps I'm a little sensitive regarding my chosen genre. It's not really my thing, but I had to give it a whirl, as part of my project. All this talk about 'beach fiction' and it's not even a recognized genre."

"It isn't, but it takes in thrillers, crime and adventure stuff, anything light and full of plot."

"You seem to know a fair bit about literature."

"I dabble," he said.

"Even before your recent forced dabbling in hospital?"

"Yes. I've always been a reader, those Hardy Boys grabbed me and never let go."

I laughed, in spite of myself and asked who his favorite author was, and what genre he liked.

"Mostly sci-fi to be honest, though anything good, is .... good. Azimov has a lot of interesting stuff, but there really isn't one author, maybe John Brunner too, its mostly title driven for me."

Theresa chimed in distractedly as she watched another shopper ruminate on her clothing rack. "I prefer titles as well. It seems to me, that most authors only have a limited scope of real high-quality stuff, though they can build a shelf of solid work on their way to and from their best stuff."

"Does that count for clothing designers, too?"

"Probably. I've never really thought about it that way. I guess everyone in the arts can hit upon a touch of greatness, but it is very difficult to find the magic over and over."

She kept her eyes on the far corner of the store, trying to pick up some visual clues to the success of her clothes. And then the man holding the jacket up, swung it around his shoulders and quickly did it up, holding his arms out and down, he checked for sleeve length and roominess.

"I'd really like to talk to him about what he is looking for in clothes."

"So do it. Look, he's heading to the cash, looks like a buyer."

"Wait until he's paid."

"And don't act like a pollster."

The man eyed a few other things on his way to the cash, where he paid. Theresea was getting ready to accost him as he left the store, but a nod from the cousin, and the man turned to look in her direction, and gave a crooked grin.

"They mentioned me at the counter?"

"Yup," he said. "Asked if I'd care to comment on what I bought and why."

"That's about it. I designed the jacket and other men's clothing over there, and wondered why you liked it enough to buy?"

"Color and fit, first, and then I really need a light jacket. As for the design, I like it, I suppose without really thinking about it. Deep pockets are good. I like to keep my hands warm if necessary. The little pocket on the breast is good for a card or earbuds, and the inside pocket for a wallet or phone."

She nodded unsure of what to say next.

"So there you go. I hope that helps you." And he turned and left the store. Theresa mumbled thanks and squeaked out, 'Have a nice day' before cringing at her lack of eloquence.

"I gotta work on that stuff," she said loud enough to be heard.

"Think of it as an interaction at a trade show."

She asked that the clothing display be spread out a bit, mostly for visibility, and suggested he take one of the corner display wall sections and put her most popular items there to be seen. The cousin agreed and even suggested a mannequin be dressed in a whole ensemble.

"I know it's a men's store but some of the women who shop for their guys have commented that they would like a matching jacket or shirt."

"Really?"

"Well, two. But if two people are asking, then 200 are thinking. Can you do something like that?"

"I have such things already. It would be easy to send a rack down here and see what happens. I'm not so convinced that there is enough walk through traffic of women to justify the retail space."

"What about telling anyone interested where women's equivalents might be found?"

"I don't want to do that. I might drive my business elsewhere."

She nodded, "Okay, I'll send some stuff down. In the meantime, think on how we can maximize sales on it."

"The truth is, a lot of women come in here looking for gifts for their guys. I've noticed in most malls, there are no stores geared to guys. Even we aren't geared as much to the men who shop for themselves, as we are to the women who shop for them."

"That's interesting."

"Men know what they want and rarely go out of their way to get it, or think about something hyper-specific, like, beer glasses are good, but spending extra time to get ones with logos and such, just isn't a thing. Believe me, we have conducted a number of surveys to try to reach our target audience."

As if on cue, we all looked at Markus, who was eyeing a pair of athletic shoes nearby. "Theresa raised her voice, "Do you need shoes or did they catch your eye?"

Markus lifted his right foot, "I need shoes, but I hadn't really thought of it until I saw these here."

The cousin looked triumphant.

We all looked around the store, with Markus trying on a pair, which he decided to buy, "No time like the present." Theresea and the cousin disappeared into the back office so she could sketch out an idea for the wall display.

Dinner that evening was mostly about Brandon and his family and we decided to linger a bit downtown before heading home the next morning.

Once home I was not in a funny mood, but I had put off the comedy genre long enough and sat down to try my luck.

I scaled through humorous situations before realizing I had just flipped through every television sitcom plot for the last 50 years. I wanted something funny, edgy and universal. Family, office, love, school, rivalry, it had all been done to death. So I just plunged in.

And then I began . . . .

Chapter Thirty-three – The Ad-man Laureate

As a young man, he decided he would become a poet. He admired the great poems, loved lyrics in songs and contrived to study them, seeking out what made them work, or fail.

After deciding the tune and melody was the key to what made seemingly nonsensical song lyrics sing, he focussed on literature. Poems required their own meter, pacing and melody, built into the words themselves, and of course their order.

He was heir to small but lucrative business, but had little to do with the everyday operations of the plumbing company his father and grandfather had built.

He didn't care for running water, unless he didn't have it. He wanted to plumb the depths of emotion, and write in rhythm and rhyme, iambs and metre. He managed a few halfway interesting stanzas, and a lot of crushed up paper, with a number of entirely forgettable odes and meditations he hid in the bottom of his sock drawer.

He was feeling sort of low. The poetry market was tiny. It favored blank verse, which he did not like, and it barely paid even if he managed to land a publication.

He did manage to sell a poem on King Arthur in one journal. He cashed the cheque for $50 and used it to buy a bottle of scotch, thinking that to build character, poets should lean towards strong drink.

He considered tequila, but decided that tequila was too ethnic and not subtle or weighty enough for a serious writer. Tequila was fun. Scotch was character building.

Introducing himself at parties, he quickly dropped his identification as a poet, as that usually left him isolated, mocked, and not invited to the next one.

A second sale to a poetry magazine netted him a cool $25 and while it made him feel a bit better, it also made him realize there was no real future in rhyme, at least not in print.

He tried putting together some rap lyrics, but felt ridiculous and unable to master a suitable beat pattern to go with his rhyming. He did perform once or twice but wondered if he was considered a novelty act in the hip hop clubs.

"That guy is hilarious," was the tip off, when he overheard someone in the men's room, after he did a rap on government secrecy and taxes.

Wandering downtown one blustery winter day, he saw a sign in a window for a copy writer. On a whim he ascended the stairs to a small office and asked after the job. They gave him a test and asked him to write a slogan and short ad copy to go with it for a fictional product.

A little rhyme and a bit of metered blank verse and he handed it to the receptionist, who asked him to wait, while she took the page he'd been working on into an adjoining office.

"Who did this?" screeched a sweating man in a shirt and tie, patent leather shoes and black rimmed glasses. His neck bulged over a too-tight collar. He looked wildly at Benjamin Brody.

"Was it you? Of course it was, who the hell else would it be?"

Ben looked scared, the wild man flailing his arms around, and his face flushed. There was every chance there was not enough oxygen reaching his brain.

"It's genius, utter genius. Who are you?" he asked with an exaggerated stretching of the question.

"Benjamin Brody and I've been writing for a number of years."

"It's melodic, memorable . . . it's an earworm."

He was hired. And two days later started in the ad business, creating slogans, jingles and short, sweet ad copy. It came naturally. At first, he was amused at his ability thinking he was slumming. But he became obsessed with the perfect slogan. He studied all the great, successful ad campaigns and tried to understand what made them work.

"Artemis Ginger Ale, it's all you need now and all you will ever need."

"Good god, where do you come up with this stuff?"

"It's just there," he answered, unwilling to admit he was mining classic poetry for his ideas. He knew he needed to stay far enough away from the source that he would not be suspected of repurposing literature. Sleuthing literature students would be his undoing.

Once he'd come close, when Mr. Rattanger's secretary said, "I've heard this somewhere before. It's like an echo."

Ben didn't want to admit the secretary Ms. Holling, likely remembered a snippet of Keats from high school English class, so he took the warning to heart and kept his sources at a distance.

After a year, the small agency was bought by a bigger industry fish and then he started going to work in an upscale downtown tower. He had a reputation and quickly re-established himself in the new company.

"Listen to that grating roar, now in the dust bin. It's the cadence of yesterday's combustion. Atlas Electric Vehicles are here for all our tomorrows."

Atlas People Movers loved it. And Ben Broady's reputation was fixed. Now he would take on anything and ruminate at length before finding a bit of Byron, or Pope or even Kipling to mine for gold. His collection of poetry anthologies was unmatched in the tri-city area, and maybe in the whole state. And he didn't stop there, oh no. He began to read lesser-known poets of yesteryear, even some of the wartime rhymers.

His father was impressed with his ability to hold a job, and then with his success at the downtown firm. He'd been secretly pleased at his success in the upstairs office of Rattinger's Standard and Standard Advertising. Though he had been shocked and somewhat taken aback by his son's new direction, he couldn't be unhappy.

"I'm so glad you've dropped that poetry stuff, there's no future in it."

Ben looked at his father rather sadly, a decided not to come clean and explain that it was the poetry that gave him his advertising voice. Secrets are secrets among the successful.

"Well, it was a young man's dream, I guess. I learned from it."

"Learned that real work and toil make money. Airy fairy dreams and conjuring make debt. Turns out my fears for you were much ado about nothing. So, all's well that ends well, as I've often said."

Benjamin nearly choked. "Um, well, there are applications of many things in our speech." He burned to slap down his father's arrogance but he did not want to embarrass the old man, nor best him in such competition.

"Sometimes I wonder what Shakespeare would have said. That helps me formulate my ad copy."

"Really? Shakespeare would likely have said, 'Forsooth, I am confused, ere I kill my king."

Ben laughed, as much at the joke as at his father's take on literature. But there was no value to him in one-upping the old man. "Perhaps you are right. Shakespeare has little to contribute to our modern world."

"Now you're talking. It was confounding bullshit when I was in school, though not as much as Latin, another pointless subject."

"Maybe they used those subjects to teach you how to think?"

"Bah!"

"Well, father, there wasn't as much to know back then. Science and discovery have crowded up the fields of knowledge. We now teach more and more things without teaching how to think critically, like they did in your day."

"Think critically? Sure, I hated Shakespeare and Latin among other things. I was very critical of them."

"Well, you like to work with your hands. Machines and gears and stuff make more sense to you than they do to many people."

"Damn right. I should have gone into electrical. A bit more dangerous, but the pay is better."

"So why did you end up in plumbing?"

"Money and opportunity, I suppose. There was a shortage of plumbers. It's a messy business, water being what it is. Go for the money, like you have, finally . . . I mean, now."

"I must admit, earning one's way is satisfying, even if there is no reward beyond the weekly paycheck."

"Maybe you should start your own agency. Business isn't that hard. It's just organization. Of course, you'd been spending more time on that aspect of your business, but maybe its time for that."

Ben thought about it, but didn't want the hassle and preferred an employee's life. He wondered if he could freelance, just do some of the work himself, but the agency provided a lot of extras, like artwork and mockups that he would have to arrange and pay for.

And then there was the truth that not everything he did was immediately accepted. Often times there were modifications and edits. And even some outright rejections. The clients would never know they turned away Wordsworth, or some other laureate.

And then the agency hired a new young gun. The man was introduced to Ben but seemed to avoid him.

And then he realized why, the guy saw through him and was using his technique. It was blindingly obvious with his first success.

"Walk where Kings have walked, but keep the common touch, experience Tuscan Travel Tours."

He had used Kipling before, but saw right through this newcomer's gambit. He couldn't expose him, without exposing himself. They passed in the hall, where Ben congratulated the new man on his success. Did he detect a glimmer of a look that passed flashed his way?

The competition was on. Clever uses of classic poems were twisted into ad copy. Once or twice, he thought his upstart rival strayed too close to the source, but he didn't want to say anything, though it gnawed at him that their secret might be exposed.

One more error, and he would have to say something. And then it was, "Alas poor Yardley, he knows it all." It was the copy of an ad for men's fragrance. The photo showed a well-dressed man getting the attention of three models who seemed particularly keen on him. The male model grinned through the fourth wall.

But this was too much, too obvious to anyone familiar with literature. He'd have to say something. Eventually, he had his chance and decided to be subtle.

"You've strayed a bit close to Hamlet in your Yardley ad? Shakespeare would sue you. You have to be more subtle."

"You think? What about your ladieswear spot, 'She walks in Verasly, in all the best of dark and bright.' That was hardly subtle, now was it?"

"You are right. I slipped up there, though nobody seemed to notice."

"Nobody noticed? All the guys on the seventh floor were talking."

Ben stood stricken. His secret was out. The seventh floor was the Visuals Department, if they knew, everybody knew. His career ruined and his reputation was in shambles.

"They all know?"

"I don't know what they know, video guys aren't the brightest bunch. I do know that one of them raised the similarity and the others did not dismiss it."

"Oh god, I'm ruined."

"Look, keep the charade going. It works. I noticed some of these slogans for years in various ad campaigns. Frankly, I thought that it was just the way it was done, until I did a bit of background checking and found out you were behind all of those campaigns."

"Well, don't give it away by being so obvious. A high school grad could pick up some of your references."

The younger man flashed a touch of anger, "Remember, I was in school still when I saw the pattern in your copy."

"See. I was right." Ben's blood boiling, but the young guy was sharper than most. He had been riding the poetic twist for many years, perhaps that was over now. He needed a new source to mine.

But poetry, and literature was all he knew. Maybe he could stray into familiar lyrics. His whole world seemed to crumble around him.

He was still a relatively young man, but he needed a gimmick if he was going to get to retirement. Maybe it was time to move into a new field. Thinking of who or what had a need for sales copy, or copy of any sort he decided to explore politics and canned copy for newspapers.

He set up an office, hired a few people, made a few inquires, became a Democrat and plunged in without quitting his day job.

He managed to get a gig as a freelancer for a US Senator who was facing re-election. A few of his pieces were used in campaign literature and he was asked to write a lengthy piece supporting the Senator's bid for re-election. At the same time, he had his two hires writing fluff pieces on medicine, autos and gardening, which they sold into a canned copy farm where they were offered to huge numbers of local papers and magazines.

"Okay boys, we need to generate enough of this stuff that we can set up our own canned copy service. He joined them by writing puff pieces on a number of subjects.

"Got a tough one for you Ben," said his boss at the ad agency. "It's a make or break for us. If they like it, we will get their business for 10 years, if they don't, we get nothing."

"Okay, what's the company?"

"Not a company. It's the pork marketing board. Sales in pork are down."

"And they want us to fatten them up?"

"Something like that. You've got a month. Slogan, a radio ad, a television spot and some print."

So off he went thinking about the slogan, as that would dictate the whole campaign. He cycled through the various kinds of pork: chops, ham, tenderloins, roasts, bacon but figured that taking on all of these separately would produce a campaign that was everywhere and not focussed enough.

He tried classic rock lyrics but came up with nothing. He tried some phraseology, 'Oh noble hog . . . ', but that didn't go anywhere.

"This little shopper went to market, this little shopper stayed home, these hungry children ate fresh and the other family had none."

'It's crap,' he thought to himself.

And then he had a brainwave, it's not about the meat, it's about the satisfaction.

"Don't burp, Johnny."

"But it tastes so good mommy."

"That's what you said last night."

"It was good then too, I love ham. Those sandwiches you made for school today were really good."

"Did you burp at school like a little piggy?"

"No mommy, I wouldn't do that. But the bacon tonight was too good."

He thought he was on the right track but it all sounded crazy.

"So you liked the bacon with your eggs, Timmy?"

"Yes mommy, all most as much as I liked the ham last night."

"They both come from the same place, you know."

"Of course they do mommy, farms make our food."

The mother smiles and nods indulgently. "Maybe tonight we'll have pork chops. They're your dad's favorite."

'Just gotta work this a bit,' he thought. 'Massage it.'

After several weeks of refinement he presented his ad campaign, with two sets of spots in print, radio and television. All worked on the same theme and varied in length.

The client went with another firm.

Two months later, "Get your pig on!" was everywhere.

"What the hell kind of slogan is that?"

He was furious. The inelegance of the slogan and the campaign seemed boorish and uncouth, until he realized that pigs were boorish and uncouth. He shook his head, thinking that some elegant bit of verse that he'd been searching for, was never going to win this contract.

"Eat a pig. Toss the bones. Eat another." That's what I should have done. 'The wonderful pig has thee in thrall', was not going to score."

His boss commiserated with him, "Who knows what these marketing groups want. Pigs are not classy and we produce classy, memorable campaigns. I'm going to guess we never really had a shot."

He did use the experience to assign his own puff shop with a series of articles on how to prepare various cuts of pork. He used that to move into other meats and foodstuffs. Pretty soon they had a complete kitchen series they could sell to prospective newspapers.

'Well at least the pig stuff wasn't a total loss,' he thought.

Back at the agency he was assigned a number of new clients, ones that were right up his alley, perfume, women's clothing, watches and women's shoes. He hit all the notes and made a killing.

If the perfume was sold like pork, it would have been 'Smell it up!' or 'Eau d'Odor' he thought. 'It's all about the product, isn't it.' He vowed to refuse an entire class of products, until he was confronted with Schmitt baseball gloves.

He wanted very badly to refuse the challenge. He knew it was out of his league, but he couldn't help himself.

"The outlook wasn't brilliant for the old leather that day. The team was tough and put scorching balls in play."

He liked where it was going. And at this point the use of well-known verse was an advantage. “And then his glove was broken bad, the leather, it was split, and with a game that night, he needed a new mitt.”

“If only I could have a Schmitt, then Casey couldn’t hit.”

Okay, okay, he knew he’d have to work on it. “With a Schmitt on his left hand he would own the finest in the land.”

“And then there is a shout. With my new Schmitt, I made the final out.”

“Not bad,” he thought. He worked it into a radio spot and a print ad and presented it to the client who loved it. In the mean time he’d come up with another, a play on ‘Who’s on first?’ It pointed to the Schmitt brand glove that was ‘on first.’

The people from Schmitt lapped it up. And Ben realized that disguising the source material, in certain cases was a mistake. Instead celebrate the source, as long as it was public domain. Firmly attaching a product to cultural touchstones was a brilliant stroke. Don’t hide the source, swim in it. Make it obvious.

He felt as if he had a new lease on his career. But he soon realized that approach was limited mostly as it all came off the same in multiple campaigns of different products.

Not having an approach he could bank on, left him adrift. His younger rival had left the firm, at first taking his classic approach with him and then abandoning it entirely as it seemed worn out.

He thought about ditching the day job and moving into his own copy shop entirely. It seemed to him that the days of his kind of ad copy were coming to an end.

The constant refrains of ‘Sell me! And ‘get the sale’, were little jabs that his way was old fashioned.

And as he thought about it, more and more small newspapers were closing shop, done in by technology.

The websites needed canned copy, if only to fill out the reading available to those who ventured to the local news sites. So, he pushed for more generic copy on activities found in every community. It paid the bills, and he hung on to his job but now as a consultant and occasionally as a full adman when specific products came to the agency. He was unofficially semi-retired as his compensation was shifted to the success of a campaign, rather than a salary.

He wracked his brain for some niche to fulfil. “Greeting cards, yeah, greeting cards.”

“Except nobody buys greeting cards anymore. Idiot!”

Newspapers were dead, greeting cards were passe and most advertising had gone to video and was moving into Artificial Intelligence. The world had changed and left him in the dust. Even a comet pulled along its own debris trail, but the change in communications in the 21st century had obliterated everything that came before. Even the dust was changed.

“How do I get into AI in a meaningful way?”

He thought about a slogan generator, but that seemed to be too much of a niche to what AI could do. He needed something broader. Movies? No, AI generated ads! He liked where this was going. But he had no computer skills. No matter, he could hire some.

The world was changing and he would change with it. How you do it may change, but sales are forever.

Chapter Thirty-four

Two weeks later Theresa was sitting in the downtown coffee shop waiting for me. I waved as I entered and headed straight for the service counter ordering an extra-large dark roast with cream. No sugar this time. I was experimenting.

Sitting down, Theresa seemed lost in thought. We exchanged pleasantries and I asked after her date with Markus.

“Oh, it was fine, you know. We went out again a few days later. Very comfortable. It’s nice having someone you can bounce things off.”

“What am I?”

“Oh, you know, not male.”

"Okay, I guess. Do you see any future there?"

"Maybe, I'm not sure where it goes next. I haven't heard from him for more than a week."

"And your business. How is that all going?"

"Wonderfully. I've picked up a few more outlets and larger orders from two I was already in with. I have had a few calls to add to the line and perhaps innovate. I'm trying to dream up a way to tap into the desires of my clients without giving away what makes my stuff desirable and unique."

I shrugged. Unique? Clothes are clothes. Unique might be a bit of a stretch, but I figured she knew what she meant.

"How about a survey on your website?"

"Done. And so is a little questionnaire attached to each garment. The return rates on these things are terrible."

"When you buy something and see one, do you respond?" Theresa stretched a toothless smile across her face.

I sipped my coffee and decided I wanted something sweet to go with it. My experiment was unsuccessful. Coffee without sugar was kind of gross. I ruminated a while as Theresa talked about another show and another date with Markus, though both were speculation. I decided on an apple fritter, sweet, with a touch of healthy fruit, I thought, smiling to myself. Theresa declined to join me.

I gave her a copy of my 'light humor' piece but she tucked it away, saying she'd read it that evening and give me a call. "You really seem determined to finish the genre thingy. Haven't you generated a new idea for a novel yet?"

"Are you kidding, I've got about 15 so far."

"Really? Not too much of what I've seen appear to have 'novel' in them. Short stories or novellas maybe, but full-blown novels? Not so much."

I was chastened. I'd been working hard to try my hand at many different types of stories, hoping to find something that inspired me to a longer piece, but Theresa was right, at this point I just wanted to finish the cycle, with the original purpose buried. There were a few I might pursue as novels.

"This week I'm going to try a rags-to-riches piece. You know, city girl finds a niche in comfortable surroundings and maybe love at an out of the way inn."

Theresa laughed, "So you are writing a Valentine's Day Movie of the Week?"

"You know, I really should probably try screen writing. The whole publishing world is a mess and there seems to be no money in anything but mass appeal video stuff. I could write it and flog it to studio people."

"Do you know any?"

"No, not yet. But I could start hanging out at fancy restaurants and fashion shows and stuff and maybe find myself rubbing shoulders with these people."

"It's a plan, I'll give you that. Need a sidekick to join you?"

"Absolutely. But someone not too interesting as I need the spotlight to remain on me. Know anyone?"

We both laughed and sipped our coffees in comic tandem. I took a bite of my fritter to break the cycle.

That evening Theresa called and said she'd read the comedy piece and enjoyed it. "There is definitely no novel there. I still like the idea of mixing genres."

"Humor is hard to sustain. Maybe that's why television comedy is only half an hour."

Chapter Thirty-five - Rags to riches

I sat on the stoop, one large suitcase at my feet, waiting for the taxi. At least it had wheels. I had already delivered the keys through the mail slot and no longer had a home. I had deposited a few things at a friend's house with the promise to pick them up once I'd found a new place.

It had all gone bust so quickly. Well, maybe not so quickly, but that's how it felt. I had been scrambling for months, juggling the books, paying the longest outstanding bills only, but still driving a BMW, still dressing well and hanging out in expensive places, hoping to be seen and maybe drum up some business.

And then, a month ago, it all crashed in on me. My car was repossessed, the landlord demanded payment of back rent and the bank wondered if I was ever going to make a principal payment on my business loan.

I had to pull the plug. I could no longer keep the balls in the air. So now I was broke. I'd sold everything I could, everything that might fetch something near its retail value, stored some of my furniture with Carolyn, an old friend, and packed my clothes into a large suitcase. It was more mobile than me.

I was dressed in torn jeans, thinking I could pass for fashionable but deep down knowing the tears were not in fashionable places. Nor was I likely to be hanging out in fashionable places, at least for a while.

Carolyn said I could stay with her for up to a week, to get things together, but I was numb and didn't want to admit I had pushed too hard, assumed too much, and failed.

Sitting on the stoop of the house I had rented, my mind was just a jumble of failure. I tried to take stock of my situation and realized if I was going to leverage my business connections, I needed a solid plan. In the mean time, I needed money to live. I had put out some feelers and had two interviews in a couple of days. Management jobs in my field, consumer computer equipment, and hoped to catch on with one of my former competitors.

I wasn't holding out much hope for either job, but I had to try.

The taxi rolled up, and stowing my case like I was going on holiday, I rolled away from my former life. Carolyn took me in with a sympathetic look. One day of moping, led to two and then the interviews went awry. Her husband Avery avoided me, but was kind and deferential when we crossed paths. I stayed in my room as much as possible, not wanting to shake their domestic bliss. As I had thought, my former competitors really had little interest in hiring me, afraid I would steal their business secrets.

In the interviews they were just trying to steal mine. Funny though, mine had led to ruin.

Another morning of feeling sorry for myself and I managed a resolve. I couldn't stay with Carolyn, I had to move on, and leaving earlier than she had agreed, gave me back a touch of dignity.

Now I was living on the street. Well, not technically. I found a shelter, leaving most of my things with my furniture in Carolyn's garage. My little stash of cash was dwindling rapidly, and my efforts to secure some kind of job slowly backsliding to taking anything I might get.

Three days of getting raggedy, showering at the shelter, in fear of my soul, I landed a retail job at an auto parts store. I downplayed my background, but peppered the interview with detailed anecdotes demonstrating my familiarity customer service. I knew nothing about cars and faked it as much as possible. Thinking I'd failed I left the place leaving Carolyn's number as my contact.

"Miss? Tara?" A voice trailed after me. The interviewer caught up to me. "We'd like to offer you the job. I just spoke to the company owner. When can you start?"

The truth was, I could have started right then, but I wanted to keep up the façade, "I give me a day to make some arrangements and I can start day after tomorrow." I intended to take a crash course on Auto parts. Thank God for libraries.

I spent the rest of the day and most of the next reading auto magazines, parts manuals, and anything which outlined the thousands of parts on a car. I needed to know which ones were required the most often and how different parts were for different makes of vehicles.

I knew I was overwhelmed, and likely to make mistakes in even the most basic things. But at least I wouldn't simply stare into space at the mention of a manifold or gasket.

The first week was tough, but I fell into a rhythm and soon the paycheques gave me a chance to get out of the system.

By now I'd learned a number of ways to leverage government and charity assistance to keep my costs low, and I was able to bank most of the first two months of earnings. That got me into a student rooming house, near the university as I fobbed myself off as a mature student, doing a graduate degree. I wasn't so young anymore.

My costs were low and the job at the auto parts store was looking up as I was given a promotion to parts supply and inventory. Six months had gone by but I was only a tiny way out of my fall.

I had become familiar with the owner of a used car dealership, who often came in to buy parts to upgrade the cars he bought so he could sell them in good working order. He came in often. A burly man with a scratchy, thin beard, I figured it took more work to keep the beard at a wild half growth than it would to just maintain it properly. He always came in in a shirt and tie, sales being the most important thing.

"George, nice to see you. What are you looking for today?"

"You know Tara, I'm not sure. I just got a couple of BMWs as a trade in and I need to get them into sellable shape."

"So what's wrong with them?"

"Nothing really, just miles."

"I can't help you with that."

"I think you can." He bought a few leaf springs and suspension struts, saying he could upgrade the ride that way, without spending too much. "A few bucks and the car will ride like new. BMWs are nice that way."

I came to look forward to his visits and we soon had a banter up, with him pretending to consult me on which part would add the most value to a resale. Not that he didn't know what he wanted, but by asking he got a sense of what was selling. I could see his business was fairly lucrative. Cheap cars and generic parts in, a bit of labor and polishing, and more expensive cars sold out at a profit.

I started to ask questions, and looked beyond the manufacture of name brand auto parts, to understand the industry better. The whole wrecking yard industry was out there and I was only barely aware of it.

George came in one day and enquired at the cost of a new radiator. He often asked the prices of larger parts but he never bought them. I finally asked why. It turned out that he was buying for the wrecking yards which was a huge source of parts to retail home mechanics and even regular dealerships. The parts were cheaper than new but carried a huge mark up as whole cars were purchased for small amounts, and then the cars were stripped of parts, with each thing bringing back a large portion of the original purchase price of the whole vehicle. George wanted to know the retail prices so he could drive a harder bargain.

Once it became apparent that George and other clients were buying most of their parts at wrecking yards, I considered trying to enter that business. But the cost was prohibitive as such businesses needed a huge number of old cars to provide an inventory of parts. The guys who ran these places were parts savants, knowing which models held parts that could be used in other models. And they were perpetually oily, both as grease monkeys and as resellers. My retail job was eating at me, but there were no real prospects. However, it was clean, required me only to work the inventory listings and the cash. My dealer friend had hinted I should come work for him, but he had not voiced an offer, nor had I enquired.

Something had to happen, but I was running out of patience. Fortunately, I never ran into any of my former clients or friends. I kept in touch with Carolyn but wanted to maintain a distance until I was back on my feet. We would meet occasionally in the mall food court and chat.

I was still living in the rooming house, pretending I was a student and was prepared to keep the place for another year. The landlord didn't seem to care, as long as I was quiet, they didn't enquire, even though they were firm on only renting to students.

I had fallen into a good routine with the rooming house and was pleased when it got much quieter in the summer when many of the students were gone. It took me a while to put two and two together and then to realize a new crop would enter the house in September when the new school year began.

"Why don't you just go home? Surely your folks would take you in?"

"Carolyn, Carolyn we've been through this. I'm not on stellar terms with them. They live in the middle of nowhere, so prospects are few and I simply cannot imagine letting them have the 'I told you so' moment. I have my dignity."

"Living in a rooming house, sharing a bathroom with who knows who, is dignity?"

"Yes, when viewed against the alternative. If I went home, I'd be pushing to get out within 24 hours."

"So go for a visit."

"Why? I'm still paying rent."

"So what's your plan?"

"At this point, I'm thinking of hanging out at the docks and meeting a guy with a yacht."

Carolyn made a face. "Come to my place in two weeks. We're having a BBQ with some friends. Some singles too. Who knows?"

"These are people I've never met?"

"Yeah, I think so. You can tell them you are a student. Explains your living quarters."

"Well, nobody is going to know where I live."

"They will if you tell them the area. It's all student housing there for blocks."

"You know, I don't mind the auto parts warehouse. People are nice and unpretentious. In my former life I certainly had little enough of that."

"So you no longer subscribe to success?"

"Stop it. Of course I'd like to win in life. I'm just less sure what winning looks like. What about you Carolyn, do you think you've won at life?"

Carolyn's smile faded. She looked down at her food, swirled her drink as she thought. "You know, I'm not sure I've thought about it. Avery is great. Our life is good. Challenges, financial concerns, sure, but nothing overwhelming. In fact, without the ups and downs, life might seem dull. So, I definitely haven't lost at life. Right now, it's a tie, with overtime on the horizon."

"You aren't that old. Why is it a tie?"

"Not sure why I said that. I'm thinking there is something missing, but I'm not sure what it is. We aren't financially secure but unless there is a big change we are on the path to a good place."

"It's kids, isn't it. You want a family."

"Maybe. We are so fixated on getting ahead, mounting one challenge after another that we haven't even gone there yet."

"And you aren't getting any younger."

"Oh stop! I'm not old and in fact I have always held a belief that older parents are better. You know, more patient, more understanding, kind of past their own dramas and able to focus on the next generation."

"That's what they say. Once you have a kid it's all about the kid or kids. And it should be. You take one step back down the line."

"If that's true, I'm not sure I'm ready. I'd like to travel a bit, while I'm young enough to enjoy it. Being the support system for some snotty nosed kids, isn't on my dance card. Not yet."

"It will be Carolyn. I can see right through you. What does Avery have to say?"

"We haven't even talked about it yet."

"Sure you have. In little comments, side notes when children are present. His actions among nephews and nieces."

Carolyn thought for a moment. "I guess you're right. Avery seems to enjoy those things, but he makes no effort to become involved when they are present.

"I knew a guy once, who was the same. Totally uninterested in kids, especially babies. But once he had his own, he shifted completely. Took to the kid like a duck to water."

"Who was that?" Carolyn and I knew many of the same people.

"Tony. Remember him, Tony Agnotto. We went to school with him. I used to see him and his wife Lisa, from time to time. Wonder where he is now?"

"I remember him. Kind of a quiet guy in school. Never said much, never did anything unusual, but he was always around. Met Lisa in our senior year and they just hit it off. She was super quiet too. Always wondered what they talked about."

I laughed, "Well it must have been something as they had three kids, last I heard."

"So come over. If nothing else it will be a bit of a break for you. A touch of normalcy."

"So I'm abnormal. Thanks, Carolyn."

"Oh come on, you know what I mean. Just a bit of suburbia for your urban mind."

"Okay, you've convinced me."

Of course, Carolyn wasn't really out in the suburbs. I think she and Avery would have been mortified by the real suburbs, where success was measured by how many cars could fit on your driveway. They lived more in the inner burbs, the first expansion of the city outward just after World War Two. Single car garages, lots of mature trees, street parking. It was only a lengthy subway ride and a bit of a walk and there I was.

She and Avery had a small but functional backyard which she had turned into about as private an oasis as was possible when the houses are 10 feet apart.

I knew Avery of course, and had met one or two of the others, friends of Carolyn who brought their husbands. Two guys were there alone. We all sat around and chatted about this and that. Once it was established, that I had owned my own assembly business one of the guys opened up.

"We are looking for an operations manager in our manufacturing facility uptown. Not sure if you'd be interested but I can pass you the info if you want."

"Sure, I'll take a look at it. It's all about the money though."

"And for us it's all about the performance. What happened in your last venture?"

I shook my head, "Mostly supply chain issues. If it wasn't one part, it was another. That delayed production which caused problems all down the chain. Eventually creditors wanted cash and didn't care about the problems.

I had to pay for orders while I waited for other necessary parts to come in. I pulled the plug because it seemed hopeless between supply problems and government regulations."

"What was the business?"

"Computers. Well specifically servers and digital infrastructure. Sourcing from Asia and having loads of problems with spyware and the like."

"Well, my company is a bit more pedestrian. We retail furniture and household goods. Often sourced in Asia but really from anywhere we can get quality for the right price."

I agreed to look into it. Eventually I took the job and was back in the saddle but without any equity in the company. A year later they were looking for some capital, and having seen the company operate, I borrowed a bit, pooled my own savings, and jumped into a 20 per cent ownership stake, all while keeping my job. I had graduated into the additional responsibility of assistant buyer for the group and persuaded them to open two retail outlets in outer suburbs, away from our usual partners.

Business took off. We moved into basic appliances and fashioned our retail outlets as the place to go when establishing a household. Beds, couches, chairs, tables and fridges, stoves and dishwashers. There was no fluff, only the essentials and all at a great price with reliable service.

I was flying high, but my previous failure kept me grounded. I knew that this company was tied tightly to the rising housing market and any reversal in home buying would crush our bottom line. I could smell a downturn. Just as I was formulating a plan to get ready for a poor economy, the board asked me to sell out to them. They had a major investor who did not want to split the ownership more than two ways.

I was almost giddy with excitement when I signed the papers and received the cheque. I was free and clear of the company, still had a job but had privately decided to look elsewhere or use the cash I'd earned from the sale to begin my own venture. I just had to decide what to look at.

When the economy collapsed, I was ready. I had a bundle of cash and bought real estate. I was familiar with the student housing and managed to buy four rooming houses and made a plan to slowly upgrade them into the modern world. In addition, I bought a few destressed stocks and decided to hold them for a couple of years hoping to double my money.

I found an older guy who could repair or install just about anything. He worked his own hours and at his own pace, but he was very reasonable and reliable. I gave him as many hours as he wanted and slowly he came to see me as a one stop shop for work. I knew he had other clients but I tried to stay out of the way and not be too demanding. I pitched in where I could.

A couple years of sweat equity later and my properties had been improved, repaired where necessary and the real estate fall seemed to have bottomed out. I had taken an apartment in one and upgraded it into something passable in which to live.

My stocks had risen so I was in the black but not by enough to rejoice. Holding them for a while longer was possible and so I did.

By now I had a lot of equity. Not so much real cash as significant equity in the properties and could get my hands on that money if needed, but frankly real estate too, had taken a long while to recover.

My business ventures had paid off, but I was burnt. I hadn't had a vacation in years as I did not have a property manager so I had to be around if there were problems with my tenants. I toyed with the idea of selling out, but I couldn't as I'd survived the worse of the economy and need to hold on through the rise in values if I wanted to cash in.

I did meet regularly with Carolyn and a few other friends. Her friend's husband who had put me onto the housewares company was into something new, as that company had undergone a significant restructuring, essentially shedding all the tenured employees who cost a lot, and bringing in new, younger people who worked cheap.

"I'm happy to be out of there. It's not a sinking ship but they appear to be treading water. The new management is trying to maximize profits but reducing quality. They sold off their manufacturing and now buy exclusively overseas. They are riding on their reputation and once they lose that, they will be hurting."

I nodded sagely. "That's too bad. What are you doing now?"

"I got in with a few friends on a digital start-up, mostly developing applications for cell phones."

I had heard of such things. They were extremely lucrative, or could be but they seemed very limited in the scope of the opportunity. I had given that business some thought, and had decided that a mirror app for your phone would be what every woman needed, only to be told by one of my nephews that simply turning on the reverse camera would accomplish the same thing. He had tried to supress a side-eye look indicating my complete unawareness of technology, but I saw it, and took it to heart. High tech stuff was no longer my thing, I had moved on. Or high tech had.

Carolyn announced that she and Avery were going to be parents. She seemed positively giddy at the prospect. I was happy for her but tried to remind her of the practicalities. She waved me off.

"We've got the space. I can get my hands on hand-me-down furniture, clothes and toys to last for years. Money isn't a problem. I just have to re-orient my time."

"Easy," I said. "But we are talking all of your time."

"Yes, I'm ready. I will go down to part-time working from home mostly. Avery does well, so we will keep that going."

"We are talking about all of your time for the next 20 years. And then just a lot of time, but it will feel like very little after the previous 20 years."

Carolyn smirked, "And how do you know all of that?"

"My brothers and sisters have let things slip you know. And my mother. She was never afraid to tell me what she sacrificed for us all."

"That doesn't seem very nice."

"It wasn't I guess, but I never thought of it that way. More of a call to straighten and have a good life to justify her choices."

"Oh, in that case, she can lean on you all, no problem. I'm not sure I want to put too much expectation into a family."

"You can't help it. It becomes the reason for your life. Rewarding and heart-breaking, and largely out of your hands. Or at least that's what my mother would say."

"I can only focus on one thing at a time. The now and the near future."

"I think, based on what my brothers have said, that you take the way you were parented and try to fix the mistakes, or at least the things you thought were mistakes. And you try to do at least as well as your own parents on the things they did well. And neither one of these things is easy."

"There might be some truth to that. None of it is easy."

It was about this time that I decided to take a trip. A long trip. I decided to remain in contact with my tenants in case of emergency. I got my handyman softened up for any possible emergency, and knew I could make more substantial arrangements over the phone if needed. The cost of overseas communications was far less than hiring someone or paying them to be on call.

It wasn't until I landed in London that I realized how badly I needed the change.

I had travelled light, with about a week's worth of clothes, and a plan to hit laundromats as needed.

Arriving on the red-eye at the early hour of 8 am, I found my hotel, The Royal National, a block from Russel Square, left my bags at check-in and wandered out into the city. Knowing I'd never be able to concentrate I went to the National Gallery at Trafalgar Square. Leaning against a fountain I took in the city, finally able to breathe. I could feel all the tension in my body, tension from years of battling, fighting to succeed and fear of poor living conditions, just shed itself from my body. At first I didn't know what was happening but when the last of the tension had flowed out of my shoes I felt light and wonderful. It didn't last. My phone rang. It was one of my tenants and I tensed, but she just wanted to know if she could drop her rent cheque early as she was going away for a few days.

I was almost giddy when I told her that would be great, and said I was also away, and the cheque would not be cashed right away.

I rang off and the feeling of calm washed over me, now tethered to my own reality at home. I walked into the National Gallery and moved slowly from room to room, beginning to slow down from the overnight flight. I realized I had not eaten and so I managed to get a spot of tea and a scone from the cafeteria.

"Well luv, where's your boyfriend?"

I looked up from my tourist book and saw two young guys leering at me. "He'll be along presently," I said trying to come off as somewhat posh. One looked chastened the other still leered.

"I didn't see you come in with anybody. How's about us showing you around?"

The guy looked like a punk, but we were in the National Gallery, not a likely place for a punk, unless this was how he targeted his victims.

"Not a likely place for your sort, is it?"

"What? Everybody likes the Gallery. Don't they Eddie?"

His companion seemed surprised to be addressed. "Um, sure Al. Everybody."

I got up to leave, my senses uncomfortable, especially given that I was not fully alert.

"What's say luv? We can show you around. We know places that the regular tourists miss."

I shook my head, "Thanks, no. I'm off to meet with my friends. Bye."

I could feel their eyes on my back as I went out. I resolved to dress less like a tourist, shedding my casual appearance. I decided to go and buy a few clothing pieces to extend my tourist wardrobe into something more respectable. Shoes, it's all in the shoes. Tourists wear sneakers.

I could only think of Harrods as any kind of a shopping experience and made my way there by tube. A few purchases secured, I reversed course to my hotel and crash landed. I lay down for a moment, entirely aware of the issues of falling asleep and I was awoken by my alarm. I had dozed for an hour and now I need some real food. I found the closest pub, on the ground floor of the hotel and ate while studying my tourist book. I decided that a nice walk was the best approach and left Russel Square for Trafalgar Square again, hoping to avoid the punks.

From there I wandered through the Admiralty Arch and down the Pall Mall to the Victoria Statue and Buckingham Palace. A big building set far back of the roadway, it really wasn't much to see. So I followed the road down the Green Park and across it, sitting at a bench to consult my tourist book.

I did have a plan and decided on three full days in London before renting a car and doing a wide circle of London taking in St. Albans, Oxford, Stonehenge, Salisbury, Winchester, and Canterbury. From there I would ditch the car and take the Chunnel to Paris.

A week later, England was nearly behind me as I sat in the St. Pancras Station awaiting the call for my early morning train. I sat near a small group of people, obviously together, and from what I could hear, graduate students from the States on a vacation. They all appeared to be about my age, okay near my age, so I listened in, while keeping my head in my book.

On the train, they spilled across both sides of the aisle and I decided to take one of the empty seats beside them.

After a time, one of the girls looked me in the eye and asked if I as travelling alone. I admitted I was and then she began to include me in their conversation, eventually finding out about me, and I them.

Soon I had been introduced across the aisle and we compared notes on what we had seen in London. I was relieved actually when one of them suggested I tag along with their group.

As it turned out they were staying in a hotel in the Latin Quarter and I was not far away. The group consisted on five guys and four girls, two of which were tagging along as girlfriends of the students. They attended Penn State University and were studying business, hoping to get graduate degrees or professional designations.

When they found out what I did, they were very interested in the real-world experience I had. I didn't want to give too much away or become too familiar with them, so I held back a bit, but it was hard as they were all so friendly and welcoming.

One of the guys was familiar with Paris, having travelled there with his parents' years before. He took the lead and everyone else chimed in with their suggestions, culled from their own tourist books. Determined to avoid that, I suggested ditching the book and just walking, so we moved off as a group from our hotel, through Notre Dame, and then to the Louvre.

“I wanted to explore a different side of Paris but here we are following along the standard tourist trails.”

“I can attest to that,” said Matt, our unofficial guide. “This is the exact route my parents took us on. There is a lovely old church with serious stained glass just down here,” he said, pointing down a street once we’d left Notre Dame.

“I am sort of disappointed not to see Quasimodo, swinging out from one of the towers,” I said.

“Quasi-whodle?”

“Quasimodo. The Hunchback of Notre Dame.”

“Was that his name? Doesn’t seem particularly French.”

The group laughed a bit and we entered the courtyard of St. Chapelle, where we were completely underwhelmed by the undercroft and stunned by the upper church where we were surrounded on all sides by 30 foot tall stained glass windows.

We went to lunch at a restaurant on the Blvd St. Germain and I had decided to pick up the bill as a thanks to the group for letting me join them and as a bit of a celebration of my successes. I had not done anything so extravagant in years, if ever. I did make sure to scan the prices at the restaurant before deciding that this was the day.

When I interrupted Matt, who was going to ask the waiter for separate bills, and insisted upon only one, the table went silent.

“Hey, I’m going to get this. Thank you all for taking me in and providing me with friendship and laughs. I didn’t know how much I needed it until you all generously welcomed me.”

“It’s okay you know,” said Cindy. “You’ve been good to have around as well. Without you we’d all talk incessantly about our professors.” A few others chimed in suggesting I didn’t have to do it.

“Actually, I really want to, and its completely on me, without any payback needed. Believe me, after this, it’s separate bills all the way.”

We had a great lunch and moved on to the Louvre where we spent the rest of the day. After heading out to dinner and back to their hotel, I needed to get to mine and was determined to walk the three blocks. Cindy looked at Matt and Matt volunteered to walk me to my hotel. I wasn't about to say no in the middle of an unfamiliar city and surrounded by a language I barely understood.

"I'll be back in a couple of minutes," he said.

"I'll come with you," said Peter. "You know, so you won't get lost on the return trip. It's dark out there."

So the three of us made our way down the block and up a side street. It was dingey and poorly lit but we made it without being accosted.

"Thank you, gentlemen. I will see you all tomorrow. What time are we off in the morning?"

"Talk was we were heading for Versailles by bus at 10 am. Meet us at the hotel and we can walk over to the main road, or Rue, where the bus goes by. Hey, I'm getting the hang of this."

I smiled. "Oui, mon amie."

Peter looked confused which made me laugh. Matt managed to remain stoic and I disappeared into the hotel lobby.

A few more days in Paris went by quickly. I had not heard from my old life, so presumably everything was going along well. I was pleased with my new friends but they were all ready to move on and I had to decide if I wanted to follow them, or go where I had planned.

The group was slated to visit Normandy and then reverse course and fly home from Paris. I had it in mind to go to Rome for the final leg of my trip.

"So, we pick up the van from a rental agency near the Dome Church near the Eiffel Tower. Our first stop is Chartres and then we are on to Caen. A couple of days tripping around Normandy and we head back to Charles De Gaulle and home."

Not wanting to be a burden nor even knowing if the van had room, and what their travel and hotel arrangements were, I explained my trip was going to finish with a visit to Venice and then Rome.

They all seemed sad, and we exchanged contact information and Matt and Peter escorted me to my hotel as they had been doing.

"It's been nice to have you with us. Are you sure you don't want to come to Normandy? You could head to Italy after we come back to Paris."

"I don't want to become a burden. Frankly even you walking me to my hotel is unsettling to someone who prides herself on her independence."

"It's no problem really, just a couple of blocks and the girls insisted."

"Thank you and them. It makes for one less thing to worry about."

"So why did you come to Europe by yourself?"

We continued walking and I looked at the sidewalk trying to think of a way to avoid the question.

Matt asked again.

"I needed a break from working hard for years. Failure and success have left me pretty much alone, and I just wanted to decompress and think about my next steps."

"What are they? Have you decided?"

"Not really. Meeting all of you made me think I'd missed something, friendship, laughs, and stuff and frankly, I've forgotten to think about my own future."

"I'm not sure if we should be happy about that, or sorry."

"Don't be sorry. I fully intend to look you all up once we are back. We've got pictures to share."

"Absolutely. Of course we don't all live together in Happy Valley, but call me and let me know when you are coming so I can pull everyone together."

I slipped into my hotel and immediately felt unburdened and alone. It was not a great feeling but the sense of no responsibilities was a good one.

The next day, I considered going to the van rental agency to see them all off, but we'd had our goodbyes the night before, and I didn't want to be tempted to go with them.

I decided on one more day in Paris so I left the hotel and was going to walk though some of the areas on the Right Bank which we'd ignored. I exited my hotel and standing on the street was Peter. I was taken aback.

"Did you get a late start? They will be waiting for you and not too happy."

"No, I decided if you wanted to go to Italy that I would go with you," he said with his voice running dry. "If you'll have me."

"What about the others?"

"They wanted to come too, but their return tickets are fixed. Mine was open ended so I can change it to leave from Rome."

I laughed. "If you really want to come with me, sure, I guess. I could use an escort. Italian guys can be pretty pushy."

Peter smiled broadly, "I wasn't sure if you'd be mad. You seem to like to be on your own."

"I do. I like the independence. I have lived much of my life making my own decisions. And you know, having you all make them for me was actually quite liberating."

"So when do we leave for Venice."

After a day in Paris, we took the train to Venice and marvelled at its quiet streets, devoid of engines, where squawking birds drown out the sounds of the odd Vaporetto as they plied the major canals.

A couple of days there and we were off to Rome. Both of us lamented the fact that we were not travelling to the small cities and towns but once in Rome that was forgotten as I had only a few days remaining and so much to see before flying home.

At the Pantheon we ran into Cindy and Matt.

"Peter said you'd be here. We were able to change our flights as well but decided to come straight to Rome."

"I'm so glad to see you." And I was very touched that these people, who I'd known for only a few days changed their plans to meet me.

"When you mentioned Rome, well, we'd been talking about it and, so here we are. It wasn't that hard to co-ordinate with Peter. We were going to hit Venice but by the time we could get everything rearranged there wasn't enough time. And frankly Normandy was pretty cool."

So we walked Rome as a group, from the Vatican to the Piazza Navona, The Spanish Steps and then the ancient center and the Capitoline Hill. We covered a lot of territory. We hummed and hawed and eventually decided on a day trip to Pompeii, where we walked the cobbled quiet streets.

Well, we had to imagine them as quiet because the squawking tourists made the city seem alive and their ringing cries of discovery reluctantly pulled us toward whatever marvel they had discovered. At the end of an exhausting day, we were back in our hotel.

We all parted at the airport as we were on separate flights. Peter was heading to New York and then by bus to State College. And I, was going direct to Toronto. Cindy and Matt were flying on from New York to Chicago where they would spend a little time at home with Matt's parents.

Once in Toronto I was happy to get back into the swing of my life. There were minor issues to attend to, rent cheques to cash and accounting to be done.

And as I sat down filling in the last of the accounting notes, I realized that I was rich. Not so much rich in material or cash, but rich in experience, rich in new friendships and richer for my entire experience of losing, working hard and winning.

And I speculated on where life would next take me. If I was rich, what more did I need? And I realized that to stay rich, I had to continue to have successful experiences. Marriage and children were certainly not close but for the first time in my life I saw them as positive experiences. Who knew what was next? Well, certainly a long weekend in State College, Pennsylvania, sometime in the near future.

Chapter Thirty-six

Was Theresa right? Was I focussed on the genre so much that the whole novel was out of my reach. I had managed some good ideas but nothing had caught fire and now I was fixated on completing the cycle. I had struggled with trying to write complete stories that were really the opening chapter of much longer, novel length fiction. I hated leaving things open ended but that was the point, I guess. The lack of finality, of polish, annoyed me when I thought about it.

And what was worse, was I was running out of choices as I had managed most of the genres and several of the story archetypes. I had completed the ones that most appealed to me and the ones I had always avoided. Theresea's idea of mixing genres seemed a bit of a life saver as I took to considering the mixed versions to make it easier to complete the cycle.

We met for coffee as usual and she told me she liked the comedy while stuffing the pages of the Rags to Riches story into her bag.

"So what's next?"

"I'm leaning to a voyage-and-return or a quest archetype."

"That sounds full of possibilities."

I wondered about her and Markus, but she had ignored my hints, not even stalling to give me a 'don't go there' look.

"Have you heard anything about Brandon?"

"Yeah, he's back to work. Still a little ginger on his feet, but doing really well."

There was a pregnant pause but she declined the chance to go any further.

I took a few sips of my coffee, determined to let her say something or choose not to.

"Everything is chugging along, you know."

"Business is like that, I guess. Same for me. Same old clients, same old requests, same old money. But it works. As much as I'd like a change from the routine, every Friday about noon, I begin to see the charms of modest success. No drama. Bills paid. You know?"

'Yeah, I guess. But after working so hard to make a go of it, I wonder what's next. Do I grow this business, do I try to control my niche or expand?"

"Moving away from your successful products, I think you'd need a very strong brand presence. You've spent so much time and effort to build that market presence it would be a shame to dilute it before its really strong."

Theresa nodded. "Yeah, I've heard that. I'd like to extend my product line, just a bit. Gives me the creative joy and hopefully adds to the brand appeal."

"That sounds good. Staying on brand is important at this time."

"What about you?"

"I am seeking a brand. I think this process has been good for me. Finding a niche is what its all about, but I hate to box myself in. I really like your idea of mixing genres. The more I think of it, the more it seems to be the right formula."

"I'll read the Rags-to-Riches thing," she patted her bag, "and let you know."

Chapter Thirty-seven – Voyage and Return

The ship bobbed on the swell. The two-masted ship was large for the day. On a government commission its captain was more concerned with completing his mission rather than speed. Violent weather of the last several days appeared to be over.

For most of the last two weeks, the ship had cut through the waves with a constant motion, until it was forced to pull in the sails and ride the storm. Overnight the sea had calmed in the wake of a second, sudden and violent storm which rose in the dark and buffeted them for one whole day, finally petering out before the second dawn.

Now, the sea had changed. The air was crisp and the salty smell a bit stronger, with a hint of something else. No storm lurked on the horizon, but always beyond it. The crew scurried about making repairs, cleaning up debris and unfurling the large sails. The swells were still there to be ridden but they were small and broad with the rise and fall almost soothing after the pair of storms.

"Aye, Captain, aye, ahoy there," came a voice from above. The Captain had been walking the deck, taking his spyglass to the bow and returning to walk to the stern again. He was just about to give up for the day when he heard the call.

“Aye, you there in the nest, what of?”

“There’s a smear on the horizon, land I’d say, but we need be closer to be sure.”

A broad smile creased the captain’s face. They’d been a week longer in the crossing than he’d expected, due to the weather. He directed his first mate to take a reading. Latitude, their north-south position, was not the issue as sextants could provide that knowledge with some precision. Longitude, the measurement of how far they’d come, was much more difficult. Seeing land was the best measure.

Aboard he had 300 settlers, mostly former indentured servants and their families, who had agreed to take the King’s commission and form a colony to the glory of the King and the Lord. A formality really, as these people had nothing and had nothing to lose. There were a few dissenters among them.

He gazed east to the three other ships sailing with them, “Signal them, that we’ve seen land.”

A few hours later it had become obvious that they had indeed spied land. And before that the first mate had reported their position, they appeared to be much north of where they had been headed.

They came upon a fair land and sailed around capes and into bays. The captain had consulted with the settlers on whether this land was suitable or they should head south to find the islands for which they had aimed.

“Well Captain sir, I for one am happy to find something a little less tropical, if you know what I mean. My experience is growing things in England.”

Another colonist disagreed, “We are prepared to grow sugar cane and have little in the way of shelters, should we choose a harsh land.”

They sailed along a coast line which seemed lush but when they put ashore, they often found swamps, sand and only hardy, coarse vegetation, although, lots of it.

"We cannot search for the perfect spot for too long. The colony needs to get a good start early in the growing season. Waiting could endanger the whole project."

"Aye Captain, a ship. A ship is approaching from the south."

"To arms, my lads. And pray it's one of ours."

The Spanish were in the south in large numbers, but they often sailed their ships with the current up the seaboard before heading across to Spain. English ships were rare in these waters and the two nations still held an animosity for each other, in no small part because of the English determination to steal Spanish cargoes. And the Spanish attempt a few generations before to steal England.

The period of tension grew but was quickly abated as the ship hove to with an English flag. It was a warship, sent on patrol to ensure the safety of British colonies in Eultherium, a group of islands off the Florida coast.

The warship beckoned the captain to board.

"Aye, Captain, are you Sir William Grenaud?"

"I am, and you, I'd guess, are Sir Arthur Chandles."

"The same. Nice to see a friendly face out here, so far from home."

"Aye, dear Captain, I had the same thought."

"Where are you going?"

"We were headed to the sugar islands to start a new colony, but were blown in a storm somewhat north."

"That happens. I would advise against those islands at this time. The Spanish are aggressive. I have only just repulsed an attack and was looking to land and replenish our water and food stocks in Massachusetts."

Captain Grenaud looked lost. Upon returning to his ship, he told the colonists of the problem and suggested they consider somewhere nearby to settle. Chandles told him that only a day or two's sail north provided some fine land to cultivate and existing colonies to help ease the transition.

They sailed in tandem until Chandles indicated they should sail due west of a head of land, while he continued north to its east.

Sailing up the bay, Grenaud followed the directions he'd been provided and sailed into Jamestown with great fanfare. The colonists exited his ships on strict orders to return forthwith as their journey would continue. After consultation with the governor of Jamestown the settlers sailed up the James River looking for a suitable spot to tame.

At Middletown they were directed another few miles north and came to a lovely spot on a bend in the river. They debarked and immediately began to parcel out the area among themselves. No natives showed themselves and those in Middletown said the Indians who had been in the area had not been seen for a few years.

The river was wide here and on the north side, where they settled, the land was watered by two small rivers providing everyone a water source. The colonists spread along the two rivers and filled the shore of the larger one they had sailed in on, and began felling trees, clearing land and building shelters. Experience taught Grenaud that the first season was crucial to the colony, as survival was paramount. Some colonists began permanent shelters on their land, but most of the effort was confined to constructing a communal building which would be converted to a warehouse once more permanent individual homes were built. They did some planting but far more clearing of land for the following year's growing season.

It was frantic, back breaking work, and the colonists knew they would reap the rewards of this effort a few years down the road. But a short planting season, native incursions and weather had a strong call upon their supplies. They did know that the existing colonies a few miles away could provide a bit of help if necessary.

Grenaud stayed with the colony for several months, administering the King's justice, taking land claims and settlement boundaries and generally governing the area. He made frequent visits to Jamestown and Williamsburg a few miles to the north. He set up a common council and was pleased when his choice for leader of that council was accepted by the vast majority of settlers.

Armand Cornelius was not a typical settler. A watchmaker in Bohemia, he had followed his uncle to England, as business there was booming. He was a master craftsman specializing in table top timepieces powered by a precision spring. He had brought many of these springs with him to America. He had dabbled in building smaller watches that could fit in one's pocket, but they seemed too much of a luxury in colonial America.

But it wasn't to make watches that Cornelius had come on the voyage. He had been accused of tax evasion and popery and decided to leave England rather than continue to fight the smears. Cornelius expected to become a farmer and build clocks in winter.

He was a precise man. His eyesight was poor, from years of hunching over the small workings of clocks, and he was not strong, but he was organized to a fault and determined. He had won the trust of the colonists and Sir William Grenaud on board ship, when his calm approach to the storms, had given everyone hope.

"Embrace it man. You will never likely do this again. This is a story you will tell your children and grandchildren," he said raising his voice above the wind as the rain slashed down.

"Only if we live, can we tell the tale."

"Fear not death. Fear a life without achievement."

"Survival is achievement? I was surviving in England but there was no achievement to be worthy of."

"Aye, my friend, survival is achievement. And without survival you do not exist to proffer more deeds worthy of remembering."

Grenaud liked the man. He liked his fearless spirit and direct approach to getting things done. On several occasions he had intervened to stop endless, circular debates and cut the talkers to the decision point. He had served to sway most of the colonists to their present location pointing out that no matter how much they wished for the sugar islands, they were no longer a choice, given the circumstances.

Grenaud had led the survey missions, or at least been quick to dispatch surveyors to impose some kind of organization to the hodgepodge farms springing up. On a survey mission to the north west of the settlement area, two of Grenaud's men happened upon several natives. Both groups were surprised to see each other and their meeting was gracious but not friendly. The natives indicated they often came this way as the hunting was good. When Grenaud's man expressed his pleasure at that thought, the Indian grew tense.

"We have been pushed away from our places of hunting."

"Surely there is good hunting, better even, further inland? We only seek places to live near the river."

The native admitted they had fine hunting areas other than this one, but wondered when the English encroachment would end.

"See all the river valleys here, see all the sea sides, see all the little creeks, bays and niches. We cannot fill them all up. There is plenty of room here for all of us."

"But, we have enemies in the hills. If you push us that way, we find them, and they are not happy sharing their hunting grounds."

"Plenty of land, plenty of land. How far into the hills does the land run?"

The native shrugged. "Far enough that the tribe in the hills will not go further as they will find another tribe that does not want to move from what they know."

The natives made their way west but the English did not drop their guard. Williamsburg had a palisade across the space between the James and York Rivers but the new settlement was west of it, beyond the protected area.

His work establishing the colony done, Grenaud made ready to return to England. He would bring a second wave of colonists the following year or perhaps two if enough people could be found willing to brave the journey. He was also charged with providing for the settlements at Jamestown and Williamsburg. He would also visit Boston.

The English presence in America was firmly in place, though as the colonists learned more about the area, some things changed. Jamestown was found to be a poor place to settle and eventually the capital of Virginia was moved to Williamsburg away from the swampy river. The colony at Charlestown survived but never grew in size, remaining a shipping port for the local farms and plantations which grew out of the original settlements.

Life in the new colony was frantic with new buildings and fields popping up frequently.

Two years later, rigging appeared down the river and the call went up. People crowded around the wharf as the middle-sized, two mast, ocean-going vessel hove to, and tied off at the quay. Those at the quay saw the ship and recognized it. A few men hopped off to inform the governor that Sir William Grenaud had returned and was bringing news, supplies and 234 new settlers. They would need 50 to 70 new farms. Some of the settlers were craftsmen, much needed carpenters, blacksmiths and masons. And even these men wanted farm properties to help grow their wealth.

"I'm amazed at your progress sir," Grenaud said, sitting and sipping watered wine. "We were delayed in Bristol, with the usual tangles, so I took the opportunity to visit Court in London. By the time I had returned and gathered everything necessary to embark the weather closed in and we had to wait. The King shall be most impressed when I tell him of your progress."

"We have been lucky sir, the natives have moved off and we assiduously do not provoke them, nor they, us," said Cornelius. "Those resources have been redirected into building and cultivating. We can send you back to England with a full hold."

"Excellent. And what of the new settlers?"

"A bit of a concern my lord. We do have some plots already staked off and ready for farmers. The land here is rich but the heat of summer means there are some crops which do not do well here. Choices are necessary and crucial."

"And the others?"

"Well, we can extend the colony. Certainly, some farmers can create new plots within our area of control. But that will leave a large number to be accommodated outside of our current jurisdiction."

"Can't the Indians be bought off?"

"They have no use for money, what they want is weapons."

"We can't have that, can we?"

"We'd like to avoid that, but they really want them to attack their enemies, not necessarily us. I have toyed with the idea of providing a few, mostly as a gesture of good will and a test of their sincerity. They have no means to make their own and would be beholden to us for ammunition and powder. A valuable point of control."

"Sensible. What do your fellows think?"

"There is a divide. Though there is on any question. I think the majority believe it a gamble worth taking. As for some of the other new settlers it might be wise to see if Williamstown and Jamestown have farms available. There is no need to provoke the natives."

"But what if we could provoke them to fight among themselves?"

"An idea sir, and one that has been considered. They claim our presence here has resulted in friction between native tribes. We have thrived with the natives at peace with us. The farmers fear a native uprising, as much for their property and progress, as for their lives."

"I have been authorised by King George, the First of that name, to provide you with several cannons for your defense. I also carry with me a black-smith, his forge and two apprentices."

The Governor looked up, astonished at the riches that were on offer, "God be praised. Long live the King."

"I believe when good King George hears of your progress, he will be even more generous."

"We will send back a nearly full ship of furs and a large consignment of tobacco."

"It will please the King."

"Now what of our enemies?"

"If you speak of the Spanish, they are still agitating but we appear to have unofficially agreed to stay apart here in America. We have entered an alliance with France, and the Netherlands to hold back Spanish expansion and the Germanic people in Central Europe seem interested in joining us. As for the French, they are very much occupied with the lakes to the north, and have explored a large river flowing south. Quite an unexpected direction."

"How are things in Massachusetts and New York?"

"They are progressing. Like you they had an understanding with the natives and have been able to thrive, which of course draws more settlers."

"And how do we deal with the natives? If we keep bringing settlers here, we will be forced to push west, to expand into other areas and even to threaten the Spanish to the south."

"The King is very much engaged with these thoughts. He has beaten the Jacobites and their Pretender, pushed off an attempt by the Spanish to engage with the Scots and has secured the Kingdom, enough to begin considering our position here in America."

"He is more concerned with defending the islands to the south as they are rich with sugar but several of his sea captains are convinced the true wealth of the colonies is here in Virginia and other colonies. Free land, a chance to work for your own advantage and a lack of oppressive historical antecedents is a powerful draw for people. Once the word of your successes begins to seep into the imagination of those who have been passed, by the progress in England, they will flock here. Or so I am convinced."

"Are the former Swedish and Netherland colonies peaceful?"

'Yes, they are also growing rapidly. The winters, while harsh, are short and the tolerances of customs and religions have led to people flooding in from places in Europe where such tolerances are rare."

"Sir William I do have two men, boys really, who want transportation back to England."

"Really, why? Have they failed in settlement?"

"No, the opposite. Their families have thrived so much so they want to send their sons back to England where they have family. In both cases they are hoping to set up a lucrative trade."

"Do they not need these boys to work the farms?"

"In both cases the families have grown substantially. The younger members will remain and grow into their farm work."

"It is not unusual for some colonists to give up. This is a new development, and a welcome one. Especially if new farms are difficult to obtain."

"Of course, we can always find new farm lands, but we risk agitating the natives."

Grenaud remained in the colony for several months before returning to England with the two young men. Later that same season he returned to the new colony with five ships brimming with colonials and goods to sell and trade to the farmers and trappers. Pressure was on to push settled lands to the west in several areas along the Eastern seaboard.

And agitation brought with it a growing unease with the natives who were beginning to realize that the colonization was not going to stop. Continued voyages back and forth by Grenaud and others brought more colonists, more firepower and more guns.

Several skirmishes with the natives turned deadly and armed red coats were sent to parlay with the natives to convince them to move west. Of course this meant that they were impinging on the lands of rival natives and that provoked more strife, much of which the English only heard about, but were secretly unconcerned.

Raids to kill livestock and burn farms only agitated the colonists and caused them to be distrustful and violent in their retributions. The Indians, careful to not use the few firearms they possessed, were slowly pushed away from the sea and deeper inland as the colonies grew and prospered.

Just as Grenaud was preparing to leave to return to England news of a large raid on some distant farms reached the Governor. Grenaud had brought with him a regiment of Red Coats and significant arms. He organized a retaliatory strike on the Indians.

Scouts had found a major Indian settlement 25 miles from Williamsburg. The armed English swooped in at dawn and slew hundreds of Indians, burned the villages and pushed the women and children to disappear into the forest and take news of the English anger to any and all natives that wanted to continue to fight.

There were skirmishes in the next few weeks but the Indians seemed to have disappeared. Grenaud congratulated himself on his bold action and left for England.

When his ships sailed into Bristol harbor there awaited a message for him from King George himself. He was to report to London and bring news of the Virginia colonies.

Leaving his ships and giving his men an extended liberty, Grenaud made his way overland to London. Before he went to Westminster Palace he made several social calls.

"Ah, Sire, so pleased I am to see you."

"Sir William Grenaud, you exploits precede you. I have heard of wanton destruction of farms and livestock in Virginia. I have heard many things I want you to spell out in detail."

And Grenaud told the King the entire tale of his voyages, the thriving economy of the colonies and their rapid growth. He told of the problems with natives.

"I would have you bring me some of these savage men. I should like to treat with them. Show them my court and perhaps they will become allies rather than thorns in our plans."

"Yes, your Grace, I can do that. On my next voyage I shall return with some who are willing."

"Sir William, bring some even if they are unwilling. Let us hope the ocean voyage with make them docile. I would like to demonstrate our benevolence."

"As you wish, my lord."

Back in the New World, Grenaud decided to take the task head on. He sent a regiment of soldiers into the forest seeking the natives.

They happened upon a band fishing on the river and approached them loudly to let them know they wished to speak and did not bear them ill will.

The natives quickly took up defensive postures but one of Grenaud's ship captains, David Mulberry, approached with empty hands, palms out. He had with him a native interpreter and they greeted each other in peace.

"I should like to treat with your Chief as I have a proposal that will be to your benefit."

The natives were naturally suspicious and nothing in their contacts with the English had been to their advantage. Sitting in a native circle, after an hour of walking, the Chief of the tribe entered the clearing, and sat cross-legged in an open place. He bowed his head and his interpreter spoke after him.

“You, invaders of our lands, people of misery, what can you possibly have for us that is to our advantage, other than news that you are leaving for good?”

“Great Chief, greetings. I am here to extend to you, greetings from my own Chief, my King, the leader of my people, who has heard of you and your people and wants to know more.”

The Great Chief said nothing.

“My King, George is his name, would like several of your people, people of your choosing, to come with me, back across the open sea, to my homeland, to speak with him, so he can better understand your people.”

“And how long would these people be gone?”

“It is hard to say, Great Chief, sailing our ships can be difficult in winter and there are other possible delays. However, I am usually able to make the journey at least once each year.”

The Chief looked around the circle and saw there was interest there from some of his warriors to see the homeland of these English and determine their strength.

‘I will consult with my circle. Go now, remain in the village. I will send for you.”

The English were given a dwelling in which to wait, though they set guard as some of their people took shelter. They were called back within two hours.

“I have warriors who would like to sail on the large ships. Four of my people shall go. I trust you that they will be well cared for and not hindered in their exploration of your land.”

Mulberry agreed and set a time for the warriors to present themselves for the voyage. At the appointed time, a contingent of natives arrived at the city walls of Williamsburg and were escorted to the wharf. They looked about with some amazement as they had not seen such workings before and certainly not at close quarters. One Englishman was assigned to teach them English, and in turn, learn their tongue, and to translate their language to several men on the ship.

Grenaud's ship slipped from the wharf and made its way north to Philadelphia.

"This is your kings' home?"

"No, no, we just make a trading stop here to take on goods for the long journey."

The Indians remained on board but looked out at the small city, growing on a grid of streets and bursting with settlers, merchants and laborers.

"The ship sailed down the big bay, and swung up the coastline to the port of New York where it began the journey eastward. Once out of sight of land the natives were very quiet. They all had trouble keeping food down due to the swells, and they all seemed much happier below decks.

Three weeks of this, and the Indian who spoke the best English came forward. "How long must we live like this? How long until we reach your lands?"

"Perhaps another six or seven moons. We are at the mercy of the sea and its moods."

They sighted land seven days later, but turned into the channel to make for London directly. It was decided that the overland journey from Bristol would be too difficult. And besides, Mulberry had been instructed to awe the natives where possible. Travelling through cultivated lands and visiting multiple towns might show the Indians the extent of the English empire but it wasn't the ultimate show of their power.

The natives took to the top deck when the ship finally reached the Thames. The sheer number of boats, quays, wharfs and buildings astonished them. And as the river narrowed, and the ship neared London, the large stone buildings, and huge numbers of people swarming the banks of the river on their own business, kept them quiet.

They docked and disembarked, and were granted a place to stay in a regimental building on the south side of the river, within sight of the Tower of London, still the tallest building in the city, even if the spire of St. Paul's up on Ludgate Hill, loomed over the city.

The Indians were awed, entirely mesmerized by the hive of activities that was London.

"And this is what you wish to bring to us?" said one of the Indians.

"In time, yes. We are builders. This is but our central city. We have many others, and dozens of smaller ones, and then villages like you, save made with stone and timber."

"And the French, your rivals?"

"Yes, they too have many stone cities, as do the Dutch, the Spanish and others. French lands were visible as we entered the Channel before we turned into this river."

Two days later the natives were brought before the King. They were asked to remain in their native dress for this meeting, even though they were given English style clothing for their own comfort. The idea amused them, but they quickly realized how they stood out in English society.

King George sat on his throne in the Palace of Westminster, his crown atop his head, his sceptre in his hand, with advisors and court lackeys surrounding him. The four natives were brought before him. They were in awe of the huge stone hall, its large span roof and decorations. Seeing the English bow to the King, they bowed, wishing to give this Chief his due.

"Great Chief, greetings from my Chief Powatan, leader of my people."

King George, put his hand to his brow and made a gesture for them to continue.

"We have some grievances with your people who have invaded our lands and we have heeded your desire to speak with us."

"Your Great King did not come himself?"

"No. Would you have come to see him if he had asked?"

The King raised his eyebrows. These men were not afraid of him. And they made a significant point.

"Have you had liberty of the city, yet?"

"No Great Chief, we have only survived the journey here over the great sea. It was a longer trip than we had believed."

"I should like you to see our capital, spend time with our people and perhaps we can speak at length of our mutual doings in America at that point."

Meet with me, at St. James Palace in three days. We will speak again at that time. The King remained seated and the Indians were escorted from the room.

They were taken to the wharfs, to some manufacturing halls, to a black-smith shop, to a horse and wagon stable, to St. Paul's and to Westminster Abbey.

By now they were familiar with the rhythms of the city and its wonders. They had spoken to each other, and had been spied upon by their handlers who listened into their conversation.

"We have no ability to hold back the tide of this world," said one of the warriors.

"But if we can push them back into the sea, perhaps they will not return. If we let them gain a foothold they will never leave and will defend their great works, like we do our own villages."

The conversation went on.

They returned to see the King, this time in an alternative Palace, the more sumptuous St. James Palace.

"Oh Americans, what think you of our London?"

"It is a great village, Great King. But with it and its wonders, why do you try to take our peaceful lands?"

"Your lands are peaceful? That is not what my ministers tell me. They talk of battles with other natives, squabbling among yourselves and the inability to build anything permanent."

The Indians looked at each other, uncomfortably. "Great Chief, we move with the seasons, we move to where the game is plentiful. We fight with our neighbours much as you fight with the French and the Spanish."

Now the King looked at some of his advisors uncomfortably.

"We seek to invoke the peace of our Kingdom upon yours."

"Your offer is most intriguing but peace has not come from your presence in our lands. Our young fear that you will continue to gobble up our hunting grounds. That you will set fields for your crops and push ours away."

"Surely, you would seek to join our colonies. They offer riches, protection, prosperity and a future for your people."

"Again, an interesting offer, but no such advance has been made. There is animosity among both our peoples and a history of violence and fear that is hard to overcome."

"Have you not overcome such thinking since you've been here."

"I have, but I also know your purpose. You want us to go back to our people with the news of your stone villages. For us to instill awe among our people. I have seen the possibilities of co-operation between us, but we are still escorted everywhere, we are still followed and guarded."

"It is early days in our mutual relationship, and much you do not understand. Without escort you would certainly lose your way, you would have trouble conversing with our people, and they, not knowing you, might fear you unnecessarily."

"Ah, but Great King, we have known you long. For many, many turns of the moon. And we still fear you."

"So how do we find peace?"

"You return to your stone villages, and we to our homes across the water."

"Great Chief, we are out of room here. It is in our nature to seek new things. And, if it is not the English coming to live near you, there would be others. The French, the Dutch and Swedish and even the Spanish further south have all tried, and more will."

The two parlayed for some time, continuing with mutual admiration among the seeds of distrust.

"You will push us away. And we will face war with out enemies, as we take up their lands, much as you have taken ours."

"Great Chief, join with our people. Do business with us. We seek furs and food. And for that we will give knives, cloth and credits to buy things of your desire."

"We desire the fire sticks."

"I understand that, and with the demonstration of trust, we will sell them to you. I would like more of your people to come here and learn our ways and take back to America what will benefit you."

So the warriors travelled some of the land seeing the vastness of the English territory and the swaths of farm fields and animals tended. And then they returned to America and told of their experiences, to an awed and disbelieving circle.

The travelled warriors formed a powerful circle within the tribe, advocating peace and co-operation but remaining aloof from their English neighbours. It was difficult to get their people to understand the extent of English society.

"We do not want to lose our ways," said one young warrior.

"Nor shall we if we stand with the English. Yet, if we oppose them, they have the ability, should they choose, to destroy us. Keep our ways, fight the English in spirit, for they are determined to hold their word, to keep the peace. They only become violent when violence is used against them. If we appeal to their sense of honor they can be pressed into whatever shape we desire."

And so the Virginia Indians worked with the English, bringing furs from the interior, and helping them with food stuffs, planting techniques, and harvest times. Word from other settlements suggested the Indians were being more friendly and easier to deal with all up and down the coast.

The French had benefitted from alliances with natives, but they too had difficulties with tribes determined to remain independent. More natives travelled to Europe to see the awesome power of these usurpers, and bought back tales of things barely understood by the natives.

"I have travelled over the water, eaten their odd food, seen their villages and know that we cannot compete with their ways. We can join them, or move away and keep our ways of life for another lifetime."

"What if we determine to remain apart from them?"

"Then we would do so only at their pleasure for they can force us to do their bidding. We can keep our way of life as long as we run from theirs."

"There is no compromise?"

"Of course there is, but it will take many generations of warriors to find that peaceful place, to know they are no longer pushing us."

"We will never be free of them. We must join them or forever be at their mercy. We can flee into the setting sun but then we face other tribes and should be forced to make peace with them by joining their tribe."

Chapter Thirty-eight

"I need a quest."

"Don't we all."

"I mean that's the archetype of my next story."

"I'd like it to be the focus of my own story."

"Okay, I'll ask. How are things going with you and Markus?"

"Okay I guess. We speak frequently and have gone out a few times, but it seems forced to me. I think we need to have 'the talk' but I'm guessing its not going to be pleasant."

"Does he seem invested in your relationship?"

"I don't know. He's playing it cool, not in terms of temperature but rather as someone who is happy to have a friend."

"So maybe the talk will just establish that neither of you are really into it. That's okay. Friends are good. You have to admit that Markus has helped you out a lot."

"He has, so I don't want to make him feel bad."

"You two have to sort things out."

"I haven't really sorted them out myself yet."

"So, you like him?"

"Of course. Don't you?"

"Sure, but he seems more interested in you."

"And that's where it seems to fall apart. If he was more interested, you'd think he'd be more enthusiastic."

"Well, maybe he isn't getting a strong vibe from you."

Theresa sat for a moment and then looked down at her bag. "I read your Voyage and Return story. I like it, but it seems very male oriented. I recall you saying there isn't much of a market for male-friendly fiction."

"There isn't. Don't forget, these stories aren't meant to be full novels. They are sparks to help me get my game back. I think they are working. I go into each story without any preconceptions or worries that I'm just writing the same old story again and again."

"Have you got any ideas for your next real project?"

"Not yet, but I'm optimistic."

"I like optimistic. Optimistic is good. Right?"

Theresa mulled over her second cup. "Back to the grind soon."

"Me too. But I thought we'd decided the grind was good."

"Yeah, it is. I'm finding it a bit subscribed, if you know what I mean. Orders in, product out, juggle here, juggle there. Phone a retailer, try to get feedback on sales and on the designs. Same old, same old."

"There are precious few careers which offer unlimited exhilaration every day. And most people hate that level of unknown more than they hate the routine. Just be thankful you aren't on an assembly line somewhere."

"You have quite the magic touch to make me feel better."

I giggled, "It's my job you know. Coalescing the essence of things and putting them down in memorable phrases."

"Any new clients?"

"Yeah, two. One I met with last week. A computer hardware retailer. The other I'm meeting later today. They are looking for some copy for their website. A dressmaker."

Theresea started, rattled. "Really?"

"No. I just wanted to wake you up from your funk. You never know when a rival will come along. I mean, you did it to others in the industry. Someone might do it to you if you don't stay sharp."

"I hadn't really thought of it like that. I just figured I was filling a niche that nobody else saw. So, who is the new client."

It's an insurance company; they have an ad campaign in the works and are looking for a fresh voice. I get to pitch a few ideas and get paid if they take them or not."

"You might morph into an ad agency."

"Maybe, I already do some of that on a small scale. Maybe this will be a game changer. One never knows what kernel will grow into something big."

Theresa took her leave. I stayed as I had some time to kill before my meeting. I wanted to know what would come out of her conversation with Markus, but I wasn't sure why I wanted to know. I put it down to clarifying the status of our friendship. If he and Theresa were off-sides with each other, how would that affect my friendship with him and Brandon?

What I really needed was an excuse for us all to get together, but I couldn't think of one, not with my mind deep into insurance, home and auto. I smiled to myself and rose to leave.

"Oh hey! Don't forget your bag."

I had turned from the table with a tray of garbage in both hands, looking to dump it before returning to gather my things. The weather had finally turned so I had taken off my light jacket and laid it on top of my purse, with the small portfolio bag leaning against the table leg.

"Thanks, I'll be back, just dropping this first," tipping the tray in indication.

I looked back to the voice and saw a well-dressed guy taking a sip of coffee.

"I've seen you and your friends here before. I work just around the corner."

I smiled nicely, not sure of what to say, before I turned to take the tray away.

Upon returning to the table, he looked up at me and I thanked him for his concern before gathering my things and leaving.

My presentation went well so I had a lot of work on my plate and was unable to put any attention to my next fiction project. It turns out that insurance is complicated and boils down, at least to me, to peace of mind, safety and comfort with potential claims. I tried to work that into my ad copy.

And when I compared it to other insurance ads, which I decided I should pay attention to, my approach was the same as everyone else. So, three days later, I had the same amount of work to do, though I convinced myself that my failed effort was not a waste. My mind constantly wavered between fiction genres and archetypes and ad copy standards. My previous story about the ad writer who stole from great poets was starting to sound more and more legit.

I imagined a dystopian future event, saved only by quality insurance. Of course, insurers did not cover acts of God. I then imagined a horror story and a crime story and a thriller with the plots all saved by necessary application of the wide variety of insurance products.

It made me laugh and though I was dismissive, I couldn't quite let the ideas go.

The next week I went to meet Theresa as usual, and this time I noticed the guy I had spoken to, sitting at a table about as far away from our usual table as was possible.

I kept looking over at him, over Theresa's shoulder, but he never looked at me. He was reading something. Theresa noticed my looks and asked.

"Last week that guy over there made sure I didn't forget anything when I left. I didn't think much of it at first, frankly I thought he was a bit odd, but the more I thought of it, the more I'd wished I was nicer. He's sitting against the wall. Says he comes here often, and had noticed us, but he hasn't looked my way."

"Well, that's something, let me know if he does." She started to turn around, but I stopped her.

We fell into a conversation about my adventures with insurance and I was just about to ask after Markus when a suit stepped to our table and a voice said, “Hello, I’m David. I made sure you didn’t leave anything at your table last week.”

I must have looked annoyed, as David began to back off, but Theresa invited him to sit down. “Nice to meet you David. My friend Cassandra here, mentioned that you were looking out for her.”

Now I was outright flustered. David softened completely, mumbling something about leaving a package behind once, and being careful in the future.

“She said you come here often.”

“I do and I believe you both come here often as well.”

“Every week or two barring natural disaster or an important appointment.”

“It’s terribly convenient for me. I work around the corner at the hospital, in administration. The hospital coffee shop’s brew is pretty good, but the lines are horrible, so I come here.”

“Well, I live downtown, actually a bit east of it, and Cassie here lives uptown, so this is a good meeting spot for us. We are old friends from school.”

“University or high school?”

“Both,” I said.

“And what school did you both attend?”

“Fordham University, our fathers both went there, and we attended the same high school. Theresa also did a year at the Fashion Institute of Technology.”

“So you both grew up in the city.”

We both nodded. “And you?”

“I’m a transplant from the far suburbs, but I went to Columbia.”

I must have made a face, because he launched into a defence of Columbia University.

“Was hospital administration your goal or something you just fell into?”

"I'd always been interested in health but frankly none of the care disciplines really appealed to me, so I sort of aimed at administration fairly early. There is something new every day."

"Well, we were just discussing that. How to keep the routines of work from wearing you down."

"I don't have that concern, at least so far. I guess I'm still learning. I've only been at my current job for a year. There are endless things to think about, and once you've got them all corralled, the government or science throws something into the works and it all changes."

We finished our conversation and Theresa suggested we'd likely see each other again the following week. David said he looked forward to it, but couldn't be sure he'd make it as his meeting schedule was very changeable.

"Don't you worry, my dear, he'll be here," said Theresa, once he'd left.

"Worry? He seems like a nice enough guy, even if his approach is a bit creepy."

"A figure of speech. We've now met and we will see if he continues to be aggressive."

"Well, I have to refine my insurance approach. Lots of work to do. See you next week. Call me if you want to go somewhere this weekend."

Theresa nodded but I could tell she was busy and didn't want to say.

In the mean time I was anxious to get my quest story started. The sun was setting that evening when I finally sat down and opened a new file.

Chapter Thirty-nine – Who is who?

I was stunned. I had a half brother I knew nothing about. And sitting in the solicitor's office my life had changed even more.

My father's death had been traumatic, not because of its timing or method, but because we had been close and I was very much like him. Both businessmen, leaders and not followers and very on point.

He had died a week before, after a cancer diagnosis, some treatments and attempted cures all done without my knowledge. But when it became obvious that he could not win the battle, he told me he wanted to go on his terms, while making sure his wishes were followed.

There was a considerable estate, and, given some recent business losses of my own, I really needed it. I could pay back some debts and put some money into my company, a real lifeline despite the source. I also had to wind up the loose ends of his life. And as it turned out, one was a half brother.

According to the will, I needed my half-brother's signature before I could complete the estate dispensations. The big problem is, the will did not specify who this half-brother might be. I would have to find him. Okay, there were clues but my father had not spelt it out. So much for him being organized and on point, I thought. Then I figured he must not have known the details.

First, I searched through my father's papers. In his keeper drawer there was a small, unlocked wooden box. Inside was his passport, some foreign currency, his birth certificate and a few odds and ends, most of which made little sense to me. A few German Marks and French Francs told of a trip I knew nothing about. There was a photo of my mother and father together when they were young and happy. My mother had died of breast cancer when I was 14.

Also in the box were a cache of other items, mostly bits of memory for my father, and a scribbled note from someone named Peg. The note asked if he was happy and thanked him for his letter. There was no envelope or return address. The letter mentioned a road trip to Boston, a birthday party for Jamie, and man named John.

So I figured this was a place to start, John and Peg and a little boy named Jamie, some where near Boston. A day later I started to comb through adoption records in Massachusetts looking for the combination of names. That led nowhere. I decided to register with biological parent search organizations and tried the combination of names. Nothing.

The solicitor called to ask if I was ready to seal the will and dispense the estate. I asked him if he knew anything about my apparent half-brother, that might help me find him.

"Surely, Don, you must want to complete this process as much as I do."

"I was given a name," said the solicitor. "James Robert. I understand he went to school in Hartford Connecticut."

"Do you have a last name?"

"Yes, your father issued a bank check to a James Robert McCandless. Two checks actually, one to the University of Connecticut and the other to Mr. McCandless directly. It was about 25 years ago. I'd have to look up the date to be sure."

"Well that's something to go on. In the mean time, please rack your memory for any other detail. I have a business to run and have already spent considerable time trying to find this person."

I called an old friend and arranged to meet him for lunch. He had been adopted at a young age but we'd never really broached the subject.

"So, I have to ask you a difficult question, so please stop me if you have to."

I explained the situation and asked how I should go about searching for this long-lost half-sibling.

"Well, there are two possibilities. One, that this person has no idea they are adopted, or two that they know and are either happy and not curious, or they are actively searching for their heritage. In my experience, the urge to search gets stronger as you age. So, I would check adoption registries and parent birther sites. Most adoptions were closed back in the day, meaning the records would never be revealed, but now many of these closed adoptions can be opened if both parties agree."

"And you are okay with talking about this?"

"Yeah, my parents were up front with me and I knew I was adopted from an early age."

"Well, you never made a big deal about it."

"But you knew, didn't you. You know how kids can be. So, I didn't say anything. How did you find out?"

"I have no recollection. I imagine my mother must have told me, she was a great friend of your mother."

"Well, my mother didn't go around saying anything, but she didn't hide it either, she was just sensitive."

I accessed the UConn database and searched for a graduate named McCandless. There wasn't one. I decided to visit the school and explain that I was looking for any information they might have as there was an estate bequest to this person.

Initially I met with some resistance but when I finally was able to speak with the manager of alumni affairs, he was sympathetic. His assistant came back with the record of a James R. McCandless who had transferred out of UConn to The University of Kentucky right about the time the bank check was issued.

And so I visited the UK site and found my man. He had graduated two years after transferring to Kentucky in electrical engineering.

A search of the name in engineering associations turned up a few possible leads. I sent inquiries as if I was an old college friend trying to find someone who attended UConn and Kentucky.

I also decided to chase down Peg McCandless, or at least look for someone with that name.

Sure enough, there was a person with that name living in Nashua, New Hampshire, a short road trip from Boston. I made enquires and found she was in a nursing home. Corroboration was going to be difficult.

I flew to Boston and rented a car. Arriving in Nashua I found the home and made some enquiries, explaining myself to the attendants. They were unsure of my visit and insisted upon notifying her family.

I was actually happy to do that as it was her family I was trying to locate.

"Okay, I contacted her next of kin and was told you could speak with her, but if she gets upset, I am to end the contact immediately."

I had no choice but to agree and was ushered into a small private lounge with a television that the attendant turned down low.

"Mrs. McCandless? I have been looking for a Peg McCandless for some time."

"I'm Peggy, or more formally Margaret McCandless, though my friends have always called me Peg."

She seemed quite lucid as she sat in a wheelchair, her head scrunched into her shoulders and sitting at an uncomfortable angle. She wore a golden chain and wedding rings on her finger. There was a broach as well pinned off her shoulder.

"I am looking for your son, Jamie – James Robert, as I have some money that I owe him."

"Jamie? Jamie moved away. I haven't heard from him for a long while."

"Where is he living now? Is he in San Jose?"

"California, unless he's moved again. A restless boy if there ever was one. How do you know him?"

"Well, I don't. I don't want to upset you, but I've reason to believe he is due some money, as his father died and he is included in the will."

"His father died 10 years ago."

"His real father? What about his other father?"

She looked at me in shock. The attendant looked up sharply and appeared to be ready to end the visit. However, Peg McCandless did not get upset. She looked a bit confused.

"Is Jamie named in this will by name? Who is the deceased?"

"No, he is not. The will names a child of the deceased, William MacDaniel. My research suggested that child might be James Robert McCandless."

"No, James is not adopted. He is the natural child of my husband and me."

"Oh, I am sorry to have troubled you." I thought to leave but then decided to take one more stab, "Did you know a William MacDaniel? He had a picture of you and your family in his keepsake box."

"William MacDaniel?" She shook her head, but her eyes tightened like she was thinking, "No, but I knew a Billy Mac. Long ago. Long ago. Come to think of it, and I haven't thought of this for a long time, he asked me to place a child with foster parents and arrange for a foundling adoption, back when I worked with the County."

"You were a social worker?"

"No, I was a secretary to the Director of Public Works. One day a man came in in work clothes, dirty, like he had been in the fields. He had a baby with him, a newborn, said he found it at a job site and asked if I could take care of it, put it up for adoption, you know."

"And you did."

"Yes, it wasn't uncommon for such things to happen in those days. Foundlings here and there. There was a procedure. The man asked that he be kept out of the reporting on the foundling. He said he was just helping out and didn't want any unnecessary complications. I asked around later and they told me he was Billy Mac and worked for the County."

"You contacted him?"

"Yes, I looked him up and asked that he come in to pick up some papers that he needed. There were no papers, I just wanted to let him know that everything was taken care of. He was happy, relieved in a way and said he was happy to have been a help that day."

"So why did he have your family photo in his keepsakes?"

"Now that's something I don't know."

"I couldn't get past the idea that she may be lying but I didn't want to accuse her directly, especially with the attendant nearby. I gave her my contact information and asked that she let me know if she remembered any other details.

"I am trying to find this foundling as there is some inheritance due from the MacDaniel estate, if the foundling turns out to be the person I seek."

I still wanted to contact James Robert and found a few responses to my inquiries when I returned home a day later.

One was particularly promising, and in our back and forth contact it appeared that this James Robert was in fact the son of Peggy McCandless and her husband. He offered Peggy's maiden name, Robert, as a corroboration, but I had failed to get that from her. It did square with James' middle name, again a common practice in those days, to give a maiden name of the mother as a middle name of a child.

Why my father paid for Peggy McCandless's kid's schooling, I had no idea. Either Peggy was lying or she had been paid to keep quiet.

I called Larry looking for a little advice.

"Well, you are probably right about Peggy McCandless. But I will say these things have a way of being far more complicated than you can imagine. Especially adoptions from those days. Things were done more quietly as transgressions by young women were much more of an issue."

"So where do I go from here?"

"You can approach the kid, James Robert, and see if he'll give you a DNA sample. With money on the line, he might. Failing that you might try to get a bit of his DNA on the QT."

"So I'd have to root through his garbage."

"Something like that. Get him to lick an envelope. Maybe hair from a brush. That kind of thing."

I was quietly cursing my father who could have just been up front about all this, even if it was only revealed after his death. I'm guessing he didn't know the answers himself.

"Hey, can you talk to your folks for me, you know pick their brains about where I should go in my search?"

"I guess I could try. My mom is notoriously quiet about most things and really uncomfortable speaking about adoptions. I think she's just been trying to protect me."

"Did you ever find out about your natural parents?"

Larry looked at me but his eyes were far away. "Yeah, it wasn't pretty."

"Sorry to have brought it up, we can just drop it. Weather's getting better recently."

"That was about the worst segue I have ever heard," he laughed. "No, I don't mind telling you. But my mom would not want to know I was speaking about it. My parents were not together. I am likely the product of a one-time liaison, between a drifter and a naïve local girl. I got most of this out of my father, but he didn't want to say much. He struggled with my need to know and my mother's discomfort with the whole thing."

"It seems like this is going to be hard. And frankly I need to settle this quickly, I can use the money."

"Business not good?"

"A little slow, but suppliers want their cash, and buyers are scarce."

"It will turn around."

"Oh I know it will. Half my job has been to find ways to smooth out the markets, to flatten the boom and bust. In the mean time, to keep my head above water, a little cash would help tremendously."

Larry called me to meet for coffee a week later saying he'd spoken to his mother and father. He recommended the direct DNA approach and said his father hummed and hawed about the issue and his mother had largely shut him out, eventually admitting the DNA approach was best.

"She hates this so much, she just wanted it to all go away. But I really don't need protecting. I know what I know about my own origins and have no interest in pursuing anything more. Even if I wanted to, I'd never find the drifter. And apparently my bio-mother came from out of town somewhere. I just thank God that my adoptive parents had the kindness in their hearts to take me on. They were great parents."

So I tracked down James Robert McCandless and made the direct approach. He dismissed me, unaware that he may have been adopted. I appealed to him about the money and the possibility that we were half brothers. It didn't work.

Or, it didn't work for a week. Then I received a message asking for my address and saying a snippet of hair would be sent to me ASAP. Jimmy had had a change of heart and wanted to know. It turned out Peggy McCandless had been telling the truth, there was no match. Of course I wasn't there when he read my message, so I will forever wonder if he was relieved or upset there was no money forthcoming.

Thinking of the possible negative test result, I had already accessed the adoption data base for the State and found a few possible matches of male children who had been adopted in the four counties near our town in the two months around the date that I had for the adoption.

"So James Robert McCandless was not the kid? Funny, but I've heard that name. Did we go to school with a Jimmy McCandless?" Larry sat, looking into space with his eyes all scrunched up.

"I could look that up too, I guess. But it doesn't appear to matter. I'm back to square one. Now I wonder if my dad gave him the McDaniel name and whether that had been changed as some point."

"Not likely, but try there, maybe you'll find something."

And I did. There was a Frank MacDaniel adopted into a family in a nearby city. The mother was listed as a Margaret, with the last name redacted. She was only 15 at the time. The father was my dad.

And I was lucky the adoptee had issued an open call for contact by either of these people or any relations and had a DNA sample on file.

I made the necessary contacts and found out two weeks later that the former Frank MacDaniel, now Frank Forrest Farthingham, was my half brother.

I made contact and we had an awkward conversation, and soon after a strange meeting, where we seemed to circle each other for some time, slowly comparing notes about our lives. Of course, Frank wanted to know if my father, our father, was still alive. I had to inform him that he had recently died and it was because of that, and some clues he had left, that I have begun the quest to find him, as I had not known about the existence of a half brother until the will was read.

"Was he a good guy?"

"Yeah, he was a good father, almost doting, I think, and I can clearly remember him forcefully backing off on things when he started to smother me," I laughed a bit. "Perhaps the best of both worlds. What did they tell you about your natural parents?"

"Not much. Their names were redacted and I still only know my mother's first name. I was told they were much too young for a child, were unmarried, and moved far away to avoid a scandal. I was not adopted through the county or state channels, it was privately done, so the information was scant."

"Well, perhaps some good news for you. My father named you in his will. That is why I've been looking for you."

"That's nice. He did give me money for school and stuff. It was all done quietly, through a third party."

"So the State was not involved?"

"No. I'd just get a letter once each year during my college years and a cheque. The writer was careful to say he's been asked to do this on my behalf by my bio-dad and that he, the issuer of the checks, had nothing to do with the adoption, save as a messenger. The name on the checks was McCandless."

I jerked my head up. Stunned. "McCandless? Are you sure?"

"Of course, I thought maybe he was the natural father. When I enquired, he was quite explicit that he was not, and was only a delivery man."

I rolled it all around in my mind. Frank Farthingham looked at me strangely, "What of it? Why is that name so shocking?"

I explained the McCandless connection saying Mrs. Peggy McCandless had been approached by my father to privately arrange for an adoption of the baby. They had their own child who at first, I thought was the adopted baby, but DNA ruled that out."

"Peggy is short for Margaret."

"It is, but your mother was 15 when you were born and Mrs. McCandless was working for the county when my father, our father approached her to arrange the adoption. But Margaret is not an uncommon name, especially then."

I told Frank that he was in for a cash dispensation once the Estate of our father was processed and taxes paid etc. I said it was hard to know the exact amount but his share would likely exceed $100,000 depending on the final value of investments, the sale of the family home, less taxes and other costs.

He seemed pleased and I reiterated we were half-brothers and there would be a copy of the will sent to him and an accounting of the dispensations in it, once everything was put together.

He seemed to want to continue contact with me, and I was only too happy to oblige. I had few relations so a fresh one seemed ripe with possibilities. We arranged to play golf together a few weeks later.

I had lunch with Larry Donovan and brought him up to speed. "I'll pass that on to my parents, they were asking and seemed interested in your progress. My mother, for all her standoffishness about the whole process actually wanted to know how you found Frank."

"Having my dad's name and a range of dates and places where the adoption likely took place, and it wasn't that hard. I am looking forward to wrapping the whole thing up in a few weeks. The house will go up for sale, stock shares are being sold this week and I am arranging to empty the house and have a few minor issues taken care of before the sale."

I kept in touch with Larry as we had renewed our friendship over these issues. And of course I staying in contact with Frank, even playing golf with him and sharing a dinner or two as the process played out. We were friendly but still guarded as the whole thing was so fresh. I was looking forward to issuing him the check and seeing how much interest he had in maintaining contact.

And then that done, some months, even a year later, I received a phone call from Larry's mother. She introduced herself and in a flash I knew. I answered her questions about Frank, and I agreed to keep our conversation private.

"These things, meant to help people and make lives smoother, have a way of becoming huge issues."

"Yes, Mrs. Donovan. But all's well that ends well."

"Its not ended yet. My parents forbade me from even talking to your father. We were young but I never thought of it as a mistake. I was sent away to live with my Aunt and Uncle and they asked Peggy McCandless to arrange things. Your dad dropped off the baby. My parents and the McCandlesses were friends. Well, everybody in town was friends of a sort. They all knew each other. My parents were mortified when I met and married Chuck Donovan who worked in the steel foundry just outside of town. That brought me back. I did see your father again, though we never spoke, usually in church or across the street. He looked at me in a way nobody else ever did. I'd like to think he knew I saw him the same way. Did he ever speak of me?"

"No, Mrs. Donovan. I knew nothing about this until I read of a half-brother in his will. I wonder if my mother knew?"

"I can't answer that. There aren't many who do. My husband has no idea, and even though it was long before we met and married, I'd like to keep it that way. There is no value to anyone in knowing. Even Larry. I'm not sure how knowing his mother had a natural child would affect him, as he was adopted and all. I certainly treated him as I hoped Frank's adopted parents would have treated him. Oh, what a tangled circle."

"Your secret is safe with me. I have renewed my friendship with Larry over my searches. And it appears, I now have a relationship with Frank, but I don't know where that is going. Am I sworn to secrecy even after your passing?"

"Yes, please," she pleaded. "Never let on or even joke about it. Even the fact that Frank knows my first name scares me. I was wondering how to handle it in my will, so I am very glad that your father owned up to it in his. I will try to make some dispensation to him, but anonymously and through a third party when the time comes."

I hung up the phone and was determined to keep the secret for Mrs. Donovan's sake and for the sake of all the people who would be affected by the truth, a truth which nobody seemed keen to uncover.

So it appeared Larry's Uncle had used Peggy McCandless as a go between to set up the off-record adoption and my father had paid her, years later, with some money for her son as he went through school. Larry's Uncle, had my father deliver the child to Peggy, probably to keep his family out of it. The baby had been adopted by the Farthinghams and raised by them.

A complicated web. However, I was pleased to finally arrange for the inheritance and get on with my life. Frank Farthingham seemed pleased at first, especially with the check. He made a half-hearted effort to keep in touch. He seemed to know that I knew much more about him than I was letting on, but I had sworn to Peggy Donovan that I would say nothing.

It struck me a few months later that I was Larry's half brother. A revelation for a moment, then I realized I was not, but Frank Farthingham was his step brother. I racked my brain for anything telling my father might have said years before, but I couldn't recall anything.

I managed to pay my creditors and predictably business picked up so I had weathered the storm. At least in business. However, the whole Donvan – Farthingham – McCandless arrangement didn't seem right some how. It all fit together and I was certain there were details I did not know about. Perhaps it was better that way. The estate had been settled, and everything fit into place, even if the picture the puzzle showed seemed askew, once the last piece had been placed.

I wondered if my mother had known, and decided that because it had happened long before they met, it was unlikely. That would make Frank Farthingham several years my senior. Peggy McCandless was the only loose end, and she was in a nursing home rapidly losing her memory.

I decided that James Robert McCandless, living on the west coast, was also a loose end, but he was far enough away that it didn't seem likely he would spill the story to anyone who might be affected.

And sure enough, Frank came to me wondering who his mother was. At first, I denied knowing, but Frank came back to me, saying that without the mother's name it was unlikely that I could get the will probated. I told him that the DNA sample had proved paternity so the legal process was satisfied.

And then Mrs. Donovan died and in her will there was a bequest of shares she had inherited from her maiden, great aunt, years before, which had grown substantially in value. The will was cryptic, saying a trust should be set up to administer the shares, with the annual proceeds going to a scholarship fund to be given to girls who return to post-secondary education after their 21st birthday. It was to be administered by the eldest living member of the Donovan family, and the McCandless family and the McDaniel family, all family friends in prior years.

Mrs. Donovan's husband had died before her, so his knowledge of the situation did not compromise anyone. However, Frank Farthingham, while not technically a McDaniel, was in fact the eldest living member of the McDaniel clan, he and the Donovan's solicitor didn't know it. I did. He was also the oldest living member of the Donovan clan, but nobody but me knew that.

To protect Mrs. Donovan's secret, I would have to fail to make this knowledge public and lie if asked.

So the trustees were named, Larry, myself and James McCandless. James for his part seemed interested in helping out, but his distance from us and his peripheral inclusion led to him dropping out as the trust was about to award its first bequest.

"Hey Larry, have you had a chance to review the papers? The lawyer just called me. They want to proceed with the scholarship award."

"Yeah, I did. It all seems okay to me, Jack. Though I still have the nagging feeling we should award two scholarships. Both the leading candidates seem inseparable in terms of need."

"We talked about this Larry. If we award two, we necessarily reduce the amount of the scholarship."

"I'm okay with that. Listen, there is no need, according to my mother's will, to award a scholarship each year. We could award two, and then let the principle grow back to the base amount required to award further scholarships. In some way, because this had taken more than a year to arrange, giving two scholarships just makes up for the year we missed while the details were being worked out."

"Larry, I don't want to be a hard-ass on this. But I feel a real strong need to do what your mother wanted. If you want to proceed that way, then let's just do it. As long as the legal trustee agrees."

"Thanks Jack. I feel better about it that way."

"And what happens the next time, where there are two qualified recipients?"

Larry didn't say anything. I was trying to see how this trust set up through Mrs. Donovan's will was going to benefit Frank Farthingham, who she had told me, she hoped to help when she died. I had a funny feeling the trust was placed in the will before the death of her husband, with the expectation of changing the terms once he passed. She never did.

Even though I rolled this around in my mind often, I always came to the conclusion that waking the truth from the dead, served no one. And so I helped Larry in a trustee role for many years.

As we got on, it became apparent that the trustees in the scholarships would change once we passed on. My own son and Larry's daughter would take on the roles. However, passing on the nature of the scholarships opened some uncomfortable questions. We kept our story to Larry's adoptive nature and my father's finding of a foundling in the fields and passing it on to the county as the genesis of our involvement.

I received a note from James Robert McCandless, saying his mother had passed. And a few weeks later another note, saying the will named me, Jack McDaniel, and could I attend a conference with the lawyer to draw up the necessary papers.

I was unsure of what my name might portend inside the will of Peggy McCandless, but I agreed to go.

"Ah, welcome Mr. McDaniel, do come in and sit down."

I entered the solicitor's office, in a town just outside Boston, with James Robert McCandless already there. I turned to a third attendee and was shocked to see Frank Farthingham. I think I managed to not give away my surprise.

We all shook hands and asked after each other. We had kept up our contacts but only on rare occasions, especially between me and James Robert McCandless as we appeared to have little connection. After all my father had paid for much of his schooling as a thank you to Peggy McCandless in helping find a home for the baby Frank Farthingham.

"Down to business gentlemen. I understand you all know each other?"

"Yes," said James. "Our families had contact many years ago."

"As you know James, there is an interesting codicil in your mother's Last Will and Testament. One that affects Mr. McDaniel here."

James nodded. I stirred, even though I knew this much, but tried not to lean toward the desk to show my interest.

"Mrs. McCandless says in her will, that as a County Clerk, she often handled delicate situations for people in town, and her husband often acted as the third party in these proceedings to shield those involved."

"Yes, she acted as such for my father, as did her husband."

"Apparently she acted more than once for him."

The revelation was a shock, and then an impossibility, as my father had not named anyone else in his will, many years before.

"How can this be? He let on about her involvement in placing my half-brother Frank, but said nothing else about anyone."

"It seems that your father had a second child with Peggy Donovan, nee Carlock, not long before her marriage. Somehow, she kept the child a secret from her husband to be, travelling to visit relatives in Pennsylvania for a lengthy stay, when she was near the delivery time. The delivery was difficult and she was unable to bear children after that."

"That's why Larry was adopted. I guess."

"Seems like your father was a bit untamed, shall we say," said James, shaking his head.

"No, probably just in love with Peg Donovan or Carlock."

The solicitor looked down at the will. "I want to get this right, reading it precisely."

"Okay, read on," said James.

"And it is my intention to clear the air regarding the paternity of all the parties involved. We did each other good deeds and those good deeds were rewarded. I acted in good faith and with the knowledge of all the parties involved. Frank Forrest Farthingham is the first child of William McDaniel and Margaret (Peggy) Carlock, later Donovan. James Robert McCandless is the child of John McCandless and Margaret (Peg) McCandless."

"Well thank god for that," James Robert said.

The lawyer looked up, "To continue . . . Larry Donovan is the child of Charles Farthingham and Margaret (Peg) McCandless. He was given up for adoption to the Donovan family once it was determined that Peggy Carlock was unable to have children, in consideration for the Farthingham's adoption of Frank. And, the second child of William McDaniel and Peg Carlock was given in adoption to the McCandless family, for their help in the whole affair. She was named Lilly McCandless."

Frank Farthingham spoke up, "So Bob, your friend Larry is my half brother and Lilly McCandless is my full sister. And Lilly is not a blood relation of James Robert McCandless." We all needed time to process this, as until now, Lilly's parentage had not been questioned. She was the full sister of

Frank Farthingham, even though they had been raised in different families.

"What a tangled web, between needs and wants, social pressures and the desire to do the right thing by babies and people and the future," said the lawyer.

"Why isn't Lilly here?"

"I believed it better to break the tangled news to all of you first. To continue . . . I bequest to my natural and adoptive children, John Robert and Lilly Rosamond McCandless, my home, and all my worldly possessions, with the exception of the following . . . to John (Jack) McDaniel the locket his father gave me and which I was unable to wear. Know that the pictures in it, were very hard to arrange."

The lawyer handed me a locket on a chain which I opened.

"I've seen that. My mother wore it all the time. She would touch it when she was thinking, like a magic lantern."

The locket contained a photo of my father and Peg Donovan when they were very young. On the other side there was a photo of three children, a boy and a girl sitting on a two-seater, and holding a baby, me.

"In addition, I bequeath to Larry Donovan, my natural son, a family bible from my mother's side, a table from my father's side, and want him to know, I watched him from afar his whole life. Be it known that this whole convoluted arrangement was the best solution we could determine at the time. I have many regrets about it, but believe our choices were the right ones.

Larry was stunned, his eyes unblinking as he tried to take in the truth. Peggy McCandless was his mother and Frank Farthingham's adoptive father was his biological father. He had never met the man who had passed years before.

I was unaffected except for the doings of my father who was a much different man than I had believed. And Peg McCandless was also woven into my family history. I could only wonder if my own mother had known any of this.

Chapter Forty

Theresa had begged off our usual meeting so we didn't go back to the coffee shop for two weeks. I was anxious to catch up with her as she had apparently been out with Markus.

"There you are. It feels like a month. So, what's the latest?"

Theresa put her things on a chair and went to get her coffee, coming back with a pair of Boston Cream donuts as well as her usual Café Americano. She shifted her things and sat down, sipping her coffee, pushing a donut my way and saying nothing.

"Out with it, I can't wait any more."

She smiled, "There's really nothing to say. Markus and I went on a couple of dates but there is no spark. I like him well enough but that's it."

"A couple? What about him?"

"I'm not sure. He calls and we chat, but there is nothing deeper, no intimate conversation. It's like our dates are just between friends."

"Are you disappointed?"

"No, not at all. There is no spark to ignite any disappointment. How has your week been going?"

"The usual. Clients, work, presentations, rewrites. Got a couple of corporate speeches to write. One very formal and the other a Ted Talk, which should be fun."

"Topics?"

"Increasing international trade with third world countries, er ah, developing nations, and the Ted Talk is odd, about the new telescope in space and what it's finding. Very cutting edge and a chance for a little speculation. It's got to be grounded in science; it's for an astrophysicist at the request of his university. Some conference or something. Grants are on the line, and so it has to be informative and engaging. I'm off to speak to him right after this, get some background and a sense of where he wants to go. I'm fully expecting at least three rounds of edits on this one."

"That sounds different. How did he contact you?"

"One of my other clients is his brother-in-law. Convinced him that a professional approach to the speech would work for his career advancement."

"What about your own writing?"

"I'm actually not too far from the end of this exercise. And you know, I've actually begun to speculate about a new novel. Early stages, but I caught myself dreaming about things, like how people of modern temperaments and skills would fit into long ago historical times."

"A time travel story?"

"No, more a human development story. People have had the same skill sets for millennia but the times they live in dictate the use of these skill sets and even personalities. Some times might be better suited to specific skill sets than others. It speaks to human development and our shared humanity."

"Is that how you start formulating a story?"

"Well, I think it can be. I'm in the very early stages of anything, but the germ is there. No plot, no characters, just the idea that a tradesman today might have been a tradesman of yore, but might not have been, as today's trades require different skills than they did centuries ago."

"Good luck with that."

"It may not go anywhere. It's just the germ of an idea. My Quest story turned out pretty good. It still needs another rewrite to get it clean, but read it and tell me what you think." I handed over a small sheaf of paper.

"You know I like everything you write. I feel like my input is weak. Frankly I'm afraid to tee off on you as I do generally like what you've given me."

"Hey, I want the truth, maybe sugar-coated truth, but the truth in any event. It's hard to hear criticism, but usually upon reflection, I can see the kernels of truth in the comments."

"I've been trying to do that, but I can't help that my input all sounds the same."

"Well, try being a little more specific, if you can. Did you like a certain character? Was the story too predictable? What I've given you are just the rough drafts of the story lines. The exercise is to loosen my brain and not necessarily to complete each story perfectly. I mean what is perfection anyway?"

"In art, there is no perfection. Someone will always not like it, or criticize. I've always said, there is no universally loved art, paintings, books, movies, anything."

"Clothes?"

"Absolutely. I'm sure there are people out there who would not be caught wearing anything I've designed. It's not their style or something. As crazy as that sounds," she laughed.

"As I'm running out of genres and architypes I'm having to focus. This week I'm going to try a 'buddy story' or a 'tragedy'. I'll go with whatever pops out of my brain."

At that moment David came through the side door of the coffee shop, the closest approach from his office building. He spied us immediately, and without shame was obvious in gauging our willingness to have him.

"Speaking of which," Theresa said.

"Mind if I have a seat? Didn't see you two last week."

Theresa gestured for him to sit down, and took the opportunity for a second bite of her donut. I sipped my coffee, trying to decide if I should return to what we had been talking about or shift my focus. Neither one of us were keen on him sitting down but our conversation had reached a tipping point for change.

"Well, you missed it here last week. Two guys were sipping their coffees over by the window there, and the next moment they both stood up, with one guy giving the Heimlich Maneuver to the other."

He had a big grin on his face. We both stared at him, waiting for him to continue.

"All ended well. But it was really crazy. Everyone in the place was looking, but nobody moved to help. I guess we all thought the second guy was on it. And the Heimlich is a one-person maneuver. I wondered if it was a bit of performance art. The guy doing the squeezing didn't say a word. And when it was over, everyone sat down and went back to their own worlds."

Theresa and I looked at each other, not sure of what to say.

"So, the people behind the counter didn't go over to see if everything was alright?"

"I don't think so. At least not right away. The two guys sat down and continued their conversation as if nothing had happened."

"Life in the city, I guess. Things move fast. No harm done, and on to the next thing."

"I guess. I looked around at the other tables and nobody else was looking back at me. The whole thing seemed invisible."

"Other than that, how have you been?" asked Theresa, nakedly changing the subject.

"You know, sick people coming, treated people going. It's a living."

"Not healthy people?"

"Not always. Once people are ready to be released from hospital, they inevitably have some recovery time of their own to deal with. We really don't like readmissions, but it happens."

We chatted a bit about the day to day as David managed to find out what we each did, though he had no connection to either of our professions. He warmed up when my Ted Talk subject was brought up.

"That's interesting. I've been reading about some of the things that telescope has found. Things that cannot be explained by our current model of the universe. It's funny but physics and science seems to act differently at the local level than they do on a larger, universal scale. Go figure."

As we prepped to leave, David said he would walk with us as we dispersed. I was headed to the university and decided a walk in the sunshine would do me good. And Theresa had her usual short hop and subway ride to her business premises just outside the downtown.

"A few people I work with are meeting for a drink tonight at the Earl of Sandwich, a couple of blocks from here. Guys and girls. You are welcome to join us if you'd like."

Both of us begged off. Me because I would be heading uptown after my meeting and didn't want to come all the way back, and Theresa who said she had an important phone call in the early evening with a retailer in Virginia.

David shrugged, and said he and his group would be there for several hours if we changed our minds. And with a little wave, he walked off at the corner heading west, while Theresa started across the street for the subway station and I continued north, with a 15-minute walk to the university still in front of me.

The Earl of Sandwich was a pub in the financial district. Usually full at lunch time but not too busy on a workday until later in the evening. I had been there a few times. There were several 'Earl' pubs scattered around town, all different, and all the same.

Back home I put in a few hours on my Ted Talk, after getting the lowdown from the professor. He was actually a fairly engaging guy, several years older than me, and fixated on the idea that he was a very dry speaker.

I assured him I would take a light approach to the subject and was expecting at least one complete rewrite to get the details correct and to match up to his presentation style. He reminded me that the reason he hired me was to improve his presentation style. I had to laugh, though I must confess the science and detail of the telescope were a bit hard to grasp.

The next night, wanting my telescope project to stew a day, I launched into my next fiction project.

Chapter Forty-one – Buddy story

Frankie and I had always hung together. Since we were little kids. He lived just around the corner and we met the day my family moved into the neighbourhood. I was four and he stood awed by the size of the moving truck and the never-ending pile of stuff that came out of it.

We spent a couple of weeks together at the end of summer and then found ourselves in the same class. That worked well for us, but at Christmas the classes were mixed and we were in different rooms until June.

It's hard to say if one of us was the dominant friend. We just seemed to agree on everything and had a very similar set of interests. We played whatever sport seemed in season, roamed the woods two blocks from our street and played games and stuff when the weather was bad.

The woods were a small thing really, though they seemed huge at the time. A suburban block left undeveloped as an urban greenspace, it was maybe 150 yards by 200 yards in size but heavily forested. A little oasis for dog walkers but the great wide open to a pair of exploring kids. We climbed trees, threw things at one another, checked out the wild life, dug for treasure and built stick forts.

Of course, the other kids in the neighbourhood were there too, but Frankie and I were a team, and everyone knew it. A few of the other neighbourhood boys, classmates and others would move in and out of our doings, but we always seemed to be on the same page.

One day I went to his house to fetch him but his mother said he was sick and would be for a few days. She seemed worried. The next day my mother wondered why I was hanging around our house and I told her that Frankie was sick. Later that day she had the same expression as Frankie's mom.

I didn't see Frankie for a week. And by then I knew he had polio. I was told to avoid his house and everyone in Frankie's class had to go to the doctor.

I would walk by his house and in the third week saw him sitting in the window looking out at the street. He waved, and I waved back with a big smile. He did not smile. I pointed to the ground, wondering when he could come out to play. He shook his head and shrugged and then held up a finger. I must have looked confused and then he held up seven fingers.

I didn't really want to go, but I had no idea what else to try to say, so I waved goodbye and went to the woods, but there was nobody to play with, and the idea of building a fort alone had no joy.

I went home and asked my mother what she knew.

"Frankie has polio and it takes a while to clear his system. I have heard he has been in bed. Polio can waste away your muscles and you become crippled."

"Is Frankie going to be alright? I saw him today in his front window."

"I don't know, love, but if he was up and about that's a good sign."

It took several more weeks but Frankie returned to class. He said he woke one morning and couldn't move his legs. By the next day, things were improving but he had to stay quarantined for a time. Some of the kids stayed away from him but my mother said once he was better it was okay to be with him.

He walked with a limp. Not a bad one, and it got less and less noticeable, but he forevermore favored one leg.

I got used to his limp, and so did he, so much so that neither of us noticed it, or at least he never mentioned it. We went through high school together, with a wider group of friends and doing much the same things, but it was still always Frankie and me at the end of the day.

As we neared the end of high school I got to wondering what Frankie was going to do next. I hadn't really decided myself, but college or university was a given in those days.

"I don't know Ben, my parents have been pushing me toward engineering, saying it's a good future, but I hear it's just a lot of math."

"But you're good at math."

"Yeah, but math is pretty boring."

"I wish it was boring to me. I look at a problem and have no idea what to do. Teachers say, apply this formula or break down the problem in a certain way and I ask, how do I know that that is what's required? How do I know what steps to take? They look at me sideways, 'you just do,' they say."

Frankie looked at me sideways. "It just depends on what you are trying to accomplish."

"Well, I have no idea. Trying to solve the question but I have no idea why, or what the question is trying to answer."

"That seems like a problem. Maybe its like me in English class. They are always talking about symbolism and stuff and I can't figure out why they don't just say it straight out. What the heck is everyone hiding?"

I laughed, "Quite the pair we make eh? What school are you looking at?"

"My dad says I should go to a good school, and one not too close or too far away. You know, establish some independence."

"I don't know. I haven't thought about it yet. Maybe I'll go to the same school, but in business or something."

"I heard that Larry is thinking the same thing."

"It would be nice to have a friend or two nearby. It's a big step."

"And only temporary. Four or five years and then the real world hits."

"You sound like my dad."

In the end I went to a state college a few hours away by car, and Frankie did the same. I wouldn't admit it but I chose that school knowing that Frankie was likely going there too.

Once school started, we spent some time together, but soon our different class schedules and newfound friends started to eat into our time together. It wasn't a bad thing and we were both able to spread our wings a little. We still saw each other once a week or so for dinner and when one of us was heading home for a weekend, the other usually caught a ride.

Only one incident stuck out during our time at college. We both signed up for an intra-mural slo-pitch league. We were on different teams. In our one game against each other, Frankie hit a ball deep into the right center gap. I prayed he didn't try for third, but he made the turn around second going as fast as he could, his gimpy leg becoming noticeable.

The throw came in from the right fielder and it was perfect. I wanted Frankie to have his moment so I dropped it, in what felt to me like the worst acting job on the planet. Frankie slid in safe. I think he knew but didn't say anything.

"Why did you try for third?"

"The bases are 60 feet apart. In real baseball they are 90. So a double in real baseball, a ball getting to the fence is 180 feet, but in slo-pitch a triple is 180 feet. Why not go?"

"If I'd caught the ball you'd have been out. And besides smart guy, the fence is only about 300 feet from the plate, not 400 feet like a real baseball field."

Frankie looked chastened. "Good point. Well, I was safe, no harm, no foul, right?"

"Right. It was a nice hit."

My teammates looked at me a bit oddly. I think they picked up on the purposely dropped ball.

"We had that guy. You were talking to him. Do you know him?"

"Yeah, a bit. We're from the same home town. I asked him why he went for third. He said he thought it would take a perfect throw to get him."

"It was."

"It bounced funny."

And that was it. Frankie had his triple. And I had little piece of my integrity peeled off. I thought it was for a good reason, and I would never say, either to teammates or to Frankie. Still, the whole episode did not sit well, but I had no choice other than to move on, a choice made in the moment. It was such a small thing really. Or so I thought.

Once we graduated, we hung out together playing golf, some slo-pitch and grinding through weekends. Soon enough Frankie met a nice girl, actually re-met her. We'd gone to high school together. She was working in an office not far from where Frankie worked.

I had a series of short-term girlfriends. I'd meet one, go on a few dates and realize, usually mutually, that it was not going to work out, and the cycle would repeat itself.

Sure enough Frankie and Kimberly married and settled in a small house a few miles from where they worked. Of course I didn't see much of him, and that was okay, he had other interests and responsibilities, especially when his son came along. And when we did run into each other, it was like we'd just spoken the day before.

And eventually I did settle on someone, or she on me. I was fairly non-committal but she was determined to start a life. She was nice, her family was nice, and I went along for the ride.

During this phase I often wondered what I wanted from life. I'd been lucky so far, I thought. A good friend, family, a job I didn't mind, but I felt as if I was settling into something that provided no challenge, not that my life had been filled with challenges to that point.

And we dutifully married, and soon there were two kids, a pair of daughters. My wife was very family oriented, spending a lot of time with her mother, and centering much of what she did on family holidays and birthdays.

I went along with it, bringing some friends into the circle including Frankie and Kimberly, who seemed to hit it off with my wife, Beth.

And then, out of nowhere, Beth died. She gave birth to our third child, a son, and didn't survive the childbirth. I never realized that could happen. I mean, I'd never heard of it.

So at that point, I'm 28 with three kids under four years old, and an absolutely terrifying future. I took a year off from my job, knowing that it probably killed any career enhancement, but having no choice.

At the end of that time, I went back to work, and relied on a network of family to mind the kids five days a week. I agreed to help with their kids on evenings and weekends to balance things out. All in all, it was a god-send. Inexpensive and available, the only cost was my own life, even if I was resigned to putting that all on hold at least until my youngest was in school.

And then my son entered grade school and Frankie came to me with an idea. He had it all worked out. He and I would do a cross-country road trip, while the usual suspects would take care of the kids, who were remarkably independent already.

Of course, I resisted. But the seed had been planted and two years later Frankie was going out to California for a month-long assignment with his company. He was a process engineer and had skills in virtually all aspects of engineering.

I continued to resist but my mother pushed hard, saying she wanted to spend some time with her grandchildren, up close. I knew she was lying, not that she didn't want contact with her grands, but she'd already had plenty of it and had for years.

I got in the car and was very reluctant to leave. It just didn't feel right leaving my responsibilities behind. But Frankie had secured a live-in hotel for the month so there was space and no additional cost. He assured me, that having someone out there with him was almost necessary.

Despite that, the first half of the trip was full of anxiety for me. I couldn't help but live on my usual schedule of my kids lives. To Frankie's credit he indulged me and only gently pushed. We planned a route west through Colorado, Nevada and into southern California before heading to the Bay Area, where Frankie's contract job was.

Once past Denver, I loosened up. I don't know if it was the mountains, the new vistas, that I had never set eyes upon, or the constant reassurance from my mother or the excited voices of my kids, who seemed to be having a good time without my constant scheduling.

Maybe this trip did everyone some good.

In Denver we took in a Colorado Rockies game and looked around the city for a day. Utah seemed an interesting place until I realized the highways followed some of the more livable places and avoided the deep desert.

Then on to Las Vegas where we spent another day looking at everything and marvelling at the desert lifestyle, which was so different from our own. We played a round of desert golf. The course, like the lifestyle, was completely different from what I knew, but the change seemed liberating. I kind of wished we had another day.

But Los Angeles was calling and if we were going to be in San Francisco on Frankie's work schedule we had to move on. The topography of California was amazing, with hills, low mountains, lush valleys and dead, dry deserts one right after another.

As we neared Los Angeles I was happy to leave the desolation behind, until it was behind us and the sprawling city swallowed us whole, making the desert seem inviting.

We did a few tourist things on the one day we'd given ourselves and then headed north to San Francisco. Through Hollywood, a studio tour, down to the beach and just generally noticing small things that were the backgrounds of television and movies we'd been watching for years. Our destination was actually San Jose where Frankie's assignment was.

We settled into a long stay hotel where we had a small suite. When Frankie went to work each day, I looked around. I did some grocery shopping and became a bit of a domestic. I was used to it with my own kids. As I moved around the area, it was amazing to me the number of places I had heard of, Cupertino, Sanford, Palo Alto, Menlo Park, it was almost like New York, in that so many things had happened in these places that they were all familiar.

Frankie and I went in to the mountains east of town and did a few minor hikes. His polio injuries were almost non-existent but I could tell that a lengthy hike was not something he looked forward to. We played some golf on weekends and I started to fit in a bit, developing a routine. In the back of my mind, I was looking forward to heading home, but I was determined to enjoy this slice of freedom from responsibilities. And that's all it really was, just a time away, with the grind of life just over the horizon back east.

We went out to play golf at a small local course on the weekend and got paired with a couple of girls. It turned out that they had a corporate golf day coming up and both were beginners wanting to play at least reasonably well so they wouldn't embarrass themselves.

"Why couldn't it be a tennis day," one said. "That I can handle."

The other smiled, she had her own clubs and said she had played as a teen, but drifted away from the game. It was evident in her swing that she'd done it before. Her friend, the tennis player was a different story, she couldn't keep her feet still wanting to constantly adjust her weight distribution like she was timing up a forehand.

"Vanessa, the ball isn't moving."

"Thanks Em, I can see that. That makes it harder."

Frankie and I watched with bemusement not wanting to interject unless asked. He and I both hit competent drives down the middle and then moved up to the ladies' tees. It was going to be a long day, I thought.

Emily sliced a drive off the toe of her club, but it went, even if it was as much sideways as long. Vanessa took two mighty swings and missed both times. Then she slowed it down and managed to top the ball about 40 yards.

I pursed my lips and refused to look at Frankie.

"Okay you guys, how do you do this?"

"Emily, care to help your friend out?"

She shook her head. "I'm just going from muscle memory and it's a bit foggy. Frankly, I could use a refresher too."

We let them duff their ways through the end of the hole, watching everything they did and did not do.

Frankie stepped up at the next tee, demonstrating a basic set up and push off and follow through on his drive. I did much the same but without comment.

Emily stepped to the tee and Frankie adjusted her alignment, explained why she should adopt his suggestions and told her to take a more controlled swing, to stand with her weight on the balls of her feet. She hit one straight, if not too far.

"Well, that felt better."

"The swing or the result?"

And then Vanessa stepped up and Frankie went through the same routine with her, calming her feet by telling her to stay stationary but keep her weight on the balls of her feet while taking the club back slowly and low, to avoid chopping at the ball. It worked like a charm, and she sailed one down the middle about 230 yards.

"Wow?" We all spoke in unison. "Okay, Frankie, what am I doing wrong?" I joked.

The round proceeded with the girls getting slowly but noticeably better. Interestingly, both Frankie and I played well, considering we gave our own games no thought.

At the end we shook hands, they thanked us and we agreed to meet in in the clubhouse for a drink.

Once settled we found out that Vanessa and Emily were childhood friends, who had taken jobs at the same software development company about six months apart. Vanessa was a computer engineer and Emily was in sales.

We told them about ourselves, Frankie making it very clear he was married and only in the area on a job assignment. We'd both be gone in a couple of weeks.

Vanessa was engaged and Emily had just broken up with a short-term boyfriend. "He was a nice enough guy, but it just didn't work out. Too much baggage." But she didn't specify whose baggage it was.

We chatted about the area and our jobs, me being in the backseat as my job was 2,000 miles away.

"I'm so sorry about your wife," Emily said.

"It was a tough time," I said. "I guess it still is, but it was a while ago now. My youngest is seven and in school. My family has been very helpful. In fact this is the first time I've been away. They insisted I take a break."

We drained our glasses and took our leave with a wave. "We are coming back on Thursday for another run through," said Vanessa. "If you are around, we could use some more pointers."

Frankie had a meeting that afternoon and I remained non-committal, trying to invent some non-existent thing that needed doing, but it rang pretty hollow. I didn't care, as I'd likely never see either one of them again.

Two days later I dropped into a coffee shop for a bite to eat before going shopping to fill our fridge. I was engaged in folding down the newspaper to read at the small table when someone stepped up in front of me.

"Oh, it's you," I said. "Emily. What are you doing around here? I thought you worked in Cupertino."

"I do, but I was on a sales call, this morning. Thought I'd stop for a cup of coffee and a rethink of my approach."

"It didn't go well?"

"No. It did not. I think things are changing in the computer world. The old tried and true seems stale."

"So, what's the answer?"

"I thought maybe coffee could tell me."

I laughed. "Coffee speaks to me too, but usually in Spanish and I can't understand it. Keeps me awake at night too."

She smiled, "Mind if I join you?"

She was already pulling out the chair. She placed her coffee on the table, her portfolio on a third chair and sat down. "Thanks, so much for helping Vanessa and I the other day. Well, I just needed a few reminders I think, she needed a full course lesson."

"It was coming nicely at the end. You are back on Thursday? When is your event?"

"We are supposed to play on Saturday. I'm not too keen on work taking up some of my weekend time, but it's expected. Looks like Thursday is out; Vanessa can't make it now."

"Hopefully your career doesn't center around your golf game."

"In sales it sometimes does." She sipped her coffee.

I could feel myself being pulled in, and didn't want to be. Oh well, you'll have other chances."

I could see the wheels turning in her mind. "Can you help me out? Like no pressure. Just friends you know. I need some help. Bring Frank if you want."

"He's working."

"Please. You helped me get better, and I need to get better as the golf course seems to be the place to do business these days."

I could see no reason not to help, as I was running out of things to keep me occupied. Frankie and I were due to return east a couple of weeks later.

I agreed and we set a time to meet. Emily thanked me and we set off in different directions.

Thursday afternoon I dutifully arrived at the club and noticed Emily already on the practice green, working on her putting.

"Good plan," I said, "That's where you can save a lot of shots." I gave her a quick tutorial on pace and rolling the ball, with the major focus on keeping it close to the hole to avoid a three putt.

We played our round and to be sure I really didn't offer too much help, save on chipping around the green. She seemed to have remembered everything else.

On one hole she hit a ball into the woods and we went looking for it. We were separated by maybe 30 yards when I pretended to find it. I suggested dropping it in the fairway to get her back into the game and told her there was usually a penalty associated with the drop but that in the spirit of fun, we'd not bother with it. I really wanted her to break 100, and she still had a chance at it.

She looked at me oddly, but trudged out of the long brambles and dropped the ball. We finished the round a few holes later.

"You're a tennis player?" I asked as we sat down for a drink after the round.

"No, Vanessa is the tennis player. She played in college. Her family is big on it."

"So, you're not into tennis or golf, what's your thing?"

"My thing is trying to find a thing." I looked at her for an explanation.

"You know, I have tried almost everything but cannot get interested in anything enough to pursue it for any length of time."

"Oh," I said, not wanting to judge.

"Tell me, how did you know that was my ball in the woods?"

"Umm, ah, I noticed what you were playing one time when you teed up."

"Oh, okay. What if I changed balls?"

"Then I would have been wrong. Did you?"

"What was my final score?"

"98. You played really well."

"Thank you. What's the penalty for playing the wrong ball?"

"Two shots."

"So I was really 100."

"No, you took a penalty for the drop. So you were 99."

"Okay, that's good I guess."

"Truth is, the rules of golf are odd sometimes, and in that case, you probably should have gone back to the tee and played your third shot. One for your first shot and one for the penalty. We just took a short cut."

We sipped our drinks and pretty soon it was time to go. I asked her if she was ready to play the company tournament and she nodded saying she was unlikely to get any more ready, save for the obscure rules she did not know. I agreed with her saying I really didn't know all the ins and outs of the rules as circumstances and ground markings sometimes affected the rulings.

Frankie and I were due to leave 10 days later. I wanted to get to Yosemite on our way home and maybe head back by a different route. Frankie mentioned that he might have to stay an extra day or two as his business stuff was piling up. That would leave us less time to get back home if we wanted to keep the original schedule.

I went to the same coffee shop I had been to earlier in the week. Grabbed a paper and buried myself in it as I didn't want to think about anything.

And too my surprise Vanessa appeared at my table.

"Mind if I join you?"

"Sure," I said, folding up the paper. "First, I run into Emily here and now you. I thought you worked in Cupertino?"

"I do. Came up here for a product demonstration. Emily mentioned she ran into you here, so I figured I try it. You know, she was really happy you helped her with her game."

"And you, I think. And Frankie. Helped her, I mean."

"She really likes you, you know."

"Really? That's nice I guess, but I'm heading home in a few days. Back to my life of responsibilities. Three kids are a handful," I said to remind her, or at least scare her off. "Frankie and I are planning out the route tonight."

Vanessa seemed lost for anything to say.

"When is your wedding? Planning that usually takes months."

"Yeah, it does. But my mother is all over it. It's like she is on a mission. I can barely get anything in when we speak. So far, she's not determined to do anything crazy, so there is no friction. At least no combustible friction."

I laughed. Then Vanessa asked me for my phone number.

"Like I said we are going back in a few days, we won't be at that number."

"Then give me your home number, I can pass it on to Emily."

I took a deep breath, "Okay, I said. There is no harm in that."

Vanessa gave me two of her business cards. "Write your number on the back and keep one, in case you want to get in touch with Emily. She'd probably be mortified if she found out I'd asked for your number. I'll have to invent some reason you gave it to me."

"You better tell me what the excuse is, or I might say something you don't want me to."

"I have a conference out east coming up, I might give you a call for help navigating the city."

Frankie finally finished up his work commitments. For a bit it seemed like he might be flying back while I drove or something, as he was being tabbed with hanging around for a few more days. Just when I figured that was the likely plan, his schedule cleared and we were off.

"I told them the hotel reservation was up. The idea of ponying up for another month was enough to push us on the road."

"They really seem to need you. Might they offer you a transfer?"

"It crossed my mind, but with the speed of us getting out of here, probably not. Anyway, I'm not sure I'd take it. Though, I must admit California has its charms. Weather, opportunity, you know."

We decided to hit the road the next morning, mostly so Frankie's company couldn't change its mind. We had five days to get back east. That was going to be a lot of hard driving and little, if any, sightseeing. The quickest route was the best and our plan to meander back through Yosemite and Yellowstone was tossed.

"It looks like Reno to Salt Lake to Cheyenne and back to the real world."

Both of us were looking forward to getting home. Our trip had its moments but the world we were both familiar with was calling us home. My mother wouldn't say, but I could tell from her voice on the phone that she was nearing the end of her ability to cope with three children. The leisure time had done me good, but I was eager to get back to my routine and I expect the kids needed that structure in their lives.

Frankie mulled over some of the problems the California branch of his company was having, admitting they needed an experienced hand but remaining determined that it was not him.

"They have engineering schools in California? Right? Just hire from there, I told them," said Frankie.

"It's the experience they probably can't get. You know, I think you need to decide what you would do if they offered. As it was, we just barely escaped."

"It's our failure to go surfing that really sticks in my craw."

I laughed. "Surfing? Really?"

"Yeah, we had a chance to live differently and we did not take advantage."

"So maybe you really do need to transfer to California."

"I'd hate to pull the kids away from their friends. And the whole lot of us away from our families."

"Everyone has their price," I said.

"Even you?"

I shook my head, agreeing with him about the need for family, and reminding him that I'd be lost without it.

Strangely my crew seemed more mature when I got back into our routine. They were more helpful and seemed to do little things without asking. I mentioned it to my mother and she just tilted her head, in a way that told me everything.

"Your kids are wonderful, but they needed a little dose of reality. Everyone does. How was your trip?"

I gave her a quick description of our time mostly centering on the trip to and from San Jose. In between I thanked her often for stepping up.

"Did you meet anyone out there?"

"Oh, for sure, hundreds of people." I wasn't ready to admit to anything more than that.

"You know what I mean."

"Oh mom, I hope that was not the reason you pushed me out there?"

"One of the reasons, maybe. You are young still."

"With three kids. Not too many girls are keen on an insta-family. And anyway, I have far too many responsibilities to get mixed up in any of that. Too much drama. By the way, I think that Frankie's company might offer him a transfer out there. They are in great need of experienced people. As it was, I think we just escaped a longer stay."

A few months later Frankie called me, "You weren't wrong. They've offered me a major role in the company's western operations."

"You going to take it?"

"I don't think so, but I agreed to think on it for a couple of weeks. It is a great opportunity. My kids are excited by the prospect of California, but I don't think they fully understand the implications."

"Your kids are a bit older than mine. High school is a tough time for them. And what? You have two in high school already?"

"And one on the cusp."

"What's Kimberly say?"

"Not much so far. I think she sees the future clearly, or at least more clearly than me. We'd be giving up a lot of our roots here, but it's the way to advance my career, and that's important too. I'm guessing, she will just make do with either decision. I just wish the whole thing was more obvious."

"You can always take it and make a deal to return here if it doesn't work out."

"I suppose, but you know big companies, reversing course is difficult. Oh, I should let you know. I heard from Vanessa, you know the one from the golf course in California. She is coming to a software symposium here in a month and wondered if I could show her around."

"How's Kimberly feel about that?"

"She doesn't know. I don't want any awkwardness, so I'd like to suggest you show her around and keep me out of it. I don't want to stir the pot."

"I guess I could, as long as its geographic and not work oriented. My familiarity with the computer business is limited to where your office is located."

He laughed, "I'm sure its just about having a connection out here. Oh, and she said Emily was coming too, apparently there is a sales conference at the same time."

Word got around that I would be meeting two girls from California. At a bar-be-que, Kimberly mentioned it as an aside.

"You and Frank met these two in California?"

"Actually, I did. When Frank was working, I'd sometimes go play golf. Got paired with them as they were practicing for a corporate golf event." I didn't want to lie, but I didn't want to stir any odd feelings, either. Kimberly seemed okay with my explanation. The more I thought of it, the more I realized she would likely try to corroborate my story if she ever met them. And somehow, I knew she would contrive to make that happen.

I mentioned it to Frankie. He seemed unsettled. "Of course, stories that don't line up, just make me seem guilty. I try to keep everything on the up and up, and I still get jammed."

"Why don't you just tell Kim the truth?"

"There is no truth. I'm going to have to speak to Vanessa and let her know what's been said. I mean, we don't even know them very well and here we are dancing around trying to cover up that we even spoke to them."

"Well, Vanessa might be doing this to get Emily and I together."

Frankie's eyebrows shot up. And I told him about my conversation with Vanessa and admitted that neither she, nor Emily had been in touch with me since.

"Well, maybe I could use that if Kim keeps pushing."

"You might have to. I just worry about tangled webs and weaving and stuff."

In the end nothing came of all our machinations. I took Vanessa and Emily on a tour of the city, and we had dinner. Frankie stayed firmly planted at home. I think the whole episode was the final straw in his decision to refuse the transfer.

Emily did call me the evening after the tour and wondered if we could meet for dinner. I had to make a few arrangements, mostly paying a sitter and exorbitant sum for short notice, but I managed it and found myself sitting across from Emily that evening.

After we exchanged some pleasantries and I enquired after Vanessa's wedding plans. Emily wondered why Frankie had not come with us the previous evening. I confessed he did not want to encourage his wife into thinking our acquaintance was anything substantial.

"Frankie is about a straight and narrow as anyone, and Kim, his wife, would not normally be suspicious, but a month away and a stray comment or two and everyone gets upset needlessly."

She nodded. "I'm in for a golf game tomorrow if you can do it. I have the day off and only have to go to a speech at night."

Again, I'd have to make some expensive arrangements, but by this time I was warming to Emily. I made sure to make mention of my kids, often. Of course, if my mother found out about our golf game, she would jump to conclusions and the whole thing could snowball into Kim thinking we were more closely connected to these two girls than we really were.

I toyed with the idea of having Emily come to my house for dinner to inflict my kids on her and scare her off. I wondered if I should include Vanessa. My mother didn't need to know, but I was certain my kids would spill the details and my mother would wonder why I had kept quiet about it.

Being nice was complicated. Everyone thinks there is some larger agenda at play.

Our golf game went well. We shared a cart and had a chance to speak. I tried to keep it mostly to our golf game, and Emily's improvement. She kept harking back to local things, mostly about my kids. I took the plunge and invited her for dinner. We could do take out. My kids would like the treat. She agreed. I decided to leave Vanessa out of it, as that's what she would likely want me to do, given our California conversation.

I wasn't sure how I felt about the dinner, as Emily would see the stark reality of my life. And that was okay. If I was going to see more of her, she had to be good with my responsibilities. I just prayed my mother did not stop by.

Emily made an effort to speak to each of my brood, and agreed to join in a game they were playing. I used that time to clean up after dinner, suggesting they go and watch television when the game was over. I knew if I shooed too hard, they would never leave.

"It's amazing that you have everything so together," she said.

"I have a lot of help and frankly now that they are older, they are much easier to handle."

"They seem like nice kids."

"They are on their best behavior."

Chapter Forty-two

"So what did you think about David's offer?" I said into the telephone.

"I don't like doing things on very short notice. I'm a planner, not very spontaneous, I guess."

"Well, I got to thinking that maybe expanding our social circle a bit would be a good idea."

"Last time you tried that, you had so many friends you couldn't keep up with them all."

"You're right, though I do try to keep up with a few of them." I held the phone to my ear, and watched the interplay of shadows on the wall. "It's not easy you know. Some people are footloose and others got married and settled down. Once they had kids they were just in a different space."

"If David offers again, I'm going to go. I'd be happier if you came too."

"Let's see what happens. I'll see you at the coffee shop tomorrow. What did you think of the 'quest' story?"

"It was good. A bit different from most and the twist fit in nicely, not too obvious, though I was expecting something to happen."

"I'm not done my next one yet so you will have to wait on that. It's a buddy story. I'm getting close to the end of this exercise."

"Has it helped?"

"Oh yeah. It's really loosened up my creative juices but I don't feel any closer to a really good idea for a new novel."

"Keep going then. What's left?"

"I'm going to write a 'tragedy' next and after than there is 'rebirth', 'overcoming the monster', 'adventure' and 'young adult'."

"Good luck, let me read the buddy story when it's done."

After the conversation, my mind blank, I went to make a cup of tea to settle in for a few hours in front of the keyboard. I kept thinking about David's offer to mingle with some of his work colleagues and thought maybe something different would be good. My life had devolved into a lot of sameness. Or so I thought, until I realized I'd been to Philly, done some trade shows, dealt with my own clients, and lived a dozen lives through my keyboard, filtering new ideas into stories.

So why did my life feel so routine? I took a sip of tea, put the teapot in its usual place, just so, but couldn't focus. I sat in front of the screen watching the cursor blink, its impatience mirroring my own inability to move ahead. My rut did not feel like a tragedy.

What would I do if I knew I was going to die? Break the routine?

Chapter Forty-three – Tragedy

The heralds had completed their musical call with all the orchestral instruments booming, the kettle drums rumbling, the giant gong providing a counterpoint, and the wind instruments playing the triumphal tune on top of the pounding bass.

I stood on my high dais, specially built for this ceremony in front of the castle wall, in a forecourt between the barbican and the tallest corner tower of the fortress. Paved with intricate inlaid patterns, the forecourt spread from the curtain walls outward in a large fan shape. It was meant for large spectacles, especially ones where the inner castle could not handle the crowds. A second stone paved area, three steps down from the first, held it in place like a buttress, as the ground sloped down to a broad river.

I had come to my coronation in what was generally thought of as the standard way. My father, the Great King Bartholomew, had died after a long reign, having provided a steady rule and holding the affection of his people. In the days leading up to my coronation, I thought back to Kings before my father and realized that a direct handover of the crown from father to son had not happened too often. Intrigues, legalities, early death, rebellion and competing claims to the throne seemed to derail the process much more often than not.

The pleasure the populace seemed to have in a simple, uncontested succession was evident in the large crowds and the general happiness that seemed to emanate from the gathering. As my father had aged, I had taken on many of the responsibilities of rule and I was familiar to the subjects of the realm.

I had decided to keep the coronation portion of the festival short and simple, as I needed no introduction to the masses, nor did I need prove anything to them.

I was the youngest child of my father, but as his previous issue was a parade of girls, I was first in line. Only one of my sisters seemed to have any interest in statecraft. Diane, the third girl, had gravitated to my father and his concerns, eventually giving advice and providing a trusted sounding board as issues and concerns were addressed. Much of my father's reputation for fairness and geniality stemmed from my sister's ability to persuade.

I had no doubt she would be valuable to me as well. My two eldest sisters were married and had moved with their noble husbands to their estates. Both were on hand for the coronation and stood behind me on the dais.

My own children were there as well. Princes of the realm and now the oldest, Tristam, the heir apparent. He was a natural leader and his brother Tyrus, a willing follower, being five years younger. They were both in the bloom of adulthood, my father having lived to a rich old age.

On a lovely spring day, the freshness of the air reflecting the new administration of the realm, the Bishop intoned the words of commitment and placed the high crown on my head. It proved hard to hold up given the weight of it. No wonder this thing was ceremonial, I thought, with the king wearing a circlet only, when dealing with the public or his ministers.

"I present to you all, King Anzia," said the Bishop.

I had a smile on my face as everything had gone perfectly to plan. I held the crowd in my hand as I spoke words of fealty and honour to them. As I spoke, men of my house directed those I had hired to set their machines.

As I concluded my speech, telling everyone my reign would be peaceful, hopeful and wonderous, the first of the fireworks boomed from a cannon. The crowd at first gasped at the sound fearing the worst.

"Behold," I said. "A golden age."

And the firework exploded in the sky, sending bright yellow golden shards in all directions, and then a huge chrysanthemum in white. And as the shards twinkled and slowly fell, a second boom, built anticipation from the onlookers. And now a flower of red filled the sky.

The castle was built along side a swiftly flowing river, broad and deep enough for all but the largest ships, but with a powerful current, especially in spring as it carried the melt water of the surrounding mountains. The stream ran clear in spring but the rest of the year it was a smoky cauldron of water and eroded earth and stone carried down from the ringing peaks.

The booms cascaded out one after another, with differences in the fire show in the sky. And all too soon it was time for the finale, when multiple shots were projected even higher than before and they all exploded together creating a wall of colour and spectacle, all over the top of the orchestra playing familiar music.

As the embers slowly fell toward the river and the lights faded, and people were being beckoned to tables of food and drink, a low rumble could be heard that seemed to be coming from everywhere. The onlookers, intent on getting their victuals before the tables were picked clean, paid little attention, though those who had waited for the crowds to thin looked up, as if the show might continue.

At first, I thought the rumbling was merely the movement of many feet making ready to eat, and the scraping of tables and chairs being moved into place for the oldest of the onlookers.

But the rumble continued, low for a time and then louder. It could not be ignored and people looked in all directions for its source. Then someone yelled and some of the crowd began to point. They were indicating a disturbance high on the mountain across the river. It looked as if some storm had disturbed the top of the peak, snow swirled and caught in the last of the sunlight. As the settling sun was now behind the line of mountains, it provided a spectacle almost as wonderous as the fireworks.

And then a hubbub of voices rose, as below the snow light, there appeared to be movement. It was perhaps two miles away and up the mountain and soon became apparent that it was a snow slide. The visual hardly changed as the slide was obscured by the dim light on the east side of the mountains. However, the sparkling snow at the top remained and even suggested to some that the avalanche was occurring on the other side of the range.

The rumbling continued however and people seemed satisfied enough at the explanation of sound that they went back to their merriment with only an occasional glance to the mountain.

A few minutes later there was a scream and then quickly a general tumult of the massed crowd that rose above the music. People pointed, though most remained in place as across the river, and through the foot-hills of the mountains, the slide was obvious. Even in the dimming light one could see rocks rolling down the hill, pebbles they seemed in advance of the distant wall of snow, gliding serenely down the slope. But they were not pebbles.

The power of the slide was evident as it covered trees and then consumed several buildings on hills some distance from the river.

The crowd grew restless and some began to move with haste away from the forecourt, either around the castle to where the town center lay, or, into the castle itself if they had the ability and right. The town itself hugged the banks of the river a mile in each direction, and the centre of town lay behind the castle.

“Fear not,” said senior statesman Earl Craigarnoth, to those who stood around me. “This has happened before, the river always consumes the slides and has for generations.”

The Earl was right. We had seen these slides in the past. Spectacular, but the mountains were far enough away that they posed no threat to the town or castle. It was Craigarnoth who had proposed the fireworks portion of the ceremony in an attempt to make memorable the orderly transfer of power.

“Calm. It will soon be over and we can proceed with the feast and merry-making,” I added, trying to project my voice to those around me.

I stood resolute, not wanting to appear afraid. But the rocks, some the size of carriages, were now hitting the river, and they hit with enough force to smash huge plumes of water skyward. And then one bounced over the stream hitting the bank on the castle side. Though its progress was halted by the riverbank it had smashed into, it quivered with energy remaining to be spent.

And the rocks were no mere pebbles, they are huge boulders of stone, the size of a room in many cases, and they crashed into the stream. That barrier seemed to still the unease in the crowd, many of whom stood and watched the wonderous spectacle. Their eyes on the stones, one of which took the royal boat launch completely off its foundations, and then first one, then another destroying a bridge across the stream, as they smashed into the arches with an unexpected fury.

A gasp escaped the crowd and some people were trying to move away from the castle wall.

And on the heels of these shocking events the snow, obscured in the low light, and providing a path for the stones, glided down to the river and filled the stream. Then the snow crossed the river and more and more snow, mixed with stones, and trees and other detritus, began to advance up the slope from the river. Of course, the rising bank on the castle side of the river forced the snow and debris outward where the rubble filled more and more of the river. And though it seemed in slow motion, it all happened fast.

I was standing rapt, still not believing there was any danger, when the first of the snow, mostly a thick cloud of white mist and ice, rose above the bank and filled the forecourt. Some had escaped in various directions but the sheer size of the fall made outrunning the slide very difficult.

My sisters and mother, the bishop, the Earl, my two boys, and several close companions and high-ranking nobles, stood with me, as I directed them to get under the raised platform and out of the on-rush of snow and debris. I had hoped to be able to make a run for the castle itself, but the distance to the barbican was too great and the howl of the moving snow too loud for my commands to be heard. My boys thought other-wise.

"Father, I can make it to the barbican if I go now," and off he sprung, my oldest son, not waiting for approval. He was followed a few steps later by his brother. I yelled after them to remain, but they were nimble and quick and the sound of the rushing snow too loud, and they were gone.

"I tried to stop them," said Earl Craigarnoth, with a sheepish grin.

All the rest of us could do was retreat under the stage platform and wait until the slide finished its movement. The unholy noise, punctured with screams and grinding sounds became muffled and then died away completely, as we were buried by the snow. We were safe under the dais. Perhaps two dozen of us were now in complete darkness, without any sound save the whimpering of my sisters and several of the other female attendees.

"I don't know if its over, but we cannot stay here," I said to whoever wanted to hear it.

"Well, this is not the way I expected your coronation to be concluded. And now we have a trial to contend with. What do you suggest we do?"

"Those in the castle will begin to dig as soon as they realize what has happened. I suggest we do what we can to dig out and make their jobs a bit easier. We do have some space down here in which to house the ladies."

I removed my cloak and laid it over my hands and began to clear away the snow from behind the dais nearest the castle wall. My childhood friend Viscount Allenby had sparked up a flint and provided a little light.

"Use it sparingly my friend, it generates smoke and consumes our air."

Seeing what I was doing, several of my companions, men I'd been friends with for my whole life, and my two brothers in law, joined me.

Digging above our heads wasn't easy as we were concerned of a major cave-in as we hollowed out a rising tube. Soon it was difficult to dig as the ceiling of the tube was taller than one could reach. Several of the diggers marvelled that the snow could be so deep.

My brothers-in-law found a solution as one rode of the shoulders of the other giving several additional feet to their ability to pry out the snow. Soon there were three teams in the tube doing the same thing. My head was spinning as the air seemed thick as we worked. A few minutes as the holder and the teams would switch positions.

"Oh, no," said my brother-in-law Earl Neverage. And he gave a mighty pull and a body fell to the ground. One of the older nobles pulled it aside.

"He yet lives, my lord."

Engaged in my task, urgently now as the air seemed thick, I said, "Do what you can sir. If he lives, pump his chest and maybe he will breathe more deeply."

We were near the maximal height we could reach as pairs and I contemplated the possibility of a triple stack of people but fortunately my long-time companions beside me yelled, "The snow is thinner, I think I am near the surface of it."

Our cloaks were ruined. Finery bought especially for the coronation lay soaked and torn and was of no further use. There were two pieces of wood underneath the platform, that someone had stumbled on, left over from their construction. I called for them to be brought and two pairs of men, using the wooden planks poked up through the snow.

Immediately the air cleared and we all collapsed from our vigor. "How much more snow is atop the hole?"

"Perhaps six inches, maybe less." As I dug, I patted down the sides of the tube so they would not collapse upon us.

The flint sparked up some damp cloth acquired from one of the ladies' headdresses. It spluttered and caught but only barely provided minimal light.

"I do not think we will receive much help for a while yet. We can continue the dig, with an occasional yell up the shaft to alert any rescuers, or we can carry on and extricate ourselves from this tomb."

"You ask me? I'm all for getting out of here as fast as we are able."

Despite the situation I had to laugh, "My thinking exactly, my friend. As we rest momentarily, does anyone have a good idea how we should do that? The shaft is unstable and I'd guess at least a dozen feet high."

"We might be able to lever one of us up to the top, and with luck the snow will hold his weight."

"We could wait until the snow melts. The day was fair when all this began."

"This amount of snow will take a time to melt enough, even in the warmth of the day."

"I'm thinking we boost up one of us to fetch help. I suggest one of the ladies, they are lighter, a boon both to us lifting her, and for her to traverse the snow without causing a cave in."

The other looked at me, a mixture of considering my madness and an appreciation of my bold and unexpected plan.

"First let us try one of us. Failing that we will select the likely female candidate."

The decision made, I nodded and we all rose, with weary bodies, some stretching their bones to bring them back to life. I looked around and my eyes settled on my lifelong friend, Lord Nethercott, as he was the slightest among us. He was tall and thin, light and hopefully able to extricate himself if we pushed him high enough. He looked willing but dubious.

We went into a double piggy back set leaning against the curtain wall of the castle, and encouraged Nethercott to climb the human tower we had created.

Two of the ladies giggled. I turned saying, "You had better hope this works or one of you will be asked to try something similar."

Nethercott found footholds on bent knees, cupped hands and shoulders. It took much effort but soon he was at the top of the pyramid trying to rise to his feet on the shoulders of the top men. Some snow cascaded down.

"It's just me, clearing the top a bit and packing the snow together. I'm above the snow level and can balance against the castle wall."

"Can you get out completely?"

"I will try, though I think I should lay flat and spread my weight out."

"Do what you must. Before you try it what can you see? Is anyone about?"

"Tis bleak. All the snow mist has not settled, though it is clearing. I see some movement, principally down by the food tables, or at least where they should be. But mostly it is a changed landscape. The river has disappeared. The moon has risen so there is some light. It appears that getting ourselves out of this hole is only the first problem we must overcome. I will try now to reach the barbican and pray the entrance to the castle is not blocked. I will return with news and hopefully help."

My companions and I settled in, unsure of how long we might wait. Some time later, hours perhaps, I heard Nethercott's voice, "I am back. The barbican is blocked but there are people digging it out. I did manage to get a ladder tossed down from inside the castle."

He lowered it down, bracing it against he castle wall and claiming that the snow was packed enough to walk on, with care. One by one our tomb emptied and a line of people made their way to the barbican.

Once there I met the castellan who was directing efforts to clear the way into the castle.

"Ah my lord, your Grace, I am so pleased you were able to survive this. We have almost cleared a path inside and you and your companions will be able to rest."

Thank you, good sir, if someone can lead the ladies inside, I would be most grateful, as I will stay here to help in whatever efforts are devised."

"I have men surveying the snowfall looking for anyone who can be extricated. I am told the snow is blocking the river and water is building up behind the dam. It is warmish, even now in the night, and the snow will melt. Though I am afraid of what we might find when that occurs, and remain fearful of any floodwater damaging the upper town."

"We must do what we can as we watch what God has in store for us. Keep working and the morning will provide some answers."

The new King directed some of the diggers at the barbican to move toward the river and the festival reception area looking for survivors. While the court yard was open to the onslaught, there were a large number of tables used to display the feast and for people, particularly the aged, to sit and eat.

Sure enough, a few of these tables were found buried not too deeply thanks to no obstructions, which allowed the avalanche to spread out at an even depth. Several people were rescued but they showed the early signs of suffocation, gasping for breath, stiffly moving away and unable in most cases to help with the rescue of others.

The castle wall, where the coronation dais had been built, was piled high with snow and some stone debris as the castle itself contained the slide and allowed it to pile up as it spread along the curtain wall.

Fairly confident that no one would be found near the castle walls, as all who had been there had hidden and been rescued, the King pushed hard for the clearing of the snow in the court yard.

A few more survivors were found accompanied by whoops and calls for medical help. And then the first of the dead was found. Apparently safe under a large serving table, three people were crowded together in a small pocket of air. It had not lasted long enough for them to be found. Their faces were contorted in hideous grim expressions, as they faced their deaths rapidly and unexpectedly.

Having found a few buried tables, the location of others was revealed as the onslaught had pushed the tables away from the castle's outer court. The tables, many of which had remained upright, were pushed toward the castle and spread in both directions, though most of the tables were to the south as the snow slide had followed the flow of the river.

The king asked after his sons, but none had seen them.

Two days later much of the snow had melted away, the river had resumed its course although it still trapped a large lake behind it. Several cannon shots had been fired in vain at the snowy blockage. The cannon balls were simply swallowed up.

Rescue work had turned into recovery of victims. Most but not all of the attendees at the coronation had been accounted for. One thousand guests had been invited, of which, nearly all attended. The King's party had all survived, but 665 of the guests had not. Innumerable nobles, family members and distant relations, had succumbed to the avalanche.

"We have not yet accounted for all the attendees."

"What of my sons?"

"Not yet my lord. We are hopeful they have been rescued and are recovering somewhere."

"That is not likely though, is it?"

"No, my lord."

The three hundred survivors either found a pocket of air in which to await rescue or they fled at the first indication of trouble. Several who had been in the court yard near the barbican were able to scramble into the castle at the moment the slide breeched the river. At that point anyone who was near enough and determined enough would make it to safety. Hesitation or bad luck consigned those in these categories to death.

"What is to be done Diana? What would you have told our father to do at this point."

"Issue a decree, lamenting the dead, show determination to rapidly award estates to their heirs in natural succession, and call a King's council on how to proceed. Your own men largely survived but a newly constituted king's council, bringing in some of the newer lords from distant provinces, would be wise."

"Should we erect a monument?"

"No! Remind not the people of this tragedy. And quash any speculation that the fireworks triggered the slide. People are talking and those that do not want to blame you are often thinking that this is a poor omen of your rule. People will talk, but give it no air or credence."

The King pursed his lips, "There is talk that I caused this?"

"Yes my brother. You cannot stop that, and any attempt to crush such speculation will only make you seem more guilty. Simply ignore the issue and hopefully it will slowly fade away."

"But what if the fireworks really did trigger the slide?"

"You cannot prove that, no one can. And we will never know. Accept no responsibility directly, but do what a sovereign should do for his people. Bestow aid where appropriate, smooth the legal processes for inheritances and announce a public works project which will include the rebuilding of the bridge."

"Perhaps you are right, my sister. What of any other damage to farms and homes between here and the mountain?"

"Accessors have returned and there was little damage, there are two instances where the crown should help the affected landowners. In both cases we should arrange to rebuild but insist much of our help needs to be repaid, though at a vastly advantageous rate for the landowners."

The king's two sons had been found buried in snow and debris, crushed up against the castle wall about 30 feet from the barbican. The funeral rite had been solemn and the new king seemed to age in the few days between the discovery of his sons and the burial.

At first the rebuilding efforts and advantageous terms offered by the king were taken up with enthusiasm. But there was an undercurrent of blame that still lingered, and it was fueled by those who saw the Kings concessions as a guilty admission.

Men continued to look aloft at the encircling mountains wondering if another avalanche would descend upon them. But the weather rapidly warmed and the tragedy was put behind them. Two stone arches of the new bridge were completed with five more to go. Builders used blocks from the original bridge which saved on quarrying costs and helped to clear the river of any reminders of the tragedy.

“And now an heir must be appointed,” Diane said. “A painful duty though it is. Given our father’s great age and your maturity, you are unlikely to produce another in direct line.”

“Four of the probable heirs, those in line after your sons, were killed in the event. And I believe you are aware of the other three likely candidates.”

The King had been told of a group of noble cousins who had been found sitting in a circle under a serving table. Nephews of the King, cousins to each other, two each from the families of his older sisters.

The possible choices of heir were not optimal as the King had daughters but as his own sisters had been passed over in succession. Changing the customs and appointing a ruling Queen seemed to be detrimental to the foundations of the kingdom.

Another was one of his own sisters, but they were all facing the same gender challenges and they were all older than he was. The last, was the young son of his father’s brother, the issue of a second marriage to a much younger commoner.

His father’s brother, Uncle Edward, had died several years before in a self -imposed exile, due to the irregularities of his life. Never expecting to have any royal duties or ambitions, Edward had taken all the pleasures of life each day, forgoing responsibilities until the pleasures, as common as they were, ceased to provide any joy.

The young boy, his son was now only reaching maturity, a generation younger than his cousin, the new King. He had not been in attendance at the coronation.

"I cannot see my way clear to appointing any of them as my heir. There is no suitable family available."

"Edward's son is the likeliest choice."

"And an impossible one. We cannot go from hiding the boy, barely acknowledging his existence, to appointing him the next King."

"Then provide me with another choice."

"I shall have to. Give me some time to think on it."

And the new king knew that he would have to engineer an heir. That meant sidelining his wife, the new Queen. "There are some things more important than faith and fairness," he told himself.

Meanwhile his great uncle, Earl Craigarnoth came to him with a possible solution. As the son of the second son of our great king, your own father's sire, I am in line of succession," he said. King Anzia raised his eyes at the brashness. "But I renounce any claim for myself. There is however, my own son, your cousin, Michael."

"The son of a second marriage," I believe, said the King. "The line of succession has passed him by, I'm afraid, my uncle."

"Your choice is limited, think on it, I beg. Whatever you decide is chosen."

He anguished over the choice but in the end, Queen Isabella was offered a choice, die by poison or renounce her marriage and enter a convent.

She very nearly had the former imposed upon her as her ravings began to be a distraction, but in the end she succumbed to the latter. She was taken away to a distant abbey church and provided with four attendants, guards really, to insure she remained.

The King wasted little time in finding a suitable girl. Married in a quiet ceremony the young girl had little idea of the tumult surrounding her affairs and was chastened by the King on more than one occasion. When she failed to produce a male heir, she was promptly shunted aside and another took her place.

This young woman had been groomed by her family for such a moment and was demure and quiet even while those she knew schemed around her.

She produced a strong and healthy baby boy and then another one. Her mission complete she was sidelined, though treated with respect. The two boys grew strong, the eldest acknowledged as the heir to the throne on his 13th birthday. His father the king had, in the ensuing years, aged rapidly. Now in his middle 60s he walked like a man much older. His young son was brought up with statecraft in his blood. He was taught to be respectful of his advisors and teachers but to always remember he was their superior, even if he was to never, save in the most extreme circumstances, to exercise that power over them.

One of his father's most trusted advisors, Earl Makomby was charged with the youth's training and disposition. With the King aging rapidly, Makomby saw an opening he was determined to exploit before anyone else could. He brought the boy into his own circle making sure he was well acquainted with his own daughter, especially when they were quite young.

As the boy passed the age of 13 King Anzia introduced the boy into the King's councils and began to think of a mate for him. Once that job was complete and the line of succession set, the old king could cease to be concerned.

Makomby's daughter, Isabel, was often in the royal presence. However, King Anzia had never considered her as she was a fixture in the court. Until one day, he stumbled upon his young son and Isabel speaking together in the castle. He saw them from a distance and was about to say something, when Isabel with a tender smile, reached up to touch his son's face. His son smiled back and said something that made Isabel laugh. Before he could be noticed having seen them, King Anzia made a show of stumbling into the large space. Anzia's entire hopes were wound up in this boy. Though it struck him that he did have a younger, second son.

Chapter Forty-four

The sky was dark even though it was mid morning. They'd called for a thundershower and the weather front that contained it was advancing. I was glad to reach the safety of the coffee shop and just as pleased to see Theresa already there sipping on her coffee and looking at her phone.

I slipped in to my seat and she looked up.

"Oh, it's you."

"Who were you expecting?"

"Could have been anyone. Markus said he might come by. David is likely to be here at some point. Maybe someone else entirely."

"How about Brandon?"

"I haven't heard from him or about him in a while now. I should ask Markus about him. I take it he's still in recovery mode but it's been months now. Maybe he's just busy catching up with his life."

"So, I wrote a tragedy this time around."

"You must like it. It's the first time ever you've volunteered the genre of your project."

"Yeah, it turned out reasonably well. No wonder Shakespeare was so big on them. It's relatively easy to hurt and abuse characters."

Theresa smirked, "Don't we all know."

"So why is Markus coming by. I thought that was all over."

At that moment a light rain started outside, easily seen through the huge windows. The heavy stuff was sure to follow.

"I never said it was over. It's just simmering. Frankly I think he's moving on as well and just wanted to stop by to keep the friendship up. He said something about an appointment somewhere around here."

The rain came harder, followed by a punctuation of thunder, so loud and compact that everyone in the shop jolted. It sounded like gunshots.

"If he shows up, we can get the lowdown on Brandon. This rain might slow him down. So how are things in the clothing business?"

"I'm not sure. I'm getting calls for fall fashions, which certainly in keeping with the seasonal nature of the business. Thank god, guys don't think the same way. A little thicker fabric and perhaps a different collar and they are good for the winter."

"Any trade shows on the horizon?"

"There's a big one out in California but I'm not sure I'm ready for that. Different climate, and distance for shipping and stuff, I'm inclined to just stay small and workable for another season before considering that market. I'm toying with just going to the show as an observer. I can get a look at the stuff on offer, talk to a few people and maybe get some things in place for next year."

"Sounds interesting."

"You want to come?"

"Interesting if you're in the business."

"We could make a holiday out of it. It's not for two months, in LA, well just outside of LA."

"Isn't everything in LA, just outside of LA?"

Theresa grinned. She took a deep sip of her coffee. "I never understood how the coffee can be so hot one minute and almost cold the next."

"You talk too much. Does it happen at home?"

"I don't drink much coffee at home, so I can't say I've noticed it."

And then Markus swept into the shop and gave us a wave as he moved to make his order. The hard rain had slackened and no thunder had followed up the first crack.

"Maybe things are heating up," I said. Theresa gave me a look. He collected his coffee and three fritters and sat down.

"Ladies. Bit wet out there."

"You managed to dodge it. You seem almost dry."

"I confess, I took a cab. Managed to get this wet on my run in from the curb."

"We were just talking about Brandon. How is he?"

"Funny you should mention that. I was just talking to him; seems he's been busy."

"Catching up on work?"

"Catching up with an old girlfriend who moved back to town."

"Oh! That's news. Is he past his injuries?"

"Yeah, I think so. Still moves a little gingerly but you would hardly notice it."

"And this friend?"

"He used to date her in high school and she moved away and then attended college in Kansas, but she's back with a job in the city."

"So what have you been doing?"

"Oh, not too much really. Work has me bogged down and some family stuff. Mostly helping my younger brother to move. I am something of an expert in packing. Just saying."

"Where's he moving too."

"Moving from actually. Coming back from college in Ohio. Took two trips to get everything. I managed to turn some of it into a work trip. Visited a few companies we are preparing IPOs for."

David appeared in the shop doorway with a quizzical look on his face. Theresa waved him over. She quickly made introductions and David excused himself to get his coffee.

Markus seemed interested in the hospital where David worked, and they chatted a bit.

David mentioned that he was again going to the pub after work with his colleagues and invited the whole table to join him.

"I'll be there David, what's the story exactly?"

"We just head over in ones and twos after work, about 5:15 or so, and have a few drinks and maybe some appetizers and off we go when ever. I think the whole thing is done by 10 if you stayed to the bitter end."

"I will join you as well," I chimed in. "Markus?"

He looked a bit pensive but nodded, "Why not?"

After my appointments I spent some time just wandering around the shopping district before heading to the pub, making sure to arrive about 5:30 pm so David would be there before me.

I need not have worried. Theresa and Markus were already there and where chatting with someone I did not know.

"There she is. Hey this is Susan. She works with David, who is here somewhere."

We nodded to each other. "So how many of your colleagues usually come by?"

"Sometimes its as many as a dozen. There are a lot of us around the same age."

She went on to say she was an insurance administrator within the hospital, matching treatments to payments and such.

People kept swinging by our table and we exchanged so many introductions I couldn't keep track. David was back and forth between two groups and seemed happy we had all come, saying it was nice to have somebody to talk to who wasn't connected to the hospital. Susan excused herself and it was just Theresa, Markus and I.

"Perhaps we should mingle a bit," I suggested.

"We have, they just come to us. Works perfectly." And with that, two people detached themselves from the other group and sat down with us. Smiles and introductions were made and Tal, a tall red-headed guy said he'd heard we were David's friends from the coffeeshop.

"He loves going by there. Do you go every day?"

"No," I said, "we are usually there only on Wednesdays. Theresa and I are old friends and make it a regular thing."

"That's nice. David goes at least three times a week. Says it clears his head. I've gone with him once or twice. Perhaps I should make it more often."

"Well, if we can join your after-work group, then surely you are welcome to join our Wednesday coffee."

"Wednesday has been a good day to do this. The weekend is in sight but most people just want to socialize a bit, without any pressure."

"I'm not sure why we ended up on Wednesdays."

"It was you. You had a regular client meeting near here for a long while. That's why we picked the spot," said Theresa.

I nodded. She was right and I still visited that client about once a month. Retainers are lovely things to freelancers.

I was hopeful that we wouldn't get into our work situations as I was uncomfortable talking about my side projects, but of course it came up.

Susan had been fascinated with my communications work and asked a question or two about my fiction. Somehow, she knew not to get to into it. Maybe I gave off a 'don't go there' vibe.

Tal and Gerry, Gerry being his girlfriend, showed some enthusiasm for novels and we talked about our favourites.

"For me, I loved 'The Count of Monte Christo' never mind how long it was. I didn't want it to end," said Tal. Gerry, who was a sales rep with one of the pharma companies, said she really loved 'Jane Eyre' and that type of story.

We mentioned a few other classics and it seemed that the pair were typical among those who were reasonably well read. Tal like the books aimed at men and Gerry like the romances and stories about manners. I mentioned that and wondered aloud if there was any common ground.

They both looked up as if the answer would appear on the wainscotting, and then looked at each other.

"You know, I've never really thought about it, before."

"I think about it a lot as I'm caught between trying to write something popular and something that might appeal to a wider audience."

"What about 'The Hunchback of Notre Dame' or 'Vanity Fair'?"

They both shook their heads. They hadn't read them. Gerry moved into movies and we got talking about that. Tal loved the old black and whites.

The gangster films, the westerns. Gerry said she had a love of Casablanca but mostly the black and whites threw her off. She had trouble watching a movie without colour. I found that odd and said so, but she shrugged and Tal defended her, saying he'd heard of that approach to films before.

"Okay, what about 'A Hard Day's Night'?"

"Funny you should mention that," said Tal. "I just rewatched that and picked up a chat group that was talking about it. It's a brilliant film, even though it has been dismissed for years as just a vehicle for the Beatles."

"I agree," I said. "Some of the scenes still resonate today, not only with the vagaries of popular culture but with the raw energy of the music. It's funny but the cultural impact of that film seems to grow."

"In the chat, a lot of people said that exact thing."

And then we started talking about music. I had really warmed to Tal and Gerry and soon David was back listening in.

During a lull in the conversation he said, "I hope you've enjoyed yourselves. We meet every Wednesday. Feel free to come when ever you'd like and bring Markus or other friends who might want to come."

I left at that point, not wanting to get home too late. I even thought about my 'rebirth' story, as I must admit the whole evening left me feeling like I'd opened a new door.

There were no revelations in any conversation but it was nice to get outside of my own world even for just a few hours. I was going to go back, but I figured I'd wait a couple of weeks.

The next evening, I had the chance to start in on a new story.

Chapter Forty-five – rebirth

I had always painted, since I was small. Well, I drew first. My mother had been an amateur artist, and had even managed a few minor commissions among friends. It was not unusual to go to a relative's house and see one of her paintings hanging on the wall. She was a realist, drawing what she saw, or what she wanted to see.

I certainly shared in her innate ability, being able to sketch and get the necessary details in a face, so you knew who it was. I never thought about it, figuring that everyone could do it.

At some point I realized it was a fairly rare skill, though, not so rare that it made me special. Like athletic ability or smarts, it just marked me as part of my tribe.

Oh sure, I once wished I could turn that ability into a paying job, but it wasn't meant to be, not really. I took some graphic arts classes and worked for a while in an ad agency, doing mock ups, and stuff. At least that way I could do something close to what I loved.

Of course, after a time that got stale, I was promoted into an agency project manager job, then technology changed and I was largely out of the game.

One day I was just doodling at my desk, awaiting an important phone call, when I sketched out a pair of characters. They amused me and I took the sheet of paper home and began to doodle some more, placing them in a situation and drawing the next thing that occurred. Before I knew it, I had several panels and a bit of a story line. I was drawing a cartoon. And later it evolved into a graphic novel.

My subjects were two cave men who took on their challenges, planned their days and then drew significant events on the cave walls, cave man style.

I loved it and kept at it in my spare time, taking these two on adventures, hunting, having fun, and meeting other cave guys in scary and eventually friendly ways. Having just been to northern Italy, I set the story there and one day had my guys stumble upon the ruins of Rome. Now my story had moved into dystopian science fiction, with science that the main characters could not know or likely understand.

Meanwhile at work my job had become pretty routine. It paid the bills and kept me engaged with the world. I had a vacation coming up so I decided to go to Rome, partly to check it out for the benefit of my cave men, but also to discover great art, and I decided, to play the part of a street artist for a day or two, just to see if I could do it.

My Italian wasn't great, but it was passable and I figured most of the potential clients I had wouldn't be locals, anyway. I got into a conversation with a couple going to Rome for a vacation and I let slip my intention to do some street art. They were both enthralled and asked all kinds of questions, most of which I didn't have answers to.

They wheedled out of me where I was likely to set up, and said they would come by and see how I was doing. We said our goodbyes and I didn't expect to see them, as I was planning many other locations for my drawing than I had let on.

Wanting the evocative but unusual, I scoped out the city for two days, doing the usual tourist things. Then I took my heavy art paper and easel to The Baths of Caracalla, a huge but often overlooked ruin south of the Forum.

I found a spot and started drawing, thinking I'd go with a simple pencil sketch first and then try something a bit more ambitious. I had much of the stone work done when a group of people entered the largest space and began to set up a stage. I'd heard of performances taking place here so I figured I'd dig in.

Once the stage was set, I began to sketch in the performers, difficult for me, as they kept moving. I think the organizers figured I had been hired to provide a picture of the proceedings as no one bothered me.

When the performance was done, I gathered up my things and moved to leave. One of the performers asked me when I would complete the picture. I shrugged an artist's shrug, saying it would be done when there was nothing left to paint.

He gave me a knowing look and a slowly forming broad grin. He turned and left with a nod. Back at my hotel I did add a few elements, the backs of audience member heads, a bit of stage scenery and it was done. I considered donating it to the performance group, but of course I had little idea of who they were or how to find them.

The next day I first went to the Piazza Navona and set up in a far corner, trying to capture tourists entering the piazza rather than the famous fountains. This time I went with a more impressionistic style, which I thought suited the subject matter. I must confess I was not all that satisfied with the result. I was more a realist, like my mother. However, an incident as I was setting up, gave me an idea.

A pair of young tourists, Americans I think, approached me and asked what I charged for portraits. I dismissed them as I was not drawing with that in mind.

And so, on the third day I ended up at the bottom of the Spanish Steps with my pencil drawing from Caracalla on my easel. I quickly took my first commission as a street artist, drawing a pair of young people sitting on a plinth at the bottom of the stair. They seemed pleased with the result and happily paid my price.

So, I decided to double it. Eventually another pair came by and engaged me to take on essentially the same picture, but they wanted it painted rather than drawn.

I doubled the price again and we agreed on a slight discount after I said it was likely to take at least two hours to do properly. This was pretty good money for a few hours work, doing what I was going to be doing anyway.

I set the Caracalla picture down, leaning against the back of the easel, and started the basic sketch, and quickly moving to the painting portion of the job. The picture was done in largely light tones, the marble steps, the people, the clothing of passing tourists and the like. I threw in a touch of colour in the flowers and on some of the clothing and things people carried. Then I concentrated on their faces, the key if my customers were to be happy.

They sat patiently and I worked away, occasionally having passersby stop and watch me at work. Pretty much done, I glanced at my watch, and decided to add a few details to the buildings and steps to push me toward the two-hour mark.

They were very pleased, kept thanking me and happily turned to go, deciding to take their treasure back to their hotel before continuing on the day. A wise choice, I agreed.

That success spawned a few others looking for a similar memento of their trip. The first person balked at the price, the second wanted a third person in, so I increased the price. The man grimaced but agreed to pay. And so I began the picture all over again, this time having the subjects sit on the steps rather than the plinths of the flower beds.

I figured I'd do one more, as that would put me into the middle afternoon. And the money I had earned was a nice bit of extra cash. One of the other street artists wandered over to me, saying he'd never seen me around. I tried to ease his concerns that I was elbowing into his territory saying I would only be here for the day. That seemed to satisfy him, and he wandered off.

A third picture painted and I decided to stay at it until any requests dropped off. Two more pictures completed and a bundle of Euros in my pocket and the Steps seemed to thin out as the day was winding down. I wondered if I should stay around as the Italians were notorious for late suppers, but I decided I'd had enough and wanted a rest before I ate. It would give me an opportunity to figure out my next day's plan.

I was gassed. Once I lay down, the heat of the day slowly began to rise and I dozed, thinking without any concrete form, about the next day.

Not wanting to deal with the prying eyes of Italians who loved to go to restaurants in large groups, often with family members, I elected to eat in the hotel room. I had collected a few easily consumed items for just such a choice.

The next day I wanted to draw for myself, but I was torn between trying to set up in the Forum, not knowing, but expecting push back from the authorities, or maybe doing a street scene near the entrance to St. Peter's Square. I chose the latter and found a place to set up where the square would be in the background.

I wasn't too pleased with the outcome as the oval of pillars which defined the square simply didn't come out right, or at least was less pleasing to my eye. Instead of the curvature of the pillars opening the space up, they seemed to close on each other forming a wall of sorts. I repositioned myself inside the pillared square and drew the front of St. Peter's through the pillars at an oblique angle. It had probably been done a million times, but I liked it. While drawing, I had the brain wave of going to The Appian Way, a road leading to, and I guess, from Rome, and lined with monuments of ancient Romans.

It took a bit of doing but I managed a taxi ride a few miles out of Rome and found a nice spot where three substantial monuments were situated near to each other.

"Well, there he is. We checked out the Coliseum and the Trevi Fountain but you weren't there. Fancy seeing you way out here."

It was the couple from the plane. Both with grins on their faces, I asked how their trip had been thus far.

"Wonderful. Rome is . . . . Rome is, special, unique I guess. I'm still taking it all in."

His wife nodded. "How has your painting been?"

"Good, I guess. I found some uncommon spots to draw from and managed a few sketches that I liked."

"We are headed to the Forum and the Capitoline Hill. If you are free, we could meet for supper back near our hotel. You did say you were staying near the Pantheon, didn't you?"

"I did, and I am. Sure that sounds nice. Italians look at you strangely if you dine alone. What time?"

"There is a nice restaurant just down the street from our hotel. We could meet there at say 8 pm, to be fashionable. We are trying to do things the Italian way."

I agreed, and they gave me the name of the hotel and the street it was on, all familiar to me as my hotel was only a few blocks away.

Sitting down with them, still a little wary of unknown people, I began to open up a bit, needing the human contact, realizing that my own countrymen, even those very different from me, were closer to my understanding than Italians who lived much differently.

I described my day as a street painter, and the pair were very much engaged, pointing out my courage, chutzpah and apparent skill, to have a steady stream of customers.

"I didn't think of it that way, at least at the beginning, but drawing the Steps half a dozen times made me feel like singers who tour and give the same performance over and over again. I enjoyed the street painting but I'm in no hurry to do it again."

"Would you paint us? We'd pay you and we'd have a great souvenir."

I hesitated but I was stuck. I told them what I had charged at the Spanish Steps and my dinner companions immediately agreed, in fact they insisted upon paying for dinner as well. So I had to ask them where they wanted to be painted. With a moments thought, she suggested a café across the street from the Pantheon. They would be paying customers and I would be situated just outside the café itself on the walk.

It was a nice idea, and I asked them what style they wanted it in. They were sort of confused by that, not being artists and all so I just asked if they wanted a simple sketch or a complete painting.

"A painting please. I expect we will have it framed and hung in a prominent place at home."

I had a few canvasses left so I used one of those and the next day, late morning I met them there and commenced. The café owner gave me a dirty look and the couple intervened to say they had arranged the picture. The proprietor grimaced slightly, waved his hand and left us alone.

It took me about an hour and a half, as I drew in some of the nearby people to their table and in fact, used someone crossing the square as a bit of a double focal point, keeping my subjects in great detail but a touch smaller and off center in the resulting painting.

She loved it immediately. And he seemed taken with the image and his wife's pleasure in the result. He insisted upon paying for dinner again that night and we agreed to meet at the same restaurant. In the mean time I had several hours to go about my own business.

I was weary of painting and decided to make the afternoon a tourist time, heading to St. Peter's Basilica and the Castel Sant Angelo, nearby.

I toured the massive church unable to shake my painter's eye, constantly looking for interesting subjects and angles. I thought back to my day to day at the ad agency, and marvelled how much I had changed in only a few weeks. I remembered my original premise for coming to Rome, was to give some depth to my dystopian cave men, but it had morphed into so much more. The idea of going back to my job seemed like a bit of a death.

I toyed with the idea of changing my life, but kept coming back to paying the bills, and having the social advantage of my colleagues.

I decided I could think on those things later, I should enjoy my time in the Eternal City. I looked critically at the architecture of the great Basilica, noting particularly the huge rounded arches which formed the nave, so different from the Gothic cathedrals I was more familiar with.

I walked into the ancient Castel, which had served so many functions over the centuries, a mausoleum, a jail, a fort, and now a tourist attraction. It's ancient walls, and strange construction made an impression on me. I headed to my hotel to wash up and rest before dinner. Surveying some of the work I had done, I wondered how I would incorporate it into my cartoons. It was at that moment that I thought I could use those characters and create a graphic novel. The idea consumed me, but the execution seemed hazy, as I really didn't have a plot, or anything beyond my two cave characters and a ruined Rome.

I headed off to the restaurant, thinking on my next day's adventure, as my Roman holiday was nearing its end. Meeting my friends they gushed about my painting and tried to get me to tag along with them to Naples and Pompeii the next day. I declined saying I had little time left and did not want to spend it travelling, when there was so much of Rome left to explore.

"I wish I had time for Pompeii as I'm sure it has a number of interesting drawing locations, but I'm on a plane back home in two days, so I've got to spend my little remaining time, here."

They were flying out a week later, and would first take a train to Florence after their trip to Pompeii. I made the appropriate comments on how nice that would be. We talked of other trips they had taken and what they hoped to tackle next.

Between the lines, it appeared he was a hugely successful finance man who had experience in stocks, bonds, banking, business and real estate. He and his wife had taken to travel a few years before as he had scaled back his professional responsibilities. She had some of the same background, mostly in business acquisitions and reorganizations.

I mentioned my own ad agency business ties and said I was toying with publishing a graphic novel. He had no idea what I was talking about, but she knew what they were.

"I've seen them in book stores. They seem quite popular, mostly among younger people."

"Comic books?"

"No," I said, "well, yes, I guess. But they are more substantial stories presented in a comic form, more detailed art, deeper stories and published like a large picture book."

"Oh, Herb, sometimes I worry about you. You need to broaden your horizons. Not everything is the same today as it was 50 years ago.'

"I liked comic books."

"They've evolved. They've been reborn, into something with more staying power," I said.

"I don't know. I understand the old one's command huge prices now."

"For collectors yes. It's all about condition and collectability. It's not about reading them, sadly."

"An investment vehicle?"

"Yes. The graphic novels might do that someday, but most of them are not a series, they are stand alone books, if you will. Given the lack of interest in publishing among the young, I'm going to guess that nothing currently will capture the popular imagination like Superman and Batman of old."

"You aren't in it for the money?"

I laughed, "No. More for the challenge. I have to look into it more, as my idea, is just an idea at this point. But I'd be talking about producing hundreds of pictures of various sizes and details. Such a project would take me several years, even if I was dedicated."

Herb shook his head, largely unable to square the effort with the lack of renumeration.

She scribbled an address on a napkin and said I should contact them if I managed to finish the project as they would like to buy a copy.

I glanced at the address. It was in midtown Manhattan. I lived in Brooklyn, and commuted to my agency job several days a week.

"I know that neighbourhood," I blurted. And then wished I hadn't. "That's on Park Avenue not too far from the Met."

"That's right. You must be a New Yorker."

"Born and bred. I live in Brooklyn, a straight shot into Manhattan."

"Perhaps we can meet for dinner at some point once we all get back?" she said. I was naturally skeptical but Herb seemed pleased with the idea.

It wasn't a surprise when I received a note to join them for an evening cocktail party they were having about a month after I returned from Europe.

Not sure about the way this was going to play out nor sure about the size of the party I decided to dress in a nice suit but without adornment. It would be easy to take off the tie and jacket if the occasion called for it.

It did not.

I arrived at the Park Avenue address to find an older, brick and stone, New York apartment building long ago switched over to condominiums. I gave the doorman the names of my hosts and was directed to a specific elevator. I rose a number of floors, I'm really not sure how many, as the elevator was fixed on only a single floor other than the lobby.

Once out, there was a small desk set up in a short, but wide hallway. The attendant, a young girl in her early 20s, and well dressed, rose to greet me. She checked my name against a list and walked me to a doorway. She entered first and announced me to the gathering.

There were perhaps 20 people inside, gathered in small groups and scattered around a fairly large reception space. At its center was a sunken sitting area which could easily accommodate 10-12 people. There was a bar against the back wall, a television area to the left and a kitchen area to the right. Perhaps the most impressive thing to a New Yorker, like myself, was the staircase in one corner leading up to a second floor.

Given the address and the size of this place, it was worth a fortune. Now I wasn't entirely surprised. While they had not hidden their wealth, they did not flaunt it, when I had known them in Rome.

"Oh there you are, Alan, I'm so glad you could come. Let me get Herb, he wanted to know when you arrived," she said, turning and finding her husband a few steps away.

He looked up from his group, excused himself and they both approached. "I hope you have no trouble finding us?"

"None at all, I'm pretty familiar with New York. This is a lovely building."

"It is. We've been here since forever, actually getting this apartment from Herb's mother when she passed."

"It's been in the family longer than that. It was my grandparent's and I was raised here," he said. "The building has been done over twice, mostly to modernize it and such."

Before I could say anything, Betty pointed out a painting on the wall. My painting of them with the Pantheon in the background was hung on a wall just outside the kitchen area. I was pleased and frankly a little embarrassed when Herb called out to everyone in attendance.

"Hear, hear, my friends," he said to settle the room. "As you know Betty and I have recently returned from Italy where we met an exceptional young man. He is the skill behind the painting you can see between the kitchen and the staircase." Herb gestured to the spot.

"Please, when you get a chance take a close look at the painting and the skill it took to get it right. We are very pleased with the result."

I had a permanent smile on my face, which I could feel redden. Everyone looked at me and I felt the need to say something. I nodded, "Thank you sir, it was a pleasure. But I really must give most of the credit to the exceptional light in Rome and of course Marcus Agrippa who built the façade of the Pantheon."

A ripple of laughter bounced off the walls.

"If anyone wants to engage our painter, I will be taking a commission," said Herb.

Another ripple of laughter.

"Seriously though, Alan here is working on a 'graphic novel' which I am told is not a comic book but a more serious work of fiction, accompanied by many panels of artwork." Herb spoke and Betty nodded.

I encourage you all to buy an advance copy of his work as it is sure to be a good investment.

Now I was in deep. I only had a few pages of the graphic novel done and even those were tentative as I had no real story line set up. "It is some time away from publication," I said weakly.

"I have a surprise for you. A good one. I have spoken to your agency and they have agreed to hold your position to give you time to complete the work. And I have talked to a good friend, a senior acquisitions editor at Simon and Schuster who has agreed to publish the finished work."

I was stunned, and while I tried to recover my wits the editor, Frank Monifor was brought over to me and introduced himself.

"Herb can be very persuasive. Have your agent speak to my rights department head," he slipped me a business card, "and we will take care of the necessary paper work. Celia will be expecting a call."

Frank looked pretty smug, either thinking he'd scored a coup by getting my work, or more likely created a favour from Herb, who appeared to be a bit better connected than I had thought.

So now I was an artist, an author, and in up to my eyeballs. Part of me thought I should cancel the whole thing, but at a quieter time. Another part of me figured I was in for the test of my life, and one I was secretly yearning for.

The rest of the party was a whirlwind to me as I met a number of people that any artist would kill to know. Patrons of the arts, people who had provided endowments to large museums and educational institutions, and others I had never heard of and who liked it that way.

As the party began to dwindle, I thanked Herb and Betty for a wonderful evening, chided them gently on putting me on the spot, and thanked them again for pushing on my behalf.

"I have no doubt son, that you will succeed brilliantly. I only wish you have been in Pompeii with us. The late afternoon light coming off the ruins was quite .... something," he searched for a word.

"Ethereal, dear. It was ethereal. I was astonished and have never seen anything like it. Any painter that could catch that light would have opened the doors to heaven."

"I envy you for having seen it, but I think I'm glad I was not faced with the challenge of capturing it."

We parted and Betty suggested I accompany them to the Metropolitan Museum of Art in a month's time where they would be dedicating a painting they had donated. Given their generosity I couldn't say no.

Two days later I went to work and was met with the agency owner. "I hate to lose you, but Mr. Monifor was quite persuasive. You have mightily impressed him."

"That's what I'm afraid of. Matching his expectations will be difficult."

"Now don't be so modest, I've seen your work, and haven't I always said it was exceptional?"

He was only partly right. He had complemented me on a drawing I had made for an automotive ad in a major magazine spread. But that was three years ago, and it was the only praise he had ever offered.

"Thank you, sir."

"Well don't forget your job awaits you here if things don't work out." I nodded and at his direction began to collect my things. He suggested I box all my personal effects and he would have them delivered to my Brooklyn address.

I never went back, except once to visit some old colleagues.

I finished the graphic novel in about 10 months of gruelling work. After bouncing around with no real plan, I established a work schedule and kept working away, chipping through the drawings and story line, until I realized much time would be saved if I had a solid, completed story before I started drawing.

Once I did that, and found the rhythm in the work to keep on it, the novel and accompanying graphics came together quickly. As I worked, I modified the story a bit here and there.

It was published as promised and Simon and Schuster got behind the book in a way unprecedented among graphic works. After a year I found out why. They sold the rights to Panavision Pictures for a movie version. Panavision could not decide whether to film the picture in animation, keeping the graphic details exactly like the published version, or, to make the film in live action. I got a nice check.

They went round in circles seemingly trying to time the market for one of the other. Finally, someone broke the log jam and they made the film both ways. They wanted to see which version would do better and justified their decision on the amount of animation work that needed to be completed for the live action film. In making either version of the film, they covered much of the production cost of the other, just in the prep work, or so I was told.

By now I was working on a new graphic novel but the success of the first one found me fielding calls for a sequel. I was determined to complete my task before moving on to a sequel, though I must confess having that project already in the works allowed me to consider the details of the sequel before I even began.

Strangely there was little resolution between the two formats as neither seemed to outdo the other in the public mind. Studio people kept rebuffing my inquiries as to the preferred format.

I resisted the pressure to work quickly, determined to produce an equally compelling product as my first work.

I had found success, or at least professional success, and mostly on my own terms. Of course, the publishers made certain decisions when it came to marketing, cover, and reselling into the movie market, but that was okay by me. I received royalties and they never did anything without at least consulting me on the impact any action would have on the integrity of the work.

I tried not to shrug about this integrity, figuring, as a graphic work, I had already covered the visual and editorial aspects of the art. They did give me an opportunity to visit the movie studio and watch the magic of movies being put together. Some of it was fascinating but most was just tedious prep work, not unlike my own creative process.

I finally figured I'd made it, when I saw a play on my dystopian cave men in an advertisement for tires. If my characters were that well known, I had accomplished something. Meanwhile my second graphic novel came out and it did okay, but the pressure was building to provide the sequel to the first.

I toyed with the setting, thinking of two new cave people in a different ruined city, but it seemed too contrived and besides, people kept saying how they loved the first two characters, who were knowing and ignorant at the same time.

I had a bad feeling that I was not going to be able to meet the production timeline. And I struggled with getting something done and keeping the quality up. At first the studio stopped pushing when I said I was working hard to keep the level of work up, but after a few months they just wanted something completed, saying the audience would drift away if we waited too long. I countered saying they would be gone permanently if the story was bad. That bought me a few months.

Four years after the first one, my sequel was released. The studio took up my idea of reviving interest by releasing the original in short runs across the country opting for large audiences in only a few performances. They even talked about a Broadway show but that seemed a long shot.

I was booked for several talk shows just before the second film was due to hit the theatres. The studio was all bluster about it being another big hit, but I could detect an undercurrent of fear that it would bomb. Apparently, that was standard issue in Hollywood, but I only found that out later.

The movie went over well. Really well among those who were fans of the first. And there was talk about a third. Having exhausted the Roman setting I again retreated to the same concept in another major city but at that point I was stymied. Meanwhile another graphic novel idea came to me and I casually started work on that, more to keep the ideas alive as I went back to my cavemen part three.

And soon enough I was dedicating much of my time to the new project. The publisher had followed the film with a graphic novel version of the sequel, backwards to the original approach. So this time I concentrated on writing a film screenplay rather than put all the effort into the artwork of a graphic novel. So now I'd morphed from an ad man, to an artist, to a graphic novelist and now to a screenwriter.

Was I happy? Sure, on some levels. On others I was terrified and on still others I was bored. The cavemen concept was an almost limitless back-story, but the concept was just repetitive. Of course, the business end wanted it that way. Much easier to sell something people are already familiar with.

Chapter Forty-six

Back in the coffee shop, Theresa seemed far more interested in my next project as this one was winding down.

"I'm feeling a bit less blocked as a writer," I said, "but I don't have any plans for a novel just yet. I'm keen to finish what I started."

I asked after her business.

"Oh you know, business, business, work, work. Sometimes I feel as if I've lost the connection with why I started in this business. And then something happens that brings a bit of joy."

"Did you meet anyone at David's office thing that seemed interesting?"

"They all seemed pretty nice, but first impressions you know, they all seemed like they were on their best office behaviour."

"I thought they were a lot less guarded than people in an office. They brought their spouses and partners. That must mean they all get along pretty well."

We were expecting David or maybe even Markus to join us, but neither appeared. Theresa detailed her plans to go to California for the trade show, her admission seemed to be dangling the opportunity to come and help her, but I wasn't biting.

"Your staff should be able to help you get the booth up and down, easily enough. Is this the start of the trade show season or the end?"

"I think this is going to be the last one for a while. In fact I'm thinking of moving from the trade shows to the fashion shows, or maybe hang back a bit and see where my business is after a year. Fashion shows are not quite suited to my product. But then again, I've wondered if I should try to revive my couture brand as a compliment to my more mainstream designs."

"Ah, the struggles of success."

"Success so far. Who knows how long I can sustain this. There are so many things that could knock things off track. Markets are fickle."

"So make your money while the sun shines."

"That's why I'm going to California. I wasn't going to, but there are lots of people out there, a good climate for my designs and a chance to go national in my branding."

"Have you thought of doing any advertising beyond point of sale?"

"Not really. I mean you never see fashion ads on television and the ad market is so broken up these days, it's hard to know where to focus your dollars."

"I hear you. I face that everyday. Some of my older clients pine for the days of just a few potential ad outlets. I have to remind them that things can be more precisely targeted these days."

"So tell me about this precise targeting?"

We chatted a while about particular You Tube channels, various platforms and other forms of modern marketing.

"So what's your next story?" she asked, tucking my European painter tale into her purse.

"I'm down to the last few. Looks like a 'Young Adult' story. I've been tinkering with something in my head."

"What I don't understand is how Young Adult seems to have characters that are early teens."

I thought about it a moment and nodded, "Yeah, I guess that's when people move into adulthood. It's a key time for the readers of that genre. Life choices abound and decisions, hard decisions about your life have to be taken then, often when people are not really ready."

"I guess. I always knew what I wanted to do, or at least what I wanted to be dealing with."

"And has it worked out?"

"I wasn't quite prepared for all this business stuff. But frankly, I'd prefer to make those decisions myself than farm them out to some corporation."

With that I drained the last of my coffee, "Off to my meeting. You going to David's pub crawl tonight?"

"I think so. I have a meeting of my own at 4 pm not far from here. So maybe I'll see you there?"

"No, not me, I don't plan to attend this week, too much on my plate."

"If anything interesting happens, I'll give you a call."

We parted, Theresa heading for a streetcar and her crosstown offices.

I managed to dig into my official work, and had a very satisfying day, cleaning up a lot of stuff that needed to be done. I wondered if I should go a grab takeout for supper or just scrounge around the fridge. In the meantime, I made myself a cup of tea, planning on drinking it slowly to wind down. Sipping it I started to form the 'Young Adult' story in my head.

I resisted at first, but decided scribbling down a few notes would not be a problem, but as I did, I found myself starting the process. It took me about 10 minutes before I fully succumbed.

Chapter Forty-Seven – Young Adult

I didn't want to come across as aloof, but I couldn't help myself.

I'm sure these people were nice. Most were. And I had a lot of experience with that. A lot.

I didn't actively avoid new people, but I reigned myself in from becoming too enthusiastic. And that purposeful distance, born of good reason, cast me as detached, uninterested and even snooty. Of course I craved friendships, who doesn't. But I had been burned too often and had learned.

My father was a serial dream chaser. He moved on to the next great thing with regularity. Sometimes he hit big, most times it blew up in his face, because his timing was bad or the idea held no water. That didn't seem to matter to him, getting the idea, and working the possibility out of his system was more important. We moved around a lot, chasing the next big thing.

We lived well enough, though there were some lean times, mostly hidden from us kids. And I understood from my mother after this roller coaster of ups and downs that she put her foot down. After my father hit it big with a computer security application, he sold high and at my mother's insistence, banked the money to keep the family afloat as he bounced from idea to idea.

From my perspective, the upshot of all of this was that I could never really make a friend. I was in perpetual fear of our next move.

When I was younger, we would move, and my parents would bring a former playmate to our home for a day or a weekend and then I would never see them again, moving on to new people in our new home. I can attest, when you are young it's not such a big deal. Friendships among grade schoolers tend to be of convenience and proximity rather than ideas and shared passions.

I already had developed my standoffish personality before I went to high school, thanks to seven moves in my life. Seven that I could remember.

High school would be different, I hoped. My mother pushed hard and insisted we remain in the same place once I enrolled in Franklin High. My father carefully concocted his move with the idea of remaining in the neighbourhood for some time. Even if his job changed.

So he brought us to Dallas, a major regional city, from where he could manage a wider business umbrella, should he need to.

He took on a networking project, one he could manage remotely, and we settled into our new home.

Texans, the real Texans, are hugely open and friendly people. Fortunately for me, a lot of our neighbours were transplants. Some were refugees from California and some, like my nascent friend Amanda, were from back East.

Now I was from the East too, but I was also from the West, North and South. But for Amanda's sake I was from New York. Partially because I had some memories of that city, more than most we had moved through, and partly because I wanted to have a connection to her, and she loved New York.

"I went to High School on the Upper East Side, Jefferson High, just off Third Avenue, a bit north of the Met."

"I was expecting to go to Nassau County High, but we moved here."

"That's on the island, right?"

"Long Island, not Manhattan."

"Oh," she said, seemingly disappointed. "We never went to Brooklyn. Well, maybe a few times. My mother loved Manhattan."

"I miss it, I must confess," I said, "The speed that everything is going is mesmerizing."

"Not like here. In Dallas, things are so spread out that you can never feel the momentum."

"Except for Cowboys games."

"Yeah, my Dad likes them. I think he's just trying to fit in. He used to be a Jets fan."

"My Dad isn't really into any sports, at least as a spectator. He does play golf sometimes. Usually with clients as such. He takes me out once in a while."

Amanda seemed to pine for New York, in a way much different than I would think. She never mentioned her former friends, mostly centering on places, or events that she remembered with her family. Parades, Central Park, the Met (which she loved), and Fifth Avenue shopping.

Amanda and I remained friends through our junior year, but just when I thought things were solid, she moved away. Her father had been transferred to San Francisco. My heart sank. I wished my father would move us too. If I had to start over again, I'd rather have a clean slate.

I tried to expand my friend network but I just couldn't put my heart into it. I was too afraid of losing my emotional investment. And college was looming. It was then that I realized that the only way I could make a life long friend was mutual determination to keep that ball in the air.

I had kept up a loose correspondence with some of my former friends, but they all drifted away, as we no longer shared common experiences. As long as I lived at home, I was going to suffer disappointment. Strange though, my family was tight. I guess we had to be, as none of us could maintain relationships with anyone outside the family.

My mother came into my room a week after Amanda had left. I'd been in contact with her but it was fading away, as she had a whole new world to explore and Dallas, to which she had never really taken, was dissolving in her mind.

"Hi honey, everything okay?"

"Mom, I have no friends."

"You have me."

"It's not the same." And then I realized my mother was in the same situation I was, and always had been. I could feel the heat of shame well up in my face. Of course she understood, she lived it too.

My mother took no offence to my remark, "Honey, I have told your father that we must remain here in Texas until you go away to school. So don't be afraid of making friends."

"But you just said it. I will be going away and the same thing will happen again."

"Go to school in Dallas. There are a number of fine universities here."

"I hadn't really thought about it yet. Do you still have friends from grade school or high school?"

My mother looked up at the ceiling. "One, and we try to keep in touch. But it's hard. I went to school where Grandma lives, in Tampa. My friend Lilly lived there a long time, so I could see her when I went to visit Grandma. But now she lives in Atlanta with her own family and it's harder to make a connection.

"I know it's been hard on you. "But you know, those people who don't move around in their youth, want to go far away to university. And those who did move around often want to stay nearby. Funny that.

"Life is a balance. A never-ending balancing act between an infinite number of wishes and desires, wants and needs, hopes and fears. If it were easy, it would be boring," she said.

"Sometimes I wish for boring. Having a solid friend, a place I can call home and a different way of looking at the world is very appealing."

"Start thinking about yourself, where you want to be, and the who of that will eventually fall into place."

I chose The University of Arizona but I'm not sure why. I thought long and hard about going to California, or back East, but I think I chose Arizona because we had never lived there, and somehow the desert appealed to me, another blank slate, or something.

I made a few freshmen friends and those predictably morphed into other friendships until I had become a character in a circle of friends, male and female, who hung around together, played sports, socialized and commiserated when necessary. I had a boatload of understanding the end of relationships, so they did not bother me. A few in our group fell into deeper relationships and then inevitably fell out and removed themselves from our circle of friends.

And I wondered where I would end up after school. I wanted to find my place and set down some roots after my disconnected existence. Once my younger brother finished High School and went to college in Tennessee, my parents left Dallas. They settled in Tampa near my grandma, and my father returned to his remote work, travelling now to California, flogging his latest business ideas and apparently loving the relentless change of focus.

In my senior year he came to Phoenix to visit me.

He called once he landed and gave me the address of his hotel. We met in the lobby and went to dinner.

"I think I just scored a coup," he said. "My presentation went very well, and I signed a lengthy contract to manage their video streams."

"Good. Can you do that from Tampa?"

"I will as long as I can. Your mother deserves a place she can call her own. She liked California but your grandma is getting older and needs a little help. Plus, we have a few good friends there now."

"And what does that feel like?" It came out more harshly than I intended. My father looked at me, surprised and then a little miffed at first, which morphed into concern.

"I have friends all over the country," he said. "I keep up with them just fine. For me, a little bit of most people, is enough, I guess."

"Maybe it's easier when you are old," I said. He looked wounded.

"Okay, not old. Older."

His face brightened a bit. "I've often wondered about the age gap these days. When I was young it seemed huge. My parents' experiences and lives were much different than mine. And my parents, most parents, allowed that indulgence to occur. I think for them, their parents turned them into little adults at a young age. In the end our generation coped with a lot of change, a lot of turmoil as we were very aware of big brother in our lives."

"But that is small compared to today."

"Yeah, I guess honey. Technology has altered life profoundly. Things we had to deal with back in the day are simply not a thing anymore. You kids conduct your lives completely differently than we did. Most of our communications were face to face. Now, hardly any. I would have thought you'd be in touch with many, many friends from all the places we lived. I am."

"No, it's not like that. I guess when you are young your friendships fade easily."

"Well, you aren't wrong. I have one friend left from High School and two from university. Everyone else is either an old neighbour or someone I've worked with."

"So they aren't deep friendships?"

"I guess it depends on what you mean by deep. I can call any of them up and have a nice conversation."

"Usually about family?"

"Yeah, I guess. And our golf games. Travels and stuff. My oldest friends are probably the deepest, as I feel we have remained friends through a lot of changes."

"Dad, I don't know what I want to do after school."

"I think there are a lot of people in that boat. And frankly, for your generation, the pace of change makes staking out a spot in the world, much more difficult as our world evolves."

"That's not comforting. I want a little continuity. Something solid. I've never really had that."

"If you like Phoenix and the University maybe you should stick around here."

"I've thought about that."

"What are your friends thinking?"

"Nobody has really said much yet. We all have at least another year to go. Some have talked about a Masters Degree."

"That's something to think about. Keeps you rooted here a bit longer. You could always come to Tampa. I know your mother would love that."

"I've thought about that too. But it seems temporary."

"Things have a way of working themselves out. If I didn't like the nomadic life, I would have stopped it. If you want roots, you will grow some where ever opportunity presents itself. Life has a way of funneling our choices into that which we truly want."

"Yeah, but the choices we don't make, the path's not taken, do they haunt you?"

"A good question. Not really. I made the choices I made for good reasons at the time. They didn't all work out spectacularly, but thinking back, and I have, I'm not sure any other choice would have worked out better."

"Just different?"

"Yeah."

It was the best conversation I'd ever had with my father. It helped me understand his motivations and desires. He was fixated on creating something that people would pay for. Failure, was part of the equation, and he chalked it up to knowledge and experience gained. He'd had enough success and a smart wife, that his future was secured. By now everything was just a challenge to his mind.

"So are there key choices you made in your life, ones that really made things better?"

"Yeah, I guess. Mostly luck on my part rather than calculated choices. I met your mother. That worked out well. I'm not sure too many other people could have managed the frequent moves. My first big sale of a company. I wanted to flip the proceeds but your mom insisted we use the money to secure our future. That set me, and us, up for life and gave me a lot of freedom from the grind of the rat race. But if forced me to remain in the smaller ventures as I didn't want to risk the cash of going big. Smart move, and your mother's doing. And I chose to take a course in computer networking back in the day. Mostly because it fit my schedule in senior year, but that turned out to be the key to the digital future. Who knew?"

"So, what's the plan for retirement?"

"What's that? I have no plan. Keep on going as long as it's interesting. And frankly, it's still interesting. At some point we will likely find a place in Florida or even here in Arizona. My mother liked it here, the dry heat and cool evenings."

"I'd forgotten Grandma and Grandpa lived here. They left before I came."

"Yes. Grandma, liked it, Grandpa did not. He was too used to the seasons, so they went back East. You probably remember them living in Virginia."

"Was that the house with the horses and the long driveway in the trees?"

"That's it. They had lived in the Washington area when Grandpa was still working for the government but when they moved back, they decided to get out of the city, but still be close enough to it. Virginia was a compromise. He leveraged some of his contacts and got some consulting work and appointments to government agencies and boards to keep him busy and in clover."

"I have a year to figure it out, I guess."

"You have your whole life to figure it out. One of my best friends from school is in his 50s and says he is still trying to figure out what he wants to do when he grows up. His words."

"So how did you know?"

"Sort of the same. I just liked moving from thing to thing. As a developer and entrepreneur. I always had ideas. Working for someone else and not getting to take the plunge nearly drove me crazy. Not all of the ideas worked, but enough did that we've lived pretty well. I know your mom didn't like all the moves, but there is a price to be paid for success."

"She might have thought the price was too high."

"She has never said. I guess it depends on what would have befallen us if I'd stayed still. I learned from watching my father that you have your own life, even if it is compromised by the responsibilities you decide to take on, like a spouse, kids, a lifestyle you like. It's the responsibilities that tie people down, but they are almost always taken on by choice, so they become part of the life you choose. I have always said that choices should be reversible, the ones that are not, you need to be pretty sure of, when you take the plunge."

I shrugged. "I guess I'll just focus on finishing my degree and then decide."

"School is never a bad choice. A few extra credentials can open doors."

"Yeah, but I don't want to be 25 and have no direction. Or 50 like your friend."

He laughed. "At 25 my direction was just to make some money. Opportunities and the like come as you make your way. Don't fret it. If you don't go for a Masters, come back to Tampa. Grandma and your mom would love it, and it is always a reversible decision. And a year at your stage in life seems like a long time, it's really just a blip in your time."

He went on to California and a few months later I received the terrible news. He'd had a heart-attack on a flight back to Florida and they could not get him to a hospital in time, despite an emergency landing in Dallas, of all places.

I saw my mother a few days later and she was blank-eyed. If it was not for her own mother directing her around, I think she would have been classified as a zombie. My brother was there, and while he dug in for two days, he could not wait to return to school in Tennessee. My father's nomadic existence meant there were few of his circle at the funeral, but plenty of my mother's newer friends. Even though he wasn't retired, my mother had become friendly with a huge community of retirees or near retirees. They came out in force.

Of course, I didn't know anyone save my immediate family and a couple of distant uncles, though we had nice conversations after the ceremony.

And dutifully, after I graduated, I moved back to Tampa, largely because I had nowhere else to go. I wandered around for a couple of weeks, spending time with my mother and grandmother and learning the city and the usual shopping holes.

One of my father's clients called to commiserate but I got the feeling he really wanted a lead on where to funnel his work. With nothing to do, I took a look at his file and figured I could do the job myself. The design work was completed and all that remained was the marketing campaign. The client seemed relieved and skeptical at the same time.

It came off fairly well, the client was happy and I was paid. So, I began to work my father's contacts and complete any outstanding contracts. Next thing I knew I hired two coders and a computer engineer and I was in business.

I was determined to keep the business rooted in Florida and for the most part was able. As the nature of work was moving to a more hybrid model, I was able to deal with a few distant clients on-line and with a short site visit or two. Two days on site seemed a small price to pay.

After a year, I began to become aware of my mother's gentle pushing to have me find a place of my own.

And so, I was torn between a condo in Lakeland or one in Sarasota. I was trying to stay away from the big retirement communities, which in Florida are everywhere. Both of those cities were close enough to Tampa and far enough from retirees that I figured they were good choices. In the end I went with Lakeland, well somewhere outside of Lakeland, in a very new development not far from Interstate 4. My choice was reversible, right. It would only cost me money if it was the wrong choice.

I never really thought about moving anywhere else as my employees lived in the Tampa area and even though they worked mostly remotely, we did get together during large projects for some face to face.

I remember distinctly saying goodbye to my mother as she left my new place once all the stuff had been moved inside. I sat on a kitchen chair, too tired to right one of the more comfortable armchairs, still on it's side, and grabbed a soda from the fridge and slumped.

"Now what?" I asked my self out loud even though I knew the answer. I had three projects on the go, my office space to set up and a bed that needed sheets. I sipped my soda wishing the television was connected but too lazy to get up and do it. I flopped on the mattress and slept.

The next morning, I was a ball of energy, moving things around, kind of like someone doing a Rubic's Cube, a whirling dervish of action where everything I touched got closer to its final resting place, in a tornado of activity.

The bed found its starter spot. Sheets were tossed on top when the box they were in was opened. Eventually the bed was made. Kitchen stuff was piled on countertops, a couple of coolers of food found the fridge and freezer. Eventually plates found their way into likely shelves and glasses and cups as well.

My television was hooked up and placed on a table, wires askew, but in working order. I'd tuck them away later, once I was annoyed enough from looking at them.

Clothes and recreational gear found their spots and I sat down, this time in a comfortable chair, to assess my progress. I was torn between doing a bit of grocery shopping or just taking out. I decided to do both and cruised the nearby major streets for probable stores and fast-food places.

Back home I put away the groceries, mostly consisting of items used occasionally, but necessary to cooking. And I popped the containers on some Chinese food, standard American style stuff, but delicious.

My friends Carly and Charlie, who lived near my mother in north Tampa said they were coming through the area on their way to Orlando, and would drop off a few forgotten items. I awaited their arrival while checking my emails.

The next day, I started to catch up on work. I took an early evening walk, something of a tradition I'd started in Tampa as a way to separate the work day from down time, though of course I answered emails and other queries when ever they came through.

Walking through the neighbourhood, I was toying with the idea of a vacation, a real break from my busy life, but figured the move was almost like a vacation in that all my usual routines were broken.

It struck me as I walked, that people say when you are young, that you have lots of time, but if you make too many mistakes that time shrinks and the tail of success, where a good choice pays dividends, is very short. Yeah, young people have time, but it is not unlimited.

The streets wound past a school and a small neighbourhood plaza, which seemed out of place and looked like a remnant of some long past configuration of streets.

I stood with my hands on my hips, stretching my back and considered the old plaza.

"The pizza in there is the best for miles around."

I turned and saw a man carrying a set of golf clubs. There was no golf course nearby that I knew of. People in Florida are odd.

Caught for something to say I mumbled some minor affirmation so he wouldn't think me stuck up or something.

"You look like you've never seen it. Are you visiting relatives? We get a lot of that around here."

"I was just thinking the whole plaza seems out of place."

"Yeah, it is. If you look carefully, you can see how its not lined up with the current road configuration. It used to sit on Florida State Route 822 but the land was developed and now it's just a neighbourhood convenience, a throwback to another time."

"You must be from around here, then?"

"I am. I grew up here and went to that elementary school," he pointed back the way I'd come. "And you must be new here."

"I am. Moved here a few days ago from Tampa."

"Well, welcome to the neighbourhood. I'm Todd. I just live around the corner, in my parents' old place."

"Who retires and moves away from Florida?"

"Not them. They died. Before they could retire. They owned much of the land around here. It was a farm, started by my great grandparents. My own parents died in a car crash not quite 10 years ago."

"And you took up golf?" I wished I'd not said that, as soon as it passed my lips. "I'm sorry. This is all just a lot to take in."

His face had tightened at my remark, but it softened again as I quickly apologized.

"Well, with no farm to manage I had to do something."

"I'm sorry for your loss. It must have been a shock."

"Yes. I had planned to move to Atlanta for a job, but found myself stuck here winding up their very complicated estate. I had to bail out on the job offer and while I got things settled, I took a job at the golf course a few miles from here. A friend from there just dropped me off on the main road and I'm walking home. I fix and build golf clubs on the side, regripping them and such."

It was my turn to come clean but I didn't really want to. A lifetime of distance from people had taught me to stay quiet.

"I run a small remote business out of my home. I was walking through the neighbourhood to check it out."

"Well, perhaps I'll see you around," he turned and began to walk away with a short-armed wave, the golf bag slung across his back.

"I'm Amanda."

He turned, still walking away, backwards now, with the clubs over his shoulder, and his hand steadying them. "Nice to meet you Amanda. Good luck getting everything sorted out." He turned and was too far away to say anything else.

I had intended to go the same direction he was walking, but I didn't want to seem strange, so I turned and retraced my steps home.

It took me a couple of weeks to find my feet. A place for everything and everything in its place, happy clients, busy staff and a comfort level with my choices. I had taken to walking through the neighbourhood, like I did in Tampa, as a good way to end the work day. On one of these walks I again ran into Todd. As soon as I saw him, I realized I had not gotten his name when we first met or rather, I'd forgotten it. As soon as he mentioned it, I remembered. Fortunately, in the quick hello, he referred to himself in the third person, which I wondered if he'd done on purpose.

"I thought you said you walked through here often, have you been away?"

"No, I'm right here and I do walk through here most days, kind of a way to end the business day."

"I am here after work every day, and I've not seen you."

"We must be just missing each other. Sometimes I dodge into the pizza place for a slice."

"Me too."

"Well, I was thinking of doing that today, or maybe ordering a whole pizza so I'd have some left overs."

"So, you don't want to share as there would be no left overs if we did?"

"I could just order an extra large."

"Ah, a non-linear thinker. What's your business?"

"Computers and stuff."

"I knew it."

"Today, I think I'll just get a slice and a soda. Come with me if you want."

He did, and we got pizza and sat at one of the two tables just inside the door of the mostly take out place. He admitted that while he ran the golf course, gave lessons and worked on equipment he catered mostly to the morning crowd of seniors who lived in the area.

"That's a side of Florida I only really see in the grocery stores," I said, "and on the roads."

He produced a lopsided grin.

He suggested I come by the golf course, asking if I played.

"I have. I used to play with my father sometimes. It did not come naturally. I'm more of a hiker."

"Golf is just like hiking. You just stop to whack a ball every few hundred yards. Or less. And you even get to wander among the trees once in a while. More often if you can't hit the ball straight."

I laughed. "Never thought of it that way."

"Come by in the afternoon. The course is quiet then. I can take you around."

"I don't have clubs."

"That's okay, I have access to a lot. Mrs. Peabody will never know. I clean them up good after I regrip them."

So, despite my reservations about golf and Mrs. Peabody, I found myself on the first tee with a new ball and a determined attitude. I knew enough about the game to just try to make good contact rather than perfectly smash one off the tee. It worked and it actually flew further than I thought.

"I must be stronger than I was the last time I did this."

"When was that?"

"Oh, maybe 10 years ago. My dad loved golf. He took me a few times, but I didn't warm up to it."

"Where does he play?"

"Heaven, I guess, or hope. Or not at all. He died a few years ago. Heart attack."

"I'm sorry. Was he a good player?"

"I have no idea. I know he like it because of the business connections it provided. He loved business, and was always selling one and opening another."

We played nine holes, with Todd gently encouraging me on the basics of the swing and the set up. I wasn't sure I liked Mrs. Peabody's clubs but then I had little experience to compare them to.

Todd had to stay and close the club that night so I wandered home by myself not sure if I wanted to play golf again, but happy for the connection with Todd. I had a business meeting in Charlotte the next day. It wasn't for a week before I stumbled on Todd again during my evening walk.

"Hey, there you are," he said as he emerged from the pizza place as I walked past.

"Hi, I've been out of town on business a few days."

"Oh yeah. I'm just doing my usual when I don't have to close the pro shop. You might be happy to hear that Mrs. Peabody loved her new grips. Of course, she usually does, as she gets her clubs regripped every six months or so."

"How often should they be regripped?"

"Most people wait years. The process of wearing them down is so slow, most people never notice. Like Mr. Peabody. He has never regripped his."

"That you know of. Maybe he goes somewhere else."

"Maybe, but you'd think if I was good enough for the Mrs. I'd be good enough for him."

"Does he play at your club?"

"You've got me there. Yes, he does, but I think he plays at Coral Gables with his friends more often."

"And Coral Gables has a regripping service?"

"Most likely."

"There you go. Who knows how often he gets his clubs regripped. Maybe Mrs. Peabody is simply following his lead."

"Are you inclined to play golf again? You showed some promise."

"I don't know. I didn't dislike it, but there seemed little point."

"Like most sports or past times."

"At least with hiking, the non-ball chasing kind, I get some exercise and clear my head each day."

"Golf is much the same, and you get to take out your frustrations on the ball."

"Or you create more frustrations if you can not hit it consistently. And besides, I can't count on Mrs. Peabody's clubs. I'd have to get my own and that's an investment I am not sure of right now."

"We have clubs for rent: daily, weekly, or seasonally."

"If I rent for a week, I'd have to play at least three times to justify the cost."

"As you wish. Say Monday, Wednesday and Friday. I'll be waiting for you, about 3 pm."

Now I was stuck, though I didn't really mind.

Chapter Forty-eight

Theresa had gone to California but I went to the coffee shop for a morning break, thinking maybe I'd run into David. I had vague plans to go to the pub that evening since I had been working hard all week, either for pay, or for myself.

I mused a bit as I sipped, not wanting to get too far into anything in case I was interrupted. I was down to the last couple of story archetypes and my project would be complete. I was beginning to sweat about my next project, especially as I didn't have anything in mind.

'Overcoming a monster could be almost anything', I thought to myself. Monsters come in virtually any form. I did not want to just write the standard monster story so I mused on a possible plot.

The monster might be an addiction. It could be a powerful humanoid force. Maybe a ravenous, demonic animal. It could be my own fears. What could be compelling enough to write about?

Lost in thought I hadn't even seen David come in, perhaps because he was not alone. When I noticed him, he gave a quick wave and eventually directed is friend to my table.

"You don't mind if we join you, you seemed lost in thought? Is everything okay?"

He looked around expecting to see Theresa while I explained she was on a business trip and I was just thinking about my next story.

"Hey, this is Noah, we work together. He's a numbers man."

"That I am, Dave." Noah looked a touch annoyed to be reduced to a single attribute, but he rolled with it.

"I don't recognize you from Wednesday pub night, are you new to the hospital?"

"Yes and no," he said, "I worked at another campus of that august institution but was recently transferred. I'm an accountant and have been assigned to review the hospital operations."

"It seems the other campus operates more efficiently than ours and Noah here, is going to find out why."

"In my experience, limited though it is, large institutions are riddled with odd choices and ways of doing things that simply hang on even in the face of significant change."

Noah nodded, "So you've worked in forensic accounting?"

"No," I laughed. "I'm a writer, a freelancer, and I see the insides of many corporations. Getting paid by them often reveals things."

"Are you going to come tonight?"

"Yes, I'm looking forward to it. Theresa won't be back until next week, but I'll be there at the start."

"Wonderful. I think there will be a few newbies. Tal said he was bringing a few friends along. I'm beginning to think we should get a few freebies from the pub as we fill it every Wednesday."

I returned from my meeting and decided to at least start the new story. And it struck me that while I usually wrote my novels in third person omniscient, I had written almost all of my shorts in first person narrative. I decided to wonder why when I had some chance to reflect. In addition, virtually all my protagonists were single and most were women. Strange, I thought, then realized that married people just weren't as interesting as people who had options and less responsibilities. And the shorter formats lent themselves to a single perspective.

'What would I do if I knew I was going to die?' I thought. Make amends, travel, say nice things to people I loved? Then it struck me hard. I am going to die. I already know that. I've known it since I don't know when, as soon as I was sentient, I guess. We all know we are going to die and yet we rarely act like it. I guess it's the difference between dying soon or just dying at some future point, yet to be determined. Is that the monster?

Chapter Forty-nine – Overcoming the Monster

It was uncomfortable. But as soon as I made the decision to just go to lunch, I felt better. Calmer. Of course, my resentment would just begin to grow again, but for this moment, I was content.

I slipped out of the office and decided to walk to a nearby café to buy lunch. I had a book with me, and could read and eat in peace. As I walked, the feeling that something needed to change crept up on me. I couldn't go on forever in this manner, but in the past, I had just waited out making a tough decision, or taking any concrete action and just let events wash over me.

It had to stop. I was a spectator in my own life. But I was frozen into inaction by previous mistakes. I knew I had a huge capacity for overthinking things. And I did it without even realizing until things went sideways.

Was it a lack of confidence? Or discomfort with change? People who changed jobs every couple of years seemed hugely foreign to me. I had had precisely two, two jobs in 23 years after I graduated from college. And I only left the first one because they left me. The company went out of business.

I guess I was not ambitious. It wasn't happiness, it was more just an acceptance of my lot, save for the gnawing feeling that I should be more, and do more. I had tried to take my ambition to hobbies, first sports and then other activities, painting, collecting and hiking. The latter a nether-world between an activity and a sport. It was essentially impossible to be an ambitious hiker. Unless I decided to go hike in the Himalayas. That seemed extreme and expensive.

A Novel Idea

I wasn't terribly good at sports and I tried a lot of them. Maybe that was the problem, I lacked the ability to remain focussed and get better. And now, a touch past 40, anything new seemed impossible.

'Maybe I should do something crazy, something completely out of character, to expand my horizons?' I thought while taking a bite of my bagel. "Of course that would just invite the wrong element into my life," I said aloud. Well, I was alone even if people were sitting all around me.

"Excuse, me, did you say something," said an earnest man, dressed in a suit with his tie loosened, as he looked up from something he was reading.

"Um, no, nothing," I said, "Sorry."

He nodded and returned his attention to the paper. And I to my book. He looked at me and I could see his eyes reach for the spine of the paper-back I held. He went back to his paper.

Soon, he got up, and with a glance in my direction, collected his things and left. I still read my book, though I'd come up for air upon hearing the scrape of his chair. He exited the café and turned to walk up the street. I felt oddly relieved and bereft at the same time. He seemed pleasant enough but one of thousands in the streets each day.

And yet we had shared more than I did with the other thousands that crowded the sidewalks.

I thought of the oppressiveness of the city. When I was younger, the excitement seemed interesting, thrilling even. As I aged, and understood the city a bit more, I cringed at the slices of life I saw there. The city became dark and its merry-go-round hurdy gurdy of life, just sapped the energy out of me. Maybe I should quit the city and find a better place to live. It wasn't the rat race I needed to absolve myself from, it was the rat's nest.

"I'm not a rat," I said aloud, again attracting the attention of a few of those waiting with me on the corner for the light to change.

I marched a few blocks back to my desk, and by-passed it, went straight to human resources and quit. And then I regretted it, and almost went back to change my mind. But I didn't.

My boss came up to my desk an hour later with a concerned look on his face. “So, you’re leaving us?”

I nodded, tongue tied.

“Can I ask why? You’ve been a wonderful member of the staff.”

I was on the verge of unloading on this man, whom I’d known at a distance for 10 years, since he replaced my former boss. Unloading all my worries, fears, insecurities and inabilities, but I held. “I just need a change.”

He nodded. “You will be staying two weeks? That’s standard.”

I nodded back, “Yes.”

“You will be missed,” though I could tell he was already plotting to replace me.

When I arrived home at the end of the day, I gave my notice. I had now set in place a series of actions that gave me six weeks to find a new job and home.

My mind went blank at the thought. I couldn’t even get past the ‘what have I done?’ phase. It was like my mind was static. Where four hours before there was a feeling of an unendingly long tunnel with no end, now there was nothing. A void. Not even walls to define the space. At least the tunnel was safe.

I slept the best I had ever slept that night. And when I opened my eyes, I was instantly wide awake, a feeling I had not had since I was a child.

I decided not to dress for the day, but to lounge around the entire Saturday, without a care in the world. Save by lunch time, I was thinking about the process necessary to move into the next phase.

“I cannot even enjoy it for one full day,” I said aloud. With nobody there, nobody noticed, except me. I did have a predilection to talking to myself. “And that’s okay,” I added.

Without thinking about it, lunch was a purge of left overs in the fridge. No time like the present to start getting ready for my move.

Trying to decide where I should look for a job, I picked up an old paper map of the Eastern Seaboard. A smaller city seemed the right choice, but of course where I ended up would be determined by what jobs I might land.

I looked at the map in ever increasing circles from New York. I wondered what living on the Island might be like. It's more suburban, especially east of Brooklyn, but no, I wanted a bigger change.

Boston? Albany? I could probably get a job there. Springfield? Hartford? Jersey? Philly? Baltimore? Nothing jumped out at me. I called up a job board and started scrolling through. Office jobs abounded but none that seemed interesting. I poked out a couple of applications and decided to update my resume more completely. It seemed more productive than light housework.

Back at work on Monday I was called into my boss's office.

"You say you want a change, perhaps I could interest you in a new position here?" he said.

"Well, I had hoped to get out of Manhattan but I'll certainly listen."

"This might work for you. There is a small company we now own in Durham, North Carolina. We need an administrator there, reporting back here. They make a number of items we ship to our retail clients. When the original owner decided to retire, we bought the company as we are its biggest client."

I thought only a moment. "I think that could work for me. Tell me more."

And he did. Considerably more responsibility, I'd be acting as the owner did, hiring, firing, doing the books, sourcing raw materials. I liked the idea of stretching myself past the office work that I had done for years. We quickly reached an agreement and I was tasked with going there for two weeks, before making the move down permanent. In that time, I would learn the business from the former owner, I would find a place to live and then I would arrange to move there.

I cleaned up my former job, passing on a few outstanding items to others, and rented a car to make the trip. Leaving Manhattan I felt a curious sense of relief and weight drop from my shoulders. I had lived and worked there for 23 years and only now did I find the familiar seemed so weighty.

Snaking my way into New Jersey, and down through Philadelphia, Wilmington and Baltimore I skirted Washington, marvelling at the sprawl of it all. There was a sniff of suburbia on my way to Baltimore but it took until I emerged in Virginia before the countryside finally became the norm. South, south through Virginia I passed Richmond and saw the signs for Virginia Beach, which tugged at me, as it sounded like a nice place. And Norfolk which had a nice colonial ring. But I had a mission and continued south itching to get off the interstate highway, and feeling slightly smug when I switched to I-85 from the larger, better known I-95, the main route down the Eastern Seaboard.

Trees, tress and trees. Who knew there were so many trees, I thought. So many that for miles you couldn't even see the northbound lanes. I had been expecting farm fields but they were invisible to the travelling eye. Even as I approached Durham the trees did not let up.

I made for my hotel, arranged by the company for a two week stay and located a few miles from the plant. I checked in, and decided to get something to eat and then do a bit of grocery shopping. I would head to the plant the next day, though I kind of wished I had a day or two to explore.

When the time came, I picked my way through unfamiliar streets and found the plant. It was a derelict looking conglomeration of buildings at the end of an industrial block. It sort of looked like a gothic pile, held together by rust and hard packed dust.

"Not a promising start," I said aloud, before exiting the car, straightening my skirt and marching in though the only door.

As I entered, the bright sunlight gave way to semi-gloom and my eyes adjusted. Two employees were stacking up a flatbed and they stared at me, without straightening up from their labor. As my eyes adjusted, I glanced around. I propped my sunglasses on my forehead. There were two haulers parked on the main floor area. And the walls were lined with large metal shelves that reached to the ceiling in four tiers. Out of the sun, it was decidedly cooler here, and I looked around for someone to speak to.

"Oh, you must be Lilly Stevens, the new boss-lady from New York," said a tall, lean, older man, who strode up to me from my right.

I nodded, still taking in the whole of the building. As I turned to the voice, I saw a series of office spaces stacked on each other with a wooden stair leading up to another space wedged into the corner of the metal frame building.

"Lance Devershire," he said with his hand stuck out. "We've been expecting you."

Devershire had owned the company. He introduced Lilly to the two men loading the hauler, and then escorted her into the lower office space.

"This here is Edna, she is the main clerk and her assistant Sally should be back with coffee in a few minutes."

They chatted, apparently waiting for Sally who blustered through the doorway about five minutes later. "Good thing those guys were out there, this tray is heavy. Oh, hello."

Devershire introduced Sally and explained that Lilly was the new boss. "As they probably told you, I'm here for another week and a half, to show you the ropes, and then I'm on the phone should you need me. Don't hesitate, the boys in New York are paying me to be available."

Devershire walked Lilly up to the office above, rising up a rickety staircase and entering a strangely messy office. "I'll be clearing most of this out as you learn the job. This is your office. You can see the entire building from here," he gestured to the window.

Lilly took a deep breath.

"Not what you expected?"

"I'm not sure what I expected. They didn't tell me much back in New York. I wanted a change, and this is certainly that."

Devonshire smiled, he seemed to be enjoying her discomfort. "Of course, Telluride Corporation is not our only client, just our biggest. I gotta say, them buying the whole shebang made my life a bit easier. Though I wasn't expecting to be out of my routine for a while yet."

"So you are retiring?"

"Yeah, I guess you'd call it that. I am leaving the day-to-day and I will just be a gentleman farmer at my place a bit north of here. Got plenty to do there, though."

Devershire took out a thick file. "This needs to be cleaned up, but here are our orders for the last couple of years. Telluride is in another file," which he then pulled out.

"We have a bunch of regular clients, with standing orders, and we have a few one-off clients, who order from time to time, but without a long-term contract."

He opened the file and began to pick off the pages, reading out the company names and orders, and saying if they were regulars or one-offs.

Lilly nodded. Job one, was getting more organized. Job two was cleaning up the detritus of Devonshire's ownership. She sincerely hoped his move would accomplish most of that.

"I'm going to suggest we tour the whole facility." She nodded. "This is our offices and warehouse and shipping dock. The other buildings are supply, processing and a mechanical shop, some employee space and our vehicle shop.

"Oh, before we go, here is the file of our suppliers. They all have contracts of various lengths and amounts. I'm going to have to add myself to that file," he chuckled. "My farm is a supplier. I expect you'll give me a good price?"

Lilly shrank a bit, overcome by his insider knowledge and his larger-than-life personality. Answering her question, he told her they had 28 employees, six of whom were part time and formed a pool of workers that could be called when orders were due.

She had researched the company after accepting the job, and saw that they provided Vaping cartridges that Telluride Corp sold to convenience stores across the northeast.

She was aware that the tobacco came in to the plant, was processed and cartridges were filled and shipped out. The other clients sold to stores across the country, with large orders in the South, in California and smaller ones in other locations.

Sally spent the day with Devershire poking around the buildings in the back and seeing all the aspects of the business. The employees were deferential to her, but saw her as some sort of Big Bad Corporation type. She tried, mostly unsuccessfully to counter that notion. Her appearance, a skirt, high heels and a matching hand bag did not help. She took note of what Edna and Sally wore.

Back at her hotel, she had brought a fast-food dinner with her and she sat on the bed wondering why hotels did not provide a more comfortable experience. There was always a hard chair for the desk, and the bed piled with far more pillows than were necessary. Only rarely was there a chair that offered a bit more comfort. She flipped on the television, and passed the time reading the hotel's amenity booklet. There were a few tourist attractions nearby, some interesting university campuses, a few minor professional sports teams and a listing of the hotel offerings.

Normally not interested in the hotel details as her usual experience with hotels was as a place to sleep, this time she'd be staying a while and wanted to know about laundry facilities, local restaurants and other things of day to day living. There was a pool and she determined she would use it, especially as the heat of North Carolina was something she was not used to.

The next day she found herself in Edna's office, dressed down a bit, with a pile of employee records in front of her. Edna gave her a running commentary on each employee, outlining their personalities, personal histories and strong points. She was trying to soften up the new management, and Sally decided she would try to enlist Edna as an ally.

"Mr. Devershire told my bosses back in New York that you were the key to the whole operation. They have authorized me to give you a raise."

"Well, that was mighty nice of him, and them. Course he could have done that when he owned the company, but I'm not complaining."

"I'll be leaning on you pretty hard to learn the business, especially in the early going."

"That's okay, truth be told, I run most of the day-to-day around here, making sure everything runs smoothly.

"I just want you to know that I'm not some corporate shill out of Manhattan. The reason I took this job was I wanted something different. So if this is different, I'll be happy."

"Never fear, Miss Lilly. This and all of Durham, North Carolina is going to be different from New York. I'm pretty confident in that prediction."

They both laughed and Edna continued the running commentary on each of the employees as their files were revealed.

"Mac George is the foreman. Essentially, he is a mix between me and Mr. Devershire. He works the entire plant floor area from the product processing, to manufacture, packing and shipping. It may sound like a lot but generally its just very steady work. Our supplies come in, they are processed in fairly modest batch sizes, the product is put together, packaged according to our contracts. For instance, company branding is added, and then we ship it out. We do include some point-of-sale displays, which we source locally."

"Are there busy times?"

"Yes, but they are fairly predictable. Instead of adding more daytime capacity, we just add a few overtime shifts to get the additional orders out. The guys who have worked here, know when they are likely to be called and are usually quite accommodating in taking on the extra shifts. Of course, we pay a premium and everyone is happy."

"Happy is good. So, my next question. Are there any problem employees?"

"No." She said it a little too emphatically. "Well, no, not anymore. Two of the guys in production were agitating for more money and Mr. Devershire said they could have it, if their productivity went up. It did, so he gave them a raise until he found out they'd been cutting corners. Mostly it was the inspection of the packaging that they neglected. He pulled their raises and was on the verge of firing them, but they talked their way back in. Since then, we've had no troubles, but I'd wager they will try to get raises out of you, since you are new."

I nodded as I had remembered a break in the delivery of product to our company that was blamed on a production problem. It had only lasted a couple of weeks and was largely forgotten as none of our retailers had gone short.

I spent the next couple of days going over those things I had already been introduced to, trying to make them sharp in my memory.

I reported back to New York and everything seemed to be falling into place. My job was new enough not to be boring, not yet anyway. North Carolina wasn't New York and was quirky and fun even though I had to get used to the idea of driving everywhere.

I began to look for a place to live, enlisting Edna's help on where to look and how to negotiate with Carolinians.

"We are way more reasonable than South Carolinians," she said. "My sister lives near Charlotte and the stories she comes up with are unbelievable. And strangely only occur when she is dealing with people out of state. You know Charlotte is really close to the state line. Pretty much right on it, actually. Didn't used to be, but it is now."

The early part of my second week was spent talking to suppliers. They all seemed wary of me, a bit standoffish, but I tried to be open, accommodating and reasonable, which was easy since there were no real issues to deal with, and we all got along fine.

I had some time left in the hotel and decided I would use it all, especially as the hotel stay coincided with the end of the month, likely the time any lease would start. That gave me a few days to decide where to live.

I liked the first place I saw but refused to sign on the spot telling the rental agent that I had only just begun my search and wanted a few other options to compare. She was genial and said I shouldn't wait too long as the best places were snapped up quickly. 'A hard sell', I thought, 'remember, I'm from New York'.

A few other places and it was obvious the first was the best, but there were other options, and it wasn't a clear-cut choice. I went to bed determined to call the agent in the morning.

"Oh, I'm so sorry, but a couple took it last night."

I hung up after the appropriate 'too bads' and determined to be more aggressive the next time. However, even the determination to be more aggressive was an issue with me, it just wasn't my nature. And the commitment, making the final determination without all the facts, seemed a bridge too far.

The next day at work I determined to meet with everyone who worked there, deciding after a couple of meaningless greetings, to use the opportunity to ask people what they thought about their jobs and the methods employed to do them. I tried to keep it all informal, meeting people on their turf.

It all went fairly well until I met with the two men in production who had agitated for more money. I think they saw me as an opportunity, and they weren't far wrong. Above all I wanted to establish good relations with everyone to help the transition. Devershire had warned me so I went in at least knowing they would push.

And push they did. We had a little back and forth about a raise, and I said that if I gave them a raise in pay, I would have to consider a raise for everyone, unless they could demonstrate more productivity, not just in harder work, but better outcomes for the company bottom line.

To his credit, the older of the two admitted that the attempt to gain productivity by not securing the shipments as well as they had been in the past, was a mistake.

"Can we do it better and especially cheaper? That's a productivity gain."

The younger one looked away, obviously unhappy with the task, but the older guy, Matt, sucked on his teeth and said, "Leave it with me. I'll see what I can do."

Two weeks later he approached me with an idea. "I found this cellophane wrap that is twice as strong as the stuff we've been using. And they have an automatic dispenser that wraps the pallets faster."

"What's the cost?"

"Okay, we gotta spend a little money, but there is savings in the smaller amount of wrap necessary and the quicker turn around of product. I did a bit of math and I think we'd pay for the upgrade in a couple of months." He looked hopeful.

I mulled the issue over and checked out his sources. He was right. I wanted to sleep on it but I decided to give the two guys the good news.

"Okay, we are going to make the change to the new wrap product. And because you guys found it and helped to improve the bottom line, I will authorise a raise of $1 per hour to your wages, effective immediately."

Matt broke out a grin, but looked away, not wanting to show his pleasure, "Thank you."

"No, Matt, thank you. I very much appreciate team members who don't just put in time with the company but actively seek to improve our business."

And this had the effect I had hoped, with other employees working to make improvements that would save us money or generate more. In a few months I had doled out several raises. The improvements were small but the cumulative effect was seen by the new owners in New York.

I believed I had found my element, where I could let go of the passivity and take new challenges. The justification included how it made me feel and how I would be perceived, but in the end the choices were determined by measurable qualities. As I well knew, measuring quality was almost impossible, but seeing one level of quality as better than another, was easy.

I settled into Carolina but still came up against the lifestyle differences from New York. I needed to make friends with people who were not in the office so I took on a few hobbies, joining a book club, starting to play golf, and following college basketball, which was the talk of the town.

The book club came naturally, and I was lucky to find it, on a supermarket bulletin board. I didn't know such things still existed, but there it was. I guess that people who read books still post on supermarket boards. A natural reader, I was interested in reading less New York things. My old book club usually just went with recommendations from the Times Literary Review. They had a sameness to them, a New York state of mind, something I was working to avoid. Even a seasoned New Yorker like myself, had begun to find some of their author interviews quite unintentionally comical.

Golf was in my family, if not in my blood. My own father and brother were keen on the game, and played regularly back home in Connecticut. I had played once in a while, not loving it, but finding its rhythms soothing. Once I moved to the Big Apple I had forgotten about it.

College basketball was a different animal. It was huge in North Carolina, with several major teams coming from nearby universities. I watched when I could, mostly so I had some reference point when people around me talked about it.

I found myself watching with some interest, mostly to see who among my acquaintances was the most schooled in the sport. I did like the fact that the college players were different from the professionals, in that they made more mistakes, seemed to try harder and were soaked in the collegiate atmosphere. Not that I saw these things independently, but when people spoke about them, I saw that they were right. I hadn't attended a game, but I would have if I'd have had anyone to go with.

As for the golf, I signed up for a Wednesday evening women's nine and dine and made several acquaintances there. Some were drawn by my New York accent, and others were repelled, but I soon had even the most anti-Yankee at least being cordial.

I had almost beaten the beast of my life, my willingness to leave well-enough alone, but I still was slow to make changes, thinking that my reticence could be best attributed to giving new things a fair chance before moving on.

I cottoned on to the Durham Bulls minor league baseball team as one of my book club friends was a big fan. We attended a few games together. Never a huge fan, I did like the game and the entertainment aspects of attending live.

Chapter Fifty

I paperclipped the pages together and tucked them in my bag. Theresa was back from California and said she had big news.

I arrived at the coffee shop to see Markus sipping on a coffee and looking at his phone. I slid into a seat opposite him and asked where Theresa was. He shrugged, "She told me to meet you both here today. Big news of some sort."

A few minutes later she trailed in, wheeling a presentation case behind her. She waved, got her coffee and sat down. "First, your story. I really liked it. You might consider expanding it into your next novel."

"What's the big news?"

"It can wait. I want to talk about you two first. I really liked the story of the man who went to Italy to paint."

"Well, thank you. I have a couple more since then," I rummaged in my bag and brought out a couple of paperclipped sheaves. "Just the beginnings, just so you get a feel for it. My next story is the last one in my genre and story archetype cycle. Then I'm done."

"Then you're done?"

"Done the cycle. I think it has helped. I'm now able to launch into something almost immediately and once I've established the main characters and set the scene, the plot seems to suggest itself. Beginning with a base in mind, seems to be the key."

"So they could all be novels?"

"Let's not jump the gun. Some are decidedly short stories, unless larger rafts of characters and necessary subplots crop up. And I hate adding subplots just for the sake of length."

"Maybe you should collect them all into a volume of shorts?" suggested Markus.

I wrinkled my brow, "Maybe, I hadn't really thought of it that way. That idea keeps coming up. For me it was just a writing exercise, a prompt if you will. I really try to keep away from the tropes and the standard story lines. But given the sheer volume of fiction being written, that's hard to do."

"How about 'War and Peace' set in America, during the Revolution or the Civil War?"

"Been done, that's 'Gone With The Wind' and probably several others."

"Maybe you should find a way to teach this stuff," said Markus. "There's money in the support structure. Like selling camp gear to gold miners."

"An idea, but I write for more reasons than simply making money. If that was my motivation, I'd have stopped long ago."

"Well, whatever you decide, I want to read it and do my part to help out," said Theresa. "And Markus, what's been going on with you?

Something's cooking. I heard it in your voice on the phone last night."

"Nothing too big. Brandon's life is falling into place. I managed to land an account to watch over the Initial Public Offering of his company's stock. It's a nice bit of business to be involved in, and might lead my career in an interesting direction."

"How about your brother?"

"He's back home now, looking for a job. In fact, I might use him for some of the busy work that needs doing in advance of the stock offering. He's got some background in that, and it would help his employability if he has some experience."

"I'm glad everyone is doing well," said Theresa. "My California trip was successful. I have a number of orders and an offer for a West Coast branding of my clothing lines, with some additional pieces and design modifications."

"How was California? I've never been out there."

"Well, Markus, it was wonderful. It's a paradise. Weather, urban populations, a mix of life styles from Hollywood chic to suburban summers to beach parties to desert cool."

"You had a chance to travel around a bit?"

"Yes, as it turned out the show I attended was really two shows, or the same show picked up and plunked down into two cities on back-to-back weeks."

"I think I sense the big news coming," I said.

"Okay." Theresa pursed her lips, and made ready to speak.

"Come on, out with it," I virtually yelled, exasperated by the drama. A few people in the coffee shop looked up. And then David walked in.

The air was let out of the anticipation of whatever Theresa wanted to say. She put a finger in the air indicating we'd wait for David, accompanied with a sly smile. I knew she would chat with him for a while.

"So, who is going to the pub tonight?"

All of us, hummed and hawed, making mild excuses we could lean on later, or, if we chose, we could ignore.

"Well, I'd encourage you to come if you can. Sharon and Georgio have convinced Tal to sing and they will perform a set of popular music."

"I didn't know they played. Tal never said anything, though he did confess to a real interest in popular music. Of course he likes movies too. Is he going to act as well?"

"Until a few weeks ago, none of them knew the others played. Now they've formed a combo, with Tal singing and the pub allowing them to perform. I'm assured it will be a short set, maybe half an hour, and they will not be playing too loud, as they only have a few small amplifiers between them."

"Well, I hope I can juggle my other commitments and be there," I said. The others nodded. "But we've been waiting for Theresa to spill the beans on her 'big news' and I refuse to wait any longer."

Theresa pulled an exaggerated smile and sat ramrod straight in her chair. She took a sip of coffee and gazed at the donut display. "I wonder if the Boston Crème is fresh?"

"Theresa!"

"Okay, okay. I'm moving to California."

I gasped. "When you said it was nice, I didn't know how nice."

"It's not just that. Though I did see some difficult places, run down, social issues and the like, but the vast majority of the State is a huge open door for me. I was offered several options which I haven't decided between yet. I can sell my company outright. I can go into a full corporate partnership, or I can set up a second company just for the West Coast. Likely with shared ownership."

"So, you've decided to move to California?"

"Well, it appears to me, that every option requires me to be there, on the ground for some considerable time. At least a year."

"When do you have to decide?" asked Markus. His voice cracked as he spoke, but his eyes belied no other indication.

"I have some time. First off, I sold a large amount of merchandize to a couple of regional ladies' wear stores. A sport chain also was interested in some of my men's collections. It was a successful trip before I received the major offer."

Markus seemed a bit uncomfortable and I sensed he and Thersa would have a long telephone call tonight. Or a very short one.

David had financial questions and asked after the retailers who were interested. Theresa said the merger, or outright sale of her company came with a number of caveats but either way it was financially advantageous.

"If I sell outright, I have to sign a non-compete agreement for 10 years. So, I would be effectively retired, At least, from the clothing design business."

"What would you do?"

"That's the issue. I'm not sure. And unless I can come up with a viable career, I am shying away from an outright sale. The partnership is more my style, and I would be encouraged to stay around in a management role or as a head designer. That's the way I'm leaning now, but I have a month to think it over."

Theresa smiled broadly, but I noticed, she did not look at Markus, even though he was staring at her.

As we left the shop, I noticed Markus falling into step with Theresa as she peeled off to catch the subway. Their talk might not wait until the evening. David headed to the hospital and I to the subway to get back uptown.

I'd left the 'adventure story' genre to the end, wanting something easy to finish my cycle. I thought about what kind of adventure story I could write as I followed my path back home. And while nothing crossed my mind, I decided to sit down and get started despite having nothing to start with. The 'overcoming the monster' had not turned out quite the way I expected, as the monster wasn't evil enough, not that a passive nature cannot kill, but it does so without blood or danger. It made me realize why the tropes that I avoided were so popular.

'Well, Theresa is on an adventure, so there is that', I thought. And I sat there noodling adventures as the sun hit its high mark, and started to fade. I decided to get something to eat to break the block I appeared to have, smiling ruefully at myself that my writer's block had come back at the moment I was supposed to be triumphing over it.

I had to boil it down. What's an adventure? Everything. It's a trip into the unknown. It can be as simple as walking out your own door. Exploration, action, a trip, even something in your own mind?

I began to type, erased it, and began again.

Chapter Fifty-one – Getting in tune

It wasn't really a rehearsal, rather a jam session. I had idly mentioned that I'd been noodling around on the piano when two of my after-office companions said the same thing. The next thing I knew I as in a basement with three other people and a raft of musical instruments.

It turned out that only one of us could actually play, and he alternated between bored, annoyed and fascinated when we struck up a number, something we'd made up on the spot. All three of us noodlers were huge music fans with a range of interests and all of us had made things up on an instrument. Not quite composed, but invented for sure.

And the one person who could play, had not. His mix of snobbery and envy was evident.

I launched into a series of chords on the keyboard which sounded good to me. The experienced guitar player Gord, stared at me a moment and then joined in, at first just playing what I was playing and then moving around it, altering it and adding to it. I just played the loop. Certainly, his weaving around my theme was a form of writing. I was in awe. I couldn't do that; I didn't have the background. I had no idea where to take it, but Gord did. Apparently formal training was important. Who knew?

The other two sort of looked on. Barry with a bass guitar, started plucking out a line that sort of matched the chords I played and Artie, short for Artemis, tapped the drums. He struggled to provide a beat, especially one that was not too loud given the large drum kit and the small space.

Barry had a grin from ear to ear, and I matched him. I think if he could have he would have yelled, 'Hey there, watch me.' Artie looked like he was working very hard and Gord was staring at his strings. We played the same set of chords over and over again, Gord being the only one who seemed to be able to advance the sound.

We all stopped. "This is almost as much fun as I thought it would be," said Barry. "I must confess, I had no idea how difficult it was going to be."

"Come on, plucking the strings is not difficult."

"No, but plucking them in a meaningful way is nigh on impossible. Let's try one of mine," he said.

And so he began to pick out a growling tune on his bass. Gord immediately strummed into it, something that sounded a lot like 'The Beatles' 'Day Tripper' pushing Gord to croak out the words.

"Shit. Who knew," said Barry.

"Look, a lot of popular music is similar. I could have played something a bit different on top and you would never have known. Let's do it again."

And he did. The bass parts of 'Day Tripper' sank underneath a guitar progression that sounded entirely different. I could see the yawning rabbit hole where this was leading. I resisted the desire to immediately sign up for music lessons.

"I'm going to suggest we finish up tonight and then we all take some basic music lessons, and return in a month. The best musicians in the world are practising and working at their sound and technique all the time. I'm going to take a few lessons myself." Gord had hit the nail.

We all nodded enthusiastically.

Artie never came back. He said he was too busy with his family to pursue anything else that demanded his time. I toyed with buying a drum machine. A cheap one. But there weren't any. So I suggested to the others that we keep learning, keep playing together and either try to find a drummer or rent a low-level machine.

"The drumming is way more important than most people realize," said Gord. "For now, I agree with you. But we really need a drummer. Someone with a bit of experience."

And we had advanced to playing some rudimentary songs, with one or two of us croaking out the lyrics. We even worked up a couple of our own compositions into short pop style songs.

"I think I have someone, someone to play drums."

"How much experience does he have?"

"A lot. He played in a college band. Five years there and some in high school."

"Well, that's something," Gord conceded, "As long as it wasn't the marching band."

And Nolan was introduced to us all. Someone Barry had met at one of his kid's soccer games.

"So where is all this going?" he asked after his third session with us.

We all looked at each other. "Going?" asked Barry. "Well, right now, it's staying in the basement. I really like doing this. It's fun and I take a certain joy from it. I look forward to it. It's partly the technical requirements to get better but its also the creative element. It's an outlet."

Gord nodded, "Nolan isn't wrong to ask though. So far you guys have never felt the joy of playing for other people."

"Or the unmitigated fear. I think I need to be a lot more confident if that is going to be a joy."

"True enough, but I've played at parties, and the appreciation is strong. Especially if they are drunk."

We all laughed, "Do you think we could ever do that?" asked Barry.

"If we want to aim for that, it's a goal. I've done it. I can let you know when we are ready. We'd need to work up a short set list. And keep our eyes open for gigs."

"We have a couple of songs that are pretty polished."

"Correction, we have a couple we are working on polishing."

"So how long is it going to take?"

"At our present pace, maybe a year. If we step up our sessions, then less.

And then we have to find a place to play. A pub maybe. Someone's party."

I nodded, prepared to put in the extra work. Barry just played a familiar bass line and Nolan tapped the drums, ending with a cymbal flourish.

"If that's our answer, then let's get to it."

The year went pretty quickly, especially as we upped our practice time with an extra session every two weeks. I really looked forward to this time, though I don't think Gord's family did. He went to the extra level of sound proofing our practice room. We built baffles and installed them in the ceiling and on two of the walls of the basement room. It was an improvement or so we were told.

"Okay, okay, I got us a gig."

Barry, Nolan and I all stared at Gord. "Are we ready?" someone croaked out.

"I think so. It's a pub downtown. They are trying to introduce live music on Thursday nights, an experiment really, to see if it's popular. I'm thinking they figure friends of the band will push sales."

"How did you convince them?"

"It wasn't hard really. They are looking for amateur bands to play short sets, not so much as a background distraction but more as a performance. I got us two, 30-minute sets. If he likes us, we get a second Thursday."

"Are we going to be judged on our music or how much our friends can drink?"

Gord laughed. "Don't kid yourself, this guy isn't a music empresario, he's in it for the money."

We had two weeks to polish our act. Gord insisted we perform as a band, all facing one direction, rather than in a circle as we usually did. We compromised on a semi-circle, mostly because Barry said he needed some visual cues from the drums.

The big night came and it went okay. Gord had taken up the mantle of front man, introducing the songs, taking charge of the timing and stuff. We were all singers, though Gord or Barry usually sang lead and I chimed in with background noises.

The first thing we noticed was we needed a sound man to handle the board, modulating the instrument levels especially as the venue was very different from the low-ceilinged basement room where we practiced.

A couple of adjustments in the first two songs and it was all good, or at least passable. We did a few Beatles tunes, a couple of Crosby, Stills and Nash harmonies, a Stones song and finished our first set with King Crimson's 'Epitaph'. It was ambitious but it was one of our best.

The second set went well too. Keeping the songs short and well-known bought us a bit of good will in the room. Most of our friends had never heard us play and seemed impressed. There were a few cringes, as well worn pieces were modified slightly to fit our skill level, but Gord managed to keep it all together for us, finishing with the short solo from the Abbey Road medley, as a sure show stopper.

At the end of the second set, I was elated and happy it was over. I was sweating heavily and wanted to do more, but maybe another day.

We all smiled at each other as the last chords wafted away. The big finish was kind of quiet, until the applause washed over us. I hadn't really expected it, and the feeling was magical.

Gord just smiled ear to ear. Barry was stunned and Nolan wasn't quite sure what to do with himself. As we disassembled the instruments and electronics we shared a few snippets of elation.

"Wow, that went better than I thought."

"I was scared the entire time, but now I want more."

"I told you it's hard work. Our efforts paid off."

We reconvened in Gord's basement a week later, and everyone wanted to know if the pub owner wanted us back.

"Indeed he does. He said our friends are drinkers."

So back we went a month later, as the pub was using all sorts of amateur bands to pull in local music fans. Another month of practice helped as well and we swapped out two songs from our first go around. Now we had encore music. Rush's 'Subdivisions' and Van Halen's 'Jump'. And while the applause was enthusiastic, an encore was not part of the structure of the event.

Pub goers who were not interested in the music could be assured that their quiet conversations would be restored to them after 30 minutes. The pub owner liked it that way. We worked to find the right levels, loud enough for the subtleties to be heard and quiet enough that tight conversations could still occur under the music.

I suggested that we put together a set that gave everyone a featured song.

A month later Gord announced he had secured us a spot playing at a local 'music in the park' event that happened every year in town. "It's all amateurs you know. Though some are pretty polished."

By this time, we were feeling fairly confident and decided to enlarge our repertoire. Two more covers and two more original songs. This gave us about a 90 minute set if we wanted to use it all, including about an hour of covers.

The band was turning into a significant hobby, taking up two to three nights a week, between music lessons, band practice, performance and composition. Gord and I seemed fine with that, but Barry in particular was feeling the strain.

"You know I love this but I'm having trouble committing the time," he said after one practice session. Gord was fiddling with some equipment that we had just bought, and I was sitting at my keyboard, noodling a few chords.

"Well, you could cut back on anything but our weekly practices and any performances we get."

"I've been doing that. But my wife and kids are feeling sidelined."

"Hey, man, you have to decide what works best for you. Remember, we aren't pros, there isn't any money in this, and isn't likely to be, unless we push out original stuff."

"Okay, what I'm thinking is that we really go after the original stuff, and maybe see if we can record it. You know, make it available and see if it goes anywhere."

I looked at Gord. He shrugged. "Okay," he said, "I'll look around. We might even be able to record it on our own, at least to the level of a good demo."

"Hey you never know."

A few weeks later we were ready and Gord had called in a favour with an old friend who had connections with a recording studio in a nearby town.

We decided to dig in and take a couple of hotel rooms so we could work longer and later. We had the studio for four days wedged between other contract bookings. We were on our own and though we were told that the management guy from the band following us, might show up to scope out the space before they arrived.

Barry didn't say it but he had gone out on a limb with his family to make this work. It seemed like his swansong to the band, one stab at glory. A wild stab.

I reasoned we'd gone from amateurs with an appreciation, to playing badly in the basement, to creating some original stuff, to playing for small groups of people. No matter what happened we could post for sale whatever came out of these sessions.

I saw it as an adventure, Barry as a do-or-die final effort, Gord as the next step and Nolan as an experience and experiment. We spent the first day setting up and getting familiar with the studio, mostly playing what we knew and getting the engineer familiar with our sound.

I found out later it was the engineer's first attempt at being a producer, which he acted in tandem with Gord. They both indulged my contributions and not expecting much, I was fairly content having made them. Nolan was fascinated by the way they miked the drums and set up baffles to reverb the sound.

The second day was a serious attempt to record. We had picked out several songs, hoping to get as much completed in the four days as we could. It was a tall order as Gord had to push his co-producer to lighten up on perfection so we could get more accomplished. I could tell the guy was unhappy as he wanted whatever came out of our sessions to be his calling card for his next gig.

On the third day the next band's management guy came around. I saw someone in the control room who I didn't know, and found out later it was him. Mostly I was annoyed that we didn't have the full attention of the engineer, who seemed in fairly deep conversation with this unknown guy. Probably angling for some work.

That day of recording went well and we managed to complete six songs and had another six or seven ready for the final day of recording.

It was not a 9-5 operation. We had arrived at the studio each morning around 8 am, mucked around until the co-producer showed up and worked all day and into the late night to maximise our times. I was exhilarated and out of gas at the same time.

On the final day we worked until 1:30 am to get the last few bits dutifully recorded. Gord arranged to go back a week later to do some mixing and asked us all if anyone wanted to come. I volunteered but the others backed off.

A month later we had 15 professionally recorded original songs. Not perfect mind you, but to a standard that we were at least pleased. We threw in two of our more popular covers just to have options.

At our first band practice after the ordeal, Gord fessed up that the management guy for the band who came in after us, had asked about managing us. He had put him off, not wanting any distraction but now we had to decide.

Barry grimaced. He was hanging by a thread with the band and now had a significant decision. I was happy for the recognition but prepared to do whatever Gord thought was best.

“If we take him on, I don’t care about the money, I just don’t want to get ripped off,” I said.

“Care about the money, because that’s all they care about. Don’t think of it as business. Think of it as a scorecard for your effort. And right now, you and all of us have put in way more effort that that guy who wants to cash in.”

We practiced a bit, sometimes annoyed that something we discovered had not made it into the recording.

“We’ll need a name,” I said. “If we go with that guy, we’ll need a name, something better than ‘The Four Suits’ that we’ve been using.”

“Hey, I like that. We wear suits at work and our four aces logo seems good to me.”

"It's not bad, but can we do better."

"It's served us so far. Why change? Especially if our posted stuff is already under that name, and our huge pub following knows us that way."

We decided to keep the name and get some footage of ourselves performing to post on-line. It's about marketing and promotion, you know, that's what a manager can do for us. Gord was pushing. I wondered what else the management guy and he had talked about.

I found out soon enough. We all decided to take a break, mostly to sooth Barry and to give everyone a chance to do things they had been putting off. After two months of nothing, Gord called to restart band practices, one a month for a while, just to keep up our skills, he said. Barry had said nothing either way but had happily showed up to practice and seemed to be enjoying himself.

The second month Gord ushered us all into the practice space and excused himself. He returned with his hands filled. He handed out Compact Discs. It was our recordings packaged into an album.

I was sort of speechless, though I croaked out that I would have liked to have been involved in the process.

"Me too," said Gord, "Sid, the recording company guy, did this. He got the masters from our co-producer who was told it was all on the up and up."

"You guys haven't noticed that two of our songs, that we posted to the web, have had a significant number of streams, especially considering we have done no promotion. Sid noticed and pushed the envelope. These are just demos. They are not for sale or anything. But they could be."

"Significant streams? What does that mean? Like, what kind of numbers?"

"Both had around 50 million streams."

I nearly choked.

"Now 50 million isn't that many actually. But for something unknown and unpromoted it catches the eye. According to Sid, people found it as the title of one, is similar to the name of an up-and-coming group. People found us by mistake and apparently liked what they found."

"So where does that leave us?" Barry asked. He almost seemed to be dreading the answer.

"Sid wants to sign us. Put some promotion money behind us, release the CD and send us on a tour, small venues, but intense."

"That sounds like an adventure, good or bad," I said. Nolan stared into the ceiling. Barry looked haunted. Success or the sheen of success was a precipice, and I didn't know if we were at the bottom looking up, or on the top, looking down.

Chapter Fifty-two

It appeared that Markus and Thersa had their long talk. Markus didn't want her to go, but was unprepared to suggest anything that would stop her. For her part, she told me later, she was open to continuing her friendship with Markus but didn't see any future there, especially as he was unwilling to get excited at the prospect of anything more substantial between them.

She decided to move to California. She cut a deal to sell a majority position in her company but retained a management job with the new owners and a 10 per cent share of future profits. After five years they would revisit the arrangement with an option for her to remain or sell out completely.

"It's the non-compete thing that has me worried," she confided. "I'm not sure what I would do with myself if I couldn't be involved in the industry. It's what I know."

"Surely, you have enough experience that you could fit into a CEO spot with a number of companies, especially emerging ones?"

I had begun the arduous task of revising my previous stories and had started to think of publishing them. Or maybe taking on the most promising for a lengthier treatment. It was a huge task as I could barely remember some of them. So, each story was an exercise in editing and revising beyond anything I'd tried before. But it was satisfying. And that, is what life, especially our chosen activities, is really all about.

I realized that time is the most precious commodity anyone has. Killing time, wasting time and filling time, is a crime against life. Imagine what Shakespeare, Beethoven, Newton, DaVinci and others might have achieved if they had more time. Thinking of them waiting for something to happen, someone to take action, to jump start their activities, is laughable. And I realized I was on the same path as they were, striving hard, pushing to have my voice heard in the future. But with no guarantees. Some of the most successful books, movies, music and paintings had faded away with time. And others, buried in obscurity, eventually found the light and were widely known.

I sat at my desk, looking out over the block I could see from my window. If I was higher up, I could see farther. But higher up, meant more money that I'd have to make to pay the rent. And higher up, meant that the details of the view would be lost.

How high could I go? How high did I want to go? Money has its charms I thought, but comfort in your own competence and level of accepted responsibility, does too.

Theresa had reached up and won, apparently. I reached up but nobody appeared to notice. I smirked at the thought. If they did, I'd probably be mortified. Celebrity is not all cake and icing, there is an ugly side.

A cab rolled along the next block. I could see it between the buildings as it passed. It slowed and lurched forward a few times, and then passed out of sight. Somebody trying to get somewhere but unfamiliar with the neighbourhood, I guessed. How many people are going somewhere but don't have the address, they just go by memory or the feel of what is right?

I wondered if Markus would continue to stop by the coffee shop, or even if I would. A chapter seemed to be closing, but the story would go on in its various threads. And maybe it would become interesting again.

In the meantime, I had my own business, my own clients and my little side gig. I was getting more proficient but really gaining no traction among readers. I thought several of my short stories could easily be expanded into novels but I also wanted to try something completely new.

Like my fictional band, doing covers was satisfying only to a degree.

Branching out, coming up with my own sound and learning how to get it into people's hands was my next great challenge. And of course, writing the Great American Novel was not something you could decide to do with any chance of success.

I found myself back at the coffeeshop a few months later. Partly out of familiarity and partly because I hoped to run into someone I knew, I had a meeting nearby so in I went. And who should be there but Theresa and Markus.

I marched right over to them, smiling but indignant, and only realized I was likely intruding once I was standing at their table.

I had already blurted out a greeting and expressed my annoyance that they had failed to contact me, when I realized why. I begged off and prepared to leave.

"No, no Cassie, sit down. You aren't interrupting anything," Theresa said. "We decided to meet here because it's familiar. California is not everything I thought it was. I've decided to sell out completely. Working for someone else after building my own company is awful."

"Nice to see you again Cassandra."

I nodded to Markus and mumbled something about niceness as well.

"I just got back into town late last night," Theresa said. "It was a bit of a whirlwind breakup. They pushed too hard, I pushed back and they offered to buy me out early, and I accepted. I have to go back and pack up if I decide to leave the State and of course, complete the necessary paperwork. I called Markus because he understands that stuff and said he'd help me out. I was going to call you tonight."

Somewhat mollified I sat down, then got up to clear my head and get a coffee. I decided to get three apple fritters as well, passing them around without fanfare.

"Well then, I don't want to interrupt the business talk."

"Don't worry, we will have to thrash about the details for a couple of days. I'm just thankful that Markus, here, has offered to help put things back together."

Markus had a twinkle in his eye, like a reprieve, a second chance, and this time he knew his own mind.

"Brandon's getting married. To that girl he's been seeing. Not a surprise really, they seemed very happy."

"Any details?"

"No, nothing yet. Probably a moderate sized affair held somewhere in the suburbs."

"What about you?"

"Married? Don't even joke. Gotta meet the right person and then everything has to fall into place. You might have noticed that that hasn't happened yet."

"Yet? So there is a glimmer of hope?"

"Always a glimmer," he said, "always something that seems probable even if there is nothing material on the horizon. You never know when lightning will strike."

"What about thunder?"

"I guess you need that too before you can even think about lightning. What about your fiction project? Are you done? What's next?"

"I have never seen as bald an attempt at changing the subject as that, Markus." I laughed, and he did too.

"How about your love life Cassie?" he asked, a slight edge to his voice. "Don't worry, rhetorical question only. Nobody wants to talk about it, as it's complicated or non-existent and the most private thing we have."

I nodded. Theresa nodded. And Markus, comically, nodded as well. "So now that we have that cleared up . . . ."

I mentioned that I was going to fish through my fiction stuff and give it all some consideration, possibly cherry-pick a story or two to develop and perhaps quietly close the book on a few others that were more exercises in experience than real efforts to write a tidy, tight, memorable tale.

I invited Theresa to stay with me if she was looking for a place, that is, if she decided to come back at all. She asked if we had attended David's Wednesday night soirees.

And we had, though we had not bumped into each other, Markus was at the two I'd missed. In any event only a few months had passed since Theresa had gone west. It just seemed like a lifetime.

The ground had shifted. It appeared that Markus' IPO had gone very well, and he had moved up a bit in the company pecking order.

"The big boss, said I'd likely get another one before the end of the year. It all seemed very natural to me. All the details and stuff were easy, so easy that I was deathly afraid I'd forgotten something, something big."

"Well, it seems as if the three of us are at the end. The end of something."

"And the middle of something else," said Markus, with a nod to Theresa.

"And the beginning of what's to come," said Theresa. "I just wish I knew what that was."

An excerpt from

‘The Cup’

© F. Bradley Reaume

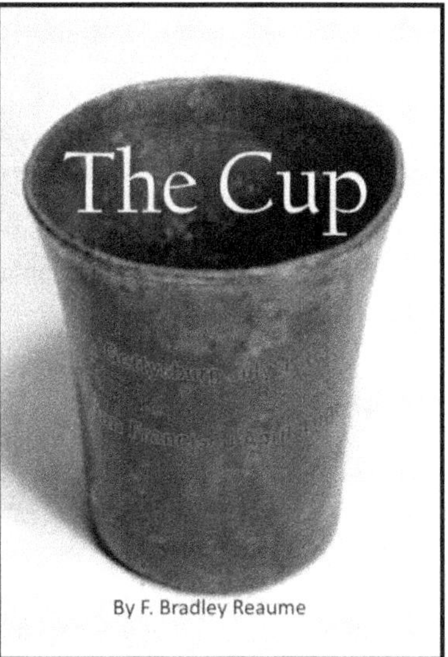

Castian resolved to attempt to speak with the natives. He took his entire party of armed men, leaving only a few camp attendants to guard their things. The men were all on horseback with their rifles visible as a show of strength. They made for the native camp taking care to approach it from the east so as not to surprise the natives, nor be surprised themselves.

Cantering into the open about a half mile from the natives, he had his men sing a popular song to insure they were spotted from a distance and they approached at a trot, slowing down to give the natives time to ready for their arrival and so they could see how their arrival might be taken.

Two natives quickly mounted their horses and slung rifles over their shoulders, and trotted out to meet the railway group.

The lead native spread his arms out at his waist with his palms open indicating a peaceful approach.

Castian held up his own right-hand palm open in an answering greeting and to halt his large group of men. He moved his horse forward and asked the two men on either side of him to approach the natives with him.

Castian was agitated. He did not know what to expect.

"Hello. I am from the Central Pacific Railway. We are wondering what you are doing near our railway line?"

The native narrowed his eyes and cocked his head to the side as if to try to hear better. Castian repeated his question.

The native arched his back to sit tall on his horse. He spoke in a clear and unmistakable tone. The language was unknown but the tone forthright. He pursed his lips and stared right at Castian. Seeing the railway men look uncomprehendingly he again spread his arms wide but low with his palms out. Then, turned the palms down and patted the air, unmistakably indicating the natives were intending to camp in this place for some time.

Castian was unsure what to do. He wanted to impress upon the natives that there would be significant repercussions should they interfere with the railway. However, he could not communicate such a detailed and obtuse idea.

"Stay away from our railway line and we will have no difficulty with you." He knew it was futile to speak a language they did not understand but he felt better having tried.

The natives looked at each other to see if either of them understood the white man.

Sensing his point was not entirely understood Castian held a single finger in the air asking the natives to hold and wait, vacillating between pointing up and fanning all his fingers with his palm down. He had three of his men on horseback walk in a line and instructed the first in line to throw a handful of dirt into the air while making a whistling sound.

As this was being arranged a few other native warriors had moved from the camp to stand a few yards behind the two natives to whom Castian was 'talking'.

The railway men laughed as they got into position. The natives laughed when they saw the result. But they nodded that they understood.

Castian pointed to the natives and then the train of men and shook his head and waved his hands palms down across each other trying to indicate the natives should have nothing to do with the train.

The natives nodded vigorously. Then one put his hands up and made like he was shooting an arrow down towards the ground. He then held both his hands to his mouth and made chewing motions and licked his lips with a grin.

Castian nodded. He then pointed to the natives and with both hands made sweeping motions to the north away from where the track lay to the south. The smile slipped from the native's face. He patted the air with his palms face down. The natives were planning on staying. The hunting was good in this place. Castian had been instructed to remove the threat. And even though this group did not seem threatening, he believed he could not leave it in place. He repeated his pointing to the natives followed by emphatic waves to the north.

The native shook his head and pointed to the ground. Sensing his position was not what the white men wanted to hear, he then pointed at his own chest and waved with both hands to the south west. That direction would take the native band right over the rail line somewhere west of Great Salt Lake.

Unsure what to do, Castian figured he could remain and monitor the band for a few days, returning if they did not move off and demanding that they move away immediately.

He nodded and indicated to his group that they withdraw to the south. Once away from the native camp, still under the watch of the natives, they changed course and moved to the west. Castian wanted to explore that territory and look for any signs of the missing scout.

The men picked their way through a forested area generally following a creek which flowed to the south and east. Leaving the creek valley, the group moved to the west. If the scout had become disoriented, he would have used his compass or the sun to make his way south to intersect with the railroad and make his way back to camp.

Finding no sign of him the group moved to the north. A rustle in the trees suggested they were being followed, but Castian figured it was only a single warrior who tracked their movements and was unconcerned. He would have arranged the same thing had their positions been reversed.

Castian was on the verge of sending most of his troop back to camp when the forward elements gave a whoop. He trotted forward and saw a body tied to a tree, bloody and pierced with many arrows. Only the clothing made it unmistakably one of his party.

Castian was stunned. The natives had seemed peaceful and while determined to plot their own course they did not appear threatening. This suggested otherwise.

He took a deep breath. To buy time he instructed that the body be taken down, slung over a pack horse and taken back to camp. His men assumed they would all go.

"We cannot let this stand. And we cannot wait. They have been tracking us and may attack in the dark of night."

Mulling the situation over in his mind and constantly returning to his instructions to remove any threat, Castian resolved to immediately attack the native camp. He decided his own camp was not particularly defensible and feared an attack on the native's terms.

The men removed any excess baggage from their horses. They would return to retrieve it should they be able. They split into two groups, and decided to approach the camp from the high ground behind it while feinting an approach from the lower ground to the east.

Moving quickly into position they attacked. The natives were waiting, likely tipped off by their scout that the railway men were returning. The native's secondary camp was in an uproar with teepees being taken down and people moving off to the northwest in an attempt to get into a forested area where they would be less vulnerable from an attack.

Castian sent out a whistle from high on the hill. The force of 20 armed men began to charge the camp from the east. As soon as they were engaged Castian called on his group of 60 men to charge down the hill and through the camp. The natives were waiting.

Halfway down the hill a shot rang out and Castian's horse fell. He was pitched forward and landed with the downward slope cushioning much of his fall. He rolled down the hill clutching his rifle. The horsemen swept into the camp and shot as many natives as they could at close range. Having guns used against them, the railway men showed no mercy nor any inclination to choose their targets. Castian himself was still on the lower part of the rise carefully taking aim and squeezing off shot after shot. One of the attackers went down. Two horses reared and fell. Arrows found their mark and several attackers were unhorsed. The men from the east continued their charge into the camp and did much the same on a smaller scale.

As the battle was fought there was a steady stream of natives leaving the secondary camp and moving away west.

Soon the resistance faltered. Natives had taken all their shots and had moved off toward the women and children taking horses where they could.

Fearing the natives would reach the other camp and rearm, Castian waved his men in pursuit. He searched out a horse for himself and followed.

The former military men had swords which they unsheathed as they chased after the natives who were mostly running away on foot. Riding hard, the men swept their swords across the backs and necks of those they pursued, dropping them as they ran. Not knowing the men from the women, they continued the slaughter in pursuit of any native save the very smallest.

It dawned on Castian that he had best leave no one to speak of the massacre lest other natives revolt and cause far more damage to the tracks than anyone had thought possible.

'The Cup' is the story of the settling of the frontier West as told through the eyes of former Union soldier Galahad Lake, shopkeepers Gwen and Lance Hopkins, Irish immigrant and newspaper man Percy O'Hagan and a slippery and dissatisfied Morton Castian.

An excerpt from

'A Turn of Pitch and Toss'

© F. Bradley Reaume

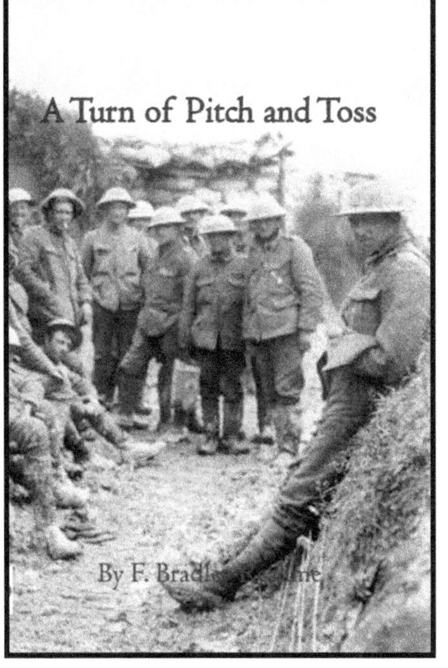

The newspaper headline, printed in large letters, jumped out from the news seller's stall as Bernie and Oliver walked through central Salisbury.

'Kaiser invades Belgium.'

"I can't see that going over well," said Bernie nodding toward the display.

"At least in Belgium."

"What an odd little country. I should like to know more about it."

"What's to know? They are half Dutch and half French and don't seem interested in being either. And they really don't want to be German."

"Seems like everyone wants a piece of it."

"It's a commercial crossroads so I guess that's the attraction."

They walked along Silver Street and had proceeded across the river. Suddenly, around a corner, there it was, the ancient Poultry Market, a small, heavily ornate, gothic styled, stone built covered space, and the centerpiece of a biweekly market.

Bernard nodded toward it, "I've seen pictures, but the real thing is more impressive, and less, if you follow."

Oliver had often heard that description when he showed visitors the historic site.

"Yes, it is more ornate than the pictures suggest but also much smaller."

"Hard to believe they'd house an entire market there. A couple of turnip stalls and it's full."

"At least it's still intact. There were others, apparently, for fruits, vegetables, but they are gone now without a trace. At least Old Sarum is a ruin. Do you still want to go there?"

"Most definitely. It's all in the imagining, isn't it?"

"And speaking of imagining, that headline back there was ominous. What have you heard about the Germans?"

"My father says there will be war. The Germans are itching and the Prime Minister has made noises about Germany being keen to finish the job of Bismarck. We can't have that, apparently."

"Oh, there's a coach," and he made to wave it down looking for transportation north of the city.

"No, we can walk. It's only about two miles. You can use the exercise."

Bernie made a face, but Oliver was right, living in a city, his friend hardly had occasion to stretch out. "You want to be a bit more prepared for our games of rugby and football than you appear to be. Maybe we should run?"

"It's easy for you. You get strong just by doing your daily chores. I still don't know how you manage, just helping you with the feed yesterday practically finished me off."

"And it does me too, when I first come back from Oxford. I have to rebuild the muscles. And it is exhausting. My sister-in-law cannot believe the amount of food I need."

They wound their way north to spend a few hours trundling about the ancient hill fort of Old Sarum with the remains of a small castle and the foundations of a cathedral on its crown. It really wasn't large but could have housed several hundred tightly packed residents, once upon a time. More than likely it was the administrative center of a more spread-out semi-urban area, with a castle, church, monastery, and some other buildings including residences for the nobility, churchmen and servants. Yet, all that remained were foundations, as the other stones had long ago been pillaged for newer building projects.

What was left, sat on a rise, carved out of the hill, making an easily defended flat-topped cone above the plain. It was especially impressive in height from the north, and more of a slope to the south, where ancient Britons had dug out the hillside to form the cone and a sort of deep dry moat where once there had been a constant rise. Realizing it had all been dug out by hand was impressive as was the foresight the ancients had to achieve their defensive high ground.

"Funny, this is such a good idea, chipping off the hillside and making a fort, you think you'd see this kind of thing all over England."

Oliver thought a moment, "I suppose, but there are examples of other hills where they fortified the whole thing, rather than chipping off a piece." Bernie shrugged. "Other towns were more ambitious, I guess."

Looking south, the city of Salisbury, through which they had trudged, was plainly in view, the center only a few miles away. Through the mist and above the treetops they could make out the spire of Salisbury Cathedral.

"That would be one mighty bow shot from here, my friend."

"A longbow or crossbow? I have no experience with such things."

"Who knows, but it's a legend, and a good one."

"How so?"

"It endures. The legend has remained firmly fixed in our history. Wonder how they found the bolt so far away? It might have stuck halfway up a tree."

Oliver laughed, "So like you, to think of the practical side."

Bernie nodded. It was part of his personality he could not escape, and frankly he liked that people noticed.

"It's all about what you can actually do, accomplish, not about things that are not attainable. I would have counselled against shooting the arrow. Why waste it? Just go down into the valley and find a suitable place."

"That's probably what happened. Amazing that the arrow found the high ground next to the river."

"Amazing that they found the arrow at all."

"Is it even possible to shoot an arrow two miles?"

Bernie shrugged, "We should try it sometime and see," he grinned.

They spent the next day in Salisbury, poking around the Cathedral. A few more days doing tasks around the farm and they were ready to take their leave, catching a train to make their way to Winchester, the next leg on their procession to Oxford.

Even knowing Oliver's plans, Daniel had grumbled when he specified the date of his trip, as those tasks Oliver had been doing would have to be taken on by someone else. Only Fred seemed pleased for him. And maybe Sally too, as it was one less mouth to feed and clean up after.

In Winchester they met another friend who was also heading back to school. They stayed a night before boarding the train for Oxford the next day.

Archibald (Cappy) McLintock was heading to Oxford where, like the others, he attended Magdalen College, dipping his considerable abilities into many subjects, including divinity studies. The many hats he wore due to his range of interests, produced his nickname. McLintock came from a prominent Winchester family with a strong thread of in the Scottish Presbyterian church in their veins, despite their Church of England faith.

Owners of a colliery, the family had emigrated from Glasglow a few generations before, when one of the clan had been elected to the House of Commons. They slowly converted to Anglicanism over the decades but retained a sympathy for the Scots sect of Protestantism. Cappy had found the whole thing fascinating and resolved to study it, but without any desire to take orders or serve the church. Like his father, he was interested mostly in business and the business of coal, to be more precise.

The McLintock's had worked up financial interests in English coal mines, and Cappy's father William was dabbling in oil and refining.

"Coal isn't going anywhere, at least not in our lifetimes," he would say. "But oil is coming. It's the next big thing. That strike in Persia back in Ought-Eight is the turning point."

"How do you know that?"

"It's the Admiralty my boy. They decided, not long ago, to convert the British Navy to oil. And oil is cheap compared to coal and not quite as messy. Too many men end up with coal dust cough, which slows them down."

"You mean it kills them."

"Occasionally."

The elder McLintock had accompanied the boys to the train, waving them off, "Prepare for the future lads, just don't get too far ahead of yourselves. Money doesn't jump in until long after the thinkers have seen the future. Investors want a sure thing, but once it is really sure, the money pours in and an instant later, the opportunity is lost. It's all about timing."

The elder McLintock's words stuck with Oliver, as he was wondering about his own future and his growing fascination with automobiles and internal combustion. If the Admiralty was keen on oil, then the future of transportation fueled by oil was likely assured, he thought to himself. If oil was the next big thing, then how would it's use affect British society? Certainly, automobiles appeared to be taking over, though horses, even in the cities, had not yet been pushed out.

They settled on the train, Cappy looking out the window to wave to his father, but the old man had vanished.

"Your old dad is certainly interesting."

"He knows stuff. Being in business he is first to see changes in attitudes and buying patterns. When the Admiralty decided against a lengthy contract for coal, it became obvious that the future of oil was immediate."

"Funny but my father never mentioned it and he's in deep with the shipping lines out of Bristol."

"Does he run the ships or just use them? Commercial barges, or British Navy? Commercial interests are likely a step behind the Admiralty. All their existing ships are coal. Look closely when they build new. Commercial interests don't lead the way, they follow on and buck up changes already in place. At least that's what my accounting professor said last term. Kind of squares with what the old boy was saying. Imagine what you can learn if you just listen to what competing interests are saying."

They all nodded sagely, quiet for a moment, with grins at the echo of the elder McLintock. Bernie imagined a future in Bristol as the coal industry declined. Oliver saw the rise of personal automobiles and Cappy wondered how much money his father had invested in oil, which still seemed years away from widespread common use.

The train released its brakes with a hiss and shuttered forward as each car strained its connection to its neighbours.

"We'll be in Oxford in less than three hours. We secure our rooms and meet for lunch. Who's in?" They all nodded.

"Too bad we couldn't get that engine to work."

"It was a close thing," said Oliver. "I'm really not sure what we were missing. It should have worked. If I had to guess, I'd say the tolerances on the metal work were not good enough. I worked that and reworked it. We couldn't get enough internal pressure. That old forge is a bit primitive."

"Perhaps you should find a job making engines after you graduate?"

"I'll need to be better at it. But who knows, maybe I will. That seems to be the coming thing if Cappy here is to be believed. It seems important to be on the cusp of change, but not too far ahead or your efforts will come to naught."

"The Gospel of William McLintock. So, you've taken Cappy's dad's comments to heart?"

"I guess. I had been thinking about such things without actually putting a finger on it. And my own Dad just doesn't have experience with that stuff. Certainly not enough to see the future."

“I’m thinking about the army. Get myself a commission and off I go.”

“Bernie, you will be coming in after the war, assuming it happens. They don’t expect it will go on very long. Not sure how that works for opportunity”

“I could go now . . . “

“Before you graduate? Don’t be silly. We only have a couple more terms.”

“Anyway, I figure if things go badly, there will be opportunity and if they go well, I can always make another choice. Engines and automobiles, there’s the ticket.”

Oliver laughed, “Flexibility will take you far my friend.”

‘A Turn of Pitch and Toss’ is the tale of men born in the late 19th century whose lives were defined by world war, and profound social and technological changes. It is inspired by Rudyard Kipling’s poem ‘If’.

F. Bradley Reaume

Brad has written his entire career, first as a newspaper reporter and columnist, and then in the political and government world before pursuing fiction. Brad lives with his wife and children in Ontario, Canada.

'A Novel Idea' is his 11th novel.

Also by F. Bradley Reaume

A Picture of Distance (2014) - a family saga

All Fall Down (2016) - future history after a nuclear attack on New York

Casting Giant Shadows (2017) - story of Americans in The Great War

Past Immortal As We (2018) - story about alien first contact

Becoming (2019) - baseball team players and coaches face their future

Reckoner (2020) - odd occurrences at a huge gothic manor house

The Cup (2021) - the American frontier shapes those who tame it

The Queen's Keys (2022) - a reluctant WW2 spy sparks oddities in the war

American Elegy (2023) - American idealism explodes at turn of 21st century

A Turn of Pitch and Toss (2024) - Living in the first half of the 20th century

Other Books

A Wander Within Wonder (2021) - verse and prose telling of an epic tale

Other Skylines (2015) - short stories

Other Skylines, Too (2022) - more shorts and the novella 'The Rising'

The Wonderful World of Wogs (2014) - illustrated stories for pre-schoolers

*** As Brad Reaume / Illustrated by Nicole Flax